G000269499

John Cowper Powys, novelist, poet, criti[...]
1872, the eldest son of the Rev. C. F. Pow[...]
descended from the families of the poets [...]
brothers, Theodore Francis and Llewely[...]
Educated at Sherborne and Corpus Christi College, Cambridge, he was a
lecturer in America for many years, and many of his most famous novels
were written away from the England he loved so much. He died in 1963.
His other books include *Wolf Solent*, *A Glastonbury Romance*, *The Brazen
Head*, *Autobiography*, *Owen Glendower* and *Weymouth Sands*.

Also by
John Cowper Powys in Picador

A Glastonbury Romance
Owen Glendower
The Brazen Head

Maiden Castle
John Cowper Powys

Ar yr echwyd ethyw gwall!
A vyd vyth Uryen arall?

The Red Book

published by Pan Books

First published in Great Britain 1937
This edition first published 1966 by Macdonald & Co (Publishers) Ltd
First published in Picador 1979 by Pan Books Ltd,
Cavaye Place, London SW10 9PG
Special contents of this edition
© Macdonald & Co (Publishers) Ltd 1966
ISBN 0 330 25598 3
Printed and bound in Great Britain by
Richard Clay (The Chaucer Press) Ltd, Bungay, Suffolk

This book is sold subject to the condition that it
shall not, by way of trade or otherwise, be lent, re-sold
hired out, or otherwise circulated without the publisher's prior
consent in any form of binding or cover other than that in which
it is published and without a similar condition including this
condition being imposed on the subsequent purchaser

*Dedicated
with
affection and admiration
to my sister
Philippa*

PREFATORY NOTE

Owing to the delay in publishing the first English edition of *Weymouth Sands* as *Jobber Skald* (1935), it is often supposed that the writing of that novel immediately preceded the writing of *Maiden Castle*. In fact the writing of both the *Autobiography* and *The Art of Happiness* intervened between the two novels. From his cottage called Phudd Bottom at Hillsdale in New York State, John Cowper Powys wrote to his brother Llewelyn on 24th July 1933, "I have got off *Weymouth Sands,* sent it off yesterday on the day of St. Mary Magdalene." On 29th August following he wrote, "I have begun my 'Autobiography Without Women' and am enjoying writing; and writing it fast. I have already finished the 1st Chapter."

He finished the *Autobiography* before he sailed to England in June 1934, having sold his cottage at Hillsdale and decided to settle in Wales. He went first to a farmhouse called Rat's Barn at East Chaldon to be near his brother Llewelyn, who had been lying dangerously ill since the previous August. There on 11th August he made a "rough tentative beginning of a new story." On 8th October—his sixty-second birthday—he moved to lodgings in Dorchester at 38 High East Street, where on the 12th he received from his New York publishers, Simon and Schuster, a proposal for a book on "the art of happiness", with the offer of an advance too good to refuse. "This is the first time in my days that I have received an offer of this sort," he wrote; "I have written to say I would certainly do it, putting aside my Dorchester Romance—just begun—until I have finished it."

On 2nd January 1935 he finished the last chapter of *The Art of Happiness,* posted the revised typescript on the 14th, and by the 25th was "pondering very seriously on the First chapter of my new book which is a Romance with Dorchester as a background. I have already begun this book and have got the main plot and the chief characters in my mind. I began it at 'Down Barn' but though I shall use what I began—about fifty pages—I shall make a completely fresh start because I want it to begin in

7

Dorchester itself. I am going to bring in local places but be very careful about any *libel danger* after all these terrible libel suits."

In his important study of Powys's work, *The Saturnian Quest,* Professor G. Wilson Knight has remarked that in *Maiden Castle* "we are little aware of Dorchester as a town." There is no such vivid evocation of the story's setting as in the South Somerset of *Wolf Solent,* the Glastonbury of *A Glaston-bury Romance,* the cliffs, beaches, and streets of *Weymouth Sands*—perhaps partly because Powys wrote those novels in America, where he felt the need nostalgically to evoke for his own satisfaction the atmosphere of scenes he had known so well in the past. By contrast he was living in Dorchester while he wrote much of *Maiden Castle,* and at any moment he could, like Dud No-man, take up his stick and walk to Friary Lane, to the Hangman's Cottage, to North and South Glymes.

But his brother Llewelyn's involvement in a libel action in January 1935 was a reminder of his own bitter experience. Following a libel action against *A Glastonbury Romance,* his London publishers had changed the title of *Weymouth Sands* and required the substitution of fictitious place-names for all the scenes described. Besides avoidance of particularity in local description, discretion dictated his choice of less realistic names for his characters in this last of his novels with a contemporary setting, the writing of which occupied a full year. At 7 Cae Coed, the newly-built cottage on the hill above the town of Corwen in North Wales—to which he moved from Dorchester at the beginning of July 1935—he recorded on 23rd January 1936, "Tonight I did finish Chapter IX and my book." He completed the revision on 18th June following—a few days before beginning "my anti-vivisection story", *Morwyn.*

Readers of his *Autobiography* know that Dorchester was the home of Powys's boyhood for six years before his father left the curacy of St. Peter's, Dorchester, to become vicar of Montacute in 1885. As Powys himself would have said, he was "a great one" for memories and old associations, and coming again to live in Dorchester at the age of sixty-two, he must often have looked back over his life to his boyhood. Certainly he thought often of his mother : "she dominates my dreams with more than Oedipean persistence," he wrote from Hillsdale on 23rd April 1932; "where is that illumination that lit up those brown eyes

8

... so beautifully and magically?" (No-man in the novel will be found reflecting, "And after all, fathers are nothing! It's who your *mother* is that matters.")

Such thoughts must have reminded him of the need for repairing to some extent the most obvious omissions in the *Autobiography*, which he wrote "Without Women", not because women had mattered little in his life, but because they had mattered too painfully and he feared both wounding them and bringing further trouble upon himself. He happened to have a woman as agent and manager for his lectures when his brother Llewelyn urged him "to take his affairs in hand" and he replied on 23rd December 1922 : "I can no more see myself having that kind of drastic competent conversation with Jessica than I can see myself in an aeroplane." Again, on 1st April 1923 : "These women with strong natures and shrewd brains and so on are very terrifying to me! I feel like the Tsar of Russia in the hands of Queen Victoria ... I get so terrified of these formidable women, you know! Margaret, Jessica, and Frances too, they've all scared the life out of me at one time or another. I have the tendency to get a sort of morbid fear of them, as if they were so many Alisteir Crowleys."

Two of the five chapters of *The Art of Happiness* discuss "Woman with Man" and "Man with Woman", for "to neglect the power of sex in any question of this sort is like trying to make bricks without straw." The problems of man and woman living together begin "when first love is gone ... when the state of being-in-love is over." Woman has to contend with her impulse to self-assertion and that possessive instinct which may result in "her devouring and swallowing up, like an insanely possessive python, both her offspring and her mate." Man has to rationalise "his impersonal masculine lust" and find refuge in a "mental life"; "men are more imaginative than women," but ironically "the more imaginative a man is ... the more complicated will he find his life with any one of them," for he is then the more vulnerable to a woman's moods. Each must seek understanding of the other without the fatal habit of futile argument.

After working two days "slowly" on Chapter IX of *Maiden Castle*, Powys remarked (30th December 1935), "What I want to do is to justify my planetary idealism by convincing domestic details." Thus *Maiden Castle* derives as a corollary from *The Art of Happiness*, with which it comprises in some sense a complement to the *Autobiography*. Wizzie Ravelston, Jenny Dearth and her sister Thuella, and Nancy Quirm are all women with different backgrounds of past suffering which have moulded their characters, and the story reflects the conflict of their characters upon each other and upon their menfolk. The power of feminine influence is further shown in No-man's being still affected by the personalities of his mother and his wife long after their deaths. *Maiden Castle* is indeed the story of men and women whose characters have been made or marred by the loss of their first loves and first faiths, of their struggle to readjust themselves, and of the devastation created by the struggle. Above all, it is a study of the destructive powers of feminine emotions.

MALCOLM ELWIN

CONTENTS

CAST OF CHARACTERS

Time, the Present: 1935

D. No-MAN *or* NOMAN, familiarly called "Dud," a babyish nick-name—for he was never given *any proper name*. . . . "D." stands for "Dud."

He is the Hero of the Romance. A man of about 40 (with rooms in High East Street), an historical novelist engaged in composing an historical novel dealing with Mary Chan-ning—a woman who was executed and burnt before 10,000 spectators in the Amphitheatre at Dorchester early in the 18th century.

WIZZIE RAVELSTON, an orphan from a Catholic Convent taught to be a Circus-Rider and seduced by the Ring-Master of a strolling Circus. She is the Heroine of the Romance, a girl about twenty, with an illegitimate child born when Wizzie was seventeen. She becomes the companion of D. No-man.

LOVIE RAVELSTON (aged three), Wizzie's daughter by Mr. Urgan.

PROFESSOR TEUCER WYE of South Glymes—a student of Plato.

Teucer Wye's daughter, THUELLA WYE, who supports her father by painting modern pictures—mostly of clouds. (Her name in Greek means a Storm-Cloud.)

Teucer Wye's other daughter, JENNY DEARTH, older than Thuella, a divorced woman, living in Platonic friendship with Mr. Cask, generally known as "Claudius," in Friary Lane.

MR. CASK, *otherwise* "CLAUDIUS," a well-to-do ascetic Philan-thropist with a passionate devotion to Communism.

MR. ENOCH QUIRM, of North Glymes, otherwise called Uryen. He is a mysterious and rather sinister figure (of Welsh origin) who desires to get into touch with the old gods of *Mai-Dun,* or "Maiden Castle," the great neolithic earth-work near Dorchester.

13

Mrs. Quirm (*Nancy*), wife of Enoch Quirm, but twenty years younger than her husband and the mother of a boy who is dead.

Dunbar Wye, commonly known as "Dumbell," a young Fascist, son of Professor Wye and brother to Jenny and Thuella.

Mr. Urgan, known as "Old Funky," the father of Lovie Ravelston.

The Spiritual Presence of Mona Smith, ten years deceased, D. No-man's first wife.

PART ONE

1

ALL SOULS' MORNING

The morning of All Souls, November the second, opened in a not very remote year of Our Lord, for the town of Dorchester with a sunrise out of a clear sky.

But such complete freedom from clouds at that early hour was not a sign of a day without rain. As the sun rose over the roof of Fordington Church experts in the weather predicted at once what sort of day it was to be. It was to be what is called a "pet" day, that is to say a day that must quickly be made the most of, a pettish day, a petulant day, a day prepared to fall into a "pet" the moment any atmospheric event occurred that threatened the obscuring of its glory.

The old thoroughfare called High East Street descending the incline from the centre of the town to the London Road bestirred itself slowly as befitted the dignity of its long history, to meet this beautiful but treacherous morning. One by one the great chimneys above the old brick roofs, many of them fronted with massive slabs of stone, sent forth their smoke. One by one the prentice-boys appeared, opening the shop-doors and sweeping the pavement. Milk-carts made their pleasant clatter; while the sound of the hoofs of the horses that drew these reassuring equipages, echoing between the walls, seemed to gather the centuries together with a familiar continuity of unbroken tradition that was not disturbed when an occasional bus or car came down the street.

The homely sense of a recurrent satisfaction of old human necessities found another expression in the pleasant chiming of the clock in the tower of the Corn Exchange situated at the head of the street, a chiming that seemed in its perennial cheerfulness to purge the very mystery of Time of its tragic burden and divide the hours to the tune of some secret knowledge of its own that "good hope," in spite of all evidence to the contrary, still abode "at the bottom."

15

Under the sloping roof of one of the older and taller houses on the northern side of the street a man of about forty lay listening to all these early morning sounds, lay watching the yellow sunlight flow like liquid gold over the various objects that surrounded him. Fully awake was this man, even while many of his fellows in High East Street were still unconscious of the horses' hoofs, of the chiming of the clock, of the passing of the buses and cars.

This man now raised his knees under his bed-clothes, gathered his pillows under his head, and set himself to stare intently at the rose-patterned paper which covered his sloping ceiling and at the massive whitewashed beams which intersected the angle of its descent. These beams took the shape, as the man stared at them from his bed, of an elongated and distorted cross.

To the right of this cross a small deeply gabled window with a broad wooden sill overlooked, on the opposite side of the street, the roof of a cheerful stationer's shop, above which could be seen a couple of tall elms that lifted up against the sky three or four ancient rook nests, whose adaptability to the distant nesting season seemed on that particular morning to be the subject of a clamorous investigation by a group of black-winged birds.

The writing-table of the man on the bed stood in front of this deeply embrasured window, while the whole width of the wall, from window to door, was filled with a series of capacious cupboards solidly built into the masonry of the room.

To the man's left was a small ancient-looking fire-place, full at this moment of cold cinders and powdery ashes, while between this fire-place and the wall to the left of the man's head, where stood his chest of drawers and his mirror, was a shallow alcove filled by an overcrowded bookcase reaching from floor to ceiling.

The room was homely and unpretentious, but it could not be called lacking, as the morning light flooded it, in certain pleasing qualities. There was, for instance, a reddish rug in front of the fire-place, that although very worn gave the hearth a welcoming air, and several small rugs in front of the cupboards had a cheerful look, while the cupboards themselves, in their old-fashioned mouldings and panellings, endowed the place with a tone of old-world dignity.

16

The most agreeable aspect of it was the wall-paper, which was covered with little pink roses, though there was one small spot, where, as if there had been no more roses in the world, a fragment of a much older paper hung disconsolately in tattered shreds.

After making use of those whitewashed cross-beams as a background to his first waking thoughts the man lowered his uplifted knees and concentrated his gaze on the foot of the bed. This bed was clearly a very ancient structure. It was large and massive but its bed-posts didn't match each other. One of them was lacking a something that its fellow possessed. This something was a grotesque head of heraldic carving and it was upon the ambiguity of this object, an ambiguity rendered still more obscure by the manner in which the narrow stream of sun-motes from the window passed it untouched, that the man's cogitation was now absorbed.

For the thousandth time he asked himself to what conceivable body could that extraordinary head have been attached : was it a lion's head, a bird's head, a dragon's head, or a human head? Or had it, as happens sometimes with ecclesiastical gargoyles, elements of each one of these natures, of the bird's, of the beast's, and of the man's? What he was so intensely wondering just then with regard to this heraldic head was whether it was really possible, as he had been so often assured, that its companion, its mate, its fellow, was hidden away in one of the many old curiosity shops of this unique town.

The bed had some connection with his mother and it was connected in some way with his mother's lover, a mysterious personage to whose existence the woman had only twice in his life, and then on very confused and agitating occasions, made the faintest allusion. "The woman from Wales," (for this had always been the way his supposed father had expressed any momentary grievance against his mother), must have found in this mysterious head some token, some symbol of her concealed past; while the head itself, whatever it carried of old, dark, heraldic, or even mythological significance, had been the object round which more than anything else the brooding imagination of his childhood, playing with the notions of both good and evil, had constantly hovered.

There was good in it, for *him* anyhow—else how could his

17

mother have made so much of it?—but there was obviously evil in it, too. What most of all he seemed to detect in it was simply *desire*, that Faustian "desire" to penetrate and enjoy—even in forbidden directions—the huge mystery of the Cosmos.

And yet, for all that, it had become a fancy of his that to his mental dalliances in that bed with the spirit of his dead wife, who had died a virgin, this head was, in some queer way, inimical.

And there was something else too about this relic that closely affected his life. This monstrous fetish of "the Woman from Wales" was mixed up vaguely in his mind with a singular reluctance of his, the reluctance to have a name!

It has not often happened, even in the most primitive times, for a man to have no name. Such, however, by a singular concentration of circumstances, was actually the lot of this lean, hook-nosed, clean-shaven individual who lay staring pensively at his bed's head.

There had been, indeed, throughout all his forty years, only two modifications of this singular anonymity. The first of these occurred during his infancy and gave him a substitute for a "Christian" name. As a baby this tall man had been accustomed at frequent intervals to give vent to the babbled syllable "Dud," and it was not long ere both his mother and himself began to apply to his small and querulous identity the monosyllable "Dud." His substitute for a surname did not attach itself to him till later, not, in fact, till he reached years of discretion, and was entirely his own choice.

After an agitating domestic scene when he had drawn from his mother the disturbing fact that Aaron Smith, the organist in a West-Country town at some distance from Dorchester, was not his real father, he had refused to use his simple patronymic, and casting about for some substitute for an ordinary name, hit upon the appellation, "No-man," and henceforth always signed himself, and indeed thought of himself, as "Dud No-man" or "D. No-man."

In using this name that was no name, he had not been thinking of Odysseus's encounter with the Cyclops, for he was at that time unacquainted with Homer. The phrase had come upon him, in his sulky reaction against his parents, as an inspiration of pure misanthropy.

This was only the second morning of Dud No-man's life in

Dorchester. He had spent the previous day unpacking his books and arranging his furniture. Yesterday night there had been nothing in his attic except this ancient oak bed, but now he was able to survey with satisfaction his snug quarters, and to ponder with pleasure upon the familiar domestic utensils which awaited him in his tiny kitchen across the small landing, along with a white-enamelled sink and an unpretentious gas-stove.

He had already discovered that this little kitchen, on a winter's day, was extremely chilly, but he made up his mind that independently of closing its door against the draughty staircase he would light the oven of his stove and get the place thoroughly warm on all the occasions he had to make use of it.

Dud No-man had been lucky enough to get two historical novels published, and though their sales had not been large they had been enough, combined with an occasional article on some kindred subject, to supply his needs. He was thus able—though he had inherited nothing from his parents—to live an independent life, and he had taken this attic in Dorchester, with a view to gathering material for his work in a region charged with so many layers of suggestive antiquity.

His thoughts, as he watched the yellow sun-rays, from above the opposite roof, strike first one object and then another in his little room, began now to wander from the heraldic monstrosity at his bed's head.

He thought of his putative father, the music-absorbed organist, and of his silent, equally absorbed mother, whose everlasting pleasure it was to be perpetually embroidering, in carefully selected coloured wools, flamboyant covers for everything that lent itself to be covered. He had kept only one of these covered objects, a small cushioned ottoman, which now occupied a place to the right of his attic hearth where there was just room for it. In this ottoman he kept the manuscripts, written in his own vigorous hand, of both his lengthy novels, and he had retained this specimen of his mother's devotion to her wools because she had worked upon it the picture of a stately manorial gate, ornamented by *two* heraldic heads identical with the one now before him.

One of his earliest memories had been of his mother working at this ottoman-cover, and since she always kept it in her own room the sight of it brought back her reserved personality more

19

distinctly to him than anything else—except this bed of hers on which he now lay—that he could possibly have preserved from the past.

But No-man's thoughts as he lay there, enjoying the morning sounds that came to him from the street, did not remain long with his mother. They moved to the figure of his young wife. All three of them—his parents and his wife—had died in one of those virulent epidemics of influenza that swept over England at a certain date.

No-man had lived with his wife for only a year, or rather *she* had lived with the three of them for only a year—for at that time none of his writings had been accepted—before this disease carried her off, but she was still, after a lapse of ten years, by far the most powerful influence in his life. It was not that he had ever loved her, this girl that their neighbours called "young Mrs. Smith"—with a normal love, for it was Dud's misfortune to be rendered nervously incapable of consummating his marriage, but his bride's startling beauty and singular character had made a deeper impression upon him than anything in his life; and for all these ten years Mona's personality had stood between him and all other emotional impressions. Now that it was too late, now that she had died a virgin, the vision of that beautiful body, ready to yield itself and yet so terrifyingly immaculate, had come to absorb every amorous instinct he possessed.

All feelings of that sort, such as now and then were stirred in him by casual encounters, invariably ran, like subservient tributaries, into this main stream. The glimpse of a lovely ankle, the turn of a soft neck, the swing of a girl's figure as she walked, if such things were ever dwelt upon in his thoughts, were always caught up and transformed and preserved in his memory to make part of his enjoyment of that terrifyingly beautiful body.

He had decided to come to Dorchester for several reasons, but as he pondered over his motives now, he tried to idealize them into a longing to solve, if he only might, on the spot where his own dead lay, the ultimate meaning of death itself. The phrase "where his own dead lay" was already a pregnant one to No-man, for living as he had done for the last ten years almost entirely in the thoughts about these two women he had come by degrees to link up his whole conception of our dim human chances of immortality with their two figures.

If our survival of death, he had come to feel, depended on the intensity with which we lived our individual life, the intensity with which we grasped life's most symbolic essences then it was "the Woman from Wales" who was more likely to dodge annihilation; whereas if our chance depended on the power we develop for sinking our individuality in others' lives, why then it was the dead Mona who had the better start.

He shifted his limbs uneasily and crossed his hands behind his head. He began wrestling in his mind with the old insoluble question. Already a premonitory cloud had materialized for a minute between the sun and the town, tossing against his window, ere it went its way, a spattering of thin rain.

"Dorchester means," he thought, "the town of water," and then he thought : "How queer that sorrow and sacrifice in men and women should draw water from behind the eye-sockets of their skulls !"

"I haven't cried for her once," he mused, "since she died. All Souls' day it is! The right day for me to go to her. *Are* they gone forever—those two, or is one gone forever and the other, by some magic in her way of life, *not* gone? Why should survival of death be universal? Why shouldn't there be an 'art of survival' to which some souls find the clue and others not ?"

And there came over him, as the sun of this "pet" day once more shone into his room, the old dark Homeric conception of death, with that terrifying multitude of the spirits of the dead surrounding us in their pitiful half-life and liable, on this day of their Cimmerian remembrance when the minds of the living turn so desperately towards them, to rise thronging up : *ethnea myria nekron*—"the myriad tribes of the dead, with a terrible cry !"

But it *could* not be like that, not just like that, he told himself. Anything were better than that, even total and absolute annihilation !

Drawing up his knees again in the bed till his skeleton under his flesh assumed that huddled posture of the as-yet-unborn in which so many ancient bones are discovered, he now began to wonder whether it hadn't been this superhuman disinterestedness in Mona that had given her beauty that detached and unapproachable quality that used so to freeze his desire.

On this particular morning, his second morning in the place

21

where she was buried, he caught himself in a very startling thought: the recognition, namely, that in his cerebral love-making during all these later years he had furtively turned her into *a different girl*, a girl with erotic vice in her, a girl with wayward caprices and wicked moods!

Full of thoughts of this kind, thoughts that, now he had dared to let himself go, grew momently more monstrously sacrilegious and dangerously sweet, he jumped quickly out of his bed and proceeded to walk round the foot of it with the intention of closing his attic-window. As he did this he lingered for a minute beside the questionable bed-post, and he seemed to catch an almost human expression upon that monstrous face, but an expression as much beyond his interpretation now as it had been in his childhood.

Dud washed and dressed more quickly than usual that morning. He was as pleased with his kitchen on the other side of the small landing as he was with his bedroom; but his head was full of various important purchases that he would have to make that day before he could consider himself really settled, and he felt impatient to get his breakfast over and go out into this unknown town.

Anyone watching Dud light the fire in his bedroom and the gas-stove in his kitchen and begin making his preparations for breakfast would have thought him extremely lucky to be able to obtain his living by something different from manual work; for it was very clear that his bony fingers, though as "long and lean" as the dwarf's in Scott's *Lay*, were so awkward as to seem scarcely under the control of a rational mind.

People regarded it as a wonder that his handwriting was so legible, but no doubt this was due to the intense childishness of a certain aspect of Dud's nature, his power of being transported with a pleasurable glow of pride in the accomplishment of the very smallest physical undertaking. Helpless though his bony fingers were he derived extraordinary satisfaction from gathering up the cinders out of his grate and transferring them to a pail. Where, however, almost every day a malicious observer would have been tickled by Mr. No-man's antics was when minute bits of his sponge—and his sponges remained in use till they fell to bits—were observed floating in the basin after he had sponged his face. These infinitesimal objects he always pursued with finger and thumb round and round the basin, and it was a recurrent wonder to Dud's mind why these wisps of submarine life should apparently desire so intensely *not* to be saved. He "saved" them by putting them into his pocket, where they mingled with indescribable fluff and vanished from the roll of recognizable objects into that obscure limbo of not-existing existence out of which all comes and into which all returns. What he saved them *from* was going down the drain-pipes into the nearest *cloaca maxima*.

No-man got extraordinary satisfaction from lighting his fire. He made a point of having a fire in summer as well as winter—it was his one luxury—merely for the pleasure he got out of it! His fire had been literally the landscape of his heart's desire during these ten lonely years. It had been his Lost Atlantis, his Eldorado, his Fountain of Youth, his Mountains of the Moon, his Coasts of Latium, his *Urbs Beata*, his "bed of crimson joy." But though he derived such delight from devoted service to his fire, Dud was the worst maker of fires in Dorset. He had no notion of the natural laws that regulate this Promethean activity and after ten years of blundering he still made the same mistakes as he had made when his mother and his wife first deserted him.

Nor was it much better—such a fool was he with his hands—in the matter of the various culinary tasks and the various kitchen utensils into a struggle with which destiny had seen fit of late to plunge him.

He had brought to Dorchester with him what pots and pans and kettles he possessed. They were not many, and they were old and dented, but he had unpacked them tenderly the day before, and now with his gas-stove lit and his kettle boiling for tea and his saucepan boiling for his eggs, as he went to and fro between the two rooms, arranging his breakfast things on a little folding table in front of the fire, he began muttering aloud—much in the manner of an aged religious recluse—and talking to his pots and pans as if they were human.

Dud had come to cherish, as a result of his researches, several strong historical prejudices. One of these was a quite personal hatred of Henry VIII. Another was a somewhat unusual animosity against the Stuart kings. And he had gratified both these hostilities by naming his kettle "the Royal Martyr," his saucepan "James II," and his refuse-pail "Henry VIII."

23

Short of having kings for scullions it was gratifying to No-man to see them making his tea and boiling his eggs; and it eased his rage against the destroyer of monasteries and the founder of county families to throw his tea-leaves and his egg-shells into that great belly.

For the House of Hanover, on the contrary, Dud had a strong *penchant*. Especially did his heart warm, as an unsuccessful his-torian, to the royal reception of the triumphant author of *The Decline and Fall*. "What? *Another* volume, Mr Gibbon? Always the same I see—scribble, scribble, scribble!"

He knew very well, as he now proceeded to turn out the gas-jets and carry "the Royal Martyr" to the fire in his bedroom that these lively sensations of his first experience of his new abode would never repeat themselves.

With the steaming kettle in his hand he leaned first across the broad sill of his kitchen window, looking due north, and then across the even broader window-sill of his bedroom looking due south. He was enchanted by the view from both these posts of observation. Who would have supposed that you could see so many tree-tops and so many rooks' nests over the roof of a busy stationer's in the High Street of a prosperous town? And as for what he saw from his kitchen window it simply astonished him. It was a pure pastoral scene! Just a few slate roofs, a few tiled roofs, a few warehouses built with the solidity of churches, a few carefully cultivated little gardens, a few flagstone paths, ancient tool-sheds, disused privies, fowl-runs, cat-haunted stone walls, just one single row of artisans' houses, and then beyond all these the veritable country, lovely in its dewy repose as if it had been miles away from any town!

As the man uneasily shifted his kettle from one hand to the other to avoid the steam he allowed his gaze to follow the rising uplands till they lost themselves in a downlike horizon, topped by clumps of trees. But what was that line of shining silver in the middle distance, that curious strip of metallic brightness dividing the water-meadows of the immediate valley? Dud knew well what it was, though this was the first time he had realized that it was visible from his own dwelling. It was the river Frome! It was the river which shines so bright in its swift, clear, gravelly flow that the great Wessex author has compared it to a tributary of the celestial Water of Life.

Eating his breakfast at last close to his fire—and he was delighted by the amount of warmth that emanated from that old-fashioned grate—No-man decided that he would postpone washing up, postpone buying ink and paper and the few other necessities he required till he had visited his dead in the cemetery. This was one of his motives in coming to Dorchester, that he might, by means of the familiarity of propinquity, overcome a singular reluctance that had possessed him, all these ten years, about visiting those graves. He had been ill himself of the same epidemic when they died; and when he recovered and ought naturally to have gone he found he could not bring himself to do it! The very fact that Mona was such a constant presence, that she was with him every morning and every night, made it hard for him to think of her body—that body which had become the object of all his idealism as well as all his satyrishness—actually lying in a coffin under a mound of turf.

It was even now with not a little trepidation that he made up his mind that he *would* go, go at once, go that very morning, to find the three graves. Aaron Smith's relatives had been buried there from the time when the cemetery was first used; so that he did not anticipate any difficulty in finding out from the officials where to look for the spot. His mother, as a waif from the Principality, with no known relatives at all and with no desire to go back to "the land of her fathers" (unless those armorial gate-posts showed such a desire), was naturally buried with her husband.

As for Mona herself, he well remembered how, when he thought he was going to follow her, he had insisted that they should be buried together; and he had a vague memory of seeing her parents by his bedside through a cloud of delirium and of imploring them to keep a place for him in her grave. Such a place, he took for granted, *had* been kept—not in the same grave, but between the girl and his mother—but Mona's relatives in their distant home had contented themselves with rarer and rarer visits to the Dorset cemetery.

Had Dud's businesslike landlord in his little shop below been of an inquisitive turn of mind and on the alert for the goings-on of a crop-headed taciturn lodger he might now have been surprised to hear a ferocious oath descending the stairs from the landing at the top of the house.

25

A sudden realization that he was going to visit within an hour the grave of the girl whose spiritual substitute he had embraced in his amorous perversity every night for ten years, caused Dud's clumsy hands, when, his breakfast being finally over, he was carrying his kettle back to his kitchen, to become twice as clumsy as usual, with the result of the spilling of no little boiling water.

"Damn and blast you!" he cried in a fit of nervous exasperation. "*Spill* then, if you want to!" and swinging "the Royal Martyr" in the air he brought it down into such sharp contact with the sink that he made a dent in one side of the one and a chip in the edge of the other.

A second later he felt ashamed of this performance, and he set himself to do more tidying than he had intended. In his penitence he even made his bed. He could not, however, endure to wait for water to boil again so that he might wash up; and shaking the tea-leaves and the egg-shells and the crumbs into "Henry VIII," he began pulling on his overcoat. His hand shook with excitement as he possessed himself of the oak cudgel he was wont to use, a support more like the club of an ogre than an ordinary walking-stick; but with this in his hand he leaned forward once more across the window-sill of his kitchen, which was as deep as the window was high, as if to give himself strength by a last glance at the view.

As he stared at the water-meadows he detected on the further side of that strip of glittering silver, that he knew was the Frome, a most singularly-shaped willow-tree. This tree grew in an isolated position in the midst of the ditches and as he surveyed it now he could distinctly make out two white objects in a stationary position beneath it. What were these? They were evidently living things. They must be white birds. Surely, they were too big for ducks? Too big for geese even! Could they be swans?

Dud, grasping his great oak cudgel by the centre, and leaning over the broad window-sill while he stared at those water-meadows, let his gaze wander now from the mysterious white objects. He could see on the right of the willow-tree a large medieval-looking straw-thatched edifice, a cottage and yet more than a cottage. This building was now illuminated by the risen sun, to the rays of which its ancient masonry and its great

26

thatched roof responded with what seemed quite a special sort of congruity. The southern end of it had apparently suffered long ago from some disaster, and looked as if it were uninhabited; but the bulk of its massive stonework seemed nobly solid and secure, and there was a wisp of smoke ascending from one of its spacious chimneys.

The sight of this building gave No-man an indescribable thrill, a sensation which, as he left the window and returned to his bedroom to make sure he had put the "guard" in front of his fire, he could not precisely analyse. When, where, and how had he seen a building like that before, a half-ruined cottage that was so much more than a cottage? The strange glow of elation that the impression of it gave him remained with him as he descended the three flights of narrow stairs.

"I am glad," he thought, "that I can see that house from my window!" And the fatality that clings to these accidents of what we chance to see from some new day-and-night abiding-place fell upon him as he emerged into the street with a feeling that for a while distracted him from his thoughts of Mona. It was queer to come bolt up against the rush of traffic in this lively thoroughfare after giving himself up so entirely to the mysterious serenity of those water-meadows. The difference came to him in one of those swift mental shocks the full significance of which is so often obscure. It was as if he had been initiated at that small window into some level of life, older, deeper, less transitory and vulnerable, than the surface-appearance of ordinary reality. Glancing up and down the street with a view of taking the nearest turn southward, for he had already discovered in what direction the cemetery lay, he noticed a turn a few steps down the descending thoroughfare, the wall of which seemed literally covered with friendly instructions. Crossing the road and following the pavement down the hill, he soon reached this turn. Yes! The directions on the wall told him that this street led to the Palace Cinema and the Y.M.C.A.; and finally informed him that this narrow road itself, winding gradually southward, bore the name of Icen Way.

"God! I am in the right place!" muttered the history-obsessed Dud, as he contemplated these romantic syllables. "To think that a stone's throw from my own door I can enter the Icen Way!"

27

As he followed this turn, up a picturesque narrow street, he was faintly aware of a queer feeling that he was being treacherous to his substitute for Mona by thus setting out for the first time to visit the real Mona's grave.

He had discovered on the previous day how the town was surrounded on three sides by ancient avenues of trees—mostly chestnuts though a few other kinds are interspersed—and he found that the avenue down which, forsaking the Icen Way, he now hurried, was formed entirely of chestnuts and made, though their branches were bare, an interlacing roof, like that of a cathedral cloister, over his head.

Turning southward again at the foot of South Street No-man followed the Weymouth Road, which itself for at least a mile was another avenue of trees. He passed the Dorchester Brewery, with its immense chimney. He passed one of the town's two railway stations. He passed the County Constabulary. And a few seconds later found himself in sight of the low iron railways that separate this southern highway from the Roman Amphitheatre. Of this extraordinary legacy of the classic Empire Dud had already caught a glimpse on his first arrival. He had heard his mother's husband speak of it as "Maumbury Rings." Indeed, it had been one of the taciturn musician's favourite problems, on the occasions No-man could remember him in an expansive mood, to speculate whether the Durnovarian legionaries confined their sport to the slaughter of wild beasts, or whether certain among Cornelia Smith's Cymric ancestors—for Aaron was never weary of malicious gibes at his wife's Welsh origin—had reddened that turf-covered enclosure with their blood.

For some while before reaching Maumbury Rings, Dud had been aware of a considerable though somewhat desultory activity going on in a much-trodden expanse of ground on the right of the road he was following. The Amphitheatre, like the cemetery, was on the left of his road, as were the railway station, the brewery, and the Constabulary. Thus his attention, absorbed in a mental image of how the bones of his unravished bride would be lying, separated from him by the merest parcel of earth-mould and grass, was kept automatically turned *towards his left,* and he had only realized with the most vague consciousness that there was some sort of small travelling Circus even at this early morning hour open to the public, *on his right.*

28

He had been tapping the ground steadily with his great cudgel as he went along, and his awkward figure with its long arms, bony countenance, and close-cropped skull might have belonged to some necrophilistic Cerne Giant, intent on playing the werewolf in a civilized graveyard, rather than to an innocent antiquarian recluse.

But ever since he had passed the railway station Dud's abstracted senses *had* just been aware of certain lively sounds, gay strident gala strains and whirligig shrieks, combined with a confused babble, animate as well as inanimate, proceeding from a much-trodden open space, away there to his right, flanked by whitewashed pens for live-stock, and by wooden booths, and by counters for poultry, eggs, vegetables, and fruit. But this smallest of all possible Circuses was not at that early hour in full blast, and only a few stragglers and a sprinkling of young people on their way to school seemed at present aware of its existence. Several large stationary caravans, too, and a row of agricultural machines, apparently on show, made it difficult to observe from the road much that was going on.

When No-man did at last take in what was behind those caravans and agricultural implements his first characteristic feeling was a confused sense of the queer continuity of things. Here in front of him rose the grassy outlines—just as they had remained for nearly two thousand years—of the Roman Circus, where scattered legionaries from Gaul, from Spain, from Africa, from Asia, and a few perhaps from Italy itself, after due libations to Mithras, to Venus Anadyomene, to Diana, to the great goddess Isis, gathered to watch the butchery they loved, whereas now the most exotic excitement that these school-boys and school-girls hoped for, before their morning repetition of a prayer to the new "Saviour," was the sight of a Fat Woman or a Legless Dwarf, or a lady in spangled tights turning somersaults on a pony.

What had worked this change of heart in men "who eat bread upon the earth"? Just the shaking of the atomic dice by purposeless chance?

Dud sighed, swallowed his saliva, broke some thin cat-ice, that was already melting in the sun, with the end of his great stick, and hurried along by the iron rails.

It certainly looked a harmless spot to-day, that turf-ramparted enclosure, and yet such was the imagination he had inherited from "the Woman from Wales "that if he had been a Catholic he would have crossed himself as he shuffled past its high grassy bank.

He crossed a bridge over the railway now, and here he was at last at the gates of the cemetery! For a moment he was fearful lest these gates should not have been yet unlocked; but he found they were, though his hand shook as he lifted the latch, and he entered with something furtive and surreptitious in his manner, as if his errand had been a sacrilege.

He was surprised at the extent of the place. What a lot of people had been carried here since the burial of Aaron's grandparents! "Who would have thought death had undone so many?" Well, it was no use hunting for them; he must get hold of an official guide.

He had not far to seek; for one of the caretakers, an elderly man with drooping moustaches, was already burning weeds outside his ornamental lodge. By good hap the man had been at his job for twice the number of years Dud's dead had lain in their graves, and after a brief colloquy he threw down his rake, stamped on the smouldering heap he was tending, and led the visitor down a winding gravel path towards the southern end of the cemetery.

The further they went, the older and more time-worn seemed the monuments, though Dud noticed that there were a considerable number of these horizontal mounds with no headstone of any kind upon them. But he was gratified by the care that was evidently taken in Dorchester of the "green coats" of this invisible population and also by the number of yew-trees between which his guide led him.

"How black these yews are!" he thought, as he moved between them. "Dark green flames, with separate up-struggling fire-tips, but all one underneath!"

All at once he found he was trembling from head to foot. "This won't do," he said to himself. And then he thought: "How the devil am I to get rid of this fellow when—when I get to where they are?"

But the caretaker was one who understood the needs of the living as well as the needs of the dead. He suddenly stopped short: "Do 'ee see thik 'ooman, sir, down there," he said. " 'Tis she's young 'un her have got down there and a fine lad 'a were—I knowed 'un, to pass the time o' day, afore 'a fell sick. 'A used to come by here to school; and 'a used to ask I about they Circuses—I do mind he whenever I do hear 'un."

No-man allowed it to be realized that he did see the woman in question; but for his life at that moment he couldn't have uttered a coherent sound.

"Mr. Smith and Mrs. Smith be 'atween where thik 'ooman be and where thik wall be. Some likes to be nigh thik strong wall and some dunna'——— 'Tis our fancies, I reckon, living *or* dead. 'Tis a fancy-world, sir, look at 'un as us may. Thank'ee kindly, sir, though I weren't looking for't."

Touching his cap and pocketing the half-crown which the visitor held out to him the old gentleman turned his back and retraced his steps; nor did he so much as look round till he reached his heap of smouldering weeds.

No-man hurried forward. He had a sensation as if his legs might any moment grow numb and refuse to obey him. He felt as if his whole nature were suffering some overwhelming revolution. He passed, as he had been directed the woman in question, who did not even raise her eyes to see what kind of intruder he was, and there—under the wall—were the graves he sought! They each had a plain headstone, the girl's being the outer one; and a space *had* been left, wide enough for a fourth mound, between her and his mother.

It was upon this empty space that Dud, with his cap and stick clutched in the same hand, found himself staring. It was not, however, that he was visualizing his own resting-place. It was that between him and that fragment of level grass there hovered the familiar bed-post with its heraldic head, and leaning against this object there wavered dimly, as if about to vanish forever through the wide gates of Hades, the form of his unravished maid.

Without the least movement, just as if he had been himself turned in the Portland stone of the surrounding monuments, No-man watched the familiar vision fade slowly away. Not till it was quite gone did he step forward to the girl's actual mound. Here he stared downwards. There she was, the bride of his last ten obsessed years! *And what was she like now*? He had one quick hideous vision of the unthinkable possibility. He saw her bones. He saw horrible blotches of decomposed flesh and wrinkled skin

31

upon those bones. He saw her long hair still clinging to her skull. But this was only for a second—savagely he flung the image away and turned to the girl's headstone.

This was marked by a small block of the same grey stone as the others, and he set himself to read the inscription. MONA SMITH he read—so they had disregarded his request to put "Mona No-man"—THE WIFE OF D. N.—they had at least humoured him there!—WHO GAVE HER LIFE NURSING THE ABOVE AARON AND CORNELIA SMITH.

And down at the bottom, in type so small that some of it had already grown obscure, were the words :

GREATER LOVE HATH NO MAN THAN THIS.

Dud glanced at the mound next to his girl's as if to make a fatuous inquiry of "the Woman from Wales," whether it was true that Mona had given her life for her.

"What else could she have done but what she did?" he asked his mother. But of course gravestones always lied. "Greater," he read again. And then it struck him for the first time—and he thought afterwards how queer it was that he hadn't noted it at once—that this scriptural anonymity it talked about was himself : "Hath No-man than this." So what the Eternal really announced was that there was some rare mysterious species of love "greater" than "giving up your life." And that this "greater" love, whatever kind of thing it was, was the prerogative of poor Dud!

And *this*, in the equivocal way she did everything, Mona, under this turf, had waited for ten years to tell him! "Damn it, though!" he thought, "it's not you, Mona No-man; it's your relations who've put this quotation here!" And once more Dud turned upon "the Woman from Wales" a look of almost imbecile bewilderment.

"Did she give up her life for you, *did* she, or was it that the four of us just caught the plague and went down like ninepins?"

Cornelia Smith made no reply to this question, but No-man's thoughts had suddenly rushed off at a tangent. "Why are there *two* graves for you and Aaron?" And then a startling idea came into his head. "Did you arrange your life with Aaron on different lines than anyone guessed? Was Aaron complaisant all the time about—about *him?* Oh mother, why didn't you confide in me just a bit more?"

He stared down at a small cluster of freshly-budded snow-drops that were coming up in that empty space between the two women's graves. "Perhaps," he thought, "they didn't leave this space for me at all, but for *him*! Perhaps he's an old man now and has made all his plans, and one day I'll come here and find him buried by her side!"

He looked hurriedly across Mona's mound to see if there was a place for him on the other side. No! There was a newly filled-in grave there, with an elaborate headstone in honour of some aged lady, "the daughter," it said, "of Alderman Carroway, to whom this town owed etc., etc."

Dud's gaze came back to the snowdrops. "I'd like to find out," he thought, "who he was or who he is! It can't be often that a person—I wonder if he knows of my existence?"

Once more he forced himself—he thought of it afterwards as a significant thing that he had to *make* himself do it—to read over again every word on his girl's headstone: "Greater love hath no man"—but at that point the devil in him, or it may have been the nervous agitation of the last three or four hours, burst forth strangely enough, and he gave vent to a loud, jarring, unpleasant howl, a sound like that of a person making a forced imitation of a howling dog.

Thinking of this later, he came to the conclusion that if he hadn't uttered this malicious sound he'd have done something more hysterical still—danced a real *danse macabre* perhaps over his girl's grave! But its sacrilege shocked his own ears, and for the first time since he'd come to the spot he glanced hastily at "thik 'ooman," his fellow mourner of this sunshiny day.

Yes, the woman *had* heard him, and the moment their eyes met she moved straight towards him.

"Don't do that," she cried earnestly, hurrying up to him. "It's terrible to lose everything, but we mustn't let——" her sentence hung unfinished, for Dud had taken off his cap with an exaggerated bow of malicious deference, and she could see from his quivering lip that his whole nature was drawn out like a piece of elastic.

"I beg you pardon, sir—of course I have no right——" Her face, as she spoke and as she quietly turned down her eyes and fumbled at a faded wreath she was carrying, had a queer effect upon No-man. It must have been her face, for the little soft

33

brown hat she wore was so brimless that he could see her forehead for inches above her spectacles whereas the rest of her person was concealed by a long, faded, tweed coat, which left nothing exposed to impress an observer except a pair of athletic ankles in grey woollen stockings and a pair of sturdy brown-leather boots.

"I beg *your* pardon," he murmured apologetically. "I was bothered, you know, by what——"

Dud's countenance became quite gentle and relaxed as he looked at her. He even smiled as he used the word "bothered," for this word seemed to protect his pride, to push away his trouble, and to make a querulous little appeal for sympathy.

The woman raised her left hand, for her right was still clutching the wreath, and made a motion as if she were trying to pull down her brimless hat over her forehead.

"It's my only child I come here for," she murmured, disregarding the airy flippancy of his word "bothered." But when she had spoken she bit her underlip with annoyance at herself. "I lost him last June. He was as healthy as could be till he got wet one day at Upwey."

No-man gave his own dead a casual nod, glancing furtively sideways at the three little upright stones at their feet, then proceeded deliberately and carefully to put on his cap.

"Are you going straight out?" he said.

The woman made no reply, but she scrutinized him from head to foot with a friendly interest as they moved away together.

"Don't you find that stick heavy?" she asked.

"My wrists are very strong," he replied.

"Do you live in Dorchester?" she asked.

"Three flights up," he answered laconically, "over a shop."

"I don't think I've seen you on the streets, have I?" she said; but Dud was silent. He liked this woman, but some obscure force within him kept saying, "Let her go! Let her go!"

But this irrational warning didn't prevent his stealing several hurried glances at her face. He liked those features under the brown hat better and better each time he looked at them. "She's about my own age," he thought, "or a *little* less. What I like in her face is its endurance. It's a patient, gentle face, but very enduring. It's a sweet face but a rather dilapidated face."

34

They were walking together in silence when they came to the caretaker's heap of weeds. The man was visible a little distance off gathering up rubbish. Dud called to him. The woman murmured something, drew away with an inclination of her head and made as if to seek the cemetery gate.

"Can't we," he whispered hurriedly, "walk back together? I've only got to ask him one little question!"

The woman discreetly moved away while he asked this "little question," but Dud did not even wonder how it would have struck her had she heard what he said.

"I notice," he began bluntly, seizing the bull by the horns, "that there's an empty space between my mother's grave and my wife's. Do you happen to know if any steps have been taken to retain that space for me?"

The elderly man with the drooping moustache gave him a sudden startled look, a look that made No-man feel as if he suspected him of intending to rush upon death in some way that interfered with the established order.

"You must go to 'They' about *that*, sir," he remarked gravely. Dud's mouth opened; and so tense were his nerves that he felt on the point of repeating that sardonic sound—like a man imitating a howling dog—that had burst from him before. In his effort to control himself he glanced away from his astonished interlocutor to the figure of "thik 'ooman," who was still standing by the cemetery gate.

The sight of her enduring yet ravaged face under the brown hat had once more a calming effect upon him.

"All right," he muttered. "I expect I'd better do as you say." But as he left the man—and he always remembered the peculiar sourness of the thin smoke that came from that heap of cemetery rubbish—he felt an unsurpassable barrier of distaste for the whole subject.

"What the hell does it matter *where* they bury me?" he thought. "And what does it matter *whose* son I am?"

He had indeed an obscure sensation, as he hurried to join the woman, as if to go a single step further on this graveyard quest would really be a kind of suicide.

"Damn this whole business!" he thought. "What does it matter?"

"I'll write my books and I'll live in the present! No-man is my name and my business is No-man's business. My girl is my girl, and my mother is my mother. To hell with these graves!"

He felt when he joined the woman and looked in her face as if he had scrambled out of the earth and carried the smell of it in his nostrils.

When they were on the path by the side of the road she spoke gently to him as if she knew what he was feeling.

"I couldn't bring myself to go to my son," she said in a low voice. "But it was wrong of me. It sets them free when you go to them. We oughtn't to hold them back."

Dud's countenance must have expressed his inability, in his agitated state, to catch her meaning; for she went on in a firmer tone. "He was with me too much at first," she explained. "It was like madness. I lived with him closer than when I really had him. But it came over me that I was doing him a hurt; and something made me go to him *there*—to set him free. I've——"

And the woman gave a sigh the like of which Dud thought he had never heard from any mother or any wife.

"We've got to live. Don't you feel like that?"

But No-man had been deeply disturbed by what he heard. "But doesn't our thinking of them so much, so long," he protested, "*help* them—wherever they are?"

The woman shook her head. "It's of them we must think," she said firmly, "not of ourselves. We ought to set them free." And then she added, in a voice so low that he could hardly catch her words, "Life is for the living. Death, whatever it is, is for the dead."

They crossed the railway bridge and were soon level with the Amphitheatre. No-man looked at its emphatic outlines with gloomy attention.

"It's queer," he said to his companion, "that a thing made for cruelty should last so long."

The head in the brown hat turned towards the steep bank beyond the railings. "Those are daisies, aren't they?" she said. "There! Near the top. It's all this rain and warm weather."

It was No-man's turn to sigh now. "But I suppose," he went on, "if the race of men was gone, and one spirit pointed out to another spirit our whole planet, it might say the same! The only comfort is that pain can't last forever. Thank the Lord there *is* death to end it." But it clearly was not easy for the woman at his side to take these spacious flights.

"You won't think me rude," she said, after a concentrated silence of a second or two, "if I ask your name?"

"D. No-man," he replied hastily. "Stop! I'll put it down for you and my address, too. I'm a writer. I've taken a room here so that I can get the quiet for my work. I don't know a soul in Dorchester.

"*My* name is Nancy Quirm," said the woman. "I live on the other side of the town, about a mile out. I hope you'll come and see me one day. You'll be interested in my husband and in Teucer Wye. For the matter of that, you'll probably be more interested in Thuella than in any of us."

It was a peculiarity of Dud's—and one he had had from his childhood—to be forced to stand still, when he was out-of-doors, if he was to take in any important remark. He now stood still opposite the trim, well-manured garden of the Dorset Constabulary.

"Say your name again, lady, will you?" he remarked, speaking in an unnecessarily loud voice. This was another peculiarity of his to address people as if they were deaf the moment he felt embarrassed.

"Quirm, Nancy Quirm. My husband is a reader. In fact he probably has got your books somewhere about. Our place is nothing but books."

"I'll write down my address," said Dud, fumbling in his pocket for pencil and paper. He felt that Mrs. Quirm was watching him with amused sympathy; and this increased his impatience. Finally he did not hesitate to deposit the whole contents of his pockets on the top of the Constabulary's thickly-grown, evergreen hedge. But no pencil was forthcoming. "It's in High East Street—you'll have to learn it by heart." He twisted his head round and frowned at her in vexation. But suddenly, as he began returning the things from the top of the hedge into his pocket: "Did you say 'Quirm' or 'Squirm'?" he asked.

The woman smiled. "It will certainly be Thuella who'll interest you. She does things just as you do; things like emptying your pockets."

Dud turned towards her such a blank and bewildered countenance that she had to explain. "The Wyes live next door to us, in fact, under the same roof," she said, "and Thuella is Mr. Wye's daughter. He has a son and a daughter-in-law, but *he* only comes on visits, and another daughter who lives in the town. Mr. Wye doesn't like history, and he hates fiction. He never reads anything but Plato. We've found that it's useless to lend him books, for they stay exactly where he first puts them down when you take them to him. I took him a novel once, and he leaned it against the side of his clock. A fortnight later it was still there. Mr. Wye said it shook when the clock struck."

"Is it in the country you live?"

"A mile out of Dorchester. It's half-way to Stinsford; but of course you don't know where *that* is. But anyone will tell you, and I know you'll like Thuella. You'd better say you want to go to Mr. Wye's. You'll have no difficulty! Yes, I'll remember yours quite easily. But come soon; come any of these days. Some of us will be sure to be in. Thuella will be thrilled to meet you."

A sly and almost malicious expression crossed No-man's face. "Well! I expect you're in a hurry to get home, Mrs. Quirm, and I mustn't keep you." With this he turned again to the Constabulary hedge. A letter, or some piece of paper out of his pocket, had slipped down between the evergreen leaves.

"Let *me* get it out," said Nancy Quirm, stepping forward. Her gloved hand proved more efficacious than his bare one; but No-man felt irritated rather than grateful.

As they moved on together he kept glancing, not altogether sympathetically, at her profile. "She's one of those maternal women," he said to himself, "whose sympathy for me is a kind of——" But he checked himself in the middle of this thought. Something within him, far deeper than his spleen, responded to the character of this stranger, and he had the wit to recognize it. "She isn't good-looking," he thought. "She's very pale, and her face is very lined, and I hate to see them with spectacles. But I like her and I think she likes me."

Once more she began referring to Thuella, as they walked on, and how nice it would be for Mr. No-man to meet her; but he heard all this as one who heard it not. His nerves, however, were growing much calmer as he walked by Mrs. Quirm's side. He liked her face, as he kept glancing at it, more and more.

And yet she had no dominant feature. Her nose, her mouth,

her brow, were none of them, what might be called "distinguished." Nor was it exactly a strong face. It was pale and her eyes under her spectacles looked blurred and dim though they were of a soft and friendly grey. Her face had lines of tragic suffering, but No-man came to the conclusion that what suffering it showed—and he could not forget how it had looked when she spoke of her son—had been, and *was*, under the control of an extraordinarily gallant spirit. Her mouth and chin were not in the least masterful. They were morbidly sensitive, he thought. But her whole countenance possessed a poise, a dignity, a curious kind of grace, that he found very charming.

Once or twice indeed—as for instance while she had teased him about resembling this damned Thuella, when he had emptied his pockets on the Policemen's hedge—he had detected in her look something girlish and roguish, something challenging, something almost flirtatious, which strangely enough did not displease him as he recalled it now, though at the moment, perhaps because he was irritated by his own clumsiness, it had struck him as "maternal" rather than provocative. But when she began talking again about this confounded Thuella—what a name for a woman, and how he disliked the thought of her!—he decided that it wasn't "maternal" at all, but something quite different, something that was extraordinarily sweet and appealing, and yet light as the touch of a butterfly's wing; and something too that appealed to a vein of personal response in him that had not been reached for years, not for ten years!

In spite of these feelings, and yet perhaps because of them, there was a tone of sly malice in his speech when he suddenly interrupted her: "I don't believe you yourself like this Thuella at all. I believe you *hate* her!"

Nancy Quirm's sensitive mouth opened in astonishment. Her grey eyes seemed to blink, as if he had actually hit her, under her spectacles.

"Oh!" she gasped. "What *have* I said to make you think that?"

No-man looked her up and down. He had already noticed with approval how slight and girlish her body seemed under her rough coat.

But this gasp of surprise made her slighter and more girlish still. "She has very slim haunches, I'm sure," he thought shamelessly, "and quite slender hips, too!"

39

He had no time to reply to her startled question however; for a loud discordant shriek of some whirligig-engine behind the caravans on the other side of the road made them both look round.

"Let's go in there for a second! Shall we?" the woman said. The last thing that Dud wanted to do was to investigate the activities of this intrusive Circus. He had secretly been promising himself to offer his new acquaintance a cup of "something hot" in one of the South Street confectioners. However, he had come to like this woman so well—and, after all, this was the first time in his life he had made friends with anyone in this unconventional way—that he felt ready to obey any caprice she might have.

"Come on then," he said, submissively though not very eagerly, "there's nothing to pay, to go and look!"

Nancy Quirm's smile, when she heard this somewhat unchivalrous remark, was a flicker of that same charming challenge "more flirtatious than maternal." Inspired by that smile he felt more adventurous and, boldly taking her arm, led her across the road.

There were more people about now than there had been a couple of hours ago, and Dud soon began to be amused at the oddity of the occasion. He certainly had never foreseen, when he passed this place on his way to the cemetery, that he would be entering it in so short a time in company with a strange woman! They were soon watching the "roundabout" whose engine had made such a demoniac shriek, and though there were only three diminutive little girls on the backs of extremely dilapidated wooden horses, the sound of the lively music and the gay up-and-down giddy revolutions gave them both the familiar revival of long-forgotten childish emotions.

Dud fancied he saw in the animation of the face under the brown hat that his companion was on the point of suggesting that they should join those three small riders! To avoid having to refuse such a wild whim, he hurriedly proposed that they should visit the chief place of entertainment. This was a not very large and anything but new tent; but there seemed to be something of interest going on inside. To this they accordingly advanced, and the magnanimous Dud was already surreptitiously trying to calculate—with the tips of his fingers in the leather purse in his pocket—the limits of his financial resources,

40

when they became aware by the sound of raised voices of some sort of altercation going on at the back of the tent.

Drawn by a mutual impulse they proceeded to the spot whence these sounds came and found an old man and an old woman—both of them obviously connected with the show—trying in vain to persuade a young girl, in absurdly grotesque stage attire, to enter an aperture in the discoloured awning, through which was visible the lower rungs of a small step-ladder. The upper portion of the girl's body glittered with tinsel chains of the most preposterous sham jewelry, while her lower limbs were clothed in very dirty lavender-coloured tights.

The old woman, evidently in a state of malignant helplessness not unmixed with alarm, for she kept glancing furtively round in dread of intrusion from the public, was listening to a torrent of wild abuse addressed to her from the excited girl.

The old man, whose bald head was topped by a red wig and whose crooked person was tightly covered by a long, greasy, greenish-black tail coat, kept making feeble conciliatory clutches at the girl's brocaded sash, which looked, in its gaudy disreputableness, as if it had once adorned the body of a performing dog.

"I tell you this is the end!" the girl was crying in a voice at once husky and shrill. "Don't you understand English? I say it's the end—the end—the end! It's one thing for me to do it when there are decent people in there, and I've told you I'd do it for them. Do you think I care what I do? But to this handful of grinning kids who don't know anything, who don't know me from a monkey, I won't, I won't, I won't! You're a money-licking old bitch, that's what *you* are, and I don't care who hears me say it! I'm done with you, do you hear? I've done with you! A set of damned grinning kids—and me acting like a monkey, a monkey, a monkey!"

Her voice rose to such a pitch at this point that the old woman, scowling savagely at the old man, as if he were responsible for this scene, rushed herself into the aperture and let the awning fall behind her.

The old showman now became aware that a "gentleman" in a shabby coat holding a formidable-looking stick and accompanied by a tall white-faced lady was standing not far off watching them intently, and he promptly made a sort of caressing gesture to the girl in tinsel, stroking the piece of dirty plush she wore round her hips and whispering in her ear.

"*Damn* you!" cried the young woman, repulsing him with such a violent push that he nearly toppled over. "Damn you all! I tell you I've had enough of it!" With this she rushed off towards the row of caravans that separated them from the road and scrambling up the steps of the nearest of these disappeared from view.

Simultaneously with the girl's departure, the old woman, who looked like a bathing-machine attendant now that her weather-beaten countenance was no longer distorted with anger and fear, emerged from the aperture in the awning and stared about her with blinking uneasiness.

"She's a gone, Mother," said the man in the wig. "No need to diddle wi' *she* till dinnertime. Be young Popsy in there, hearting of 'em up?"

But the old woman had caught sight of "the lady and gentle-man" and walking straight up to them began a voluble explanation of all that they would enjoy if they would only pay for the special and peculiar privilege of a front seat in the tent. "A bob apiece, dearies, only a bob apiece," she chanted to them earnestly, "and ye'll see what no Christian eye have seen, since the Romans was drove from Darset."

Nancy Quirm, taking no notice of this professional chatter, began questioning her at once as to what she had done "to make that poor girl so angry," and No-man took the opportunity, when the old woman launched into an unending rigmarole of grievances in the course of which the name "Popsy" attended with lavish praise and the name "Wizzie" attended by compli-cated blame kept entering and vanishing in confused succession, to walk towards the caravan steps up which the angry girl had fled. Seeing the ominous direction "the gentleman" was taking, the bald-headed showman hurried after him and caught him up just as he appeared to be actually meditating an ascent of these steps.

"All right," muttered No-man gruffly, when the red wig and greasy tail coat appeared at his side : "All right, I'm no relation of that girl. I've never seen her before. But she's somebody's girl, isn't she? I take it she's nothing to do with you or with your wife either? She's a hired performer, I take it. One of your dancing-girls, eh? Perhaps your only one! Yes, I can see that's it. She's your only one. And you and your wife, I suppose she *is* your wife," and Dud nodded his head towards the old woman, "are working her too hard. No, I'm not a relation of hers : and I've not—not to-day anyway—any authority to interfere with you. It's only that—well! I saw how upset she was and I thought I might, I mean I thought I'd *like*, just to see—you know what I mean—just to see she was all right again. I'm not a doctor, of course, and I'm not a clergyman; but when—you know what I mean—when a person sees anyone so upset as that girl was, he can't help——" Dud broke off suddenly, for he perceived that instead of looking displeased at what he was saying the wizened countenance under the red wig brightened, and to Dud's dismay he saw with perfect distinctness a small grey louse making its way gingerly and tentatively along the thin line of demarcation between the wig and the skull. "Well, at any rate," he flung out again, and as he spoke he deliberately sat down on the bottom step of the caravan and took out a packet of cigarettes, "at any rate she's *somebody's* girl, even if you and your wife don't give a damn what happens to her!"

Uttering this vague truism as if it had been a drastic ultimatum, No-man lit a cigarette, and perceiving that Mrs. Quirm was still engaged in conversation with the man's wife, he offered him one too, deliberately taking care, as he did so, not to puff his smoke near the louse on the fellow's cranium.

The old man accepted the cigarette and Dud noticed a most curious expression come into his face. His small gimlet-like eyes gleamed with an unholy light. A *mental* louse had evidently been engendered inside that unattractive skull, the glowworm glitter of which was like the passing of a taper across prison-bars. "Us be sick to death of she in there," the old rogue whispered suddenly. "Our new gal be worth five of she—— Her in there were a horphan, *her* were, what me and the missus took for charity whereas 'tother one be coom of old Darset stock. I tell 'ee, sir, and may me liver be thunderbit if I'm lying, it were a Christian charity in any well-wishing gentleman who'd take she." He glanced over his shoulder at the caravan door and twisted his mouth in a most unpleasant leer. "Gentlemen *have* ere now, let me tell you, spoken to we of taking this crazy bitch off of us. Her be young, look 'ee, and her be of a 'lurin' figure

43

spite of her tempers. There were an old gent in Bristol, where me missus comes from, that would have given she I don't-know-what if she'd a let 'un. 'Twas her tempers and such-like frightened the poor man away or maybe he'd have 'dopted she or made she his lawful. He told me missus—and a man could see it with one eye—that he was main gone on the bitch. 'Twas her figure I reckon, for her face ain't nothink—some likes 'em for one thing and some for another; and this old gent was struck crazy, I shouldn't wonder, by what he'd a' seed of her figure. You've a-said, sir, in me hearing, sir, that she in there were some man's gal! but I tell 'ee, sir, with her tempers and carryings-on and her 'I will' and 'I won'ts,' she be no man's girl and never will be nothink else. 'Tis to Wokkus, 'tis to nothink but Wokkus thik bitch belongs. I tell 'ee, sir, if it hadn't been for her figure and for our old hoss being so daft over she, we'd 'ave popped her into Wokkus years agone. Missus and me have no sponsoring for she, ye must understand—no sponsoring for she at all. Us picked she up for charity and us have picked up a wiper! That's what that bitch be, for all her airs and her 'lurin' figure. Her be an ongrateful wiper! I tell 'ee, sir, if some gent what likes 'em with a 'lurin' figure, and knows how to 'andle 'em, and not to 'ave no bloody nonsense from 'em were to say to missus and me to-day: 'Mr. and Mrs. Hurgan, you've a-done godsends for this here chit and in return her've treated 'ee cruel. But seeing as her *has* got a 'lurin' figure—with or without they pretty jingles what you've been put to expense of perwiding, though there weren't no sponsoring for it—I be minded to take she off of 'ee, and do it legally too; legally, lawfully, and all according.' I tell 'ee, sir, I should say to 'un: 'Take she, quick, take she to Mother Carey's Home for Horfinch! Us don't want to see her, *nor* her bloody figure—never no more!'"

The old man now noticed that his wife, standing beside Mrs. Quirm who was apparently examining the contents of her purse, had begun making him private signals to join them. "Excuse me, sir, I'll be back in a jiffy!" cried the fellow, jumping up; and off he went, walking with a hop-and-go one-step in his tight shiny tail coat, till he reached the two women.

No sooner was the man out of hearing than, moved by a sudden overpowering impulse, Dud ran up the steps of the caravan, gave the door one sharp, loud knock, and boldly flung it open. The place was so full of steam from a great pot boiling on the stove that it took him a second to get his bearings and see anything clearly; but there she was.

There was the " 'lurin' " figure. She sat crouching on the bed with her heels under her flanks and her staring brown eyes so wide open that to Dud they looked as round and as big as two shining pennies. She had torn off her bangles and chains. She had flung away the unpleasant plush thing she'd been wearing round her hips, and it was impossible for Dud not to be struck by the curves of her body in that crouching position.

Her face, however, was what really hit him to the heart, though he must have noticed *everything* about her, more than he realized at the time, for he recalled afterwards that her lavender tights had a stain on one of the knees, a stain like the skin of an orange when it is peeled off and takes the shape of the figure 8. But her face went clear through him. It went through him like the reflection of a face in a mirror that suddenly appears to a particular person after a long miraculous retention in the chemical substance of the glass.

It went through him as some drowned face through fathoms of water. She certainly was not in the remotest degree pretty. Daddy Urgan had been perfectly right there. And yet he had been right too—oh, so fatally right!—about the sensual attraction of her figure.

Of course her body was not perfect, any more than her face! It was not—and Dud found himself comparing his wife's limbs to those he now saw before him, in this dirty finery—in any sense what you could call a classical body, which is certainly what Mona's *was*.

It is a deep and magical mystery, reverting to the fragilities and slendernesses of flower-petals as well as to the love-candles of glow-worms, the secret of these indescribable touches that have been bestowed by the artistry of Nature on the limbs of some girls, and not of others.

As men go, Dud was the reverse of amorous. He was indeed morbidly fastidious. But when he saw this queer, wild creature crouching there in her fantastic attire, he felt, mingled with his outraged pity, and in part *compounded of pity*, a shivering awareness of something more troubling to his senses than he had ever felt before.

45

What ravished him so in this girl's figure, what pierced his heart in this girl's desperate face, was nothing less than that troubling thing that he had added *out of his own perversity* to the personality of his dead wife.

It was not that he had time then to feel more than the overpowering beat of fate's terrible wings. It was only later that he realized the nature of his feelings. Something in his obscurist being was roused and stirred as he saw the girl crouching there; but the pity he felt for her so completely dominated his conscious mind that it was as if he had to wait till he was alone, to puzzle out the cryptic response of his subterranean senses, a response in which they indulged independently, like famished demons.

Thinking of her afterwards he found that that blurred stain below her knee, that stain which resembled a bungled outline of the figure 8, was the particular thing that brought back with a fearful rush the subtle thrill that his senses felt even while his conscious mind was so preoccupied.

But it was of her face—only of her face—that he thought at the moment, and the expression upon it melted the bones within him. What a desperate face it was! As he saw it now in that dim place, with the thin strawlike hair falling straight down—and there seemed so little of it—falling each side of her hollow cheeks, he was struck by its pinched sharpness. Every feature of it seemed in that half-light so contracted and long and pointed! Her nose was thin. Her chin was thin. Only her eyes, looking larger than they really were, seemed so desperately dark and round!

For quite a perceptible moment Dud stared at her with stupid embarrassment and she stared back at him from beneath the wooden wall behind her, with terrified bewilderment. Then her eyes grew less preternaturally round. Something, swift as a breath, passed between them, and like a released bowstring her tense muscles relaxed. She sank back a little against the wall. Her thin fingers unclasped themselves from between her knees and fell loose at her side, the bare arms above them looking childish and piteously grotesque.

Suddenly she leaned forward listening intently. Then her young breast heaved with a deep-drawn sigh and she lowered her eyes and frowned. She was evidently thinking rapidly, thinking intensely, desperately.

46

At last she raised her head, looked straight into his face, and quick and fast, her voice sounding as husky as a thin gust of wind through a patch of stubble, began speaking to him.

"I was listening to Old Funky. I heard all he said to you about that man in Bristol and their wanting to get rid of me. It's all lies! They don't want me to go. They want to keep me till I'm dead. Everything he said was lies—except about the horse. I don't know who you are and I don't care. I like you! You're good. I can *see* you're good. And you're the first one. Listen! we're going to Yeovil to-morrow. We're going to the fairground there. But I'll go to the post-office, and ask for a letter. If there's not a letter I'll run away. If there is a letter *I'll run wherever the letter says*! They always have tea at six and I can run away then. I heard what Old Funky said to you—every word—about 'legal' and 'lawful' and all that. But I don't care about 'legal,' and 'lawful'. If you haven't a woman I'll be your woman. I'm a grown-up girl. I'm not a child. You heard Old Funky say what a good figure I have. I'm not mad either, though they think I'm mad. I can be your woman as well as another, for I know what men want and I won't say a word. *Yeovil*, mind! And I'll go to the post-office and I'll run wherever the letter says. No one shall stop me! If there's no letter I'll disappear; but there *will* be a letter, there *will*, there *will* be a letter!"

The tone in which she uttered this final appeal gave Dud a particular kind of twinge, a twinge that he had not had since a garrulous nurse told him Mona had died calling for him to come and thinking he was afraid to come.

But now they both stopped and stared at each other. There were voices outside. The girl jumped to her feet with the leap of a wild animal, and her eyes grew round again.

But Dud's good angel gave him an inspiration. "For Christ's sake," he whispered, while they heard someone coming hastily up the steps, "*tell me your name*!"

Her eyes twitched and a scowl of anger distorted her face. For a moment he thought she was too angry to answer. But she did get the words out. "Wizzie Ravelston," she murmured as if she were tearing the syllables out of her bosom and handing them to a bandit. Then she turned away and with the cunning of a wild animal flung herself down on the bed. Here they found

47

her; lying with her face to the wall, when the old man and the old woman entered together.

"It's no good, I can't get this girl to utter a word," pronounced Dud, in a stern authoritative voice, as if he were at least a Royal Commissioner. "So I am afraid I shall not be able to make a complaint *this time*—to the proper authorities. But I can assure you that if you don't treat this poor girl———" He stopped and turning his back on them, contemplated for a second the form on the bed.

"Good-bye, Wizzie," he swore to himself, "and if I don't meet you in Yeovil may I die howling!"

He moved to the caravan door, turning a deaf ear to both the violent protests of Mrs. Urgan and the obsequious innuendoes of Old Funky. With his foot on the first step, and emboldened not only by the reassuring sight of Nancy Quirm in her brown hat, but by the reckless and cynical strains of an American tune that just then floated across the market from the fair-ground, he turned round again upon them.

"Your name, I take it, is Mr. and Mrs. Urgan? That's what I thought; only I wanted to be quite certain in case we ever needed—for any reason—to communicate with each other."

"Yes," cried the woman, breathless to get the last word, and she pushed past Old Funky who was winking and leering as if the authoritative tone taken by the visitor was a pure pretence for the benefit of the lady outside, and to cover the little masculine understanding which they had established between them.

"Yes," the old woman cried. "Yes! We'll send for you when we want you!"

With this retort ringing in his ears Dud rejoined his new friend. He could see she was anything but deceived by the offhand and laconic manner with which he now proceeded to dismiss the whole subject, hinting that he *might*, if he felt uneasy about it, after a night's sleep visit the Circus again.

"I'm afraid you won't be able to do that," she said. "It appears they don't own the Circus; and the woman is more anxious to get rid of her than her husband, though he pretends to want to get rid of her; but he taught her her job. She says they're off to Salisbury to-morrow."

For the flicker of a second Dud felt he could have seized Nancy Quirm and shaken her, until the teeth chattered in her smiling face—— But *Salisbury*? Oh, damn them! What was he to do now? His present companion must have been used to being queerly treated by erratic persons, for she went on "carrying it off" without asking him any questions. She apparently accepted his laconic waiving of the whole episode, only remarking on her own account that from what she'd seen of the Urgan pair she preferred the old woman to the old man.

When they reached the bottom of South Street where the South Walks begin, he felt that he couldn't, in the turmoil of his mind, endure to go a step further with Mrs. Quirm. "I *must* be alone," he thought. "I *must* get rid of this person, so as to think it out!"

But as chance would have it the poor lady now began showing signs of physical distress.

"I am sorry," she murmured. "It's silly of me. But I've—I've done more than I should to-day and—I feel—I feel I *must* sit down—just for a minute, if you don't mind!"

No-man cursed her to himself bitterly and unkindly. He glared round him distractedly. They were now standing by the side of a War Cenotaph, and the woman was leaning helplessly against the rails.

He could see a stone slab under one of the chestnut-trees where there evidently had been a seat, but they had taken it away for the winter. What the devil was he to do with her? He couldn't leave her leaning against iron rails. Was it his destiny to take her somewhere, or fetch a doctor? He looked blankly at her. She had the appearance of a person who might at any second sink down on the ground. He stared angrily at a handsome wreath that some one had placed at the foot of the cenotaph. He visualized Mrs. Quirm prostrate on the round with her head against this wreath. He felt a curious hostility even to her brown hat. Why had she come all this way if she wasn't fit for walking?

He moved towards her and made a clumsy gesture as if to substitute himself, as a support, for the iron railings; but she feebly pushed him off.

"I'll be—I'll be better in a minute," she whispered. "It's really nothing—if I could—if I could—only—sit down."

In his effort to help her his fantastic oak cudgel fell down at her feet and as he stooped to pick it up he noticed that one of her shoestrings was hanging loose. For some reason this made him more angry still. "She didn't even trouble to dress herself properly," he thought, "before setting out. She's a hysterical fool!" Her hat too had begun to tilt sideways in a ridiculous was and he now began indulging in the ignoble thought that the people passing by might suppose she was drunk.

But making a great effort Nancy Quirm straightened herself up and lifting one of her hands adjusted her hat.

"There's a bakery—just there," she murmured looking vaguely towards the street. "Perhaps—you could—take me there—and then—I won't—I won't trouble you any more."

He took her at her word, and with her hand clutching his arm they moved slowly into South Street. Here to No-man's immense relief they did soon find themselves at a place where refreshments were sold, and where there were little tables and seats.

At one of these tables they now sat down and Dud got her some milk and a biscuit. Here, as she drank the milk, she showed symptoms of recovery. Her eyes behind her spectacles began to have more "speculation" in them and ere long she actually smiled at him.

"I'm quite all right now, Mr. No-man," she remarked in her ordinary voice. "I'm *so* sorry to have been such a bother. You must wish you'd never spoken to me! And it was I, too, who made you go into that Circus-field. I've brought you nothing but bad luck this morning. I'm almost afraid to beg you to come and see us. You'll think of me as a person of ill omen. But please go now! I'll rest here for a time before I start back. I beg you, don't let me waste any more of your morning. My husband will be shocked when he hears I've taken up so much of your time."

With the recovery of her equanimity, however, Nancy Quirm's original effect upon him came back. "She really is nice," he thought. "For a very little," he thought, "I'd tell her about Wizzie Ravelston."

There was a mirror near where they were sitting; and as he was wondering whether he dared take her at her word and just leave her here, for he had already begun to compose *two* letters to Wizzie, one to Yeovil and another to Salisbury, he gazed at the reflected image of their figures sitting there side by side.

"What kind of a person did I seem to Wizzie?" he thought, as he surveyed his dark, closely-cropped skull, his hooked nose, his weak chin, his protruding upper lip. "How old are you?" he began to wonder as he gazed at the image of his companion, but the next second Mrs. Quirm's pale lineaments in the mirror became merely the plastic material wherewith his senses repictured that girl's expression as he heard her say: "I'll be your woman. I'll make your bed."

He turned to his companion: "If you promise not to move till I come back," he announced suddenly, and then rose so abruptly as nearly to upset the little wicker table with its blue cloth, "I'll just do a couple of errands. But I won't be more than a few minutes; and if I don't find you here when I return I'll be so angry that I'll never meet your precious Thuella!"

"I'll be here!" declared Mrs. Quirm emphatically.

"Do you promise?" he reiterated; for oddly enough he now felt protected in some way in her company, while outside, beyond her protection, were the dirty lavender tights of that " 'lurin' figure," a hubbub of Circus-fields, and all Yeovil and Salisbury mixed together in one terrifying crowd of unknown streets.

"I hope you *will* be all right," he called back to her from the door. His tone had unmistakable concern in it, but though Nancy Quirm may not have been subtle enough to detect all the nuances of his childlike appeal to her, he felt something that was not just simple gratitude in the smile she gave him.

Hurrying up South Street he rushed into the post-office and buying a couple of letter-cards, each with its comforting rim of good, secretive, conspiring glue, he took possession of a partition at the desk for telegrams and wrote two communications. The first of these was addressed to the Yeovil post-office and ran thus: "Dear Wizzie, meet me at the entrance to the big parish church, or just *inside,* between six and seven to-morrow Thursday; and if we miss I will be there again on Saturday; and I will call for a letter too. My name is D. No-man. Tell me in your letter where and when to meet you if we miss. Your friend, D. N. P.S. I live at — High East Street, Dorchester."

And the second was addressed to the Salisbury post-office and ran as follows: "Dear Wizzie, meet me at the entrance to the cathedral between six and seven on Friday. I will be there again on Sunday and I will call for a letter too. My name is D. No-man. The woman said 'Salisbury,' so I chanced it! Your friend, D. N. P.S. I live at — High East Street, Dorchester."

Having licked his longest finger with meticulous scrupulosity, Dud fastened up these missives, glancing round savagely at a portly commercial traveller who was fumbling across the desk to reach the ink-pot. He then addressed them both to their respective destinations, angrily hiding what he wrote from the totally uninquisitive eye of this worthy man: "Miss Wizzie Ravelston —*To be called for*."

Hurrying out with these fatal communications, he dropped them one after the other, with infinite care into the orifice marked "Posting." He even went so far, in his anxiety that they should get safe to the bottom, as to follow them with his hand, groping so much like a thief in that dark aperture that a passer-by glanced suspiciously at him.

Then he gave a deep sigh and walked back to the little bakery. As he walked he was conscious that the pulses of both his wrists were throbbing violently and that he had a clutching sensation in the pit of his stomach, while the whole of South Street was completely obliterated by a vision of lavender-coloured tights with a stain on them in the shape of the figure 8.

His mind was in a turmoil. He knew well what a revolution this was, what an insurrection against everything on which his emotional life had fed for ten years; but from the moment he had seen that figure crouching on the caravan bed he had no second of hesitation. His whole being leaped towards that luck-less girl in one desperate upheaval. If he was conscious of the least back eddy of remorse or shame it was no more than a handful of bubbles on the furious tide of his impulse. "If I don't find her again," he said to himself, "I shall be——" And at the thought of the absolute desolation that such a thing would mean, this new self within him with its leap towards life buried in ashes, he grew cold all over.

He received an unpleasant shock, not a very deep one—for having got those letter-cards off he was beyond any serious concern as to what happened to Mrs. Quirm—but still an annoying shock, when he found her leaning back in her wicker chair in front of the blue table-cloth in a half-fainting condition. The

52

woman of the shop was standing by her side with a glass of water, and as soon as No-man entered she informed him that she had despatched a boy to call a taxi.

"She told me to get one," the woman explained, "before she went off. She felt it coming on. How do you feel now, madam?"

Mrs. Quirm made a feeble gesture towards her hat which the woman had removed.

"I'm—*such* a—bother!" she gasped hoarsely, recognizing Dud, "but—I must—I fear—ask you——" He divined her meaning. "Of course I'll go with you," he said hurriedly. "She lives at the end of some lane," he added for the benefit of the shop-woman.

"I know," that lady said. "She's told me. They call it Glymes. There are two houses there. It's where Mr. Wye lives. Tell the driver it's Mr. Wye's. He's lived there for years."

It thus became Dud's destiny to find himself, about twenty minutes later, supporting "the cemetery-woman" on the seat of the biggest and most luxurious taxi he had ever entered. It appeared to be necessary for this conveyance to make a wide circuit to reach the lane in question, which turned out, when it *was* reached, to be a narrow road, sometimes running between hedges and sometimes through an open upland, but following in its main direction a ridge of green pastures that looked down upon Dorchester from the north.

Readers of this meticulous chronicle who know the district will look in vain to-day for any relics of Glymes, for not only has the plough passed over the spot, but ashes have been sprinkled where the two cottages stood; and where Mrs. Quirm at that time cultivated her little flower-garden there is now a gravel pit.

But Glymes, when Dud saw it that day, represented a conglomeration of low slate roofs, irregular gables, and brick chimneys, that from a distance looked like a small farm-house, but was in reality a couple of adjacent cottages, the abode at that time of the Quirms and the Wyes. These two dwellings stood side by side, so that all their front windows shared the same extensive view. The view was indeed one of the finest in that part of the county, comprising in its scope the whole of Dorchester, together with the wide-stretching downs to the south of the town, downs which, beginning to rise beyond Fordington

53

Great Field, and sinking for a space where Came Church and Came House stand, mount up to the far-seen tumulus-bearing ridge, where Culliford Tree—really a monumental *clump* of trees—overlooks the expanse towards the channel.

His charge once safe in her own house and in the presence of her husband, it might well have been supposed that Dud would have hurriedly departed; but such was far from being the case. His excitement about Wizzie, the thundering beat of his pulses, as if with the release of a sobbing flood of ten years' suppressed feelings, his anticipation of what to-morrow might bring forth, threw him into a mood of wild recklessness in which he only wanted to take the slow-moving hours by the throat and strangle them one after another and rush over their dead bodies to the train for Yeovil! He would get the earliest morning train. He would spend the day at the Three Choughs. He had been there before and remembered the name well—but aye! he would be outside that church, or inside that church, or straddling like Apollyon across the path to that church, long before it struck six by the clock!

"If that old bitch," he thought, "wasn't lying and it *is* Salisbury, I'll take some late train from Yeovil; and if there's no letter at the post-office there—and it's mad to think there would be, for how *could* there be?—I'll go straight to the Salisbury fair-field and *insist* on seeing her!"

So far he had caught only a glimpse of Mr. Quirm, as that gentleman helped him getting the lady into the house; and since then it had been his role to sit by her side as she lay on a faded and dirty couch, in a room that he heard them describe as "the study," though it turned out to be their only living-room, while her husband prepared some medicinal concoction for her in the kitchen. The woman's eyes were shut now and she lay breathing so softly that he fancied she might be asleep. She had roused herself to murmur some question about Mr. Quirm and had smiled with what looked like weary amusement, when Dud explained where the man was.

His own thoughts, as he watched those tired eyelids under the blurred spectacles, had suddenly taken such a drastic leap that it made the whole fabric of Glymes with all its inhabitants melt into insubstantial vapour. "Why don't I go round to that market field to-night and find out for certain where they're going to-morrow? I'd surely find *someone* to ask, without being seen hanging round by Old Funky?"

With what seemed like the reasonable part of his mind he decided that this is what he *would* do, but he had an extraordinary shrinking from it that he couldn't overcome. He had a blind fear that he *might* be seen and that if he were, the girl would be somehow spirited away! He glanced at a plate of cold meat that had been laid at his side among the piles of books.

"It's funny," he thought, "that I'm not a bit hungry. It must be that girl. I don't believe I'll eat a morsel till I'm safe in the train for Yeovil. How long that chap is! What the devil is he doing? I must have been sitting here for at least half an hour."

But several more minutes passed, and he had begun to feel sure by her breathing that the woman *was* asleep, when the door opened and the man came in. He was holding a steaming bowl with a big wooden spoon in it and he stood solemnly in the doorway stirring the bowl's contents. He was a big heavily-built man, a good deal older than Dud, and what chiefly impressed the latter about him were the majestic proportions of his head and of his swarthy features. Mr. Quirm's features were indeed nothing less than tremendous. Brow, nose, mouth, chin, all were modelled on a scale of abnormal massiveness that would have been awe-inspiring if the man's eyes had been different. But Mr. Quirm's eyes were dull, lifeless, colourless, opaque. They were empty of every gleam of human response. They neither softened nor warmed; they neither lightened nor darkened—they were simply *there*, as if someone had found a great antique mask with empty eye-sockets, and had inserted a couple of glass marbles into the holes. His head was covered with small, stiff, black curls, and so low did these curls grow on his brooding forehead that Dud was reminded of some gigantic bust he had seen once, but whether Greek or Roman he could not remember. His dominant impression of the man, as he recalled it afterwards, was of a half-vitalized corpse, a being that "but usurped" his life, a semi-mortuus, an entity only "half there."

"Thank 'ee for playing sentinel, Mr. Newman," the man remarked. "Why, you haven't touched that meat! Don't you eat lunch? I don't myself, to tell you the truth. I think it's a miserable, pestilential meal. Now my Nancykins, now my sick kitten, your old conjurer has brought you your jorum! Here you are

55

". . . sip it carefully now. Not too fast, my dabchick! That's it. Just a little more, my snowball! The whole spoonful now, and my seraph will soon be well again!"

Treating Dud as if he didn't exist, the big man had knelt down by the dilapidated sofa and had begun feeding Mrs. Quirm with the wooden spoon. Never did our friend forget the convoluted unpleasantness of that scene! Indeed if he hadn't been protected from the whole atmosphere of Glymes by his obsession for Wizzie Ravelston, he would have incontinently bolted. He felt convinced that the dabchick on the horsehair sofa gave him several glances of ironic deprecation as she lapped up that precious concoction.

"It's made of nettles," Dud thought, "nettles and camomile and some kind of fungus. Yes, I certainly smell fungus in it!"

But the complicated irony of Nancy Quirm's expression, as he caught it over the great hand of her "old conjurer" and his wooden spoon, mitigated the unpleasantness of the scene. "There's something in that woman's soul that's *invincible*," he thought, "something strong enough to defy this welter of anti-quarianism, this great imbecile's bullying, this plate of cold mutton, this 'jorum' of stinking funguses, this disgusting sofa, and all this horrible 'dabchick' talk! There is such a thing as 'the Irony of the Mothers' that can cope with all the Devils of Hell! This fellow's tone is sickening. It's like the jolly badinage of the Lemurs who buried Faust! The chap's face would be as pale as his woman's, only his complexion's so dark. He looks as if he never took any exercise. I believe he reads nothing but these books—God! It makes me ashamed to be a writer—'Scribble, scribble, scribble!'—And he reads 'em all day and night, lolling on this awful sofa like a great sweltering toad, like 'the fat weed that rots itself at ease on Lethe's wharf'! The chap has an unpleasant smell too. It's in those clothes of his. I am sure he sleeps in them. No wonder his woman has a bad heart!"

It must be confessed that Mr. Quirm's ancient and frayed broadcloth trousers and his jersey that had once been blue and now was an indescribable colour, were not calculated to evoke pleasure in normal human senses; nor, as he knelt close to Dud, with the steam of his bowl circling round his head, was his proximity altogether free from a sweetish-sickly odour that really did have a faint resemblance to the smell of a corpse.

56

But to our friend's surprise this repulsive concoction thus indecently administered—for never in his life had he heard such a string of fondling endearments—had a magical effect on the patient's condition. Dud began to think there must have been some aphrodisiac drug in it, or at least some powerful juice charged with alcoholic fermentation, for at the end the woman not only swung her feet off the sofa and assumed a sitting-posture, but actually snatched the bowl from her husband, and tilting it up, drained it to the last drop.

Our friend had the kind of imagination that always seized upon the grotesque and even monstrous aspects of things. If he had not been of an extremely sturdy nature in other respects this tendency might have made him a savage pessimist, but it was a tendency well under control. He now observed, with a fantastic mixture of discomfort and satisfaction, in fact, as if he were being *physically tickled*, the singular effect it had upon Mrs. Quirm's appearance when her face was concealed by this convex object.

Mr. Quirm with a totally impassive countenance leaned forward and deliberately flicked, with his forefinger and thumb, the back of the upheld bowl. "Good girl!" he murmured approvingly. "Now you're my precious quillety again, now you're my dandipet, my linky-love, my dilly-darling!"

It produced a weird effect to hear this fond babying issue from that majestic and impassive mouth. The man turned his tremendous countenance towards our friend even while he was still murmuring this gibberish, and the newcomer at Glymes experienced a sensation that was nothing short of uncanny when he met the unmoved stare that accompanied such intimate endearments.

But Nancy Quirm stood up now and seemed completely recovered. She smiled at Dud in that same mischievous challenging way that she had made use of in the cemetery. "I'm now going to keep my promise to you," she said airily, "and introduce you to Thuella!"

Dud consulted his watch for the second time that afternoon. "I am afraid," he murmured, "I must be off very soon. I have only just—only just come here, you know."

"Are you going to stay long?" she asked, picking up, as she spoke, both the empty bowl and the plate of cold meat.

57

"You needn't answer if you don't want to, Mr. Newman," interjected her husband. "Women's curiosity can't always be satisfied."

"His name is No-man," protested Nancy Quirm and with her free hand she straightened the collar of his filthy jersey, smiling at him tenderly. "But of course I don't want to be inquisitive," she added in a low voice, giving Dud a quick, intimate glance.

The man surveyed them both with a look of weary indifference. "He'll stay if he wants to say I suppose!" reiterated the master of the house, "and if he doesn't want to stay he'll go. He has his own affairs, I presume, as we all have."

With this Mr. Quirm seemed suddenly to retire into *his* affairs so completely as to become oblivious of both of them. He fumbled about among the books on the table while his wife looked at Dud as if he were visiting her in the cage of the strange beast of whom it was her duty to take care.

"He'll turn round a few times and then lie down," her look seemed to say, "and when he's asleep we can go."

The great unwieldy man did, in fact, soon find the volume he sought and, sinking into a deep armchair by the fire, lit a cigarette and began to read.

He looked up, however, when he found that the couple hadn't yet gone out of the room.

"Have you told Newman what to expect?" he said. "People don't like to be taken by surprise."

Mrs. Quirm went over to him, and bending down kissed him lightly on the top of his coal-black head. Dud noticed that the man's hair, in its tight little curls, grew so closely to his ponderous skull as to resemble some species of dusky moss. He was reminded of the way certain similar growths look upon old tree-stumps. He felt himself almost as uncomfortable when the wife kissed the husband as when the husband called the wife dilly-darling.

"They oughtn't to act like this before a stranger," he thought. "There's something indecent about it."

But the Beast in the Cage was evidently quiescent now and likely to remain so.

"*Come,*" she whispered, opening the door and beckoning Dud to follow her.

She took him first into the kitchen, a room that opened on the back of Glymes, and that proved the only tidy and clean place he was destined to enter in that portion of the two houses. Here she deposited what she was carrying and then led him to a closed doorway at the end of a passage. This doorway possessed that peculiarly secretive, disconcerting, and even menacing aspect that doors have which are neither "inside" doors nor "outside" doors, but doors between separate establishments!

Before opening this barrier between the two families at Glymes, Nancy Quirm turned round to him.

"What did you think of Uryen?" she whispered with her challenging smile, that smile that had the power of annihilating a score of years, and making a woman of forty into a girl of twenty.

"I beg your pardon. Do you mean?——" stammered Dud.

"I mean *him, he,* my man in there," she cried. "Why don't you exclaim over his handsomeness? Why don't you cry out that you've never seen anyone like him? Why don't you tell me what an enviable woman I am?"

Dud could only open his mouth in helpless bewilderment as he contemplated her expression of furious sarcasm outlined against that unpromising door.

"Hasn't everyone in Dorchester told you about him?" she continued with mounting excitement. "Haven't they begged you to go and see him as their greatest wonder after Maiden Castle and Poundberry and Maumbury Rings? Haven't they assured you that in the future people will come to Glymes as if to a shrine?"

Poor Dud could only shut his mouth and uneasily moisten his lips with his tongue, as a lap-dog does when uncertain about his mistress's temper.

"Why didn't it surprise you?" she went on while he thought to himself: "What *is* there about women's sarcasm that hurts so? It certainly isn't its subtlety. God! I don't envy that great hulking stinkard. Good luck to him, with his 'dilly darling'!"

"Surprise you I mean," she concluded, "like something monstrous," and he could see a swollen vein in her white throat expanding as it would burst, "when I called him Uryen just now?"

"Why should it," protested Dud feeling less and less sympathetic, "why should it, if it's his name?"

59

Nancy laughed a rasping little laugh. "I suppose *you* didn't mind his calling you Newman then? But I saw you *did*. And so you can imagine what *I* felt when he started calling himself Uryen when his name is Enoch! Enoch Quirm's *his* name, just as my name's Nancy. They're old west-country names; and of course Enoch's out of the Bible. But simple things don't suit *him*. No! *He's* not a simple man. He's *more* than a man! There are too many Enoch Quirms buried in Dorset churchyards to suit *my* Enoch. He must be something greater and grander! And if he can't be great in his life—and you see what he is! I can't even keep him *clean*—he'll be great in a name, and not his own name either. He'll steal a name for himself, and then will swell over it and swell over it——" she broke off with a groan, but still stood gazing at what she could see of Dud's bewildered face in that dark passage, keeping her hand on the unopened door.

"Damn this Glymes!" our friend thought. "What are these people to me? I've got to keep my wits about me; or I may be making a mistake I'll regret till I die—yes, I believe I'll go back to that place to-night and insist on seeing her! They may change their mind completely, and go neither to Yeovil *nor* Salisbury. And I never told her my name or address!"

But Nancy Quirm was speaking to him again and in a different tone. "I really don't know," she said, "why I'm letting myself go like this with you, Mr. No-man, I expect it's because I live such an unnatural life out here, and see so few people. I oughtn't to have said such things about Enoch. Of course he has a perfect right to call himself what he likes, or think of himself as he likes," she paused and letting go of the door-handle began straightening her blouse, stuffing it tightly under her waist-band. "He's wonderful with his herbs. I must allow *that* to him. It's that stuff he made me take that's cured me. I suppose it's gone to my head too. We're a queer set out here at Glymes. But you'll find us quite different another day if you bother to visit us again. I oughtn't to have said what I did and I wouldn't have if we hadn't met *out there*!" She leaned forward quite close to him and clutched at his sleeve. "He was Enoch's stepson," she whispered. "They couldn't get on together. *That* was at the bottom of everything. Enoch couldn't change and Jimmy couldn't change. I oughtn't to have talked like this but I always feel I *must* burst out to someone after I've been to the cemetery."

"Oh, it's all right!" murmured Dud in an absent-minded voice. But the woman had let go the door-handle now. She seemed too excited to know what she was doing, and kept fumbling with both hands at the rim of his coat.

"I'll never come again to this damned Glymes," he said to himself in a fever of impatience.

"I don't want you to think," she went on, "that I blame my husband—I understand him as no one else understands him. I venerate him as no one else venerates him. You can see how he cured me just now! My heart's been so bad since Jimmy left us that I wouldn't be alive now if it wasn't for his knowledge and his healing power."

"Oh, it's quite all right!" repeated the wool-gathering Dud, and he thought to himself : "They *couldn't* stop me from seeing her! She's of age. She's her own mistress. Suppose I *did* risk it and go to-night? I know one thing; the bottom of my life'll fall out if I don't get hold of her!"

"Whatever anyone says against him," went on the excited woman, and in complete unconsciousness of what she was doing she still continued fumbling with the frayed edge of his coat, "no one can deny, *with my heart as it is*, that he is a miracle-worker with his drugs! But then—don't you see?—if I'd never married him, Jimmy would be alive to-day. A woman can only save a life when she gives herself wholly. Without Enoch I could have saved him. *With* Enoch I couldn't. So I am the one!—That's what I always say to myself. I am the one."

"These are—hard questions," murmured the preoccupied Dud, and then with a jerk of his shoulders and a high-pitched creak in his voice he suddenly cried : "You won't think me rude, Mrs. Quirm, if I—if I put off—*going in there*—till some other time?"

Mrs. Quirm's weakness disappeared instantaneously. Her whole expression changed, and letting go his coat she turned round sharply and gave that unpromising door several vigorous taps with her knuckles.

It was then that Dud realized how calmly he had been taking for granted that Mrs. Quirm had been "affected" by the contents of that bowl and was in an unnatural state.

61

It was on the contrary in a competent woman's most normal manner that she now declared: "Oh, certainly you shall go. I fully understand you must go. I only want you just to set eyes on——" But at that point the door was opened by the very person whose name she was on the point of uttering.

Dud's first impression of the notorious Thuella came from a pair of the most painted lips he had ever seen! These scarlet lips belonged to a tall and incredibly thin young woman, dressed in a long, old-fashioned black silk dress that might have been her grandmother's. Her hair, of a reddish-gold, was drawn up tight from the back of her neck, and her neck itself, below these smooth strands of gold and above her lace collar, was white as a magnolia petal. When she turned her head towards him and gave him her hand he was startled by its feverish magnetism. Her fingers communicated to his nerves something that resembled an electric shock. He became aware too not only of her dark blue eyes but of her soft white neck that was as slender as a flower-stalk, but seemed to pulse with the vibrant livingness of the neck of a swan.

Beneath that black silk gown he felt, rather than saw, the extreme thinness of her form. Her chest, her hips, her legs seemed to be thinner than the thinnest boy's, so thin as to resemble the fancy of some perverse sculptor who had turned in fastidious loathing from every normal curve in a woman's body!

But the girl had painted her lips so red that her mouth in her white face seemed like a wound, a wound that struck him at once as the outward sign of a complicated tragedy.

From this crimson mouth there now poured forth a stream of high-pitched words, words that seemed like the *spiritual blood* of an infinite grievance. Her diatribe was addressed to No-man's companion. Of himself, as she ushered them through a little passageway into a room that looked like a mixture of a studio and a boudoir, she took only the barest notice.

Mr. Teucer Wye, who had risen from his chair by the fire when they entered, bowed politely to Dud, nodded in a friendly manner at Mrs. Quirm, and asserted himself sufficiently, in spite of the girl's angry mood, to get the visitors seated.

But Thuella refused to sit down. Like a black-and-white insect, with a crimson mark upon it, she kept fluttering about the room, until to Dud's imagination, she dropped her blood-spotted insect role and became the Lamia of Keats's poem, her white neck in her wrath acquiring the disturbing curves of a beautiful snake.

It was only by degrees that the drift of her grievance against her father became clear. It had been obvious from the start that she was anxious to drag Mrs. Quirm into her quarrel, and now she seemed ready to drag in the stranger too.

From between those crimson lips she was, in her grievance and her passion, trying to direct against that little old man in his neat clothes and black skull-cap, some jet of vengeance that was beyond her own frail androgynous being to call forth.

Some of her allusions were cryptic to a newcomer and Dud's mind kept wandering off to Wizzie on her caravan bed, but finally the girl reached a point that made him very much alive.

"It's just like you, and just like *all* men," she cried, "and Nancy knows it is, to say because you took me to the 'Picture' yesterday you won't take me to the Circus to-night !"

It may be believed how Dud's attention quickened when he heard the word "Circus." He was confused by the confederate glance that Nancy Quirm gave him at that point, but so lively had the reference to the Circus made his wits that he now gathered that the young woman had just completed a small oil-painting—he saw it resting on its easel—and was in desperate need of distraction after this arduous undertaking. It also appeared that the income of herself and her parent largely depended on her activity as an artist.

As soon as he got these facts into his head Dud surveyed the picture on the easel with more interest. It was a picture intended, so far as he could make out, to represent either waves, or clouds, or spirals of smoke, but to his untutored mind it was like nothing so much as bales of fluffy and rather dirty cotton being projected through space on a pair of artificial wings.

"It's in the modern style," he thought. "That's why I can't make head or tail of it."

There was no more reference to the Circus in what the girl was now saying, and her grievance, whatever it was, began to subside and finally died down altogether.

Dud had at first been constantly rehearsing in his mind variously-worded excuses with which he would get up to go; but the reference to the Circus seemed in some mysterious way to

63

carry through the air, clear from the Weymouth Road to Glymes, that is to say across the whole town of Dorchester, some voyaging essence of Wizzie's personality and to make this adhere in a good deal more of a vaporous form than Thuella's clouds to Thuella's own person !

The two girls were not in the least alike, and yet—and yet they *were* alike! But perhaps it was only that he had stumbled upon them both in their fits of anger. Yes, this psychic metamorphosis, this transubstantiatory grafting of the one's identity upon the other's, must have come about, he said to himself, from the fact that all feminine revolt has something in common.

Wizzie's anger had been, it is true, rather addressed to Mrs. Urgan than to Old Funky, and it had to do with much more serious issues; but how queer that *the Circus* should bring them together !

Thuella was furious because she hadn't seen the Circus, while to Wizzie it was a matter of life and death never to see the Circus again. He certainly had the Circus on his own nerves just now, for he suddenly began to tell himself a story about the wearer of that black dress, for all her lovely face and the braids of shining hair coiled round the top of her head, being discovered by him as the Thin Woman in some sideshow of Old Funky's !

The girl, anyway, was now standing in front of Nancy, looking in her weird slenderness exactly like the Lamia of the poem. She kept twisting and untwisting her fingers behind her back as she stood listening to the story of how Mrs. Quirm had had her heart-attack at the Cenotaph.

"I think if you don't mind," Dud began, "I ought to be——" but his mouth was stopped by the fascination with which he felt compelled to watch the motions of his host. The old man was taking two thin battered volumes out of his capacious side-pockets, glancing at them, exchanging them, replacing them; and then even after giving both his pockets a complacent pat, falling into the throes of some new and still more troubled dilemma about them, which led, against his will, to his having to begin the whole adjustment all over again.

"What *are* those books, sir, if I may ask?" inquired Dud.

"The *Phaedrus* and the *Timaeus* in old school editions!" replied Teucer Wye. "I'm not comfortable if they're not in my pocket. Only I like the *Phaedrus* in the right one and the other in the left one; and I'm not comfortable till I know for certain that I've got 'em where they ought to be!" The man now came over to Dud and began to talk eagerly to him.

"They're my only books," he said rapidly. "You see what this room is!" he gave an expressive and rather Gallic movement with his shoulders and hands—"the girl's room; entirely hers! And it's the only room we've got, except the kitchen, and the bedrooms upstairs." His words grew faster and more confidential after a glance at the women to make sure he was not overheard. "It's fate of course that she is as she is. Of course she *does* sell her pictures. She has an agent in America who sells them for her. They like the kind of thing she does over there; and besides —well! we need the money."

Once again he made that expressive French gesture. "But it's fate of course," he went on. "I called her Thuella, out of Homer. Thuella means a storm-cloud; and so, *aisimon ergon,* the clouds of the sky, the dew of the dawn, the waves of the sea, and all other elemental beings are her passion. I read Homer in *those* days, when her mother was carrying her, and I was always quoting him—well! perhaps it *was* an infliction; at any rate she used to hold it against me—the mother I mean—but I thought she'd at last have a boy I could talk to, for I couldn't talk to the boy I had, though my God, he talks to me! But instead"—the little man's skull-cap was now on a level with Dud's chin— "instead of a boy it was Thuella!"

During this speech Dud's mind kept wandering back to Wizzie but he did hear enough to be sorry for this girl-ruled Platonist. Teucer Wye's forehead was so capacious that it compelled respect for his intellectual power, and there was something at once spirited and touching, at least so Dud thought, about the way in which his white silky hair—was it red-gold like his daughter's once?—hung over his brow in a feminine fringe.

Dud had time for an extraordinary number of conflicting images as he sat listening to Teucer Wye. Sometimes he was in the caravan, looking at the stain in the shape of the figure 8 on Wizzie's lavender-coloured tights. Sometimes he was in the cemetery, looking at the skeleton-shape, still covered with horrible patches of decomposition, that was his lost bride's new legacy to his mind.

But his senses returned by fits and starts to the curious room in which he sat. It was certainly a feminine room! Apart from the cloud-picture on the easel everything he could see was feminine. The magazines were, the cushions were, the books were, the ornaments were, the decorations were, the very tidiness was! And in addition to all this as he glanced about, with his nerves as taut as if they were a bowstring Wizzie Ravelston was violently tugging, he became aware that there were actually certain objects from Thuella's toilet-table here and there, not left by accident or from untidy haste, but evidently in constant use, things like cold-cream pots and elegant scent-bottles, and indeed, on one small writing desk, a silver hand-mirror and a brush and comb.

When at last Mr. Wye walked over to the fire-place and stood with his back to it, Dud took in the fact that the man, though of low stature and very slightly-built, possessed considerable dignity. He seemed indeed almost a distinguished figure as he stood there, making an obvious effort to overcome his mania about the volumes in his pockets, and talking to his visitors with lively eagerness about a new head of Aphrodite that had recently been discovered.

Wizzie's would-be rescuer came to the conclusion that Mr. Wye had lost all his teeth; for when his mouth fell into repose he had a habit of pressing his lips together in such a way as to form a perpetual grin, a grin hardly less sardonic than the one reproduced in Houdon's famous bust of Voltaire.

This nut-cracker mouth made a queer contrast to the man's transparent blue eyes and the silky hair under his velvet cap; but to Dud's grotesque and rather malicious imagination his whole personality, as he stood there in his elegant light suit and with a wisp of greenery in his buttonhole, resembled some final touch of feminine bric-à-brac, a Meissen-china figure perhaps in the "biscuit" stage, wherewith the young painter of clouds had adorned her studio! In fact the sight of this figure with a cigarette in its mouth, its hands fumbling at its pockets, and its lips murmuring some sentence of Plato, had something about it that struck even Dud's preoccupied intelligence as not a little shocking. Had Thuella, with her mediaeval swan's neck and her painted mouth, feminized even the words of Plato himself till they whistled between his toothless gums like the sighing of a virgin's lute?

66

For about the twentieth time in these **Glymes** *ménages*—and he found as he met Nancy Quirm's questioning smile from across the room that this "cemetery-woman" still had a friendly influence upon him—Mr. D. No-man took out his watch. But on this occasion—on the strength of Mrs. Quirm's look—he had the courage to announce the necessity of his immediate departure.

"It's nearly four o'clock," he said emphatically. "I really must be getting back to my work."

The thin black form with the swan's neck rose hastily and began murmuring something about tea; but Nancy Quirm was on her feet too and proceeded to make things easy for him.

"I should be jealous," she protested, "if Mr. No-man's first meal at Glymes should be anywhere but with me! I must be off too, for Uryen will be wanting his tea; but you'll come over often, won't you, Mr. No-man, now that you know the way? I believe we're all going to like you ever so much! Thuella—may I tell him, my dear?—says that you make her think of a gladiator."

At that point Thuella herself audaciously and impulsively lifted up her small head and fixing him with eyes full of animation cried in a caressing and cajoling tone : "Won't *you,* since Dad is so crusty, take me to the Circus this afternoon?"

The human mind is a strange thing, or at any rate the mind of Mr. D. No-man was a strange thing; for instead of being aghast at this startling proposal, Dud actually felt an astonishing shock of pleasure. The chief element in this rush of pleasurable emotion that brought the blood to his cheeks was—at least that is how he interpreted it to himself—an immense relief to his cowardice. Down deep in his nature he had already been planning to go back to those people that night. He felt if he didn't go he might lose sight of Wizzie for ever; but he felt thoroughly scared; scared of himself, scared of Wizzie, and above all scared of Old Funky and that detestable woman.

But such was the nature of his nervous system that the idea of going there with this remarkable young person, the idea of facing those people in conspiracy wih a youthful Circe who could reduce Homer to a harpsichord and Plato to a pianola, seemed to him quite different from the madness it really was, seemed to him in fact just *what he needed* to make the adventure, with all its wild possibilities, feasible to his timidity.

67

Mrs. Quirm, who had been observing this scene with a look like that of a skilful playwright whose most secret intention has been caught by her puppets' representatives, now put in a decisive word.

"Mr. No-man is already interested in a performer there. The Circus is a foreign one, not a regular one," she remarked, "and since we've learnt that this special little troupe of ours may lose its job any minute, he was thinking of going there to-night himself."

Dud stared at her with open mouth.

"Have you—told her—what—what we saw?" he stammered.

Nancy Quirm smiled at him, her most subtle and provocative smile, and, as she did so, came nearer to him. Then she repeated that impulsive gesture she had made in front of the closed door and caught at the edge of his coat.

"I only told," she murmured softly, "how I held that old woman back while you went to the caravan. I couldn't tell her any more, could I? But I'll make her tell *me* everything when she comes back to-night!"

If Dud had been less obsessed by Wizzie's desperate face he would have been dismayed at this publishing of his infatuation. But as it was he felt as if this subtle ally of his, knowing his timidity, had deliberately involved Thuella in his daring quest. He felt like a "haggard knight-at-arms" who on the verge of his great adventure was being led to the threshold of his desire by tender confederate hands.

Teucer Wye left his place by the fire, at this critical moment, and came up to them. His clear blue eyes were radiant with relief. It was evident that he anticipated with immense satisfaction a long uninterrupted Platonic evening.

"By Jove!" he cried. "Are you really going to be so kind to us, Mr.——" He paused and glanced at Mrs. Quirm.

"Mr. No-man," murmured that lady.

"Mr. No-man," he echoed, thrusting both hands hurriedly into his side pockets. "For I assure you, Mr. No-man, it's more than—more than—I mean it's a great kindness to my daughter—and—*and to me too*," he added, allowing his patient mouth to relapse into that *l'homme qui rit* grin, which was so disconcerting. "She's been working so hard lately," he recommenced, noticing the agitated frown of indecision that convulsed

68

our friend's countenance, "and I'm—well, to tell you the truth, it's an effort for me to go out in the evening."

Never in his life had so many conflicting thoughts, so many turbulent impressions, whirled through poor Dud's brain. At his feet, on that smooth polished floor, he detected a little drop of blood-coloured paint. Upon this object the whole machinery of his soul seemed compelled to concentrate. For the flicker of a second he recalled Mrs. Quirm's words in the cemetery. "If you come to 'Them,' you set 'Them' free; and 'They' must be set free."

"It's all right," he blurted out lifting his head and relaxing his frown. "Don't mention it, sir! It's nothing. It's a pleasure to me. Shall we"—and he looked straight at Thuella; not into her eyes however, which were fixed upon him then with a slow questioning gaze, but into the soft obscurity of her white neck—"shall we start at once? You won't mind if we—if we call at my place first? But of course——" At this point he looked away from the girl to the elder woman, as if asking for a new lead. "Of course," he added, now at last meeting Thuella's eyes, "You'll want your tea; but there are"—he flung this at that scarlet mouth as if it were a snowball—"plenty of little shops!"

"I should think there are!" laughed Nancy Quirm, looking from one to the other with her successful puppet-manager air. "Oh, you'll make quite a sensation, you two, wherever you go! But don't be silly, as I was," she added, smiling at Thuella. "Don't faint by that cenotaph!"

A quarter of an hour later the figure of our friend carrying his great oak cudgel, and the figure of Miss Wye in a long ulster-cape and a cloth cap, might have been seen making their impatient way across the narrow river-bridge leading to what all Dorchester knows as "the Hangman's Cottage." They spoke very little as they went; though, at one point, where the path between the ditches was impeded by an overflow of water, Dud had felt impelled to offer his companion his hand.

To his surprise the fingers the girl slipped hurriedly into his own were ungloved, and he found them as feverish and electric as when he had first greeted her. Was she consumptive, he wondered, or was she morbidly sensitive to a man's touch?

The sun had disappeared for the day when they reached the Hangman's Cottage; and Dud, who as yet knew nothing of

69

Dorchester, hesitated whether to turn to the left, along the river-path under the prison, or to go straight up the hill between the overshadowing walls and trees.

"Do you want to go to your place," his companion whispered, "*before* we have our cup of tea?"

Recalling this moment later, and of how they stared at each other's faces while the sound of water rushing through an up-lifted sluice became an integral part of the dusk about them, he wondered what it had been that had made them both speak in whispers. All he really wanted was to get to the Circus, and to the devil with the rest, but what he actually said to her was that he had to get some money from his lodgings.

Thuella pondered a moment, wrapping her cloak so tightly round her as the cold airs from the sluice-gate invaded them, that he thought : "She *is* thin! She's horribly, shockingly thin!"

Then she exclaimed : "Why! that must be half-way down the street! We'd better go *this* way then. It comes out by the bridge near the White Hart."

"What's that building up there?" he whispered as turning eastward he felt several drops of rain.

"Oh, I don't know," she returned. "Some nice comfortable house I suppose!"

They went on a little further. "What's *that* building?" he whispered again.

"That?" she answered. "Let—me—see. Where have we got to? That must be the Governor's, I think. No! I'm really not sure!"

The sound of running water never ceased, and with the rain the twilight seemed to be falling more thickly.

Dud kept feeling as if there were some subtle confederacy between the flow of the water and the descent of the dark.

In the accumulative gathering of the one it seemed as if what the Bible calls "the water below the firmament" were rising to meet its mate, while in the accumulative sinking of the other what the Bible calls "the water above the firmament" had begun to precipitate itself in a vaporous diffusion of reciprocal attraction.

Dud felt as if this house his companion called "the Hang-man's" and this other she thought was "the Governor's" were both guarding, like two insubstantial elfland warders, the one above and the other below, this mystic encounter of water with water.

"Is that the prison over there?" he asked presently.

"Yes," she replied. "Over there and *up* there."

Certain lamps on the slope of the prison hill had already been lit for the night, though it was still far from being really dark, and these threw long, wavering light-paths over the ripples of the flowing water, light-paths that moved as the man and the girl moved, sometimes lengthening themselves and sometimes shortening themselves as the two advanced. There was a deep ditch on the side of the path opposite this flowing stream while the path itself was flagged at the edge next to the brimming water by grey flat stones which showed whitish in the faint light.

"What a place for running water this is!" Dud murmured to his companion. His tone was still low, still subdued to that muted key into which they had seemed compelled to sink when they first stopped by the Hangman's Cottage.

"Yes," she returned. "Dad's always talking Greek about it." She shivered and hugged herself, twisting her cloak still closer about her. "There's a great underground river," she whispered, "as well as all the rest. They get their drinking water from it. There's always water! Never an end to the water!"

Dud noticed as they moved on side by side under the precipitous prison-garden that one of her hands was still ungloved. It was with this one that she kept dragging her cloak round her. What *did* she make him think of at that moment? Was it of one of those queer dark *posts* that he had seen in pictures of the Grand Canal in Venice?

Presently they came to a spot where a strip of concave flag-stones crossed the path. A thin stream of water was flowing over this, from the river to the ditch on the other side, and once again he offered to take her hand.

As she slipped it into his he realized even more vividly than on the first occasion how full of magnetic life a girl's ungloved fingers can be! It was as if a small naked creature, trembling with the secret pulse of its own separate identity, had yielded itself up to him.

When she drew it away he could not prevent the thought rushing into his head: "Will Wizzie Ravelston's hand be as electric as this one's?"

71

But he struck the ground, after dismissing this thought, with the end of his stick. "I'll leave her in the street," he said to himself, "while I run up to my room and get my money."

2

ALL SOULS' NIGHT

IT was quite dark when No-man and Thuella stood together outside the Circus-field. Dud could clearly make out behind his companion's figure the curved outline of the Amphitheatre against the not-yet totally darkened sky. He got a sudden feeling as if a part of him were entirely detached from this agitating crisis, this cursed need of decision, and as if this part of him, like that dark bank against the sky, were so immersed in the fatality of matter as to be ready to face whatever happened with easy acquiescence.

But Thuella was addressing him now in a brusque, rather harsh voice. "The thing to do," she said, "is to take this woman, if she really wants to leave them and if they'll let her go, to my sister's in Friary Lane."

"Your sister's?"

Dud felt, as he looked past her head at that dark bank against the sky, as if he and poor Wizzie were being pushed through a damp mist—she still in her lavender tights and he with his useless cudgel, into a narrowing perspective of irretrievable destiny inscribed "Friary Lane."

"Yes, you didn't know I had a sister living in the town, did you? She and I don't hit it off so awfully well; but *you'll* probably like her better than you do me! Her name's Jane, Jane Dearth; but she's separated from Tom Dearth and lives by herself. Dad dotes on her but she's too hard-working to be much with us. She disapproves of me and when we're together I can't help being more—you know—of what she disapproves. They say she has some kind of an affair with a fellow next door—an idealistic chap. But she's the one to take this woman. She lives

72

alone. She has a spare room, I know, because my brother comes and stays with her. But the real point is she makes a cult of helping girls like this, and if you——"

But even by the light of a remote station lamp she could see that Dud's face had suddenly become stony. She broke off at once. "Oh, it isn't what you're thinking!" she cried hastily. "Jenny isn't a social worker. She's a feminist, if she's anything! She'd make no difficulty about *that*. You could be together at her place as much as you liked. You could live together there if you wanted to. You and Jenny are birds of a feather in those things. She despises marriage. That's why Tom went off! He was far too conventional to endure her ideas. Of course, she's terribly good herself. I don't believe she lets her friend next door make love to her. But she likes to befriend the bad, while *she* stays good. I'm just the opposite. I hate that kind of moral immorality. I like to do as I like; but it bores me to tears to make a principle of it. Where's the pleasure of anything if bad and good are the same? But Jenny says——"

Dud tapped the edge of the platform with his cudgel. The last thing he felt equal to at this crisis in his life—let Thuella's white neck show never so inviting against Maumbury Rings—was to get embroiled in her dispute with her sister.

"Well—let's go!" he said brusquely. "Perhaps it *might* be best for her to stop at your sister's to-night. Of course, we don't know yet for sure that those Urgan people will let her go. But I *am* grateful to you for your——" he stopped, and his face suddenly clouded with anger; for Thuella was smiling in the most teasing manner.

"Oh, that's nothing, my dear!" she murmured. "Come on; let's get out of here. We'll soon see what happens!"

Dud had the peculiarity of being able to see the sardonic roguery of life's situations with an ironic substitute of his own for that physical response to it that people call "showing a sense of humour"; but if he refused to respond to her smile, he liked her calling him "my dear." Nor did it fail to strike him as they went out of the station that, though Dorchester was under the water-sign and himself under that of earth and air, his coming to this town coincided with the lifting of a great sluice-dam in his emotional fate. For here was he on the point of making himself responsible for a completely unknown Circus-girl while at the same time he heard himself called "my dear" by an almost equally unknown painter of clouds.

"What do you think the time is?" Thuella asked, as they entered the market-field.

Dud's watch had grown to be as accessible as a woman's powder-puff, but at this moment it was too dark to read its face. "Damn! and I never looked at the station-clock as we came by! But it must be about a quarter after six."

"There's nothing going on here," said Thuella. "The music's stopped."

Dud looked round. *There* was the big canvas tent. *There* was the caravan where he had found Wizzie crouching on the bed. But save for a few fruit-stalls and ginger-beer stalls where there was a handful of young people, there seemed to be nobody about.

Then he remembered what Wizzie herself had said to him about their having tea at six.

"They're all at tea!" he cried excitedly. "This would be the best time to find her with them. Come on! Let's go up the steps. I'm certain they're in there. That's the one for sure! I know it by those things hanging on that rail. Come along! Quick! Before anyone comes out. I'll knock and walk right in, eh? Not give them a chance of dodging, eh?" He was so agitated, and he took Thuella's confederacy so entirely for granted, that it was the merest chance that he didn't call *her* "my dear" in the same way she had done with him.

They moved to the foot of the caravan steps. Yes! there were voices inside. "This *may* be," thought Dud, "the most fatal moment of my whole life! And I could still dodge it. I've only to go off with the 'Venetian Post,' and nobody would know I'd been here!" But to himself the satisfactory thing was that though he could dally with thoughts like this he did not feel the remotest serious temptation to relinquish the quest.

When Wizzie had uttered the words: "I'll be your woman," and they had stared at each other through the steam of that pot, something very crucial and important—the drawing-back of some tremendous bolt—had occurred within him.

But here they were—with the sound of voices on the other side of that door—and they had only to run up the steps and fling the door open to be face to face with the Urgans and Wizzie.

74

Dud was conscious now of a sickening feeling of nervous cowardice. He shivered as he stood by Thuella's side; and he fervently and shamelessly prayed that when matters came to the pinch the girl would show her mettle and prove herself a powerful ally.

He knew well how frightened he was, for his fear totally transformed, as they stood there at the bottom of those steps, the normal processes of time and space. His fear had the effect of making each single second, each tick of the eternal watch in the pocket of the Creator, transmute itself, like a vision in a magician's mirror, into a shifting impression that was composed of space as well as of time. The "space" of this transmuted experience, this vision over which a psychological magnifying-glass was being projected back and forth with every breath he took, was the trodden grass and clinging mud of the fair-field; but the time-element in these magnified *fear-seconds* extended itself so far beyond the present as to throw a magical desirableness over both a past and a future that were free from the engrossing panic of the moment. He was even able, while his feet were still on the steps of the caravan, as much did the nervous fear he suffered extend the content of the passing seconds, to tell himself a story about living in unruffled peace forever, with the "eidolon" of his wife visiting him daily while both Wizzie and Thuella melted into thin air.

But they were both on the top step now; and with a quick knock, just such an one as he had intended, and a quick turn of the handle, he opened the door and they both went in. He couldn't see Wizzie at first glance, for she was sitting cross-legged on the floor with her plate on her lap; but when Old Funky and Mother Urgan rose from their seats he saw her, and their eyes met, and he experienced for the second time that impression of *recognition*—there was no other word for it—as if he had known her time out of mind. In that one look he knew that he had been right, he knew that all his *other* thoughts, his recoils, his hesitations, all the recent flutterings of the rational soul within him, had been but ripples on the surface of his being.

All this passed in a flash; and as soon as it had passed his mind felt clearer, more formidable than it had felt since she had said to him that morning : "I will be your woman." It was only

75

by degrees, after they had begun talking, that he took in the exterior appearance of things. Wizzie wore nothing but a cotton "slip," not over clean, and as she stared at them above the bowl on her lap she kept making childish attempts to pull her garment over her ankles with a thin white arm. A strong light from somewhere—he couldn't remember afterwards whether it came from the stove or from a paraffin lamp—made it possible for him to mark the tiny hairs on one of the legs she was trying to hide and even to note the soft curves of the flesh of the other as it lay bent against the floor. Old Funky was attired in the same greenish-black frock-coat as before, but Dud noticed as the old man was speaking that his wig was perceptibly awry which gave him a repulsively comic and even a tipsy air. Mummy Urgan's attire was more ordinary, for she wore a red woollen petticoat that appeared to be a replica of the one hanging on the rail outside, and the upper part of her short body was clothed in some black stuff, heavily ornamented with glittering black jet beads.

"Well, Mr. Urgan," said Dud boldly, but in that unnaturally loud and rather hectoring voice that his agitation had caused him to use in the morning: "I've come to relieve you of your troublesome young charge!"

Old Funky screwed up his eyes and performed the automatic movement of sucking in his thin lips till they nearly disappeared. Then No-man caught him giving the girl on the floor a glance totally at variance with any desire to be rid of her. It struck him at the moment as almost a tragic look.

"I be glad to hear what 'ee do say," the fellow began, "and if us can come to terms over 'un, happy be all and mare's bosom take us! Mother and me were only considerin' about you and your kind offer this wery arternoon and us said—didn't us, Mother?—'If the kind gentleman be ready to indemnity we for all the hexpence us 'as been put to regarding she, us'll be more thankful to behold the scut of her tail!' But 'twas good red gold us spent and Mother over there knows how much it were!"

"I'd—like—to—say—one—thing!" This simple string of monosyllables unexpectedly uttered by Thuella caused a curious change in the tension of the group.

"Sit ye down, lady! Sit ye down, young man," threw in Mummy Urgan, indicating the bed and a couple of shaky chairs.

But Dud's mind was far too disturbed to let him sit down. He found himself mechanically repeating the curious invocation Old Funky had indulged in—"happy be all, and mare's bosom take us!"—and he had begun to be disturbed too by the way Wizzie was looking at Thuella, her brown eyes beginning to assume that dark *round* look that he had seen in them this morning.

"No, no, sit 'ee here, pretty lady, sit 'ee here, for 'tisn't often a beautiful one like what you be have stepped across whit stone of our old van!"

"It doesn't matter where I sit," repeated Thuella, "for I shan't be here long. But I would—like—to—say—one—thing!"

As she spoke she *did* sit down on the edge of the bed which, as it chanced, was directly facing Wizzie and so close to her that the point of one of Thuella's shoes came within an inch of the Circus-girl's knee, over which—for the latter had put down her bowl on the floor—the not very prepossessing cotton "slip" was at once indignantly and fiercely stretched.

Thuella's magnetic presence, red lips, and startlingly white skin were the things most calculated of all the advantages any intruder could have had to disarm Mother Urgan whose passion for beautiful girls was at once vividly professional and intensely personal. It had been Wizzie's pinched face and thin colourless hair far more than the girl's touchy temper that had finally come to create that "lodged hate" and that "certain loathing" in the old woman's breast; while the discovery of Popsy, whom she made into a pet but who could never manage the circus-horse, added the element of bitter jealousy to the situation.

Neither Dud nor Mother Urgan seemed inclined to sit down; but Old Funky, who always preferred to make his "sorties" during an explosive situation from some convenient retreat, squatted down upon a wooden stool between the stove and the wall of the caravan.

"What—I—want—to—say," continued Thuella in an emphatic tone, throwing upon Wizzie's bare arms, and upon the garment the girl had dragged so fiercely over her knees, a quick satirical glance, "is simply this : Mr. No-man here is a friend of my father's, Mr. Teucer Wye of Glymes, and any misunderstanding about"—she met Wizzie's suspicious stare with a proud tilt of her eyebrows and substituted the pronoun "you" for

77

whatever it was she was going to say—"about *you* leaving the Circus so suddenly can be referred to him. He understands a little about the law, and he's lived in Dorchester a long time and he isn't badly known here. I only mention this," she added, glancing at Dud, "because I know that Mr. No-man feels rather like a stranger in this town."

"I want to go with *him*; not with *you*!" cried Wizzie rudely.

"You *shall* go with him, girl! He'll take you to Friary Lane where you can see him as much as you like. His place is just round the corner."

"I want to *go* to his place! If I can't be with him I don't want to go at all! He and I will meet in Yeovil where we'll be alone without anybody. We've arranged that ourselves! You didn't know we'd arranged that, did you, Grummer Urgan?"

The first portion of this outbreak was attended by a fierce glance at the girl on the bed, and the second by a yet fiercer glance at the old woman. This latter immediately retaliated. "You see what she is, beautiful lady!" and she turned her black-beaded torso to the girl on the floor. "If you call me 'Grummer' again I'll tell them how you scratched poor old Mr. Tenterhook at Weymouth, and what you said to that nice Father Bones at Blandford, and how you pushed Mr. Catchpole down the stairs of his own house in Bristol, and how you threw a jug at my husband, and how you pulled poor little Popsy round the stable by her hair."

Wizzie appeared delighted rather than horrified by this re-cital. She put out her tongue at the old woman. "Grummer! Grummer! Grummer! Grummer!" she cried. "That's what you are, and that's what you'll always *be*. If you killed me I'd go on saying it.

> "*Grummer Urgan born in Gloster,*
> *Without father, without foster!*"

There seemed to be something about this jingle that con-vulsed the old lady with fury. For a second Dud thought she was going to fly at Wizzie, but Old Funky's voice, from his hiding-place by the stove, brought everybody back to the main issue.

"The pint is this, Miss Wye, and please give our respects to Mr Wye, for though I can't say *for sure* as I've set eyes on he,

78

to the best of my 'umble belief I *have* had that privilege, and anyone could see by the cut of his cloth how respected he were. But the pint is this. Mother and me have spent more'n ten gold sovereigns, late and soon, on Missy Ravelston's stage-dizzeries; and in addition, ye understand, 'tis mighty upsetting to business —legal, lawful, *and* according—for she to leave we without notice and for this 'ere I must in duty to ourselves put down another ten pounds. That'll be a nice round twenty pounds to settle *all*, mister; and without *that* us can't let she go."

Dud ceased his pacings up and down between the stove and the bed—*twenty pounds*! He had imagined that he would be able to purchase Wizzie's release for a couple of five-pound notes. In fact he had transferred just that sum from the ottoman into his purse. Well! he would have to give them those notes and write a cheque for the rest!

But Thuella spoke up again. "I think that's far too much, Mr. Urgan," she cried indignantly. "No! stop a minute, Mr. No-man!"—for Dud was already holding his cheque-book in his hand and looking vaguely around for pen and ink.

"What," she went on, "will she," and she turned her scornful eyes, that showed almost blue-black in the lamplight, upon the girl at her feet, "want with your circus-finery? You can dress your next girl in it, can't you, Mr. Urgan?"

There was an uncomfortable pause, during which they all stared at Wizzie's purchaser, or rather at the cheque-book in his hands, which he kept absent-mindedly rolling up and unrolling.

But his own mind had taken a great leap from the whole scene. The preposterous jet-covered blouse, which wasn't a blouse at all but the top part of a heavy black dress, looming so near him above the red flannel petticoat, suddenly became the *point d'appui* for a dance of exciting ideas.

"I am buying her! I am buying her!" he thought; and then he thought, "Mona's been dead ten years. Mona is 'free.' What was it the Glymes woman said? 'Free' and far away from all this!"

But the glittering jet beads he kept his eyes upon gave his thoughts a still further projection. "Mona is free and I am free," he said to himself, and a strange, wicked, heathen exultation began rushing through his veins.

He felt like a monk who having once decided to break his

vows gave his sensual fancy full range. It had troubled him a little when Mummy Urgan brought out that spiteful list of Wizzie's misdeeds. It had troubled him a little to see Wizzie put out her tongue at her enemy; but in this new rush of wicked exultation he had ceased to care. The girl's " 'lurin' figure" remained. That look which had passed between them remained. She was his. He was *buying* her! And how beautiful the "Venetian Post" looked just now, lifting up her scornful voice on his behalf! He would never have dared it, he would never have faced them here without her support! But he felt exultant now. His mind seemed clear—clear and strong.

His senses might be in a whirl, but his mind had never been more steady, never more compact, never more ready for what fate should bring.

"Death is for the dead: life for the living," the cemetery woman had said. And then all at once his ardour sank. Wasn't he to be alone with Wizzie that evening? Wasn't she "to be his woman?" Wasn't he to make love to her now, very now, in an hour or two? Weren't they to sleep together that night? Why couldn't he have a confidential talk with his landlord and propitiate and get round him? Surely if he paid a higher rent there'd be no objection to Wizzie? Damn this Mrs. Dearth of Friary Lane! He didn't want any Jenny Dearth interfering between him and his girl:

But Thuella was now addressing a sort of personal appeal to Mummy Urgan. As Dud watched the two women's faces he could see why it was that the unknown Popsy, of whom he kept hearing, had got round the old crone to such a tune!

Mrs. Urgan's face was indeed a map in which "you could read strange matters."

Avarice struggled in it with a positively maudlin attraction towards the red-gold hair, the white skin, the crimson lips before her. She kept picking at the jet ornaments of her half-dress, and while she leaned forward her red petticoat, as it pressed against the rough caravan table, slipped down a little from her waist and caused a dingy strip of dirty linen to manifest itself above the table's edge.

"Make it eighteen sovereigns, Miss Wye," she gasped at last. " 'Tis a screwing of us down; but I want 'ee to be satisfied and maybe them things *will* do as second-best for Popsy."

"Us'll take eighteen, as Mother says," cried Old Funky eagerly, and hurriedly getting up from his stool he shuffled to a cupboard and produced a pen and an ink-pot which he placed on the table in front of Dud. "Eighteen pounds, Mister, and she's yours; and us'll never"—here he gave Dud a sly, black-mailer's leer—"meddle with she or with thee again!"

Dud looked round for a chair and saw none; so kneeling on the floor he began with meticulous nicety making out the cheque for eight pounds.

"What's your Christian name?" he inquired of the old gentle-man, who in his anxiety to assist this laudable undertaking was tilting the ink-bottle towards the point of the pen.

Old Funky answered this question almost before it was out of Dud's mouth. It was as if the pen had answered it in an im-patient squeak, or as if the ink-pot had replied to it in gurgling haste. But to Mr. Urgan's vexation the important word "Ben" remained still unwritten; for the signer of the cheque felt im-pelled to glance at the girl on the floor.

During the whole of this singular debate Wizzie had been casting quick nervous looks at her rescuer. Dud too felt "in his bones" a vivid awareness of her presence. At some moments, while the others were speaking, it was as if he and she were really alone in that caravan, and yet separated, separated by troublesome phantoms, that kept materializing and unmateria-lizing like faces at a séance.

He had become aware that the girl was intensely shy of him, terribly afraid of encountering his gaze. She always looked away hurriedly, when there was a chance of their eyes meeting.

At this moment her shyness of him seemed to mingle with his own consciousness of the unusual nature of the situation. From somewhere deep down in his soul a feeling arose as if all this had happened before, ages and ages ago! He *did* meet her eyes now, as he held that pen, and it was as if out of the remote past of that long-historical spot some reincarnated Bronze-Age in-vader were selecting from among the girl-captives of the older Stone-Age the particular one that appealed to his erratic fancy, the one, out of them all, that no one else would choose!

He now repeated his question about Mr. Urgan's Christian name.

"Ben," was the comprehensive reply. "Just plain Ben. Bee,

81

hee, hen—*Ben!* With great oneyers like 'eeself I tells the bare truth, so strike me gawd! 'Ben' for Birth and Ben for Death, though in the Hin-between, as you might say, a person like me gets called all and sundry!"

Dud was spurred on now, not only by the help of the tilted ink-pot but by his impatience to escape a strong smell of burning fowl's dung which, at this crisis, seemed to emerge from the perspiring skin of Old Funky, and he was soon putting the final flourish to "D. No-man." He was in fact just completing this, and the silence was broken only by Mummy Urgan whispering something to Thuella that he couldn't catch, when all at once Wizzie jumped to her feet and approached the tall young woman.

"So you think I'm not worth twenty pounds, do you!" she cried. "You're happy now, aren't you, now you've beaten down my price? You think he'll always hold it against me, don't you, that I wasn't worth twenty pounds? I suppose you think you'd be worth a hundred to him, only he can't afford *you*; he can only *afford me!* Oh, yes, you can lift up your eyebrows, you can turn down your mouth, you can look the lady! I've—a great—mind—to give—your lady's face—and I would too—yes, I would!—if it wasn't for him."

Mummy Urgan now caught the angry girl by both elbows and pushed her in front of her until she projected her behind a screen of sacking which hung on a cord from the roof.

"Get your clothes on, you crazy bitch! Get your clothes on! And put in everything you've got—do'ee hear?—*everything*! Us don't want nothin' of your'n and Popsy don't want nothin' of your'n. Us wants the *scut* of 'ee; that's what us wants, and never to see your ugly phyz no more!"

Wizzie's only reply to this was to thrust forth her head, without letting any portion of her neck or shoulders be seen, and make a savage grimace, a grimace that distorted her countenance much more than the mere putting out of her tongue had done.

Thinking it over afterwards Dud found it astonishing that he didn't feel the slighest flicker of a reaction against the girl when she extended her head and made that horrible face. What he actually felt was a curious pleasure at the way that pinched little countenance, with the thin, straggly, straight hair falling, like straw from a hedge after a wagon has passed, on each side of the hollow cheeks, seemed for a moment to hang suspended against that piece of sacking. Dud felt as if he could gather up that small head in his two hands and carry it away—quite independently of the rest of the girl!

And then he began wondering if he ought to find out who the foreign employer of these people was. But no! The lad he'd talked to had answered him they were all just transients, taking the place of the Circus-owner's real troupe. "They be like gipsy folk," the lad had said, "come to-day—gone to-morrow!"

Besides, the chances were against this foreigner's being in Dorchester at all. Likely enough he'd slipped off to the Continent, now that they were so near the coast.

His abstraction was interrupted by Old Funky's anxiety about the other ten pounds. Dud became aware that the man was in desperate fear lest Wizzie's purchaser should go off leaving nothing but the cheque for eight pounds. He was actually tugging at his coat like an excited ape.

"Sorry, Mr Urgan," he said. "I wasn't going off with them." On receiving the two bank-notes the old man religiously and solemnly spat upon them both, and then, with a hurried glance to make sure his wife was absorbed in Thuella, and with a wink at Dud, he hid them in the same little cupboard out of which he had got the pen and ink.

It was at this juncture that there was a sharp double knock at the caravan door.

"'Tis Popsy," cried Mummy Urgan. "Shall us have she in, Father?"

But Old Funky was so occupied in the effort to carry things off and make out that he hadn't hidden the bank-notes in his private cupboard but was even now leisurely engaged in putting them away along with the cheque, between certain particular pages of the caravan Bible, that he made no coherent reply, and Mrs. Urgan allowed Popsy to enter.

Dud was not tempted to share the woman's partiality for Popsy, though he did recognize her as strikingly pretty. She was short and plump with a satiny skin and small dark eyes. She had long eyelashes, which lay when her animation gave them a chance, like the softest and blackest pansy-petals against her cheeks. She was dressed in a dazzling costume; not in tights as

83

Wizzie had been, but in a spangled vest and glittering skirt, while her plump muscular legs jingled with little silver bells. Her appearance brought into the caravan a real "aura" of the Circus. She flirted with the old woman, jested with the old man, kissed the tips of her fingers to "the gentleman," and clapped her hand to her mouth in mock solemnity when she learned that Wizzie was dressing behind the curtain.

Dud now became conscious of a weird sensation that he had once or twice before in his life; namely, the parallel existence of quite different layers of reality. It was a disturbing sensation and it made *all* reality a little shaky, as if there were yawning gulfs of Not-Being under every particular manifestation of Being. Even while he watched Popsy's antics and heard what he fancied were suppressed imprecations from behind the sacking, this wedge of unreality made the old lady's jet beads grow fantastic, like the ornaments on the poop of a fairy ship; made the greenish mould on Old Funky's frock-coat grow diffused and undulant and floating and wavering and uncertain, more like a strain of music than the fungus of time settling down on a fragment of ancient broadcloth.

But these evidences of the insubstantiality of *all* reality were only accessories to its chief mutation which left him with the feeling that Popsy, with the silver bells round her knees, and a blue feather in her cap, was on a totally different layer of reality from the one in which he, with his eyes on that bulging bit of sacking, and Wizzie struggling into her clothes in that narrow space, were now occupying.

"Just one wee *leetle* drink, Mummy darling," Popsy was now imploring, with her plump hand on the wrist of the infatuated old woman, "and then I'll go on! The music's started; listen!— and tent be filling up! Just one leetle tiny wee drink, and I'll draw silver from Maumberry Old Stone!"

With a melting softness in her blinking eyes Mrs. Urgan shuffled across the caravan floor to what was apparently *her* private cupboard. Here, with her broad black and red back, like some great woodpecker at its accustomed hole, turned square to the company, she poured something into a tea-cup, and then swinging round handed it with a doting grin to her favourite.

"Here's luck!" cried the young woman emptying the cup in a couple of impatient gulps.

She was in the act of returning the receptacle to the old lady when Dud became aware that Wizzie had come out from behind the sacking. She was attired in a normal grey dress and a plain dark coat and hat, and she carried a small hand-bag in one gloved hand and an old umbrella in the other. She walked straight up to him and stood erect by his side.

With a proud, dignified docility she slipped one gloved hand between his elbow and his side and clutched tightly at the stuff of his coat-sleeve.

Dud never forgot to the end of his days the thrill of exulta-tion that rushed through him when he realized, without actually feeling her touch—for her hold on him was like the impercept-ible clutch of a small animal—the tragic pathos of this mute gesture.

It was clear that there was a sublime confidence in her un-questioning acceptance of what had been done. For a second, as they thus stood side by side, while Popsy, jingling her silver bells and putting her plump arms akimbo, began a little *pas seul* in front of them, the monstrous thought came into his head: "Suppose I was to thrust her away, take Thuella's arm, tell them all I was only fooling, that they could hang on to the money for the jest's sake, and clear out?"

What he really said to Miss Wye, however, was simply, "Shall we go then? I'm afraid we're keeping this young lady's audience waiting."

No aristocratic prisoner of the Old Régime leaving her jailers for liberty or the scaffold could have turned on Mummy Urgan and on Popsy a haughtier and more indifferent glance than Wizzie bestowed on them as she and Dud followed Thuella out of the caravan.

Of Old Funky she took no notice at all. He might have been the pen or the ink-pot, he might have been one of the bank-notes now secreted in his own cupboard, for all the awareness she showed.

As they went down the steps however, the old gentleman scrambled after them. Dud heard him behind them and glanced round as they were leaving the caravan but could not decide whether it was to say anything particular that he was following them, or simply from an innate tendency to play the satellite.

Just behind him, jingling briskly down the steps, and whistling as she went, came Miss Popsy; but *she* made a lively dash straight for the back of the tent, and the last he saw of her was the fluttering of her skirts as she skipped up the little step-ladder and vanished into the dark interior.

But still, as with Wizzie's gloved fingers clutching his coat-sleeve he walked off between her and Thuella, he had an uncomfortable intimation of the proximity of Old Funky. At last, swinging round so abruptly as almost to disengage Wizzie's hold upon his arm, he turned and confronted him.

"What is it? What do you want?" he rapped out, speaking crossly and sternly.

"I wanted to say one word to you, mister, afore you went off," panted the old man, "not more than just one word to you!"

"Don't—let—him," whispered Thuella. "He's up to mischief."

"Don't speak to him," whispered Wizzie. "I'd kill myself before I went back!"

But Dud hailed him again. "What do you *want*?" he cried.

The old man stood stock-still in the trodden November mud. Then he lifted up a shrill unpleasant voice, a very different voice from that of his previous obsequious cajolery. Both the women made repeated efforts to get Dud to move away, but he refused to budge. He felt a fascinated desire to hear every word the old man was saying in this surprising access of fury.

"You think you've seen the last of Ole Ben, don't 'ee? That's all I've got to say to 'ee," Old Funky shouted. "You think you've paid he off and done with he, don't 'ee? Ole Ben's easy to see the last of, ain't he? Ole Ben's one to be whistled down wind, ain't he, and gone and done with, ain't he? Ole Ben's no better nor dirt, ain't he? But I've got to say this to 'ee, and to she too, so pussy-quiet by side of 'ee. There be some what calls 'spectable people bad names, some what calls the missuses what employs them dirt names. And Ole Ben what be so easy to see the last of, Ole Ben what's so soon *laid,* same as dust be laid, Ole Ben what don't know, do 'ee, how to blow here and blow there through cracks and crannies, through keyholes and windies, through Pleasures and Palaces, from Journey's End to John-o'-Groat's, Ole Ben have got to put up with hearing his missus called Grummer by a bedlam! I do know 'ee, Mr. D. No-man! ye be an indulgent gent, a 'good luck and good-bye to 'ee!'"

gent, a gent that can walk and talk pat-a-cake tender with a mind-your-step maid at his side. But look well to she, mister, *look well to she*! Her've deceived an old 'ooman. Her've a-flouted an old man; and let me tell you you'll wish, afore she's done with you, you was buried under Pummery, rather nor got she scrabblin' at thee's vitals."

But at this point even the unbelligerent and propitiatory Dud could stand no more, and he advanced towards Old Funky in a manner which—though not exactly suggestive of physical violence—induced that gentleman to turn his back and shuffle off. He had not got far though, and our friend had only just rejoined his companions, when the old man swung round to fire off a final verbal challenge.

"Her've deceived an old 'ooman," he shouted. "Her've flouted an old man: and let me tell 'ee this; afore she be done wi' 'ee thee'll wish theeself buried under Pummery ash-pit rather than have she lodged in thee's bussum!"

With this the old man really did take himself off and Dud was left with nothing to do but to look as indifferent and self-possessed as he could while he escorted the two women to the road.

"We *are* going to my sister's then?" said Thuella Wye as they passed the lamp over the entrance to the station.

Dud glanced at Wizzie. The girl had remained completely mute and quiescent during the old man's vituperation; but now she cast a quick anxious appealing glance at him.

"It's like this," said Dud nervously; and as he spoke he experienced an uneasy feeling that he was falling into the traditional hypocrisy of the lecherous male dodging responsibility for his pleasures. "My landlord's an oldish man and a very pious man, and I *know* he'd only chuck us out if I took you up there; whereas Miss Wye says her sister——"

What it exactly was that stopped him there, just as if a hand had been put over his mouth, he could not have told; but he suddenly felt that whatever he did or didn't do with Wizzie it was essential to get rid of Thuella and get rid of her at once.

"But we'll have," he said, fumbling at any delay that might serve to give him breathing-space, "a glass of beer together somewhere and talk it all over."

Whatever it may have been—whether a desperate gesture

that he caught in the darkness, or a telepathic wave of passionate protest from the girl—he felt now that the one thing he must *not* do was to go with Thuella to this sister in Friary Lane. But what *was* he to do? The "Venetian Post" at his side had merely murmured her acquiescence when he suggested a glass of beer. "What on earth has she got in her mind?" he wondered. "She's had no tea. She'll be wanting her supper. Why doesn't she say that she must get back to Glymes?"

And then, as he glimpsed once more the stone front of the now too-familiar cenotaph, the disturbing thought came to him that he could hardly allow this girl to walk back alone to Glymes.

"What I fool I was," he thought, "not to take her to the station and put her in a taxi!" But simultaneously with this idea he suddenly remembered that except for a few shillings he had no money left. A taxi would empty his pocket!

Characteristically enough, as the three of them moved slowly up South Street and passed beneath the Almshouse clock, which informed him that it was already after seven, he made a mental attempt to detach himself from these absurd little worries. "I've got Wizzie," he reminded himself, "and that's the great thing. Somehow or another it'll work out and we'll be left alone!" Alone—*that's* what he wanted to be, alone with this silent girl in her grey dress and quaint black jacket. What was she thinking now, what was she feeling, as the three of them moved up that crowded street, full of lively housewives come in from the country by late conveyances for their weekly marketing?

He began to be conscious that some of the people they met regarded them with puzzled curiosity; and this, though present to him only as a vague half-felt annoyance, was another teasing irrelevance.

They were nearly at the top of the street now; and since Thuella made no sign, and Wizzie walked at his side—he was still between them—with the automatic docility of a person who had been drugged, he began looking desperately round for some escape from the crowd.

At last, though they were on the opposite side of the street, he caught sight of the friendly old-fashioned entrance to the Antelope Hotel. He stopped and called Thuella's attention to this welcome refuge. "Let's go in *there*!" he said.

The tall girl nodded without speaking, gave him a quick, fleeting, ironic smile, and at once took the lead in crossing the street.

They entered the historic archway, under pleasantly lighted windows, and pushed open the door. Here in front of the office-counter, No-man began to feel decidedly nervous. He glanced quickly to left and right; and making a bold plunge led his companions through a closed glass door into what turned out to be the private bar.

It being so near the dinner-hour he was rewarded for his temerity by finding the place less crowded than might have been expected, and he had no difficulty in selecting an inconspicuous table, neither too far from the cheerful fire nor too exposed to the public eye.

The young women sat down, Wizzie's bag by her side, Wizzie's profile turned away from the table as she stared frowningly at the blaze which threw an added gleam on Thuella's bright hair; while, under the table, the girls' two pairs of shoes seemed as anxious to avoid any sort of contact as were their two pairs of eyes.

No-man, standing at the bar, ordered three large glasses of beer, which, when he had brought them to the table and taken his own seat, remained for a perceptible moment untouched, while the foam ran reproachfully down their sides.

After a glance, however, at Wizzie's averted face he stretched out his hand and pushed her drink towards her.

"Come on," he blurted out impatiently. "Here's to us all— my first drink in Durnovaria!"

Both girls fixed their eyes on him as they raised their glasses, and he noticed how curiously alike the expression in them was, an expression of forced indulgence, that seemed to say to him, "Well! This is a man's game. What is the next move, when we've followed you in *this*?"

He had had no food himself since his breakfast that morning, and while he recklessly drained his glass in hurried gulps it occurred to him that since he had no money to treat them to a decent meal, he might at least have ordered sandwiches.

Instead of doing this, however, he simply replenished his own glass, not only once, but twice, before his companions, who seemed to be sipping beer as if it were some rare wine, had finished half of what their glasses contained.

But the effect of all this drink on **Dud's** empty stomach was to throw him into quite a new mood.

He began to grow not only reckless and free from hesitation, but, privately, to his own inmost soul, simple and emphatic in regard to the twist he wanted to give destiny that night. The more he drank, the clearer did his desire—and his purpose under the urge of his desire—define itself within him. "Damn these delays!" he said to himself. "I've got my girl. I *must* find a room for the night and get rid of this other!"

"I *like* the Antelope Bar," remarked Thuella, taking another little sip of her beer and turning her head slowly round so as to survey the room. "I've never been here before. It's odd how you don't find the right places till you're with strangers!"

Rendered incautious by his drinking, No-man now looked straight at Wizzie and made a mute and helpless appeal to her, the sort of appeal a man makes when a situation is growing totally beyond him.

"Are—the rooms—here—*very*—expensive?" Wizzie murmured in a low voice. "I've got ten shillings in my bag."

Confused and excited as he was No-man could not help catching the expression of absolute astonishment with which Thuella heard these words issuing from that pinched face with its constrained frown. That she should refer to her ten shillings was evidently as surprising as if she had suddenly spoken French.

"Just one minute," the tall girl cried, rising from the table. "Don't decide anything for *one* second—I'll be back in a jiffy!"

Thuella's appearance as she walked to the door must have arrested the attention of a couple of elderly gentlemen, of the country-squire type, who were drinking at the counter, for Dud, who for all his eccentricities was morbidly sensitive to social embarrassment, caught one of them whispering something to the other, while they both glanced at him and Wizzie. "They feel it's odd," he thought, "that the 'Venetian Post' should be mixed up with such funny ones as Wizzie and me!"

He pushed the girl's scarce-tasted glass aside along with his own empty one, jingling them clumsily together, and then leaning heavily over the table he tried to address her in a tone so low as to make it impossible that he should be overheard. "We'll get off somewhere; only I've *got* to think a bit. But I'll find a room somehow all right. I've a few shillings left, and we'll certainly use your ten if we have to. It'll be all right, my dear! Don't 'ee mind too much. This waiting about is awful. It's *damnable*. But you'll see! I'll get rid of her somehow : put her in a taxi or something. It isn't far where she lives."

The girl muttered something he found it difficult to catch. "Say that again, Wizzie. I couldn't hear you."

"He—said—you'd—be better—*buried under Pummery*—than to have me for your woman."

"Oh, *that* old rascal! I see what you mean now, my dear. But, God! what nonsense!" He drew away from her and leant back in his chair. "I don't think", he said, speaking with an exaggerated nicety and choosing his words out of respect for the Antelope Bar, "that *that* gentleman's prognostications need worry us."

But as he saw her frown again, and heard her sigh, and watched the weary submission of the way she once more turned her head and resumed her forlorn staring at the fire, he longed desperately to make her realize how good he intended to be to her, how fond he already was of her, and above all—only that would be very hard to explain—about that feeling of *recognition*. "That's how all real love affairs begin, Wizzie darling," he would say to her as soon as they were alone. "It's like that queer feeling that you've seen some place before, or heard something uttered in a certain tone before. They explain it"—he would tell her when once he got her to himself—"by some trick in the time-sense of the brain; but I believe——" oh, he would confess to her all his wildest fancies as he undressed her by his fire in his attic-room.

But, curse it! he wasn't to be allowed to have her in that room! No, it would be no good, he knew it well, no possible kind of good, trying to cajole his cautious elderly landlord. What he noticed in himself, however, was that he did not feel really indignant about the impossibility of having her up there. "It must be that bed," he said to himself, "and that head on the bed-post."

And at once, after his fashion, he began telling himself an elaborate story about Wizzie and that bed-post head, how she would try to propitiate it, and, when she failed, how there would be a permanent quarrel between her and it!

Wizzie had turned her head away from the fire now. She was fidgeting in her chair and looking down at her hands on her lap. He wondered for a second if she didn't want "to wash her hands," as he had taken for granted that Thuella had gone to do; but he decided she would not have hesitated if such *had* been the case. Then he wondered if she were not secretly studying the "lines" in her hand. She was looking down now with a more intense frown than ever, and he noticed that she had crossed one leg over the other and kept making various little physical movements with her shoulders and with her chin, lifting the former a little and letting the latter sink low down into her chest.

A great rush of tenderness for her thrilled through him as he looked at her.

The little movements she had just been making, as if she had been doing what he himself so often did, *hugging herself to herself* with a shiver of thankfulness that at least she had herself to take refuge with, gave him a sudden stab of delicious awareness of the mystery of her identity.

"I have bought her, I have bought her!" he thought, and then he thought how the relation between them, at least as far as he was concerned, and perhaps for her too, was a far more exquisite one than if they had been ordinary lovers who had known each other in and out for years and were now calmly anticipating their bridal night. For one thing it enhanced the difference of their sex to a far greater extent than if they had had time to know each other well.

"This is how men and women met in the old days," thought the historic Dud, reverting again to his original vision of the Bronze-Age wayfarer with his Stone-Age paramour, "and to have found Wizzie in Durnovaria and for us to sleep together the first day we meet has a beauty that makes an ordinary love-affair—such as I might have had with the 'Venetian Post'—seem tame!"

Dud's pulses began beating with so much excitement as he watched that sallow, oval little face with its chin pressed low between its owner's breasts and its gaze studying carefully—at least so it seemed—the magic of destiny in heart-line and life-line, that it began to grow intolerable to him that it was still uncertain what would happen to them that night.

It seemed to his excited senses just then that it was no less than a miracle that he should be allowed by fate to see that long thin nose, that mute, pitiful mouth, that straw-coloured hair whose stray ends stuck out so comically over that tiny little ear—he could see only one of her ears from where he sat and it really was like a shell, the old simile for a girl's ear, usually so pathetically remote from the truth—that heart-breakingly neat grey dress, her only armour to face the world now that she had discarded her lavender-coloured tights and her performing-dog's cincture of red plush, and, above all, those nervous hands in her lap.

He got up and fetched himself yet another glass of beer, and as he stood over her before resuming his seat, he became aware that it wasn't after all at the fate-lines in her palm that she was looking so intently with lowered eyelids. All she was doing was passing the tips of the fingers of one hand backwards and forwards over the knuckles of the other. "This must be a nervous trick of hers," he said to himself. "She's just thinking, and she's shy of looking at me."

As he drank this last glass, his wits, instead of growing more muddled, suddenly became preternaturally clear.

It seemed to him that never in his life—certainly never with his dead Mona—had the mystery of a woman's identity held him under such a spell! As he gazed at her in this ecstatic trance, all his nerves sensitized and his mind whirling with vivid thoughts, he decided that it was her muteness, her passive submissiveness, the fact that she had never once opened her lips to smile all the hours he had known her, that made her so wonderful to him.

As for her putting out her tongue at those people, he liked her the more for it. Over her mute lips with their pitiful acquiescence, over her lowered eyelids, over her thin fingers that kept up that unceasing nervous movement, hovered, without troubling him at all, that savage grimace she had made at Mrs. Urgan when she called her "Grummer." Those words of hers that morning, "I will make your bed," turned even that ugly look into something that gave him a grim satisfaction.

"Wizzie," he murmured, leaning towards her with an almost imploring note in his voice, "don't 'ee think any more about what that old rascal said! It was all his malice at your going.

93

He can't hurt us. How can he? I don't suppose we'll ever see his face again."

She did lift her hands from her lap now, and she rubbed her face with them, as if trying to obliterate some nervous tremor. When she dropped them after this she let them rest helplessly on the table, and he could not help noticing the difference between *her* hands and Thuella's. Hers were as thin, but much rougher and less tapering, and if Thuella's had struck him, when he was with her on the river-path, as living things with an identity of their own, Wizzie's now lying here looked even more detached from their owner. They looked as if the girl might have got up and gone away, leaving them on the table.

But it was she now who looked round the room to make sure she was not overheard.

"I—am—trying—not," she began in a slow emphatic voice as if she were laying down each word by the side of her hands; but after a second's pause, during which she drew in her breath with a gasp, she finished her sentence very rapidly, giving it that peculiar intonation with which schoolchildren recite a lesson. "Not to think about what he said of me being a burden and a curse to you so that you'll wish you'd been buried under Pummery before you ever saw me or took me away from them, but I can't forget what he said, and I can't stop thinking about it." She uttered these words so much as if she had learned them by heart that they did not strike his ear as tragic, or even solemn.

He went so far—for, for all his romantic sensationalism, Dud had it in him to be a sardonic realist—as to accuse her, in his heart of hearts, of having been composing this sentence all that time he had imagined she was reading the "lines" in her hand.

He looked round at the bar-counter now. "Why doesn't she come?" he said crossly, speaking his thought aloud. "She said she'd only be a second. Has she gone back to Glymes?"

Whether it was that Wizzie's circus-training had given her an unusual command over her expression or whether it was that her jealousy of Thuella had been, all that evening, only skin-deep, she did not show any sign of distress at his concern.

"Didn't she—say—to wait for her before—before we——" she stopped, evidently nervous of being overheard. Their eyes met, however, and this time, although she still did not smile, and he began to wonder if she had completely lost the power of

94

smiling, it was the closest exchange of their real selves that they had had since their first meeting in the caravan.

But her wrists were soon on her lap again and her eyelids lowered, and he could see without seeing that she was once more drawing the fingers of one hand over the knuckles of the other.

Dud refrained from teasing her with any further questions.

"I can enjoy her," he thought, "by simply looking at her, as I am now, and not touching her at all! By looking at her I can seduce that personality in her which says : 'I am Wizzie Ravelston. I belong to Mr. No-man who bought me from Old Funky for eighteen pounds.'

"By looking at her I can seduce that personality in her that makes her hug her knees alone in bed, as I do, and become an embryo again, as I do, and put out her tongue at the 'Grummer'-Universe, as I do."

But he was disturbed in his egoistic thoughts by Wizzie making an unexpected movement. She crossed her legs, giving the table a little push in his direction. She actually stooped down and arranged the position of her bag on the floor. Then sitting up very straight, as if she had only just entered the Antelope Bar, she gazed with interest at a woman who had just come in, and who was looking quietly round the room.

The woman for her part was quick enough in returning Wizzie's stare; and presently it was Dud's fate to see that very smile, that smile that was to have been such an important symbol to him, given not to him at all but to this woman-stranger! The smile, when it did appear, went on flickering over the girl's lips, and Dud could not help noticing what an elfish, even eldritch look it gave her face.

Meanwhile the newcomer, answering Wizzie's mute recognition, came straight up to them, and standing squarely by their table spoke to them both, easily and naturally, looking first at one and then at the other.

"Pardon my bothering you," she said, "I'm Jenny Dearth of Friary Lane, and Thuella told me you wanted a room. I myself sometimes let rooms—to transients—under particular conditions, and I'm always glad to oblige friends of Thuella's. So I thought I'd come round and see if I could catch you before you'd made any other arrangements. I expect you'll want something else later on, but Thuella seemed to think"—here Mrs. Dearth lowered her voice—"that you'd be glad for a night or two to pay the three and six for my double room, which is all I charge when I like people, and I'm sure from what Thuella says I shall like you two—like you ever so much!"

"I knew it was you, directly I saw you come in!" These surprising words from the lips of Wizzie, whose white cheeks now carried an unmistakable flush, were a complete bewilderment—and, it must be confessed, not at all a pleasant one—to Dud No-man. It would certainly have spoiled the fine edge of the whole situation for him had it turned out that Wizzie already possessed respectable friends in Dorchester; and it certainly looked, from the way Mrs. Dearth was now leaning over the girl and whispering to her, that this was precisely the case.

But it turned out otherwise, to Dud's immense relief. Taking a seat between them but refusing any refreshment on the ground that she'd left her supper on the stove and must hurry back, Jenny Dearth soon explained that she and Claudius had been every night to the foreign Circus and though they hadn't spoken to "the young lady on the horse" they knew she noticed them and had appreciated their being there and had been surprised and delighted by the interest they took in her horsemanship.

"That fellow isn't your husband, is he?" Wizzie now inquired rather rudely of this friendly lady.

No-man was unpleasantly affected by the girl's words; but it was clear the lady from Friary Lane did not mind this familiar tone.

"Oh, dear no!" she said with a chuckle. "My husband and I are separated. That fellow's Mr. Cask, my neighbour in Friary Lane. His real name's Roger, but I call him Claudius, because he's so Roman-looking. Mr. Cask and I thought this young lady was the loveliest thing we've ever seen at any Circus. It's a shame—and I should say that to you if you were a nobleman carrying her off"—here Mrs. Dearth discreetly lowered her voice again—"it's a shame that her power with that horse, the way she balances and all, should be given up! But there it is! When young people fall in love——" She looked from one to another as she spoke with such a glow of maternal sympathy that Dud could not feel annoyed. He noticed the tact with which she linked them together, and he saw clearly that this attitude of hers was wonderfully comforting and reassuring to his companion.

"What's become of your sister?" he inquired.

"Oh, she went off home," Mrs. Dearth said. "Father's getting the supper to-night—he often does—and he would have kept it till midnight if she hadn't come."

"She said——" began No-man.

"Oh, yes, she told me! But she *had* to get back to Glymes. I promised her I'd come round. I couldn't lose such a chance of letting my room! You'll both love it. There's a big double-bed, and it'll be a real treat to me to have such romantic guests. Do *try* it, anyway, Mr. No-man! If you like it you can keep your other place as a room to work in. It'll be an escape from us women when you want to be alone!"

Dud's feelings were extremely complicated as he listened to all this. Destiny had certainly answered his prayer! Something about this woman, her gaunt angular figure, her rugged bony face, like the face of an affectionate steed—no wonder she was struck by Wizzie's horse: she was like an old circus-horse herself—made him think of the great Phrygian Mother. Hadn't he heard of some image of that mysterious divinity that had a *horse's head?*

It was a pleasure to him to see his companion look so different, so much less nervous and embarrassed, *and yet,* beneath this pleasure, in the under-sea penumbra of secret feelings that encircled his thought, as an old moon encircles a new one, he was conscious of a definite "let down" in the vibrancy of the situation.

Wizzie had smiled, Wizzie was more at ease, but her consciousness was no longer entirely absorbed in her relation to himself.

The "Stone-Age captive with her Bronze-Age rescuer" was no longer the unmixed note of the occasion.

They all three left the Antelope together; and as they turned down High East Street and passed side by side beneath the pillars of the King's Arms, No-man could not help being aware of the contrast between this moment and the former one when Thuella was their companion.

It was quite clear to him that Wizzie tended a little to "cling" to this friendly image of the Phrygian Mother with the horse's head, and though he did feel ashamed of such a thought it was impossible for him not to wish that it was still his "Venetian Post" who was walking on the other side of the girl. But he could not help being delighted by the picturesqueness of Friary Lane as they now turned into it, passing on their left the tap-room and stables of the King's Arms and, on their right, an ancient wall.

It was at a door in this wall that Mrs. Dearth finally stopped, a massive and ancient door, leading into a small but solidly-built house.

Readers of Dud's veracious chronicle must, however, be warned that they will look in vain in these latter days for the house into which Mrs. Dearth led him, for solidly-built as it was then, it has long since been condemned as unsuitable for human habitation, nor are there any features left by which it could be distinguished by the curious. But it was down a little bare hall-way with a stone pavement that their guide led them then, and opening an inner door ushered them straight into her parlour, a retreat she always spoke of as "the dining-room."

Here there was a warm fire, a supper-table laid for four persons, a wicker armchair on the left-hand of the hearth, and, covering almost the entire wall opposite the fire, an enormous map of the county of Dorset printed in Dorchester in the early days of Queen Victoria.

A man got up from the chair by the fire as they entered, and Dud surmised at once from the tone of his greeting that this was the friend of Mrs. Dearth whom she told them she had nick-named Claudius. "Mr. Roger Cask" was the way, however, she introduced him as they shook hands. Mr. Cask held Wizzie's fingers so long and praised her horsemanship so warmly that the girl listened with the look of a complacent child who had won a prize at school, but it was a relief to our friend that at least she did not smile this time.

While the men were talking, Mrs. Dearth, who quite startled Dud when she removed her hat by becoming more like that Phrygian goddess with a horse's head than he supposed was possible, conducted Wizzie, along with the latter's bag and um-brella, to see the double-bedded room she had told them about in the Antelope.

It was bitterness to him to lose the sentimental-sensual pleasure of seeing this room in company with the *soi-disant*

Madame No-man; but while in the case of both Nancy Quirm and Thuella he had felt very sure of himself, somehow with this horse-faced personage he felt at a disadvantage. "Do I like her or don't I like her?" he asked himself as he was conversing with Claudius. "I don't think I do; but I can't yet quite tell why. I must talk to the 'Venetian Post' about her." And he suddenly found, in his malicious jealousy of a rival who had taken by storm what was to have been the subtle reward of a complicated siege, that he was impatient to draw out the "Venetian Post" on this topic. "She'll explain to me quickly enough," he told himself, "why I don't like this 'Horse-Head!'" For a passing second he found himself wondering how Thuella and this woman could possibly be sisters; but the question had little interest for him, and it left his mind as quickly as it entered it.

The two women were absent for nearly a quarter of an hour, but when they made their appearance again, he found that whatever his grudge was against Jenny Dearth for her unlooked-for interference with the tone of his situation, he *was* impressed by the way she had brushed and combed and generally *thawed out* her young *equestrienne*. He got that impression of half-shock and half-beguilement that men so often get when they mark the difference between a woman in hat and jacket and the same woman with her head bare and in her indoor dress.

Though it *was* the work of the "Horse-Head," as he kept maliciously calling her, and though he still felt jealous that it had been *her* hands and not *his* that had removed Wizzie's outdoor things, he did become aware of a delicious sideways thrust when he observed the intimate indoor softness that now characterized the girl's appearance.

"Why! she's made her change her shoes and stockings," he thought, as he noted the neat black indoor slippers, with a strap over the instep, that the circus-girl now wore. "Did she have those things in that bag?" he wondered.

The supper whose preparation had been disturbed by Thuella, and which apparently had been saved by the discretion of Claudius, proved to be quite a substantial one. Though intended for only two people it had been successfully enlarged for the complete satisfaction of four, and Dud discovered that he was ravenously hungry.

Wizzie herself, whose pale complexion was never of the best, but whose cheeks did now display a faint flush, ate very sparingly, but Claudius ate everything before him, ate it in rapid hungry snatches, while he did his utmost to amuse them all by his lively discourse. "He certainly does look Roman," thought Dud, contemplating the man's long face, his high bald forehead, his heavy-lidded prominent brown eyes, his obstinate chin. He had very little hair, and the chief impression left by his countenance had to do with the weather-beaten skin of his high narrow skull, and with the wrinkled lid-folds above his prominent eyes which gave him a pronounced hawklike expression, both when he half-closed his eyes, which was a trick of his when speaking, and when he fixed the point of his gaze upon any particular object. In this latter case his expression became so *outward* that it was as if his whole intelligence was completely absorbed in the mere act of looking until every reserve of personality *behind* the look ceased to exist.

He had been talking to them for some while in a vivid, lively manner, not exactly humorously, but rapidly and shrewdly, about some semi-official tour he had recently made through the Channel Islands, when it occurred to our friend to ask him point-blank what his particular work was.

At this Claudius stopped abruptly, lifted up his chin, a movement which had the effect of causing the lamplight to illuminate the tip of his small aquiline nose and the creases of his wrinkled, half-closed eyelids, and proceeded to reply as gravely and carefully as if Dud had been an official at a landing-stage.

"I'm a reformer, sir, a reformer," he said; and then, with a half-glance sideways at Mrs. Dearth, a glance that made Dud think of a bald eagle, with moulting feathers, that he had once seen at the Aquarium in Brighton, he proceeded to explain that he had no official job, that he lived on his private means, but that he spent his life meddling with social abuses. "Have you ever," he asked our friend, "read the life of Lord Shaftesbury? The turning point of *my* life came—didn't it, Jenny? But Jenny's tired of hearing about it!—when I reached that passage in one of his letters where he uses the expression: 'I have to grub where the mischief is worst!'"

At this point Claudius shut his eyes completely and lifting one of his hands to his mouth fell into a muse, while he ponderingly bit the nail of his little finger.

"You old liar!" murmured Jenny Dearth, regarding him with what seemed to Dud a stare of doting attention. "He's always been the same!" she pronounced turning earnestly from Dud to Wizzie. "Always, always the same! He talks of living on his 'private means.' As a matter of fact if it wasn't for me he'd have been in the workhouse years ago! He gives his money away before he sees it—before he's *touched* it! He wouldn't even have the pleasure of doling it out if I hadn't—and by a dirty trick, too—got hold of some of his capital. I'm the one who doles it out now—*to him*! And even that's not safe. Oh, what a liar you are, Claudius!"

It was impossible to believe that Mr. Cask hadn't heard what his friend said; but, if he had, no actor in the world could have played better a complete mental abstraction that rendered him stone-deaf.

When he woke from his musings, gave up biting his finger-nail, and lowered his chin, it was upon Wizzie that he fixed his raptorial bird's gaze. "I hope that old horse," he said, "won't suffer too much from missing you. I suppose," and he turned his moulting eagle's gaze on Dud with a little appraising nod that made our friend feel as if his own head were growing horse-like, "I suppose you'll give this one so much pleasure that in the general balance it'll be worth more than the pain of the horse."

The faint flush upon Wizzie's cheeks deepened. "It isn't that he doesn't like Popsy," she protested earnestly. "You mustn't think that! And you mustn't think Popsy does like *him*." She kept looking at Mrs. Dearth as she spoke. "He really *does* like Popsy. He's proud of having her on his back! It's only that he knows me better, and I know him better, and we've been so often miserable together and happy together. He always snuggled up to Popsy. When she goes in to his tent. He did it when she first——"

Wizzie paused for a moment and frowned in deep thought. "Come on, child—out with it!" cried Mrs. Dearth. "When she first *what*?"

No-man was astonished to see how good-naturedly the touchy girl accepted this friendly brusqueness.

"When she first came," she went on. And then she smiled with a most confidential smile at her hostess. "I think," she added, "he likes to be sad with me and happy with her, and I expect that's what—what's only natural!"

Roger Cask looked a good deal more Roman than any existing bust of the real Claudius as he concentrated his birdlike brown eyes on the circus-rider. "I've had occasion once or twice," he began, "to investigate the treatment of animals in our small travelling shows and I've often been agreeably surprised to find——"

He went on at some length to relate his impressions; but, since Wizzie was now only an interested listener, No-man's mind wandered to other things.

He began, for instance, to take in the general appearance of Mrs. Dearth's sitting-room. He noticed with some surprise that the "Horse-Head" kept her place scrupulously clean. As far as the furniture went the room might even have been called austere. What pictures there were seemed to be old-fashioned oil-paintings, no copies of masterpieces, but the sort of stiff quaint, original pictures one sees in farm-house parlours, and there was a complete absence of all touches of feminine softness. The room indeed might well, Dud thought, have been the dining-room of an impecunious elderly bachelor, possessed, not of a wife or daughter, but of a shrewish housekeeper.

"But the devil take the dining-room and the whole house!" Oh, how enchanting his girl looked sitting so sedately by the side of "the Horse-Head!" "I've saved her from Old Funky," he thought, "saved her and *bought* her for eighteen pounds!"

As he looked at her now in her grey clothes he felt suddenly as if he had never seen a woman before: yes, in relation to this girl he was a real *No-man*; or rather he was a Man without a Name, encountering, for the first time in his primeval wanderings, a Woman without a Name! Oh, how the mere fact of their being strangers to each other, not "lovers" in the ordinary sense, enhanced this miraculous feeling!

An ordinary lover, an ordinary betrothed man, could have no notion, in comparison with what *he* felt, of the divine mystery of these things. Everything about Wizzie transported him with a thrilling reverence, with an *awe* even, such as he had never known. Her submissiveness, her mute acceptance of their extraordinary relation, gave him an ecstasy that made him feel almost faint. Yes, her phrase, "I will be your woman: I will make your

102

bed," had been as much of a covenant between them as his signing of that cheque in the caravan. The thought that he alone in the whole world had the right to undress her, had the right to break down that sacred barrier between a man and a woman, which was the screen between tedious illusion and all the prismatic enchantments of reality, made him dizzy in the pit of his stomach.

If she hadn't been so silent and quiet, if she hadn't lain back upon destiny like this, if she had been flirtatious, if she had chattered, the whole spell would have been broken. His ignorance of what her feelings were all this time was one of the deepest of the *notes of silence* that gathered between them like a mist of thin sweet rain. Were ordinary girls of the street like this? If so—but of course they weren't! They chattered, they drank, they flung out cynical obscenities, they ogled and leered, they told fabulous stories.

How much more exciting it was in the old days when you rescued a woman from the oppressor! She was quiet then. Perhaps she did not even know your speech or you hers. And it was like that with Wizzie. What was she wearing under that nursery-maid's grey dress?

The glamour of her muteness, the glamour of her relation to him, turned everything she wore into a delicately withdrawing mystery. He felt as if he wanted to make love to her boots, her stockings, her waist-band, her funny hat! The mystery of her evasive inscrutability flowed through all these things, flowed *inwards* through them into her infinite feminine soul, receding, receding, yielding, yielding, so that of their heavenly "seduction" there was no end!

How unimportant this business of "beauty" in women was about which men made such a fuss! Men who only wanted "beauty" had no idea of the ineffable mystery.

Damn this dining-room and that map of Dorset! Would this meal never come to an end? He now began to wonder what kind of pictures would look down upon him when he had Wizzie to himself in the chamber upstairs.

And then, all suddenly and uncalled for, a vision of his familiar bed-post rose up, just above the table-lamp, between himself and the girl.

All Souls' night had come! And here he was, plunged into a

treachery to his past, which, if he had been told of its possibility when he awoke that morning, he would have laughed at with incredulous indignation. But he had from his earliest days suffered from the savage perversity of a morbid imagination. Indeed, he had by degrees built up an elaborate technique against the loathsomeness of the images that the demon in him was liable to conjure up against his will. For some reason to-night, however, he felt too excited to make his accustomed *immediate* use of this technique. He felt so strong in his exaltation at the prospects of his night with his Stone-Age capture that he was ready to dally a while with the old disease before uttering the magic word that dismissed it. He knew it was a dangerous thing to do; but there is nothing like the moment when cerebral lust blends with romantic idealism to make a morbid nature reckless, or to fill timid nerves with abnormal courage. And the demon of his bed-post—that sub-human entity so fatally dear to "the Woman from Wales"—took full advantage of Dud's moment of pride. It began making love to the pitiful shreds and tatters of Mona's unthinkable state under that cemetery-mound. It became something that resembled the terrible "Devourer" of Egyptian judgment scenes, only to our friend's monstrous fancy it was immersed *in*, and yet emerging *out of*, the unspeakable dissolution upon which it fed.

The horror of it was, as the man's excited mind still refused to dismiss his torturing demon, that the idea began now to enter his head that by leaving the poor eidolon of his frantic worship alone that night with the solitary bed-post, he was deliberately giving "her" up as a prey to the thing.

All his recent reasonable view of the invisible odalisque of his last ten years, as something quite different from the real Mona, as something transformed, in fact, to a Being created by desires in him that Mona herself could never rouse, only left the un-lucky wraith more pitiful. He seemed to hear the unhappy phantom crying out to him for help! He felt a sudden impera-tive to rush from this alien house, to let this alien girl sleep as she might in her "Horse-Head's" bedroom, and fling himself between the "Devourer" and this helpless wraith. This would be the first night for ten years that he had not slept in that bed of "the Woman from Wales." What would *she* think of his de-sertion?

His thoughts became more and more unbridled, more and more frightful in their monstrous inventions and at last things went so far that the fever of the unnatural exaltation that had brought it all about began to drain away. He began to feel weak and inert.

Matters had reached this point, when he became aware that the monotonous voice by his side, whose steady sound had been the accompaniment of the madness of his thoughts, had ceased; and that a quite different voice was speaking, and speaking to him.

"You're tired, Mr. No-man," Mrs. Dearth was saying, "and I'm sure your little lady here has had enough of our chatter. Don't let Claudius and me keep you up, if you want to go to bed." She paused and exchanged a quick feminine look with Wizzie. "But don't you men move *just* yet," she went on. "I'll take *you* upstairs," and again she looked at Wizzie, whose eyes, Dud could not help noticing, were fixed upon the hands in her lap just as they had been at the Antelope, "and when I've made sure you're comfortable I'll come back and break up this—what do you call it?—this happy symposium!"

Thus she spoke and rose at once from her chair, while Wizzie, without giving No-man so much as a single glance, got up quickly too, and bidding Claudius a nervous but self-possessed good-night, allowed herself to be led from the room.

No-man mechanically did as their hostess had suggested. He turned his chair towards the fire, refused the more comfortable one offered by Roger Cask, and bending over the grate lit a cigarette with a torn envelope from his pocket.

"Oh, by the way, Mr. Cask," he said, "*would* you mind telling me where the lavatory is?"

"Certainly—certainly," responded the other and went to the door; but when he reached it he paused and turned: "I generally go out myself," he said "for ordinary purposes, to the back of the King's Arms. There's a nice place there. Ours is next to the spare room where your"—he hesitated a second—"where your wife is, and the 'flush,' for I saw to its plumbing myself is rather—rather violent, but, of course, do just as you like!"

Dud moved past him ungraciously with the barest nod and went out into the street.

Roger Cask followed him, pointing with his hand, and exclaiming: "There, over there! You can't miss it; it's just out-side——" But the man's words were drowned in the musical voice of a youth selling the local paper. The tune to which he sang, "*Ech ... o! Ech ... o!*" would have charmed Dud at any other time; but on the top of Mr. Cask's aqueducts and plumb-ing it was too much. He had not gone many steps in the direc-tion indicated—and it had begun to occur to him that since he was so close to his lodging he ought to inform his landlord that he would be out all night—when he came upon a musician standing in a stable-arch and accompanying his singing on a concertina. This man looked at him—a wistful supplicating look —and Dud, feeling superstitious about refusing anything to any-one on this night of nights, fumbled in his leather purse for a piece of silver.

"I was a double-dyed fool," he said to himself as he produced a shilling for the singer, "not to take a room at the Antelope. Between us we'd have had enough. I feel as if I were going to my girl in the temple of Vesta!"

Vesta or no Vesta, Dud certainly felt, as he emerged from the yard outside the tap-room, that he could not even spare the time to go and speak to his landlord. "I *must* get to her," he thought. "The 'Horse-Head' may have scared her. She may be lying there now, wondering why I don't come."

As soon as Dud returned to the room, Mr. Cask fixed his caged-eagle's eye upon the visitor and asked him quietly if he didn't want to go to bed.

Not waiting for an answer, he mounted two or three steps of the narrow staircase and called out: "Jenny! Jenny! come down!"

"*Coming!*" came the faint reply from that upper room; and a second later, with the opening and shutting of a door, Mrs. Dearth descended. "You'll find a good fire up there," she said to our friend; and then, for on her appearance Claudius had re-treated to the dining-room, she came up close to him. "Be nice to her," she whispered. "She's feeling shaky after all this."

The dining-room door shut behind her, and Dud mounted the stairs. There was no question about what room to enter when he reached the top, for emerging from the spare room the fire-light was flickering into the small dark landing. For two or three seconds he stood there, breathing heavily, his eyes fixed, not on

106

the door, which was ajar, but on the flickering light on the landing-wall. He felt as if this crucial moment, with all it contained, with the darkness round him, with the cry "*Ech . . . o! Ech . . . o!* with the faint murmur of voices in the room below, with his little unlighted attic in High East Street, with those three mounds out there in the cemetery, with that foreign Circus in full blast behind the farm-implements, was totally *unreal*. He had a sensation in his legs as if, were they to take a single step, they would find nothing beneath them but empty space!

And then, without a second's warning, the enormous sallow countenance of Mr. Quirm of Glymes materialized between him and the open door. Vague, nebulous, darker than the darkness, the man's lineaments wavered, fluctuated, solidified, and then faded away. But even as they faded Dud's original impression of the fellow's eyes returned upon him. They were devoid of every kind of expression. They were part of the feeling he had had just now, they *were* that feeling, that the whole place, with his whole day, All Souls' Day in Dorchester was *unreal*, unreal with a dissolution that would turn it to dust under his feet if he moved an inch.

He made a desperate interior motion of his whole being—a motion that, in a blinding strain of shivering tension, resembled a motion he had once made when "going under gas" at the dentist's; and he *did* move an inch. He moved more than an inch, for he moved straight to the lighted door, opened it, and entered the room.

Wizzie was in a white night-dress, her thin, colourless hair tied back with a black ribbon. But she was not in bed. She was seated in front of the fire. She neither moved her head nor changed her position as he closed the door, and he noticed that her wrists were between her knees, and that she was rubbing the knuckles of one hand with the fingers of the other.

PART TWO

3

CANDLEMAS DAY

Three months had passed since Dud No-man came to Dorchester. It was now Candlemas, the second of February, and our friend, with his round skull cropped even closer than when Wizzie first beheld it on the pillow by her side in Friary Lane, sat writing at the window of his attic.

The rooks, flapping about round those ancient nests in the high elms above the roofs, were hardly less clamorous than in the autumn, though cleverer naturalists than Dud might have been able to detect from their sounds and movements that winter had not only come but was nearly gone.

His fire was burning well, his shelves of old books responded warmly to its pleasant glow, his coloured sketch of Nuremberg beckoned him with its accustomed benediction to follow its easy track among the richly-mingled walls and towers of that ideal city. But on the thick western wall of his own deeply gabled attic window there lay no sunlight to-day, and if he wanted to conjure up any token of the approach of spring all he could think of were the hothouse daffodils in the greenhouse by the bridge at the foot of the street.

He had not yet washed up his breakfast things. "The Royal Martyr" was still simmering over the gas-jet on the stove in the kitchen. The belly of "Henry VIII" still bulged with the refuse that must presently be taken downstairs.

He himself was smoking only his second cigarette. But he had left his armchair by the fire the moment he had eaten his meal; for he had been in haste to get to his writing that morning. His hand was moving now at top speed over the white paper, directing the pen-point that did the work, that indeed sometimes went on doing the work when its director's attention had drifted away. But fast as his hand crossed the white paper that Candlemas morning his mind went faster still, beating against one barrier after another, flying down one open vista after another, losing itself in infinite perspectives, creating and destroying one landscape after another, each one leading to variable and vanishing horizons.

"I've got my work," he kept thinking to himself. "Whatever happens I've got my work." And indeed in all this exciting and agitating time since he snatched Wizzie from the Circus he had displayed an almost savage resolution in his concentration on his writing.

Morning after morning with an obstinacy that surprised himself he left the girl in bed at Mrs. Dearth's and came over to his attic, got his own breakfast by eight o'clock, and settled down at his window to work.

Mrs. Dearth humoured him to the limit in all this. She herself got into the habit of carrying up Wizzie's breakfast long after she had had her own; and this went on till it seemed as if the little circus-rider would soon fall into the role of a privileged toy of the older woman; the Friary Lane establishment becoming a doll's house, and the girl's self-centred oblivious reveries resembling the natural passivity of a cherished doll.

The "aura" of this old Roman-British town, with its layers upon layers of human memories, semi-historic and prehistoric, seemed to have a magical power over Dud's imagination. He began tapping levels in his consciousness that he had not known he possessed.

The moment he sat down at that table in front of those old roofs the spirit of the past seemed to obsess him. Sometimes he actually wrote so fast—especially when his more analytical faculties were in abeyance—that it was as if he became a medium, writing, he scarce knew what, under some unknown "control." He knew he was living an unnatural sort of life, sleeping with Wizzie at night, living with her half the day—for after he returned to Friary Lane, early in the afternoon, he never saw his attic again till the next morning—and he knew that all the customs, habits, crotchets, peculiarities, in which he had indulged himself for the last ten years, had been devastatingly infringed upon, some of them outraged. He knew that he was living, as it were, from hand to mouth, from day to day. He knew that the old meticulous continuity of his existence was completely shattered.

112

And yet no one could have persuaded D. No-man that he was anything but happy. He had come to accept his relations with Wizzie as his unquestioned fate, as the trench in the great cosmic battle-field up and down which it was his destiny to march, making the utmost of every "view" it offered and escaping every morning to that secure "dug-out" of his own, where he kept his resolutely guarded tablets, and where he became an obsessed *hand*, covering sheet after sheet of paper with intimations reaching him out of the air.

Every now and then, while his pen automatically went on moving, he became aware of the noises of the street. They had come to be curiously dear to him, these sounds. Best of all it was when the bells of Fordington Church, away to the east, reached him over the roofs. These sounded only on certain days, and even when they were ringing it needed a favourable wind to make them clear to his ear; but when he *did* hear them they seemed to have the power of transporting him to a city as ideal as his pictured Nuremberg, a city charged with the rich, sweet residue of centuries of human life, life from which the suffering and bitterness had been winnowed, and only the long, dim deposit of humanity's afterthoughts, its intimations of hope against hope, lived on, in the air-motions of that far-carried sound.

He had come to like the noise of the great busses too, rolling up or rattling down the street with their reminders, so pleasant to his history-loving ears, of the old coaching days. Even the rumble of the ordinary motor-cars and lorries, as he caught their unseen passing from where he sat, seemed to come to him through a delicately muffled mist, softened by the ghosts of earlier, less mechanical sounds, and interspersed even now, especially in the morning hours, by the friendly beat of horses' hoofs and of the rattle of milk-carts.

It pleased him to think of "the winding mossy ways" along which all this London Road traffic through the town from Weymouth to Salisbury, and from Salisbury to Weymouth, had to travel ere it reached its destination. He had grown quite attached to the two Dorchester bridges over which these vehicles had to pass; the little one at the foot of the street, by the White Hart and the Bridge Hotel, and the big eighteenth-century stone one, beyond the filling-stations, known as Grey's Bridge.

But what he liked best of all after the ringing of the bells was the clatter of human feet on the two pavements. Never had the poetry of the anonymous human tread struck him as poignantly as it did here. He found himself recalling the famous passages in Keats about this sound, as the poet imagined its rising among the classic towers of Corinth or the gothic arches of Chichester. He would even try sometimes to distinguish the tread of a man from the tread of a woman when a chance hush in the stir of the thoroughfare threw into special emphasis the steps of some solitary pedestrian. On this particular Candlemas morning, windless and warm, though grey and cloudy, Dud had propped open a little the lower portion of his old-fashioned attic-window. For this purpose he had not scrupled, in the absent-minded impatience of his fast and furious work, to use a large edition of Malory.

His burst of inspiration, such as it was, having exhausted itself, and his pen having lost its magic, Dud felt ashamed of what he had done with this particular book, and he proceeded to substitute a piece of firewood.

As he made the exchange, and in the process opened the window wider, he was conscious of a particularly refreshing breath of air coming in. "From the southwest it comes," he thought, "from Maiden Castle." And he remembered how Claudius had been speaking lately of taking him over there and of showing him the site of the last excavations. "But I must see it by myself first," he thought. "I'm damned if I'll go with *him* to such a place till I've got my own impressions of it!"

Since his childhood Dud had obscurely linked his mother's bed-post demon with Malory's *Questing Beast*; and still seated in his chair by the window, he now began hurriedly turning over the pages of the volume, searching for the familiar passages relating to this legendary being. Deeply implicit in the old dark religion of his mother's people, the hunting of this monster was apparently confined to one particular family, of whom Malory only knew two, Pellenore and Palomides, who might have been father and son.

Dud soon found the passage he wanted and read for the hundredth time the following words: "And this meanwhile there came Sir Palomides, the good knight, following the *Questing Beast* that had in shape a head like a serpent's head, and a body like a leopard, buttocks like a lion, and footed like an

114

hart; and in his body there was such a noise as it had been the noise of thirty couple of hounds questing, and such a noise that beast made wheresomever he went; and this beast evermore Sir Palomides followed, for it was called his quest."

"For it was called his quest," Dud muttered aloud, and returning the volume to the bookcase, he left the room and went into his kitchen. Here he lit the gas, set "the Royal Martyr" on the flame, and added a few crusts he had overlooked to the tea-leaves and egg-shells already overburdening the belly of "Henry VIII." While he did this he tried to recall the obscure arguments, drawn by Professor Rhys from a gnomic allusion of Taliessin's, that identified this *Questing Beast* with the ambiguous word "Dor-Marth," meaning the Door of Death.

Then he remembered how that morning as he came along beside the stream which flows between Orchard Street and the meadows, striking it to the east of the prison as he came down the hill, he had met an elderly gentleman with a dog. He had at once started telling himself a story about this elderly gentleman, whom he imagined as retired from some simple business and leading an absolutely harmless, happy, and selfish life. Dud had decided, as he went along between this stream and the meadows, and finally turned up High East Street by the bridge, that he could not have identified himself with this old man if he had not been at bottom *like him*, if he also had not been absolutely harmless and absolutely selfish.

He had decided then that he would certainly get on well in Dorchester if the psychic weather of the spot were of this kind. Had the place always been like this? Was a blameless propitiatory self-centredness the characteristic of the ancient Durotriges?

But he had also met, down by that river-path, an extraordinary number of babies in perambulators. Never in his life had he seen so many harmlessly selfish babies. Elements that went deep in Dud's solitary character responded instinctively to both these extremes of egoistic harmlessness. He had always been something of an old man, he had always been something of a baby; and in these daily walks from Friary Lane to the brick bridge, and thence up High East Street to his lodging, he had come to derive a mystical satisfaction from identifying himself both with the placid infants and with the placid old men.

115

This very morning he had been privileged to witness a singular encounter between one of his philosophic infants—only this one was out of its perambulator and on the steps of its dwelling—and a ruminative dog of an inquisitive turn of mind. This particular baby who could *just* walk, was only faintly concerned by the fact that the door of its home had by chance been shut, nor was it much more concerned over the approach of the dog, who stood on its four legs almost as high as *it* did on its two. Dud was fascinated by the manner in which this young egoist guarded in one hand the crust of bread it was holding, while with the other it pointed out to the dog, with a sagacious forefinger extended the desirability of its seeking its fortune in a distant meadow.

After finishing his breakfast and resuming his place at his writing-table, No-man was annoyed to discover that his inspiration refused to return. He was accustomed to these lapses in his magnetic contact with his sources of inspiration but as a rule after waiting for a time with his ear attuned to the murmur of the thoroughfare the breath of the spirit would return.

But on this occasion it refused to do so, and laying down his pen he stared in a sort of indolent trance at the rooks' nests in the opposite trees. He still was conscious of a faint delicious stirring in the air from the southwest, and it seemed to him that it came in stronger gusts than before.

"No!" he thought, "I'll have nothing to do with Maiden Castle till I can go out there absolutely alone!"

Turning away from the window he swung half-round and cast a malevolent glance at the dark, cracked, worm-eaten visage on his bed-post. "Dor-Marth! Dor-Marth!" he muttered vindictively; and then he came near chuckling aloud as he remembered the similar tone in which Wizzie had spat out the word "grummer" at Mrs. Urgan.

"Is Rhys right," he thought, "in flinging this old word of Taliessin's at you? What a word it is! 'Hunter of Dead Souls'—but Malory says you have the head of a serpent. You don't look like a serpent to me, Dor-Marth!"

Dud realized he was behaving like the baby he had watched that morning; but the truth is that his ten years of contact with this piece of obscure wood-carving had endowed it with all that was least admirable in his own nature. The thing had become a sort of "sin-eater" to him in the course of these years, and even if it had been just a block of wood with no connection with any mythic creature, it would have imbibed something, as a child's doll might have done, of its owner's perversity.

"This would be a good day," he said to himself, "to slip off to Maiden Castle." And he wondered vaguely what it was that kept bringing Maiden Castle into his head this Candlemas morning. He now heard the clock above the Corn Exchange strike eleven, and with this sound there came a ring at the house-door downstairs. He listened idly for any sequel to this signal, but without much concern, for as a rule such a sound meant only a visit to his landlord, who, being a vestryman of All Saints', was frequently having calls on church business.

But he got up quickly with some interest when he heard steps ascending the last two flights of stairs. The mere sound of these steps disturbed him. They were shuffling steps and they kept halting, as if the person ascending stopped to breathe, or to look round, or to listen. There was a long intermission of this sort when the visitor reached the top. What was he doing? Was he peering into the small kitchen?

No-man went to his door and opened it with an abrupt jerk. To his amazement, and it must be confessed to his extreme disgust, there stood Old Funky. "I—be—come——" began the old man who was dressed in a shiny broadcloth coat from below which, when he finally turned to depart, the coat-tails of his official attire were just observable.

In one hand he carried his own ancient bowler hat and in the other an almost equally battered woman's riding-hat with a cord twisted round the brim.

"Come—Mister—for to *seech* other."

Biting his lip with annoyance No-man made a sign for him to enter; and as soon as he was well in the room closed the door behind him. He then swung the chair round he had just been sitting in. "Sit down, Mr. Urgan," he said.

Old Funky hurriedly touched the chair with the tips of his long fingers, as if it was necessary to bewitch it first, or unbe-witch it, and did as he was bid.

"For—to—see 'ee, Mister, just for to *seech* other, Mister!"

This running together of the syllables "see" and "each" into the single syllable "seech" was, No-man felt, exactly characteristic of Mr. Ben Urgan. The man must have felt this himself too, for he repeated the phrase with unctuous satisfaction. "For to *seech* other, Mister." No-man glanced angrily round the room. The only thing that gave him an ounce of comfort was that he had waylaid Old Funky and got him safely seated before politeness compelled him to offer him the armchair by the fire.

As for the "sin-eating" bed-post, which now appeared anxious to catch his eye, he was conscious that it had never looked better satisfied with the general trend of events.

"This 'ere riding-'at," said the visitor, tapping the object referred to with the brim of his own bowler, "be her'n what be with 'ee. Me Missus can't-a-wear'n, nor Poppy can't-a-wear'n. And me Missus said 'twere a tearin' pity that such a 'at, a 'at might have been a Honourable's 'at if not a Ladyship's 'at, should be gived to a scarecrow so I takes the liberty, and pleasure, as 'ee might say, of killing two spadgers with one brick. I've brought 'ee she's 'at, and *us* be able to *seech* other!"

As he uttered these words he turned to No-man's table at the window and with meticulous nicety laid down his bowler on the top of Dud's last page and the riding-hat beside it.

"Be that the book you're making?" he asked when with his alert roving eye he noted the manuscript. "Bain't about these 'ere parts, I suppose? Bain't about Darchester, be 'un?"

"I never tell anyone a word about my writings, Mr. Urgan, till I've got them quite finished."

"Fear they'd steal 'un, eh? Mare's bosom take all, but I can't blame 'ee, Mister! Them blighters from Ameriky be in *our* line of business too, and by crick they've a' stole all. I warrant there be some even now, if all were known, skivvying about this sober street, who'd as soon snatch up these here papers and hide 'un under their vesties as pick lice from a dog!"

"Well, Mr. Urgan, this is my time for work and I'm afraid I must bid you good-bye. As to Miss Ravelston's hat I can assure you she has no use for it just now. But if your good lady doesn't want it—and I can see it can't be called a very *new* hat—you needn't bother to carry it away. I'll dispose of it somehow. You can leave it here."

But Old Funky made no move that promised any submission to this dismissal. He gave No-man a look of the most equivocal

118

blackmailing subtlety that our friend had ever beheld. There was a thin trickle of indescribable malice oozing from this look which fell on every word the old man uttered, soaking it in venom.

"Me and *her* what now bides along of 'ee, Mister, know'd each other better, looksee, than be natural for she to tell 'ee of! There were a time when her and me were wondrous confiding. 'Twas about that time—'tweren't so very long ago neither—that her told Majesty's Spectre a plumbing great lie about a axidint our hoss had. Her were afeard 'twould have to be destroyed—that's what made she do it—destroyed, see? put out of way you understand, but what her didn't count on was Ole Ben looking out for his wone self, and not forgettin' nor forgivin' like most silly ole men what have grown confidin' with a young woman what has a 'lurin' figure."

"What—on—earth—are you talking about?"

And then Old Funky gave him a second extraordinary look. It was primarily a look of a furtive rat: "How far can I go before this dog springs?" But it was also a look of what might be called the "adhesive plaster" of hatred, a look whose hatred "clung" like the fabulous shirt of Nessus to the very soul of its victim.

But a shirt—even a poisoned one—is after all inanimate, and Old Funky, in his role of the avenging parasite, seemed to flit like an insatiable mosquito round all the undefended places in No-man's nature, seeking the spot where he could, with safety to himself, settle and suck. "I be come so us can *seech* other," he repeated. "Me Missus have spoke ere now of calling in the Law"—he spoke of "the Law" with an unctuous veneration, as if it were a sort of super-Funky, a kind of arch-mosquito of bloodsucking—"but in course as 'twixt an Ole Ben like me, what means no 'arm, and a chit like *She* what do now bide along of thee's self, 'tis best, and so I tell my Missus when her do carry on about thee's gall and me, 'tis best to *seech* other, 'tis best to come to 'appy 'rangements. The truth be"—here Old Funky actually extended a furtive wrist and a confidential hand, and lowered his voice to a whisper—"that thee and me with 'eads together and a few gold sovereigns to make the poor 'ooman's 'eart rejoice, can settle this 'ere trouble smooth and sweet, without calling in no lawyer, nor no bloomin' jurycourts."

Dud advanced a step towards the seated figure, his eyes fixed not on the man's face, but on the sharp line where his reddish wig met his bald scalp, and even at that crucial moment he found himself quite vexed that there was no louse there to-day to emphasize the nice distinction.

"Come now," he said in a low clear voice, "Don't beat about the bush! What actually *was* there between you and—and Miss Ravelston? What actually *is* there between you now, eh? Speak up! Tell me every *single* thing. Have you ever—have *any* of you ever—taken—liberties with her?" He felt as he said it, that "liberties" was an outrageous word to use, but Old Funky's insight into his character was so deadly that he began to feel sick with alarm and disgust. How could the old rogue have known that he wouldn't act like a normal man and kick him incontinently down the stairs? How could he have known that it was one of D. No-man's deepest peculiarities *not to be able to fly* into a normal rage. How could he have known it, although like Othello "not naturally jealous", he *had* grown to have, in everything where Wizzie was concerned, an almost insane curiosity—not jealous curiosity, but what might be called erotic curiosity—carried to a disturbing degree? How could Old Funky —except by throwing a Nessus-shirt of appalling comprehension round his adversary's soul—know that this man, instead of indignantly cutting him short, as a gentleman would, as any man of honour would, would plunge instead into a detailed inquisition that clearly caused him extreme suffering and that would have thrown Wizzie, had she known what he was doing, into a fit of furious indignation?

At the time, after his babyish fashion, snatching at a glitter in the air—though that glitter was the ambiguous phosphorous of his girl's secrets—No-man thought only of his own desire to learn at all costs, even at the cost of not kicking Old Funky downstairs, what exactly was the kind of lies *possible* for these people to invent about Wizzie's life with them. No sooner had Old Funky departed than it did occur to him that the mere listening to these lies was a gross treachery to Wizzie. At the moment, however, it seemed the opposite to treachery, for wasn't he "drawing out" the old man? Wasn't he craftily discovering what dangers there might be, for both of them, in this game he was playing? Of course if instead of being D. No-man, an individual who lacked the divine right of losing his temper, he had been a gentleman and a lover—— But our friend was neither of these. He was a nameless bastard, whose mind was so morbid, and whose virility was so weak, that he could neither "love" as other men or feel angry as other men.

"Of course, Mister," went on Old Funky, "I be only come *this* time to *seech* other. But I'll drop in again to-morrow about this time—for 'tis agen me principles to hurry a gentleman— and if so be to-morrow ye *happens* to have a 'fiver' in yer pocket, what us could give to me Missus, her won't think no more of calling in the Law."

"So you won't tell me," said Dud sternly, "what I ask you? Come on! You'd better tell me. Out with it now! What *is* in your mind about Miss Ravelston? What have you got against her? Did you or anyone else in your damned Circus take liberties with her? What do you mean about that inspector and the accident to the horse?"

Without replying Old Funky rose to his feet. There was not a shade of disappointment, not a shade of confusion in his manner. Apparently his gentleman had acted in complete accordance with schedule.

"*Seech* other to-morrow, Mister. A 'fiver' ain't much. But it'll do wonders with me Missus. No more talk to poor Old Ben about the police and the jury-courts. A 'fiver' bain't much; but I can tell 'ee, private and confidential, 'twill do the trick."

Saying this Old Funky moved to the door, skirting the bony figure of his antagonist who stood as if petrified, half-leaning against the bed-post that lacked its top, and gazing not *at* his tormentor but *through* him.

"Us'll *seech* other to-morrow," the man murmured as he went out. "Arternoon to 'ee, sir."

Dud abode in the same position for some seconds after the fellow was gone. Then he pulled himself up, and threw a ferocious glance at the heraldic monster between him and the fire. "Dor-Marth!" he flung at it. "That's what you are. Dor-Marth!" He tossed aside the chair, where Old Funky had been sitting, with a gesture of disgust and leaning across his table looked out of the window.

It was a mental device of his—for in these last three months of his life with Wizzie he had out of self-protection contracted many such tricks—to throw aside the immediate trouble and

121

force himself to realize his situation in general terms. "Here am I," he forced himself now to think, "looking down on Durnovaria! Beyond those elm-tops are the South Walks. Beyond them is the Amphitheatre. When they killed Mary Channing in 1705, with ten thousand people looking on, did she look *this* way in her last moments, or far off, towards Maiden Castle?"

His thoughts, when he reached this point, ceased to be transcribable in definite words, but their gist was that some kind of sympathy—some friendly Influence beyond the power of that blood-thirsty crowd—may have reached the dying woman from the great earthwork!

A sick disgust with all the material happenings that had ever taken place in this town of such tragic roots seized him now, and he made an effort to think of his soul as altogether detached from matter, detached from all movements of matter, for they were *all* hurting and cruel. Matter couldn't be stirred without pain; and he tried to think of his soul as if it floated in a clear calm sea underneath the whole turbulent business.

"I must talk to that Mr. Wye," he said to himself. "Doesn't Plato teach *how* you can sink down into this sea of untroubled Being, below all the fever of the world?" He went over to his fire and seating himself in his armchair threw some more coal into the little grate.

A blue flame, and then an orange-coloured flame, rose up to welcome this offering, and the light flickered on his cropped skull, on his bony knees, on his powerful wrists, as he leaned towards the blaze. "I'd better tell Wizz," he thought, "but it'll upset her. It'll make her angry."

He realized, as he thought of this, how much everything in his life had come to depend on Wizzie's moods. "Will it vex her, will it please her?" had become, if not his dominant motive, at least his perpetual preoccupation.

He leaned back in his chair now, still thinking hard. "She never talks about those old bad days," he thought. "But *that's* natural. It's still too near and too painful. Aye, what she must have gone through!" He began plumbing all the deep-sea fathoms of what he had learnt about a girl's mind in these last months. But after all how little he knew! Mona had been obviously an exception. But wasn't this one an exception too? Perhaps *every* girl was an exception!

122

Perhaps there was no such thing as the normal woman, or woman-in-the-abstract. What was it that Old Funky had been hinting at and hovering round? The horse was clearly a side issue. But what *did* he mean about Grummer Urgan being jealous? It was inconceivable that Wizz had allowed such a repulsive old man to make overtures to her. She would certainly be justified in getting furiously angry with a lover, however jealous, who for one second played with such a thought. But what did he know about the real conditions of her life with those terrible people? Old Funky may easily—it was exactly what he *might* do—have tried to play the pander with regard to her. "What a thing it is," he said to himself, "that I can listen calmly to a person like that! What is it in me that makes me so—so detached? It's not cowardice, and it's not that I'm so inhumanly philosophical. What the hell is it? Anyone else would have stopped the chap's mouth in a second, and sent him to the devil!"

Dud suddenly felt as though by reason of some lack in his character or in his mental vision, some want of a natural instinct in him to strike back, a clean, straight blow on a ticklish occasion, he was being pushed down a spiritual *cul-de-sac*.

He loathed that old man. He felt a profound suspicion of him. Why, then, had he let him sit in his chair and talk like that about Wizzie? Then it came about, as his mind turned the thing over, that he went so far as to ask himself point-blank whether it was possible that for some convoluted reason he *wanted* Wizzie to have been involved in some squalid and revolting situation! The mere floating into his mind of this insidious doubt made him feel as if there were abysses of dark notions within him whose nature he hesitated to plumb.

The idea was so disturbing that he got up from the fire, went across to the "Questing Beast," and gave its obscure worm-eaten physiognomy a sharp flick with his finger-nail. As he did so another thought came to him. Wasn't it only too likely that what had filled Old Funky with so much gall was a rebuff he himself had suffered from the girl? Wasn't that what women often did—accuse a man of assaulting them who in reality has rebuffed them? Full of this illuminating idea—and he reproached himself for not having thought of it earlier—No-man began pacing up and down his small attic, bending his head mechanically, and even giving his body a sideways twist, when he was in danger of striking his head against the sloping beam.

"I daren't ask her, though," he thought, "whether anything like that happened. The man's such a disgusting specimen that to suggest that he dared to approach her at all would be an insult." Or *wouldn't* it be? Dud felt he was much more capable of entering into the feelings of that infant he had seen, protecting her crust, or her doll from the dog, than into the feelings of a grown woman.

He had just reached this point in his recondite speculations when he heard much heavier steps than Old Funky's ascending his staircase and ere long there followed a bold decisive knock at his door.

When he went to open it, there stood Mr. Roger Cask, looking as if he had been working hard all that morning on a technical committee for the restoration of the old subterranean water-pipe between Dorchester and Maiden Castle.

Claudius was panting a little from climbing the stairs; but he seemed to display an additional nervousness beyond his dislike of being caught out of breath. He appeared glad, however, to sink down in Dud's chair by the fire, and he willingly accepted a cigarette as soon as the latter had gone through the particular formula, the terms of which had been taught him by Mrs. Dearth. All Claudius's more intimate friends were, in fact, implored by Mrs. Dearth to asseverate to him that they got no pleasure from smoking alone. Dud in his gross way had sometimes wondered whether Claudius saw through this little "formula" but was so damned thankful to enjoy a cigarette that, as Shakespeare would say, he "jumped" this bit of casuistical "cat-ice" so quickly as to give the frozen fish, Conscience, no chance to lift its protesting head.

Mr. Cask's desire was to get rid of desire, to become, in fact, an automaton of self-sacrifice, and he had gone further than many saints in this direction; but if there was one physical sensation that seemed absolutely essential to his restless disposition it was the sensation of smoking; and thus it came about that Mrs. Dearth, whose role in his life was that of the benevolent temptress, was driven to invent this "formula" so that the poor man might have a *little* pleasure.

"Certainly—if it makes you feel more comfortable, No-man,"

Claudius now remarked, sinking back in the chair, and drawing long luxurious inhalations of this desirable nepenthe.

"Oh, I mustn't forget——" he began with a start, for though his memory was like the Tables of the Law in the sphere of social reform, it was liable to lamentable lapses in social intercourse. "I've a message for you. Jenny's going to take Miss Ravelston to tea at Glymes this afternoon and since she—they, I mean—had a late breakfast—or Miss Ravelston had a late breakfast—and they, *she*, I mean, doesn't want any lunch, they thought you might get a bite of something indep-endent-ly, and come round about three, and we'd all go out there together."

Claudius uttered the word "independently" with an odd kind of reluctance, as if to his social-conscious feelings the partaking of anything "independently" was a sort of debauch.

"Are *you* going out there?" inquired No-man with surprise, for anyone less addicted to such jaunts than Mr. Cask it was hard to imagine.

The question seemed to destroy the blessed moment of repose in which the man had been indulging. He threw the end of his cigarette into the fire and pulled himself together with a jerk, sitting straight up.

"I'm collecting subscriptions—for the excavations," he said wearily; and then, with an obvious effort to get the interior wheels of his energy working : "The excavations at Maiden Castle next summer—there's a great deal to be learnt about those early races, gaps—large gaps—in the history of Evolution that must be filled."

"But Mrs. Dearth told me," said No-man, "that you didn't get on with her father, that you couldn't bear that chap Quirm."

Claudius's brown eyes seemed to gather a film over them, and a look of worry came into his face. He frowned in a vexed, troubled, bewildered way. "I can't—go—into it—now," he said, "but I've heard from many quarters things I don't like about that woman's life. It isn't only in slums that there's wicked 'mischief'; and wherever mischief is I've got to 'grub' " This final word he rapped out with the flicker of a smile.

No-man surveyed him with interest. He looked so much more like one whose destiny it is to pounce than to "grub," that our friend was conscious of the presence of an almost ghastly *tour de force.* If the man were an "automaton of sacrifice" he was one that required a great deal of cranking. "She told me of the loss of her boy," Dud remarked carelessly. "I met her the first day I was here—in the cemetery." He spoke without intention, but there came over him, after the words were out of his mouth, a wave of profound sadness : "Three months," he thought, "and I haven't been back there. I've certainly left them what that woman called 'free.' "

Claudius gave him one of his most raptorial looks. "That boy——" he began, "that boy ought never——" But he stopped short, turning his head away, as if his decision not to go on was too sudden even to give him time to lower his great eyelids. "It's only," he said, hastily, evidently anxious to turn No-man's thoughts off the subject of the dead boy, "those—excavations. I haven't been to Glymes about it yet."

"I should—have thought," remarked Dud, looking sharply at him, "that there would be a—a prejudice against meddling with Maiden Castle."

Claudius turned his eyes upon him. "That's just what I mean," he said. "It's one of those cases when virtues are as bad for Progress as vices—Evolution means Scientific Excavation at one end and Scientific Experiment at the other. The more you know about what *was*, the faster you can create what *will* be. We must undermine *all* prejudices!"

An hour or so later Dud, his head full of his interview with Old Funky, entered the Friary Lane house. Claudius had retired to his place next door, announcing that when they were ready to start they could give him a call.

No-man found Mrs. Dearth hard at work getting her house in order. "Our Wizzie's a bit nervous this morning," she said. "I expect it would have been better if I had just let her go on sleeping—she said last night, when Mr. Wye was here and invited us, that she'd like to see Glymes. He asked her himself, but I don't think he made much of a hit with her. And she seems to have woken up feeling a bit scared of us all. But you'll see how she is. She's up and dressed—sitting by the fire." Jenny Dearth paused, and then added, when Dud's foot was already on the stair : "We must be very indulgent to her, my dear. But you *are*. I think you're wonderful!" and she gave him a slow, rich, deep smile that transformed her equine countenance. He went on up, and softly opened the door of their bedroom. He had got into the habit of approaching Wizzie's chamber in a sort of tiptoe manner as if he were treading on a velvet carpet.

And now, once in her presence, he closed the door behind him with as much care as if it were the entrance to a sick-chamber. She was no longer dressed in what he had thought of as her "nursemaid's costume." Mrs. Dearth had helped her to get through quite a lot of shopping during these months of their life together. He himself had been ungrudging in supplying the funds for these enterprises, though the cost of feminine attire, even at the less expensive establishments, had been to his bachelor mind something of a shock. Black was what she seemed drawn to as to the colour of her clothes, while in their texture she evidently leant to the softer and less rustic fabrics.

He himself had only interfered in one single particular; and, as might have been anticipated, for it needs the strongest of all human urges to inspire a man with the gall to interfere with his girl's taste, this had to do with a substitute for the lavender-coloured tights. It was in fact in long black stockings he had insisted that the loveliness of Wizzie's legs should be emphasized. The decking out of all other portions of her person he was content to leave to Mrs. Dearth and herself.

He found her now seated on the stool by the fire, hugging her black-stockinged knees. This was the position he had found her in, on the evening of All Souls' Day—only she wore no stockings then. Her hair at this moment was tied up, but apparently not yet "done" for the day, for several untidy wisps of straight straw-coloured locks stuck out in woeful disorder above her lace collar.

She was frowning when he closed the door. She was frowning when he stepped hurriedly to her side. Indeed, Dud was so cognizant of the dangerous mood which this expression signified that when he did reach her side he was afraid of worrying her by any sort of clumsy caress, and instead of kissing her, leaned up against the chimney-piece and addressed her from that position.

"They've told me about our going to Glymes, Wizz; and that though you didn't like Mr. Wye you'd agreed to come with us. I'm afraid old Claudius is not best pleased at the prospect; but I shall get great satisfaction—won't you, Wizz?—from seeing the fellow quarrel with Thuella's father? What'll happen between

127

him and that extraordinary chap Quirm remains to be seen. I challenged him about that Glymes boy, but I couldn't get a word out of him. He sheered off, the second I alluded to it."

"I—am—sure—it's very—kind of your friends to invite me along with you," remarked Wizzie. "*You*, anyway seem as pleased as Punch about it!"

"Wizzie!" he protested, and his mind began whirling round to discover what her new grievance was.

"I haven't seen you," she went on, "in such good spirits for weeks. I expect you're thinking how wonderfully good of them it is to be so nice to your pick-up."

"Wizz! Wizz!" he pleaded in a supplicating voice and with a solemn, rather foolish expression, "Wizz, how *can* you talk like that?"

The girl's eyes flashed with indignation. This particular martyrlike countenance which he had recently assumed when he felt she was treating him unkindly, always infuriated her. Whether it seemed to her inconceivable that any human being could really give up the natural violence of our race to the tune implied in that portentous expression, or whether, while believing in its reality, there was something about it that exasperated her nerves to such a pitch that, as she would have put it: "She could have screamed," Dud had no idea; but he very quickly found out that the way he behaved when his feelings were hurt and he was trying to pretend they weren't, and that all his concern was for *her*, was peculiarly irritating to the girl.

"Don't go now and put on your grieved face," she burst out, jumping up from her stool, and confronting him, "because I won't have it! If *you* think it's so splendid of your friends to treat me as if I existed in the same world as they do, *I* don't! What's wrong with you, Dud No-man, that you're so humble and so grateful to these people? My mother was as good as any of them, though she *was* so poor! You're a bastard, and so am I. But I've seen enough to know that your father was something just as my mother was something—better, I warrant, than any of these Glymes idiots! What's wrong with you to make you act like you do?"

He was indescribably relieved at the unexpected turn her anger had taken. It was a turn that started his mind off on a completely new track. He began telling himself a childish story about his father being some great Welsh nobleman, who claimed to be descended from Sir Pellenore. He looked at his watch. This was a habit of his the moment he got excited about anything, as if all events in Time were an unwinding scroll of mist through which the peaks of a higher reality could be seen. This higher reality just now concealed itself in the form of three minutes past three; and as he put his watch away Wizzie's anger became a thin vapour crossing this triadic symbol.

He pulled one of the chairs close to the fire and sat down. He made a gesture to get her to sit on his knee but she remained aloof. Her eyes, however, ceased to flash with that terrifying revolt against her life, against him, and against the whole cosmic system, to which he was becoming so accustomed in her.

"Can you remember those days, Wizz," he inquired of her, "when you were in that Catholic institution? When your whole world was made up of those nuns? You told me how your mother died and how they put you into that place, and how you got out of it, but I'd give anything to know——" He paused and drew a sigh of relief, for she had resumed her seat on the stool and her frown had disappeared.

"Wizz, why are you always so silent when I ask you about those nuns?"

She was silent now, staring placidly and not unhappily into the heart of the fire, and Dud had a curious feeling as he looked at her as if all that he could do or she could do in the sphere of practical life would always land them again in this passive situation, she waiting and he waiting, as they sat opposite each other, waiting for they knew not what, but being in some way spellbound by their isolation from the rest of the world and by the fact that they were still complete strangers to each other.

Ignorant of women as he was, Dud had never been blind to the fact that while he apparently satisfied certain dominant romantic cravings in Wizzie, she did not, for some obscure reason, respond with any warm, amorous reciprocity to his intermittent caresses. "She's a virgin," he was always saying to himself. "She's a virgin not only physically but spiritually." Sometimes he even asked himself whether it might not be that the sterile viciousness of the pleasure he got from her was the real bed-rock cause of her growing irritableness. "Am I tantalizing her," he said to himself, "in the same way I did Mona?"

129

But Mona had shown no sign of revolt against the absence of normal passion in him. Mona had completely dominated both himself and his supposed father by her inviolable spirit, and she had seemed almost as detached as he was himself in the matter of a couple's impulsive "give and take."

A faint quiver of diffused sensuality began now to disturb Dud's senses as the two of them sat there in silence. This was brought about by no conscious provocation on the girl's part, for Wizzie seemed more devoid of the desire to excite desire than Dud had supposed was possible in a young woman. It was purely due to her childish trick of exposing her knees to the warmth of the fire as she sat over it.

"If I go over to her," he thought, "and pull her up by her hands, could I get her to sit on my knee?" He had found out by experience—and oh, dear! there were so many little discoveries of a similar nature yet to be made before he could feel that his knowledge of her had properly begun—that if he could get her to sit on his knee by the fire when she was absorbed in her thoughts he could go on holding her and enjoying his contact with her for long periods of time, without her displaying any annoyance, or apparently any consciousness, of the pleasure he was taking.

Dud used sometimes to fancy that his amorous propensities, in their long atavistic history, must have skipped over the quadrupeds and the birds and gone back to the reptiles! It is true he had never been permitted the privilege of seeing the claspings of snakes, nor did he know if biologists could reconstruct "the ways of love" of jurassic lizards; but he always imagined that there must be something about the cold-blooded protractedness of his own erotic joys that resembled the love-making of these saurians.

With the dead Mona—in the one single year of their life together—he had never got anything of the secret pleasure, half-mental, half-physical, that alone satisfied him. With the "eidolon" of Mona, on the contrary, his wraith-girl of the last ten years, it had been totally different. But however strong a person's imagination may be, a wraith *is* a wraith, and to find his Stone-Age captive passive and not cantankerous under his cold-blooded ways was a heavenly delight.

"It's monstrous," he thought, as he looked at Wizzie hugging

130

her knees over the fire, and wondered if he dared pull her up to her feet by those thin wrists, "it's monstrous how few people in this world are allowed their precise, exact, particular, and most secret delight! If it isn't a cruel one, if it's only a sterile and peculiar one, every 'way of love' ought to be encouraged to the limit! I must talk to Claudius about this. I'd like to tell him that if Evolution's to make successful machines of us in his Roman-American-Russian life, it had better give our amorous eccentricities all possible satisfaction. *Satisfied Senses make docile Servants*—yes! I must suggest *that* to Claudius as the motto of his ideal state."

But while Dud's thoughts wandered to Claudius, Wizzie, seated there before him, began to give way to *her* primitive peculiarity which had to do, apparently, with the abandonment of her "'lurin' figure" to the caresses of the fire-god, for she began to treat her skirt with the same contempt as she used to treat her Circus finery and to hug her shins in quite alarming closeness to the flames.

But suddenly her frown came back and she turned her head with a jerk towards him. "You're paying Jenny *enough* for me, I hope?" she said sharply. "I *won't* be dependent on her, so you must remember that! It makes me feel she's making a pet of me—like Grummer Urgan did with Popsy!"

Dud hastily did his best to explain that the amount he paid Mrs. Dearth every week, though not very large, was sufficient to give a businesslike independence to the girl's position. "A pound a week, Wizz? Don't 'ee think that's enough? You know how often we have our lunch out. Or do you think I ought to make it twenty-five shillings? I'm a bit at a low ebb just now. That's why I'm writing so fast at my book. But you wait, young lady! This book's going to sell much better than the last. It's a *lovely* book. It's a *terrible* book. You wait, Wizz, my angel."

He was surprised to see the long, grave, penetrating stare she fixed upon him now. She pulled down the skirt over her knees and began tugging at it, just as she had done in the caravan when Thuella came near her, and in this hunched-up pose she swung round and faced him.

"I—want," she said slowly and emphatically, "to go—to work again. I don't like being her pet. If I'm not going to have a child, I want—no! Let me go on!—*I want to help*. That one

131

isn't the only Circus, and my old horse—oh, I hope he's all right!—isn't the only horse. I used to think sometimes I could do more, more than they let me do, in a bigger show. It was never the work I hated. I was doing it easier all the while. It was *them*. It was her and him, and the men they made me meet. The tent-boy always used to tell me I could better myself in a bigger concern. He said he knew a girl, not near as good as me, who made three quid a week. I want to help, Dud No-man, don't you understand? I want to *do* something in our life."

He achieved now, in the boldness of sheer tenderness, what a few minutes before he had helplessly contemplated from a more primitive motive. He pulled her up from her stool and took her on his knee.

"Jenny Dearth thinks," she went on—and it always enchanted him the way she perched on his lap as if he were her Circus horse—"it would be a pity for me—as things are—to let my work go. I should have to shake myself into it of course. A girl gets soft and lazy living like this. But it would soon come back. After a few rehearsals I'd be all right. Besides, there's plenty of time—more than a month before anyone's on the road again."

"You're a darling, Wizz," was all he could discover in him to mutter. "You're a darling. But I swear to you we'll get on all right. There are all sorts of ways we could economize—much more than we've done yet. Besides—Circuses mean travelling all the time. God, my dear, I'd never see you! No, no, Wizz. It's darling of you to think of it—but good Lord, no! I wouldn't let you do it for anything. Do—you—propose—that—I——" His tone had suddenly changed. His voice took on a harder, less sympathetic, almost ironical accent. "Do you propose that I should go round with you, stopping at the inns in the places we visit and always having a seat free, to see the performance?"

The reason of this change of tone was that the real weight of what she suggested began to sink, with implications of an extremely upsetting nature, into his rational consciousness. He began to recall his conversation with Old Funky. But curiously enough this flicker of a change of feeling increased rather than lessened his pleasure in holding her. He kept her on his lap—she was always as docile as a doll when he caressed her in this protracted saurian manner—but he effected a change in her position so that she no longer had her feet tucked beneath her.

He held her closer and closer, however, enjoying with an almost vegetative contentment the pressure of her flexible body.

By holding her like this he seemed to drown Old Funky's suggestions and even to fling into a momentary Lethe her proposal to go back to her circus-life.

"Darling," he gasped as his embrace slackened, "what—put—it—into—your—head—to think of such a thing?"

Now although Nature has denied to women—and no doubt for a sufficient reason—the power to discriminate between the "lust" in a lover's embrace that is alien to love, and indeed may be *the opposite of love,* and the other "lust" which is an excess of tenderness, she has made her feminine creation abnormally sensitive to the tone of a man's voice at such a crisis; and Dud's tone betrayed to the girl in a flash that something was wrong.

"What's the——" she began, and then finding that he still continued holding her, she frowned angrily and her limbs grew stiff.

Now the least suspicion of anger against him in *her* heart—it was a different thing when *he* was the angry one—always reduced his feelings to the coldest chastity. The second he became aware of this stiffening he released her and drew back.

The suddenness of this movement and the look which he gave her were enough to exasperate her nerves to the breaking-point.

"It's just what Jenny said," she burst out. "She said men hated us to keep our jobs after they—— But I'm not married to you *yet*, and I'm glad I'm *not*, when you look like that after what I've said and after my wanting to help. No, I'm *not* married to you— and I never will be either, now I see that look on your face! You only wanted me just like all the rest. That's all you did. Just like all the rest! I—was—going—to—do—this —for—*us*—to help us, to help *you*; but now—you'll see. I'll do it for a different reason! I'll do it so as not to have anyone looking at me—like you're looking now! Yes, it's just what Jenny said you'd do. She said——"

"*Damn* Jenny!" cried Dud hurriedly fumbling for a cigarette. When he'd found one and had looked about in vain for a match he finally lit it from the fire with a piece of paper picked up from the grate.

In this procedure he scorched his fingers and the smart remained with him, like a little drop of the girl's indignation clinging to his skin, as he sat down and smoked in silence.

Meanwhile Wizzie had rushed over to the dressing-table and standing in front of the glass began with trembling hands to tidy her hair and put on her hat. When he saw, through his clouds of smoke, what she was about, a deadly chill went through him. Unused to women's ways, he regarded this move on her part as a kind of desperate ultimatum. He visualized her putting on her cloak next, and then her shoes, and then packing that bag of hers which stood at the side of the dressing-table, and then running down the stairs without a word!

A whirling sequence of violent thoughts pursued one another through his distracted mind.

Again his eyes glanced to the foot of the bed, as if looking for the Welsh woman's demon, as if prepared to vent his confusion by muttering "Dor-Marth" to it. He recalled, as he watched the girl's back and the fierce way she was struggling with the obdurate ends of her hair, that feeling of *recognition* which had given him such a thrill when they first met. His Stone-Age captive? And was this the pass they had come to!

And then, as often happened with him when he felt driven to bay by the malice of chance, his mind tossed overboard at one fling all his cherished imaginative superstitions. Below these romantic dallyings there was in No-man, as has been hinted, a grim vein of savage bed-rock materialism, all the coarser and grosser, all the more stark and more brutal, for its contrast to his poetical fancies.

It was only a short while ago that he had allowed himself to play with the idea that his mother's lover was some great Welsh lord who "deduced his lineage" from the mythical pursuers of the "Questing Beast"; but now, as through the cloud of his cigarette-smoke he watched his "Stone-Age" girl putting on her hat, a hat bought in Durnovaria for five shillings, he felt as though the real reality of things was much more simple and much less pleasant.

Here they were, a man by the fire, a woman by the mirror, confronting the mystery of each other's angry personality, and it seemed most damnably likely that the quarrel between them had more to do with the confused chemistry of Claudius's confounded evolution than with heraldic heads on bed-posts, or mystical "recognitions" from neolithic times.

134

He threw his cigarette into the fire and rose from his chair. "Wizzie!" he whispered gently.

She turned at once. "What?" she murmured.

He moved a step towards her. The whole room became in a moment terribly hushed, as if it drew in its breath to listen. The coloured print of a young woman in a barge surrounded by water-lilies was suspended above their bed and sought in vain to detach itself from these deplorable goings-on.

A singularly malicious portrait of Mr. Wye by his daughter—full of Thuella's contempt for the poor man—that hung above the fire-place, tried pitifully as it stared at them, to utter the words : "Stand up to her now, stand up to her, or you're lost!"

The mirror from which Wizzie turned as she swung round to face him became all eyes and ears. And as for their bed—that "double-bed" that had sounded so magical to him when he heard of it in the bar of the Antelope—"Now for it! Now for it!" it seemed to gasp.

"You misunderstood me, my precious," No-man began. "I think it's *very* dear of you, *very* dear, to think of helping me like this. It's only that I—that I want to live with you, Wizz, all the year round, and not only in the winter when there is no business on the road. Do you know, Wizz, that old Urgan chap came to see me this morning?"

The result of these final words was startling. The girl gave up her fumblings with her hat, left it as it was, all sideways and disordered, and approaching the bed sat down and gazed in panic at him, her eyes assuming that queer effect of being round, that had been his first impression of them.

And now it must be confessed of Dud—such is the baser element in the hearts of the kindest among men—that it was not by any means unpleasing to him to tell her about Old Funky's blackmailing demand for a "fiver" and how he had mentioned some incident about an accident to the horse which gave him some mysterious legal claim against her.

"Why haven't you told *me* all?" he kept thinking to himself as he continued his story of Old Funky's blackmailing demands.

But her palpable agitation as she listened to him gradually assuaged his disturbed nerves; and by degrees his normal tenderness towards her began to flow back.

Poor little Wizz! Yes, he'd more than revenged himself for

135

that stiffening of her limbs under his lecherous hug; and since his anger with her—and he was sure he was fair to himself in this—was a mere automatic response to *her* anger with him and not due to sexual jealousy, he was resolved to restrain himself, even now, from teasing her with any questions about Old Funky.

"I don't care," he said to himself, as he related every detail about the "fiver" that he was to have ready by to-morrow, "what liberties she allowed. I don't care how jealous she made Grummer Urgan; but what I *can't* understand is why she's been so secretive about it all and why she's so upset now. There's nothing she could possibly tell me that would shock me or make me turn against her. The more she's gone through of that sort of thing, the better she suits me!"

Such were his thoughts as he dilated on the smug obsequiousness with which their persecutor had bowed himself off.

"Well?" he murmured when he'd finished. "Do you think we'll have to fork out that five pounds, or shall we tell him to go to Hell and just see what happens?"

The way she raised herself from the bed's edge, the way she stood facing him, still with her ridiculous hat—what bad taste all women had in hats!—clinging so disorderly to her head as if she were tipsy, the way she pressed her hands together across her stomach, and began, though with her eyes still staring into him, her old trick of rubbing her knuckles, the way a particular vein in her neck, that always looked knotted and swollen, started pulsing as if of its own accord, suddenly thrilled him with such a rush of affection that he sprang forward and hugged her to his heart.

"Don't!" she gasped, "don't! I can't—I can't"—and she tried ineffectually to push him away. Whether she would have softened, or whether she was so deeply agitated by what he'd told her and by what—beyond his knowledge—it meant to her that she *could* not soften, he never knew. He knew only that he held between his hands at that second all that really really pierced his heart in this phantom-world. Looking down at her disarranged hat that now scarcely adhered at all to her poor wisps of hair, feeling her reluctant body throb against his ribs, Dud became aware that he was prepared for anything that Old Funky might do, for any crazy scheme she herself might launch

136

upon, for any feministic chatter of Jenny Dearth's, *as long as she was his,* as long as she turned to him against all the world!

But a quick, light knock on the door made him release her with a start.

"Come in!" he called out while Wizzie fled to her dressing-table.

"All ready?" inquired their hostess briskly, entering the room.

"Must—I—really?——" began the girl with her arms lifted to her head as she turned to her protectress.

"Of course you must! How on earth could you imagine any-thing else?" retorted Jenny Dearth. "Claudius is here. He's just come. I've been waiting for him. How nice that hat looks! Where's your new jacket? Oh, you men, you men!" she added, taking a step towards the fire. "She'd have been ready hours ago; yes, I can see she would, if you'd left her alone. But I don't blame you. She looks perfectly sweet in that hat."

"Damn the hat, and damn you!" muttered Dud to himself, and it suddenly occurred to him as an illuminating revelation that it had been all the time for this expedition, and never to run away, that Wizz had been attiring herself at that looking-glass.

"I *must* learn," he thought, "not to take too seriously what they say. They go on with their practical obligations *just the same,* while they are bursting out like fireworks with the most terrifying ultimatums!"

It could not have been more than half an hour after the appearance of Mrs. Dearth that our four acquaintances were pursuing their way beneath the prison rampart, below the slop-ing garden of the Governor's house, past the Hangman's Cot-tage, with a view to crossing the Frome on their way to Glymes. They had to cross by the bridge that Dud was at last learning to call the Blue Bridge, though its present colour seemed to him unmistakably black; and so narrow was the path leading to this bridge, between the ditch and the small brook, that it became impossible for them to walk four abreast as they had been pre-viously doing. Thus it came about that the two women walked ahead while Claudius and Dud followed a few paces behind.

Glancing at the ditch on his left as he went along by Claudius's side he suddenly stopped with a sharp spasm of delight. *There was the first celandine!*

137

He forced himself to walk on by Claudius's side, but that pallid embryonic bud had taken possession of his consciousness.

"I don't believe," he murmured carelessly, "that you'll find any of those Glymes people sympathetic with your excavations. But what—*are* you—looking at?"

The interjection was amply justified, for Claudius was the one to be caught out of himself now. He was staring frantically and with an expression of positive illumination at some unknown object above the grassy ramparts of Poundbury.

"Don't you know what *they* are? Don't you know *them*?" was his excited reply.

He spoke in the adoring tone in which Homenas in Rabelais talks to his Pantagruelian visitors about the Pope.

Completely nonplussed, No-man swept his gaze over the bare crest of the prehistoric, Romanized camp, searching for some unexpected marvel. His companion's tone of worshipful awe gave him the feeling that if he only looked close enough at the top of Poundbury, and at the air-spaces beyond, he might be privileged to catch Evolution itself in the very act of creation!

By God! he *did* see the things now; and they certainly were incredible, standing out there against the far distance. "You *do* see them, don't you?" repeated Claudius with infinite satisfaction. "They're the Wireless, man, the Wireless! I never knew you could see them from here."

"Yes, they're remarkably clear," responded No-man vaguely, his mind full of the celandine-bud. "I suppose it's the station for the Far East, or something like that." But Claudius went on. "How they shame us out of our petty feelings! How they tower above our personal sensations! How they point to the great Future!"

No-man was silent; and they moved on to the Blue Bridge and pushed their way through its two turnstiles.

Skirting the edge of Frome House Garden, they reached a stile leading into a big sloping meadow; and here they caught sight of their women, already halfway up the grassy incline.

In those days the lane at the top of the sloping field was called Glymes Lane, though few remember that name now since the plough has passed over those two houses and their very foundations have vanished.

As the two men crossed this field there followed them from

some tree in Frome House Garden the unmistakable notes, gallant and clear and high-pitched, of a thrush's song. But Dud's private feeling as he listened to this fearless artist was that the pale celandine-bud he had seen by the ditch held some clue to this dim Candlemas Day that the lively thrush-song missed. There was something in the very bravado of this voice, and it was an artful bravado too, each note so deliberate in its defiant life-praise and so full of stoical self-consciousness, that seemed to him discordant with a day that hovered between winter and spring like a soul between two worlds.

That chilly yellow-green bud, piercing through darkness into birth with such tremulous and pallid sharpness, was much nearer the mystery of this day than the clearer-throated musical challenge. The bird defied a winter not yet departed, it triumphed in a spring not yet begun; but to No-man's exacting senses as those gallant trillings followed him there was something missing. To him the day was poignantly abortive, a thing of small measure and faint margins, of intimations drawn back as quickly as they appeared, of unfulfilments and frustrations. Nothing but the sharp, sickly yellow-green of the celandine-bud could have expressed the tenuous image of this day of half-birth as it reflected itself in mist and water. There was that in its pallid prematureness that suggested the dim population of some Limbo of life, wherein all the abortive vegetation-births which had ever taken place on this spot were reiterating their appeal, in tender unreproachful supplication.

And this low-pulsed Candlemas Day—was it not conspiring with the subtle tragedy of what he was doing himself, taking from Wizzie both her chance of a child and her chance of a career?

Claudius and he soon gained on the women, as they advanced up this long field, and it gave our friend a shock of curious pleasure to watch Wizzie vault so lightly over the rails at the top, into the lane that led to Glymes.

"What a supple body she has!" he thought. "Damn! Perhaps it *is*, as the 'Horse-Head' says, a wicked thing to snatch her away from her natural destiny and turn her into a single person's plaything." He and his companion were so close behind them now that he felt tempted to call out, simply to make Wizzie turn round, but Claudius had plunged into one of his diatribes against the cult of "the simple and poetic" and he hadn't the gall to interrupt him.

"We've got to obey Evolution now," the man was saying, "just as we used to obey God. And our duties under Evolution—the thing's moral exactions as you might say—aren't easier than God's, but very much harder! Under God we had to suppress a few of our lusts; but under Evolution we'll have to shake off what's not only innocent but praiseworthy. All this 'quiet life,' of which we English are so proud, will have to be changed; and, changed into——"

No-man's upper lip trembled. He didn't often get angry in argument, but something in the man's tone gave him the feeling that Claudius had sharply and deliberately kicked his shins. He felt as if the very root of his whole life-allusion was being maliciously threatened.

"You'll have to change us physically then!" he cried fiercely. "Celandines and the rest of it are in our blood; and 'blood's a damned mysterious juice,' as it says in *Faust*! Blood refuses to give up its celandines for any scientific future!"

They were in sight of their women again now, and Claudius, who had opened his mouth for a crushing rejoinder, closed it with a sigh.

Dud suddenly became conscious that a vivid image of the monstrous countenance, dulled by its dead eyes, of Uryen Quirm was floating before him. "Glymes will settle this chap's evolution," he thought, "Glymes will do his business. Wait till he talks to those Glymes people about his damned excavations!"

The women were awaiting them now, at a closed gate by an extremely muddy pond in the centre of which a mottled cow was nervously holding her broad mouth against the water pretending to drink, but really waiting till the coast was clear. The grey Candlemas weather, as it worked its will upon this cow, and upon the troubled mud into which the animal's cloven hoofs were sinking, seemed to our friend at that moment as if its circumambient presence, extending to all the air "above the firmament" and to all the "water below the firmament," were resting exhausted after having given birth to that single celandine-bud.

This feeling was intensified by the look of several time-worn posts, with twisted wires between them, that stared down into

140

the disturbed mud, as if waiting for some glimpse of their patient reflection to re-form in the rippled surface.

But what was that? Could it be true that Wizzie's little pinched face, under that deplorably smart hat, had actually broken into a smile at his approach? Did she care for him then in *some* kindred approximation to the way he cared for her? Oh, damn these mysterious hearts! Could a man never read their secrets? Had she meant it when she said she was going back to the Circus—to some Circus—or was it only a momentary burst of anger? And was he, or wasn't he, to greet that repulsive old man with his "fiver" to-morrow, and if he *did* give it him how could he be sure?——

But the four of them had met now. Claudius was opening the gate, standing in mud almost as thick as that which was liquefied in the water, and the cow was laboriously dragging herself, each separate mud-bound hoof after each separate mud-bound hoof, out of the pond without having done more than wet her nostrils.

Wizzie's frown came back as soon as they were all through the gate. "She *will* get that line fixed on her forehead if she's not careful," he thought; and then, as they all moved on together, the shameless puzzle entered his head—it was the sort of thing Dud was always thinking about : why did his "wicked" pleasure in Wizzie's figure, when her back was turned, invariably change into a chaste tenderness when their eyes met? Of course he *could* turn his gaze then, if he wanted to, upon her girlish bosom, that object in all the old amorous poems, of a lover's most consecrated idolatry.

As he lowered his eyes to the front of her jacket now, so much more worthy of the "Horse-Head's" skill than that awful hat, it came to him that it was a weird thing that he, D. No-man, should have the power, by yielding to his nervous manias, of actually preventing a woman from bringing to birth a living, conscious, and perhaps immortal soul! The old idea came back to him now, the idea, which had troubled him when he first ascended to her room, namely, that if he went on only tantalizing her with his half-love *someone else would take his place.*

In his fancies about his Mona-wraith he had imagined "Dor-Marth" taking his place in that deserted bed of his mother's. Who now would take his place in the Friary Lane upper room?

All four of them fell silent when they actually reached the place. The two houses, as they existed at that date, at the junction between the lane and the road leading to Piddletrenthide from the London Road, were certainly not inviting in that grey weather. No tramp would have selected Glymes, as it showed itself this particular afternoon, as a friendly habitation at which to pause. No derelict boots, no ruined castaway shoe, would have been tossed in the purlieus of Glymes informing the traveller, in the language of mendicants, that here was a possible welcome.

Wizzie's expression twisted itself into something a good deal more strained than her usual frown as Jenny Dearth opened her father's door. Even Claudius looked a little put about as he stood aside for the others to enter. As for Dud, so powerful was the place's "aura" and so strong was his animal instinct of distrust, that he received, as he went in behind Wizzie, a peculiar chill that he had not known since the publicity of his marriage to Mona.

"God!" he thought, as he watched Mr. Wye's two daughters greeting each other, "the old 'Horse-Head's' quite fond of Thuella. But of course the 'Venetian Post' hates *her*!"

Mr. Wye himself greeted our friend very amiably and involved him at once in serious conversation, while Thuella, giving him only the most casual of nods, made Wizzie sit down by her side on one of the elegant sofas in this superboudoir and, with malicious furtive glances at her sister, began plying the girl with a regular siege of impulsive cajolery.

Our friend was not so deeply absorbed in what the nervous Platonist was telling him to miss the manifest distress of Mrs. Dearth while her sister was throwing her whole soul into this prolonged cajolery of the young circus-rider.

He noticed too that even Claudius himself, who had at once begun engaging Mrs. Dearth in a complicated interpretation of Thuella's new picture, kept looking at her sharply, as if he detected something that interfered with her usual infatuated absorption in his remarks.

But it was hardly less agitating to Dud than to Mrs. Dearth to watch the beguilement by which the beautiful cloud-painter was trying to seduce Wizzie. "What *is* the name," he thought, "of that Frenchwoman, who paints pictures of girls, that Thuella talked about the other day? She said they were like depraved hares. Is she trying to turn _my_ girl into a depraved hare?"

"Yes," he replied aloud to Teucer Wye. "I _have_ read him a certain amount; but I take Plato in a way peculiar to myself. I take him as an absolute sceptic, so uncertain about everything that he could afford to turn God and Immortality into poetry, and the Soul and Love into fairy-tales."

Teucer Wye's sensitive mouth twitched so galvanically at this, and his two hands began to grope with such electric intensity at what Dud supposed to be the _Phaedrus_ and the _Timaeus_ in his side pocket, that it was natural for our friend to feel that politeness compelled him to look away; to look, that is, in the direction of Thuella.

Thuella's slenderness was accentuated by an extremely clinging olive-green gown of fine silk. If it hadn't been that she was so deliberately setting herself to cajole Wizzie, Dud would have been fascinated by her appearance. With that silk gown clinging to her body she looked exactly like the Lamia of Keats's poem; while from the expression on Wizzie's face, an expression of almost idiotic satisfaction, he gathered that the seduction was complete.

"Does she do it on purpose, to drive the 'Horse-Head' to frenzy?" he wondered, observing the look of desperation on Mrs. Dearth's face. But the odd thing was that what really was bothering his mind at that moment had nothing to do with Wizzie. What he found so disturbing was the simple and natural fact that at any second the door of this superfeminine room might open, and Mr. and Mrs. Quirm come in. He knew that Mr. and Mrs. Quirm had been invited. He knew they were expected. It wasn't a matter of the usual vague uncertainty, whether they would be there or not. It was a matter of certainty. How was it that this group of people could go on behaving so naturally, so spontaneously, so casually, when there was nothing in the whole stream of Time, nothing in the infinite past, nothing in the infinite future, that could stop Mr. and Mrs. Quirm from coming into that room in one minute, in half a minute, in a second?

Seated on the sofa by his host's side in this ladylike room listening with polite attention to the man's Platonizing, who— poor dandified devil!—seemed relieved to be talking to anyone

143

who wasn't a *daughter*, No-man tried to explain to himself why it was that his pulses were beating such a tune in expectation of the appearance of these people. He had seen them once or twice—not often, because of his shyness of Thuella, but enough to have kept up a sort of rough intimacy with Nancy Quirm. No, no, it wasn't because of *her* that he experienced this singular excitement. It was because of her husband. Him he had hardly seen at all, never at any rate to speak to since that first day; but it certainly was over him, not over the cemetery-woman, that this coil in his nerves was growing to such a pitch. Was it because the man was the only person in Dorchester who knew him as a writer?

He felt anything but easy with regard to those two forms on the other sofa, his girl's figure in her black dress, and that shining-headed Lamia at her side, whose long limbs shimmered so insidiously as she leaned over her. Nor did it give him any pleasure to see the poor "Horse-Head" suffer so as this curious seduction proceeded.

But, for all that, he kept turning to the door. He couldn't keep his eyes off the door. The truth was that a most singular sensation had begun to steal over him, as if he, and he alone, knew the real significance of the entrance into their presence of this man who called himself Uryen. . . .

"Don't you want me to bring the tea in for you, Ella?" Jenny Dearth cried suddenly and Dud felt as if her voice had broken *his* trance without disturbing the one which the green-and-gold serpent had cast on Wizz.

"No hurry, no hurry," murmured Teucer Wye, anxious not to lose a second of these precious moments with a masculine listener.

Dud thought to himself: "Nobody seems to understand what's happening." He felt more and more, as the windows darkened and twilight filled the room, that they were all involved in some obscure transaction of momentous importance.

After her hopeless attempt to break up that scene on the sofa Jenny Dearth evidently resigned herself to her role of devoted disciple; but her deep-set eyes, out of her bony visage, seemed all the while to be crying pitifully to Wizzie: "Shake her off, shake her off, for the love of God shake her off!"

It was certainly amazing to Dud to see how Wizzie permitted the long electric fingers of the cloud-painter—and Dud could remember the precise feel of those fingers—to rest on her knee as the tall girl murmured her whispered beguilements.

Thuella's seductive murmurings were inaudible, so that the monotonous droning voices of Claudius and Mr. Wye were the only sounds in the room. These two sounds seemed to move about together among the mirrors and the cushions, like a pair of obstinate bluebottle flies who ought to have had some window opened to let them out.

"He's coming along that passage now, between the houses!" Dud thought. "Now he's got to that wretched door where she told me about her boy's death. Now he's standing *just behind that door*! Why doesn't someone go and get up and go and open it for him?"

Dud sat up straight on his sofa, glancing anxiously from one face to another. He only nodded now in reply to Mr. Wye's remarks but this seemed quite enough to keep the Platonist from falling into silence. No-man began to see through a filmy mist the fellow's dandified clothes, his hair smooth in front like a woman's fringe, his clean cuffs, caught at the wrist outside his side pockets, a couple of faded daisies in his buttonhole, and his shoes gleaming with polish. But it was clear that Mr. Wye had been doomed to discourse so often to women as they searched for their cigarette or their thread, or their thimble, or their scissors, or their palette, or their eraser, or their novel, that he only increased the emotional pitch of his tone when his hearer gazed at him as if through a thick mist.

Dud's own mind still ran upon Mr. Quirm. "He's tired of waiting. He's got his hand on the knocker now. He's still in those disgusting clothes. His hair's still like dirty black moss on a rotten log. *There!* He's dropped the knocker again. He's waiting for Nancy before knocking; waiting with his dead eyes on the door, waiting without moving a muscle. The door, the door, the door!" Yes, No-man couldn't prevent the word "Dor-Marth" from rushing, like a flat-nosed bullet, into his brain; and when once this had happened he couldn't stop himself from beginning one of those endless droll tales he was always inventing, a tale in which he imagined himself finding out that this man at the door was the living incarnation of his mother's "Questing Beast."

"The soul remains pure as a drop of dew," Mr. Wye was now saying, "in spite of all its experiences", and to Dud's mind as he sat waiting for the sound of Mr. Quirm's knock to break up the unreality into which they were all sinking, a ridiculous little problem came into his head totally unsolicited, and entirely unconnected with what Mr. Wye had just remarked about the soul, the problem, namely as to whether the soft human hairs that Nature—unless the girl were a real Lamia underneath her green-and-gold gown—must have permitted to grow upon the long thin forearm that now lay across Wizzie's knees, were of the same colour as the hairs that gleamed in the fire-light at the back of that slender neck.

"Do you mean to say you really didn't ever feel *at all* frightened when?——" He actually caught this whisper now from Thuella herself as his problem made him concentrate upon what he could see of her.

"It isn't mere historic curiosity that makes these excavations," were the words Claudius was uttering into the poor "Horse-Head's" ears. Into her ears—but the woman's eyes were fixed, just as Dud's had been, on that long thin arm lying, like a green branch from a golden bough, across Wizzie's lap.

There! Surely that was a knock at the door. Why doesn't someone get up and open it?

"When people say," went on Mr. Wye, "how can the soul remain a pure essence and yet retain a memory of its earth-sensations? I answer——" And in his eagerness, while his hurried movement carried to his interlocutor the peaty smell of his clothes, the man actually twitched out of his pocket one of his little school-texts and began turning its pages.

Dud saw Thuella at that second give her father the sort of look that an animal trainer gives a dog when, at the wrong moment, it stands on its hind legs.

He himself sat up straighter than ever, listening intently. The idea crossed his mind as he glanced round at the little group and saw how the twilight perished in those Glymes windows, that this is how they might all have been found, if some cloud of volcanic ashes were to bury them as they sat.

"Is her feeling for Wizz," he thought, as the word "excavations" reached him again, "going to kill the 'Horse-Head's' love for that chap?"

The woman's expression was certainly just now more like that of a much-enduring wife than an ardent disciple.

"Thuella's doing this," he thought, "either to tease *me* or to tease *her*. Which is it? She's up to something. I've never seen Wizz in such a state. The child looks positively drugged with complacency."

He suddenly felt a grim disgust for the whole situation in which he had landed himself in Dorchester. "I've got out of my element," he thought. And a picture of himself as a solitary writer, walking to the end of Lover's Lane every afternoon, and putting "the Royal Martyr" on to boil the moment he got back, rose up in his mind; and as it rose it seemed to collide with the bruise left in his consciousness by Old Funky's blackmailing visit.

"Wizz isn't happy with me," his thoughts ran on. "She never looks like this when we're——"

The door of the room opened abruptly and Nancy Quirm entered alone. "So sorry, my dears!" she hurriedly began. "Uryen's gone to Maiden Castle, and he's not back yet. I've left a note telling him to come straight over the moment he——"

"Come and sit here, Nancy," cried Thuella jumping up. "Jenny and I'll get the tea now you've come. We won't wait for your husband."

4

CANDLEMAS NIGHT

The presence of Mrs. Quirm at what Mr. Wye had called "Thuella's cloud-party" did a lot to break up—at any rate for Dud—the uneasy tension that preceded the appearance of tea.

Nancy was all on the *qui vive* over Wizzie; and her lively concentration upon her seemed to please the young girl. It didn't turn her head, or cause her funny little pinched face to assume that idiotic look of satisfaction that it had worn on the sofa, but it evidently gave her confidence and reassurance. Wizzie, indeed, under her close contact with Thuella, for the cloud-painter managed to wedge the girl tightly against herself at the round table where they all sat, and the sympathetic encouragement she got from Nancy, became quite voluble. She talked more freely than our friend had ever heard her talk before. She told them all in a quite easy and assured tone all sorts of details about her Circus-life. These included many little matters that were of absorbing interest to him, but about which he had never dared to question her.

But it wasn't only on Wizzie that the tea had an enlivening effect. Dud himself drank several cups quite rapidly, one after another, and the glow that diffused itself through him dissipated in a very short time all his nervous feelings about the only absent one of the Glymes group.

It was Mrs. Dearth who poured out the tea. "That's why," our friend said to himself, for he was seated between her and Mr. Wye, "I'm so lucky. Thuella would have let me whistle for all these cups!"

The effect of their all sitting so closely together round the table seemed in some subtle way to change the whole key of the occasion. Thuella's magnetic energy, no longer absorbed in seducing Wizzie, expressed itself in wilder and wilder speeches. Dud noted at first that Wizzie's hands, when not occupied with her plate or her cup, instinctively sought her lap, and were, he was sure, occupied in the accustomed trick of playing with her knuckles.

As time went on, however, and Thuella began to dominate the conversation, he became convinced that the elder girl's electric fingers had surreptitiously sought those nervous hands. An occasional flicker of something approaching a smile on Wizzie's mouth and a heightened flush in her cheeks showed that, whatever the effect of the other's touch was, it was not disagreeable to her.

Both Mr. Wye and Claudius rose to their feet. There was a general movement then in that Glymes room. Cigarettes were lit; and encouraged by Mr. Wye, who after exchanging a word with Thuella began rearranging the chairs, they all moved nearer the fire.

No-man seated himself between Wizzie and Nancy, and feeling relieved when Mrs. Dearth brought up a chair to Wizzie's end of their sofa and engaged her in conversation, he began to do what he had been wanting to do for some while, that is to say, question her about her husband. He had begun to do this

148

and she was telling him, neither eagerly nor wearily, but in a casual, half-amused tone, about Uryen's mania for visiting Maiden Castle, especially at certain particular seasons of the year, when he heard Mr. Wye suddenly remark to Claudius as they stood together by the fire. "Did you hear *that*? The wind's getting up!"

Nancy caught this too, and a look came into her face that was at once perplexed and faintly exultant. She and Dud stared in silence at each other, and he fancied that something passed between them that he would have been puzzled to express in words. "He knew it would rise by the evening," she whispered. "That's why he's so late. He'll be back soon now! He waited there for the wind to get up." They both paused to watch Thuella go to the window. It was open a little at the top, and the dainty curtains, for there were no blinds in that studio-drawing room, had begun to flap and shiver uneasily. "It's all right, Dad," the tall girl cried over her shoulder. "I can do it!"

"How lovely she is!" whispered Nancy, as they watched that thin figure in its clinging gown raise its arms and close the window with a deft movement.

"He'll be here soon now," she repeated, sinking back into the sofa. "The wind must have touched Maiden Castle long before this."

"He didn't look much like a walker to me," Dud hazarded after a moment's hesitation. The woman sighed: "Oh, that's because of his clothes and all. I *can't* manage him! Often for days he sits reading—But when he does set off——"

Their attention was distracted by a sudden argument. Claudius had apparently said something to Mr. Wye about the superiority of Roman "morale" over the speculations of Plato, and Thuella with a tray in her hands turned on him before her father could reply.

Dud never forgot how she looked at that moment with the gleam of a lamp on her white skin and shining hair, as the weight of the tray emphasized the lines of her figure as she drew herself up under the stress of her feelings.

"What I want from life is pleasure! Yes, strange as it may sound, simply a little pleasure, before I die! It's what *all* women really want—Nancy does herself, only she won't admit it. And Jin does too, only she has to be a copy-cat to Mr. Cask. It's where women suffer from you all," and she swept her indignant glance from the men at the fire to the man on the sofa. "You *know* I'm right, Nancy. You and Jin have given up the struggle, that's all; and what have you got out of it? Yes, what have you got out of it? No, it isn't that Wizzie and I are younger. *That's* nothing! We'll be like this when we're old. We won't give up, like you two have, we won't, we *won't*!" She swung round with her tray to go to the door.

Something about the way the shining strands of her hair were caught up, tight and smooth, above the nape of her neck proved agitating to Dud, but he forced himself to turn his eyes in another direction.

"My dear child," said Claudius calmly, "you know very well that when you were painting that fine picture over there your head was full of something that wasn't pleasure at all. I don't say it was my ideal of life or your father's. But it was something very different from this 'pleasure' you're talking about."

The fact that she had to release one hand from her tray to get the door open encouraged the girl to turn on all the men in the room with her final retort. "Uryen will stop your mouths for you!" was what she flung back as she left the room; and our friend noticed how even in her fury she avoided being rude to Claudius by including instinctively her father and himself in this threat.

Teucer Wye was so disturbed by his daughter's outburst that under the shock of it he hurriedly went to his bookshelf and removing from his pockets *both* his little school-texts deposited them on the top of a row of Loeb Classics.

"Sit down, man, sit down!" he said to Claudius indicating the only chair in this lady's room adapted to masculine comfort. "You must excuse her, you know—and you too, Mr. No-man. A spoilt child, gentlemen, needing, you know, a mother's authority. But she's really a good girl, isn't she, Jenny?—and besides—well, the truth is—but you all know *that* already—if it weren't for her pictures—by Jove, I don't know where I'd be! In the workhouse in Damers' Road, probably. But Jenny, listen my dear——" and he stepped quickly up to Mrs. Dearth who turned to him from Wizzie.

Dud took the opportunity of putting to this latter young woman a domestic question about the comfort of her shoes, which were her last purchase in South Street, but he felt instinctively that both she and Mrs. Quirm were straining their ears to catch what their host and Jenny were talking about.

Enticed into the same eavesdropping by his companions he caught the word "Uryen," and he caught, too, certain revealing glances that the father and daughter threw at the door. He could hear only snatches of what they were saying, but he gathered that they were concerned lest Thuella and the man from Maiden Castle should be staying too long together in the kitchen. But how the devil had the fellow got into the kitchen; that's what puzzled Dud. He had heard no sound of the opening of the door between the houses, no sound of that knock or ring which he had been awaiting with such accumulative nervousness. How on earth had the man got in? Had Thuella found him in the passage? Was Mr. Wye aware that he was even now talking to her out there? Did they suspect her of giving him his tea in her kitchen? The girl had flung at them like a magic weapon her appeal to Uryen as she went out. "She must have heard him knock while she was scolding us," No-man decided, "and that's why she ended by throwing him at our heads."

Teucer Wye was evidently anxious that Jenny should follow Thuella into the kitchen and break in on this undesirable tête-à-tête, but Mrs. Dearth appeared reluctant to undertake this commission.

At last the little man made as if he were resolved to do it himself, but Jenny, tugging him back by his coat, addressed herself to Nancy.

"We don't want Ella to steal Uryen from us *too* long," she said. "Dad says he heard him come just now. Did *you* hear him come?"

It was easy for Dud to satisfy to the full at this moment his new mania for dissecting women's souls; for with everyone—Mr. Wye, Wizzie, and Jenny—staring so anxiously at Mrs. Quirm it was natural he should do the same. He gathered from the woman's expressive face that she had realized for some minutes that her husband and Thuella were together out there, but she had not the smallest intention of disturbing them.

"What are you all whispering about over there?" remarked Claudius in a complacent and even luxurious voice. To "please Mr. Wye" he had just accepted a particularly delicious

151

cigarette, and he was enjoying it with ineffable contentment, enjoying it as a hermit of the Thebaid might have enjoyed a taste of "Flora and the country green, dance, and Provençal song, and sunburnt mirth."

"Go over and talk to Claudius, there's a good girl!" said Mrs. Dearth to Wizzie in reply to this amiable challenge. Wizzie submissively obeyed; but Nancy Quirm was now on her feet. "Let *us* go," she said to Dud. "He hardly knows *you*. You'll be a distraction. He can't be angry with *you*. Besides"—and she forced a somewhat hollow chuckle—"nothing wakes a man up more than our appearing with another man! Come on! It's all right, Mr. Wye, you and Jenny must have lots to talk about. Don't you worry about them. Mr. No-man and I will chaperon them!"

The anxious Platonist looked at his eldest daughter who smiled at him reassuringly, and as Dud and Nancy moved to the door they saw them sit down side by side. Our friend and his companion paused in the little hallway. Here was a hanging lamp that Thuella must have lit before retiring into the kitchen; and here too set up against the wall was a big iron chair with cushions on it, evidently brought in for the winter from the garden.

A soon as he door was shut behind them Mrs. Quirm laid her hand on Dud's arm just in the same way—and it brought back the whole incident to his mind—as she had done on All Souls' Day when they stood together between the two Glymes houses. There was the very door behind which they had stood that afternoon! He had not noticed this small hallway then. It seemed to him they plunged straight into Thuella's living-room.

His "cemetery-woman" was evidently thinking hard now, as she paused with her hand on him.

"One minute!" she whispered and quickly opening the door to the kitchen she held it ajar while she peeped in.

Dud had not heard a sound from the kitchen, and it gave him a curious shock now to hear a man's voice.

"In a minute, Nance!" the voice said. "Tell him I'll be in in a minute. He needn't get fussy—I'm not eating her. I'm having my tea."

Then came Thuella's voice: "Come in, Nancy dear——Don't stand there like that—come in!"

"All right," he heard Mrs. Quirm reply, "but I'm going to flirt with Mr. No-man for a bit first, out here! Dad wants to talk to Jenny. Miss Ravelston's entertaining Mr. Cask. It got so hot in there, 'Thel!' We'll be with you in a minute." She shut the door and came back to him, making a grimace like a grown person returning to another grown person from a children's game. They sat down side by side on the big garden seat, and Dud lit a cigarette. "No, no!" she said gravely. "I want to talk—I want to tell you so many things, and hear so many things. We're old friends, you know!"

Dud stretched out his long legs.

But his companion laid her hand upon his knee. It was a fleeting movement, not more than a touch, and she withdrew it in a second, but in connection with the same gesture made in their first encounter it had its effect on him. It did enter No-man's head to wonder once or twice whether Mrs. Quirm might not be attracted to him for exactly the same reason she'd been attracted to Enoch Quirm twenty years ago, namely, that there was "so much about him she couldn't understand."

But it was of Enoch, or rather of Uryen, for she always called him by his adopted name unless to his face, that she was speaking now. No-man was prepared to find proof of his contention in every breath she breathed, but it would have been difficult for an outsider to have detected in her words any signs of that craving for pleasure, or of that desire to escape responsibility, by which he interpreted her conduct.

"I'm sure I don't know why I'm saying all this to you, Mr. No-man," she said presently, after explaining to him what an uncomfortable situation it brought about—this hostility of Teucer Wye to her husband, "but you must remember——"

"*I* know why you're doing it, my dear," he said to himself, lying back still more complacently in the iron seat, and puffing at his cigarette as luxuriously as if he had been Claudius. "You must remember," she went on, "that for years and years he hasn't noticed, hasn't hardly spoken to any woman but me. There was a time before *he* came"—she always spoke of her dead son as "he"—"when it was like this, and it worried me a lot while it lasted; but then *he* was born and something quite different went wrong. Enoch took to reading all these books. Did you know that half of them are in Welsh? Yes, he was with

Welsh people when he was little, and he took to it *like that*"—
and she made a characteristic feminine gesture with her hand to
express ease and quickness—"and then when *he* grew older
Enoch used to talk to him a lot, but"—there were tears in her
eyes now and her face twitched, but she went on rapidly —"*he*
never liked him; *he* was puzzled and frightened by Enoch's talk,
and so, so Enoch lost interest in him and stopped liking him—at
least I thought he did—and it made me angry and there were
scenes between us and then—then *he* was taken from me." She
glanced at the door of the living-room and then at the door of
the kitchen and lowered her voice. "People were nice to me, but
they weren't nice to Enoch—to Uryen I mean—after that. They
thought—I know Mr. Cask thought, for he asked me terrible
questions one night—that I wasn't happy with him, that he took
drugs or something, that he was bad to me. But it was just the
opposite! He saved my life with his medicines—you saw what
he did for me that day—and I'm *not* unhappy now that I've
let *him* go free—but just lately Enoch's changed. I don't know
what's happened, but he's different! He's got a mania for going
—where he went to-day—I've come to hate the name of the
place!—and he's always hanging about 'Thel'! I don't mind
that, of course—not in itself—for in spite of what she *says*
'Thel's' a good girl and we're great friends—but it's Teucer's
attitude that worries me. I can't tell *what* may happen—he and
Uryen are both so—so peculiar!"

No-man extinguished the end of the cigarette by crushing it
against the arm of their seat. There was nothing put on, nothing
patronizing or propitiatory, about his manner now. He pulled
his knees under him and tapped them with his fists as he sat
up.

It is true that the latter part of what Nancy told him made
but a vague impression on his mind; but one thing had hit his
full consciousness—the news that half the books he had seen
littering that untidy room of theirs, *were in Welsh.*

"I'm so glad I told you!" she cried. "I felt I *must* do it; I
really don't quite know why, but I felt I must. I shall feel much
stronger to face whatever does happen now that *you* know. It's
funny, isn't it," she added after a pause, "what it means to have
someone to tell things to? I used to tell everything to 'Thel'; but
of course, now that he and 'Thel' are—what they are—I've had

to bottle it all up inside me. Well! we'd better go now and take them into the room. I don't at all want Teucer to come out—as he may any second now, for you *never* know with him—and find us here. Come on! Quick, for the Lord's sake!"

No-man got a fleeting impression that his companion, whom he now hurriedly followed to the kitchen door, actually gave it a swift tap with her fingers before turning the handle, but this may have been an illusion. At any rate neither Thuella nor the woman's husband showed the faintest sign of embarrassment at this sudden invasion. The girl was standing at the sink washing up and the man was seated by her side. At their entrance he rose heavily to greet them while she, with a tea-cup in her hand, merely turned her shining head with a half-petulant, half-playful casualness and began rallying Nancy about her new friend.

"I'll give you away to your little missy in there," she mocked at No-man, as soon as his hand had been released from the somewhat chilly grasp of the man from Maiden Castle. "You're the one whose position's shaky! Uryen here doesn't know what jealousy is, any more than Nance does, does he, Nance!" She paused, put down the tea-cup, untied the strings of a ragged but spotlessly clean apron from her waist, and while Nance was whispering to Uryen what sounded, as they all stood there together, like an appeal to him to go for something to the other house, she began addressing herself to our friend.

"You can see how it is, my dear"—"There you go," he thought, "with your 'my dears' again!"—"it's simply that I *must* amuse myself; and Dad *must* keep me like a child! You won't believe it of course, but I've only had one real love-affair in my whole life, and that was when I was sixteen and with a boy of eighteen. I scared him away with my curiosity. I wanted him to take me, then and there, out of pure deviltry, and he wanted to have a long, virtuous engagement. He's engaged still, if you want to know, to a waitress in the town. They're waiting till they can find a house. Dad was furious with me when I led him on, and more furious when I frightened him off. That's Dad all over"—and the girl's face contracted in a veritable spasm of hatred—"It's the only way he can do anything with me, by getting angry! When he's not angry I do—with—him—exactly—what—I like."

155

He had only time to murmur : "It's a shame!" and "Dear! Dear!" and "You never know *what's* going on below the surface!" when Mr. Quirm hurried off in obedience to his wife, and then Thuella turned her back to say something to Nancy.

So intelligently had Wizzie listened to Claudius and so happy had Teucer Wye been to have his elder daughter to himself that both couples seemed rather surprised than anything else to see the absent ones returned.

"I've sent Uryen for one of the best bottles of elderberry wine," Mrs. Quirm announced brightly. "I wanted Mr. No-man and Miss Ravelston to see what can be provided for visitors on *our* side of Glymes, so that I can tempt them to give *us* a chance the next time they come. You don't mind, do you, Teucer! I know my teas would fall flat after 'Thel's', but if South Glymes is the place for a perfect tea I don't want them to think—or you either, Mr. Cask—that we in North Glymes haven't *some* resources!"

Dud saw nothing but weary displeasure in the sharp-cut features of their host. Over the man's blue eyes there gathered a self-evoked film of uneasy submission, and, when he spoke, his absence of teeth, a defect barely noticeable while his face remained animated, gave him the wizened look of a person of eighty rather than one of seventy-two.

Dud, after his excitement over Thuella, was aware of a lowering of key, a muting of the emotional pedal, in the vibration between Wizzie and himself. He left her to get on as well as she could, therefore, with Mr. Wye, who began politely talking to her when the other three seated themselves side by side, but, as he talked, the disturbed scholar kept casting forlorn glances at his book-shelf, while poor Wizzie looked as if she found him much harder to deal with than her recent interlocutor.

Dud himself took the opportunity of studying the difference between Mrs. Dearth and Nancy Quirm. There they sat, these two, both of them under forty. And Dud, as he turned his contemplative gaze from the one to the other, felt curiously touched and troubled by them both.

Never before had he felt so strongly the ghastly cruelty of the passing of Time over women's lives. They both of them (he was clairvoyant enough to know that!) felt *within themselves* as young as when Jenny first lay in the arms of her conservative

Tom, and Nancy was first brought home to this disconcerting Glymes.

And what a deadly joke, practised by Nature upon her daughters, this feeling of being a susceptible young woman, eager for the flutterings, the touches, the intimations, the sweet idolatries, the airy ways, light as love's own feathers, of the butterflies of love, and yet this knowledge of the terrible fatality, like a doom engraved in stone, of the lines they carry to their mirrors, the too much flesh *here*, the too little flesh *there*, those folds, those creases, those hollows, those indents, those imprints, those furrows, those erasions, all those warnings that Time delves with its dreadful finger, "not for us, not any more for us : pass on your ways," as if Death's own head had peeped, like a jackanapes over the fence of their tender flowers !

There ! he distinctly heard the knock of the outer door this time ! The fellow must have waited on that first occasion, just as he had imagined his doing, till Thuella came out into the hall. It was not Thuella now who went to open the two doors but Mr. Wye himself. This was a disappointment to our friend as he was unable to see what kind of a greeting passed between the two men.

None of the pleasantest, he concluded, when he saw the fixed Voltairean smile on the worried Platonist's toothless mouth changed into a round gutter-pipe hole as he re-entered.

Teucer Wye's mouth began indeed to emit a sound that resembled a whistle as he followed his guest into the room. "Whew ! Whew !" it susurrated; and combined with the expression in his blue eyes the look of this whistling mouth gave our friend a very uneasy feeling.

But trouble was in the air at Glymes just then, literally as well as metaphorically; for ever since they had finished tea the wind had been steadily gathering force; and now, although the window was shut and bolted, it rattled in a most disturbing manner in its wooden frame.

"*Was there a wind like this at Maiden Castle?*" This remark of Nancy's, addressed in a subdued tone to her husband, received no answer from Uryen Quirm.

"Let's have something to scoop it up with, Thuella !" the man exclaimed impatiently. "And glasses or anything you like, to drink it out of."

Meanwhile, since Mr. Wye was apparently buried in his shelf of the Loeb Classics and was keeping his slim back, in its elegant peat-smelling coat, turned so long to the company that Dud had time to notice how high his shoulders were and how his left shoulder was higher than his right, Claudius helped Jenny Dearth to move some flower-pots from a little round table and pull it out into the middle of the room.

By this time the door had begun rattling as well as the window, and long-drawn eerie wailings became audible high up in the chimney. There began too a very singular sound at the top of the house which for a while completely puzzled No-man. It was neither as loud nor as near as the creakings of doors and rattlings of windows, nor was it so emphatic as the crying of the wind in the chimney; but it struck No-man's ears as a sound with a quality in it completely different from either of these, different indeed from anything he had ever heard.

When he first caught it, it came to him, faint and muted as it was, with the kind of shock that our animal nature receives when it touches the *Unknown*. He could not have analysed the nature of this shock, or even have said whether it was menacing or the reverse : it was simply outside his experience.

As he listened to it, it became more pronounced and then again began to die away; and it was this alternation between an increasing and a diminishing momentum that especially evoked the feeling of the unknown. As with the touch of iron in extreme degrees of frost, when it is hard to say whether you are receiving a shock of cold or a shock of heat, our friend could not be sure whether the magnetic shiver in his nerves was one of mysterious exultation or of weird discomfort.

While Thuella was arranging her table-glasses and placing some fruit and biscuits on the tea-table, and while the man from Maiden Castle was mixing the contents of several bottles in that same bowl Dud had seen him use on All Souls' Day, our friend took the opportunity of asking Nancy about this queer sound.

"Oh, that's our Glymes ghost," she said casually, neither smiling nor looking grave. "It always makes that bumping whenever the wind gets up. You can hear it in both houses. Our landlord says it's a weathercock fallen down between the two roofs that rattles against the tiles when there's any wind; but all

158

the farmpeople I've talked to say there never was a weathercock at Glymes. *They* say—you know what they are!—that the noise followed my husband when he moved here from Shaftesbury."

"Did Mr. Quirm come from Shaftesbury!" whispered our friend. This natural inquiry seemed to disturb the "cemeterywoman."

She glanced rapidly at the others; but they were all gathered round Uryen, who having seated himself to mix the ingredients of his bowl was completely hidden from her eyes. Even Claudius —though with an expression of weary indulgence, like an astronomer watching a glow-worm—was looking over Mrs. Dearth's shoulder at what the fellow was doing.

As for Teucer Wye, he still held a book in each hand and a third under his arm and was apparently hovering about his shelf, as if unable to decide which of his master's works would best lend itself as a countercharm to his ambiguous "elderwine."

"His name's an old Dorset name," she replied. "But I only met him after he came here. Do you know, I went to Shaftesbury without his knowledge once—to see—if I could—find out —something!"

They were both on their feet just then, but, as if she were on the verge of betraying a grave secret, she pulled him down upon the one of the two sofas furthest from the spot where the others were standing.

"Yes, find out something definite about him!" she concluded in a burst of nervous confidence.

"Yes, I see; definite, very definite," murmured No-man absentmindedly. He responded with this lack of interest because at that moment he became aware that Wizzie was now standing by Thuella's side and that the tall girl's arm was round her waist.

"But they told me," Nancy went on, speaking very low and with a grave impressiveness, "that he was an adopted child. They said the story was that *old* Mr. Quirm had taken him from a Welsh tramp and given him his name; but they looked repulsively malignant, at least one old man did, when they told me this, as if they knew better; but I don't know what they were hinting at. It had——"

A prolonged wail of the wind in the chimney interrupted her,

159

and once more No-man was conscious of that queer sound in the air above the Glymes roof.

"Damn this place!" he thought. "I wish to the devil Wizz and I were snug in bed under our picture of water-lilies!" No one but himself, however, seemed to be worried by the eerie rattlings and creakings that followed each other now over all parts of the building.

But as Wizz's figure swayed a little under the tall girl's embrace our friend was able to get the first steady look he had had that night at Uryen himself. "What a face the fellow has!" he thought. "And what's happened to him? His eyes look different." In fact from what he could see of Mr. Quirm's eyes, as they concentrated themselves with an almost unholy intensity on what the man was about, they no longer had that completely *dead* look which had struck him so forcibly when they first met. It was not that they had come entirely to life, but, whether as a result of the lamplight, or from his interest in what he was doing, they did show—at least so No-man fancied—a more human expression than on that afternoon in November. Yes! there *was* some subtle change in the fellow's look; but what a curious individual the chap was, and how suited to this damned Glymes!

No-man leaned towards his companion and spoke in a whisper. Everybody in the room just then, for some obscure reason—probably because of the old primitive human tendency to be silent in the presence of a transaction that smacked of ritual—spoke in a lowered voice, so that Dud's whisper had to be a real whisper. "Did you say it was with Welsh people that your Shaftesbury old man found him?"

Mrs. Quirm, who also had been studying her husband's face from where they sat, turned her head sharply.

"Don't tell a soul," she murmured, "what I've just told you. Yes, that's how they put it; but, as I've said, the old man I talked to about it—for it seems the elder Quirm's been dead for years and there are none of the family left in Shaftesbury—showed such malignity towards my husband that he made me angry, and I came away feeling suspicious of all he said. My husband himself talks to me about Shaftesbury till I'm sick of the subject. He always calls it Palladour, which he says was its old name; and he talks so much about the nunnery there that you'd think he knew every stick and stone of it—just as if it were our Glymes. He's got a mania for nuns, Enoch has, just as children have for——"

She was interrupted by Mrs. Dearth who was hurriedly pushing her way between the end of their sofa and one of Thuella's decorative cabinets with the intention of reaching her father.

As she brushed by them, Dud, after his fashion, made a mental note of the agreeableness of the scent of her body, in its rustling dress. "Dear old 'Horse-Head,'" he thought, "you smell like *pot-pourri*!" And he mentally compared the scent of Jenny's flesh thus wafted to him as she passed with that which emanated from the person of his present companion.

It must not be supposed that the two ladies had been all this while offering themselves, like a spray of rosemary and a sprig of ground-ivy, for his critical delectation, for Jenny had had time to distract her father from his books; but in any case he was now roused from his comparisons by a general move among the occupants of the room. Uryen got up from his seat, put the empty bottles on the ground, and proceeded to carry his brimming bowl to the table where Thuella had placed the glasses.

It was at this moment that snatches of what Mrs. Dearth was saying to her father reached our friend's ears though he had his back to the book-shelf by which they were standing.

"Why not, Daddy? Why on earth not? I'll be here to represent you! And I swear I'll look after Ella, and of course I'll come up and say good night before we go. There—*do* now, that's a darling! Do, for my sake. You can trust me, I swear you can trust me, about Ella." What followed, what answer the agitated Platonist made to her, Dud could not tell, but no sooner had Thuella begun carrying round this unusual elderberry wine than he heard the door open and shut, and looking round, he saw that Teucer Wye had disappeared.

He found it very easy to get hold of Wizzie, now that Mr. Quirm, liberated from his wine-mixing, was free to gravitate towards Thuella, and he beckoned to the girl to come and sit on the sofa between Mrs. Quirm and himself. With their glasses in their hands, full of a wine more deeply coloured as well as more heavily scented than any wine he had ever tasted, the party was free now, being relieved of Mr. Wye's presence, to enjoy itself entirely at its own discretion; and with an almost comical precipitancy it divided itself into couples, Claudius with Jenny, Thuella with Mr. Quirm, and himself with Wizz; only Wizz and he had Mrs. Quirm on their hands.

"How queerly the chap's hair grows," he thought, "and how black it is! And yet it isn't negroid in the least. It *is* like some kind of moss, though I'm damned if I know what kind. It's almost as short as mine. I wonder if mine looked like that when I was younger." He clinked his glass with Wizz, and, leaning across Wizz, with Mrs. Quirm. They all three lifted the dark-coloured stuff to their lips.

"It's nice!" cried Wizzie. "It's like what Sister Bridget used to give her favourite girls on Saturday nights. But it's much stronger—I can *feel* it going to my head!"

"I rather like it too," remarked our friend. "It isn't as sickly-sweet as I expected and its smell is delicious. Nancy! you're barely tasting it! You're unfair to your lord's concoctions!"

Mrs. Quirm gave him in answer such an intimately challenging smile that he put a question to her that had been worrying the depths of his consciousness for some while. "How old is your husband?" he whispered; and then leaning towards her across Wizzie's head, which the girl had bent low down over her wine, he added: "Would you say he was twenty years older than I am?"

Nancy pretended to be thunder-struck at this question. She made a silly and rather ugly grimace. "Uryen is far, far older than I," she whispered back, "and I feel as if you and I were the same age. We *are*, aren't we?"

"But he hasn't a grey hair," murmured our friend. "He *can't* be so much older. Why a man can have a son at twenty, and you don't mean to say that your husband's old enough to be my father?"

"He's old enough to be——"

But at that point Wizzie lifted up her head. "Who's old enough?" the girl inquired in her natural tone, a tone loud enough to be heard by Uryen as he sat by Thuella's side. The man must have divined that they'd been talking about him and must have even caught something of their whisperings, for he startled them all by answering Wizzie's question himself.

"I am, child, I am," he flung out abruptly. "I'm well over sixty, and Nance isn't nearly forty, so she *might* be my daughter as she says! She often *acts* as if she were." These last words were added with a faint smile.

"I wasn't boasting of my youth, Uryen," our friend's companion retorted, "and I wish you wouldn't boast of your age."

She suddenly looked from the window to the door and listened. "It has stopped," she said looking at her husband, "so you're right again!" She put so much earnestness, and even a kind of timid remorse, into these words that Thuella, who had been watching her face closely during this interplay between them, asked her what she meant.

"The wind," she said. "You're too excited to-night, 'Thel', to notice anything. But the rest of us have been listening to it ever since tea. But it's gone down now."

"*Nance!*" cried Thuella, "what's the matter? You've got a look as if—don't *let* her look at you like that, Uryen!" And the tall girl waved one of her long arms with a sort of exorcizing movement, as if to ward off the evil eye from the man at her side.

Uryen raised his hand and put the girl's arm down with a gesture as negligent as if it had been the tail of a kitten.

"I only told her there'd be a ghost-wind to-night," he said quietly. "And it's come and it's gone—that's all."

"A ghost-wind?" interjected the voice of Claudius. "I've never heard of *that* kind, and I've lived in Dorchester a good while."

"Tell him about it, Uryen," Nancy cried. "And I *will* believe you another time!" she added, with a proud awe in her tone.

"I don't know that there's anything to tell," her husband replied. "I've noticed from going so often lately to Maiden Castle that on certain days—I won't just now go into the question of *what* days—there's a wind that blows out there that's felt nowhere else—unless it takes it into its head to *follow you home*. It's probably some magnetic disturbance due to quite natural causes. I only call it the 'ghost-wind' to tease Nance who's so damned superstitious though she pretends not to be."

While he was speaking Thuella got up, and she was now going round among them filling up their glasses.

Claudius alone refused to have his glass refilled. "Talking of Maiden Castle——"

"God, it's coming!" thought No-man. "I bet there'll be a row. It's a good thing the old man's gone to bed!"

"I wonder," Claudius said, "whether any of you people want to subscribe to the excavations this summer? Last summer, as you know——"

"Old Ass!" thought No-man, "he talks to us as if we were in the Corn Exchange."

"A metal plate with a rough figure of Minerva upon it was dug up in the foundations of that Roman temple, and though that may not be important, it *is* important that we should realize how scientific, in the best sense, modern archaeology has become, getting rid of all the old romantic nonsense and studying the way our ancestors obtained their food-supply and their water-supply and how——"

It was Mrs. Dearth who had the courage to arrest this ill-timed discourse. She laid her hand boldly on that of her friend, who had risen to his feet to make his blundering appeal and was leaning against the edge of the table.

"Claudius, don't 'ee, my dear! Don't 'ee!" she cried, assuming the Wessex accent to soften her interruption. "Father's gone to bed. Mr. Quirm never subscribes to such things. Ella hates the thought of excavations, and I'm a convert already! Mr. No-man will certainly subscribe——he quite agrees with us, just as Wizzie does, but he'll give us the money later, not here, not now, not——at Glymes!"

Dud could not help being touched at the way the "Horse-Head" traded without question on *his* good nature among all these egotistical people, and he mentally resolved to subscribe a pound to the excavations. "This chap with his megalithic phiz and his ghost-winds is just as bad as Claudius. Why can't people live to themselves and let other people alone? Curse it, I believe his damned wine's going to Wizzie's head!"

"But—Jenny—but I wanted—and now you've spoilt it all!" It had been with these rather pathetic protests, for he always showed at his best when his friend asserted her power over him, that Claudius sank back with a deep sigh into his seat; but what startled No-man at that moment had nothing to do with Claudius or Mrs. Dearth: it had to do with his own girl.

The young circus-rider, who ever since Uryen had talked about the ghost-wind had kept her eyes intently fixed upon him, now leapt up from her seat and, crossing to where Thuella had just resumed her place by his side, perched herself on the sofa's arm and leaning over the girl imprinted a kiss upon her shining head.

Thuella, who seemed—for No-man caught her expression—as surprised as he was himself by this uncharacteristic action, impulsively pulled Wizzie down upon her lap and responded to her gesture in kind.

The whole episode would have been perfectly natural, and fully in keeping with the affectionate *rapport* that the evening's excitement had engendered between the two, if it had not been for the singular expression that illuminated for a moment the majestic countenance of the man at their side.

Uryen, indeed, appeared to No-man at that crucial instant to be in the act of suppressing a mighty glow of triumphant exultation, though it was obscure to our friend what there could be for *him* to triumph about in the mutual affectionate impulse of two young women towards each other. But as it looked down upon the two girls Uryen's face assumed an expression like that of some grandly modelled imperturbable idol—an expression of terrifying complacency.

"He looks," thought Dud, "as if he'd swallowed them both and were digesting them. Curse his blood, he looks as if they both were inside him!"

It was left to Jenny Dearth to interfere again now. *She* evidently had no more respect for Uryen's portentous lineaments than she had for his talk. She left Claudius, went up to the bowl of elderberry wine, and replenishing her glass, called out in an authoritative voice: "Here, Wizz Ravelston, you haven't drunk with *me* yet!"

Thuella's lovely features contracted and her eyes narrowed under their lids till they became all pupil; but her sister's appeal was such a public one that she could offer no resistance when Wizzie got up with mechanical docility and went over to Jenny; and Dud, as he watched the two standing and whispering together, decided emphatically, as he had already done tentatively on his way here, that the worst danger to his peace was not threatening him from the "Horse-Head's" quarter, nor even from Old Funky's, but from this ghost-winded Glymes.

He began asking Mrs. Quirm questions again, this time about what her husband had said with regard to this suddenly rising and suddenly falling wind.

Both Mrs. Dearth and Wizzie had now drawn up their chairs close to the discomfited Claudius; but the reformer, after a considerable pause, during which the lids drooped wearily over his eyes like those of a sulky falcon which has been put back into his cage, turned to Uryen with a less oratorical appeal.

"Jenny says I mustn't bother you now, Mr. Quirm. But I do beg you to think of it. As a lover of history I'm sure you'll agree that it *is* significant, in view of our present attempt to overcome Nature by Science, that we should find a temple to Minerva at Maiden Castle."

"There!" thought No-man, who was watching Uryen. "I believe I saw the fellow's eyes come to life!" What rushed into Dud's head as he noted this change was the curious phrase *rex semimortuus* which he had once come across in some work on the religion of the ancient Celts. "That's what he is!" he said to himself. "He's a *rex semimortuus*. He's a corpse-god!"

But the man had begun to reply to Claudius. His unwieldy bulk seemed, after his walk, to be less lethargic, though it was just as shabbily and untidily garbed as when Dud had first met him. He wore some sort of faded sweater over his waistcoat, and his corduroy trousers were so dirty as to strike an unseemly note beside Thuella's silken gown. But his general appearance— probably from his exposure to that ambiguous wind on the summit of the great Camp—was undoubtedly a shade more prepossessing, while his head, with its queer, dusky hair cropped almost as close as No-man's own, struck our friend now as if it were formed not so much of a metallic substance, as his earlier impression of it had been, as of some massed weight of cloudy mist, solidified into human lineaments.

"Yes, I've seen," he remarked quietly, but with a tone, a weight, a volume of power behind his words which made them more significant than their actual content. "Yes, I've seen that Minerva. It's clearly a votive offering; but it doesn't in the least mean that the temple was Minerva's. But why don't you speak of *the other* votive image they dug up! *That* had nothing to do with Minerva or with Rome either!"

The unusual elderberry wine had by this time so affected the whole party that there was quite an emotional tension in Thuella's studio as the man spoke. The picture on the easel looked in the lamplight as if it were a representation of some huge astronomical catastrophe.

But the two daughters of Teucer Wye now demanded simultaneously what the other "votive offering" was to which he alluded!

Uryen's massive features composed themselves like a dark stream on the surface of which an unknown animal has been swimming, leaving curious ripples. "It's a three-horned bull," he said, "with two human torsos impaled on its horns and another one transfixed on its up-curving tail. It is one of those things," he said, "that go deeper into life than anything in your Dad's Plato. *You've* had, Mr. No-man, haven't you"—and the man turned courteously, but a little wearily to our friend, as if he were tired of having to justify himself by argument—"visions of life that suggest our being impaled on the horns and tail of darkness? I don't want to frighten any of you girls—especially Nance who's so terribly superstitious—but those horns and that tail, carrying those three half-men, seem to me—— Well! It's not classical symbolism anyway, it goes back further; and when you talk of science you must remember that these things are like dark-finned fish embedded in ice. *They have life in them that can be revived.* And I must say this to you, Mr. Cask: it is *not* science that can revive them. But go on with your excavations. I saw the place last summer when your friends were at work. They, and the scratchings they made, were—but I don't want to be insulting. Go on with your excavations. But you must remember when you're dealing with *that* place you're vivisecting something different from a dog! But it doesn't matter. It's only a few hundred years against twenty thousand. It doesn't matter. Besides, the secret escapes you! What you and your kind call Evolution I call Creation: and it would do no harm to just remind you that those who create can also destroy!" His voice sank, sank like a heavy pebble thrown into deep water, and there was silence in the room.

Something about this hush, for the wind—ghost-wind or thunder-wind—had completely subsided, made our friend think of his attic-room; and then, perhaps because some piece of flooring upstairs creaked as Mr. Wye crossed his bedroom, the fancy entered his head that he could hear his own bed in High East Street creaking. And the effect of this fancy upon him was to bring his wraith-love of those ten half-insane years vividly before his mind.

It was at this point that he suddenly became uneasy as he watched Thuella and Wizzie.

What he really had begun to be conscious of, as they all went on drinking the man's wine, was some subtle undercurrent between Uryen and *both* the young women. His shameless but not very astute powers of analysis were baffled by this understanding between them which seemed to have originated in Uryen's talk about Maiden Castle, and he could not even feel sure whether its nature implied a common attitude between the two girls towards Uryen or a common attitude between Uryen and Thuella towards Wizzie.

Whatever it might be that was "up," it was at any rate something that made him feel obscurely uncomfortable. It fell in with the almost animal-like inkling of danger—of danger to his peace—which had come to link itself with Glymes; and it came over him as all four women listened in silence to the rambling argument between the two men, that his anxiety about to-morrow's visit from Old Funky was quite thrown into the background by this new and far more obscure menace.

He began to feel an unexpected sympathy for their absent host. Was it from something of the same sort, from something that puzzled and troubled his mind in just this obscure way, that Teucer Wye had taken refuge upstairs?

He began to wonder whether those creakings he had heard, which, in his whims and his fancies, had brought his own attic-room into his mind, were simply due to the distracted Platonist's sleeplessness in his room above!

Was the poor man intently listening to every word that was uttered down here? Were they all deliberately keeping a nervous scholar awake with their silly chatter about "excavations" and "ghost-winds?"

And then he too turned his gaze, as all the rest were doing, upon Uryen's astonishing visage.

"The man's still drinking that precious wine of his," he said to himself, "but he doesn't look drunk—God! I've never realized how tragic his face is! And it's not only his dead eyes. He looks as if a part of his soul were *sodden* with some abominable suffering. He looks as if he's arguing with Claudius from about a fifth of his consciousness; while the rest of it hangs suspended on some colossal cross whose very enormity keeps it from being seen."

It was at this point in his cogitations that he felt a desire to go out for a minute; and rising up rather stiffly and awkwardly —for he had a touch of what children call "pins and needles"— he apologized to Nancy and moved to the door.

As he turned the handle he caught Wizzie's eye and gave her a little reassuring nod, while he noticed that Jenny Dearth glanced hurriedly at the ceiling, as if afraid that in his search for what he sought he might disturb her father. He had hardly closed the door behind him however, when it was opened again from within, and none other than Uryen himself stood beside him.

"Come to *our* place," the man murmured. "You'll wake Old Wye if you go upstairs."

But our friend had a longing for air. "How do they get *out*?" he asked abruptly, looking at the door into the kitchen and the door into the passage between the houses.

"In there," replied the man with an approving glance at the kitchen where he had been given his tea, "and the way upstairs is there, too. It's the same with us, only we've got a lavatory down below. I'll lead the way if you don't mind." He opened the door into the passage and our friend could not help muttering the word "Dor-Marth" as he followed the fellow's bulky form across that unlively threshold.

The "lavatory" referred to by his guide turned out to be next the study, and Dud suffering a strong revulsion against the whole place instinctively turned to the front door.

"I'd sooner go outside if it's the same to you," he muttered. "I like the open air."

The impression he got from the atmosphere of the night, when he returned across the little garden, was hardly distinguishable from what he had felt that afternoon about the quality of the day. No stars were visible, no moon was visible. The wind had dropped, and all was dark and hushed. Once more Dud received an impression as of something emerging into premature birth in the warm moist air. He was anything but pleased to see the figure of Uryen awaiting him outside the door. He had already endured much more of human society that

169

night than suited his temper, and though he felt interested in Uryen, and even faintly drawn to him, what he wanted at this particular moment was only to get Wizzie away from them all and have her in bed, safe by his side, under the water-lily picture.

"Now we're out here," said Uryen, as soon as they were together, "come a step this way, will you? I want to show you something."

Dud cursed him in his heart; but, as was his wont with annoying people, he did what he was asked to do, while at the same time he made a rapid tour of his own mental fortress, pulling down portcullises, raising drawbridges, and finally retreating to his inmost keep, where he shut himself in.

Uryen led him to a small barn that had a loft above it, reached by a narrow flight of stone steps.

"That's Wye's," the man remarked, pointing to the main entrance to the barn. "We're above and he's below. That's one of his grievances that the landlord didn't let him have the whole affair."

It was so dark that Dud had considerable difficulty in feeling for the steps up which the dusky figure of his guide now mounted with the easy assurance of a great furtive tom-cat. When he reached the top he found Mr. Quirm already in the interior of the place which smelt strongly of rotten apples.

The man was busy striking match after match as he tried to light a stable-lantern—containing a burnt-down candle-end—which hung from a hook.

Dud, who tried to help him, succeeded in extricating the wick of this used-up candle from the grease in which it was drowned, and it crossed his consciousness, as they fumbled over this job with equal indifference to the risk they ran of setting the place on fire, that there was a disturbing resemblance between their methods of going to work.

When the lantern was at last really alight they both straightened their long backs and stared for an uneasy moment at each other.

Dud had never had a chance of looking at such quite close quarters into Uryen's face, and although what he saw was affected by the Rembrandtesque chiaroscuro of the lantern's rays, it did strike him that the man was much older than he appeared to be from a distance. And as they stared at each other, both a little hypnotized by the strangeness of the occasion, there moved at the bottom of No-man's mind the same wild fantasy he had dallied with once or twice before—not taking it seriously but playing with it as you might, just for sport, pass a finger through a candle-flame: what, in the monstrous madness of destiny, if none other than Enoch Quirm had been his mother's unknown lover?

Yes, the man's face *was* an old face, for all his black hair; and for all its majesty of lineaments its skin was full of blotches and creases that this damned lantern-light drew forth. It was a sodden face when you looked closely at it, a monstrous and sodden face, and yet it had touched his mother's, had pressed itself against his mother's, had sloppered its saliva over his mother's!

No! He could imagine this man his mother's lover; but when it came to—Why! this great leathery face must have lifted itself up from touching hers at the very moment—— But no! he must not, he *would* not, conjure up any more.

It was the man himself who was the first to bring this hypnotic stare to an end. He moved across to the further side of the loft and began striking a match there. The danger of this proceeding seemed more evident to No-man from where he stood by the lantern than it had done when he was helping the fellow; and he called out: "Take care, sir! You'll set the place on fire!"

At the sound of his voice the other looked up from what he was about and trampled violently on the match he had dropped.

No-man approached him and he lit another match. With the help of this tiny flame—though it existed only long enough for our friend to notice that the man's hair *was* grey above his ears—Uryen found a small grocer's box by the side of which he knelt down on the littered floor.

"Light another!" he murmured handing the match-box to Dud.

Our friend obeyed him and covering the flame with his hand held it close to the box. Pushing open the lid, Uryen extracted a roundish object wrapped up in dirty newspaper. Lighting yet another match, No-man caught a glimpse of a fashion advertisement on the paper representing a woman in evening dress. Had he known anything about ladies' dresses he would have been

171

struck in a flash by the remoteness from modern style of what this picture showed, but as far as he was concerned the gown in question might have been displayed in any Dorchester shop that very day. Tucking the object under his arm, however, Mr. Quirm now went straight to the lantern and blew out the light. This done and with a parting glance round the darkened loft he led the way down the stone steps.

"Here, my lad," he said quietly as soon as our friend had descended, "here's something that belongs to you." With this he handed Dud the package, made a sort of guttural rumble in his throat that might have been a deep-drawn sigh or a sardonic chuckle, and added laconically, "I knew your mother in the old days."

No-man took the package without a word. Again and again that night this whole transaction, and the man's tone as he said, "I knew your mother," repeated itself in every detail in his mind. But *now* standing by this man's side as they both instinctively turned, before re-entering the house, to inhale the hushed, damp, birth-exhausted air of that cloudy night, his chief feeling was one of unreality. He felt as if all that had happened had happened not objectively at all but purely in his own mind.

As he glanced at the vague dehumanized lineaments of the man beside him, every particular feature blurred, and even the general massiveness of the dark head hardly distinguishable from the superincumbent gloom, he recognized clearly enough that what made the whole event seem so unreal, what gave it this effect of being composed of mental stuff rather than of palpable substance, was the fact that from his first encounter with this fellow he had had an inkling of something in the wind in connection with him, something likely to affect the course of his own life.

It was this, then, rather than any new and disturbing *rapport* between Thuella and Wizzie, that Glymes had been hiding from him in its lap, waiting for the moment of revelation.

"What are you writing now?" The words came naturally and spontaneously from the man's mouth, but they struck No-man's ear with a sharp and naked impact, struck it as if he had just taken off a diver's helmet and along with the helmet had put away from him the humming and drumming weight of fathoms of deep-sea water!

"The truth is," he said to himself, "that damned elderberry wine has gone to my head," and he hugged the parcel closely, crumpling the pretty lady's outmoded gown mercilessly against his ribs. "I'm trying my hand at a romance about Dorchester," he replied, and his own voice rang harsh and sour in his ears, like some acrid, dusty sound on a hot early afternoon on a suburban road, "and I'm making that unfortunate girl, Mary Channing, my heroine."

He was surprised and not particularly pleased to receive a congratulatory thump between the shoulder-blades as the man commented on this. "Bravo, lad! That's the game. Give it 'em, the brutes, give it 'em, hip and thigh!"

The unconventional and familiar tone that Mr. Quirm had adopted since the exchange of that parcel—and Dud was not without a shrewd guess as to its contents—especially his use of the word "lad," thrust our friend towards that repellent vision of his begetting from which his whole nature recoiled. Had this fellow known everything then, all the while? Was it for *him* that the cemetery people were keeping that grave alongside of his lost three?

"I must keep my head," he thought as he stood there; and the extremely uncomfortable intimation slid into his mind that his mother's lover was, on *his* side, contemplating putting his great fist on his shoulder.

This nervous feeling that the man was only waiting to make the grand revelation that would bring them fatally and finally together, held No-man spellbound.

"Damn it!" he said to himself, "I've got to face it, if it *is* the truth. And after all, fathers are nothing! It's who your *mother* is that matters. For nearly a year you live inside your mother. The early races felt this. In some savage tribes the mother's brother is the—yes, and in old Wye's Plato no one knows who his father is!"

Thus did Dud seek, by one mental device after another, to dodge the disconcerting and indeed repulsive notion that this trampish medicine-man had actually slept with his mother. He began hurriedly inventing fantastic excuses for getting back to the Wyes' end of the house. None of these seemed appropriate; but this standing in silence and staring through the night towards Maiden Castle, while at any moment the beggar's hand

173

might descend on his shoulder, had reached an intolerable point. "There's something grotesque," he thought, "about the relation of father and son. It's outside nature." For a moment he struggled desperately to find a rational defence for his loathing of the process of generation.

"*Parthenogenesis* is the natural thing! That's why the act of love is monstrous and ridiculous. Lust isn't comic. Lust is grave and sacred. And there's nothing but poetry in conception. It's the act of paternity that's so horribly humorous. Monstrous and comic. That's what it is. An interference with the beautiful processes of parthenogenesis."

"Well," said the big man at his side. "We must be getting back to them, I suppose. Put that thing down here," and he indicated a stone slab at the door, "you won't forget it, I warrant. You can fix it on, *like the other*, with a little glue, when you get back to that room of yours."

No-man placed the package on the stone; but neither of the men seemed in a hurry to re-enter the house.

"I told her it would be like this—a dead calm night after that wind "

"Told her what?" asked No-man, his mind so busy with the mystery of procreation that he spoke at random.

"And that they all come to life on a night like this."

"Come to life?" echoed our friend, and he thought to himself, "Is it only my viciousness that's made me loathe the thing so, or is it really the monstrous joke it appears, the joke at the very bottom of creation?"

"Just think of it, lad," went on the other, "Mai-Dun, Poundbury, Maumbury Rings, all coming slowly back to life! I don't mean the dead in them," and the man, lowering his voice, drew nearer to our friend, drew so near, in fact, that the sour smell of his body under his seldom-changed clothes produced a physical revulsion that affected No-man like a wafture from decomposing mortality.

"I mean——"

"Let's go in," interrupted our friend, turning brusquely from the misty night as if from a graveyard. "How *could* Mother," he thought, as they re-entered the house, "have been seduced by such a person? But perhaps he was different in those days!" The impulse to go further in his thoughts, to go *the one step*

174

further, had become for him like a menace that *had* to be obliterated, suppressed, reduced to nothing. The second it heaved up, pushing him forward, he retorted by a quick mental act of deliberate negation. It was as if he set a machine at the back of his mind automatically working, with a dark, secret hammer, that fell with an interior thud—"down, down, down!"—at each stir of that suspected impulse.

Back again in Thuella's boudoir-studio, he became conscious that the atmosphere was even more tense than when they had left the room. "Claudius had been holding forth!" he said to himself, as his companion sank down by Mrs. Quirm's side, and he himself took a seat by Wizzie. "He's been agitating the poor 'Horse-Head.'"

The deep-set eyes of Jenny Dearth did indeed betray a trouble of soul that was painful to see. Whether this was due to the fact that Thuella was again whispering to Wizzie, or whether it was owing to what Claudius had been saying, our friend could not decide; but the air of the room was certainly charged with dangerous electricity. "I believe it *is* Claudius and not Thuella," he said to himself, when, with the air of a man drawing a weapon out of a wound preparatory to repeating a blow, the ruddy hawk-beaked reformer, who was now standing with his back to the fire, began talking to Uryen and himself as if they were an overflow from an already dazed and confounded audience.

"I was saying that no one has a right to call himself a Communist, or to ask to be admitted into the movement, until he's worked with his hands among other labourers and knows what manual work is. I don't say that an agitator's *not* a worker; but in my opinion no one can agitate with a clear conscience who has not known what it is to work."

It was Jenny Dearth, not Uryen, who replied to him now, and our friend was startled by the amount of feeling that her tone betrayed. "How can you talk so foolishly, Claudius? You know perfectly well that you work harder than any workman—you never rest for a moment! It's what I can't bear, this fanatical, unpractical talk. Everyone knows what your life is!"

"But he's not talking *practically*, Jin; he's just theorizing," burst in Thuella. "He's not talking about *himself*! Why do you

175

always drag people's words down so? Of course we know he couldn't stand the strain of manual work for a day. Why haven't you more sense of humour? It's what you always do, taking things so literally! He was just theorizing, as we all may do sometimes. You make everything so personal."

Claudius fixed his eyes upon the tall girl with an expression of amused indulgence.

"No, I wasn't theorizing, 'Thel,'" he said slowly and gently. "It's a serious thing to me and not an easy thing, either. Jenny's quite right about that. And it is a new thing, too. I used to feel just as Jenny does about it."

"And do you know, 'Thel,' what was the wonderful influence that worked this wicked madness?" Mrs. Dearth spoke with such harsh bitterness that everyone except Uryen stared at her in astonishment. Uryen's own eyes—it interested Dud to notice—remained fixed on Claudius. "He's wondering," our friend decided, "whether his Maiden Castle spirits want him to answer the fellow or to let him be!"

"Don't 'ee dear! ... Don't 'ee say such things!" murmured Claudius, making a quaint little deprecatory motion towards Jenny with one of his hands, a gesture that in some odd way made our friend think of a marble orator in Westminster Abbey.

But Mrs. Dearth took no heed. "It was Dumbell," she cried in a harsh voice. "That's who it was—poor little old Dumbell when he had his Black-Shirt meeting down here! Claudius went to it with his radical friends—some of them Communists—and they worried Dumbell with questions the poor dear, of course, couldn't answer. At last he got red in the face like he does when 'Thel' teases him and accused Claudius of knowing nothing about working men, because he's never worked with his hands. That's the great, profound, spiritual reason behind all this silliness, a *tu quoque* from poor old Dumbell! So now you all know! It's rankled in him—yes, it has, Claudius, and you know it, from that night on. Dumbell was staying with me, and you should have heard the way Claudius went at him after supper that evening! But of course the lad had no more idea of what he'd set going than of why he wears a black shirt."

"Dumbell's our brother, Mr. No-man," Thuella threw in. "He's only just left school but he's already married and he's

176

already high up among the Black Shirts. We all hate his wife—don't we, Jin?—and we all love *him*, but even Dad doesn't take him seriously."

"I take him seriously, Mr. No-man!" said Claudius. "I've always considered this Fascist business is much more than the last ditch of capitalism. And it's the more serious just because it is so evasive and indefinable. It springs from youth—I'm sure of that. It satisfies some craving that modern civilization has suppressed. It's as silly to say that the leaders who gain by it *account for its existence,* as to say that tyrannical popes account for the existence of the Church. We all ought to study its psychology minutely. It isn't an invention, it's a natural growth. Personally I think it's a disease, but that's only a name for something absorbing and dangerous." His hawk's eyes hovered over them all with a sad assurance. Then they settled on Thuella's picture and assumed a pensive as well as a contemptuous expression. He seemed to be seeking an explanation of Fascism in the painting of clouds.

"Sometimes I think, Claudius," cried Mrs. Dearth, "you positively love destruction. Sometimes I think that for all your fuss over our welfare you really *hate* us, and that's why you're so fond of machinery. You'd like a world of robots better than a world of men and women, for then you wouldn't have even to consider such an irrelevant intrusion into scientific problems as a human heart!"

Our friend could not help feeling sorry for the man's flushed face, as its heavy pendulous eyelids seemed almost to close as it sank forwards with a heavy droop under the woman's anger.

"I—don't—think—Mrs. Dearth, you're attacking him for the right thing," murmured Uryen in a thick husky voice, as if he were just beginning to feel the influence of his own wine. "What's wrong with him is not his changing his life to confound your brother Dunbar but not changing it enough! I would like to see Mr. Cask give up all his philanthropies and live like a hermit on Tinkleton Heath. I'd like to see him—" here Uryen's low hoarse voice gathered weight and volume—"and I'd like to see you all—especially my dear Nance here—go into a Trappist monastery for five years!"

"Why do you—" and to Dud's astonishment he found that it was Wizzie who was speaking—"want to put us into a convent?

I was taught in a convent a few years ago, and I shall never——"

"Because, child!" interrupted Uryen, and Dud was not entirely pleased when it struck him that Uryen's dead eyes seemed to embrace in some queer way both the young girls, "because the only thing worth living for is what the old monks called 'contemplation.' Not, mind you, what the mystics called by that name, but what the monks meant by it, which was quite a different——"

"Stop, sir, stop, Mr. Quirm!" interrupted Claudius, his features quivering with wrath and his voice raised high. "There's one thing I won't allow while I am present and that is the putting of mediaeval ideas into young women's heads! If you're going on with any more monastic hocus-pocus let me know it, and I'll say good-night. I can stand a good deal; but when I hear——"

"Hush! what's that?" cried Thuella sharply, leaping to her feet. Her mouth was open and her lips were twisted awry—at least that's how it seemed to Dud, as she stood listening and staring at the door.

Both Wizzie and Nance were on their feet too. He himself and Uryen were the only ones still seated, and they looked questioningly at each other, Uryen's eyebrows a little raised and his own contracted. The sounds were now unmistakeable, even through the thick walls. Someone was moving about the house. "It's Dad!" whispered Jenny Dearth, rushing to the door; but, before she reached it, it was flung open and there on the threshold stood Teucer Wye.

The old man was in his pyjamas, which had the effect of making him look even frailer and smaller than he did in his clothes. On his head was a loose white night-cap, resembling the curious head-dress worn in so many of his portraits by the poet Cowper. His feet were bare and their appearance in the lamp-light gave No-man a queer shock. Not only did they gleam with a rather ghastly whiteness on Thuella's carpet, but their size and shape were those of a woman's.

"Dad! Dear Dad! we've waked you, with our disputes! But we're going now, aren't we, Claudius? Aren't we, Mr. No-man? Wizzie and I will get our things on at once!" and Jenny moved as if to pass him in the doorway.

178

But the little man waved her back, taking no notice of her words. He advanced into the middle of the room and began speaking, addressing himself solely to Uryen, who had got up now and was standing by his wife's side.

With some vague feminine notion in her head of preventing the scene from being overhead, although everybody in Glymes was in the room, Thuella moved quickly to the door and closed it quietly.

A sulky revulsion, a sullen withdrawal from all of these people, took possession of Dud as the flood of hysterical words poured forth from the absurd little figure in pyjamas.

Uncivil though it was in the presence of his angry host he sank down upon the nearest of Thuella's sofas and tried to detach himself from the whole scene.

Wizzie alone seemed aware of this reaction of his, and while the old man gave himself up to his orgy of indignation he caught her casting a frowning and disapproving glance at his recumbent position as if he were rudely detaching himself from a situation to which she felt they were both committed.

"Isn't it enough that you should force yourself into my house when you know what I feel," the old man was saying, "without raising this disturbance and keeping me awake half the night? Take your devil's brew away, can't you, and don't come into the place again! No, don't you say a word, Thuella. I've had enough of it, I tell you! If I'm not to say what goes on in my own house, what am I? I'll tell you what I am, you proud child—no! you needn't glare at me like that, for I've done with you and your ways—*I'm your father.* That's what you seem to have forgotten, you and your friends! I'm your father. I know what you're going to say, so you needn't make that face at me with your painted mouth. Yes, I know I've got no money. I know you pay for all this. I know how long you've paid for it, too, and everybody—in—the—place"—here a choking sob made his voice inaudible for a second, but it rose again in a high-pitched wail—"and they all, I can see that, hold me as cheap as you do! I—know—myself"—here his voice broke again but No-man was able to catch his words—"yes, I do, what I am, an old man taking his bread, taking his lodging, taking his—his chair by the fire—from a woman's hand. Yes, don't speak now, Jenny, for I know what you are. You needn't tell me! I've always known you'd help me with your last penny. Oh, I ought to have come to you—only to you—long ago—long, long ago. It was—it was that"—here his voice sank so low that Dud lost several words—"my nature, my weakness, my——" his voice sank again, and what with its high pitch and toothless gums through which it whistled, something stirred in our friend's stomach that forced him to stand up, that forced him to take a step towards that grotesque figure.

And what now began to happen struck Dud to the heart, for it was one of the most pitiful things he had ever seen.

Thuella, who had been listening all this while with an angry contempt in her eyes, deliberately walked past her father and went out of the room, returning in a moment with her arms full of her sister's and Wizzie's cloaks and hats. Wizzie, though she kept her frowning face towards the little man in the middle of the room, whistling there through his toothless mouth the humiliations of a lifetime, allowed the tall girl to help her into her cloak, and even began, though without the aid of a mirror, to put on her hat.

Thuella's move had instantaneous effect too upon Mr. and Mrs. Quirm, Nancy whispering something to her husband and then something to Thuella; after which both of them went out through the door that the girl had left open. They could be heard opening and shutting the heavy barrier between the two houses.

Thuella had now drawn Wizzie to one of her mirrors. Their faces were reflected there side by side. The elder girl was helping Wizzie with her troublesome hat, while from what our friend could see of Miss Ravelston's reflection she looked extremely discomposed.

He himself felt moved beyond his wont, beyond what he supposed he could possibly feel for a person like Mr. Wye. For there was something beyond the pitiful, something that if it did not reach the tragic came very near it, in the way the old man went on with his hysterical monologue in spite of the fact that the Quirms had left the house and in spite of the fact that no one was listening to him except Jenny Dearth and Claudius.

Our friend himself found it difficult to listen with concentrated attention. He wished devoutly that Jenny, who was now standing close by his side, would stop him, but the main stream of his talk was still directed to Thuella's beautiful back and the nape of her shining head, and it crossed Dud's consciousness that it was not altogether disagreeable to the elder sister to listen to this public exposure of the old man's grievances against the younger.

There did seem to Dud something curiously shocking in the lack of moral weight in Teucer Wye's hysterical wrath. That this lack of moral weight coincided with a lack of *physical* weight was of course only a heart-breaking accident, but it certainly increased the ineffectualness of the man's pitiful emotion.

"Of course," thought Dud, "now he's got started he can't stop, as happens with us all. I dare say he's burst out like this many times before and talked to Thuella's back and Thuella's sofas and mirrors. Oh, why *doesn't* the 'Horse-Head' stop him? I shall stop him myself in a second!"

The scene indeed grew steadily more unbearable as it went on; and it soon became clear that Claudius was as much moved as our friend, for he kept raising his hand and trying to interject a word. There was something ghastly about those womanish bare feet, and that whistling voice, and what Dud found almost unbearable was the way the neatly-brushed fringe of hair on the man's forehead was all tousled and ruffled under the great night-cap. He looked like some disordered waxwork or marion-ette that had been brought to life by a magician and was now pouring forth all the high-pitched grievances of doll-life without being able to touch any really comprehending human attention.

"Father! Dear Father!" Jenny Dearth kept crying: "Thuella's not listening. Thuella doesn't care!" That the old man should come and live with them in Friary Lane was what Claudius now seemed imperatively advocating. "Oh, yes, Father dear," Jenny pleaded, "I'll work for you, I'll take care of you. Come to Friary Lane and leave 'Thel' to her pictures."

"I've *tried* to please you," the wretched little man wailed on, as Thuella and Wizzie turned from their colloquy at the mirror and stood side by side at the fire. "I've given up my life to you. I've dressed to please you. I eat what you eat. I drink what you drink. I've not a room of my own, not a table of my own. And you've—you've——"

Here Jenny cried out to her sister: "Stop looking like that at

181

him, 'Thel'! If you can't answer him, stop looking at him like that! Do you want to drive him mad?"

"You've put," he went on in the most piteous tone he had yet used, "you've put your cold cream on my shelf, *next to my books!*"

This singular accusation evidently represented some outrage to his nature deeper than all the rest, for he repeated it over again with a reproach in his voice that sounded to Dud like the inhuman plaint of all the ill-used dolls in the world.

Then and there Dud made up his mind that he would hunt through all the Dorchester shops till he found a bookcase worthy of the works of Plato. He threw a malevolent look at Thuella, but he couldn't catch her eye. She was now coolly bending over her easel, pointing out something to Wizzie.

"You beautiful devil!" he thought. "If I don't put a spoke into your wheel for this——"

But the word about the cold cream was clearly the climax of Teucer Wye's outburst. He went on mumbling a little more, but they were incoherencies addressed to himself, and he allowed Jenny to take him by the arm; but the wrong done to his books must suddenly have swept over his mind, for shaking off Jenny's restraining hand he rushed to his shelf, snatched up a piece of bric-à-brac that had invaded it, and flung it full at Thuella's picture! Instead of hitting the picture, however, the missile struck the edge of the easel and rebounded on to the seat of a chair, where it lay intact. It was a small jug, of the kind that is given a human shape, and tilted now against the chairback it cast a Punchlike eye of contempt at the little man in pyjamas who had presumed to lay hands on it, as much as to say: "I'll soon be back among your books, and, by Gad! I'll jostle them!"

For some reason there was a general feeling of relief after the old man had made this gesture, ineffective though it had proved.

It was clearly a satisfaction to Claudius, who picked up the grinning jug, and placed it on the table along with its mistress's scent-bottles; and it was while he was doing this that Dud got an opportunity to catch Thuella's eye, and he kept wondering till he got to sleep that night whether he had managed to throw into the look he gave her anything worthy of the indignation he felt.

He spoke to Wizzie then, telling her to remind him, when they were actually off, not to forget something Mr. Quirm had given him, and when he turned round, wondering if he dared to give the agitated old man a friendly good night, he found that Jenny had got him out of the room.

Their walk back from Glymes that night was a silent one. There was a manifest tendency in both Claudius and Dud to cling to their particular woman and avoid general conversation.

Our friend was scarcely surprised to find, as he held Wizzie on one arm and clutched the heraldic head under the other, that the girl took a very different view of Teucer Wye's outburst than he did himself.

Wizzie's view was that the old man's clever and lovely daughter was sacrificing her chances of being married in order to keep a tiresome and fussy old gentleman from becoming a pauper. "He needn't have come down like that just because he couldn't sleep. We all have our bad nights, and I know it's hard, but he should remember that he was the one who invited us here, and it was wrong of him to go to bed just because he was angry with that Mr. Quirm—— But do you know, I like Mr. Quirm very much! Do you know who he reminds me of? Of the priest in that convent where I lived when I was little—that priest was dirty and untidy and had funny eyes; but he had the same tone as Mr. Quirm."

"What tone?"

"Well, it's hard to tell. But I'd say a tone that goes *through* a person, if you know what I mean, and is both frightening and exciting. 'Thel' feels the same as I do about him."

"You call her 'Thel' now?"

"Why not? It's what she"—and Wizzie made a gesture towards the two figures in front of them—"calls her."

"I think Thuella must have behaved abominably to that old man for him to get so worked up."

"I hate silly old men like that," said Wizzie, hugging herself with a deliberate little shudder. "*He's* a gentleman of course, and the other's a poor man, but I'll tell you who he made me think of as he stood there with that thing on his head cursing 'Thel'. He made me think of Old Funky!"

Dud felt outraged by this remark. It was not the first time

that Wizzie had shocked him by revealing a point of view staggeringly different from his own, but this confusion of values struck him as abominable. It gave him a sense of a gulf between them that he could see no way of bridging.

"Well—what am I to do to-morrow?" he retorted. "I tell you what I'm inclined to do—just pack him off and let him do his worst! I don't see how he can hurt us."

If she had shocked him by comparing Mr. Wye with Old Funky, it was she who was troubled now. She actually clutched him with both hands and made him stand still.

"If you want to ruin us," she said in a low intense voice, "if you want to drive me away from you, that's the way to do it." Then in a different tone, a tone of shrill supplication : "Give him the 'fiver', there's a dear; give it to him, for Christ's sake! He may go then and never come back. They won't be round here again till Whitsun anyway. Maybe not till August. Give it to him for Christ's sake. If you *don't*"—and she lowered her voice to a desperate whisper—"I can't stand it. I'll run away— that's what I'll do—I'll go where he can't find me, and where *you* can't find me. None of you shall ever see me again!"

"All right, old girl," he announced to her now, in as firm a voice as he could muster up, "I'll go to the bank to-morrow as soon as it's open and get some money out, even if I have to overdraw. We'll want a little to go on with. But Old Funky shall have his 'fiver', and let's pray that'll be the last of him!"

The girl, whose fingers had been trembling with agitation as she clutched his arm, now stooped down and pressed her face in the darkness against the back of his hand, the hand that was holding "Dor-Marth's" mate, and when she removed her cold lips his knuckles were wet with her tears.

They followed their friends at a greater distance, followed them round the turn by the Hangman's Cottage where the rush of the water through the weir sounded in the still night like the rush of the waters of death. The faint lamps from above gave only the palest glimmer. The governor's house was a dim blur, and to No-man's eyes, as he glanced up the bank where the prison stood, the great red building showed as a pallidly lit cloud within the darkness.

They overtook the others at a little bridge opposite a coal-yard, where beneath a small haystack could be discerned the huddled form of a group of roosting fowls.

Together now they ascended the hill into the town. A glimmer of candlelight in some upper room of Chubb's Almshouse was their sole welcome as they passed into Friary Lane.

"*That's* the sort of place there ought to be more of!" muttered Claudius glancing at the solid stone lintels above his head and at the friendly beam of light.

"They'll sit up together and make friends again," thought Noman, as Wizzie and he bade their companions good night and ascended the stairs.

But they had hardly reached the landing before they heard Claudius's voice. "It's no good, Jenny. I've made up my mind. But we'll both sleep over it and have one more talk to-morrow."

Mrs. Dearth's reply to this was inaudible, or perhaps she didn't reply at all, for immediately afterwards they heard the backdoor open and shut, indicating the man's retirement to his own domain.

The fire in the grate of their room had been out for hours, and though with the instinct of animals come back to their lair they both drew their chairs towards the ashes there was sufficient material cause for a tension of nerves between them, and the crisis was not long in appearing.

"What's wrong with you now?" he began in an aggrieved tone. "I've said I'd give him that five pounds, though it's against the grain with me, and I don't believe we'll get rid of him by it."

She took absolutely no notice of these words. She untied her shoe-lace and kicking away her shoes stretched out her feet towards the cinders.

Now it happened that the walk from Glymes combined with the tightness of her shoes had caused the particular part of Wizzie's new stockings that covered her toes to be stained with perspiration. The sight of this stain increased Dud's irritation.

"She's a circus-girl," he thought. "Why can't she choose her shoes properly?"

There was something aggravating to him about the way she stretched out her feet instead of hiding them, now she'd made them so hot, and this indifference to his presence, this behaving as if she were alone, was accentuated still further when, with a muttered "Damn the things! I told Jenny they weren't right," she deliberately pulled up her skirt and relaxed her suspenders.

It is true that immediately after this gesture she dragged her skirt tightly over her knees, exactly as she had done in Old Funky's caravan, but the mere fact that the modest violence of this childish act brought back their first encounter only intensified his annoyance. Nothing is more teasing to the male senses than to be presented with something poignant or provocative in a girl with whom you are angry, and just as Wizzie's exposure of her limbs with such contemptuous indifference to his presence struck him as a kind of insult, so this touch of the unconsciously pathetic, where pathos was the reverse of what his anger "wanted," made matters worse.

Bending over the extinct fire the girl now proceeded to remove her hairpins and let down her straggly hair. She went so far as to pull it forward across her forehead, and then, holding her head low down over her knees, she remained motionless, save that he could see her knuckles rise and fall every now and then, like the keys of a piano, as she nonchalantly scratched her scalp.

Dud thought: "We're both tired. We're both sick of human talk. What she wants is to cry for a bit over her private troubles, say her prayers to her dead mother, suck a few lollipops, and fall undisturbed to sleep; while what I want is to make love to her for hours—delicious and yielding, but not too responsive!"

Evidently to neither of these legitimate desires were the hour and the companion prepared to be kind, and these two persons' irritation with the recalcitrancy of life, as if the cinders in the grate had been cunning devils luring them on, turned moment by moment into bitterer grievance against each other.

"I think 'Thel's' the loveliest—and sweetest—thing I've ever seen!" This remark, in itself sufficiently calculated to annoy our friend, was not made less teasing by being punctuated by a yawn which the young woman made scant pretence at hiding.

Dud's upper lip began to quiver. The fact was that he yearned to make love to this sensitized Being endowed with such rounded hips and such entrancing limbs, but, as if by an evil sorcery, with the body of his pretty Wizz was mingled the sour essence of an insulting termagant, deadly to all lust, destructive of all tenderness.

"I think your 'Thel's' a cruel bitch!" he rapped out fiercely. "She's turned her father into a lunatic; and now she treats him like a wooden doll—dressed and fed—undressed and bed—and it isn't as if she were so wonderful herself. Her painting's just a copy, you know, of this new fantastic fashion. Only *she* applies it to fogs and clouds, instead of to trees and animals! Of course some people have a mania for red hair, and to them she's a miracle—I expect Uryen Quirm has made love to her for years. He *must* have, living next door to anyone like that. But—Good Lord, her figure's thin enough to be a deformity!"

Dud had absolutely no notion, when he began to speak, that he was going to pour out all this invective against Thuella. The words seemed to shoot themselves forth, like owls' pellets, gristle and hair and bones together, from the very bottom of his stomach.

Wizzie jumped to her feet and gave him a long protracted stare, less angry than darkly scrutinizing. Then, half-turning from him, she gazed for a long while at the ashes in the grate, evidently thinking intensely.

Our friend, meanwhile, ashamed of his outburst and bewildered by the breaking down of his self-control, unwrapped the heraldic head that Uryen had given him and balanced it carefully on the mantelpiece.

"You don't think I'm going to sleep with that thing there!" cried Wizzie a little later, as she stood in her white nightdress staring at this replica of "Dor-Marth," which, free of its fashion-plate, looked singularly sleek and complacent. "What's the matter with you that you like such things? It's all right for a place like Glymes, but this is *my* room, the only room, as far as I can see, that I'm ever likely to have, and I won't have it spoilt by such monstrosities!" She looked so forlorn as she said this that No-man's imagination put into her words a craving for more than a room of her own, free from Welsh monsters.

"Poor kid!" he thought as he submissively re-wrapped "Dor-Marth's" mate in its advertisement-sheet and laying it on a chair covered it carefully with his coat and waistcoat. "What she wants is a child." Furtively, so as not to annoy her, he watched her jump into bed and heard her give a little cry: "My goodness!" as the chill of the sheets struck her.

Though he did not distinctly formulate such a thought, what

his whole nature was really feeling was: "It's all right for me with my work and all that; but she's a woman—and *they* want——" And he fell, as he hurriedly undressed, into a troubled cogitation of all that is necessary to make a woman happy.

She turned her face away from him when he lay by her side, but this had happened so often that it did not disturb him with the sense of anything seriously wrong. And she let him stretch his arm over her without the nervous protest she sometimes made. She fell asleep indeed long before he did, and it pleased him that she didn't throw his arm aside just as she was going to sleep, a thing she often did, even after submitting with apparent contentment to his protracted caresses.

The childishness of her nature always astonished and delighted him, her power of falling asleep confidingly and peacefully in his arms a minute after some furious outburst of temper. Nothing pleased him more than to hold her, as he was doing now, and to ponder, for long periods at a time, upon the enchanting mysteriousness of her identity—just as unfathomable today as it had been at their first meeting!

"I must enjoy her when I can and *how* I can," he said to himself, "for she's not happy here, and some change will have to come soon."

How well he had come to know the familiar noises of the night that entered that Friary-Lane bedroom! Intermittent they might be, but there was seldom an entirely new one. The stamping of a strange horse in the Kings' Arms stable, the cry of a wandering sea-bird come higher up the Frome than its wont, the hum of a voyaging airplane driven closer to the roofs of Dorchester than was *their* wont—such were the exceptions; but every night he could hear the long-drawn-out whistle of some heavy luggage-train as it emerged from the Poundbury tunnel, every night he could hear certain particular human steps—he never found out whose they were; perhaps they were the troubled vigil of the unhappy old gentleman whose daughter persecuted him as Thuella persecuted Teucer Wye—that passed down Friary Lane between two and three in the early morning; and finally there were the harsh-sweet rook-cries at dawn, and the chattering of the sparrows above the Kings' Arms tap-room.

It was of the flowing of water and of the peculiar smell of

water as it sweeps between dark moss-grown walls that No-man kept thinking to-night as his arm rested on his girl's hip and his imagination made of her quiet breathing a symbol of all the sleepers in the world and all the oblivion into which their trouble sank, but these soothing half-thoughts were constantly invaded—do what he could—by the disturbances to his peace that were mounting up on all sides.

Though as he held Wizzie he succeeded in keeping the figure of Uryen—with his ghost-storms and his elderberry wine and his unwashed body smelling of mortality— in the one single role of his mother's lover, even this was enough, combined with the appearance of "Dor-Marth's" mate, to fill his brain with annoying perturbations. This business of giving the "fiver" to Old Funky too, though it did not bother him as much as the disconcerting figure of Mr. Quirm, was sufficiently disturbing.

He always, at the best of times, grudged going to the bank for money, but to have to go when his account was at its lowest ebb was an extremely unpleasant prospect.

"Oh, deary I !" sighed Dud to himself, recalling the plaint of many a village granny of his childhood : "They above alone do know the worries of me wold heart !"

But he settled his cropped head comfortably on his pillow and visualized in the darkness the nape of his companion's neck. It was not as beautiful as Thuella's : "But thank the Lord," he thought, "it isn't Thuella's ! Yes," he thought, "I'll stick to my little Wizz through thick and thin. The more angry she gets with me the closer I'll stick ! What's the use of being the fool I am if I can't at least hang on to my destiny ?"

A faint stirring of air began now to tap the tassel of their blind against the sill of the open window and a breath of pleasant coolness blew across his cheek.

"I must get the essence of this old Durnovaria," he thought, "and turn Mary's tragedy into a masterpiece. That's what I must do; just work on, and let Glymes and Funky and Claudius, and the whole lot of them, come and go as they please. Hang on to Wizz and not bother with them !"

So he thought, and yet before he slept he sighed heavily again, his mind reverting to those ten years of lonely independence and to that wraith of Mona who asked nothing and denied nothing.

5

THE SCUMMY POND

Dᴜᴅ had always been one—such was the childishness of his nature—to make much of what people call "favourite" things. He had his "favourite" hour, his "favourite" day, his "favourite" season, and each particular arbitrary and wilful choice of his he would justify with an exaggerated eloquence whenever he could get anyone to listen.

Until his recent experiences in Dorchester his favourite month had been September; but as during this spring the vegetation became more and more lavish, he decided, after several struggles with his innate conservatism, to transfer his preference to May! For he found he could not remember—though he ransacked his remotest memory for a parallel—any May in any place equal to this one in Dorchester.

On the fifth, therefore, of this favourite month, just three months after what Teucer Wye had called "Thuella's Cloud-Party," our friend found himself, as he dressed and shaved in their Friary Lane bedroom, full of impatience to set forth on his morning's walk before getting his solitary breakfast in his High East Street attic.

The air that came in with the sunshine was so balmy and sweet, the sunshine itself was such a largess of golden benediction that No-man's spirits rose and rose as he completed his hasty toilet. It was his usual custom just to give a fleeting kiss to any portion of his girl's head or face that emerged from the bedclothes and then slip off without waking her; but to-day he felt impelled to take her small oval skull between his hands and press his lips against the faint wrinkle between her eyebrows that even a night of unbroken sleep seemed in these days unable to smooth away.

"Dear-est!" she murmured in response to this, and her tone increased his happiness; for one of his sweetest compensations was the tender mood to which her dawning consciousness almost invariably *first* awoke. He was indeed already at the door, when to his surprise, she called him back and he found her eyes wide open.

"Don't forget we're to lunch with the Cumbers at the Antelope to-day," she reminded him, and her words as well as her tone brought down his spirits by several pegs. "And don't wear that old coat when you come, for they'll think I don't look after you at all, and don't forget to call for me here as you did last time! I don't want to walk into the hotel alone, for it looks funny. It looks as if—oh, I don't know!—but it looks *funny*!"

"Sure, kid!" replied our friend briskly, standing by her bedside with his cap in one hand and stick in the other. "I'll be here by a quarter-to! It's at one, isn't it?—this damned lunch. Sure I'll be here! I'll be here at half-past twelve if you like, and then you can dress up, and dress me up, to your heart's content!"

Wizzie blinked and frowned as she stared at the dark form in front of her in its nimbus of golden sunshine. There was always something distressing to her nerves in the high spirits with which he plunged into the activities of a new day. She herself never felt "as if she were alive" till well on in the afternoon.

She sat up in bed now and pushed back the hair from her high forehead. Then she rubbed her face with both her hands, drawing the skin tight across it, a gesture that he loved for its characteristicness, but hated for the way it brushed off the delicate bloom left by sleep.

"Why do you groan like that over this lunch!" she asked in the particular tone that he always dreaded. "I don't have so many amusements that you need make a face like that when, once in a blue moon, we go out together!"

"But—" he protested. "But—Wizz, I've *said* I'm ready to go. A person can't like what he *doesn't* like; and George Cumber—well! you know what he is, and Sissie, too! They're a fair pair. I don't know which I detest the most."

The girl plucked at the pillow behind her head and settled herself more comfortably.

Now if there was anything that No-man disliked it was getting involved in a long discussion of their friends, when he longed to be out of doors and down there by the sun-lit stream and cool wet grass.

"Give me a cigarette," she said. "You've woke me up. Can't you sit down for *one* minute?"

He laid his stick on the bed, and fumbling with his cap sat down at her feet. The bed creaked beneath his weight.

With an impatient movement of her knees she caused his stick to fall clattering to the floor. It was a peculiarity of Dud's to like to get the fresh impact of the morning air free of the smell of tobacco. "Everything in its proper time," he would say. "Your first cigarette should be after breakfast." He uttered a whistling sound in imitation of Mr. Wye, through the barrier of his teeth.

"I really believe," pronounced Miss Ravelston gravely, "you're the most selfish man I've ever known." She closed her eyes and sighed. Dud bit his lip, and looked down at a golden pool of sunlight on the floor at his feet. He recalled how delicious it had been when he made love to her " 'lurin' figure" in the middle of the night.

The girl raised her arm with a disconcerting suddenness and flung her cigarette into the grate. Then to his complete discomfiture she threw the clothes from her and scrambled out of bed beside him.

"I'm going to dress," she cried, "and you'd better go if you can't talk more sensibly!"

Without making any retort to this Dud possessed himself of his cap, and sinking on his knees, fumbled for his stick under the bed.

"Why can't you for once," she threw out, stooping down above him in her white night-dress, while he could see in his mind's eye how contracted with anger her face had grown, "do something like an ordinary person? And what do you want with that stick at all, when you're only going up the street to your room?"

"*Am* I only going up the street?" thought Dud, confounded by the amount of floor-space his fingers traversed without encountering his precious possession. "I'm going as far as the Blue Bridge and perhaps further!" He could just feel his stick now with the tips of his fingers, and stretching far under the bed he succeeded in dragging it forth. As he rose in silence and grimly made for the door he came to the conclusion that it must have been a deliberate and vicious kick from one of Wizzie's bare feet that had propelled this inanimate companion of his life out of his reach.

"Good-bye, kid!" he murmured. "I'll be here by half-past twelve. Is Thuella coming too?"

But Wizzie, with her back to him and at her looking-glass, was now too upset to make any answer, so he contented himself by directing a sympathetic nod towards Thuella's portrait of Mr. Wye, whose pathetic glance gave him the feeling that if the poor man wasn't depicted in his pyjamas such an omission was not due to any filial tenderness.

Our friend, however, got no further than the foot of the stairs before his conscience compelled him to hurry back. How far this laudable proceeding was due to his desire to enjoy that fresh May morning with a free heart, or how far it was due to an impulse to soften his girl's mood before he left her for so many hours, he himself would have been puzzled to determine; but back he went, and finding Wizzie in a daze at her mirror haloed by sunshine like a young saint, and with her brush and comb untouched before her and her hands in her lap, he gave her a quiet kiss on the back of the drooping head, and without waiting to observe the result of this manoeuvre hurried off again down the stairs.

He walked quickly down the hill with the prison-wall on his left and crossed the bridge leading to the coal-yard where Claudius had been at work for nearly two months.

Yes! the man was there now, labouring in his shirt-sleeves at unloading a wagon. His boss was not to be seen in the small enclosure that morning, so our friend after a second's hesitation crossed the planks that had been laid down over the ditch that ran parallel to the stream and entered into conversation with him.

The reformer seemed prepared to enjoy this interruption to his toil with the same quiet satisfaction that he allowed himself to smoke a cigarette "for company's sake".

No-man was less shocked by his appearance than he expected to be, from things that Wizzie had told him of Mrs. Dearth's concern. It may have been the effect of that fresh morning with its balmy air, but Claudius seemed in good spirits.

He did look a good deal thinner though, and Dud fancied— for he wore no hat—that the scanty hair behind his high bald forehead was greyer than it had been before this experiment.

"Are your hands better?" Dud inquired.

Claudius gave him one of his most piercing "rostrum" looks, and then, evidently satisfied with his sincerity, smiled like a little boy proud of his football scars and held out the begrimed palm of his right hand while he touched his blisters with the index finger of his left.

"Better," he murmured. "I put vaseline on them. Vaseline's better than cold cream."

Dud nodded sympathetically. "Back better?" he inquired.

Mr. Cask straightened himself and looked round.

"It doesn't keep me awake now," he replied briefly.

And then, gazing up towards the prison-hill with wrinkled, screwed-up eyelids, "It's late to-day," he remarked in an aggrieved tone.

"What's late? The bugle?"

"No, no!" he replied, but with a pleased and softened look, as if Dud had made an erroneous but at the same time a very sensible observation. "It comes *before* the bugle! The airplane, I mean."

"Oh," said our friend.

"Yes, it gives you the feeling that you're in the swing of things, not just idling about and tinkering. There! That's it—it's coming now! Don't you hear?"

Dud removed his cap and leaning on his stick set himself to listen.

A faint but familiar drumming, such as might have accompanied the approach of an antediluvian monster, began to fill the air.

They were both silent, giving this well-known sound their combined attention. It soon became quite loud; then with equal rapidity it lessened and died away.

From between his companion's clenched teeth a sympathetic sound emerged, as if something in the man's very soul were automatically responding to the departing pulse of the airborne engine.

Again was our friend reminded of a small boy's pleasure in his toy kite, or boat, or locomotive. He half expected to catch the syllables "chu ... chu ... chu" issuing from that exultant physiognomy.

"Are you really happier than you——" he began. His words

194

were lost in the loud quacking of a pair of white ducks that were hurriedly leaving the coal-yard to seek the water.

Claudius took no notice of the ducks. An expression of weary resignation fell like a film across his face when he marked Dud's intense interest in the awkward manner in which these creatures conducted their plunge into the stream. The proceedings of ducks played, it was clear, no part in that feeling of "being-in-the-swing" that was the reformer's present response to the life-tide.

But Mr. Cask's oratorical countenance was clearly bothered now by something beyond the irrelevance of ducks, and with a faint darkening of his ruddy cheeks which was his nearest approach to a blush, he began in a manner that quite touched our friend to utter a tentative and hesitating inquiry as to Mrs. Dearth's state of mind in regard to him.

"You know what they're like, No-man," he murmured. "We hurt them more by deliberately disregarding their wishes than by any infidelity. I suppose it would do no good for me to make another attempt—just to see her, I mean? She won't see me at all now, you know, or answer my letters! She thinks I'm deliberately doing this to annoy her, to break with her. She's got into her head—how, God knows, for she's my only intimate friend and I shall never have another—that I'm what they call 'tired' of her. Would you, No-man, if you were me, force yourself on her, to see if—when we were together and she saw what I felt—her mood would change? Or do—you—think—it would be—a good thing, No-man, if *you* were to say something to her? You and Miss Ravelston see her every day—perhaps if you told her how I missed her—for *herself*, I mean, not for——" Here a very curious look, half humorous and half heart-broken, fluttered over the man's face : "Not for what she's done for me—those meals in her house I mean—not for 'cupboard-love', No-man"—and once more his face assumed that ravaged and bewildered look, with the eyes wide open and the contours of the cheeks suggesting, in spite of the sunshine, that they were exposed to downpouring rain—"I mean—what they like you to say, No-man?—that you're"—he closed his sentence with a desperate and yet awkward rush, like the final and squawking plunge of the coal-man's ducks into the water—"still very—very fond of them—*in love—with—them*, in fact !"

This conversion of his old friend the "Horse-Head" into the mysterious "they" of men's bewildered respect for their perplexing partners would have tickled our friend's fancy if it had not been for the image he saw in the sunshine of that lamentable expression. No doubt something of what he felt was due to the actual sweat of this elderly convert to Communism; but Dud never forgot how the man's Roman nose emerged at that moment from the troubled outlines of his face, like an undefeated standard out of a confused mêlée.

"I'll do what I can," he murmured. "I'll talk to Miss Ravelston. In these things women are wiser than we are. Yes, I'll do what I can, Claudius. I'll talk to Wizz."

The appearance of the owner of the coal-yard ended their conversation; and No-man, saluting this worthy in his most propitiatory manner, went off in haste.

He felt disinclined to go straight to his lodging; and taking the path below the prison-slope to the Hangman's Cottage he decided to follow the track between the ditches as far as the Blue Bridge. Here he walked more leisurely, turning several times to survey the line of familiar landmarks that the old town offered him from that quarter. How well he had come to know them!—the prison first, then St. Peter's tower, then the roof of the Corn Exchange, then All Saints' spire, and away in a direct line behind it the tall brewery chimney on the Weymouth Road, then the majestic outline of Fordington church, and lastly, on the extreme outskirts of the town, the sacred clump of trees planted by Hardy himself that marked the great writer's home.

Pausing to glance at these objects, he found himself defending his way of life against Wizzie's bitter attacks. After all it was the stream of human existence down the centuries that swept him out of himself more constantly than any immediate contact. It was in this, with its magical overtones and undertones, that he sought to immerse himself. This was the impersonal element in his subjective life; this was the reverse side of his cerebral sensuality. It was to this winnowed reality, a reality caught under a purged light falling on the less transient gestures of our race, that his soul responded with a feeling that broke up the limitations of his grosser nature.

He turned before his path actually reached the bridge, and on his way back he noted with satisfaction how many cuckoo-flowers were out now, growing by the banks of the ditches. "These," he thought, "and not any other flower, are the characteristic symbol of the Durnovarian meadows! What they've got in them is some magical up-welling of Nature's shyest, purest secret. They're soaked in the cold transparencies and wavering mists of the dawn; and that faint lilac bloom of their petals is like an enchanted emanation from the memories of childhood rather than a palpable colour. They always look like things seen through mist, through rain, through water. Had I been long dead and then suddenly aroused in Hades to describe the magic of life on the earth, it would be cuckoo-flowers that would rush first to my mind! They have all the grass of the field for their leaves, and all the dew of the morning for their coolness. They make me think of seashells, though of course——"

His thoughts were interrupted by the sudden emergence, from where he'd been concealed behind the woodwork of a weir out of which he was cleaning the weeds, of a taciturn personage whom he had already encountered several times, and who always greeted him with a smile of the most engaging and mysterious sweetness.

This individual's name was Droit, and his ancient and traditional occupation was that of a "Drowner." The work of Droit the Drowner was entirely confined to the damming, releasing, or preparing the channels for the waters that flooded the Frome meadows; and in his mania for omens No-man had come to regard his meetings with this personage as full of significance. Mr. Droit with his enigmatic smile made him think of the zodiacal sign of the Water-Carrier, under the influence of which astrologers declare our world is beginning to come.

Mr. Droit also made our friend think of the prophecy of Tiresias, on that Cimmerian verge, as to the oar on Odysseus's shoulder that was taken for a flail.

At this very second the man was holding the particular tool of his job, a curiously shaped weed-cutter, and No-man, for whom the whole experience of life teemed with chaotic mysteries, could not get this tool out of his mind.

All the way back to his room he was absorbed in thoughts about Dorchester. "I don't believe," he said to himself, "whatever happens I could ever leave this place. Oh, its secret goes back far beyond the Romans! The Camp on the Waters. That's

197

why it's lucky to live here when we're moving into Aquarius."

Returning to the Hangman's Cottage our friend ascended the hill to the top of the town, preferring to face the traffic of High West Street rather than risk meeting Claudius again that morning.

Arrived at his landlord's little shop he produced his latch-key and opened the street-door. Yes! there were his letters, placed as usual on the bottom step of the staircase. There was his morning paper, which he rarely opened now owing to a nervous dislike of the lively pictures it displayed, but which something always prevented him from countermanding. There too, meeting him as he ascended the staircase with the letters in one hand and his stick in the other, was the peculiar smell of this massive old house, a very agreeable smell, suggestive of burnt almonds and ancient rose-leaves.

Arrived at the top he entered his small kitchen, tossed down the letters on a shelf without glancing at their envelopes, and walked over to the window.

How emerald-green the water-meadows looked this May-morning over the roofs of Orchard Street!

Turning away from the window with a sigh, he quickly lapsed into his former complacency. He took up "the Royal Martyr," filled him at the sink, and lit the gas-flame beneath him. Then he lifted the lid of the shining refuse-can he called "Henry VIII." He found it half-full of tea-leaves and egg-shells. "But I won't take it down now," he thought. "I'll have breakfast first."

Leaving his kettle on the gas-stove to boil, he now entered his bedroom, and it came over him how different an "aura," as they say, the place had, now that there were two "Dor-Marths" at the foot of his bed.

He went up to the original one and flicked it with his finger and thumb. "You let her alone *now*, don't you, now you've got your mate?"

His eyes rested on the pillow of his mother's bed, for he had kept it, without a pillow-case, to serve as a couch when he had a mind to lie down.

"Not a sign of you for months!" he whispered. "Have you gone off 'free,' as the cemetery-women said our dead ought to go free? Or have you only gone back to her bones?"

He straightened his back and moved round the bed to the

open door. Yes! the kettle was hissing now. It would soon boil. He started laying his breakfast on the desk by the window, pushing aside his papers, spreading out a clean towel for a table-cloth, arranging bread and butter and milk and sugar with the ponderous gravity of a priest at an altar.

This had come to be one of Dud's happiest moments in the twenty-four hours. His *most* happy moments were when Wizzie, in a really receptive mood, allowed him to make love to her; but of late, for reasons which were obscure but which he vaguely attributed to her infatuation for the "Venetian Post," these moments had been rare, and the rarer they grew the more meticulous unction he bestowed on these interludes of solitary self-indulgence.

The kettle was steaming violently now, and he hastened to make his tea and boil his eggs.

Seated in front of his window which was propped open, this fine May morning, with a toy trumpet he had picked up in the Amphitheatre, he set himself to enjoy the sounds that came up from the street while he munched his bread and butter. Some-thing about the pollen-dust freshness and fragrant balminess of the air made it easier for him than ever before to envisage, as if it really were his destiny to accept such a grotesque situation, the probability that Uryen Quirm *was* his begetter.

"But if he is," he said to himself, "I must be a double-dyed Welshman!"

Dud's glance now happened to fall on one of the sheets of paper he had pushed aside to make room for his extempore table-cloth. He stretched his arm and pulled it towards him, spreading it over his empty plate, while one of its edges rubbed against his empty egg-shells.

Perusing a line or two of what he had written, he suddenly had an inspiration with regard to an important change he must make and without more ado he reached for his pen, knocking his cup into the saucer as he did so with the movement of his sleeve.

In the midst of inserting this change at the end of Chapter Twelve he laid down his pen and gazed fixedly out of the win-dow. The nesting rooks in the high elms of Acland House garden were making a fine cawing, and into this upper level of rustic clamour the town-noises ascended like voluble dust blend-ing with aerial orchestration. "Dorchester's one of the most interesting towns in England," he said to himself. "It'll be a wicked thing if I don't do justice to it in *Mary Channing*."

With this thought in his mind he fell into a muse over the various strata of social life that the place revealed, level upon level of quaint traditional differences between man and man, and all receding further and further backward, as he pursued them, into the customs of the remote past.

He had discovered already that to divide the citizens of Durnovaria into upper class, middle class, lower middle class, and proletariat, was a crude and inadequate way of dealing with the town's complicated organism. Each of these classes, the deeper he went into them, divided themselves into much subtler categories. How delicately, for instance, the town's professional people, its lawyers, doctors, clergymen, bankers, and so forth, separated themselves from the neighbouring county families, to whom in a few cases they were allied by blood! How unmistakable was the gulf between the great Dorsetshire landowners, with their immemorial manor houses and parks, and the less wealthy gentry, who yet regarded themselves, and were regarded by others, as "county people"!

Dud had come to be more and more amazed at the way, as if the tragic levelling of the war had changed nothing, as if the cataclysmic phenomenon of Russia on the horizon had changed nothing, the old feudal distinctions held on, held tight, to their deep roots in that populous soil. The respectful manner in which the humbler of these Durotriges, children at school, labourers going to work, men "on the dole," old men with pensions, touched their caps to him as he passed them down there on the river-path, many of them dressed far more neatly than he was himself—for Wizzie was not one to trim him up or spend much time sewing on buttons—often made Dud feel nervous and ashamed.

What had a nameless bastard like him, with a mere trick of book-writing, done for these patient people, to receive such honour? It must have been lodged in their blood, like a secret unescapable chemistry, this respect for a "gentleman," even for such an extremely dubious "gentleman" as himself!

It must, he thought, be the automatic issue of countless aeons of scandalous oppression, oppression of neolithic men by metal-bearing men, of Durotriges by Romans, of Romanized Celts by

Saxons, of Saxons by Normans, and, for centuries upon centuries, of all those who weren't "gentry" by all those who were!

As he stared out of the window, turning the motions of the rooks above the stationer's roof into the beatings of his thought against the mystery of custom, he began wondering in what directions, through what psychic cracks and crannies, all the stored-up retribution for these ancient wrongs was now, this very day, finding its outlet. An outlet of some sort, surely, it must find : but what, and where?

"The man of his mother's" had assured him on Candlemas night that there were times when Maiden Castle, when "Pummery," when Maumbury Rings, *came to life* again! Did they come to life "with a vengeance" for all the wrongs they had known under the sun? And was the cruelty of that atrocious "justice" that strangled and burnt Mary Channing something that must still be avenged? "And am I," he thought, "going to prove the mouth-piece of that retribution?"

Impulsively he pushed back his breakfast things, and without bothering to remove the towel from his desk, pulled his ink-pot towards him and began writing at top speed.

As he wrote, with the balmy May air blowing in upon him and the clatter of the traffic mixing with the rhythm of his thought, he felt as though he really had become a "medium" for the expression, not only of one unavenged wrong, but of a thousand, all interpenetrating one another, all overlapping and perforating one another, like separate magnetic currents within one great heaving sea of psychic tragedy!

He wrote furiously for about half an hour, letting the feeling that obsessed him pass, as it seemed, from his receptive soul into the words formed by his pen, as if he had been a bodiless presence himself, rather than a bony, middle-aged man bending over a cluttered table.

When he laid down his pen at last he gave a great sigh of relief and a wave of extraordinary well-being flowed through him, singularly at variance with the tragic nature of what he had been writing.

He got up then, and straightened his back, forcing his fists so violently into the depths of his trouser pockets that the trunk of his body came to resemble a knotted tree with a protruding bole bulging out on either side.

Then, for some reason, the image of Thuella crossed his consciousness.

"I've been more than a match for *you*, you cruel bitch!" he muttered aloud. "Yes, you vile larva, you may torture your Father and you may fascinate that Glymes man, but you'll never catch D. No-man!"

It was at this point that our friend suddenly remembered that he hadn't read his letters. He generally brought them in with him to his breakfast—gazed languidly at their envelopes while he ate—and opened them as he sipped his last cup of tea. He hurried across the landing now, only to discover that "the Royal Martyr" had boiled away and was blackening ominously above the flame. He turned off the gas with a jerk and stared round the kitchen. Where the hell had he put his letters? Oh, there they were, under that damned paper! He glanced through them; all were unimportant except two. The first of these was in an unknown hand and bore a Yeovil postmark.

Our friend contemplated this missive with extreme distaste. An uneducated hand ... the place Yeovil ... the address written in pencil ... "It's those Urgans, it's Old Funky or Grummer!"

Not only was the writing bad and in pencil but the envelope was dirty and crumpled. It looked as if it had been kept a long while in the writer's pocket before the opportunity came to post it. It was stuck down so tightly—had been licked so viciously by some venomous tongue—that it would evidently require some violent handling to get it open.

No-man laid down this unpromising communication and surveyed the other letter. God! what was this? There was no need to use any violence in opening *this* epistle, for the lady-like envelope was barely secured by the minutest dab of glue.

He did not groan out aloud the syllables "Thuella." He did not even *think* them. It was the tall girl herself—the "Venetian Post" in her green and gold Lamia's skin—who slipped out between his finger-tips and this elegant envelope and began dancing before him on that small landing and smiling at him with painted lips.

It was not in pencil, but in the clearest and most unblotted ink, that this letter was written; and Dud read as follows :

"Meet me to-day without fail by the gate a little way up Lovers' Lane where the scummy pond is and that ash you told me about, for I *must* see you before this Antelope lunch and I've told Dumbell I'll be there so it won't matter keeping them waiting but be sure to come to that gate in Lovers' Lane by eleven for certain. I'll be expecting you and if you don't come it'll be the end. Yours, *as it happens,* Thuella."

Our friend looked at his watch. It was now a quarter to eleven. What a fool he had been to leave his letters so long unread! He ought to change his clothes for this lunch—but it couldn't be helped—it was too late now—they must accept him as he was. Even now he couldn't get to that pond—he knew well where it was and he *had* told her about the ash that grew on its bank that he always thought of as the Ogre-Tree—till a quarter past eleven. She'll have to wait for him. Well! never mind! That'll do her good, the bitch! But it would be maddening if she *wouldn't* wait, for he might never know then, no! not to his dying day, what her motive was, and a person couldn't but feel intense curiosity where anyone like her was involved. She had some favour to ask him, no doubt, on behalf of Enoch before this meeting with the editor, and she no doubt fancied that the writer of a couple of romances would have a great influence on this magnate. Little did she know! He was glancing now at the stove to make sure he had turned off the gas. He was rushing now into the bedroom to close the window, lest it should begin to rain before he got back. He was imprisoning now the letter from Yeovil between his cup, which he snatched from its saucer, and his last sheet of manuscript!

This he did—heedless of the circle of tea-stain it was bound to make—so as to be sure of not mislaying such an ominous missive before he was acquainted with its contents.

Finally, with his cap pulled down low over his eyes, a trick of apparel that never failed to inform his mother that her son was on mischief bent, he was running rapidly down the staircase, far too rapidly to notice the smell of burnt almonds and rose-leaves, and was letting himself out of the front door.

And all the while he was doing these things and all the while he was hurrying along the riverside path, under the prison, by the Hangman's Cottage, round by the dam, between the ditches to the Blue Bridge, it was neither of rooks nor of cuckoos that he was thinking—though cawings and cuckooings had never seemed so voluble nor the murmurings of wood-pigeons so close to his ear—but of how he would reproach this cruel hussy, this shameless "Venetian Post."

"Oh, the sly bitch!" he thought. "She'll meet me, will she, by the 'scummy pond'? I'll teach her to be the torment of a good man! I'll Platonize her, with her sofas and her cloud-parties! Oh, the sly bitch!"

He didn't actually run but certainly his thoughts ran, as he pressed forward, swinging over the Blue Bridge, along the laurel-dark path, under the newly-budded beech-trees, till he reached the back gate of Frome House. His thoughts ran so fast ahead that they were circling like swallows round that figure by the "scummy pond" long before he had even got to the entrance of Lovers' Lane.

Few of those ten thousand moralists who crowded into Maumbury Rings to see justice done on Mary Channing can have experienced more excitement than that young woman's historian when he approached the gate leading to the pond.

He was indeed so vexed with the agitation he felt that he actually forced himself to stop for a moment to pull himself together.

With a violent effort of his will he not only stood still, but compelled himself to take notice of the fast-fading blackthorn blossoms in the hedge, blossoms that had begun to assume a reddish-brown tint before they fell, blossoms that, when they *had* fallen, lay in showers, like microscopic Milky Ways, on the rough leaves of the hedge-nettles.

"It's their stamens," he compelled himself to note, "that give them that colour. Their actual petals stay white to the last, which isn't true of the hawthorn. Why, *there are* some hawthorn buds! I didn't know blackthorn and hawthorn over-lapped in their flowering. I must remember that when I make poor Mary come along this path in her tight-fitting bodice and dainty shoes!" If any mortal resolution has ever been registered with what might be described as the outermost skin of the mind it was this resolution of Dud's about the over-lapping of the two kinds of thorn. He released himself from his botanical observations with the rush of an arrow released from a bent bow, and arriving at the gate leaned over it, breathing hard and fast.

No sign of any girl, thin or otherwise, snakelike or otherwise : nothing but the "scummy pond!" Well, *that* is not quite correct, for the ash-tree was very much alive. A pleasant-stirring air moved in its branches, but this only accentuated the upward clutch of its ogrish fingers, while it was clear from the direction of its roots that it derived much comfort from sucking up the slime of its green-mantled companion.

But he suddenly heard a step behind him; and swinging round he saw her approaching. She was coming *down* and not *up* Lovers' Lane; and he had time, as he automatically rushed to meet her, to receive that curious shock, so disturbing to human sensibility, which occurs when the person we are waiting for turns out to be, in some startling detail, seriously different from the image of them in our mind.

Thuella did not look in the least like his smart "Venetian Post!" She was less well-dressed for one thing. Her overcoat had been a tattered object for some while. He remembered how she had worn it when they went together to the Urgans' caravan. But on this warm day she wore, in place of any overcoat, the most old-fashioned, faded, frayed, cloth suit that No-man had ever seen on the back of a gentlewoman. It was of a dirty heather colour with a most discouraging effect of muddy brown-ishness, and it had a belt whch was so frayed and twisted that it looked as if the girl had used it to drag a restless animal about or was constantly using it to tie up bundles of sticks. In place of her usual boyish cap—"It's the warm weather," he thought, "that's made her bring out all these old things. It's come too soon for her, before she's had time to buy new ones!"—she wore one of those big, wide-brimmed, flexible straw hats that have come periodically into fashion, and gone periodically out of fashion, since the days of the Stuarts. This hat of Thuella's looked as if *it* individually—possibly with other ribbons or feathers—had gone in and out of fashion since the Wessex revolt against James the Second. It certainly looked as if Gains-borough might have painted it on the head of a great lady, but in the presence of that pond and that ash-tree and in combination with that brown suit and schoolgirl belt it struck our friend as the sort of pathetic hat that Wizzie might have bought.

The girl's greeting of him was as different from what he expected as was her attire. She flushed with a childish pleasure at seeing him and hastened to explain that she had "gone out at the back and over the fields" so as to avoid being seen by the Quirms. "Nancy will be there too," she informed him breathlessly, "and I wanted to get hold of you first; for they told me you were all coming!"

All the while she was speaking she held him by the hand and gazed into his eyes with a clinging confidence; and even after their fingers had separated and he was leaning back against the gate, listening to her, her form in that brown suit seemed— without actually touching him—to yield up to him without reservation the appealing warmth of her wistful youth. Anything less like the Lamia-figure of the green-and-gold gown of that Candlemas night at Glymes could hardly be imagined. She was transformed, transmuted, reborn.

The shock of this change was so overwhelming to Dud that it totally upset all his calculated campaign—he could only stare at her with a sort of puzzled indulgence, while the mixture of bewilderment and tenderness in his surrender showed itself in his face as an expression of almost foolish concern.

"What is it, Thuella?" he murmured softly. But even as the vibration in his tone drew the warm body under that frayed belt closer towards him, a mocking demon in some detached part of his brain kept repeating in a jeering singsong: "As wicked dew as ere my mother brushed, with raven's feather from unwholesome fen——" and he found himself deliberately shifting his position till he could catch a glimpse of the green-mantled water, as if the mere sight of the "scummy pond" would help him to keep his head!

"What is it, my dear?" he repeated. And the girl in the same wistful voice, childlike, pleading, and full of an absolute confidence in his sympathy, poured forth a long, pitiful story of the troubles of her Glymes neighbours.

"Their investments have gone wrong," she said. "I don't know the details, but their income has gone down to almost nothing. Do you know, I've had to help Nance from *our* larder. They've paid their rent, but that's left them with barely enough for bread and milk and butter. They're not penniless, of course. They've got a few pounds coming in every quarter but that goes in absolute necessities. Do you know, I even found Uryen was short of cigarettes, and he's a great smoker.

"They *must* get a little money somehow—even if he has to do uncongenial work. And he's ready to do anything! He wasn't before. He said he had other things to do that were more important. He never talks about what he's doing, but it's something connected with a revival of the old religions. I know *that* without his telling me. I feel it—it's a kind of instinct, you know, when you're interested in anyone! But this lunch with Dumbell's father-in-law is his grand chance. That man's got endless irons in the fire, newspapers, books, magazines—it's a huge firm!"

Dud listened gravely to every word. He felt ready to do anything she suggested, but in the hard realistic core of his being there rose up an impenetrable doubt. It was impossible to imagine Enoch Quirm writing anything saleable. It was hard to visualize him even in conversation with a real man of affairs! What would he look like at this lunch at the Antelope? Would he wear that old filthy sweater? Why, the very sight of him would choke this man off!

And yet the girl went on pleading with him. She kept assuring him that as a writer he was himself much better known than he realized, and known too for just the sort of thing that Uryen might be able to do on some smaller scale. He felt inclined to cry out more than once: "But what is Uryen to me?" but such hardness evaporated in the presence of that frayed belt, and besides, if this man of his mother's *was* responsible for his being in the world——

Thuella had already taken off her gloves. Indeed she had appeared on the scene with the right-hand one already off; but the other speedily followed. She now, with great deliberation, removed her hat and placed it on the grass by the side of the hedge. He could not help being fascinated by the way that this was done: she snatched her tortoise-shell comb from the top of her head and proceeded to smooth back her shining hair from that unequalled neck.

"You and Uryen have become more friendly than you used to be?" he hazarded at last, grown weary of all these details of domestic penury upon which she seemed to take pleasure in enlarging. She gave him a quick, tender, intimate look.

"I see," she said, "you haven't forgotten our talk in that old Weymouth road. But yes!—I *have* grown to like him better and understand him more. But, as I told you that day, it's impossible to know him *really*. He's an extraordinary being, my dear! Sometimes I think he must be one of the most extraordinary people who've ever lived. One thing is certain about him, no one—Nance least of all!—has the remotest idea of what goes on in his head. He must have talked to Nance quite a lot when he first fell in love with her—she's twenty years younger than he is, you know—but from the way Nance speaks of those days, and from what she tells me of what he used to say, I don't believe she understood a word. She's devoted to him, of course. We all must admire her for that. But it's painful to watch the way she treats him. I mean the mental way she treats him, dragging down his dignity and self-respect and turning him into a kind of boor. Of course, we known she slaves for him, but you feel it's done for conscience' sake, and because—you know—once her man, always her man. But I think she despises him down to the bottom of her soul. It began before her boy's death but it's got worse since and you feel it in the air. You feel as if she regarded him as a repulsive animal to whom in some way she's hopelessly committed."

"But he is rather—odd, isn't he? I mean in his ways! I could well understand a woman finding him terribly trying."

The girl smiled. "Never mind about his character, my dear. What I want you to do for me is a clear issue—get him some work that'll bring them some money. I know this man will do it for you. He's very keen to meet you. I think between ourselves"—here her voice sank to a whisper—"he wants *you* to do something for him; and it came over me that if you wanted to, you might strike up a bargain."

"A bargain?" echoed Dud. "Don't you see?" she whispered nestling close up to him. "You'll do something for *him*—and he'll do something for Uryen. Do you catch on now?"

D. No-man nodded. He didn't "catch on" enough to compare himself with Zeus the cloud-gatherer, but there was a maudlin unction of nervous indulgence in his gesture not at all unlike that god's attitude to the supplicatory Thetis.

"Well, that's settled!" she murmured, breathing a sigh of heart-deep relief. She gave a quick glance, after that, up and down the lane, and it presented itself to even Dud's wool-gathering wits that she was thinking of rewarding him as men have been rewarded by women from time immemorial.

"Come to the pond's edge!" he jerked out abruptly, putting his shoulder to the gate to get it open.

The deepest part of the pond had no green scum upon it, and as it happened, this portion of the water lay at the bottom of the bank under the thick hedge, completely out of sight of the lane, and even out of sight of anyone standing at the gate.

To this point of vantage, after having carefully closed the gate, Dud led the young painter of clouds. The bank had been thoroughly dried by the morning sun, and though it sloped down into water of considerable depth, judging from the ink-black surface, its slope was not a steep one and there were several deviations in its grassy descent. Some of these were ledges no wider than those made by hedgehogs or field-mice; none of them were as wide as those made by rabbits.

Down this grassy slope, offering all manner of footholds, finger-holds, and knotted supports to those who, like Dud and Miss Wye, craved a temporary isolation from their kind, stretched the roots of a couple of small hedge-trees. Our friend had only just got the girl settled in a tolerably comfortable position when she remembered that she'd left her hat on the grass by the gate.

This meant that he had to scramble awkwardly over her and make his way back to their original meeting-place. As chance would have it, whom should he see coming up the lane but three middle-aged men, persons he had come to know quite well by meeting them so often by the old brick bridge at the foot of High East Street? They were all, he supposed, "on the dole," and they were rarely seen apart, and with them, almost invariably was a little bitch terrier.

He felt decidedly uncomfortable to be caught holding such a striking-looking lady's hat; but there was nothing for it but to bid them good day, make his comment on the warmth of the weather, and assume the attitude that it was his usual habit to carry in his hand on a fine May morning this particular feminine adornment.

Treating Thuella's hat, therefore, as if it had been a bunch of bluebells, he kept the three men in friendly conversation for a minute or two, and then continued casually leaning against the gate after they had gone on.

The only trouble was that the little bitch terrier became quickly aware of the presence of Thuella behind the high hedge and proceeded to sniff and jump about and bark vociferously at the spot nearest to the invisible form.

Hearing their dog's excitement the three companions turned round and began slowly to return, which was the last thing our friend desired. The men called to the dog as they came back; and Dud beginning to find the situation intolerable, tried to drive her away, even going so far as to wave the girl's hat at the small beast's excited tail.

"Get on! get away!" he heard himself cry to the persistent dog, whose own feminine soul—though he did not go into that —was covered with a black-and-white skin, while its quivering tail, electrified by the presence behind the hedge, was of unspotted white.

But the men had got her now, and No-man watched them with extreme relief disappear at last round a bend in the lane. It was only when he had opened the gate to rejoin Thuella, and had caught a glimpse of her childish figure, for she seemed altogether childish to-day, balanced contentedly if a little precariously above the deep end of the pond, that his mind—but *this* movement of thought had nothing to do with any contemplative cult—recalled the drooping head of Wizzie as it looked when he had run back into their room to give her that reconciling kiss. This image floating irrelevantly into his head over the water-meadows, past Frome House back gate, caused him an unpleasant twinge.

As he scrambled along the bank towards the recumbent figure, his satyrish pleasure in the exposed curves of her limbs was lost in a moment's intense thinking; and yet it was not so much "thinking" as the distressing clash of two contradictory opportunities, the opportunity to be faithful to Wizzie, and the opportunity to enjoy, after his own cerebral fashion, the yielding mood of this strange young woman.

It was some plausible demon—the demon of convoluted self-preservation perhaps—that came to his rescue as he clambered over the girl's body to his balancing-place at her side. This demon suggested to him the idea of exploiting his moral disapproval of her treatment of Mr. Wye, exploiting his resentment with her for her seduction of Wizzie, exploiting in fact all his accumulative malice against her, to assist him to remain scrupulously faithful to the circus-rider, while at the same time he allowed his sense of sight to enjoy what he rigorously refused to his sense of touch!

"She will be piqued," this crafty adviser whispered, "by not being able to ruffle your self-control; and without giving her the satisfaction of making you unfaithful to Wizz you will get such pleasure from contemplating what you refuse to touch that tantalization will be swallowed up in ecstasy."

But Dud's demon betrayed him into the girl's hands. Thuella must have had the exactly corresponding feminine perversity answering to our friend's; for never since, in that old organist's house in East Dorset, he had first grown conscious of these matters had he known such entrancement, such "linked sweetness long-drawn out," as he enjoyed that morning on the bank of the "scummy pond."

"How grotesque," he thought, in the detached portion of his mind, "are the situations we get into! I must remember this in the story of my Mary. People in books are luckier than in life. Every life, if the truth were known, contains experiences of a monstrous grotesqueness."

These reflections of our friend came and went like crude "captions" on the "screen" of his sensations. The real background of what he felt must have been the edge of the green slime against the deep water, for he found himself impressed by the unevenness of this edge and by the way certain agglomerations of the microscopic green weed floated out further than the rest in minute promontories and capes. The ungodly pleasure the girl was giving him began actually to take the shape of this wavering edge between greenness and blackness; and this congruity went so deep that the satisfaction of his mental desire seemed to him then like a delirious worm feeding upon the vegetation-roots of the world, a worm rising up from that black water—that was the primal gulf of space—to feed forever upon celestial duck-weed!

It must not be supposed, so touchingly hypocritical men and women are in their love-attractions—as if this amazing vibration between the two were too sacred, too holy, too near the "el-

211

bridge" between life and death to be subjected even to the sacrilege of thought, much less to the vandalism of words—it must not, I say, be supposed that Dud and Thuella were guiltily silent during their cerebral absorption. They kept up all the while—as if for the benefit of the ash-tree and the pond—a perfunctory semblance of conversation. Nor could they bestow even what was left after that of their superficial consciousness on much rational awareness of their bizarre situation, for it was constantly necessary to keep themselves from slipping by the aid of those accommodating hedge-roots.

Meanwhile the ash-tree on the further side of the pond kept clutching at the air with its queer up-turning fingers as the soft breeze rustled through it. If it were an ogre-tree, that ash, as Dud had let himself fancy in many of his solitary walks up Lovers' Lane, it was contenting itself just now with a harmless vegetation-mimicry of what was going on opposite him, save that it was the invisible spring air and not a palpable form encircled by a brown belt, towards which its budding twigs vibrated, swaying and undulating there, as if to the rhythm of some secret pulse-throb of its life-sap.

Yes, in their pathetic, human hypocrisy Dud and Thuella went obstinately on, putting various floating fancies, unworthy of the name of "thoughts," into perfunctory words; and all the while their real thoughts were the recurrent orbits, each revolving on its own quivering axis, of their magnetic advances and retreats, while the absence of actual contact between them evoked, in place of any twinge of tantalization, an intensity of imaginative lust that was transporting.

Thuella seemed to know to a point of exquisite clairvoyance how to play on the psychic nerve of his cerebral desire; and our friend was astounded, even while he was enraptured, by her understanding of the perversity of his senses.

The magnetic interchange between them was rendered more complicated though not less exciting by reason of their dangerous position above the "scummy pond," into whose dark water it is certain that John Bunyan would have precipitated them both, and out of whose green slime it is equally certain that Dante would have called forth a cartload of horned devils, of scratching, biting, scaly devils, of foul, stinking, obscene devils, to switch them off to hell.

212

But all forms of erotic rapture—even that mysterious embracing of the cosmos known to so many of the old saints—come at last to an end, and the time arrived when our friend found himself helping Thuella, with her hat in her own hand now, to reach the gate.

Here he looked at his watch, and the very gesture of doing this, though he had not discarded it in the interval, swept his mind back to their first meeting on All Souls' Day.

"Plenty of time!" he remarked, "but I've got to call for the others in Friary Lane. You'd better come there with me—eh?—and we'll all go on together."

Thuella merely nodded and made a little grimace. She began raising her thin, brown-sleeved arms to her head and adjusting the great, flapping hat. As he saw it now beside him, it did not look so pitiably incongruous as he had felt it to be at first, and the further they advanced side by side down the lane towards the back gate of Frome House the less incongruous it seemed.

"They'll stare at her at the Antelope," he thought, "but I'm really not sure they won't think her a grand lady! She looks very fashionable to me, in spite of the belt!"

Dud's notions of what was fashionable were somewhat vague; but he *had* seen in South Street, during the morning hours when the upper class did their shopping, hats not so very unlike the one that was now fluttering at his side.

By the time they reached Blue Bridge they had passed several groups of pedestrians, and the glances of furtive awe that he had caught directed to Thuella, who was evidently taken for a distinguished visitor, changed his attitude to her whole costume.

He even decided after various surreptitious glances at the brown belt that what looked to him like its frequent use for purposes other than adornment might really be the last touch of refined dressmaking. Could this also apply to the look of genteel fadedness that emanated from the brown suit itself?

Thuella, having stolen from him a promise that he would do everything in his power to wheedle Dumbell's father-in-law into assisting Mr. Quirm, fell into pensive silence, a silence which it may be well believed gave our friend an opportunity for many lively thoughts.

Among these thoughts one at least was decidedly cowardly,

namely that Thuella would make it appear to Wizzie that he and she had merely encountered each other at the entrance to Friary Lane!

But what staggered and confounded him and led to meditations that were "heavy as frost and deep almost as life" was the fact that with their departure from the "scummy pond" all his old resentment against Thuella had returned. This was an emotional phenomenon that astonished him more than any discovery he had made in himself since he discovered that Mona's phantom was not Mona at all, but the mere creation of his perversity.

"But what a fate I've got into!" he went on. "Wizz is my girl. I had that feeling about her when I first set eyes on her in the caravan! And Wizz's figure is a lovely, natural, girlish figure, beautifully developed, beautifully athletic—whereas *yours*, my demon, yours, my cunning, lecherous devil, is an unhealthy distortion, a deformity, a sickness of nature!"

He suddenly felt a longing to see more of his companion's face than he could make out under her spacious hat. "What on earth," he asked her, "will your Uryen have put on for this affair? Will he be wearing that old jersey of his?"

He obtained his wish with a vengeance; for the tone in which he had said "your Uryen" gave her eyes a flash of fury as she turned and her red lips a twist of unconcealed contempt.

"He'll be no worse," she remarked curtly, "and no better, I suppose, than the rest of us! We're none of us so very wonderful. But if you feel like that towards him, if you're so little that you can't recognize a great man when you see him, I won't keep you to your promise for a——"

She was interrupted by a greeting from the coal-yard, where Claudius, leaning on the handle of his shovel, stood smiling and nodding at them.

It was impossible for No-man to pass him with a mere salute; so he paused by the bridge and Thuella paused with him.

"Don't forget what you promised to do for me," murmured the penitential coal-heaver across the ditch. He spoke in what he supposed was a confidential whisper, but the words were carried as far as if they had been spoken from the rostrum in Pompey's Theatre. Several Orchard Street boys, making a toy dam in the familiar ditch, stopped their game to listen. Claudius had

214

already become to the children of this district a treasure trove of delight, a jumping-jack of surprises.

"So *you've* made him promise something too," said Thuella. "I hope no more people will go and do that. If we're the only ones we can keep him faster to it."

The candidate for Communistic freemasonry stared at her blankly, and his ruddy face darkened. Dud saw that he suspected him of unsympathetic chattering.

"She knows nothing about *our* affairs," he said hurriedly. "Promises to women are quite a different thing. But I swear now that I won't promise anything more to anyone till——"

But Claudius interrupted him, letting the shovel fall and drawing anxiously nearer. "Don't offer any hopes of my changing—all *this*," he whispered solemnly. "I'm glad I saw you again. I was afraid I might have led you to think——"

"No, no!" cried Dud reassuringly. "I fully understand. It's live and let live. That's the motto! Everyone to do what's right in their own eyes, and to let everyone else do the same!"

The reformer's face relaxed. A smile of touching gratitude passed over it and he half-turned to resume his work.

Dud had an inspiration. "A cigarette?" he cried, and added hurriedly, "I want an excuse for buying another packet!"

Leaving the despiser of "the primrose path" to reconcile his conscience as best he might to this heaven-sent luxury, our friend, followed by his slender companion, began ascending the well-known hill to the entrance to Friary Lane.

The encounter with Claudius set him pondering on the indelible stamp that Rome had left upon this place.

"It's Rome," he thought, "more than the Norman houses, more than the feudal gentry, that's made all these people so patient of authority, so slow in striking back, so enduring and stoical. If that man of mother's is right, and Mai-dun and 'Pummery' ever do throw off the burden, it'll be Rome that they'll throw off at last! Perhaps ... they .... will .... some ... day. They are strange things, deep-suppressed in you, my Durnovaria, deep, deep-suppressed!"

"Do you believe in Christianity, D. No-man?" These surprising words reached him from Thuella's scarlet lips as they were passing Chubb's Almshouse.

He characteristically came to a complete stop, and leaning

heavily on his stick peered into her face under the brim of her hat as if he'd found a blackthorn with purple petals instead of white.

"Which do you mean," he asked very gravely and in a hesitating voice, "the Prophet or the magic ceremonies?"

The girl looked down. Then, in a scarcely audible voice with a scared look in her eyes: "The God," she whispered. But directly afterwards she replied crossly with an angry frown: "I was thinking of right and wrong. I don't know what you're talking about."

Dud picked up a couple of crushed bluebells from the sun-baked road and threw them over a wall. Their moist stalks left two wet marks where they had been lying, marks that resembled the slime of snails but that were less glittering.

"It's him down there," he said grimly, "made you think of *that*! But he's no more a Christian than your father!"

Thuella moved on with an impatient gesture and he was compelled to follow. He felt ashamed of what he had said. It was unkind to refer to her father, and who was he to take it for granted that this girl had no more conscience than Mary Channing?

Entering Mrs. Dearth's house he left Thuella with her sister and hurried upstairs to Wizz's room. Though he did not pause—no! not for a second—before opening the door, he had plenty of time, so fast move the thoughts of men, to wonder nervously in what mood he would find her.

As a matter of fact, he found her exactly where he had left her early that morning, seated before her looking-glass. She might have been seated there for the last four hours, except that she was no longer in her night-dress. But this time she rose at his entrance; and, Heaven be thanked! her radiant face expressed nothing but pleasure at seeing him.

"How nice you look!" he cried, holding her at arm's length. It was true. The ex-circus-rider had turned overnight into "Miss Ravelston of Ravenswood." She wore a dress he had never seen her in before. Indeed she and Jenny had kept it a secret from him. Jenny herself had helped her choose both the stuff and the pattern, and they had found a clever seamstress not many doors off who had fitted it and made it up in an incredibly short time. It was a wonderful fairy-like grey, with filmy flounces and loose sleeves, and it had a romantic touch of rose colour at the bosom, like a wound from a spear.

The girl looked a totally different person from the Wizz he had parted from that morning, and he said to himself, thinking of the changed Thuella: "They are conjurers with their clothes! And if with their clothes, why not with——" and his mind raced off down an incredible and confusing vista of feminine metempsychosis!

"Well," he said, "you'd better come down now, if you're ready, and show yourself off to your precious 'Thel.' She's down there with Jenny."

Wizzie's hands went up to her head and she turned quickly round again to her mirror. He saw her small, oval face and shining eyes reflected there and how anxiously she patted the sides of her head and smoothed her hair forward, hiding more of the hedge.

"I'd rather put on my hat first," she remarked; and then, more to herself than to him: "It isn't right. It's too large." Saying this, and muttering something else, too technical for Dud to follow, she picked up a round, black object from the table that appeared to him to resemble a priest's biretta.

"It doesn't *look* very large," he murmured, thinking of the adornment he had recently made use of to drive the terrier out of the hedge.

"It's too large," she repeated with a sigh as she put the thing on.

"It's much nicer," he said reassuringly, "than your other one."

Wizzie treated these words as if they were so irrelevant as not even to be annoying. From the faint movement she made with her shoulders he knew that he had said something with as little bearing on the occasion as if he had told her that he had found bluebells in the road.

"Well! come on down," he cried abruptly. "They'll soon tell you whether it looks all right! Where's your cloak?"

But it now appeared that Wizzie had made her toilet under the impression that the day was too warm for cloaks. She finally, however, did allow him, though with a sharp rebuke for his fussiness, to carry her cloak on his arm; and thus they went downstairs.

It may be believed that the last thing Dud wanted when they entered Mrs. Dearth's kitchen where Thuella had ensconced herself in Claudius's armchair and Jenny, already dressed to go out, was tidying things up before setting forth, was to meet Thuella's eye. But to avoid doing this he had to devote himself so exclusively to Jenny that he missed, to his great annoyance, the expression on the two girls' faces as they encountered each other in their lunch-party clothes.

He caught the intonation of their voices all the same, and it was an indescribable comfort to him to recognize that they sounded as friendly, indeed as infatuated, as ever. But it soon became hard for him to overhear anything that was going on between them because of the extreme tension of his interview with Mrs. Dearth. He had boldly taken the bull by the horns and had attacked Jenny at once in his role as ambassador from Claudius; but he was shocked at the dark cloud of implacable resentment that descended upon her when her friend's name was mentioned.

It was the first time he had dared, since her estrangement with Claudius, to approach the perilous topic, and he asked himself when he saw this black cloud of remorseless obstinacy : "Is it impossible for *any* ordinary, natural, simple kindness to play a fundamental part in the relations between the 'Ying' and the 'Yang'? Must the attraction between men and women *always* entail these abysmal angers? It isn't even misunderstanding," he thought, as he surveyed the "Horse-Head's" face, in which the blood literally seemed to change from red to black, and the eyes to grow fuliginous, and dusky wrinkles to gather between them and the nose, as soon as he referred to the man in question, "for she knows him far better than I do! She knows perfectly well how his conscience works; she knows how, after that passage with her brother, he *has* to do what he's doing. But yet she won't forgive him! He has committed the unpardonable sin from a woman's point of view. He has obeyed his conscience and not her. What they want is to possess a man's whole identity, to turn him from lover into child, to be *in* his nerves, *in* his mind, *in* his religions, *in* his conscience, so that there is no portion of his being where she isn't at home. No! No! these deep conflicts aren't 'misunderstandings,' as both sides love to affirm : they are *understandings*.

218

"They know each other too well!" Dud sighed as he looked at the face opposite him where black blood had replaced red blood. "You're a good woman," he thought. "It's the sex-demon that has entered into you. You'd be lovely to Claudius if only you didn't 'love him.' "

When the four of them, the two Wye sisters and he and Wizzie, finally entered the Antelope they found that they were the very last to turn up. All the others were talking in the comfortable lounge on the ground-floor. This was not the bar where Mrs. Dearth had first met our friend, but a room on the opposite side of the staircase, a retreat used more by residents than transients. Over and above the guests of Mr. George Cumber there was but one person in the room, a pathetically self-conscious little man, dressed in the most perfect negligence of pure gentility, whose one desire, as he sat writing at a table and shrinking into himself, was to feel his difference from this motley group of fellow creatures. Everything about this refined person seemed to be shrinking into itself along with him. Providence in depriving the poor man of every human gift but that of being a gentleman had endowed this virtue with so much magic power of its own that a palpable though imponderable circle of exclusiveness spread itself over everything within his reach. The chair he sat on became his own private library chair, the carpet beneath his feet became a compendium of all the carpets in all the rooms where he had been valued at his true value. Between his self-conscious boot-soles and this particular carpet a feudal relation had already established itself which compelled all the other boots in the room to recognise the presence of some subtle privilege.

But the poor man himself had paid such a heavy price for this advantage that his shrinking discomfort in the presence of Mr. Cumber and his guests made our friend feel quite sorry for him, and it was with relief that he watched him retire from the scene the second the clock indicated the opening of the dining-room for lunch.

"Good Lord!" Dud said to himself, as soon as Mr. Cumber, who had been standing in the full sunshine from the window and with his broad back to the fire, was made aware of his identity. "Is Thuella right then, and *am* I more of a person with people like this than I supposed?"

Certainly the moment the man gripped his hand he felt himself the subject of concentrated civility. But our friend's egoism was so subjective and his pride so averse to this particular kind of recognition that after listening politely for a while to the magnate's talk his thoughts began to wander. Civility prevented him from looking away from the countenance of his interlocutor, but each competent businesslike feature of the great man's face became the jumping-off board for his own private meditations. The man's well-cut nose caused him to remember that unopened letter with the Yeovil postmark. "Curse it!" he thought, "I believe it's Old Funky again!" And then the man's strongly marked chin served as a promontory from which he took flight to Claudius and his coal-yard.

But the most curious of the transformations that the energetic face of this unwitting patron of historians had to endure was the mental sorcery that substituted for the gleam of his small, penetrating eyes one particular look that had darted forth, at a certain point, from Thuella's soul, as they hung together over the "scummy pond."

There finally arrived a moment when the man's talk—he was evidently fishing for a sensational article on something or other —became so tedious that No-man allowed his gaze, as well as his mind, to wander; and it was then he took in the attitude of Uryen to all this.

Uryen was seated on one of the couches between their host's daughter and son-in-law, and although he *was* wearing a sweater in place of a waistcoat, it was a clean one of a dark colour and looked by no means unbecoming.

Dud himself had been greeted by Dumbell and his wife on his first entrance, but they hadn't bothered to rise. The only *rapport* he had been able to establish with Dunbar Wye since he first met him was connected with botany, for which the lad had a passion; but one could not very well plunge into botanical pedantries every time one encountered a person. Apart from botany, it was hard to imagine human stupidity carried further than in the brain of poor Dumbell, though that further point of pig-headedness *did* seem to have been reached within the fuzzy-haired skull of Sissie Wye.

The young man had inherited from his parent a high, narrow forehead, and he parted his straight locks exactly in Teucer's way. He even had the old Platonist's trick of alternately pressing his thin lips together and abruptly opening them as if to snap at a gnat. His whole nature indeed seemed to express itself in a strain of gaping intensity varied by frequent clicks of obstinate closing-down. The young man's sensibilities seemed atrophied in other directions, as if he had no natural pores to his skin, as if his sole contact with the world was through his troutlike gills which nothing but a particular kind of fly could bring to the top of the water. The face he turned to life was bloodless fish's gills, into which—our friend was forced to conclude—the "black-shirt" philosophy, whatever *that* was, had thrust a stout hook.

The little wife, on the contrary, turned upon existence the head of a cantankerous doll, all fuzz-wuzzy with flaxen hair, but quite as impervious to all but extremely limited considerations as were the hooked gills of poor Dumbell.

But what was this? Both these young people, as they sat on either side of him, appeared fascinated by Uryen! Dud had never seen them in the man's company before. Were they always like this to him, or was their behaviour just now due to their knowledge that Mr. Cumber really *was* intending to take some practical advantage of the fellow's erudition in Welsh matters?

But as he let their host continue indicating the nature of the contribution he wanted, of which the most important aspect appeared to be the precise number of words required, he took the opportunity to study Mr. Quirm's attitude to it all with a growing interest. The look of the man to-day bewildered him not a little. Was he one of those exceptional human beings whose bodily appearance depended on some secret intention of their inner will?

Our friend, as a romantic student of history, had come to explain many old psychological riddles on this ground, namely by the power that certain rare natures have been given, of changing their "protective colouring" for private ends of their own.

All his former physical impressions of "this man of his mother's" required readjustment in his mind as he saw him now in this pleasant lounge chatting so plausibly with the young Wyes. His face had subsided from the majestic and relapsed into the handsome. His features had lost—or was it that between the

221

bright sunshine and the hospitable fire this peculiarity was momentarily obscured?—that look of being formed out of mountain mist that struck No-man so much on former occasions. His dusky hair no longer resembled some queer kind of moorland moss. His eyes, though their expression remained veiled and indistinct, had no longer that semi-mortuary look.

And the man, though his corduroy trousers were by no means new and his sweater inappropriate enough to the occasion, looked quite at his ease, neither abashed nor nervous, and in no sense like a desperate suppliant for financial aid.

He caught our friend's glance fixed upon him and a natural and even mischievous smile flickered over his lips, as much as to say : "You needn't worry about me, my lad. Look to yourself!"

From Enoch Quirm Dud's glance wandered to Jenny and Nancy who apparently were as much under the spell of Thuella as the young couple were under the spell of Uryen.

The three of them were standing by the window, out of which Wizzie, preoccupied with her new black hat, to which her gloved hands were constantly rising, and seated in a large armchair, stared rather self-consciously.

Mr. Cumber, without interrupting his discourse on the nature of magazine articles, had rung a bell at his side and had ordered a variety of drinks, which a waiter was now handing round on a tray. But although Dud took in these ripples on life's surface, it was as if the old hostelry about him and indeed the whole of the town, from the chestnut-walk in front of Rothesay House to the statue of Thomas Hardy with its profile turned towards the Roman wall, were but a negligible framework to that look in Thuella's eyes.

And what did it say to him, that look? It said that their sensual nerves corresponded in a manner that linked them together until death. It said : "I can call you to me, I can excite your lust to madness, at any time I like, with this look of mine *and what it means*. You can kill me," the look said, "but as long as our eyes meet in *that* way you'll be enjoying me in your mind; you won't be able to help it. Even though you flee to the uttermost ends of the earth you'll have to enjoy me in your mind, yes, you'll have to lick me up like water forever ! Forever I'll be the water flowing under your chin," that look said, "and the mirage under your wheels, and the wind between your

222

teeth! And yet we'll have no need to touch each other! Our nerves are our gods when we're like that, and they are the same gods!

"Now that it's once happened, you'd know I was looking at you and you'd know *everything else* even if you were blind, even if we were both dead! Yes, it'll be with *that look* that I'll call you to me if I die first. Yes, yes! and you'll come quick enough, night or day, grubbing at my grave with your tongue hanging out! They'll have to put you away; but I shall be there with you all the time!

"I shall be there, looking at you—*you know how*—till they can't keep you, you'll be such a husk with enjoying me! Yes, you'll be so light that you'll blow out between the bars, and we'll float together forever over the 'scummy pond' of the world!"

While all this was swirling through No-man's brain he was accepting a glass of something from the waiter's tray and exchanging nods with Mr. Cumber.

"I have one little condition to make," he remarked slowly, "before I undertake anything definite for you. We all, down here, think so highly of Mr. Quirm, and we feel sure that if you *could*, in some branch of your publications—on Welsh matters, of course—give him a chance to show what he can do, you'll find him a mine—yes! a mine, Mr. Cumber—of untouched information."

His host tossed off his drink and gave Dud a steady, penetrating look out of his small, grey eyes. Then he smiled in a cold but not unfriendly manner.

"Mr. Quirm and I have already had a little business talk," he said, "and I hope we may arrange something; but of course I never come to any final decision until I know a man's work."

"Certainly, quite so. I understand, perfectly," said No-man. "But I'm a little—well—eccentric perhaps—in this case; and it would distress me to get—to get things taken, you know, until my friend Mr. Quirm——"

"Your friend Mr. Quirm shall have his chance," said the great man solemnly; "and as to our own little matter you'll hear from me, you'll hear from me very shortly, Mr. No-man. I am extremely glad to have had this opportunity."

Dud suddenly felt as if he had been made a fool of. Uryen

223

seemed to have gained his point independently of any assistance.

"Now, Sissie dear," and Mr. Cumber took a ponderous step or two towards Dumbell's wife, "will you lead the way with Mr. Quirm? I think we shall find our table and our lunch ready now. The room's upstairs, they tell me."

Dud found himself ascending the Antelope stairs side by side with his old ally Nancy. *She* looked exactly the same as when he had first seen her that day in the cemetery.

"I believe you've done it for us," she whispered to him as they went up. Her eyes were shining, and she gave him the usual warm pressure upon his arm. "Sissie has been sweet about it all. She likes him, you know. It's queer, isn't it? She really does! But of course it'll be what *you* say that'll clinch it. I don't think, out of Glymes, we've just realized——"

But Dud cut her short : "It just happened that this chap had heard of me somewhere. I've no influence with him whatever, or with Sissie either. What I *am* proud of is that your husband has read my books!"

She held him back for a second on the landing before they entered the dining-room. "I've come to wish very much," she whispered, leaning so close to him that the cowslip sweetness of her breath stole through his senses, mingled with the balminess of the air, and with the scent of the flowers in the big, cheerful room. at whose open door they paused, "that *he* had lived to make friends with you."

Dud was not oblivious to the poignance of the sigh that accompanied this remark.

"I am sorry for that too," he replied as they went in together.

Mr. Cumber's lunch-party began now to prove, with the help of the good wine from the Antelope cellar, quite a lively and prosperous affair.

Neither Friary Lane nor Glymes being accustomed to such luxurious entertainment, they all made hay while the sun shone, and though their conviviality was discreet it was unrestrained and free.

Except for a group of elderly ladies—residents in the hotel— who regarded our friends with amused interest, the only other stranger was the gentleman who had fled from the lounge, and though their good spirits entirely destroyed the psychic harmony which this good man felt to be his privilege, thrusting between every inch of his careful person and that decorous dining-room a wedge of discord, his sufferings were lessened by the tact of the waiter who, without anything said, protected his life-illusion with every wave of his discriminating napkin.

The least lively of Mr. Cumber's guests was Jenny Dearth, who in some sad way suggested that her black, silk dress, concealed not only a Friary Lane "overall" but also a bruised and brooding heart.

It must have been a wave of telepathy from this unappeased heart that started No-man off upon one of his favourite topics : the difference in domestic quarrels between men and women.

It was a new experience to our friend to be treated with the respect he was receiving from Mr. Cumber, and the consequent glow that suffused his lean frame was his excuse for so inappropriate a discourse.

He had begun to receive several sharp interior stabs of remorse as his eyes turned from Wizzie's little hat to Thuella's large one, and the eagerness with which he developed his improper theme was an escape from conscience as well as a response to unwonted appreciation.

"As long as men have no feeling of personal jealousy," he was remarking, "they soon learn to forgive the way women bring down their pride. But women are always vexing themselves over obstacles to their possessive instinct that have nothing to do with other women. They grow jealous over things, over ideas, over ways of life in their men that put them at a distance." Here he hesitated, catching a glance from Jenny that showed he had gone too far. "Don't you think so, Mr. Cumber?" he added weakly.

But it had become already abundantly clear that Mr. Cumber was "a man's man" and that he regarded pother of this sort about "the dear ladies" as an interruption of the practical business of life. Our friend watched him now enjoying this good Antelope fare and sipping his wine, and it amused him to note how all the vibrations quivering forth into that pleasant room from these soft feminine bodies, and from the fabrics that concealed and revealed them, fell away, as if in the presence of some non-conducting chemical substance, before the man's iron-clad virility.

Mr. Cumber treated this point-blank question as if it had

225

been a Rabelaisian joke. He chuckled indulgently and assumed an air as if this unconventional man of letters, who must be humoured in his whimsies, had introduced the levity of the smoking-room into this mixed company.

"Oh, come now, come now, No-man!" he laughed. "You mustn't appeal to me when my daughter's here. Must he, Dunny?"

Dumbell's mouth opened wide, as if a completely unknown fly, some may-fly of an extraordinary appearance, had fallen into his pool. He turned his head towards his flaxen-haired wife.

"What I would like to ask Mr. Wye," said Uryen suddenly, and something in his tone—perhaps the intonation of a man about to speak to men on the subject of politics—caused Mr. Cumber to assume his most alert office expression and grow serious, "is whether you mightn't maintain that the Fascist movement in the world to-day is a reaction from Matriarchy?"

"What I tell Dunny," intervened his father-in-law, "is that where both Communism and Fascism go wrong is in their interference with individual initiative. Capitalism has its faults. I've always said so, and my feeling is that we *must* say so; but at least it allows for individual initiative. It's based on the instinctive nature of the human average; not on our worst impulses, or on our best, but on our normal average character."

Dud's mind took rebellious refuge as he heard this, in Claudius's coal-yard. "Isn't it a little *too* average?" he protested. "Doesn't the pressure of Evolution imply—I mean," he caught himself up, "aren't Reason and Imagination more important than our average character?"

"But what about Liberty?" threw in Mr. Cumber, now thoroughly enjoying himself and squaring his shoulders as if addressing a meeting of dissatisfied printers. "I know the usual retort, 'Liberty to starve,' but with a government ready to pay the dole and to tax the rich, don't we, after all, get more liberty to live as we like in England than in——"

"But Dad!" interrupted Sissie Wye, "you remember what Dunny said yesterday about our selfishness and lack of discipline? I can't bear selfish, greedy people who——"

"Stop, little Sissie—rogue!" cried her father with the air of one putting a troublesome kitten down from his knee upon the floor. "I'm not a bigoted Tory. I'm an old-fashioned Liberal, with respect for the natural rights of man. Ask any of my employees what I am! I've got none of Dunny's blackshirts among my people, no! nor Communists, either. And why? Because I treat 'em proper! Because I know what average men want—and ought to *have* too, by God!"

Dud found himself repeating in his heart a train of crushing argument that he had heard Claudius use; but he felt sorry too, in some odd way, for this "old-fashioned Liberal." "He's not a bad chap," he thought, "and between Dumbell and Sissie——"

He continued to catch snatches of the conversation around him. Somebody—was it "that man of his mother's"?—had started them off on the subject of prayer; and Dud noticed, as a touching human trait, that the waiter showed an interest in this that he hadn't displayed before, and as for the old ladies, they listened in spellbound fascination.

"Certainly I do," he heard Mr. Cumber reply. "Not *long,* you know; but I do. I wouldn't feel comfortable, I wouldn't have the proper grip of my day's work; I wouldn't——"

"Oh, always!" he heard Mrs. Wye exclaim. "I never do, but I never interfere with *his* doing what he likes. *He* kneels down— I don't believe many men still do that."

"Does he kneel by his bed or by a chair?" he heard Uryen inquire.

Dud got a pang of uncomfortable sympathy, like a distressing blush, on behalf of the botanist who said his prayers. He got such a clear vision of that round head, bowed down in silence above a striped suit of pyjamas, while Sissie fussed round the room with her fuzzy hair about her ears.

But the conversation soon turned to another topic—whether it was possible for sounds and smells to leave ghosts of themselves behind; and our friend heard Uryen speak of an unearthly smell —a smell completely different from ordinary ones—that he had long recognized as coming at certain particular seasons from Maiden Castle.

"I think," he heard Uryen say, "they must have burnt some special kind of wood there in old days. It isn't the smell of burning flesh; but I've smelt that smell more than once, and this is quite different."

From ghost-smells the talk naturally drifted to the Glymes ghost-wind. About this, however, Uryen, for some unknown

227

reason, was extremely reserved, and it was left to Thuella and Sissie to do most of the talking. Wizzie too joined in, and the three young women's voices rose high and excited above the rest.

Our friend had taken a strong dislike to Sissie, and it gave him an extremely unpleasant feeling to see Wizzie and Thuella "reduce themselves to her silly level." The high spirits these two were in began to offend some deep instinct in him. Indeed, as he watched them across the table it seemed as if their separate identities—those identities that in their isolation meant so much to him—were actually melting together, fusing themselves in the common anonymity of "girls enjoying a party," and losing in this fusion all the mysterious and provocative qualities that were so essential to him.

As he watched their shining eyes and their enjoyment of each other and of the occasion, it came over him that *he* was the victim and *they* were the aggressors!

He had been cherishing all this time a sort of delicious guilt about the "scummy pond," but now, as he watched them, this vanished away, and he felt ashamed of having been fooled into such a crucial emotion.

In place of two mysterious worlds of evasive attraction through which he could move like a magician among spirits of the deep, or an explorer through unknown enchantments, all he saw now were two lively, young people, using a language totally alien to everything that appealed to him.

"There must be," he thought, "some curious freemasonry among women when they're together that disenchants them and divests them of their mystery, that turns them in fact into totally different creatures from those we know when we have them alone!"

Suddenly, without definite intention, he found himself on his feet, he found himself moving round the table, he found himself extending his hand to Mr. Cumber.

"Well, sir," he found himself saying, lightly and casually, as if it were a perfectly natural proceeding, "I've got to get back to my work now. We writers aren't our own masters like you men of affairs. We have to keep our fixed habits—or we're quite lost."

Either his tone really did carry it off, or Mr. Cumber himself was thinking that he ought very soon to be catching his train, for the great man responded quite naturally and easily and bade him good-bye.

"I'll write to you," he said, "and I'll have a talk," here he lowered his voice, "with Mr. Quirm before we separate. Good-bye No-man, good-bye—and good luck to you!"

It pleased our friend to note that both Wizzie and Thuella stared at him in dismay as he made a general bow to the company and walked to the door. Once again, however, he did something he hadn't known he was going to do till he found himself doing it. He hurried back to Wizzie's side, taking no notice of Thuella or anybody else, and remarked to her quietly, though not in a whisper: "I'll be back at Friary Lane by five. Let's have tea in *our* room, eh? but with Jenny of course!"

It had been one of Dud's frequent experiences in life to find certain situations—not unusual ones, but still not *daily* ones—repeating themselves in an almost exact reaffirmation of their larger outlines, and this happened to him now; for he was scarcely out of the Antelope archway than he found Uryen standing by his side.

"I'm glad I caught you," the man said. "I was only just in time! What do you say to a walk, this lovely afternoon?"

Now as he came downstairs our friend *had* thought to himself: "I'll go straight off for a walk!" But this decision had been modified by another one: "I'll go to my room first and get that letter."

Now under the pressure of Uryen's presence he decided that he'd postpone getting that letter till after his walk. He could take it to Wizzie then, and they could discuss it before tea, or *later*, if she wanted to keep its contents a secret from Mrs. Dearth!

So he expressed himself amiably, and suggested boldly that they should walk to Maiden Castle.

"That was just what I was going to suggest," said Uryen complacently. " 'Every day lost in May is a day twice away,' " he quoted, "and though it's not the exact day I would have chosen, there's nothing against it *as* a day as far as I know." They both walked with such rapid strides that it was not long before they reached the couple of isolated cottages, with a vege-table garden in front of them, that marks the halfway point to the ancient earthwork. Their road was both treeless and hedge-

229

less and around it in all directions extended wide stretches of arable land where not a hedge or a tree was visible.

In fact nothing seemed visible from that long, straight, pilgrim's road except the object of the pilgrimage. Towards this object, towards this low-lying and yet grandly rising mass of *fossae* and *valla*, this man-made promontory of earth in an expanse of natural earth, this man-made city of turf in an expanse of natural turf, this Titanic erection of the demented mould-warp man, heaved up between the roots of the grass and the highways of the winds, the narrow road led as directly and undeviatingly as if this vast Polis, for so the classical geographer designated it, this mystical City of Dunium, had been an antediluvian monster—a monster compared with whom Leviathan himself were but a field-mouse—whose long straight dragon's tongue lay supine as a strip of seaweed so that the Beings it intended to swallow might advance at ease along it, undeterred by any distraction from advancing to their doom.

Dud stared in fascinated awe at the great earth-monument. From this halfway distance it took all sorts of strange forms to his shameless mind. It took the shape of a huge "dropping" of supermammoth dung.

It took the shape of an enormous seaweed-crusted shell, the shell of the fish called Kraken, whom some dim motion of monstrous mate-lust had drawn up from the primeval slime of its seabed.

It took the shape of that vast planetary Tortoise, upon whose curved back, sealed with the convoluted inscriptions of the Nameless Tao, rested the pillar of creation.

But above all as he surveyed that dark-green bulk rising at the end of the long, narrow road he was compelled to think of the mysterious nest of some gigantic jurassic-age bird-dragon, such as, in this May sunshine, he could imagine even now hatching its portentous egg.

"I'm damned if I don't believe," he said to himself at last, "that this extraordinary ghost-smell he was making such a fuss about does come from Maiden Castle!"

He decided not to breathe a word about this smell to his companion! The last thing he wanted, just then, was to have to listen to some interminable description of all the mystical smells of the world, ending up with "the fishy fume of Asmodeus."

"I wonder," he said to himself, "whether it really *is* possible that if I'd come along this road ten thousand years ago I should now be gazing up at the Cyclopean walls and towers and temples and parapets of a great, peaceful city of a far nobler civilization than ours, where war and torture and vivisection were unknown, where neither the pleasures of life were denied nor the paths to immortality discredited?"

His companion was walking along at his side without uttering a word. Dud noticed, however, that as they passed that halfway house, the fellow removed his cap and squeezed it with some difficulty into his trouser pocket. Dud was surprised to observe that Mr. Quirm carried no walking-stick. It was on the tip of his tongue to ask him whether he never used a stick or whether he only refrained from using one on his excursions to Mai-Dun; but in place of this innocent remark a much more important question leapt to his lips.

"May I ask you something very personal, sir?"

"Certainly, certainly, lad! By all means, my boy!"

"What was it that made you change your name from Enoch to Uryen? Enoch's a good Biblical name; and I've often heard it down here in our parts just as I've heard the name Elijah. By the way Elijah was, as you probably know, if you knew my mother so well, her husband's name; the man who was supposed to be my father." *There* was the opportunity given point-blank to the Maiden Castle man to announce to him frankly and freely, and without beating about the bush, that he believed he, and no one else, was his father.

But Mr. Quirm did not reply. All he did was to clench his great fists, as if under some intense mystical excitement that had nothing to do with his companion, swing his arms more emphatically as he moved, and quicken his steps, till in the end they were both walking at such a rate that they might easily have been racing or at least competing for some sort of a wager.

But an impulsive and reckless devil in Dud forced him to continue. "I must confess," he said, "I don't think Uryen's nearly as honest a name as Enoch. There's something tricky and shifty, something fanciful and affected about Uryen to me! It's like the name of a person in a book. It doesn't sound authentic."

The man allowed Dud to finish every word of his criticism. Then he remarked in a low and perfectly calm voice: "It was your mother's favourite name. We meant it to be *your* name!"

231

So the cat was out of the bag at last, for good and ill, and the fatal word had passed between them—between his "mother's man" and her bastard son! Had Dud been expecting this all the time while he was calling up image after image with regard to the mysterious objective of their walk?

It may well have been that he had; for when the word was out, as the result of his rude attack upon his begetter's name, instead of a rush of awkwardness or embarrassment our friend felt an incredible relief.

"How long," he inquired calmly, as they walked side by side, rather slowly now, but without pausing, "has this been going on?"

"Been going on?" echoed the other.

"I mean," explained No-man, "how long have you known this? Ever since we first met in November?"

Uryen turned upon him a look which said with overpowering clearness : "I wish you weren't *quite* such a fool!"

"My good lad! What do you take me for? Of course I've always known about you. Your mother wrote to me to the last." He quickened his pace as he spoke and added in an almost querulous tone : "They wouldn't let me see her. I don't *say* I'd have cured her; but I'd have had a try. They kept me away. It wasn't Elijah; it was those doctors and nurses."

Dud *did* now, and for the first time during this singular dialogue, begin to feel a definite rebellion mounting up within him. Nothing could have outraged his life-illusion as a lonely, independent spirit more than the idea of this man's knowing him *without being known by him*, and watching his life from Glymes!

"Why didn't you tell me—after they died? Why didn't you come to me through all these years?"

"You didn't want me."

"Why do you do it now then?"

"You mean you don't want me *still*?"

"How do I know whether I want you or not? I don't know you and you don't know me."

"They told me the time had come."

"*They*? Who are *they*?"

"What you like! I don't care what you call them! The Powers created by man, but now independent of man, the Powers that have come to life *up there,* where we're going now!"

Dud came to a dead-stop, as his habit was when he had to think hard; and Uryen, evidently chafing under the delay, stood impatiently watching him, his hands still in his pockets, and as he watched him he made a sort of wind-in-the-telegraph-wire sound in his throat, a humming and drumming noise, which he apparently found soothing to his impatience.

"You don't mean to tell me," No-man began, "for *I'm* not one of your women—I'm not your *daughter*—that you really and truly believe in these superstitions? I know of course that you like playing with them, just as I do, and even half-believing in them, or trying to, just as I do, but—there—comes—a point —doesn't there?—*doesn't* there come a point, sir?—when all this playing at the supernatural, all this half-belief, this demi-semi-quaver belief, has to be thrown to the devil, and a person has to face life four-square and first-hand?"

Enoch ceased imitating the wind in the telegraph-wire. "But, lad—" he began, and then he hesitated, while some peculiar substitute for an amused smile flickered over his face, "but lad, you *can't* face life 'four-square.' That's where you make your mistake, and so many others. The back side of your square turns away from life. Life never sees it. It cannot see life. It's like the other side of the moon! And yet nobody has ever doubted that there *is* another side to the moon. No, my dear boy, you'll have to think of another metaphor for your facing of life. 'Four-square' is an unlucky one."

"But do you really believe in all this business of spirits and powers and influences and presences? Mind you, the point is not whether there may be *something* in it. I'm not Mr. Cumber. I think it's extremely likely there *is* 'something' in it. But the

233

question is—do you believe in what's in it enough to fight for it, to starve for it, to sacrifice women for it, to desert children for it? Is it as important as your lust, your glory, your peace of mind? Come, sir, come, Monsieur mon père, don't let's begin our new life by anything short of the absolute bed-rock truth. I'm not a young man any more, and I'm asking you this——" and No-man struck the stones of the road with his great oak-cudgel —"because I *must* know! Are you just playing with these supernatural influences, with these 'Powers' as you call them, or do you take them as actually real, real as this stick, real as your cap in your pocket?"

Enoch Quirm shuffled with his right foot towards a beetle who was astray on the surface of the road. Not a word did he utter for the passage of several minutes, nor did he shuffle his foot again.

"No, lad! *No*!" This "no" was so decisively and abruptly ejaculated, and with it the man looked so straight into our friend's eyes, jerking himself up and straightening his shoulders, that No-man remembered for long afterwards the impression he got at that moment of undeviating sincerity.

"No, lad, my gods aren't as real as your stick, or as the mole on your belly that your mother used to tell me about; and as to sacrificing women and deserting children I *might* do such things and I might not; but if I did it wouldn't be proof of anything. I might believe absolutely in my gods and *yet* refuse to sacrifice anything to them! They'd have their reality, not the reality of the mole on your belly, lad; but they'd have their own *kind* of reality—all that gods *can* have, or ever *do* have, or ever *will* have—and yet I might easily decide, on the strength of *another* reality, the reality, for instance, of my conscience, which also isn't as real as your fly-buttons or the mole on your belly, that I'd never sacrifice a thing to them, not even the sacrifice of 'a humble and contrite heart!' You talk like a baby, lad, when you talk of this 'bed-rock truth' for which I must be prepared to offer my life, or the gods don't exist! I tell you, lad, there are a thousand realities in life that aren't, and never *can* be, 'bed-rock realities,' and yet they're well worth pursuing. Why are you such a fanatic? But there's more in this matter of 'my old gods' than I can explain to you now. Would to the devil you *were* a girl instead of a 'bed-rock' man! Girls are satisfied with the *atmosphere of reality.* They don't need your damned all-or-nothing truths!"

But though the fellow met Dud's eyes, as he uttered all this, with a simple enough stare, our friend had an uncomfortable feeling that in some subtle way, impossible to define, he *was* fooling him and lying to him.

One impression that he got—and it may have been produced by that *semimortuus* look, which, though it was always fluctuating, never quite left the man's face—was that you couldn't get him to say anything impulsively or on the spur of the moment but only what he'd decided for some reason of his own to say.

"I'm not so particular as you seem to think," No-man remarked. "I know what atmospheres are, as well as anybody. But I can't help feeling that when you touch the supernatural it must be a clear issue—yes or no. I feel just the same about life after death. There's something teasing to my mind when people blur the issue of a thing as important as that. Either we *do* survive, or we *don't* survive. I think it *is* 'all-or-nothing' in that case! Do *you* believe we survive, sir?"

"Presently, lad—presently!" murmured the other. "I'll tell you exactly what I think when we've got on a bit."

He was as good as his word; but it became Dud's destiny to listen now to what struck him as the most confused and unconvincing rigmarole he'd ever heard. All he could lay hold of out of the man's words was that survival of death depended on three things, on your own effort, on the luck of being chosen as a favoured spirit by "the Gods," and on pure chance.

Our friend had read a certain number of metaphysical books, and it seemed to him that what he heard now contradicted the very rudiments of all intellectual reason!

What struck him about it—though his mind began quickly to wander from what the man was saying to all sorts of speculations about the man himself—was that it was simply a drift of very obscure oracles, snatches and fragments of the old Welsh books, but given by Uryen some particular twist of his own.

It was when they came to a gate across the way, with instructions on it, worthy of *Pilgrim's Progress*, about not wandering from the path, that the little polite struggle he made to open this gate for Monsieur mon père brought his mind back to what the fellow was actually saying; and it became clear to him that he was calmly assuming—which struck our friend as a monstrous assumption—that if he could tag together a sufficient weight of legendary allusions to immortality in the old books it established a strong probability in its favour; but it also struck Dud's mind as he closed the gate, only to find that he had to run after his parent as if he had been a small boy, that the way Uryen combined these floating straws on the legended tide of the soul's long history was extraordinarily clever and plausible.

"He's an old conjurer," he said to himself, as they ascended the slope to the earthwork's entrance, "but for me to assume that because 'the other world' played such a role in Welsh mythology there's a living entity under my bones that'll survive death and burial seems going pretty far."

They were passing some gorse bushes now on their way up the turfy slope, and Dud turned aside to smell a spike of their yellow blossom, the first he had seen that year .Just as with his hooked nose suffering a surprising number of pricks from the thorns he struggled to inhale the faint breath of that almondlike fragrance, he heard from over the wide valley a long-drawn whistle from one of the trains between Dorchester and Weymouth.

Now a faraway train-whistle was a sound that always gave Dud a peculiar thrill, a thrill springing from a cause exactly opposite to that which made Claudius so exultant when he heard the hum of an airplane. For the whistle of a train brought back our friend's earliest memories. It gave him that indescribable feeling we get in childhood when we see a road disappearing over a faraway hill—a road that seems to lose itself in a mystic Past, more magical than any possible Present!

A distant train-whistle never failed to bring him the sort of release that the creaking of the wings of wild swans would have brought, voyaging across the world, but rather towards some recoverable mystery than towards anything new and strange.

As he hurried up the slope after Uryen, who seemed to delight in making his middle-aged progeny run after him like a boy, the sensation he had had just then, instead of fading away, as these feelings usually did, increased upon him and diffused itself more widely till it was no longer the train-whistle and the gorse-scent but a transporting unknown sweetness that made him think of that *ghost-scent* of which Uryen had spoken during their meal at the Antelope. The few paces he had to go to overtake Uryen seemed by some trick of thought to lengthen out into a charmed duration of absolute timelessness, a timelessness that was filled to the brim with this mysterious scent. He seemed to float rather than walk after the figure striding on in front of him, and the distance between them became a heaving cloud-sea made up of an imponderable substance upon which he was borne forward.

Even after he had overtaken the man and was hurrying on by his side up the last of the grassy ascent, he still felt the same sensation of airiness and lightness, as if that unknown fragrance had taken complete possession of him.

It was not till the man actually spoke to him that the charm was dispelled. "We're at the gate now," he said with the self-satisfied sigh of a pilgrim whose journey is over. "This, they say, was the main gate; and often when I enter here in the night I can feel the chill of a great stone arch above me."

Dud refrained from asking him whether by "they" he meant his spirits or the modern archaeologists; and they went on in silence for a few more steps, till they stood in a level opening between two steep grassy mounds.

"Pardon me, lad, one minute!" Uryen muttered, as he peered quickly round to make sure they were alone. With great deliberation he now proceeded to squat down on the ground, his buttocks resting on his heels; and from this position he bent forward, all hunched-up as he was, and pressed his forehead against the turf. Many times he did this, each time for a longer period.

At first Dud followed a natural delicacy, just as he would have done had they been together in a church, and looked away; but he soon grew tired of this discretion, and with that vein in him of shameless realism which counterbalanced his subjective fancies, he fixed a detached and cynical eye upon his hunched-up progenitor. He noted that Uryen kept his hands in his pockets during his performance, which caused him at one point almost to lose his balance and roll over sideways; and he also noted, in the rumpling-up of his coat and sweater, how lean his flanks were. This latter observation was satisfactory to our friend. For some reason it was a comfort to him to find his father had lean flanks.

237

One effect all this had upon Dud was to drive out of him every intimation of the supernatural. Averse as he was from bodily self-consciousness he felt suddenly intensely aware of the bony structure of his own frame! Contemplating that hunched-up massive figure which save for the thin flanks had the heavy flesh of a sedentary bookworm, he felt glad he himself was so gaunt and bony, he felt glad his skull was cropped so close, he felt glad his cap was drawn down so irreverently over his brow, and above all he felt a great contentment in clutching with his bony fingers his solid oak cudgel.

"I've played with the supernatural," he thought, "and I believe in another dimension, but all this business of supernatural beings exercising arbitrary influence upon us—to the devil with it! Go on, you great curly-pate, eat the grass and bite the chalk! That's right. Down with you again. That's the way. Cringe before them, old grasshopper. Lick their dung! Perhaps they're there—and perhaps they're *not* there. Perhaps there's *nothing* there but this great thick globe and empty space—and then more space—and then more and more space, till it's full circle, *Monsieur bien croupé!* But better be on the safe side,

> *For who can know that They're not there,*
> *Who hasn't himself been everywhere?*

"Pray! Pray! Pray! Pray! Pray! If they're not there, they used to be there, and if they never were there, they ought to be there, and if they couldn't be there they will be there! So cringe and crouch, wallow and swallow, tumble and mumble. '*Somebody* must have made all this,' as the energetic Napoleon said. Somebody made us and not we ourselves!

"Atoms can't make atoms, nor life life, nor motion motion, so pray! pray! pray! pray! *He* made us, *She* made us, *They* made us.

"If nobody's in to-day we must call to-morrow, and if Nobody's in to-morrow we must call on Sunday. Press your head down once more, *mon vieux!* That last nod may do it. *Croupe-ton, croupeton, croupeton!*"

But Mr. Quirm rose up now, a little red in the face, but otherwise unperturbed. "Shall we go round," he asked his son, "by the street or by the wall!"

Our friend saw no sign of either a wall or a street, but he felt glad all the same that his parent didn't mention such things as *valla* or *fossae*.

"Oh, the street, by all means!" he replied.

They advanced accordingly along the bottom of the green trench. On either side of them a grassy rampart rose steep and smooth to a height of about fifty feet.

Dud had never been at Mai-Dun in anything but bad weather; and the last time he came the wind and rain had swept round this green gully with such violence that he could think of nothing but the force of the contending elements.

Nor had he ever come with Claudius, in spite of all their talks about the place. He had deliberately dodged it, being reluctant to listen in such a spot to nothing but praise of Roman civilization. For his present companion the Roman occupation might have occurred yesterday. Indeed, Mr. Quirm referred to it in exactly the same tone of indulgent contempt as he referred to last year's excavations.

Light and lovely airs cooled their faces as they advanced, drifting and eddying about them, stirring the grasses first in one direction and then in another, and letting them fall back into breathing immobility as they wandered off again.

Dud had noticed already three different sorts of butterflies : the brimstone, the common white, and the tortoise-shell; and among several minute plants in the grass of whose names he was ignorant, he marked a few that were well-known to him, especially the blue and the white milkwort.

Mr. Quirm was expatiating to his companion now on the limitations of the new methods of archaeology. No human beings, he told his son, could possibly live under the conditions "revealed," as these new students of the past put it, by "scientific excavation." Mai-Dun was a civilized *polis*, long before the Romans came, and it is only an impoverished imagination that sees them as living in miserable thatched holes, along with bones and cinders and potsherds. "You must remember, lad," he said, "we're talking of the civilization that built Stonehenge and Avebury. Why should the dwellers in Mai-Dun be regarded as wretched earth-burrowers, when their contemporaries could raise such monuments!"

It was, however, less the actual arguments his companion

kept using that affected our friend than a certain vague exultation of his own spirits, an exultation that seemed to be working both ways, intensifying both his bodily senses and his mystical supersense. The mere fact that as they advanced in their gradual encircling of the great erection they saw nothing of the outside world intensified the impression Dud got of sacred isolation.

He found himself wishing that "his mother's man" wouldn't hurry on at quite such a pace! Out there, down in the world below, was that unopened letter from Yeovil, out there was the letter, probably composed already in that competent mind, from Mr. George Cumber, repeating again exactly on what lines, and with what expurgations and discretions, his article on the social origin of the old Welsh custom of "bundling" was to be written.

And once more his thoughts ran to that unopened letter awaiting him on his desk under his unwashed cup. "I don't care," he concluded, "what there is between Wizz and those people. She's my girl, and she's D. No-man's girl, and if she's been enjoyed by Old Funky 'up hill and down dale,' it doesn't make her less mine! She's certainly got something hidden-up about those Urgans that's worrying her sick, and that she daren't confess to me. She hasn't said anything for months about going back to the Circus; but that may be it! She may have arranged it all with them by letter; or Jenny, who's certainly in the mood for spiting all men, may have been her intermediary. I wouldn't be surprised if that wasn't it! Well! if she *must* go, she must. I'm not going to hold her back by force—and after all she'll be my girl whatever she does!"

And Dud in this Maiden Castle mood of his, lifted above the earth, followed his fantastical begetter along what seemed to him like some pearl-green convolution of an airy world-shell floating in space, tried to imagine the indulgence with which he would treat the most excessive and unexpected action of his true love.

As has been hinted more than once our friend had a vein of monstrous and even obscene imagination concealed below his sentimental sensuality; and in his present state of exultation he allowed this vein its full scope, telling himself stories about Wizzie's complications with the Urgans which, though he forgave them on Maiden Castle, were, as he dallied with them,

240

enough to have shocked even a worshipper of that beast-god with a human torso impaled upon its tail that he had himself recently seen in the Dorchester Museum.

"Sir!" he cried out—for it was still impossible for him to utter the syllables "father"—"wait a second, will you?"

His guide swung round and awaited him with a friendly smile. "Let's sit down for a bit," said Dud. "I don't want to make the circle too quickly."

The pair of tall men lowered themselves to the ground, their lean buttocks resting on the warm fragrant grass that the sun had already dried.

"When I asked you just now," began our friend, "about the name 'Uryen,' you told me you and mother had thought of it as *my* name, but you didn't tell me what made you choose it as your own. Won't you tell me that now?"

The man looked at him closely for a moment. Then he looked at the butterflies on the bank opposite, and then he glanced up and down the green trench.

"If you're ready to listen without interrupting me for a bit, I'll tell you the whole thing."

Dud edged himself back a little so that he shouldn't embarrass the speaker by keeping his eyes on him. All he could now see of the man's face was the curve of his left cheek, the wrinkles at the side of his mouth, and the curious mosslike hair that above his ear was unmistakably grizzled.

"Cornie and I," and it gave our friend a most curious shock to hear his mother called Cornie, for only once or twice in his life had he heard Elijah even so much as call her Cornelia, "were cousins. We were both precocious and we were inseparable. You must understand, lad, that in Wales class-distinctions, while more tenacious in blood, are less dependent on money. Cornie and I were both orphans, brought up by an aunt at the lodge of the park-gates of the very place where in old times our ancestors had lived.

"When this woman died your mother was sent away to some distant relatives in Shaftesbury. Me these people didn't want, or couldn't have; so I was boarded out by the parish guardians, first in one place then in another. As I say, I was a precocious child and no doubt a difficult one. I don't think I grew unkindly treated, but I missed Cornie so much that I grew more and

241

more secretive and unhappy. The end of it was, when I was about ten, I ran away, the word 'Shaftesbury' being my single hope.

"I fell in with a group of tramps from our parts bound for the south, who made use of me in various ways and when finally they took different roads we had already drifted into Dorset. Cajoled by the way I talked, one of these derelicts, with hopes of something to his advantage coming of it, stuck to me, though I often tried to give him the slip, till we did eventually reach the place.

"Here my companion got into trouble for something or other. I was taken away from him, and an old childless couple called Quirm legally adopted me as their child. Cornie's protectors, for they made enquiries about them, had left the town by that time, and no one knew where they'd gone; but it wasn't till we'd both grown up, and she'd become Mrs. Smith, that fate brought us together.

"I got a job where she lived and we soon were lovers. At that time, my lad, I was crazy about women. Cornie wasn't the only one; and we had miserable scenes. In the end we had a terrible quarrel by the side of that very bed you've got in your room. I lost all control of myself—but I won't go into that—but the end of it was I left her and went away.

"But I didn't go without my *trophies*—" and here Dud was destined to hear the hoarse chuckle, in this case like that of a deep-chested Centaur, of the male triumphant—"for I left her with you, my lad, and I stole one of our ancestral beasts!" He ceased speaking, but fixed upon the opposite bank a long bemused stare, full, his son couldn't help thinking, of memories more voluptuous than sad.

"But what about 'Uryen'?" No-man enquired, while once more the bitter waters of physical distaste began to enter his mouth and creep into his stomach. He had felt something like a cold, remote sympathy while the man described his passion for little "Cornie," but the second he used the word "lovers" such a shiver of revulsion passed through him that it would have given him pleasure to have brought down his cudgel on that hairy scalp. "What about 'Uryen'?" he repeated, relieving his feelings by emphasizing his contempt for this affected and ridiculous name.

242

"I'll tell you, lad; I'll hide nothing from you, my precious poppet," and the man turned his great, handsome, swarthy, perspiring face towards his offspring, while his dead eyes drew up to their surface from the soul behind them a light that resembled the light of a lantern in the head of an up-swimming diver. "When Cornie knew she was going to have a child—for our worst quarrel didn't happen till after you were well on the way—we used to talk a great deal about the name.

"It was your mother, not I, who first got the idea of it. She woke up in the night once, she told me, and found herself repeating it aloud. It was that furious quarrel we had that really changed her mind; though I fancy a wish not to annoy old Smith may have played a part. Elijah would as soon have had his son called Satan as called Uryen and of course you passed as *his* child.

"It wasn't till long after this, not till just before your mother's death, and when I'd been married to Nance for several years, that—I—changed—my own—name—to Uryen."

The man stopped. These last words were spoken with extreme solemnity and in a very low voice; and Dud received, as he sat with his knees locked under his clenched hands, a curious impression from them, an impression that they were uttered from some level of his begetter's being much deeper than any he had yet revealed.

Until this point our friend had been suspicious with regard to everything the man said. The whole story of that house by the park-gates, of the boy's vagabonding to Shaftesbury, of his adoption by the Quirms, of his rediscovery of Cornie, had struck No-man's mind as too smooth and glib, in fact as exactly the sort of tale that a wayfarer on the highway would tell, a tale whose continual repetition turns what was originally harmless fable into a suspicious half-truth. "I shall never know how it *really* was," Dud had found himself thinking; and in a sense he was reassured by this, for the whole business of discovering "a local habitation and a name" for his solitary spirit went against the grain of his life-illusion.

It did not occur to him to connect this desire to detach himself from the mass of men, with his companion's preference for the name of Uryen over that of Enoch; but this subterranean suspicion of all the fellow said had the effect of rousing in him everything in his nature that was hard and cynical.

It was therefore in that sort of automatic stiffening by which we deliberately accentuate the qualities that have narrowed us, that he now fell back upon the starkest, grimmest, most uncompromising self he could find, a self that was almost savagely conscious of its hard mortal skull and its lean bony structure, a self that regarded every conceivable fancy about life after death with a sardonic superiority, a self whose pride it was to be a plain blunt downright unpersuadable entity, an entity that held firmly to brute Matter.

As they sat together there, both bare-headed, both hugging their knees, No-man's own mind moved faster than it had ever moved in his whole life. "Because I feel myself in bones and skull," he thought, "hostile to this man's nebulous talk, and because I don't believe in any of his ideas, *that* doesn't mean I'm a bigoted materialist. I believe, absolutely in another dimension surrounding this one; and I believe in my power of becoming a 'medium' for the life of the generations. I believe in the truth of my book about Mary Channing!"

Thus with what might be called his "official" credo did Dud justify his lack of sympathy. There was, however, a lower level of his consciousness wherein, like an antediluvian creature confronting its progenitor, he made no attempt at articulating what he felt. He simply hated the man because the man was his father.

According to what this lower level of consciousness brought to him he felt as if he and his father, isolated from all other living things in the mystic circle of Mai-Dun, were two prehistoric entities linked together by the invisible semen of paternity, but *for that very reason* destined to a struggle of measureless malignity, a struggle that could end only in the death of the one or of the other.

How natural, how inevitable it seemed to him that he should now plague, torment, and cruelly tantalize his father by keeping him waiting so long for the least word, the least sign, that he cared a fig why he had called himself Uryen!

"Call yourself Urogen," this consciousness cried. "Call yourself Urus; call yourself 'Urban of Hell.' *What is it to me?* Tell me the most ghastly, the most tragic, the most sacred secret of your life, and I'll treat it as a joke. I'll play with it as an Arab

244

might play with the Sacrament. I'll tell Wizzie about it to-night and we'll laugh over it till our bed shakes."

He noted that under his father's haunches lay a daisy, whose brittle stalk had been crushed, but whose rose-tinged petals emerged quite intact. In the process of fidgeting about to make his position comfortable Mr. Quirm had got the bottom of his coat rumpled up above the seat of his trousers, and these little rose-tinged petals peeped out from beneath his rump in a manner that was distressing to No-man.

Dud did not go so far as to entreat his parent to move, though the phrase : "Excuse me, sir, but you're sitting on a daisy," hovered on the tip of his tongue, but the presence of the daisy in that position did something to increase his nervous revolt. He had a sensation as if he could actually feel the man's huge, dusky, smouldering soul heaving and labouring there, in the centre of that hot mass of ill-smelling, sedentary flesh and blood, and in the intensity of his reaction against the seed that begat him he now thought to himself : "I'll get up and make him come on *before he's got it out*; and every time he tries to tell me about it, every time he mentions this damned word 'Uryen' I'll change the conversation."

But Dud's "mother's man" must have had a telepathic inkling of this impious plan, for he suddenly swung round on the pivot of his rump in such a way as to release the stalk of the daisy, and incidentally, too, to release a little Glymes moth from the folds of his coat, which seemed, on its emerging—for it settled fumblingly on a tiny grass-spear and began groping at the air— to find its role as a denizen of Mai-Dun totally beyond its strength.

But the face with which he now swung round and confronted his unsympathetic progeny was no little shock to our friend's egotistical soul. The man had certainly—of that there was no doubt—a tremendous face; and as he turned it on his son now in that bright sunshine there were lines about the eyelids, lines about the mouth, wrinkles above the eyebrows, a certain upward twist of the eyebrows combined with a sombre opening of the great Laokoön mouth, that really startled our friend.

The eyelids alone seemed so heavy with a dark weight that Dud's loathing lessened appreciably, not so much turning into tenderness as into a sort of outraged pity. It was as if he were

245

lifting a scab from an unhealed wound, and the foul blood and yellow pus filled him simultaneously with sympathy and disgust.

It became at last impossible for Uryen to remain quite unaware of what was going on in his son's mind.

"Why do you hate me so, lad?" he brought out. "I don't ask you to like me. Why should you? But what—have—I—done to you that you should look so stern at me, that you should harden yourself so against me?"

He stopped and fixed upon his son the full stare of his *semimortuus* eyes, eyes which at that moment were so heavy with majestic desolation that Dud found he could not bear to meet their gaze.

And there came into our friend's consciousness a queer emotion, such as he had only known once or twice before, when because of some passing mood of hers he had felt unfathomable bitterness towards Wizzie. It was an emotion of pure, blind, desperate awareness of the infinite pathos of another's identity—a feeling as if he were one kind of substance—stone, let us say—sending forth a tragic vibration that beat against a different kind of substance—iron, let us say—in a struggle to get at the heart of its alien being.

"I'm sorry—*Father*!" murmured Dud in a low voice. These words cost him a violent effort. Never indeed since his boyhood had he uttered anything that so tore at his vitals. The effort of it caused such a rush of blood to his head that his face burned; and unclasping his hands from his knees he pressed the knuckles of one of his fists awkwardly against his cheek.

"It means nothing to you, I suppose," were the words that now proceeded from the swarthy countenance before him, "what my experiences have been, any more than it meant to your mother; and I'm not telling you this as a father speaking to a son." He paused, a physical tremor crossed his face that gave our friend more than ever the impression that the man's whole physiognomy was composed of some substance that was extraordinarily malleable to the inner workings of his spirit.

And the odd thing was, in spite of his recent rush of pity, if "pity" was the word for it, the more wavering and discomposed, the more misty and vaporous, Uryen's face grew, the harder and more bony did Dud's own skull *feel* in chemical opposition.

246

"I suppose the idea of reincarnation is nothing to you," went on the face in front of him. And so independent of the words that fell from it were the wavering tremors that passed over it, not convulsing it or distorting it, but just crossing it, like ripples crossing dusky water, that No-man couldn't beat back the impression that the words that reached him came *through* rather than *from,* that dusky physiognomy.

"Now for it!" thought Dud. "Now for the grand conjuring trick of the great Illusionist!"

"I'd have you to know," continued this fluctuating visage, on which the sun fell so disconcertingly, "that there's not a supernatural Being ever worshipped, or, if you like, ever 'invented,' by our unhappy race, who does not keep on incarnating Itself, as the ages proceed. I had always guessed that what the ancients called 'the Mysteries' had their parallel in Welsh tradition, but it wasn't till I learnt to read the *old* Welsh books that I came on the track of a whole cycle of ancient gods, connected in one way and other with 'the Mysteries,' that's to say with the worship of the great goddess Carridwen."

Dud, feeling himself all bone and stone in his sullen incredulity, drew in his breath at this point with a derisive sound. "Good Lord!" he thought, "this is worse than I expected!" and his mind with one swift rush went off to Claudius acquiring merit in his coal-yard. "I've been unfair to you, you poor old beggar," he thought. "When we come to Carridwen it *does* seem about time to listen to the airplanes!"

At this moment, however, it was the shrill sound of a lark, not of an airplane, that kept up a protesting orchestration to Uryen's illusions.

It was not only the air-quiverings of the lark that emphasized for our friend at this moment what seemed to him the shocking grotesqueness of his father's talk. The amorous absorption of a pair of white butterflies, coupled in love and fluttering helplessly among the grass-stalks, struck him as bearing yet another witness to the irrelevance of his Father's fantasies. Lark-wings and butterfly-wings seemed to join with the sunshine in *outlawing* such monstrous conceptions.

"From my boyhood, lad," the man continued, in a low sad voice, "I've had a queer notion of my own. I've felt for some unknown reason that I was born to bear—well! not exactly 'the

247

sins of the world,' but the terrible pressure of that hurt of the soul when it struggles to break through."

"To break through?" echoed Dud feebly.

"To break the bonds of life's natural law! To break *out*, to break *in*, to take the Secret by storm!"

No-man watched a soft gust of wind carry the coupled butterflies out of sight.

"What I mean is this," the man went on. "All extreme emotions reach a point where you can't distinguish between pain and pleasure. The suffering is intense; but something in you rushes towards the suffering, opens its arms to the suffering. Now, lad, you must know it is not given to everyone to feel what I'm talking about. At its intensest it comes when love and hate are one. It is terrible then. It is a feeling so terrific that it often ends in madness; but if it doesn't end that way, it ends in *breaking through*. You must know, lad, that there are secrets only revealed to magic. I don't mean physical magic; I mean *spiritual* magic. And this kind only comes when the emotion of love-hate gathers to a point that's terrible. And you must know too that it only comes when the passion remains sterile. Any fulfilment dissipates its power. Nothing but unfulfilled love, love turned to hate, can beat hard enough upon the barrier of life, can beat hard enough upon what separates us from the secret, till it breaks through! It's like despair, lad, *that's* what it's like; it's as strong as despair. Of course it means abominable pain. I mean *mental* pain, of course, though there's a frightened pleasure mixed with it too, and few can endure it. Mental pain is worse than physical pain; and that is because——"

Here Dud could stand it no longer. From head to foot he was trembling with an antagonism that it was impossible to suppress.

"Physical pain's a hundred times worse," he shouted. "Physical pain's the supreme evil of life, the *only* unbearable evil! Pain in the mind can be overcome by the mind; but pain in the body is pain *in Matter itself*. It goes down to the bottom of the world, down to the roots of nature, down to the stuff out of which life's created. It's the great enemy of creation : it's worse than death!"

No sooner had he uttered these words, bellowing them forth as if his father were standing on the opposite rampart, than he became aware that he was catching the very rhythm of his

248

father's tone. He was refuting him, but he was talking to the wind, just as he did! But, though he knew all this, he seemed compelled to go on. It was as if this contact with his father were forcing him to become like his father even in the act of denouncing him.

"There's nothing," he yelled at the man, "not your love-hate or anything else—that's as strong as physical pain. I tell you it won't bear thinking on. What you're saying now is the lie of all false prophets since the beginning! Physical pain damns the whole creation. It damns God. It damns the mind. It damns religion. And what's more, if Science can cure it, if Science can drag up pain to the light, as Hercules did Cerberus——" He stopped; and to his own amazement, for once more he had a vision of Claudius staring after the airplane, he actually felt tears at the back of his eyes.

But it was not his vision of Claudius that stopped him. It was an appalling sense that his words were not his own. He was his father, arguing with his father. The harsh nervous eloquence, the curious spiritual anger, the wild ruggedness of the words he used, all belonged to this man of his mother's.

He was his son then. It came out when their souls were stirred. Nothing like talk about pain to bring forth the truth! They might differ over this mystery, but it was the same nerve, the same wolf's howl from the navel of life, the same obliviousness to every "sense of proportion."

Quite unaware of what he was doing Dud began plucking both hands at the grass beside him. As he did this his whole lean frame began rocking itself up and down as if he had been a mechanical doll wound up to bow before his father. What he began to feel now was indescribable. Not only was he compelled to talk *like* his father, but he began to feel as if the Powers of Mai-Dun were fusing him with his father. Was that what was meant by that horrible "votive offering" of the men impaled on the bull?

"So you see," his father was explaining, "it wasn't my blind instinct that showed me what I was and what I am. It came to me as the only possible interpretation of my great secret, of this destiny laid upon me to reach the life behind life. Fumbling about in the roots of the past I found what I was, what I *must* be, to be the thing I am! Everything's in the mind. Everything's

249

created and destroyed by the mind. It's the mind, it's not any devil's magic, that makes and breaks our mirrors and mirages. All's vision, lad, all, I say *all*; and the mind's the only demiurge. You think it's madness to talk of the old gods of Mai-Dun? You think I ought to be interested in their excavations, and their proofs that human beings lived in this place like hyenas in holes among bones. I tell you, lad, the truth of life's in the imagination, not in ashes and urns! I tell you *we*, I and others like me, are the gods of Mai-Dun—the same yesterday, to-day and forever. There's no one God, lad. Lay *that* up in your heart. Things are as they are because there are so many of us; and as fast as some create, others destroy; and a good thing too, as the Son of Chaos cries out in *Faust*!

"Certain masks of life *ought* to be destroyed, to make room for others; to make room sometimes for those that have lain beneath them for ten thousand years.

"Yes, my dear boy, as I talk to you now I feel the power rushing through me. You may well clutch at the grass! This bank, and that one opposite us, that seem so solid, shall I tell you what they are? They're mists and mirages and vapours! Don't 'ee feel it, lad, as I speak to you? Don't you feel this whole great fortress ready to shake, shiver, melt, dissolve? Don't you feel that you and I are behind it, making it what it is by the power of our minds? Don't you feel it floating, with all its bright grass, on the dark under-sea of our terrible——?"

He was interrupted by the unexpected appearance of three young men and a small dog advancing along the crest of the rampart in front of them.

No-man at once stopped clutching at the grass, and automatically picked up his grotesque cudgel; and then, shuffling a bit, till his legs were in a more comfortable position, held this Cerne Giant club of his tightly across his knees. It had been a wonder to him, all these months, that the people he passed in his walks refrained from jeering at this absurd stick. "These patient Durotriges," he thought, "must have got so used to the eccentricities of one set of rulers after another that they treat my stick as if it were the battle-axe of Sir Jonathal!"

His first impression when he caught sight of these three men and their little dog was that they were his old friends, the dole-receivers from the bridge. For a second he suffered that uncomfortable sensation we get when some particular chance seems more than chance.

"Am I destined to meet these three men and their dog," he thought, "at every crisis in my life?"

But he soon became aware that the men were much younger than his unemployed friends of the bridge and that their dog, though as inquisitive as the other, was of a different breed. It was indeed a Scotch terrier, not a fox terrier, and of the male sex, and it amused him to observe, when it came sniffing and gambolling to his companion's side, how disdainfully and irritably the man behaved. "He's like old Claudius with the ducks," he thought. "These people with fixed ideas can't bear it when reality barks or quacks at them."

"A fine afternoon," our friend called out to the three young fellows as he stroked the dog, "and a good day for a walk."

"Killed anything with that stick yet?" one of the boys shouted; and their giggling broke into a loud guffaw.

Dud and his father evidently struck them as eccentric persons who could be insulted with impunity. "They're not from Dorchester," thought our friend. "Those aren't Durnovarian manners." But after the young men had moved on and their dog had followed them, No-man found he'd received a fresh impulse towards resisting his father.

"I've changed a lot since living with Wizzie," he thought. "In the old days I'd have been furious with these lads. But how silly! We need these 'raw youths' and slaps in the face from them to keep our sense of proportion."

"I'm not telling you all this with any hope of your taking it seriously," his father went on. "I can see you're more interested in those young fools and that dog than in me. I'm talking because I *must* talk. A person must have someone to talk to. Nance used to believe in me; but since her boy died"—and he cast an almost savage glance towards the sky as if the sun were deliberately pelting him with lark-music—"she's changed. And the upshot of it was, lad," he went on, "I became convinced, not from any revelation, you understand, but because of this *necessity* I'm under of bearing the pain of the world, the pain of what beats against the wall, that in one incarnation after another I've been the same Power! And do you want to know *what* Power I've been, lad?" Here the man lowered his voice to

251

a solemn whisper. "I've been the Power that's older than all this damned sunshine, the Power that's older than all these new gods, the Power that's deepest of all, for it's got Death in it as well as life. It's this Power—the Power that works in me, lad, the Power that I *am*—that beats in its pain against the wall of the world. You can cry out, lad, if you like, that it's all fantasy and illusion, you can cry out that your excavations set it at naught; but I tell you that sooner or later you'll know it as I know it! I tell you it's in all the pain of the world where love turns to hate and beats against the wall! It's in the despair of all the sterile love there's ever been since the beginning! Don't you see what force there is in sterile love? Why, my dear boy, it's the strongest force there is! Rampant desire unfulfilled— why, there's nothing it can't do! Stir up sex *till it would put out the sun* and then keep it sterile! That's the trick. That's the grand trick of all spiritual life. It's the pain of Saint Derfel. It's the pain of Saint Demogorgon. Your physical pain's nothing to it. Now do you begin to see the truth about my name? I didn't change it to Uryen because Uryen's a prettier sound than Enoch, but because I found, in incarnation after incarnation, that I've actually *been* Uryen! It's all in the books. The mental pain that breaks against the barrier, the mental pain that loses itself in death-in-life, is the key to Uryen's country. This is the land of Mureif and Rheged and Cattraeth and 'yr Echwyd.' Rhys says that Skene's version of Taliesin's fragment :

> *Ac ef yn arbennic*
> *yn oruchel wledic*
> *yn dinas pellenic*
> *yn keimyat kynteic*

ought to be changed a little. I would change it to : 'And he especially, the supreme power, in the distant city, the principal companion.'

"And it's Rhys and no one else who makes clear what this Power, this 'Uryen' in me, really is. It is the old magic of the mind, when, driven to bay by the dogs of reality, it turns upon the mathematical law of life and tears it to bits! It's the old magic of the mind, the secret of which has been so often lost;

till the Welsh, alone among the races, *hid* it instead of squandering it."

Here there began again that same curious quiver in Uryen's face, as if the man's lineaments were decomposing, as if the ghastly ripples of some actual commencement of physical death were passing and repassing across his face, and not only did this occur, but simultaneously with it Dud became conscious of that same repulsive mortuary smell he had noticed on Candlemas night. "Do the man's death-thoughts," he said to himself, "produce an actual smell of death? Or is it the smell of that sterile life-seed he's talking about 'that beats against the wall'?"

"Do you know, lad," his father went on, "Rhys says that in the Triads describing my death I'm spoken of as having a crow—brān—it is in Welsh—on my breast? And do you realize, boy, that this is exactly what I *have* had since I was a child? Cornie could tell you about it! Nance could bear witness to it! It's been a peculiarity of mine for as long as I can remember that, whenever I come near anyone with that mental pain I'm talking about, I get an actual physical hurting in the centre of my chest that's like a fiery beak pecking at me and yet that's sweet as an ecstasy."

Dud now became aware that the man was actually pulling up his sweater and undoing not only the buttons of his grey flannel shirt but those of his vest. In the hurried effort to accomplish this he got up on his feet.

No-man rose too; but a quaint instinct of self-protection, as if the vision of his begetter's naked torso were a threat, caused him to stoop down and pick up his great cudgel.

"Look!" cried the man proudly, holding open his clothes.

"How hairy his chest is!" thought our friend; and as he stared at Enoch Quirm's bosom a violent revulsion against being the son of such a hairy man and a man whose sweat had such a vile smell took possession of him.

But the Glymes man complacently fumbled at his prodigious breast-bones and began with the tips of his fingers pushing the black hairs aside.

"Look! Why don't you look?" he repeated.

Dud reluctantly bent forward towards him, feeling as he did so as if he were peering into a miasmic pool worse than any "scummy pond" out of which rose a reek of corruption.

253

But even this was not enough. "Feel!" the fellow cried with a satisfaction that revolted our friend.

Dud permitted his fingers to be directed by his begetter to certain *just* distinguishable birth-marks or scaly disfigurements of some kind, that really did seem to exist beneath these damp hairs.

"Yes—I do—feel—something. Yes, I distinctly feel something there. Is it a scar?"

Dud had never seen a human face collapse so quickly from infinite complacency to infinite hopelessness as when the Glymes man heard the words: "Is it a scar?"

"I thought—it would—mean more—to you—than that, lad. What you've just touched is the——" While he muttered this in a low colourless voice he turned away from his son and began wearily buttoning up his underclothes.

The words: "Please adjust your dress. Please adjust your Dress before Leaving," repeated themselves in Dud's brain.

"What you've touched is the Crow, Brān, the Crow. I suppose you've never heard of Bendigeitvran, or Brān the Blessed? I suppose——"

But it seemed as if there was a growing hostility to the Glymes man among the larks of that radiant sky, for the solemn word "Bendigeitvran" reached Dud's ears through such a burst of lark-music that it sounded like nursery gibberish, while the rest of the sentence resembled the babbling of Nimrod in the Inferno.

"*Rafel mai amech zabi almi!*" was no more unintelligible than the words those sun-servants made Uryen utter.

"Sir John is inclined to think," Mr. Quirm concluded, in a tone of patronizing indulgence towards the good intentions of scholarly erudition, "that King Pellam, and Urban of the Black Thorn, and Yspyddaden the father of Olwen, and Uther Ben the father of Arthur, are really, every one of them, just local names for the 'Uryen' in me, as I was incarnated down the ages.

"He makes it clear that the word 'Uryen' is no Celtic word but far older—a word belonging to that mysterious civilization of the dwellers in Dunium and in the great cities about Avebury and Stonehenge and Caer Drwyn and Caer Sidi and Cattraeth and Carbonek, that was not Aryan at all, but a civilization possessed of secrets of life that Aryan science has destroyed."

Thus speaking, the Glymes man panted a little with the effort of what he was doing, made the familiar grimace that almost all mortal men make when they pull up or down pull their clothes, and when he addressed his son again it was in a more cheerful manner.

Dud was inclined to attribute this recovery of the man's life-illusion to the mere sound of such resonant words, whether Aryan or non-Aryan, as Uther and Uryen and Cattraeth and Carbonek, but he was not wholly satisfied with this explanation. Perhaps a better one was that a small compact cloud, shaped like a millstone, had rolled up, unobserved by either of them, and was now darkening the sun and taking the brightness, though not the warmth, from the green turf at their feet.

"But you *did* feel something," he said, "didn't you? It's not a scar of course. What put into your head that it could be a scar? A scar? What scar could it be? But you felt *something* and that's what was wanted! That's what's been wanting, my lad, ever since I gave you that head, and let you know who I was. You've laid your finger on the seal of Uryen, and that's the chief thing."

Dud and his father stood for a while gazing into each other's eyes. "I don't *feel*," the former thought, "as if you were out of your wits; yet no one else, listening to all this, would think otherwise."

Our friend was the first to withdraw his eyes. "Come on!" he said quietly and in the most matter-of-fact voice he could assume. "Let's complete the circle and then I must be getting home. I promised them faithfully I'd be back for tea at Friary Lane, and I've got to go to my rooms first."

By one of those phenomenal changes of the weather that Dud had already recognized as characteristic of the Durnovarian climate, quite a lot of clouds had followed the one whose shape was like a millstone till the darkened grass began to lose its warmth and a distinct chilliness fell on this citadel of the old gods.

"The wind's going to get up," murmured Enoch Quirm, sniffing the air.

"Oh, damn it, sir!" cried Dud in exasperation, "I've heard wonders enough this afternoon without any ghost-wind! Besides, if anything, the wind has dropped. Look there! The grasses were stirring when we first got here and they're absolutely still now."

"All right, lad," answered the Glymes man, in a voice so natural, so friendly, and so sensible, that No-man felt almost sympathetic towards him, "we won't call it a ghost-wind. We'll just call it 'the wind getting up,' as it usually does get up, when I come to Mai-Dun. You won't feel it for a couple of minutes, nor will the grasses, but you'll see *then*."

And sure enough, he was right. Not in a couple of minutes, perhaps, but certainly in five minutes, No-man was aware of some sudden indefinable change. It was a vast universal shiver, a vibratory stir, a low, faint indescribable tumult, a deep-throated humming in the purlieus of space. What it brought into Dud's mind was, first, the scriptural phrase "a rushing and mighty wind" and then a sense as of the beating of the wings of a vast host of invisible birds.

It pleased him that his "mother's man" took no credit for the coming time of his prediction. He did not even glance triumphantly at his son. All he did was to stand absolutely still, like a colossal rabbit who "freezes" at the approach of a pack of dogs.

Before becoming immobile, however, he thrust his right hand deep into his trouser pocket and tried to do the same with his left, but in this he was prevented by the fact, as our friend had not failed to note, that he had already stuffed that aperture quite full with his cloth cap.

They were now at the extreme eastern end of Mai-Dun, the particular portion of the turf metropolis that most antiquaries regard as the oldest.

Of this fact our friend was, of course, ignorant. Indeed, if it had not been that there was a marked difference in the contours of the trench where they had first entered it, Enoch Quirm might have led him round and round for hours without his being conscious of any north or south or east or west.

The wind that had "got up," whatever its nature may have been, came whirling over their heads from the direction of Chesil Beach; but such was the peculiar configuration of Mai-Dun that once within the circle of the place its course became arbitrary and wayward. Whether it would have been the same with any wind from that quarter, Dud knew not; but certainly this particular wind, as its force gradually increased, began to act in what seemed to him an eccentric manner. In place of leaping straight over the trench where they stood and streaming away across the centre of Maiden Castle, this wind seemed to descend bodily, just as if it were a compact and living entity, *into* their trench, and thence proceed to whirl round the whole circle, gathering speed as it went and uttering long-drawn, gasping, spasmodic sighs.

Dud had always been something of a wind-worshipper, and he was preparing now to enjoy to the full the feeling of this cold, slippery, invisible Being beating against his bony frame, when he became aware that his companion was muttering something to himself. Whatever it was—probably Taliesin's chant to the wind—the strange, elemental syllables were in singular harmony with the subhuman sounds that went sighing past them.

"This old Welsh," he said to himself, "must be the most primitive of all tongues. It sounds as if human inventions, human necessities, human thought even, barely entered into it; as if its rhythm were identical with the orchestration of the planet, whose only notes are the motions of air and water and its only burden the ancient sorrow of the earth. What he's muttering now must be what the spirits of space must have heard, rising night by night, day by day, through millions of ages, from an earth that as yet knew no organic life."

It was curious that it should have been at this particular moment that the grotesque incident of Wizzie's kicking his stick under their bed rushed into his mind. "She kicked it with her bare foot," he said to himself with the bitterness of one who has received an irremediable wrong. "She did it on purpose with her bare foot."

He was prepared for any revelation about Wizzie's obscure past. He was prepared to accept with philosophical calm the most shocking details of her life with Old Funky. But this deliberate kicking of his stick assumed, as it returned to his mind, the proportions of an unpardonable crime.

Such were No-man's thoughts as he shifted his cudgel from his right hand to his left the better to turn up his coat-collar, for he began to feel chilly; but he soon became conscious that this Mai-Dun wind was impaling him on the horns of a crisis quite as sharp as those of any bull-god. "I *must* stop this business with Thuella," he thought. "I shan't breathe a word to Wizz about

the 'scummy pond,' but I *must* stop it!" Chillier and chillier he
grew under the growing force of the wind; and there came to be
presented to him one of those searching glimpses into his in-
trinsic self that come so seldom to mortal men. "I could never
give up my life like old Claudius," he said to himself; "but I
could struggle, like this man of mother's, after the Secret. Not in
his way, not by magic of course—but I *could* drop the entire
world and live for the Spirit, as long as I was allowed my
imaginative lusts!"

But what this wind was doing was dividing him like a sharp
sword. Half of him was crying with a savage finality: "I! I! I!
I! I!" while the other half was threatening to put a leash round
the neck of this "I" and turn it into an obedient servant of
Evolution, or Communism, or the Will of God!

The colder Dud got in this Mai-Dun wind the more savage
grew the pleasure that he took in thinking of this "leash" with
which he would drag himself here and there. "If it's not my
nature to have a cause like Claudius," he said to himself, "at
least I'll hold Wizz against the ribs of my loneliness and make
people realize the tragedy of girls like Mary!"

Our friend edged himself forward a little and tried to listen to
the Glymes man's mutterings.

"Why don't you try to understand your son a little," he apos-
trophized his parent. "One live son is better than many dead
gods."

"What is your idea," he suddenly cried out, raising his voice,
"of the difference between good and evil?" His question was
carried by the wind as it swept over tussocks of grasses, over
hoof-marks of horses, over windings of sheep-tracks. It was carried sighing and swishing over the heads of daisies, it was carried sobbing and soughing between the stalks of last year's
thistles; it was carried sliding and slithering along narrow rabbit-
runs; it was carried with faint elfin screams through the curves
of snail-shells, it made sorties from mole-hill to mole-hill; it
whistled over the thresholds of shrew-mice.

But his father's answer was harsh and discordant. "What's
that, lad? What's that? What's that? What's that?" And the
man began turning these harmless monosyllables into incoherent
croaks such as might have proceeded from that crow-sign in his
hairy chest.

"Never mind now," muttered our friend. "I won't bother you now," and he thought to himself : "How bitterly alone we are when it comes to taking stock of our essential life !"

The wind had turned so cold by this time that Dud shivered. "Come on ,sir !" he burst out. "Let's go ! I've had enough of this."

His father gave him an angry look and shrugged his shoulders. "You've broken it with your cursed questions," he muttered. "Come on then. Never mind the circle ! We'll go back by Monkton and the Weymouth Road."

They clambered up the opposite bank, descended into a parallel trench, mounted thence to the crest of a second ridge, down again into another grassy channel, up once more to yet another turf rampart, and then down at last into the umbrageous valley below.

Dud remembered afterwards how vividly every detail of the way stood out before him as he came down the slope by his father's side. There was a dead rabbit in the path, in the last stage of its decomposition, and he had to force himself to do what he always did with dead things, to make the sign of the cross over it and to place it carefully in the ditch. As he stooped down for this pious act, Nature, as if unsympathetic to such proceedings, brought it about that his gorge rose to a pitch of actual retching, so that although the rabbit got its obsequies, such as they were, he himself was denied any sort of ritualistic satisfaction.

"No, no," he said to himself, "I'm going to try, more than ever, to make *Mary Channing* a book that shall—and I'm going to stop 'doing that' with Thuella ! I'm not going to care what's in the Yeovil letter. But I haven't come out of my Monawraith world to be caught by your manias, old Topknot. *There* I'm hard as a rock; but O deary I ! damn *all* these people. Why can't I be left alone in peace with Wizzie ? D. No-man and his girl . . . D. No-man and his girl . . . D. No-man and his——"

His thoughts were interrupted by a peevish and fretful grumbling from his companion, and he noticed that his father now began to manifest the same sort of symptoms of nervous exhaustion that a priest who on an empty stomach has been chanting a long and complicated Mass might display on his way back to breakfast.

He asked for a cigarette, cursed irritably when the wind extinguished his first two matches, fussed with his sweater which seemed to have gathered itself into unconscionable folds around his hips, kept searching about under his trousers for the tape on one side of his drawers which had escaped from his braces, fumbled at one of the buttons of his coat which kept slipping out of its buttonhole, and at intervals pressed the front of his wrist against his eye-sockets as if his eyeballs hurt him.

He grumbled more than our friend thought necessary about their inability to open a gate into the lane above Monkton and seemed to find the effort of clambering over it almost beyond his strength. To some remark of No-man's about the peacefulness of the little churchyard he broke out crossly against the way the enclosure had been mown.

He even displayed annoyance at the manner in which Dud hung back to get a final view of Mai-Dun between the trees. "We'll be catching our death in this damned wind," he muttered, "if you keep stopping like that!"

All this would naturally have amused, and perhaps even gratified our friend, as signs of a pleasant human weakness in the man, if he himself had not been so wrought up by his experiences on the hill that he had lost all power of humorous observation. He tried to put his father out of his mind and gave himself up to the sweetly dolorous motions of the wind in these freshly green elm-branches.

All the way back to the town, as he walked by the side of his silent parent along the Weymouth Road, the posthumous restitution of Mary Channing obsessed his mind. In some wild fantastic manner he linked the dead woman's personality with Wizzie's, linked her poisoned husband with Old Funky, linked himself with the dim figure of the equivocal gallant for whom she killed him. "I believe, if I hadn't got Wizzie," he thought, "I'd be taking Mary's ghost home with me to my room—not as a substitute for Mona though, but as——"

But even the Mai-Dun wind lacked the power to inspire our friend with any role really appropriate to this ill-used shade. He fell into a deep consideration, as they moved on towards the cemetery and the Amphitheatre, with the spire of All Saints' already appearing in shortened perspective behind the brewery

chimney, as to the manner in which he would make his Mary a
veritable symbol of all the women whose love of love, and love
of pleasure, and loathing of married slavery, had made victims
of a morality based upon property. "I'll make her so pitiful," he
thought, "and I'll describe her judges and her husband and the
cruelty of those onlookers so piercingly, that I'll burn this crime
into the bones of Wessex. I'll do *what they did to her*, only the
other way round!"

But from Mary his excited mind soon came swinging back to
his own affairs. "What *will* there be," he thought, "in that
Yeovil letter? Well! I'm ready, whatever it is!"

And then, as they drew near the cemetery and he decided
that nothing would induce him to enter that place in company
with his "mother's man," he thought how, if he were writing a
story about himself, he would make All Souls' Day, this last
autumn, appear like a new birth, the birth of a middle-aged man
over forty into normal human life. "The truth is," he thought,
"what I have to struggle like the devil to be is what normal men
are already, by the nature of things. And yet I would not
change with any of them! I'll still be myself : but I'll be myself
entering *their* life."

They were opposite the cemetery now, and our friend took
good care to look the other way, and to *think* the other way too,
lest some telepathic wave of consciousness should set Uryen
upon entering the death-enclosure.

But what was this? Yes, there was some kind of Circus—and
it looked to his eyes most startlingly familiar—being put up in
the fair-field! "I expect it's a different one, though," he said to
himself, "there must be endless ones on the road."

And then the thought came to him : "But I'm certain Wizz
told me none of them went their rounds till the summer. What
the devil *is* this then?"

Uryen made no sign of any sort as they passed the cemetery
and Dud didn't dare to take off his cap. "But what would you
think, Mother," he said to himself, "if you saw us passing you
without a word?"

It was a relief when they began to skirt the iron railings by
the Amphitheatre; and Dud tried hard to put both cemetery
and Circus out of his mind and to concentrate on Mary's execution. He had picked up some ghastly details from various tradi-

tional accounts of this event, but upon these he refused to let his mind dwell.

"That's one thing I learnt from old Elijah," he said to himself. "Aye! how I remember the way he looked on his knees at prayers when he used to say: 'And keep us all, dear merciful God, from thinking of cruel things, lest our thoughts carry food to the devils.'"

When they came past the railway station our friend remembered how he had decided during his first encounter with Wizzie not to have any scruple about making love to Thuella. "Well, I've got plenty of scruple now," he thought, with a wry grimace.

But here were the South Walks; and presently the familiar cenotaph hove in sight. "How like a figure in Hardy," he said to himself, "poor Nance looked that day staggering against those rails! It's funny how I began my life in Dorchester just as the mayor began his, only Trenchard sold *his* woman and I bought mine!"

"You won't mind if I don't come with you farther than the Hangman's Cottage?" he remarked to his companion. "It's a quarter to five I see, and I promised to be at Friary Lane at five."

Uryen surveyed the big clock on its sixteenth century façade, and nodded amiably. "Don't bother yourself, lad! Further or no further, 'tis all the same. But I'm right glad you came *up there* with me."

By a mutual instinct to avoid the crowds on South Street the two tall men crossed over by the entrance to Bowling Alley Walk and proceeded up Trinity Street. This particular thoroughfare—for when he wanted to take a walk through Came or Herringstone he generally started by way of Acland Street or the Icen Way—was less familiar to him than the other Dorchester streets. The fresh interest he took in it now as they advanced made him think how completely he'd taken all that old life of his for granted, and all the people in it for granted! Though he was a man of thirty when the three of them died it was as if he had been a boy of thirteen. It was through the thick mist of an absolutely secretive imagination that he saw his mother perpetually embroidering, his pseudo-father perpetually praying and gardening, and Mona managing them all like an angel from heaven.

262

But how different life was since he had lived in Dorchester! The old Roman town must have had in its possession some ancient classic cement of actuality, that had the power of making the real doubly real!

Nothing but his imagination had been *really* real to him before he came to Dorchester; but how palpable Wizzie was, and how terribly alive Thuella was! Claudius and the troubled "Horse-Head" too, were no mean wedges of this new verity; and as for the warm touch of Nance—— But the Glymes man and he were in High West Street now, and he became aware that it was Mr. Quirm's intention to go down Glyde Path Lane to the Hangman's Cottage. Into this romantic by-way Dud therefore escorted his companion, and he soon recognized that this road was, like Trinity Street, almost new to him. This was proved by the fact that it was left to Mr. Quirm to call his attention to a curious waterspout or gargoyle-head, that had been placed above the old brick entrance to what looked to our friend like a Quaker meeting-house. He had come upon a mention of this head in Hardy's book, but apparently it occupied in poor Trenchard's time a different position from what it did now.

In the overcast afternoon light of this spring day the stone face, as the two men paused to gaze up at it, wore a most ambiguous expression.

"Well? What about it, lad? What about it?" chuckled the Glymes man grimly.

"I don't—know—what—to think," hesitated the son.

"Doesn't it look—rather—as if—as if it hid some terrible world-joke behind that skull, some joke that nothing could——"

His father gave him a most sardonic glance from under his eyebrows. "Joke, do you say? He's grinning at his own mental pain; that's what he's grinning at. He's the face in God's motley; that's what he is. You've got to walk round your precious world, my lad, and see *the other side,* before you can talk about *his* little joke. It's a joke all right, but it's a deep one! It's the deepest, my good boy. He's the original Momus, lad, that's what he is; the face that peeped out of God's motley, when He found His creation 'good.' "

Dud struck his oak cudgel on the stones of Glyde Path Road and moved on. He detected, without being able to define it, an emanation of something so sinister from the man at that moment that it suggested things far worse than any blasphemy.

He received an uneasy impression that Mr. Quirm would have exactly that same grimace on his own majestic physiognomy when he came to die.

"But if so," he thought, "if this whole Uryen-game of his is a devilish joke, why can't someone make him stop it and set him off on a different track?"

They were soon descending the steep slope between the high walls that lead to the Hangman's Cottage. "It must have been up this hill," Dud said to himself, "that the executioner came when he met the sheriff's officers, taking Mary to her death. Oh, damn them! Damn them! But you wait—you wait. That Momus-grin is *not* the last word!"

At the Hangman's Cottage they separated, the father following the track towards Frome House, the son the path underneath the slope leading up to the Prison.

It was already chiming a quarter past five from the clock above the Corn Exchange when our friend, with the Yeovil letter still unopened in his pocket, reached Mrs. Dearth's house in Friary Lane.

As a rule when he came to this house he found the front door unlocked, but this afternoon, when he tried the handle, the door refused to open. He hesitated whether to step back into the street and call up to Wizzie's window, but there were people about, and he had no idea of Wizzie's mood, so he decided to knock and wait for Jenny to open to him.

He knocked again at the door, this time with the handle of his cudgel.

"Jenny can't be out," he thought, "the kitchen door must be shut."

But Jenny Dearth opened to him now and he saw at once that something had gone wrong. She led him into the kitchen without a word and closed the door upon them.

"Nance is up there with her," she said. "Oh, no! She's all right," and then after looking at him for a moment without a word, but with nothing but anger and contempt in her face, she announced in a low bitter tone: "And he's started writing letters to me. That must be one of *your* ideas!"

Dud began blurting out some awkward pleasantry about Mr.

Cumber's party, but he soon broke off in confusion, for the woman's face was dark with emotion.

"Good Lord!" he thought. "He must have said everything that was in his mind. Those letters must have maddened her. I wish she'd tell me what he said."

"Don't stand gaping at me like a sanctified ninny!" cried Mrs. Dearth. "You stare too much. All you can do in life is to stare."

Dud nervously collapsed on a seat by the window. He thought to himself : "Is *this* the 'dark pain' the Glymes man talks of that unlocks the secret of life?"

He looked vaguely round for a place to prop up his stick; but afraid lest it should fall with an inappropriate clatter on Jenny's stone floor, he laid it down humbly at his feet.

"What right have *you*," Mrs. Dearth cried—and he noticed that the effect of anger on her face was to make it much more human : it lost its equine nobility and became at the same time meaner and handsomer—"to meddle with my affairs? Look to your own, you idiot! They're not what you think they are. Nothing's like what you think it is in your great rum-a-drum wooden-head! He says in one of his letters that you think I'm hard on him. *I* hard on him! I, who've done more for him than anyone in the world—far more than his own mother!"

No-man shuffled uneasily in his seat. He did not dare to meet her eyes for fear of exciting her still more, and he did not dare to look at the door for fear she would see he'd heard the steps of someone coming down. He looked at his two hands, which were spread out palm-downwards on his separate knees. These hands of his looked so gaunt and so harmless as they lay there that it made him feel indignant with all these people for not just accepting him as a simple well-meaning honest man who only wanted to be alone.

"And what's this between you and Nance Quirm?" Mrs. Dearth went on. "She's been hanging about here waiting for you and her husband all the afternoon and she never waits for Uryen. She's upstairs now with Wizzie. I got weary of her talk— all about what you've done for Uryen. Have you started meddling with *their* affairs, too? Oh, you've got round Nance, sure and proper, with your sympathetic starings! She thinks you're a saint. She thinks you're the only man she knows with a really noble heart! *You* with a noble heart! You who don't know what natural human feeling is!" She gasped and choked in her emotion and came a step nearer him. "Aren't you satisfied, then, with what you've done to your own, that you're playing your games with Nance? I suppose you've told her to talk to Wizzie, just as you told *him* you'd talk to me! Oh, you're a sly one, with your roundabout ways and staring eyes! You've turned Nance's head with your dear sympathy, that's what you've done, and that's what you wanted to do! Oh, you're the one to give Enoch a lift, to help a fellow writer with the Cumbers, and meanwhile steal away his wife's heart!"

Could our friend have "stared" just then at his own visage in a mirror he would have noticed that it had its mouth open and that a tiny dribble of saliva was descending his chin. This idiotic expression of his, combined with an unruffled air of martyred helplessness that seemed to be murmuring : "Hit me! Hit me!" was evidently, of all human attitudes, the one most calculated to drive the Friary Lane lady to distraction.

"Old Claudius," he found time to think, "must have said every wrong thing that it's possible to say to a woman in love. He must have enlarged on aqueducts, he must have dragged in Marx, he must have appealed to Reason, he must have talked about forgiveness till he had thrown so much straw on the fire that when it *did* begin to burn——"

"You thought only of your own selfish sensations when you first brought Wizzie here," was what he now heard Jenny say. "It was nothing to you that you took her life away from her, yes! her life! Nothing to you that you broke up her career and spoilt her natural self-expression for ever. You and him and all of you are the same. *He* has his selfish theories, and you have your selfish books, and as long as you can hoist a woman up into your own romantic fancies, you think you've done all that's necessary. That's to be our whole life, just pleasant adjuncts to your careers—*here* when we're wanted, *there* when we're not wanted— and all the time—you mark my words—Wizzie's far more of a genius at *her* job than you'll ever be at yours! And you keep her here as your plaything, idle and useless! You're too selfish, or too depraved, even to give her a child. You take a girl who's an artist in the most difficult of all arts. I suppose she's never told you how early she had to begin, or what she had to go through,

266

to become what she is? You get round her by your damned 'sympathy' and you romantic talk, and then go and keep her shut up like a common tart. Yes! like a common tart, for your lazy-dazy lust! You don't even try to get her a house of her own. Oh, no! you can't afford that! The truth is you don't want her in your real life, which goes on in that precious attic of yours, above the church-warden's shop. You want her *here,* all fresh and prettified, for your offtime entertainment! Is that a life for a spirited girl who might be earning money at any hippo-drome in the kingdom? The truth is, my good staring friend, you don't know what real feeling is!

"And what makes it worse is your conceit, and the grand opinion you've got of yourself! Oh, you're the noble one, you're the one who'll set everybody right. And now you've gone and got round Nance. It was him in the coal-yard no doubt who told you Enoch was a wife-beater. Oh, you're a pretty pair, you two! As if we all didn't know she can twist that great idiot round her little finger!

"But you and him down there *must* be interfering! Nance must be saved from her wicked husband, and who must under-take this tender task but *you,* the sympathetic, staring *you!* That's the whole thing, my good man."

But Dud, who had by this time managed to shut his mouth and even to wipe away with the back of his hand the spittle from his chin, noted that the introduction of Nance into her diatribe had acted like a lightning-conductor and drawn off a good portion of her electric anger from its more dangerous concentration upon Claudius. "If I can keep her on Nance," he thought, "she'll soon be all right."

"Yes, I confess I *have* got rather fond of Mrs. Quirm," he murmured craftily.

"You see?" she cried, falling at once into Dud's simple trap. "It's your conceit that makes you act as you do. You'll never be any good in the world or any help to anyone till you've got rid of your conceit! I know you through and through, and what's wrong with you is simply conceit. You're a monster of conceit!"

Dud was quick to recognize the fact that this attack on his intelligence rather than his heart was a sign the "Horse-Head" was softening; and he hurriedly picked up his stick. Holding this great club in his hand he could not help pondering on the changes already produced by Claudius's darling evolution.

"It's doubtful," he thought, "whether any of the men of old time, except perhaps a few mediaeval knights, would sit as quiet as I'm sitting here now, with this Cerne Giant stick on my lap, listening to the 'Horse-Head' putting me in my place!"

"Yes, it's your conceit," she added, her face by this time wearing an almost indulgent expression. "You think you're ever so much nobler than Wizzie because she lets herself go and you never do. You think you're behaving like I don't know what because you don't let yourself go with her when her nerves are bad; whereas of course a *really* sympathetic man wouldn't be able to rest till he'd found out *why* she was like that, so that he could remove the cause."

Dud gave a deep sigh of relief and thrust his hand into his pocket to make sure he had the Yeovil letter. The immediate effect upon him of Jenny's outburst was to accentuate his usual animal-like passivity. Not that he had totally forgotten the spiritual illumination of Mai-Dun, but so far it had penetrated only the rational surface of his consciousness. A flicker of it did, as a matter of fact, come back to him even now, but so far it enabled him only to give a quick ironic inward glance at the fatal inevitableness of his idiotic docility: it did not give him the power to adopt any other method of retort!

His thrusting his fingers into his pocket, however, and their consequent contact with the Yeovil letter caused him to wonder whether Jenny Dearth knew more than he did of the relations between Wizzie and those circus people. But she couldn't, surely, have spoken in *that* tone if she had! The more she knew of those people the more she must realize what a good turn he had done Wizzie by rescuing her. She talked of the "cause" of Wizzie's nervous irritability. The cause of it was in his pocket now—her mysterious fear of Old Funky and Mummy Urgan!

He looked at Mrs. Dearth closely. The woman's anger was gone. But though her face was no longer handsome and human, it was not quite itself.

"Well, up you go to Wizzie," she said. "Tell her I'll bring the tray in a few minutes!"

He got up obediently. "I'm sorry, Jenny," he said speaking in a rather high-pitched tone, and with a sort of airy emphasis of impressive candour, "I'm sorry if I didn't do any good by my 'meddling,' as you call it. Perhaps if everyone treated my ways as drastically as you do I *would* begin to change. Perhaps anyhow I'll begin to change! I give you my word of honour I've thought of it. Something must change—I can see that. There must be *some* sort of a *Primum Mobile* and some sort of a Prime Mover, or there wouldn't be any"—he was going to say "Evolution," but he knew Jenny would take that as a piece of malice, so he said "Progress" instead, and leaving this brisk word behind him, like a puff of gun-smoke in Mrs. Dearth's kitchen, he nodded his farewell to her and went out into the entrance hall.

It was lucky that in doing this he shut the kitchen-door behind him; for to his surprise—though not to his very *great* surprise—he found Nancy Quirm standing in the front entrance apparently watching something in the street.

She turned when he came out, and in his heart he thought at once, "She's been listening!"

But Mrs. Quirm beckoned him to join her at the front door. "What is it?" he asked, for all he could himself catch from the street was that familiar "*Ech-o! Ech-o!*" of the local newspaper's distribution. This cry of "*Ech-o!*" always made him think of making love to Wizzie; for it was usually to be heard about six o'clock when they were lingering over their tea together in their upper room.

"It's the funny man!" Mrs. Quirm cried eagerly. "There he is! *There,* don't you see him, Mr. No-man! He's talking to those boys over there!"

Our friend followed her gaze and responded to her excitement with an alacrity of interest he was far from feeling. The person she called the "funny man" was indeed one of the sights of Dorchester. *He* really was a quite authentic Momus, and in his present occupation as Town Crier for the Tenth Muse, he lent himself, with his "quips and cranks and wanton wiles," in a manner almost Elizabethan to the old-world liveliness of the town.

If Dud could never help thinking of making love to Wizzie when he heard *Ech-o! Ech-o!* he found that it was almost always when he was deepest sunk in his book that the accents of the "funny man" reached him. Mary Channing's waverings between a life of her own and obedience to the grinding selfishness

269

of parents and husband gained in their human subtlety by being attuned to the "funny man's" Shakespearean fooleries as they drifted down High East Street.

"Yes! I can see him; and I can hear him too. How wonderfully he does it! It must be quite a good performance, this piece he's talking about!"

As soon as he had uttered these hopeful words and glanced into her face he knew she *must* have been listening to their talk : for she accepted his forced geniality at its face value, whereas under normal conditions she would have caught him up and protested with lively vehemence. Had she heard all? Had she heard Jenny accuse him of meddling between husband and wife? "I bet she *did*," he said to himself, noticing with nervous relief but with mental suspicion that she didn't cling to his sleeve in her usual impulsive way.

But it was his destiny to receive a greater shock to his nerves than any touch of his cemetery-woman's warm fingers.

"Come in here for a second, Mr. No-man," she whispered, opening the dining-room door and entering the room.

She turned her head as she preceded him and threw him a look which she evidently felt to be the look of a reckless courtesan.

"Jenny'll be five minutes at least," she whispered. "I *know* she hasn't spread the bread and butter yet."

As soon as the door was shut on them he knew that his cemetery-woman was in a fever of emotion. "Come over here and sit down," she murmured. "She's spreading the bread and butter, I tell you, and Wizzie's tidying up her room for tea. There's—no—chance—of anybody's—coming—no—chance—of anybody's coming—no chance—of anybody's——"

And in her excitement she actually repeated these words in a sort of infantile chant. She pushed him down into the armchair that had always been Claudius's, and with a look in her eyes that Dud had never seen before in any woman's eyes she perched herself on the chair's arm.

Our friend's thoughts became like the darting wings of a flock of swifts.

"She doesn't know that my soul's as brittle as glass and as cold as an icicle! She doesn't know that under her hot hand and heavy cowslip breath I feel as light and frail and feathery as hoar-frost! She's no more idea what a person like me really feels than she has of the feeling of the Loch Ness monster!"

And while he felt the hot magnetism of her senses rock him on its waves like a baby in a cradle, he thought how unemotional, how coldly vicious, how entirely imaginative his own sensual feelings were. "Why," he thought, "I can't even enjoy playing with Wizzie without reminding myself that I bought her for eighteen pounds! What I'm made for is quiet, *cold-blooded* lust. This hot passion's horrible to me!"

"I — couldn't — wait — to — tell — you — any — longer," she gasped in a queer husky voice, a voice quite different from her usual rich sweet tones; and he noticed that as she spoke she made a feverish rocking movement on the chair-arm, just as if her whole body burned with such passion that the mere pressure of the woodwork was a relief.

"You—don't—mind—do—you?—if I touch—your hand—it'll make it easier—to tell you."

No-man had already raised his arm and rested his hand on the curve of the soft limb that was nearest to him, across which her skirt was tightly drawn, and, when her fingers closed over his, his nervous shrinking became so acute that he gripped her with the talons of a vulture.

"I heard," she whispered feverishly, leaning forward and pressing her shoulder against his. "I heard what Jenny said about you and me. I knew it was in her mind. I knew she's been thinking of nothing but you and me ever since you first came to Glymes."

Now that the first shock of the situation had ceased to startle him Dud became so detached that his thoughts wandered away altogether from the excited woman. They reverted again to the difference between Uryen's mania for reaching the cosmic secret and the argument between Dumbell and Claudius about the Past and the Future.

"Do you know," Mrs. Quirm continued, "what Jenny's made up her mind about? That you and I are lovers! Can you imagine such silliness? Yes, she's certain it began soon after you first came." As Mrs. Quirm uttered these words she actually touched No-man's chin with the extreme tip of one of her hot fingers.

Our friend bit his lip and stared into the empty grate which

271

was still shining with the vigorous blacking Jenny had given it that morning, but into which, not content with this, she had put a small pot of yellow musk.

"Of course I know we're nothing of the sort," Nancy went on, dropping the hand she had raised, "but it's amusing, isn't it, what people *will* say? What I wished you'd said to Jenny was that I'd been your mistress from the first day we met, from that first All Souls' Day—*No-man*!"

It gave our friend a very odd sensation to hear his name, a name he had selected for its gaunt and grim taciturnity, used in a manner like this, as if it were a synonym for "sweet chuck."

"But—my dear—*you weren't*!" murmured our friend calmly. He was as a matter of fact a good deal less agitated that he would have expected by all this. The agreeable problem slid coldly into his mind as to whether it would give any sort of pleasure to pull her down on his knee.

But instead of trying such an experiment he made his voice as light and humorous and friendly as he could. "Besides, by this time, we'd have certainly quarrelled; where——"

"I seem not to care *what* I say to you!" Nancy went on, bending so low over him that she did almost, without any help from him, slide down upon his knees. "Do you know I'm *afraid* of you, No-man? You've done something to me that makes me more afraid of you than I ever was of Enoch. Just feel—No-man! "And for the first time in his extremely inexperienced life it was our friend's destiny to know what it was to have his fingers snatched at by a woman and pressed against her side. It was under her left breast that she pressed them, and he was not only made aware of the beating of her heart but of the fact that her whole body was quivering. She held his hand tightly against her side as she spoke, pouring out the words without a pause, and in the old rich mellow tones again; and the sweetness of her breath made him feel as if he were being rolled over and over in a whole field of cowslips.

In exultant and voluptuous tones, quite free now from all hesitation, she told him how she had loved him since their first meeting in the cemetery. She told him that she had at first struggled against this feeling; but on Candlemas night, when he had come to Glymes, she had decided that there was no harm in yielding to it, no harm in giving it free rein in her secret thoughts, as long as no one else knew.

"What made you decide on telling *me*?" was his comment on this. These tactless and even, in a sense, brutal words were accompanied by a perceptible stiffening of No-man's frame and by the removal of his fingers from hers and the withdrawal of his hand from her side.

But there had come a hot flush on Nancy's cheeks now, and she was doing to the limit what she had begun to do that very first day when he came to Glymes. She was telling him all sorts of intimate details about Enoch.

"Poor *old* chap!" Dud groaned. "Thank the Lord no son of mine'll ever hear such things about his father!"

But there was a yet further surprise in store for him. He had begun to take for granted that this woman hated Enoch with a relentless and vindictive hatred. But not at all! Though she told Dud things that made him shiver through the very bowels of his being she uttered other words—and entirely spontaneous ones—that proved to him that at the bottom of her heart she loved Uryen still.

"This is getting beyond me," thought our friend. "Can a woman love two men? And does she know what *our* relationship is?" On and on ran the stream of Nancy's voice. Every now and then she would give little curious indrawn gasps for breath; but all the time she leaned lower and lower over him, not touching him any more, but causing him to feel the tenseness of her nerves even more than when she *was* touching him.

He decided that this thing must stop. He must get up somehow from this fatal chair. If her feelings were hurt, well, there it was!

Then a cruel inspiration came to him. "I know, my dear!" he said coldly, pushing her gently aside and rising to his feet," I *know*; you've gone through hell in one way and another—but you're not the only one. You're not the first, my dear, and you won't be the last. Do you remember how we met at those graves, and how you told me about your boy's death?"

They were standing facing each other now, and they both could hear Wizzie's voice calling down from the top of the stairs in reply to something that Jenny was saying to her from outside the dining-room door.

And Dud wished, then, to the depths of his contrarious soul

273

that he had used any method, rather than *that* one, to end this wretched scene. The workings of the woman's face, as she took in his word about her son, were harrowing to watch. It was as if, instead of her human blood recovering its circulation after being frozen to death, all the fiery impulses of her being had been smitten at full beat by the descent on them of an avalanche of ice.

"Nance dear, *my* Nance!" he cried, laying his hand on her sleeve. He felt at the moment how ironic it was that he should be the one now to be doing this, but he spoke earnestly and with full sincerity. "If only your boy were alive," he said, "I'd show him what friends you and I are now. We're bound together now for life, my dear. I felt we were when we first met. I had a presentiment; and now I *know* it. Don't 'ee be too sad, dear heart! What Jenny said of us isn't true; but something better is true. I know you, Nance, for what you are, and you shall know me. This love-business passes away anyhow, Nance. We can begin where most couples leave off. We first met at our graves and we must make that a covenant between us. Give me your hand on it, my girl!"

As he spoke he held out his hand to her. But she did not take it. Her warm body had become a hollow reed, in the heart of which the Promethean spark had been extinguished. Slowly, and as if by some power beyond her will, her soft features returned to their normal expression; each wry curve, each wretched twist smoothing themselves out, not so much as shadows in water after their dispersal by a flung stone, as shapes in a flooded landscape when the waters have subsided.

But such shapes, returned though they are to light and air, carry upon them an indescribable film, the ashen-grey deposit of their long submersion.

Dud had many strange feelings as he watched her there, while the voice of Wizzie from the landing above cried out impatiently. "Tea's ready, you two! What's the matter with you? Are you deaf? Jenny's up here, and tea's ready. We'll begin without you if you don't come!"

He felt as he watched her, for those brief seconds, as if her soul had drawn back, down some long narrowing perspective, and was hesitating there whether to return to the tunnel's entrance or to go on and on and on, till perchance it came out on the other side! There must have been something in his eyes that showed her at that second that he was not unaware of what he had done to her, and this knowledge as it passed between them came nearer to bringing her the relief of a flood of weeping. But she swallowed her tears.

"Kiss me once—No-man," she whispered, "and then we'll go!"

He took her head in his two hands and pulled it against his chest so that her hair tickled his chin. But he did not kiss her, and she remained motionless, his hands clasped round her head. While he held her like this the voice of the "funny man" was audible again from the far end of Friary Lane. Then suddenly she broke away; and they both heard Jenny running downstairs.

Nance moved to the door and got it open in time to confront Mrs. Dearth in the passage.

"What on earth?——" began the latter but stopped abruptly.

"I can't wait for tea," Nance said; and Dud thought she said it in a purposely loud voice so that Wizzie upstairs should hear. "Mr. No-man's been telling me of his walk with Enoch, and I must hurry back to Glymes. He *can* get his tea, of course—but he doesn't like to. He'll just put the kettle on and linger about. I'll find him washing himself I expect—not having a bath, you understand, but putting his head into a basin of water, over and over again! He says his prayers while he's doing that: I don't know *what* prayers, I'm sure; but what he likes is for me to have tea ready when *he's* ready. I wouldn't be surprised," and she gave a little forced laugh, for the benefit also, he divined, of the girl upstairs, "if I got home before six and began my tea well before you three are finished! Good night, Wizzie dear!" and she raised her voice. "I'm off! Good night, Mr. No-man!"

It was Jenny who helped her on with her hat and cloak; but Dud met her eyes as she stood on the threshold.

"Listen!" she said, holding the front-door open. The old mummer must have been announcing the entertainment for that evening to a group of men in the High Street, and his resonant actor's voice gave our friend a queer impression that he too, and Nance—and all of them—were characters in a play.

"I suppose the town crier," he thought, "announced the execution of Mistress Channing in a chant just like that!" And there came over him, as he and Nance lingered in the doorway holding each other with their eyes, a strange feeling as if all the buried generations of Dorchester were murmuring in a low persistent monotone, "Pity, pity, pity, pity—none is good, none is bad; pity, pity, pity, pity!"

It struck him as very queer, while he and Nance stood there, that he should be so reluctant to let her go. As he looked into her face all his shrinking from her vanished away. That chant of the pity of the generations seemed to turn her feeling for him into something tender and precious, "all passion spent"; and he felt as if when once she was gone and he had to go upstairs with that unopened Bristol letter in his pocket he would be leaving a protectress behind and plunging into a *mêlée* of unknown peril.

"Good-bye—only for to-day—Nance! This is a beginning, my dear, not an end!" Answering he knew not what when the door was shut to some troublesome comment from Jenny, who looked especially grim and caustic in her black dress, he followed her upstairs. "You talk of our baffled desires breaking into the world's secret," he said to himself, apostrophizing his "mother's man" as he entered Wizzie's room, "but for most of us desire itself breaks like a bubble when it gets near the secret!"

Jenny's strained and caustic mood didn't last very long when their tea-party was once under way. Wizzie herself turned out to be in high spirits that afternoon, whether due to the fact that she was still wearing her pretty luncheon dress, or because she felt she'd carried it off better than she anticipated with the Cumber people, or simply because she enjoyed playing hostess to Mrs. Dearth, he could not decide, but her happy mood was not long in communicating itself to Jenny.

He had many curious thoughts below the surface of their chatter as the meal went on. For one thing he found himself placed opposite the fire-place, from which the lamentable, life-drained portrait of Teucer Wye looked down upon him. Hypnotized by the pitiful eyes of this young-old victim of the cloud-painter, and still hearing the voice of the "funny-man" in his ears, Dud began to feel as if his emerging from a life lived entirely between his Mona-wraith and the memory of his mother was something that might vanish away as suddenly as it had appeared, flinging him back upon "the Royal Martyr" and the "Questing Beast."

"But it can't, it can't vanish; it *never* can vanish! Did you think you could meddle with flesh-and-blood and go on just the same?"

It was much more than an hour after they sat down when Jenny retired and he and Wizz were left alone. Most of their talk at the end had been about Teucer Wye and the way Thuella was treating him; and Wizzie had astonished her lover, and apparently Jenny, too, by the intensity with which she stood up for "Thel."

No-man was in no mood for angry discussion and he had just listened in quiet and passive astonishment to his girl's startling defence of her friend. Mrs. Dearth herself, perhaps in the reaction from her outburst in the kitchen, seemed reluctant to protest. The gist of what Wizzie had said was that no one knew what "Thel" had had to put up with, for years, from that tiresome old man. "He looks harmless enough," Wizzie had explained, "but if I'd had to bear what 'Thel' has from him, with those old books and all, and his sneering at everything she enjoys, and her supporting him all the time, I'd have killed him by now. Yes, I would! I'd have killed him if I'd had to hang for it!"

But the moment they *were* alone Dud, without beating about the bush, brought out the Yeovil letter. The girl had lit the fire to make their tea more cheerful, and it was upon a Wizzie lying back at ease in the arm-chair, more serene and placid than he had known her for a long while, that standing opposite her by the mantelpiece No-man released the thunderbolt. "It's got the Yeovil postmark right enough," he said, holding it between his finger and thumb. "Mr. D. No-man—High Street. He's forgotten the East. Would the Urgans make a mistake like that? He's been twice to my room, too."

"Damn you, *open* it! Or let *me*! Give it here!" She was on her feet already; and she rushed up to him trying to snatch the letter from him.

But his infantile instinct to tease her, especially in the face of this "Give it here!" and his outraged regard for ritual and decency, made him hold up the Yeovil letter at arm's length out of her reach.

There was a struggle between them, and as she clung to him, growing more and more angry while he backed away from the

277

fire, they collided so violently with the edge of the tea-table that they unbalanced the milk-jug, which fell down with a crash on the floor.

She had never turned upon him a face so contorted with fury as she did now, and he was glad enough to let her get hold of the letter as he knelt down on the floor.

Crouching there, in the simple desire to escape the sight of her face, and trying to mop up the spilt milk with his handkerchief, he began gathering together the broken bits of china. That the girl's anger was short-lived, that after she had torn the letter from its dirty envelope she was frozen numb with the shock of its contents, Dud from his task on the floor soon realized. She took it over to the fire and as he gave her a sidelong glance from his crouching position he saw that the impulse crossed her mind for the beat of a second to fling the thing into the flames. She *did* tear it in half, and Dud felt no impulse to stop her, but no sooner had she done this than it seemed to him that a weight of inert despair descended on her, depriving her of all anger, of all energy, almost of all feeling.

With the torn letter on her lap and the torn envelope at her feet she sank down on the edge of the arm-chair and stared hopelessly and vacantly in front of her. He could see only the profile curve of her small face, but in his mind he knew that those unseeing eyes, gazing so straight before her into nothingness, had grown large and round.

When he did struggle up at last from the floor and take the torn letter from the girl's lap it was as if he had a tremendous weight upon him. He felt as if he were doing this, not only with the "Wizzie object" under his ribs, but with the dark globe of his book, heavy with earthworks and amphitheatres, bowing him down, as the world did Atlas.

Even now, with the two torn halves of the letter in his hand, he felt an overpowering reluctance to read it. He found himself inclined to imitate Wizzie in her hopeless apathy and to sink down in a chair opposite her and let all go.

He did sink down for a minute there and just stared at the two bits of paper in his fingers. On these two bits of paper in place of any threat of Old Funky's he saw the dispute between Claudius and Dumbell and he thought of the Glymes man on Maiden Castle. "With all your magical humbug, and your 'mental pain,'" he thought, "you *are* wrestling with the secret of life; whereas both Communism and Cæsarism are just methods of——"

But brushing these things aside with a splash like that of a fish rising to the top, one single word from the Yeovil letter caught his full attention. It was an odd word to be there. It was the word "Lovie." But it was "Lovie" who broke the spell; and jumping to his feet he puzzled out now, word by word, in the light of one of the candles under the portrait of Mr. Wye, the letter's astonishing contents.

It was, as we have said, written in pencil and it ran as follows :

MISTER D. NO-MAN, SIR.

I takes the liberty of letting you know that the child Lovie, what have been hid from your knowledge by she and me with Best Intentions, be going to be took to the 'Ouse owing to Mrs. Urgan *'aving found out all*. Never would this 'ave rizz if Her we know hadn't stopped payment. In case, Mr. D. No-man, sir, you wish to adopt the child Lovie me and me missus will say nothink save for small compensation for expenses already incurred. Hopping this finds you, sir, same as it leaves us at present,

Your obedient servant to command,

BEN URGAN.

Dud's first feeling when he had finished this communication was one of immense relief. When his eye first fell on the word "Lovie" scrawled on that dirty piece of paper, one of his wildest and most lurid imaginations with regard to Wizz and Old Funky seemed to be coming true, namely that she *had* had a child by the old man but that in her misery of mind she had murdered it, and the Urgans had been holding this over her ever since! He had thought of this possibility, and of many others equally unpleasant, for so many months, that it was a heavenly reprieve to know the worst and to find that the worst was only "Lovie." He knew Wizzie had no confidence in his behaving well at a pinch of this sort. He knew that just as she couldn't understand the *defects* of his quality, so she couldn't understand his quality.

The subject of Old Funky always divided them; so he had

279

naturally avoided approaching it; and even if he *had* approached it, it would have been hard to have said to her in cold blood :

"I don't care, my dear, what children you've had, or *who* gave them to you!"

But *as it was*—good Lord! He was ready to adopt Wizzie's child to-morrow. He remembered his thoughts about parthenogenesis in connection with his own birth. He would no more see Urgan's blood in Lovie than he was able to feel Uryen's blood in himself!

But the realities of this Roman town *were* thickening upon him. First a father and now a child! But he knew himself in these things. This was just the sort of shock he could bear with the equanimity that was the advantage of having such an outrageous imagination! The reality, when you met it, was mild in comparison.

All this rushed through his brain, as he played with the two halves of this bit of paper, separating them and fitting them together under the candle.

"Well, old girl?" he murmured coming close up to her. She listened to the sound of his voice as a suicide drowning in the sea might listen to a dialogue on the deck above, and he received as their eyes met what was the greatest shock to him in the whole episode, the feeling that the girl was—in regard to this matter at any rate—completely insane, and that there could be no rational exchange of ideas, of any sort, between them about it.

"Wizz, my darling! My life, my love!" he cried, when he caught this look, "you're my girl always, you're the same always. Don't look like that, Wizz, don't 'ee do it!" and he flung himself down on his knees by her side. "Look at me, Wizz!" he repeated. "Look at me, my treasure. It's your old Dud speaking to you! We'll go to where the child is to-morrow. We'll take her away. We'll have her always. She'll be *yours* to me—nobody else's! Of course we'll take her! Little Wizz, little Wizz, *do you hear what I say?*" And in the tumult of his anxiety he seized her by the shoulders with his two hands and shook her violently.

But the girl snatched at his wrists and flung him back with all her might. "You—fool! you don't know what you're saying.

280

There! Let me go. I tell you I've got to think this out *alone*." She swayed to her feet and drew away from him. He too scrambled up from his knees and stared helplessly at her. Yes! There was that look in her eyes that he'd seen in the caravan. To talk to her now was like talking to a person in delirium.

"Wizz——" he began desperately, but she cut him short. "You —*fool*!" she repeated. "You know no more about it than—than——" and to his dismay her voice broke into a long-drawn terrible moan, like the moan of a wild beast that has been wounded, and rushing to the bed she threw herself diagonally across it, and lay there, face down, her arms stretched out taut and stiff in front of her, and all her fingers extended.

After a minute or two that terrible moaning ceased. But her quietness was almost worse to No-man, for it seemed to draw a screen round her, like those hospital screens with which they isolate the beds of the dying. One little movement of hers was a relief to him, however. She clenched her fists. This seemed more natural. Those stiff extended fingers had been ghastly.

But he couldn't escape a sickening fear as he saw her lying there. Suppose the reaction from this business of the child were to drive her insane? He walked slowly around the foot of the bed; stepping gingerly, as if a careless movement might do irretrievable harm.

Standing close to her clenched hands he noticed how blue the veins looked and how sharp and white the knuckles were. But how innocent of the whole situation was her straggling brown hair! He longed to appeal to it—his old playmate of so many amorous nights. What had it done to be tangled and disarranged like this?

And then as he looked down at her prostrate head, which lay a little lower than his navel, he realized grimly that their two figures, the perpendicular one and the horizontal one, assumed in that position the shape of a headless cross.

He surveyed her form, extended so piteously across the bed, and he had the feeling that he was dealing with this wounded body rather than with any conscious mind. *There* was the head he knew so well, but he felt as if the curves of her back, the outline of her limbs under her skirt, her prostrate legs and upturned heels, had substituted themselves for the conscious brain

281

of his Wizzie. They were there *instead* of the girl he knew, and they were all he could appeal to!

Suddenly the sight of the inverted heels of her shoes as they lay turned up at the ceiling, stabbed him to the heart. They looked so grotesque and yet with such a lot of life of their own in them. They looked as if they wanted to dance on the ceiling. They looked as if they wanted to trip off and away and dance on many ceilings! And yet they held so much, so much more than any other part of her, of her intimate woman's life. They were what she tapped the floor with under the table. They were what she ran down the stairs on. They were what held her up, as she stretched her muscles when she was alone, as she made her secret faces in the glass.

And this body extended in front of him had given birth to the unknown body of Lovie! Old Funky had done for this woman's body what he wasn't man enough to do! But it wasn't *that* that bothered him. He felt that he now knew why she was often so sad. A piece of her had been torn away from her; and it was her fear of his knowing about this that had doomed her to her wretched half-life. The virtuous Old Funkys of Mary Channing's time had killed Mary and her unborn child together; and the wicked Dud—though he hadn't known it—had put *his* girl's child away!

What *was* it that made those clenched hands and prostrate head so precious to him? Jenny had accused him of having no feeling. What was it to "have feeling"? What would a person with "feeling" do now?

"Wizz, Wizz," he began again, "little Wizz! Look up and speak to me. I've no right to hold anything against you. I've *nothing* against you! We'll go to-morrow to Yeovil and get hold of Lovie. Jenny won't mind her being here with us."

But there was no answer from the form stretched across the bed, no answer from the tense white knuckles, no answer from that figure that Old Funky had found so " 'lurin'," no answer from the stiff girlish shape that in its prone position had become —in conjunction with his own lean frame—such a beautiful example of the letter "T"! "What *would* a person who had 'feeling'," he thought, "do at this juncture? Lift her up in his arms? Argue with her? Beat her?"

In place of doing any of these things he recommenced his

feeble murmurings, more as if they were addressed to himself than to her. "You know I do love you, Wizz, don't you? I may not be good at showing it, as some men could, but you've grown into me, Wizz, my only one; you've grown into me!"

The girl on the bed made no answer; and it was unlucky that at that second, as he lifted his head, he encountered the "humiliated and offended" look of Thuella's portrait of Teucer Wye.

"If you can't be a man," Mr. Wye's expression said, "the best thing for you to do is to read Plato."

7

LOVIE

"BETTER put on my grey dress," thought Wizzie a couple of days later, as, about eleven o'clock, she awaited the return of D. No-man from his High East Street room.

"And better put on my new underclothes with it," she added hastily to herself, as attired in nothing but her slip, and with bare arms and feet, she moved from her cupboard to her chest of drawers and back to her cupboard.

"But what's the use? What the hell's the use?" were the sentences that the girl's inmost consciousness kept reiterating as she sat on the bed and pulled on a pair of new stockings, stockings even newer than the underclothes.

In the process she was now engaged upon it was natural enough that she should note what certainly was the unequalled beauty of her limbs. "Soft . . ." she murmured aloud, as she let her fingers stray pensively along her thigh, "soft as any damned school-miss." She leaned forward more intently and passed her hands over her muscles. Then she gave a glance at herself in the mirror. For a moment she saw herself as she used to be when in those wretched tights and that loin-cloth of red plush she was ready to rush into the tent and jump on her horse's back. Those tights, and the gaudy beads she had to wear along with them, were detestable to her, but far worse was that bit of red plush.

283

When she put *that* on she used to feel as if she were going to be a mark and a mockery before a jeering crowd. But in spite of these absurd gauds she well remembered how proud she used to be of her figure. She remembered how taut and tense every muscle of her body was and in such perfect training. Yes, in those days her whole frame was as lissom, as supple, as plastic to every strain she laid upon it, as the body of a ballet-dancer. She sighed heavily as she lowered her eyes and completed the business of fastening up her stockings. "What's the use?"

Shaking down her soft grey skirt and smoothing it carefully round her hips and flanks with her fingers, twisting about as she did so with sideways glances at the looking-glass, she made little forlorn whistlings, not bothering to screw up her mouth to do it properly, but just enough to do it audibly. The top of the old-fashioned looking-glass standing on the chest of drawers had ornamental carvings on each side of it that resembled ears. It also had two carved holes in the crown of its woodwork which possessed a faint likeness to eyes.

Thus the demon-artist who, in spite of the neatest house-keepers, can give to the scatterings of chance in the arrange-ments of human rooms a mischievous twist of its own, brought it about that the glassy portion of Wizzie's mirror—that world of unexpurgated reality which is yet *not quite* the same as the ordinary one outside—should represent, as it stood there, an enormous gaping mouth.

It was in this mouth, beneath the unsympathetic leer of a pair of low-lidded eyes, and beneath the suspicious pricking-up of a pair of alert ears, that Wizzie's person had to appear whenever she made her toilet. "What's the use?" was still the weary burden of her consciousness as she presently fixed upon her head the fashionable hat of the Cumber party and smoothed back her hair below it with quick deft touches.

A glow of faint satisfaction warmed her pale cheeks as she did this, to think of the shock her ladylike appearance would be to the Urgans and their entourage.

"How Popsy will stare!" she thought. "She won't like it a bit! She'll be sick with envy—the little fool!"

When she was ready to go she sat down by the fire and slowly pulled on her gloves with her eyes on the bright flames. As she did this she glanced at her wrist-watch, her Easter present from D. No-man, and was annoyed to find that it still lacked five or six minutes of eleven, when No-man was to call for her.

"I suppose Lovie will be able to walk back," she thought. "Perhaps I ought to have let him bring the pram; but we'd look so silly wheeling it empty through the streets." And her mind reverted to a certain annoying scene of the day before, when Jenny had supported D. No-man in his insistence on purchasing this indispensable adjunct of a child's life.

"I'm not going to put up with it," she said to herself, "if he goes on making all this fuss. You'd think Lovie was the only kid in Dorchester. No, I'll have to make a stand at the start. I'm not going to have him interfering, messing about with the kid, and spoiling her, and turning her against me. If he's set on having her with us he must take the consequences. He's not her father." Her mind reverted again to the perambulator. "Silly!" she thought. "Kids of three are too big for prams."

But the consideration that D. No-man *wasn't* Lovie's father switched her mind to the man who was, and with one glove on and one glove off and staring at the fire, she became lost to every conscious thought but the sick hatred that was now, and had been for the last three years, her dominant obsession.

Up it rose, that familiar demon, that terrible "worm i' the bud" that had come to be the gnaw and the fret of all her real existence; and as she mechanically began yielding between gloved fingers and bare knuckles to her accustomed habit, and as she broke this off for a second to stoop over the hem of her elegant skirt and pick a wisp of cotton from its edge, the almost insane landscape of her tragedy took its implacable shape.

She saw herself, she felt herself, she knew herself, a real artist, after those years of unwearied labour, in the art that was her life; and she saw Old Funky, like a maggot in the rose of that life, withering her petals, her stamens, the very calyx of her being, so that only an empty husk was left, and the seed— the seed!

No one watching the girl as she sat there in her pretty clothes and neat shoes, and with as refined a lady's "purse" as could be bought in Dorchester on her soft lap, would have guessed for a moment what dark thoughts they were that made her frown. That frown had always been sometimes visible, even when, so to say, she wasn't frowning; but now it never for a moment disappeared. Even D. No-man had noticed it of late, and had said to himself, "She's frowning in her sleep." But she wasn't frowning in her sleep. Those two small lines were always there now. They were there when the image of Old Funky was completely swallowed up in kindly oblivion. Especially might such an on-looker have been deceived by the natural way she glanced at the watch on her wrist.

But perhaps a woman wouldn't have been deceived by that! So large a part do these tiny fate-hammers play in the lives of most owners of the small wrists held up to reveal their message that a girl on the way to execution might well look at her watch, *not* to see how much longer she had to live, but simply because, after adjusting her hat and smoothing out the wrinkles in her gloves, it had become an automatic gesture.

Thus though she felt no impatience with regard to D. No-man turning up—indeed her impression of her own feelings was that she would have taken it very calmly had he *never* turned up—it was inevitable that she should lift her elbow more than once in its tight-fitting sleeve to glance mechanically at her wrist. But her thoughts about Old Funky were always in the back of her brain. Whenever she had a moment to herself—unless in the middle of a blood-curdling novelette, and not always even then—Old Funky would sit down with her, or lie down with her, or stare out of her looking-glass by the side of her own face.

On the occasion of Nance's recent visit to Friary Lane Mrs. Dearth had encountered the visitor's praise of No-man by extravagant praise of Wizzie. How much Wizzie had confided in her of her past life Jenny revealed to none: but if she *had* known about Old Funky and about the existence of Lovie, what she had thought of it all can easily be imagined! Wizzie to her was a girl in whom sex-instinct and the maternal instinct were under-developed, a girl for whom the first experience of sex-violence had been a shock from which recovery, if it ever really came, would be very slow.

"Love, and love alone," Jenny would have said: "can obliterate such memories. The poor thing's ignorance of sex coincided with her whole-hearted devotion to the circus-ring, and the man must have taken advantage of that."

Jenny did reveal to Nance that in her opinion Wizzie's circus-man had been a first-rate teacher, and that, if he *did* take advantage of her, it was his hold on her *as* a teacher that had given him his opportunity. "When a girl like Wizz," she assured Nance: "has had a shock of that kind, it's like a wedge of iron in her soul. It starts a brooding hatred that can sap the very spring of life."

Mrs. Dearth's view of the case, though based on imperfect knowledge was not an unreasonable one. The birth of Wizzie's child had been to her like the madness of a fever.

No-man's wild imagination had indeed not been far from the truth when the lurid idea of infanticide crossed his mind. At the beginning in her feverish agitation, she had not been able to endure the sight of the little creature, and it had needed all the old wife's astuteness to avert worse scandal than a birth in her caravan. Nothing but the blind impulse of the healthy young animal in Wizzie's blood had kept her from complete despair.

Her hatred for Old Funky had all the same grown to such unbalanced proportions that she would spend hours inventing complicated schemes of revenge. Indeed, when No-man took her away, her mood had not been at all unlike what that quixotic sensualist wanted to imagine it. She *had* let him carry her off in the benumbed unquestioning passivity of a "Bronze-Age captive." Had the good man, however, brought down his Cerne-Giant club on the head of her enemy, it would have jumped better with her feeling than having to run away, but as it was, this lean staring gentleman with his obscure talk was at least a new "court card" in her wretched pack; and after all a man at her side *was* a man at her side, and she had no divining-rod to sound the abysses of this particular man's limitations.

If Old Funky—who wasn't, as she well knew, nearly as old as his name sounded—hadn't so fatally intertwined himself with her passion for her work her feelings would have been different.

If only she could have left the whole lot of them and started her life fresh in another Circus!

But she wasn't, herself, her free independent self, any more. In some damnable way her work and Old Funky were blent together. He had trained her too assiduously, too patiently, the old devil! Not a curve of her frame, not a muscle, not a supple-ness, not a quivering balance, not a poise, not a motion, not a

287

turn, not a twist of her young body, but he had watched develop with the eyes of a lynx! If only she had had another trainer, if only her work hadn't been work on her own body, if only she could have done it for herself without him, she would now be able to put him out of her mind and let all he had done to her go to the devil! His taking of her then would have remained as a fever-memory, a horrible unreal illness, a passing madness. All could yet have been well if only he hadn't been the one who had made her what she was. No acrobat, no dancer ever had such a training! That man was *born* to train her, and she had responded to his persistency with a perseverance that only he could evoke. He had made her a flawless—a perfect instrument. She knew it. And all for nothing!

Oh, why didn't D. No-man come? He ought to know by now that she couldn't bear being kept waiting. But it was just like him—lost in that ridiculous book! If he couldn't do anything but write to earn his living, why couldn't he write something that a person could read?

With a childish movement then, just like a little girl who ought to be doing home lessons instead of "spoiling her eyesight," she slipped her fingers—the ones bare of her grand gloves—under the cushion of her armchair and brought out a tattered story-periodical. The discoloured pages of this unliterary pamphlet she now began hurriedly to turn, wetting the tip of her first finger at her lip to expedite matters and assuming an expression of placid achievement when she found the page with the corner turned down. Then heedless about creasing the flimsy ladylike dress that was to be her revenge, she pulled up her feet beneath her and settled herself to read, holding the paper, for she was short-sighted and the print was microscopic, close to her face.

She hadn't submerged herself however for more than a couple of minutes in *The Adventures of Lily Turnstile*, when she heard the front door open and shut and No-man's steps in the passage.

Under the cushion again went Miss Turnstile, for though she knew that he was aware of her passion for such thrilling tales, she had a feeling that it was more appropriate and more in keeping with her hat and her shoes to be found idling by the fire than absorbed in such reading. It was part, too, of her instinctive system with D. No-man to emphasize her romantic desolation. It helped to make him polite and concerned, and while it stopped his asking futile questions, it kept him—or so Wizzie fancied, judging by Lily Turnstile, who drove her infatuated count to slavish obsequiousness by such a demeanour —on the sort of tenter-hooks on which elderly protectors of young ladies ought to be kept, if their interest was to be preserved.

Her glove was being hurriedly pulled on and her feet were no longer in the chair when the door opened and No-man entered.

"Good girl! You're all ready, I see," was his greeting; and then : "But I *say*, sweetheart, how lovely you look! Lovie will be simply thrilled to see you."

If he hadn't said *just* that—though by this time she ought to have grown accustomed to his stupidity which made Lily's count seem a veritable thought-reader—she'd have probably smiled and let him kiss her lips.

"I never told you, old girl," D. No-man remarked as they went down the narrow street which in her rebellious mind—so often had her companion tired her by his praise of its antiquity —she had come to call "Itching" Way, "that I saw a Circus there when I came back with Uryen from Maiden Castle; only of course I couldn't tell it was our foreign Circus, but I *thought* it might be, only I remembered how you said that none of them—— Think of our having only met each other last November! I feel as if I'd known you all my life, old thing. Don't *you* feel like that?"

What Wizzie felt—as stirred, apparently by the thought of their first encounter he clutched the tightly-sleeved grey arm at his side—was a nervous irritation that was almost unbearable. Why couldn't he see that the idea of having Lovie hung round her neck, like the albatross in *Gems of Standard Poetry*, was the last straw? And why, when he got into this mood, did he always call her "old girl" and "old thing," instead of by her name?

It was not till they were at the station gates that he dropped her arm. She glanced furtively at his profile. He was evidently pulling himself together, to do what wasn't easy for him.

"Listen, D. No-man, will you do something for me?"

"If it's not to make a row with these people! Certainly I will, my sweet."

"Do you mind. D., just for once, just for *this* time, making out we're married? It'll be easier to get Lovie away then."

The man was silent for a second. He evidently didn't want to do it. Oh, it was just like him—a little thing like that! Then he stopped, and *she* had to stop. That was a bad sign. No! he wouldn't do it. He always stopped like this when he was going to give some roundabout reason why he wouldn't do what she wanted.

"What's the idea, kid?" he inquired. "It's not their business whether we're married or not. *You* don't want to be married, do you? You've always said—at least I thought you've always meant——"

"Only to *them*, D., only to *them*! It'll make it so much easier."

"I don't know what concern it is of theirs. I'm going to adopt the child. The letter said 'adopt.' That was *their* word. Are you thinking they won't consider me respectable enough to take a child they were going to put into the workhouse?"

It was Wizzie's turn to be silent now, but as he watched her he saw her lower lip began to quiver and the familiar wrinkles appear that meant she was about to cry. "Oh, if you're going to take it as hard as that, child," he cried hastily, "I'll do anything you want. I know it's wretched for you, all this business. I don't like it very much myself; but it's only right we should have the poor little thing There, there, my darling one, my precious one, don't 'ee cry. Sure I'll say we're married. I'll say I got a special licence last November. I'll say we were married last week by the Bishop of Salisbury. I'll say *anything* if you'll only be a brave girl now, and let's get this damned business over!

"It's—only—to—say," murmured Wizzie, drawing the back of one of her wrists across her cheek, "just once—anything you like—that makes them think we're married—but if you don't want to——"

The harsh-gay noise of the Circus now reduced them both to silence and they entered the fair-field. Threading their way between a couple of gipsy-carts they soon found the Urgan caravan and with composed faces and all the assurance they could assume they mounted the steps side by side.

It was clear they were expected, for there was Mummy Urgan in her best black gown and all her jet beads, and there was Popsy in her stage finery, and there too, dressed in a manner more suited to a little acrobat than a child of three was Lovie herself! The small creature was sitting on the knees of Old Funky, who himself, attired in his usual tight-fitting green-black coat, sat on the bed.

The little girl turned her head away as soon as the strangers entered and flinging her arms round her father's neck, burst into a fit of sobbing.

It became plain at once that the child had been told that she was to be taken away by these unknown people, and Wizzie's first thought—and she was too unanalytical to be surprised at anything she felt—was a wave of dark anger with them "for making it so hard for a baby to go with its own mother." She herself was so absorbed in taking in her child's appearance—yes, thank goodness! Lovie certainly *was* very, very pretty, and Jenny would make a fine fuss of her and how nice it would be to buy her clothes with Jenny, and "Thel" would change her mind when she saw her, about never having a baby—that it was with less than half of her consciousness that she caught the look of deadly malevolence that the child's father cast on her companion.

"Mornin' to 'ee, Mister!" murmured Old Funky hoarsely. "Mornin', *Madam*!" This last word was uttered with a sarcasm so biting that Wizzie threw at No-man a glance that was at once imperious and beseeching.

"*Mrs. No-man and I,*" began that gentleman, laying down his cudgel on the foot of the bed, "have come, as you see, ready to take this little one—— That *is* Lovie, I suppose? No, no, don't cry, little girl! The man's very fond of little girls. The man will be very kind to little Lovie. The man'll give her such a lot of pretty things. The man'll give Lovie a big doll with eyes that can shut!"

While he uttered these words, to Wizzie's complete astonishment D. No-man bent over Old Funky and caressed the sobbing child, stroking its brown curls. Beneath his forward-bending figure she noticed that Old Funky had shut his eyes and was silently murmuring—without making any audible sound—some rigmarole of his own.

291

What struck her as odd was that the child, though it still sobbed quietly, dropped its hold on the old man's neck and turned its blubbered face towards the stranger.

But a still greater surprise awaited her; for not content with this advantage, D. No-man, with one bold swing, lifted the little thing bodily from the Circus-man's arms and began swaying it to and fro, hushing its sobs against his chest with a series of singsong murmurs, such as: "There's Lovie! There's little Lovie! There's the man's Lovie!" a performance that clearly had a most comforting effect.

It was Mummy Urgan who intervened now, interrupting a nervous and timid advance which the bedizened Popsy had begun to make to Lovie's fashionably dressed mother.

"Better take her straight off, straight away—there's a dear gentleman," whispered the old lady. "I've had a trouble enough to get him round to this, and if the child have took to 'ee, as seems it has, and 'tis plain you be wondrous smart with childer, the sooner you're out o' here and well away, the better for all! Give your missus the money you've a-brought, and if 'tis a 'fiver'—I told 'un a 'fiver' *twould* be—I'll say you *be* a real gent—and don't 'ee let——" By this time No-man had been hustled so hastily to the door that it was not till he was bearing the gleaming little personage down the steps that he handed the woman his precious wallet.

Nor was it Lovie who stretched out her arms to Old Funky, but Old Funky who stretched out his arms to Lovie. Such at least seemed the explanation of a spasmodic jerk, like the jerk of a frog, made by the figure sitting on the bed, a futile jerk, that ended only in the same incoherent gibble-gabble, with shut eyes and sucked-in-lips, that the old man had been engaged upon when they first entered the caravan.

"Don't 'ee let she hit her nor spend she's tempers on her, Mister!" were the last words Wizzie heard through the caravan-door as Grummer Urgan came back with the precious wallet. The girl did her best to carry off her amazement at seeing this object in the woman's hands, and she promptly opened it with the most natural air, not even concealing the fact that it contained another "fiver" in addition to the one she now extracted.

Meanwhile Old Funky had stopped making obscure noises, and had opened his eyes. Before he consented to receive the bank-note however, which his wife held out to him, he seemed to find it imperative to give weight and permanence to his feelings in some sort of solemn ritual. He rushed accordingly to the caravan-door, which Grummer had closed on her return, and reopening it sank down on his knees there and lifted both fists—the thumbs compressed within the fingers—straight into the air, where he caused them to quiver and shake with the passion of the curse he sent after Wizzie's friend.

That no one could hear a word he uttered made no difference, for had the words of Old Funky's curse been heard by everybody they would have been totally incoherent. The phrase "rats and gall" might have been caught together with something about "maggots and gizzard"; and to a very strained ear, in the midst of that whirligig din, there might have come syllables that sounded like "the worms of Herod" and "the lice of Pharaoh." But beyond a wish that No-man should quench his thirst with the urine of dogs, and have sand for bread, and that his bowels should burst with those of Judas, and his skin itch with the scabs of Job, it would have been the general drift, rather than any particular details, that the hearers would have carried away.

More articulate perhaps at the end, before the distracted old man scrambled to his feet, would have sounded his vague but reiterated prediction that No-man hadn't done with him yet, that he would in fact make him eat with Old Funky, drink with Old Funky, lie down with Old Funky, till he should pray "for 'Pummery' to cover him," and for "Maumbury to hide him," and for "the fishes of Chesil to carry him quick into the pit!"

Having got possession of the "fiver," and watched No-man's precious pocket-book being hidden away from sight in Wizzie's purse, Mummy Urgan greeted her husband's return from the top of the steps. "You and Popsy best be off to show now. What's the matter with 'ee then? Doesn't 'ee mind what us 'cided on? Hasn't us argied long enough about her going with she? What be up to then? What be mumbling about? 'Twas thee bubbled us into all this brabblement; and 'tis lucky I've got a head on me, or Lordy knows *where* us 'ud be by now! In jail maybe, for all *you* gone and done!"

Old Funky made no reply. If he wasn't by rights as old as his name he looked a deal older as he squatted down on the bed and shut his eyes. Many people when things have been too much for them, or when they've received an overwhelming shock, follow the example of Julius Caesar and hide their eyes; but Old Funky neither "muffled his face in his mantle" nor brazened it out. He just sat on that bed, the bed where Wizz had given birth to Lovie, with his lips working like a monkey's and kept his eyes tight shut. He hadn't cast a single glance at her since she entered the caravan, and this piqued her in some curious manner; and as she stood talking to Mrs. Urgan and Popsy, with the caravan-door swinging on its hinges in the wind, she edged round a trifle so as to keep that figure on the bed in sight.

"What a silly softy I am!" she said to herself. "I *hoped* he'd be funny over Lovie going, the dirty devil, and now he does this and it makes me kind of want to cry. I'd *like* to cry—that's what I'd like! I'd like to cry and cry, *and yet* take Lovie away! I'd like him to hold Lovie like he was just now every day, and me to come and take her away every day! Mercy! how he looks, with his eyes all pinched-up and his mouth working! That night when he got hold of me his wig fell off. It was like scrabbling at a slippery egg when I pushed his head away. I *could* have broken loose altogether. I *could* have thrown him on the ground and run out, just as I was. But I only kept pushing his head away and digging my nails into it till I felt all weak. He's got the marks of my nails though, I bet a tanner, under that wig, and somewhere else, too. My! I let him have it! Yes, you ugly, dirty little devil, you'd better screw up your eyes and work your chin. Yes! 'twas me, your little Wizzipeg, what you thumped and tickled and cursed and petted and made her muscles ever so, and her balance never to be beat, what took Lovie away! And I'm going to *keep* Lovie away too. Never— never—never will you see Lovie again. *See* her? Oh, well, per- haps I'll just let you *see* her. Maybe when I'm wheeling her, in her pretty pram, down South Walk one hot day, with my para- sol and my magazine, and my nice muslin dress, there'll *you* be, you dirty little devil, with your Frenchified tail and your shaky pins and your Wizzipeg's nail-marks under your wig. And you'll say to yourself then : 'O, and if I had my own child Lovie, to eddicate, like I eddicated her mummy, for show-riding, how blest I'd be!' And if I just nod to you in passing—for of course I shan't *speak* to you, and you'll know it would be impossible to

294

speak to Lovie—you'll think to yourself: 'There goes No-man's girl and his girl's girl—how happy they look!'

"My! If you're not beginning to cry, you ugly funny little man! And I could cry myself and that's the truth; for I'd sooner be in the Circus, you bald-headed old devil, with you clapping your hands and the crowd hullo-ing than walking dumb and mum along of him, and him droning on about how they burnt Mary what's-her-name, and how the history women worshipped bulls and how he and me were sweethearts before history began."

But she mustn't go on peeping at Old Funky across Grummer's heaving bosom. She must listen politely, and like a lady, to Popsy's chatter. "No," she now found the spirit to say in a clear firm voice to Popsy, "no, I never regret my marriage. My husband writes very interesting books; and we talk a lot about them, about history and the old days, and he asks my advice, though of course I don't know much *yet*, and we go walks up Lovers' Lane in the afternoons. I expect you know Lovers' Lane, Popsy? There's a gate, a little way up, that looks over a pond and an ash-tree. Mr. No-man and I often look over that gate."

Wizzie's volubility was now rewarded, though in truth she hardly knew what she was saying; for Old Funky opened his eyes and their glances met.

Once having met, it seemed to the girl that it was extraordinarily difficult for both of them to look away. They could only stare; and this they did, mute, bewildered, hypnotized. "Yes, it's a very nice lane as you say, Popsy. You said you knew it, didn't you? And it's nice leaning over that gate, isn't it, by that pond?"

But Popsy, though she knew Lovers' Lane, had apparently never noticed the pond. "Can you see yourself in it?" she asked innocently. "I like seeing my face upside down, and it looking at me."

It transpired, however, that Grummer Urgan *had* known the Lovers'-Lane pond in former days, though not for twenty or thirty years. "But in *my* time you certainly couldn't see your face in it. You couldn't see *anything* in it, but green slime. In my time girls were frightened of it. 'Twere quite a game with *our* young men to lift we over gate and pull we towards thik green pond. 'Twere only a very little pond, s'know; no more nor a girt hole in ground under thik ash-tree, but 'twere turble-deep.

"Sookey Marabout, and don't 'ee say"—this was addressed not to Lovie's mother but to her father—"thee don't mind Sookey Marabout, Father, for you were mighty taken wi' she in them days. *She* used to tell us how when her grand-dad, what lived up that way, towards Pigeon Barn, worked at bottom of thik green pond, it hadn't no bottom, but just went down and down. 'You'd have come out in Australy, Sookey,' her grand-dad said, 'if you tied your pinny up wi' quarry-stones and dived in; and what's more,' 'a said, 'thee'd have to take care, Sookey, that 'a went in with thee's head and heels fixed proper, according to geography rules, for't be wondrous, they do say, how travelling down turns into travelling up when you be going to Australy. It have to do wi' volcannies what be down there. They be turble rough with a maid, wi' stones in her pinny, travelling to Australy, they volcannies be!"

Old Funky sat up at last and said his say. "The old hoss," he began, and this word alone made the girl relax and move a step towards him, "the old hoss—have—pined—and pined—for 'ee, Wizz. *Her* can't no more manage 'un than my old 'ooman can. 'Tis—a wonder us—don't—hear 'un stamping and neighing for 'ee now! I'se warrant he knows right enough ye be in caravan!"

Wizzie's eyes opened to their fullest extent. Her mouth twisted. The old woman, watching her, evidently expected a fit of hysterics, but even she could not know how great was the lump that rose in the girl's throat.

As she struggled against that great lump, which *wouldn't* down, her heart made the maddest leap it had made that day. "Suppose I stayed here," her heart whispered, "and rode him again to-night? And rode him to-morrow, and never stopped riding him, till we were both dead! I'm proper fond of my old D., and I hate *you* to hell, you filthy old monkey, but—but—suppose I never went back? *He'd* look after Lovie and I should be gone!"

And then her body, below, oh! deep below her beating heart, must needs add *its* moan to that sobbing lump under the lace frills that Popsy envied. "At least you were man enough to take me," her body cried. "*You* didn't play doll with *me*. You wanted me, me down in here, me to the bottom of hell. And that made me weak, and you got me, got me and gave me Lovie! You were a man, anyhow, you old devil! *You* didn't care how I fought. You didn't care if you did get my nail-marks under your wig." Oh, but it would burst, that lump in her throat, in another second.

"Good-bye, Mrs. Urgan! Good-bye, Popsy, old sport! Good-bye you over there! Can't you take a girl's hand, then, who hates you so, and who'll never, *never* forgive you? That's all you can do, is it—sit on your bed and shut your eyes? I wish *I* could shut my eyes and see nothing—see nothing forever! Good-bye, good-bye, all! *Mr. No-man's waiting for me.* My husband, Mr. D. No-man, is waiting for me with Lovie."

She was out of the caravan and down the steps before Popsy had time to utter a word, before Mummy Urgan had time to shake Old Funky by the arm and tell him the "fiver" anyway was safe. She was out and down the steps just in time, just in time for the lump not to break in their sight. "Did I look hard and cold and cruel to him?" she thought. "Did he think I was *all Mrs. No-man*? Did he think I wouldn't give Lovie no meat, wouldn't let her skip and jump, wouldn't let her 'turn wheels' in her fine clothes? I hope he did. No, no, *no*, I don't hope he did. But oh, the old filthy devil, how like a monkey he looked! But *he* didn't stop because I fought. *He* didn't stop because I dug my nails into his bald head. He went on. He went on till he'd given me Lovie. So I *have* known a man, though I *am* Mrs. No-man!"

All this while, though she didn't know it, she was running so fast that her little black hat was blown all to one side. But just as she reached the exit from the fair-field the whirligig engine stopped; and in the sudden silence, as she stood there panting and straightening her hat, for everyone was staring at her and she wanted to swallow the lump and get her breath, there *did* come, quite unmistakably to her trained ears, the sound of a horse's whinny.

At this sound she swung round and started running back. Who but she knew the exact place where he was now, with the show starting? As she ran, her eyes must have looked so wild and so fixed, and her face, between the new hat and the new dress, must have looked so distorted that people nudged each

297

other and turned to stare after her. But there, where she knew she *would* find him, she found him! A lad she'd never seen before was leading him out, ready for the show, but her fashionable dress awed the boy, and he only drew back and gaped helplessly at what he saw.

For the great lump in her throat had burst now, burst at last, and as her tears rained down on the old horse's neck her arms were round him, her convulsed cheek against him. Her hat might hang disregarded now from her dishevelled hair, her purse might slip to the ground. Her life was her life again, as it had not been since All Souls' Day. The old horse kept making a pitiful bowing movement with his head, but from tail to ears he knew her, gave himself up absolutely to her, while long shivering spasms of contentment trembled through his frame.

No barrier divided her girl's body from the horse's body. Her pretty clothes were nothing. *His* gay trappings were nothing. Her shaking sobs were his, her flowing tears were his, and the wetness of her mouth, as with lips apart she pressed her face against him, mingled with the moisture and warmth of his hide.

But the lad who was watching all this suddenly seized his bridle. "Miss Popsy! Miss Popsy!" he cried. "Coom 'ee here quick, Miss! Coom 'ee here quick! Here be a lady loving thee's hoss like 'a were human! Coom quick, Missy! Coom quick!"

Wizzie's hat as well as her purse were on the ground by this time, and the lad still shouting to Popsy picked them up and thrust them hurriedly into her vacant hands. But the sight of the glittering Popsy's approach brought her to her senses. With one quick movement she pressed her wet face against her friend's nose; then letting the lad drag him round towards his approaching rider, she readjusted her hat, squeezed her purse against her breast, waved her hand to the girl, and walked steadily away without once looking back.

It was not till she reached the cenotaph—and how like No-man it was to wait for her when she might easily have gone straight up South Street and never seen him!—that she caught sight of the pair.

No-man was seated on a bench about a hundred yards up the avenue and Lovie was playing on the grass-border by his side. "He must have taken it for granted—*the fool*," she thought, "that because we came by his damned 'Itching' Street we'd have to go back by it! Couldn't he have had the wit to think I'd want to get a few things on our way, in the town? I can see already how it's going to be. I'm going to have all the bother of Lovie, and he's going to pet her and spoil her and make her troublesome!"

She got fairly close to them without being seen, for No-man's head was turned as he watched the little girl who was on the further side of him; but when she came near, it was the child who saw her first.

With one glance in her direction, Lovie, with both her small fists full of blades of grass that she had been picking, bolted helter-skelter to the man's knees where she promptly hid her face.

"Don't be so silly, Lovie! It's only me! You're not afraid of *me*, are you!"

Such were Miss Ravelston's first words in her new role of maternal authority, and Lovie hearing this querulous feminine voice behind her, in place of the indulgent chuckles of her elderly playmate, only buried her face the deeper between the man's knees, while her thin bare arms, each hand clutching its own handful of grass, lay stretched out along his thighs.

"Lovie, get up! Don't do that. Don't be so silly!" the girl cried; and when the only effect of her words was to cause Lovie's brown head almost to vanish out of sight, and to bring up No-man's arm with a careless swing into a protective position round the little girl's body, she stooped down impatiently, and shook the child's shoulder. "Lovie! Do what you're told! Don't wait for me to tell you twice. Get up at once. Didn't you hear me?"

But No-man took the child by the waist with both his hands and, lifting her from him, struggled to his feet, and held her high up in the air.

This abrupt action of his, in place of disturbing the small creature or making her angry, obviously delighted her. As a matter of fact it was the kind of thing Old Funky had done with her from her infancy; and Wizzie was soon to discover that all such rough-and-tumble games, especially when there was a touch of acrobatic daring in them, always quieted the child's nerves, quelled her naughtiness, and threw her into a trance of happiness.

299

On this occasion the man finished by perching her on his shoulder, but he was prevented from carrying her in this position by the sharp tone in which Wizzie bade him put her down, and also by the fact that he had left his great stick on the bench.

Once on the ground, however, Lovie fell into a grave and silent mood—Wizzie suspected she was beginning to feel the pinch of homesickness for the caravan and the whimsies of Old Funky—and offered no objection to walking solemnly between them, a hand in the hand of each. They advanced peacefully enough in this manner till they reached the end of South Walk and turned down No-man's favourite Icen Way. Here the little girl dragged a good deal, for though accustomed to rough-and-tumble games, she was evidently not used to walking, and it was to the accompaniment of forlorn little whinings, such as "Lovie's tired," "Lovie wants to go home," "Man carry Lovie," that they finally reached the street door of No-man's lodging.

Here—though Wizzie fancied he gave her an almost threatening look, as much as to say: "You just *dare* to treat her badly!"—he brought out his latch-key.

"Don't forget to have something to eat, yourself," he said gently, "when you and Jenny are getting her dinner. I'll do a little work, have a bit of a walk, and be with you for tea. About the usual time, eh? Well, good-bye, Lovie, my pretty! See you again soon."

So, for no more than the third time since she had become a mother, Wizzie found herself alone with the child of her womb. Queer how angry it made her feel to note the trembling lip and the wide-open frightened eyes with which the small creature saw the door shut upon D. No-man.

"I've got to pull myself together," she thought. "I'm in for it now, and *must* carry it through. Jenny'll be surprised how pretty she is. I'll take her over to Glymes in the pram as soon as I've got her some clothes. Why did he make me come this way? I meant to buy——"

But she decided since they were so near home to give up buying anything now till after Lovie had had a good meal. She had forgotten her door-key; and so, like D. No-man on a recent occasion, she was compelled to knock at the door and stand there in the narrow lane till someone should come.

She waited so long that she came to the conclusion that Mrs. Dearth must be out.

"She's run out to get something for Lovie's lunch," she said to herself. But what was she to do with the kid? It would be silly to go to a café when Jenny *must* be back any minute.

But her thoughts were interrupted by Claudius opening the door. "What—Mr. Cask!" she murmured. "Is anything wrong? I thought you were at the coal-yard. This is my little girl Lovie, Mr. Cask. Say 'How do you do' to Uncle Claudius, Lovie."

Claudius who was looking disturbed and upset, bowed gravely to the child as if she had been sixteen instead of three. "No," he replied, glancing nervously up and down the lane. "It's early closing, and he lets me go when *he* goes. He closes the yard on Thursdays, and goes to Weymouth with his wife. *She's* a very nice person, his wife is; she"—once more he threw one of his most searching glances up and down Friary Lane, for he was evidently extremely unwilling to be caught by Jenny in her house, though the connection between the two abodes was still kept open—"She," he went on, "is very interested in gold fish. She keeps them in a tank. They know her. They come to her. *You* would like to see some golden fish, wouldn't you, little girl? The Romans had aquariums of gold fish. Did you know *that*? And the Americans too, I understand, are very fond of them."

When they were inside and the street-door was shut, Wizzie saw that the backdoor at the end of the passage was wide open. This door led into the yard between their houses and it was clear that Jenny, in spite of their quarrel, had refrained from fastening it.

"I saw you from my front window," he murmured, whispering the words as if he were in church and looking wistfully through the half-open dining-room door at his old place by the fire, "and I knew she wasn't in, for I'd watched her go out."

Wizzie holding her child tightly by the hand and anxious to get her safely upstairs was all the same not quite impervious to this picture of Mr. Cask taking advantage of the early closing to watch his old friend's out-goings and incomings from his bachelor window. She surveyed the Roman physiognomy before her with more sympathy than usual. The horse-smell and horse-warmth that were still in her nostrils seemed to lend themselves to intercourse with this simple-minded man.

301

"He's got no one, now Jenny's turned against him," the girl thought, and in her present softened mood she was aware of a faint impulse to be nicer to Claudius than she'd been before. She felt he caught this softening in her, but she was unprepared for his next move.

"Come in a minute while you're waiting for her," he whispered earnestly; and then added humbly: "I'd like this little miss to see my airplane."

Normally Wizzie would have made an excuse and taken the child upstairs; but her experiences that morning had left her tender to any emotional appeal.

Holding Lovie by the hand she submissively followed the man out of the house, across the little intervening yard, and into his desolate front room.

There was his chair by the window! He had evidently been sitting at that point of observation for some time, waiting to get a glimpse of the wrathful Jenny, for the *Daily Worker* lay on the floor, and Wizzie noticed the end, reduced to the smallest possible dimensions, of this ascetic smoker's latest cigarette, lying on the window-sill.

Claudius brushed hurriedly with the flap of his coat the only other chair in the room and begged his visitors to be seated; and in her new mood of docility Wizzie sat obediently where he placed her and took Lovie on her lap.

Meanwhile Claudius shuffled across his littered room and came back with a model of an airplane in his arms. "Isn't this pretty?" he said addressing Lovie and waving the airplane up and down before the child's face so as to resemble a flight through the air.

Before very long Lovie had slipped off her mother's lap and was seated cross-legged on the floor playing some silent game of her own with the airplane, while Claudius was taking advantage of a woman's presence in his retreat to put various crucial questions to her about the preparation of cabbage, so that it should not be too unpalatable, and the washing of men's shirts, so that they should not lose altogether the shapes of their collars.

"There she is!" cried Claudius suddenly, drawing quickly back from the window out of which, for all his politeness, he had been constantly stealing anxious glances. "You'd better go," he added hurriedly and bluntly. "I don't want her to——" He stooped down and, picking up his airplane from the floor with one hand, gave the other to Lovie to help the child to her feet.

Wizzie smiled at his trepidation; and even Lovie, with one of those inexplicable flashes of clairvoyance that children display when you least expect it, looked straight into his eyes as soon as she was on her feet and said with intense deliberation: "My mummy likes it here and I likes it here, though there isn't no goldfishes."

Once more Claudius made the child a quaint little formal bow, such as he might have given to Wizzie herself. This gesture appeared eminently satisfactory to Lovie, who gave him a smile that made her small countenance resemble that of a fairy queen and Wizzie thought: "She likes Claudius for just the opposite reason from D. No-man. *He* tumbled her about while this one treats her like a princess. It must be one extreme or the other with her. Well! Perhaps I'm like that, too. D. No-man's never tumbled *me* about."

Back again in Mrs. Dearth's quarters, Jenny's behaviour to Lovie was as different from D. No-man's as it was from Claudius's. She treated the child in a calm, matter-of-fact way, as if little girls were as common as hips and haws, patting her hair, glancing suspiciously at her finery, picking up and dropping again between finger and thumb her chain of beads, and repeating in a rather reproachful voice, as if the child had done it herself, out of malice to her elders, that she was very big to be only three.

Lovie had never met anyone in the least resembling Mrs. Dearth, nor had she ever seen a woman before who was always busy about something and never "enjoying herself," and as for Jenny's calm, matter-of-fact way of treating her, it struck Wizzie that the small creature was waiting and watching to see what appalling adult vice this unemotional behaviour concealed.

What it concealed for Wizzie's own experienced observation was a gathering storm; nor had the mother and daughter been long upstairs together when Mrs. Dearth appeared at their door, her arms full of clothes.

These clothes, when they had been carefully laid out upon the bed, turned out to be a complete outfit for a little girl of three;

303

and it soon transpired that it was to make *these* purchases, and with no thought at all of the child's meal, that Jenny had been shopping for so long.

It was the clothes that precipitated the storm; for mingled with all of Wizzie's emotional reactions since the events in the Circus-field, and underlying all her softenings towards Claudius, had been the pleasurable anticipation of dressing up her daughter in pretty and suitable things.

And now, out of kindness of heart, but also, Wizzie suspected, out of a jealous desire to be the first to buy things for her friend's child, Jenny had taken the edge off this innocent pleasure.

In her vexation, Wizzie's athletic hands were more hasty and brusque than they ought to have been in removing from her daughter's person all the garish Urgan finery, and it was a pathetic little figure, with bare white arms and thin white petticoat, who was now plumped down in D. No-man's armchair by the fire.

There Lovie sat, with her legs hanging very straight and her round eyes fixed on the flames—there she sat through all that followed between "Mummy and the lady," there she sat remembering sadly what funny faces "Old Funk," as she had learnt to call him, used to make, to keep her amused when she was waiting for dinner. Her great hope now was that the polite gentleman who played with airplanes might be persuaded to substitute gold fish once in a way. But it had long passed the time for that happy moment when Old Funk and Popsy would come in, laughing and hungry, and the caravan would grow warm and snug and full of nice smells and when Grummer would tie on her bib and set her on her high chair.

Her new mummy had very grand clothes. She would like to wear clothes like her new mummy and she longed to see "them golden fishes," but "Lovie wants her dinner," and "Lovie wants to go home," she thought; but though she also thought: "Mummy'll be cross if Lovie cries," before she knew what was happening big, slow, quiet tears were running down her cheeks and dropping from her chin into her small lap.

"I thought you'd forget about early closing," Jenny was saying, "and so I got these things before the shop shut. I made sure you'd be pleased with them! *Don't* you like them? Would *you* have got different ones? You told me you didn't know—and I thought——"

"Oh, yes, they're very nice, Jenny. It was only that I wanted—— But I can get others later. These will do *nicely* now. But wouldn't white socks have been better? I never thought of stockings for her, but of course——"

"Oh, if you're only thinking of the modern fashion——"

"Yes, I know what you feel about all that—but I thought—and isn't this vest too long? She's got some sort of woollen thing on now under that little slip. Wouldn't it have been better—and I *had* thought of blue for her—though of course pink will *do,* just for now—but oughtn't her sash to go with——"

All the while this talk was going on, and the two women were picking up and laying down these little objects spread out on the bed, their nervous vexation against each other was mounting.

"I thought I'd find you *here*," Mrs. Dearth murmured presently; "but I saw where you were. He was on the look-out and made you go in. He spies on me all the time. He can't rest till he's got round everyone, and has everyone on his side. He's done it with D. No-man. D. No-man and he are thick as thieves now, whereas they *used,* if anything, to dislike each other. Anything to keep women down is their motto.

"It's funny how little anyone knows! I thought you were the last person in the world to join with him against me—but there it is! I was a fool to think what I did! It's natural enough—when a man pities himself so, and is so sure he's in the right—that he should try to wheedle a person's best friend away from them—but I *did* think—though of course I knew what D. No-man was—that you were different. I've just been a fool—that's what I've been."

As Jenny spoke, she mechanically held up in both her hands, against the light, the small vest she'd bought that morning; and Wizzie, even while she retorted, pinched it carefully with her fingers, thinking to herself: "It's not *all* wool. It's wool and cotton. I'm sure Grummer Urgan's put *all* wool against her skin."

"What put me wrong," Mrs. Dearth went on, "was not realizing all it meant, your being so sweet and submissive to D. No-man. Just because he takes his side, you must go and take his side! It's just as if you and D. No-man were married; that's

305

what I've got to learn to say to myself now. 'She's acting,' I must say to myself, 'as my Tom wanted *me* to act,' only I never would. I had too much spirit! She's acting like a good, patient, gentle, little wife!"

The two women were now examining the outdoor jacket and woollen cap that Jenny had purchased, and Wizzie, as she approached her offspring, to satisfy herself that both these things were, as she felt sure they were, a good deal too small, was worried to see the child's silent tears.

"She's hungry, the poor little mite," she thought. "I made sure Jenny would cook us a nice lunch. Instead of that——"

"Yes, it must be a funny feeling," Jenny continued, "to feel as afraid of a man and as slavish to a man as you've grown lately. But that's what a woman with any independence has to face. Her own friends desert her the minute she shows spirit."

"Well," said Wizzie with a sigh, "now that you *have* been so good, Jenny, as to buy these things for her, I think if you don't mind, I'll take her out to that tea-shop in High East Street just below No-man's place. I believe I'll go with her and see 'Thel' this afternoon. If you say I'm too good to No-man I may as well tell you what I think I'll do after we've had a bite to eat. I think I'll run up to that room of his and tell him Lovie and I are going out to Glymes if it stays fine, and may stay there for tea."

Jenny Dearth laid down on the bed the sash she held in her hand and, impervious to the fact that the child was just going to put the thing on, began scrupulously folding it, as if it were to be deposited in a cedar-chest for fifty years.

Wizzie's decision to take her daughter out was a bitter blow to her. Lovie's appearance on the scene had been more than an exciting event to Jenny. It had given her a solid new interest, independent of her grievance against Claudius. Thus the idea of being left alone for the rest of the day in Friary Lane, with Claudius free to spy on her from *his* solitary quarters, filled her with a sense of desolation.

Knowing well what her friend was feeling, but not at all inclined to spare her, Wizzie now went over to the fire, lifted Lovie out of her armchair and began to dress her on the hearth-rug in all her new clothes.

"I must say I can't quite understand," she now said to Jenny, leaving Lovie to stare for a moment into the flames while she crossed over to her dressing-table to get her big white comb for the child's curls, "what you have against Mr. Cask. I don't know anything about politics but I can't see myself quarrelling with D. No-man, even if he started calling himself an anarchist. I know how teasing men can be. Gracious! I've heard D. arguing with Mr. Quirm, till you'd have thought it was a matter of life and death, whether Maiden Castle was a town or a fort. Why do you look at me like that, Jenny?"

Jenny, erect by the table, folding and unfolding in her fingers the sash for the child's waist, had already assumed the look of indignant grievance which, according to D. No-man, made her face at once handsomer and more human.

"I'm not saying this because he was nice to me and Lovie. I'm saying it because—because we're friends, Jenny. I used to hear in the Circus, especially when they'd been drinking—and Mr. Cask never touches a drop—terrible rows all the time over politics; but it never bothered *me*! They like having their ideas, men do—it makes them feel—you know! And if you contradict them, like you must have contradicted *him,* it makes them obstinate and they go and do just what he's done, to make you feel—you know!"

It indeed seemed difficult for Jenny even to begin to say all *she* knew, and her tragic expression ruffled the maternal complacency of her friend's face.

"Neither you," she began, "nor anyone else knows *anything* about Claudius and me, so the sooner this silly talk stops the better! We've worked together for years, helping—oh! no one will ever know how many people! It's been *my life* to carry out his plans—all for helping people, and helping them in sensible, practical ways. He's been silly about it sometimes, I know, and people have been ungrateful, but we've gone on, gone on for years and years, steadily and in spite of everybody. It's—brought—us—nearer—together—than anyone has any idea of. And now—for a mere fancy, and to spite Dumbell, whom nobody, not even his wife, takes seriously, he goes and throws it all up! Do you know what he says now? No, you don't know; and none of you know, and none of you *want* to know! He says that charity's no good, that helping people's no good, that the only cure for everything is to become a Communist. And it isn't as if

307

the Communists want him. They don't! I know them. I've heard them talking to him. They're all for destroying things, for changing everything, and they stick at nothing! They don't want a man like Claudius who wouldn't hurt a fly. I tell you I know them and they're only playing with him and using him. Think of their letting him—a man like that and with a position like his—work in a coal-yard till he ruins his health. Is *that* their way of changing things? It'll kill *him*. That's all it will do. And—everything—will—be—the same—and he'll be dead. That's their precious 'Movement,' as they call it. Oh! it makes me sick to talk of it. Here were we two, working to help people, not for any silly idea, like what your drunken Circus-men quarrel about, but just to help them, and then Dumbell must come with his nonsense, that none of us have ever taken seriously—and—so—it—all happened—but what none of you understand is what it broke up. It—broke up—the most—pure —and—and spiritual friendship that's ever been. It wasn't—like —what—what people thought. We were more than just a man and a woman—we were *equals*, I tell you! He always listened to what I said. We were different from the rest of you. We were like one person! And now—just to get an advantage over a little idiot like Dumbell—all this ended! Sometimes I feel as if I couldn't——"

She broke off with a choking sound in her throat, and fell into a deep gulf of intense and miserable thinking, during which she kept winding the child's sash, like a bandage, round and round her arm.

Wizzie from her knees, as she bent over Lovie's little legs, gazed at her with puzzled astonishment.

"Sit still, I tell you, child! I suppose—Jenny—you haven't— ever—had—any *suspicions,* have you?"

Jenny came towards her, unwinding as she did so the sash from her arm, and the two women proceeded to fix it round the child's waist. Lifted hurriedly out of her chair, Lovie displayed in this transaction a good deal more concentration of mind than either of her elders. The escape of the slippery syllables "suspicion" into that thickly charged air caused the two pairs of eyes that encountered each other across the small figure standing on the rug to burn with a dangerous animation.

"*What do you mean?* Have you heard anything? I tell you if

I caught anyone breathing a single word about him in *that* way I'd soon let them know——"

"I may have heard things, and I may *not* have heard things," retorted Lovie's mother, tying and untying the sash at the child's back. "What I did was just to ask *you*, what *you* knew; so you needn't flare up so."

"I know what you're talking about," said Jenny in a low tense voice and Wizzie could see it was not easy for her to say the words. "You're talking about those Communist girls he meets at their crazy gatherings. Yes, I have some times"—here she lowered her voice so much and spoke with such suppressed emotion that even Lovie lifted her eyes from her sash and stared at her—"have sometimes thought that it *was* one of them that had got round him. But none of them come here. *That* I know, for I'm—and it's only right I should be—always on the watch."

As this crucial dialogue between her elders went on, however, Lovie's interest waned. It was the sort of thing she had listened to so often in the caravan between Grummy and Popsy, and now, looking about for something to play with—for the first thrill of the new clothes had passed—she picked up from the floor one of the torn halves of Old Funky's letter and scrambling back into the chair began tearing it into a faint resemblance to a doll. Lovie had never had a doll. The nearest approach to such a thing had been a sorrowful ape, swinging in a wire cage, but through tearing the wires asunder, she had made *something* of this, pretending sometimes it was Grummer and sometimes Old Funky, she had never committed her heart to it. But at this moment, weary of these human voices going on and on, she did sigh for "Monkey," and very soon, in a thin simulacrum scrawled with Old Funky's writing she apprehended the presence on her lap of an entity she promptly christened "Gwendolly," herself and this bit of paper becoming mother and child. It is interesting to note the physical positions that women instinctively take when their interest is absorbed, and D. Noman would have been amused to observe how Wizzie at this crucial moment stood in his own most spontaneous pose, her arm propped on the mantelpiece opposite Lovie's chair and beneath the picture of Teucer Wye.

"Why don't you get your father to come and live with you?"

she was now emboldened—perhaps by her position under Mr. Wye's picture—to fling out.

"Has No-man asked you to leave me?" was the retort to this.

"No, of course not—not *yet*, anyway—but you're always saying you'd like to have your father here and 'Thel' always says she'd like to be rid of him."

Wizzie was ashamed of herself the moment she had said this. She could feel her spiritual vision of that long self-lacerating road of her life, with the police station and the brewery chimney and the cenotaph and the Chestnut Walk, calling on her to "accept, accept, accept," receding into the distance, while this malicious remark brought her back to the very atmosphere she had renounced.

"If you're tired of being here it's easy to go!"

"I'm not tired of being here."

"What do you mean by my bringing father here, then? The only room he'd endure to be in is this one."

"I'm sorry, Jenny. You misunderstood me—I thought——"

But Jenny made no answer; and Wizzie recalled how a priest at the convent had told her once that she must never say anything that she couldn't imagine the Blessed Virgin saying. "It would have been better," she said to herself, "if he'd said 'feeling,' but what I feel now, my good Jenny, is a longing to shake you out of all this nonsense!"

"He hasn't changed one bit to *you*. It's you who've changed to him," she remarked.

Jenny stared wildly at her. "Sometimes," she said: "I wish he *would* kill himself at that yard and then we'd be at the worst!"

Wizzie removed her elbow from the mantelpiece and glanced at the girl among the water-lilies over their bed. She remembered looking at this picture that first night when she waited so long for No-man to come upstairs. How uneasy Mrs. Dearth's infatuation had made her at first! It had reminded her of Grummer's mania for younger women. In *her* case it had gradually been transferred to Popsy, though she was sure it had never quite died out, not even after *all that* with Old Funky, but in Jenny's case this quarrel with Claudius was what had ended it.

"It's my figure they like!" she said to herself as she contemplated the very different figure of the young woman among the lilies.

"It's the way I'm made, and the way I carry myself, and all that business that *he* put me through. It's not my face; for *that's* only passable once in a blue moon. Women certainly do like girls *whose bodies have been trained*, even when they're not like old Grummer was. But what tragedy-airs you do give yourself, Jenny, sitting on that table and swinging those old boots of yours as if you'd like to kick the house down!" And then, in spite of herself, Wizzie suddenly felt a stab of pitiful pathos, a stab that went through her like a bare bodkin, for she remembered how, when she'd teased her friend, as long ago as Christmas, about these old-fashioned boots of hers, which were the kind that had elastic at the sides, and might have belonged to her grandmother, Jenny had confessed that neither she nor Claudius ever bought new boots. "We get second-hand ones at sales," she told her: "and we try them on at home. He hasn't been into a shoemaker's for years, and the last *I* went into was with Dad and that's ages ago. He once came back in a pair of tramp's boots that he'd exchanged on the Bridport Road. I made him throw them away; but he wouldn't do it till I'd promised I'd stop wearing these."

"These" were the boots, with elastic at the sides, that were now being so viciously swayed up and down under the table, and something about their particular kind of middle-aged shabbiness, combined with a black scowl on Mrs. Dearth's rugged face, gave Wizzie a feeling as if—in some way she couldn't understand—Claudius *had* been cruel to her. "Perhaps all men are cruel to *all* women," she thought.

"He doesn't care now what I wear," Jenny had said: "so I thought I'd wear these boots with elastic sides—so as to save my others."

The two women, as they exchanged glances, now seemed to be trying desperately to plumb the depths of each other's real thoughts. In the silence between them little Lovie looked up from her extempore doll, and it was clear that her instinct told her that whatever their thoughts were she was left in the cold, for she suddenly burst out, in an evident rush of self-pity: "I want to go home. I want my dinner. I want Grummy."

311

"In a minute, Lovie," said her mother. "We're going out in a minute." And then, thrown into an unsympathetic mood once more by the thought of Jenny's neglect to prepare them a nice lunch, she ostentatiously stretched herself and yawned. "What *I* think is," she remarked carelessly : "Mr. Cask has spoilt you! If D. was as unselfish as he is I'd never have thought of going back to the Circus."

"I might have known it," said the other. "I was a fool to talk to you! Your life's been so different from ours and lived with such different people that you can't understand a love like ours. Love to you means only one thing—whereas to him and me, until he did this terrible thing——"

"But I can't see, Jenny, *what* he's done that's so terrible. Men *have* to have their ideas. It's like that bit of paper to Lovie. You were lucky in keeping him sensible so long, and managing him so well, but why you have to pick such a quarrel with him the moment he does anything!——"

Jenny's eyes flashed. "Well! go off to your restaurant and go quick!" She uttered the word "restaurant" with as much contempt as if she'd said, "You're a flighty circus-girl bent on dragging this poor little thing over to your precious friends at Glymes!" But she closed with a yet more palpable hit. "Why, if you've any spirit at all, you don't get a proper job on a proper stage, and show them that a woman's something better than a man's pet doll, is beyond me!"

This turning of the tables upon her own life confounded Wizzie, but curiously enough it made her feel troubled rather than angry. *Was* it possible that this noble resignation of hers was just weakness—just fear of making a struggle?

Seeing that she had made a hit with her last retort, Jenny slid down from her perch on the edge of the table and, sinking into a chair opposite Lovie's, covered her face with her hands. Her attack had one unexpected effect upon Wizzie, for that young woman, either in an instinctive desire to prove to herself that her detachment from her career was no mere negation, or actuated by a dim awakening in her of some long-suppressed feminine response to domestic life, grew suddenly aware that this room of hers, which she had hitherto treated so cavalierly and taken so much for granted, was a disgrace to the mother of a child in a new sash.

How well she knew every aspect of it, but only as she might have known a casual lodging in a town where she was working!

Hardly conscious of the complicated pressure of motives behind such a natural act, she moved over to the bed and, picking up Lovie's cast-off clothes that had been thrown across the head of it, began piling them up in a little heap and tidying up the disarranged pillows.

Catching sight of her own slippers, thrown down carelessly in the middle of the floor, she picked up these also, and placed them neatly side by side under the bed, on the very spot where, in one of their morning disagreements, she had kicked No-man's stick out of his reach.

Then she went over to the child and bending down gave another twist to the folds of one of her stockings, now converted into rather clumsy-looking socks. "Mummy's got *you* to take care of now—hasn't she, love?" she murmured, with her head bowed over the child's knees. "You tell Aunt Jenny that Mummy can't ride horses and wear tights and jump through hoops now she's got a little girl to look after."

"I—simply—can't—*understand* you," groaned Mrs. Dearth, removing her hands from her face; and her tone had more sorrow in it this time than anger. "But no one seems to care any more what I think! You used to agree to every word I said about your work and about not letting D. No-man thwart it. But of course we were friends *then*"—her voice became bitter again—"and of course that was before you went over to Ella. Well, take the pram I chose for you: put on the hat I found for you: carry your child to Ella in the clothes I spent a whole morning getting for you! It's just like what I've had to get used to in this place! He and I used always to say it took the Romans to keep the devils out of this town. He and I have always known that that Quirm man, over there, brings bad luck to everyone he comes near, by stirring up the old devils of this place. But go on—take your child to Ella and Quirm! Claudius and I used to say that if it hadn't been for that man Nance's boy would never have died. You'll find your precious Ella with him. Ella's always with him. That's what's making poor Nance run after D. No-man. But I'll say this much. If you're going to give up your life's work to look after children, you'd *better* look

313

after them. And the way to look after them in Dorchester is to keep them from people who stir up devils!"

With this as her final word, and not waiting for her friend's answer, the woman rose from her chair, moved to the door, opened and shut it quietly and went heavily and wearily down the stairs.

With the new pram waiting for them outside the shop, Wizzie and her little daughter partook of their belated refreshment in the bow-window of an upstairs tea-room almost directly opposite the house in High East Street where No-man had his attic. They shared an omelette and several pieces of bread and butter. Wizzie drank coffee, Lovie ginger beer; and they rounded off their meal by enjoying a full plateful each of bottled pears and cream.

Wizzie finished her dessert some while sooner than Lovie, and lighting a cigarette set herself to contemplate the attic-window at which the man was now sitting who had bought her from Old Funky for eighteen pounds. What a simpleton D. No-man was!

An actual smile, though it was only a faint one, crossed the girl's lips as she thought of various outstanding examples of the incredible simplicity of D. No-man's selfishness. She thought of all the nights—and there seemed five or six years of them instead of five or six months—during which at intervals that seemed to her "as regular as clockwork" she had submitted to D. No-man's excited caresses.

She extinguished her cigarette and lit another. The window of her tea-shop was not quite opposite D. No-man's house, and therefore, unless he actually leaned his head pretty far out, it was impossible to catch a glimpse of him.

"Think of his never once having asked me to go up to his rooms! Of course, I don't *want* to go. It's nothing to me what his rooms are like. But it does seem odd, and Jenny once said it proved beyond question that he didn't really love me. Jenny said that men when they really love us always want us in their rooms, so as to have the scent of us left there, and the feeling of us, and the thought of how we looked and what we said and did."

At this point Wizzie's thoughts were interrupted by observing that Lovie, having finished her pears and licked her fingers, had

314

brought out between her sash and her frock that crumpled simulacrum of a paper doll she had been playing with in the arm-chair. She was now deriving unbelievable satisfaction from pretending to make this forlorn substitute for a second Lovie, this Lovie, "once removed," whose "new mummy" was the real Lovie, lick up whatever drops of pear-juice sweetness might be supposed to remain on that extremely bare plate. "How the child makes herself at home, wherever she is!" Wizzie thought. "She might be in the caravan, with Grummy stirring the pot for supper, or she might be in"—and the girl's fancy called up, as she contemplated D. No-man's attic-window, the pleasant warmth, on that grey afternoon, of a snug little parlour of her own. Why hadn't D. No-man made an attempt to get a little home for her?

Yes, there was reason enough for Jenny's perpetual harping on his selfishness! But why hadn't Jenny herself encouraged her to press him to give her a place of her own? Simply because she wanted to keep her in Friary Lane. That was life. Everybody wanted what suited them best!

Jenny had been as bad as D. No-man in that respect. It would have been nothing less than desolation to her if they'd thrown up their room and moved. She pushed back her plate now with a gesture that she knew was an unladylike one and made signs to the young woman who had waited on them to give her the bill.

Once in the busy street she found herself to her bewildered amusement one of a crowd of young mothers who were pushing their offspring in parcel-crammed perambulators up and down the pavement of that ancient thoroughfare. She pushed her little vehicle across the street and hesitated for a moment in front of D. No-man's house. How surprised he'd be if she rang the bell, got admitted, climbed all those stairs with Lovie, and knocked at his door! She knew he had the whole top of the house to himself. She had only to get in!

While she was hesitating, the master of the house came out and stood in the doorway, talking to someone. The sight of this elderly man's placid countenance, every line and curve of which said "Thou shalt not" to all the back-eddies of existence, dissipated in a second this reckless impulse. Hurriedly she pushed her perambulator away from the door and up the street; nor did

315

she pause again till she had turned down Friary Lane, passed her own door, descended the hill, and crossed the little bridge by Claudius's coal-yard.

All the way along the path, under the steep prison-bank, she suffered from the feeling of being an outcast and an outlaw.

To Lovie's excited interest in the ducks, who as they floated in the stream kept making frantic efforts to remain head-down-wards long enough to reach the mud at the bottom, she responded with vague automatic monosyllables.

"No one knows how proud I am," she thought, and a look of hard, bitter satisfaction came into her face as she thought how she had completely hidden from D. No-man the fact of her mother's having been a "lady." The whole scene of her mother's death came back to her now, as she remorselessly quickened her pace. She became once more that white-faced young girl, with unweeping eyes and set mouth, who had deliberately buried her old life in her mother's grave and gone back with the heavily-veiled sister to the convent school.

As she pushed her perambulator now round the turn of the Hangman's Cottage, she experienced a moment of sick dizziness, so vividly there returned on her the cold, savage, insane harden-ing of her young heart under the desolation of that time.

But they were near the Frome now, and she had forgotten that it would be necessary to lift the pram over the little swing-gates on what D. No-man insisted on calling the Blue Bridge. This obstacle all the same would have been easily left behind, if Lovie, who had had to cross the bridge on foot, hadn't suddenly become naughty about being lifted back into her seat.

There was indeed a tense and disturbing struggle between the two feminine wills at that point, for the little girl, passionately bent on reaching a patch of buttercups between the railings, clung indignantly to one of these rails and refused to budge.

Wizzie had already seized her in a rush of nervous anger, when the sight of a horse placidly feeding on the other side of the field swept the taste and smell of *her* horse's warm neck into every fibre of her body. "Lovie, listen!" she gasped, and her tone at once quieted the child who turned startled eyes upon her. "If Mummy ever hits you, you must pretend you're a horse, and do this." And leaning over the top of the railing she emitted, from a face so contorted with conflicting emotions that it was fortunate the child couldn't see it, a husky and rather ghastly parody of a horse's whinny.

This sound, projected from Wizzie's agitated throat across the field, had but small resemblance to any conceivable equine utterance, and the grazing animal didn't even raise its head, but the proceeding had an instantaneous effect upon the little girl, who stood transfixed with remorse, staring at her mother in mingled terror and puzzled commiseration.

"Don't cry, Mummy!" she burst out at last; and then, actually running to the perambulator and trying to scramble into it, she murmured, more to herself than to her mother: "Lovie *hates* buttercups. Lovie's going to have hundreds of gold fishes!"

Once back in her equipage, the child, producing from somewhere about her small person the crumpled paper doll, sank back in her seat and began pretending that both she and it were riding to London in a circus-carriage to find the queen. The sight of certain scattered wind-rows by the roadside, composed of tiny fruit-seed wings, that had been shaken down from the elm-tops by the pressure of the budding leaves, minute gauzy life-sails, as it were, each with its own germinal centre, air-perambulators of innumerable vegetation-Lovies voyaging through space, started our friend's thoughts off now on a different track. Something about the lavish and wasteful fertility of Nature on this grey spring day stirred up in the girl's senses—far down below that hardened place where, with the body of her mother, she had buried her young heart—an unexpected fount of natural feminine sensuality.

At that moment Wizzie found herself longing for embraces of a passionate lover. The feeling was so unexpected and so irresistible that it sent through her a long sweet shuddering spasm. It tossed up and shook away from her, while it lasted, that lodged and settled loathing of Old Funky, that shocking memory of the madness of her submission to him; but it was not of the old man's violence to her youth that she thought, still less of the sterile caresses of her present bed-fellow; it was of some unknown lover, some ardent lover of her own age, to whom she could give herself up, as these tiny vessels of life tossed on the air from the budding elm-trees, gave themselves up to the warm breath of this cloudy day!

317

By the time she had propelled the now entirely content and preoccupied Lovie into the narrow road that led to Glymes, the whole brooding essence of that dark spring afternoon fell upon her and sank into her, as if *it itself*, the non-human presence of one unique day among all the days of her life, had become the lover she longed for! And then by degrees as she pushed her abstracted child along the winding lane, and grew vaguely conscious of the white patches of stitchwort in the hedges and the diffused scent of hidden primroses on the air, this sweet spasm of sensual craving, this craving for equal passion, for life-creating passion, mounted so strongly to her head that it swept into its train other desires. She imagined herself back again in tights and spangles—not the old lavender-coloured ones of which D. No-man used to murmur as he made love to her, as if the actual touch of her flesh was not in itself enough to stimulate his senses, just as he had to whisper, "I bought you, I *bought* you!" to turn her into what he called his "Bronze-Age girl"—but in fresh, new, beautiful, sky-blue ones, radiant as the supple limbs they covered, as she would balance herself on her old horse's back—for she would buy the horse from Old Funky—or would leap like a shooting-star, as no girl had ever leapt before, through a rainbow-circle of dazzlement and wild applause!

She even went so far, as they drew near the pond where she had to open the gate, as actually to visualize a little house of her own. But there was such a lot of mud on both sides of this gate, and the gate itself was so hard to open, and there were such formidable-looking cows—and Wizzie was always afraid of cows —close to the hedgeless road on the further side, and the pond itself, by whose edge they had to pass when they'd got through the gate, looked so grey and gaping, so like the face of Grummer Urgan when she came upon her once with Old Funky, that her heart sank just as her shoes were sinking. There! the wet mud had splashed her ankles, splashed the bright new wheels of the perambulator, while Lovie, as frightened as she was herself at the cows, began to set up a piteous sequence of tearful protests. These protests became a shrill cry when the girl turned to get the gate closed, and the cows, in place of retreating, began advancing a step or two.

It is always hard for women to believe that it is pure curiosity in these speculative beasts that makes them advance in this manner with such a formidable stare in their liquid eyes; and as she took hold of the perambulator again to force its wheels through the mud in full face of this array of horned countenances she felt tempted to join her voice to that of her offspring and send up a wail of hopelessness.

Things were in this condition and Wizzie was wildly gathering her forces together with the intention of leaving the perambulator and rushing at the cows as if they had been geese, when the figure of Mr. Quirm, who, unknown to both of them, had been slyly surveying this scene from the recess of a gate to their right, leading to the farmhouse known as Coker Frome, advanced leisurely into the road between them and the row of horns.

Mr. Quirm wore no hat or coat and carried no stick. He had evidently drifted out, dazed and confused from an afternoon's reading or writing, to get a breath of air before tea.

"Hullo!" he murmured, addressing the child in the perambulator after he'd given Wizzie a friendly smile and nod, "Hullo! Whom have we got here? Riding in state, eh? Riding to London to visit the queen? And what's *this*? Another little girl in the equipage? She's fallen out of her carriage, *this* one has, as if I were a highwayman! Hold tight to your little mother, now you're safe back!"

These last words were addressed to the tiny paper doll, which at the moment he approached the vehicle had fluttered down from Lovie's lap into the puddle at his feet; but it was not only his recovery of that crumpled bit of paper that endeared him at once to the child's heart; it was something that she alone knew, she alone, not Mummy or nobody else, namely that she was playing at visiting the queen, just as the man had said!

It never entered her thoughts to wonder how this heavy, dirty, sallow, black-headed intruder in a woollen jersey knew about this secret game between herself and the paper doll.

With an instinct beyond the instinct of any of his intimates, beyond that of Nance herself, and far beyond that of his son, Lovie had divined the fact, after one glance at that majestic, nebulous, sickly-looking face bending down to pick up that bit of paper, that here was someone who treated existence exactly as she did, that is to say, who regarded *what you were pretending* as the only real reality in your life. This being the case it hardly required explanation that he should have jumped to the right conclusion about her doll, namely, that she was the troublesome "Gwendolly" going to court in a circus-carriage with her severe mother, Lovie.

And as for Wizzie herself, perhaps never since that first day with the Urgans, when she had realized with a young girl's penetration that Old Funky "liked" her so well that nothing would stop him from giving her the best training he could, had she felt so rejoiced to meet anyone as she felt now to meet Mr. Quirm. She liked him for his evident admiration of Lovie, she liked him for saving them from the cows, and above all she liked him for looking at her as if he found her beautiful and desirable.

"I suppose," he remarked presently in a voice so casual that Wizzie thought he must be referring to that ridiculous bed-post that D. No-man made such a fuss about, "your good man hasn't yet told you what we discovered that day at Maiden Castle?"

"Oh, dear no, Mr. Quirm. D.'s never one for talking about his walks! He adores walking. I never heard of a man who loves it more than he does, but I suppose I don't seem interested enough. He's very proud, you know, though he pretends not to be—but I can't help growing a bit tired of the same old thing in the same old way—you'd think, to listen to him, that no one had anything else to do but to call a lesser willow-wren a lesser willow-wren, or a dead red nettle a dead red nettle! But D. certainly adores walking."

As with her mental picture of a beautiful daughter awaiting her in a jasmin-covered porch there was a touch of the influence of the cinema, so in the particular tone in which she uttered the word "adores" there was a peculiar girlish archness that betrayed the influence of Thuella.

Neither in the convent nor in the caravan had Wizzie been permitted to establish her self-expression on a firm personal ground. Both from the Sister and from Grummer she had learnt reticence and self-control, but no one had warned her against copy-cat intonations when she wanted to make a favourable impression in conversation.

"Then he told you nothing?"

"Oh, yes, he told me he had walked all round the ancient

British camp with you; but he said you hadn't had time to visit the excavations."

"Then he didn't tell you what *we* excavated?"

"No. He said nothing more. Was it a Roman relic, Mr. Quirm?"

"Not a relic, my dear," he said softly. "No, not a relic, nor Roman either! What your friend and I discovered together was more of the nature of—well! perhaps I might call it a biological discovery."

Wizzie was silent; but her silence was not the silence of interest. She took it for granted that D. No-man had shown this friendly person some plant, or moss, or fungus, or even bird, such as he never failed to enlarge upon when he came home from his walks and they sat opposite each other at tea in Friary Lane.

"But you haven't told me," Mr. Quirm now blurted out, "where you picked up this little one. Is she a relation of yours?"

Wizzie replied to this by leaning over the edge of the perambulator and asking Lovie, as she laid her hand on the child's shoulder, to "tell the kind gentleman what her name was."

"Lovie Ravelston," the little girl answered promptly and clearly in the automatic and yet self-conscious way in which children repeat the catechism, "and *her* be Lovie's new mummy. God bless Old Funk and Popsy and Grummy, for Jesus' sake— Mummy can say 'tish-o, tish-o,' like a trot-trot, Mummy can!"

Wizzie's heart was beating fast under her Antelope luncheon-dress as she glanced at him to see the effect of Lovie's words.

But Mr. Quirm displayed perfect composure. "Your own, eh?" he said smiling. "I guessed as much! And how does our friend No-man hit it off with his new daughter?"

"You'd better ask *her*," brought out Wizzie with much relief; and they both looked at the little girl.

"Man's going to give Lovie great big gold fishes," pronounced the child eagerly, "and Gwendolly wants gold fishes, too!"

"She's mixing up D. No-man with Mr. Cask," Wizzie hastened to explain. "He called us into his place this morning when Mrs. Dearth was out."

Mr. Quirm, who was now steering the perambulator into the common entrance of Glymes, looked puzzled.

"I thought Cask was at work," he said. "Over here we feel

321

your friend Jenny's being a bit cantankerous with her old Roman; but you know more about that, of course, than we do, By the way, it's 'Thel,' I take it, you've come to call on, not Nance, by any chance. Nance would love to see this little lady of yours. What did you say your name was, my sweet?"

Lovie fixed on him a somewhat dubious and hesitant eye, and several shades of expression crossed her face with extraordinary rapidity. It was clear to Wizzie, who was watching her with interest, that the child didn't feel as sure of Mr. Quirm now as she had felt when he picked up her doll. An indefinable unction in the tone of his voice when he said "my sweet" must have put the little thing on her guard. She turned away from her questioner and murmured a casual answer to the general purlieus of Glymes. "Gwendolly's 'tending that Lovie isn't her mummy. Gwendolly's playing this be workhouse, but Lovie bain't going to be put——"

Wizzie sharply interrupted her. "She doesn't know what she's saying, Mr Quirm. Lovie, I'm *ashamed* of you! You mustn't play 'workhouse' here. This is Mr. Quirm's nice home, and Auntie 'Thel's' nice home. You'll soon see Auntie 'Thel,' won't she, Mr. Quirm? And then——"

But Uryen had such a sardonic expression in his dead eyes when she caught his glance that she stopped abruptly.

"No, not the workhouse exactly, darling," he said, "but your mother's quite right in calling it a 'home.' We call a place a 'home' where people live whose play doesn't suit the rest. But you and Gwendolly will be all right here. *He* won't hurt you any more than I will; but I ought to warn you——"

Here he straightened his back, looked significantly at Wizzie, and jerked his thumb in the direction of his neighbour's house. "There's been a fine rumpus in there this morning," he whispered. " 'Thel' had to fetch Nance, so as to——"

But Thuella herself emerged now from the second Glymes house in her studio-smock, and rushing to Wizzie embraced her with ardour. "And who is this? And what is here?" she cried when she released her.

But Wizzie, resolute not to enter into further explanations till she was alone with her friend, offered her hand to her rescuer, thanked him for his help over the cows, and added airily: "If I *can* I'll look in on Nance, tell her, before I go; but you know how it is when a person's with 'Thel.' It's hard to tear yourself away!"

"Oh, you lovely thing!" cried Thuella, surveying her friend's attire and touching its grey flounces with the tips of her fingers. "I must give you one more kiss before we go in. Don't let's keep *you*, Uryen. I know Nance is in the kitchen getting tea."

Mr. Quirm obediently moved to his own door but made no bones about turning round when once his fingers were on the handle, to throw upon the whole little group, even down to the sacred scrap of paper cradled in Lovie's lap, a look that Thuella, in the act of embracing her friend, missed altogether, but that Wizzie, who was the passive one, and whose eyes wandered to the man as the girl kissed her, intercepted with a glow of satisfaction.

"He wouldn't mind," she said to herself, as she lifted Lovie from her carriage, "doing that to me! He likes me. I believe he likes me more than 'Thel'!" She held her child tightly by the hand as she followed Thuella into the house, while the child herself held more tightly still in *her* hand what had once been a piece of writing-paper, taken from a box with a picture of Shakespeare on it that Popsy's grandmother had given to Popsy at Christmas, but which now, having once emerged from that small chamber of limbo—for everything with the inanimate is as relative as it is with ourselves—had been permitted by fate a dim sub-reality of livingness under the creative imagination of Lovie.

"Dad's been terrible to-day," Thuella whispered, as they entered the kitchen. "The ingratitude of men, my dear, especially of fathers, passes all bearing! I bet your man's just the same, but it's worse in a man like Dad. Uryen's the only one I know who's different. Don't you think so? I'm always telling Nance how lucky she is!"

Wizzie caught only the general drift of her friend's grievance, for she was occupied in removing Lovie's coat, a proceeding that was rendered difficult by the clenched fingers of the small hand clutching the crumpled and wet bit of paper.

"Oh, she *is* a darling!" the tall girl cried with forced enthusiasm when the coat was removed and the sash displayed. "But what funny socks you've put on her, my dear! Is this a new style?"

Wizzie bit her lip. She had looked for something much more than this. Why didn't Thuella comment on the child's beauty? But the girl was off again now in a voluble torrent of telltale revelations. Mr. Wye's ways were growing daily more intolerable.

"But how selfish I'm getting!" presently interjected the tall girl, bending her shining head a little to one side and smiling at her visitor while she negligently passed her fingers through Lovie's curls.

The child was now warming an attenuated and weather-beaten Gwendolly against the front of the stove, and annoyed at this interruption she made a peevish little movement as much as to say: "Go on with your chatter, you frivolous creature, and let a busy person alone!"

"Selfish?" echoed Wizzie vaguely, wondering whether she would be allowed to run in and see Nance before they had to go, and wondering too whether, if Nance invited her to tea, she would dare to leave D. No-man alone for once at this ritualistic hour.

"Talking about my painting and my father," the other went on, "and stupid things like that, instead of asking you a word about your pretty self!"

Both the girls were on their feet at this point and Thuella threw one of her arms round Wizzie's waist and drew her towards her, running her fingers caressingly down the girl's side.

"What a lovely dress!" she murmured softly. "D. No-man *must* like this dress! It's *so* well-made and it fits so perfectly. You darling! You don't know what it means to me to have got you again at Glymes!"

Keeping her arm tightly round our friend's waist, she lifted up the girl's chin with her free hand and kissed her.

Wizzie's thoughts were extremely detached as she submitted to these endearments. For one thing she became conscious that Lovie was watching them, with eyes as round as her own were wont to grow when something serious was happening. For another thing she couldn't help an uneasy feeling that all Glymes, and every room in Glymes, was dominated by the personality of Uryen.

The tall girl seemed as if she couldn't let Wizzie go. She was dressed in a long, painter's smock, smeared with stains from her palette, and our friend felt as if she had nothing on under this thin garment, such feverish electricity shivered through her lithe body.

What she was doing now was explaining to Wizzie the picture she had been painting; but it struck our friend that she used her eloquence as a sort of wavering screen to conceal the intensity of her feelings.

She kept talking of the "response" of Maiden Castle to some mad dance of cloud-shapes she had painted above it; but Wizzie soon began to feel as if, in her disturbed imagination the excited girl were identifying herself with these clouds.

"There, 'Thel' dear," she murmured at last. "*I'm* not Maiden Castle! You'll make Lovie jealous if you make such a fuss of her mummy—won't she, my pet?"

Something in the tone in which she said this served as a chilling non-conductor to Thuella's infatuation. She let her go, and a strained silence fell upon them both.

It was Thuella who broke the spell, and she did it by a series of hurried questions as to the manner in which D. No-man had accepted Lovie.

"Did he mind," she inquired, "when you *had* to tell him about her? Did he make a fuss at your wanting to have her? Did those Urgan people make trouble? Did they get money out of him?"

"What an actress you are!" Wizzie thought. "You don't care a damn whether they got money out of D. No-man or not, or whether D. No-man was beside himself with rage or gentle as a lamb! But on the other hand *I* don't care how much your father spoils your happiness. That's how life is, I suppose!"

Then aloud: "You remember how I decided to tell him nothing, even if I *did* have to take the child in the end? Well, do you know, my dear, I wish now I had told him! He was so nice about it. You can't think how nice he was. And the extraordinary thing was he didn't seem surprised when that letter came.... Listen, 'Thel'! you didn't breathe a word to him ... did you? But of course you didn't! Well, then, I simply can't understand it. I made sure he'd throw me out. Any other man would—wouldn't he?—I thought when I read that letter: 'Well, young woman, *out* you'll have to go, bag and baggage, you and your bastard!'—but he didn't even sulk. He completely astonished me. You'd have thought Lovie was *his* child, and he was telling *me* about her; not me telling him!" She paused and then with a glance at the window and a little sigh : "Does Mr. Quirm," she asked, "help you a lot with your painting?"

The moment she had asked this question she thought in her heart : "I know what you feel about *me* with all that sort of thing—'a little outsider like her, with an acrobat's training, can't really understand such things'—but still all the same——"

Thuella gave her a quick searching glance and shrugged her shoulders; and Wizzie deemed it wiser to revert to D. No-man.

"Wasn't it extraordinary, 'Thel,' his acting the way he did? Would *you* have thought he'd have acted like that?"

"What did you do when you first read the letter?"

Wizzie shot at her a very straight glance, and one of those curious looks passed between them that will be a trouble to men till the end of days.

"You got hysterical and drew the lightning on yourself?"

Wizzie frowned. This sophisticated tone in her friend displeased her. In a flash she became defensive of her man. "He acted splendidly," she said. "I needn't have made any fuss."

"But wasn't he scared at having the child? I take it you two must have long ago decided against"—and Thuella made a little gesture of disgust at the thought of maternal responsibility.

Wizzie couldn't restrain the glow of satisfaction with which she let this natural implication pass as the truth. She knew her friend well enough by now to realize the wisdom of tempering frankness with certain basic reservations. "No, he wasn't scared. He doesn't want children of his own but he *likes* children, and he thinks it's only right that I should look after mine."

Thuella shrugged her shoulders, and to Lovie's relief ceased her perfunctory toying with that busy young woman's person. She moved to the door but instead of opening it turned sharply round, her fingers on the handle.

"Do you know, my dear," she said. "I'd give up," and she raised both her arms to the back of her fair head and clasped them behind her neck, "every pretension to good looks I've got if I could do some really good work!" From between her lifted elbows her eyes gleamed wildly and desperately round that little kitchen as if it had been transformed with all its pots and pans into one large empty canvas.

326

"You don't know what it is to want anything as much as I want to be a *real* painter! I come near it. Yes I do now and then! But just as I'm on the edge of something good, something really *great*, Dad's damned sneering contempt drags me back." She stopped, let her hands fall to her sides, and stood silent for a second, gazing on the ground.

Then she raised her eyes. "How you've given up *your* work, as you have, passes my comprehension! I've never forgotten how you looked in those things you had on, when you sat on that bed and hated me so. You looked like—oh, I don't know what!—and now here you are—with *that* little thing—and a pram at the door! You looked beautiful then, child, beautiful and *terrible*, like a woman who could dance on a bare sword—and now—I hope D. No-man enjoys the change—that's all *I* can say! Well, come on—I want you to see what I'm doing—I don't talk like this to everybody. But though you've put on petticoats and thrown your soul to the fishes, you've got it in you, Wizz, and don't think I don't know it!"

A week ago Wizzie would have been impressed and even a little awed by this outburst, but she had had so many emotional shocks of late that it was only with a narrowing of her screwed-up eyes and a contracting of her straight eyebrows that she responded to her friend's words. More reluctantly still was Lovie dragged away to see these pictures and these philosophers. The miracle was still going on at that warm stove, a scrawled-over bit of paper becoming a person with a past and a future!

Just four hours—four drops of conspiring time—had this creation occupied. And now the paper doll like the rest of us had to pay the penalty of being Something rather than Nothing. Clutched in Lovie's hot fingers this poor entity was now compelled, as were its young mother and *her* mother, to follow that tide of destiny "that sweeps earth and heaven and men and gods along" the moment they emerge from Nirvana.

And like ourselves the paper doll had had no choice. Snatched from the trunk in the caravan when it lay between Popsy's underclothes and a volume entitled *The Book of Beauty*, given to the girl by her first sweetheart, it had been forced to submit to Old Funky's scrawls, forced to submit to being torn in half by Wizzie, and now, without question asked as to whether it would prefer to remain warm and quiescent by a kitchen fire, it was

327

destined to be conveyed into the presence of a Platonic thinker at the end of his tether.

The desperate state of poor Mr. Wye must have been divined by Lovie, if not by her doll, at first glance. He had evidently just come in from a long walk, in which no doubt he had sought to recover from the turbulent scene referred to by Mr. Quirm. He had thrown down his overcoat and hat on one of Thuella's sofas and was now engaged in taking off his boots by the fire. He rose at their entrance and shuffled forward to greet the visitor with one boot on and one boot off.

The silky-white fringe across his high narrow brow was all dishevelled, and one lock of grey hair hung down almost as low as his left eyebrow and looked damp with sweat. His thin lips were sucked in in a forced grimace and from the cavity of this Voltairean leer, as he gave his limp hand to Wizzie and stared in amazement at the child, there emerged a whistling series of half-articulate interjections: "Whew!—what a pleasure!—whew!—what a surprise!—whew, whew! What little girl have we got here?"

Thuella's face hardened with disgust as she surveyed the trailing laces of the boot he still had on and the muddy aggressiveness of the one befouling the hearthrug.

"We have tea at half-past four, Miss Ravelston. I like my tea as soon as I get back from my walk. But of course, I try not to be impatient. Is the kettle boiling, Thuella? Is the bread and butter cut? I expect this little one likes cake. Come over here and let me look at you, child! No, no, don't hide your pretty face! Don't be shy. Have you got any cake for the child, Thuella?"

Wizzie risked a hurried glance at her friend; but the tall girl, taking absolutely no more notice of Mr. Wye's words than if they had been the ticking of some old hall-clock that was always wrong, was standing in front of her easel lost in critical contemplation.

Wizzie herself began to grow more and more ill at ease, but she allowed Lovie to establish herself on the floor, where the child became at once gravely occupied in arranging her sacred bit of paper so that what passed for its head should rest on a particular square in the pattern of the rug.

Mr. Wye, evidently suffering acutely from this delay in the

preparation of his meal, kept glancing alternately at the clock and at his daughter. At last with an angry effort to emphasize his patient impatience he settled himself in his chair and produced—one from each pocket—his cherished volumes.

Wizzie could see he didn't read a word, but opened first one book and then the other, balancing them on his thin knees, while little drops of perspiration trickled down his brow, causing his errant lock of hair to droop in damp misery.

But Thuella now turned her easel round so that Wizzie might see the picture. The tall girl's bright head hung sideways in intense absorption and with each broken sentence of explanation of her purpose, her flexible body seemed to quiver in sympathetic response.

"I've made the hill *conscious*—if you understand what I mean," she was saying, while from the curves of her figure as she hovered over her work magnetic shivers kept following one another in a series of spasmodic vibrations that seemed to pass into the canvas.

"I mean I've made the hill *alive*, don't you see?—not just grass and chalk—but the breasts of the earth."

What Wizzie saw was that Thuella's own small breasts were responding far more obviously than Maiden Castle to that cloud-orgy in the sky.

"It was Uryen—saying—it came—alive—on—certain—nights —that set me off," the artist went on, uttering her words in short gasps.

The mention of Uryen's name broke up Wizzie's feeling that this tension above those cloud-wraiths was like herself on her horse, and once more she found herself recalling the peculiar look Uryen had fixed upon them when Thuella was kissing her.

"He wants me! He wants me!" her thoughts repeated, and a revival of something like that delicious throb of warm sensuality trembled through her that she had felt when she imagined herself embraced by a passionate lover of her own age.

The girls were now startled by Mr. Wye letting both his books slide down upon the floor, while he rose with a bound. "You're doing this to torture me!" he burst out, glaring like a demon at his daughter.

The sight of his daughter still surveying her picture with

329

absorbed attention while she kept her knuckles pressed against her ears caused the indignant old man to devote himself exclusively to Wizzie, who groaned as she saw all chance of seeing Mr. Quirm again vanishing away.

"You wouldn't believe it," the man went on, "but your—your husband's the only person round here who takes the least interest in what I say!" He passed his hand over his forehead, pushing back his forelock, propelling his chair away. "I've been a professor in my time. My unnatural child forgets *that*! Perhaps Mr. No-man doesn't realize that I was a professor of Greek in one of our Midland colleges. Will you tell him that from me, Miss Ravelston? For I think it will interest him. Tell him— what he certainly wouldn't know from the way I'm treated in my own house—that in Derbyshire they still call me Professor! *That's* what the girl over there forgets when she behaves in the way she's doing now. Professor Teucer Wye, that's what I was when I made my wife choose Thuella as the name of our second child; that's what I was when I bought for her—in the main street of a well-known Midland town—her first paint-box."

Here to Wizzie's consternation the furious little man skipped across the room to Thuella's side, and seizing her by one of her elbows tried to pull her fingers from her ear. "Yes, a paint-box, you unnatural girl!" he shouted, "a paint-box! a paint-box!"

But Wizzie was on her feet by this time. "Good-bye, Mr. Wye!" she said in a clear emphatic voice that had, all the same, something of an uncomfortable tremor. Our friend was no longer in the tender mood she had been in Claudius's house, but the sight of the contemptuous loathing in Thuella's face as she tried to shake off her father's fingers, and the view of the back of Mr. Wye's head which looked so pathetically calm and scholarly as he struggled with her, made her feel, as she later described it to D. No-man, "funny in my inside."

"Good-bye, Mr. Wye! I'm afraid I've got to go now. Mr. No-man is waiting tea for me."

As soon as she had spoken she felt ashamed of having uttered the dangerous word "tea"; and when afterwards she told D. No-man what she had said he maintained that she'd done it with malicious intent; but her speech had at least the effect of causing that grotesque struggle in front of the picture of Maiden Castle to come to an end.

Mr. Wye hurried up to her at once and became the normally polite gentleman. Thuella too came forward; and as it worked out, the visitor's departure was attended by unexpected ease and geniality on the part of the father and unexpected awkwardness and embarrassment on the part of the daughter.

Wizzie herself was overwhelmed with shame at the end; for when the moment arrived to disturb Lovie's game on the floor and get her into her jacket it was found that her extremely good behaviour during all this unpleasant scene was due to the fact that she had pulled towards her the *Phaedrus* and *Timaeus* from where Mr. Wye had dropped them and converted them into a tunnel, in and out of which it gave her a grave ecstasy to propel the one-dimensional form of the recumbent Gwendolly.

It was indeed to Lovie herself—for he seemed to treat the child's contact with the mere binding of the *Phaedrus* and the *Timaeus* as a species of initiation—that his final words were uttered. He muttered quite a lot into the little creature's ear as he saw them off the premises, and Wizzie wondered, as she watched him turn back at the garden-gate, whether he had told Lovie that in Derbyshire he was still known as Professor Teucer Wye.

The door of the southern portion of Glymes, had however, hardly closed on the troubled Platonist, and Wizzie was formulating in her mind a lively account of him for the benefit of D. No-man, when the gate of the northern garden opened and both Mr. and Mrs. Quirm hurried after her.

"Uryen told me about the cows, my dear," panted Nance hurriedly, "and I thought I must just see this little person." She bent over the perambulator as she spoke and began to make warm hovering overtures to its occupant.

But Lovie was tired and irritable by this time, and replied to her approaches by drawing rudely back and acting like a little hawk, of whose distance from its nest a benevolent and maternal hen is trying to take advantage. And the mother was as unresponsive as the daughter. "Sorry not to stop," murmured Wizzie, pushing the perambulator forward so fast as almost to trip up the poor lady : "but I must get back as quick as I can. D. No-man's waiting for me in Friary Lane. Don't make that noise, Lovie! We're going home. Look! the cows have all gone home!"

331

"Have you seen his attic in High East Street yet?" inquired Nance hurrying along on one side of the small conveyance, while her husband walked on the other. "I'm always so interested—as Enoch knows—in a writer's study. Has he a warm fire up there? Does he have any of his meals up there? Has he got a nice view from his window?"

Pushing the perambulator faster still, and acutely conscious in every part of her person of a magnetic pull reaching her from the dark figure on the other side of her whimpering charge, Wizzie was faintly conscious of an instinctive stiffening against these interrogations.

She made up her mind in a flash not to admit that she had never ascended those stairs above the shop.

"You don't know D. No-man," she brought out, "if you think he doesn't take care of himself."

"There—there—don't 'ee cry, little one!" came the husky voice of the man on her left, and Wizzie became aware, as she hurried on, that he had laid his hand on Lovie's shoulder.

The spring sky had grown dark with heavy clouds; and a mist coming up from the river was now crossing their path with a palpable chilling of the air.

Her reply to Nancy seemed to have reduced that friendly lady to silence, and all the way down the hill till they reached the pond Uryen kept murmuring consoling words to Lovie.

To him the girl felt she couldn't utter a syllable, no! not if all the cows in the Frome meadows were obstructing their way! That warm wave of delicious response to anonymous human passion which had swept over her on her approach to Glymes began to flow more and more consciously into the channel of her contact with this living man at her side.

Little Lovie, whose pathetic whimperings had now completely ceased, like the trouble of a small bird soothed in a magnetic hand, now became a medium for the electric current between him and her, a current which she could feel tingling irresistibly through every nerve of her body.

It was out of an exquisite trance that she suddenly grew conscious that they had reached the gate by the pond, that there were no cows to be seen, and that with the opening of the gate to let her through, her companions were intending to turn back. So strangely elated, and yet so numb and passive, was her

332

mood, that the withdrawal of the Quirms hardly seemed to touch the deeper levels of her feeling. She couldn't be quite clear indeed, as she pushed the perambulator on and muttered mechanically to herself : "I must be quick. I mustn't keep him waiting," how they had left her, or even whether she had thanked them or said good-bye to them. All she knew was that she felt happier than she had felt for years, happier than she had felt since the last time, with a free heart, she had balanced herself on her old horse's back !

When she reached the turn leading to the back entrance of Frome House, an impulse that she would have found hard to explain compelled her to pause and let go for a minute the handle of her little vehicle.

Stepping hurriedly to her child's side she bent down and gave Lovie an impassioned hug and the first kiss, the first *real* kiss, her offspring had ever received from her.

"Don't, Mummy !" the little girl spluttered, under this unexpected embrace. "Don't, Mummy ! You've—made me—pinch Gwendolly." And then, without warning, something in her small bewildered heart broke down, something that reacted obscurely and wildly from all the troubled impressions of this long day, and the little girl lifted up her voice and wept. "Lovie wants to go back to Old Funk and Grummy," she wailed. "Lovie wants to go home !"

8

MIDSUMMER'S EVE

THE Eve of St. John the Baptist, the twenty-third of June, fell this year on a Sunday, and turned out to be one of the hottest days of one of the hottest Junes that the West of England had known for a long time.

Dorchester was full of visitors. The unusually warm weather had stimulated the Archaeological Society engaged in the Maiden Castle excavations to begin their summer work earlier than was expected; and in the afternoon of Saturday the twenty-second the local *Echo* announced a momentous discovery.

From the wording of this announcement it appeared that in the oldest portion of the earthworks, in a place where digging had been undertaken for the first time, the remains of an extensive stone building had been discovered, of greater antiquity than the well-known Roman Temple on the high tableland in the centre of the ramparted hill.

So important was the discovery, the *Echo* hinted, that the head people in the work had halted all further meddling with the spot until several experienced authorities could be brought to the scene, and the paper went on to predict that there would be a rush to the place from all parts of the country.

The day following this exciting announcement being Sunday, and the weather remaining as auspicious as ever, there was a pronounced tendency among local persons interested in such matters to make their way as soon as possible to the scene of action.

The astute Mr. Cumber, from his publicity watch-tower in a remote town, lost no time in making sure that the chain of papers connected with his office should have first-hand information of what was going on. With this in view he hurriedly despatched to Dorchester his son-in-law and his daughter in his own private car with explicit orders to remain at the Antelope till every aspect of the new find had been thoroughly investigated. They were bidden to keep in touch with him over the telephone, and he declared his intention of coming down in person when things had gone a little further.

Meanwhile he instructed them to get into immediate contact with both his local correspondents, Mr. No-man and Mr. Quirm, and obtain a general article on the situation from the former, and a special one on the mythological implications of the discovery from the latter.

The task given to Dunbar Wye on this occasion was the first among all the labours undertaken for his father-in-law from which he could derive any personal pleasure.

Dumbell hated office work. He was the worst possible reporter. Everyone had been amazed when Mr. Cumber consented to his only child's marriage with so unpromising a youth, though the explanation was simple, namely, that the famous widower was completely under his daughter's thumb. How the girl herself yielded to the candid innocence of such a lad no one had inquired. Her own quality of intelligence was obviously of so thin a texture that, whatever her friends *said,* in their hearts they thought: "She's lucky to have found such a good-tempered, quiet lad, free from all vice."

For Dunbar Wye was certainly untempted by either the world or the flesh. Whether the devil left him alone, too, was a question dependent on one's views of the metaphysics of Fascism; but if not to flirt, or to whore, or to drink, or to smoke, or to give way in the luxury of solitude to lascivious thoughts, was to be a good catch for a petted little shrew, Dunbar was the man. That, to top all this, he was an incredible fool was not perhaps a paradox. Many ere now have held the view that simple virtue and extreme foolishness are blood brothers and that it is as hard to be clever and good as it is to be rich and good.

At any rate what the Cumber girl suffered from in Dumbell was not his virtue, was not his Fascist devotion—it was his mania for collecting, and drying, and keeping in portfolios, endless speciments of the larger-growing vegetation of the United Kingdom. In plants, in ferns, in mosses, in mushrooms, Dunbar took less interest. His passion was for trees and bushes.

Mr. Cumber approved of this mania in his daughter's husband. He took the point of view that it was better to make love to trees than to ladies, and he used to derive a proud satisfaction from being able to say to his colleagues: "That lad of my girl's knows every damned shrub in the garden of Eden!"

But Mr. Cumber's offspring came, after five weeks of life with Dumbell, to loathe the sight of a bush. Their little suburban garden was all bushes. You couldn't plant a pansy in it, much less a row of poppies. And Dumbell's "study," as the girl strove to make her servant call the apartment where his specimens were arranged, had the peculiarity of leaking all over the house. The young woman had told herself the prettiest stories of the way she was going to run her establishment and decorate it and show it to her admiring friends; but Providence had other plans.

In excusing Dunbar's lack of the lighter touches of sociability, she would always say: "Well, at any rate Dun isn't a writer. He won't mess up the house with books and things!" Her forecast was correct. The only books in Beulah Lodge were presentation sets of standard authors; but what no girl could have predicted from such harmless evidence as a habit of plucking leaves and twigs wherever he went was that she and her little servant, neither of whom was in any sense a devotee of Nature, should come to be faced with a positive plague of vegetable debris.

The two young women in Beulah Lodge—and even the tradesmen noticed this—grew week by week under this deciduous affliction more and more alike in their ways. By contending against the same obsession they acquired a secret code of unspoken understanding, an identical pattern, you might call it, of protective colouring, so that they even began, after a year of Dumbell's arboreal researches, to resemble each other in facial expression.

Young Mr. Wye soon found it was no use to inquire of the maid what had happened to a rare specimen of a certain blackberry, or to a treasure trove among willows—for of these simple growths, contrary to received opinion, there seemed to be unending varieties—if the mistress declared she had never seen it !

Dumbell's passionate acceptance of the Fascist hostility to feminism may have had nothing to do with his obstinate pursuit of a hobby so incompatible with a tidy house, but he made no more successful attempts to get into the mind of his womenfolk the importance of collecting willows than he did to make them realize the catastrophic menace of Communism.

It was therefore a triumphant release to the Cumber girl to carry her dogmatic botanist to Dorchester, knowing that in her absence her other self, in the person of Lottie Day, would dust most vigorously and with most thoroughness where dusting was most forbidden.

It cannot be said that this son of "the professor in a small Midland college" was in the least interested in excavations; but since he had well nigh exhausted both the indigenous and the exotic vegetation in the environs of Beulah Lodge he accepted his commission with alacrity, bearing with him not only reams of Black-Shirt propaganda but the most capacious of all possible botanizing tins.

Early as was the start of the Cumber pair, it was impossible for them to reach Dorchester till mid-day; and long before that, in fact, before most of the inhabitants of the old town were stirring, considerable numbers of interested people were already on the way to Maiden Castle. Among those might have been seen—while the Corn Exchange clock was striking ten and the bells of Fordington Church were already ringing—quite a large group of our particular acquaintances setting out from Friary Lane. Both the Glymes *ménages* were represented, Nancy alone, by an arrangement with Thuella, having stayed behind to cook a combined Sunday dinner. "Don't hurry back now!" had been her last word to them all. "I'll manage somehow, however late you are."

D. No-man and Wizzie had privately arranged for Claudius to accompany them to the scene of action; and this meant—for the idealistic neighbours were still unreconciled—that Jenny Dearth found her own reasons for staying at home. And since she *was* at home, Wizzie entrusted her with the care of Lovie.

It was no surprise to Wizzie, as they all met at Jenny's door, to see the portentous face of her Glymes man, for No-man had received a telegram, and they took it for granted that the other Cumber correspondent would be stirred up in the same way.

But it was a most startling surprise to them both to see the dapper and even dandified form of old Teucer Wye, swinging an ash-coloured cane as slender and straight as himself, and prepared to be amiable and polite to everybody, not even excepting his younger daughter.

Both the pockets of the professor's light tweed coat bulged a little, for he evidently anticipated interludes in the proceedings wherein a word of the greatest of all philosophers might be appropriately snatched; but his mood was as unruffled as the weather, and he skipped about from one to another of the party with a lively volubility that astonished them all.

In the general confusion of the start there was quite a conclave outside Jenny's house, while Thuella, dutiful for once in her life, ran in to have a word with her sister.

Wizzie noticed that No-man began at once arguing with Claudius, and she gathered that it was the old topic they were debating—the topic she had heard till she was utterly weary of it—the topic that seemed to demand that you had to pit the word "subjective" against the word "objective," as if these expressions—totally meaningless to *her* mind—had been a pair of fighting-cocks.

The elated professor—for it was soon clear to Wizzie that the whole Glymes party were in high spirits—had stopped an impatient member of the Salvation Army, whose band always gathered in that part of the town for their march to chapel, and was telling him—as far as she could catch his words—that Midsummer Eve ought to be a great occasion with a sect like his, which had revived, under the Christian symbols of blood and fire, the old Dionysian ecstasy of salvation. The Salvation Army man rested his weight, and the weight of his musical instrument which the professor called by some Greek name Wizzie couldn't catch, first on one leg and then on the other, while he struggled to escape; and if the girl didn't wonder what that "college in the Midlands" could have derived from such fantastic studies, it was only because what she heard from Mr. Wye kept being interrupted by what she heard from D. No-man as he argued with Claudius.

"It *isn't* just sensation that I live for," D. was saying. "It's something that has behind it more than you think—the feelings of our race for thousands of years. For instance, this morning, warm though it was, I lit a fire in the grate to celebrate Midsummer's Eve. What are all your electrical apparatuses compared with a fire that I light with my own hands? It isn't only a sensual pleasure; it's a religion, it's an ecstasy of life."

Wizzie couldn't prevent an amused feminine smile—irreligious as the famous "laughter" of Sarah in the presence of the angel —when she heard this word "ecstasy" repeated on both sides of her. "I wouldn't be a man for anything," she thought. "*They* talk; but *I* feel. Old Teucer Wye's beating the dust up now with his stick and letting himself be happy, just because they lit bonfires on Midsummer Eve thousands of years ago!"

But if the humorous feeling that might be called a recognition of the eternal limitations of Homo Sapiens was on *her* side over Mr. Wye and D., it was on No-man's side when Uryen came up to where she stood and began to talk to her.

"I didn't dress like this for *you*," she kept saying to herself as she gave herself up to the man's formidable magnetism.

But though she repeated those chaste words in her brain, she could not prevent all her girlish senses from responding "with linked sweetness long drawn out," as she felt his dead-looking eyes stray over her figure's provocative curves.

It was the first time she had put on what she was wearing now, and she knew well that never—certainly not in the days of those old lavender-coloured tights—had the loveliness of her form had such complete justice done to it.

More than a month had passed since that day in early May when Uryen had rescued Lovie and her from the cows, and, though she had only seen him about half a dozen times since then, their attraction to each other—or, at any rate, her submission to his spell—had gone a good long way. It had not yet led to their being alone together, or even to her going—as he had asked her several times to do—with "Thel" and him to Maiden Castle. Nor had it—at least she told herself it had not—aroused D.'s jealousy; though at this very moment she could not help being aware that No-man was keeping watch on her and Uryen.

It was all done just by Uryen's nearness, just by the way he looked at her. Indeed, she risked everything, it was so sweet, so much what she had longed for all her life, and never come near enjoying. She risked the danger of D. seeing the rapt expression of her face; she risked the danger of committing herself irretrievably to her "Black Man of Glymes"; she risked the danger of killing his interest forever by abandoning herself so precipitously.

Uryen himself seemed entirely unperturbed, though he *must* have seen, just as she had, the savage look of jealousy that No-man had cast on them. But so unperturbed was he that he told her quite quietly, turning his dead-alive eyes to the door of the house, to watch for Thuella's reappearance, that he didn't think she realized how passionately Thuella admired her. "It's a rare thing," he whispered, keeping his eyes on the door, "and it *can* be a very tragic thing, for one girl to admire another as much as our friend admires you; and the truth is——"

"Oh, you're exaggerating, Mr. Quirm!" she threw in.

"The truth is," he went on, "Thuella's so self-distrusting that she's got an idea she's unloved and unlovable. Don't be angry with me for what I'm saying, but if you *could* bring yourself to respond a little more, you'd be doing—— But if you feel you absolutely can't—never mind—forget I've spoken of it. Sometimes it's the best we can do, to beat on the impenetrable; and if we go on doing that"—here he suddenly raised his voice and addressed D. No-man, who *had* left Claudius, as she knew he would, and was already at their side. "Wizzie and I are getting impatient to start," he said. "Can't *you* go in and get hold of Thuella?"

No-man made a queer little bow. "Gladly," he threw out in a high-pitched artificial tone that evidently covered a spasm of irritation; and he kept repeating the word "gladly" as he disappeared into the house.

But they were off at last; and as they passed under the projecting windows of the King's Arms Wizzie grew aware of a wish leaping up within her, that she had, after all, brought Lovie with them. Her spirits rose high as she walked by No-man's side behind Uryen and Thuella. She had at least been spared ar, awkward crisis this time. But the sun was so warm, the traffic so quiescent, the streets so deserted, that it seemed a shame for little Lovie not to be getting the benefit of it all, particularly as Jenny, who, like Nance, was going to cook an elaborate Sunday dinner, would have to keep the child with her in the hot kitchen.

"I'm half inclined," she murmured to D. No-man, "to go back for Lovie. It wouldn't take long. I'd soon catch you up."

But No-man scouted the idea. "You ought to have a holiday now and then," he said : "and besides, I *like* to see you so free and so charming in those things !"

Wizzie cast a complacent glance downward. Yes, the thin grey jersey she was wearing, the little grey cap, and above all the tight-fitting flannel trousers were by far the most becoming attire she had ever put on ! She felt deliciously at ease in them as she advanced with her springy step. If it hadn't been for thinking of Lovie in the kitchen, her elated mood, now that D. had got over his spasm of jealousy, would have been without alloy this perfect morning.

Oh, how superior she felt to Thuella ! Thuella in her yellow frock and absurdly flapping hat—which at the slightest breeze she had to clutch with her hand—was "acting silly" to put on that affected way of walking, swaying her hips and flanks like that. That was the way girls walked when they wanted to attract men. There was nothing in it but the obvious fact that you had a slim waist and a woman's back. It was all very well to sway like that on the stage. "Thel" ought to know better than to do it on the street. Oh, how she longed to jump on a horse just as she was! She would have shown them what a girl's body could do.

How slow they were to get off! They were all at the Corn Exchange now, and were waiting before crossing over into South Street to watch some soldiers, still some way off, who were marching down the hill from the barracks.

Suddenly D. No-man turned to her with a troubled face. "I've left my stick," he said. "I've left my stick in my room."

The babyish way he announced this, and his gravity about such a trifle annoyed Wizzie.

"Well, if you've left it, you've left it," she said. "You can't keep everyone waiting."

He looked at her with an expression of outrage. "But you know perfectly well——" he began. The worst of it was that the others all seemed aware of the situation, for they glanced with amusement from No-man to her and from her to No-man.

At that moment the Salvation Army band, which had been collecting its forces at the end of North Square, began to advance to where they were standing, striking up as it did so a gay, beautifully conducted tune, whose stirring sound, rolling over them and gathering weight against the tower of St. Peter's, brought a dark flush of pleasure to Claudius's face, and even caused Teucer Wye to open his mouth and tap his cane on the stones in sympathetic rhythm.

No-man made a move to be off under cover of this distraction but she caught him by the sleeve.

"What does it matter, *once in a way*?" she whispered. "Claudius hasn't got a stick. Mr. Quirm hasn't got a stick. These manias of yours can't *always* come first. You *can't* keep all these people waiting. You just *can't*! I've never heard of such a thing."

"Oh, I want the *Observer*!" cried the professor at this juncture in a piercing voice. "Paper! Paper! Have you got the *Observer* there, young lady?"

His sharp cry caused a girl who was riding past on a bicycle with a pile of Sunday papers to stop so suddenly that if she had not been a very active and limber person she would have fallen over.

"Would you like me to go back with you, No-man?" put in

Claudius, approaching them. "I'm not so necessary up there on the hill as these people, and I'd be glad——"

But a new encounter had just been affected which kept them still standing in uncertainty on the curbstones of St. Peter's. This was Thuella's accosting of a stalwart and robust old man, bearded like the pictures of Sir John Falstaff, and looking as if he could confute a whole consistory of lawn-sleeved bishops, like Falstaff's prototype, Oldcastle the Lollard!

It was this old gentleman's pastime, in the later hours of his well-earned retirement, to aid informally in the distribution of the *Echo*; but on Sunday morning, bereft of this distraction, he could only watch from a respectful distance the lively proceedings of the young purveyor of metropolitan news as she glided in and out of the old squares and alleys.

Thuella was a friend of this aged man, whose heroic, Gargantuan laugh, disposing sardonically of all human weakness, would resound from above his sheaf of *Echos* as they exchanged their badinage.

It was this old man's reiterated laugh, a laugh that certainly refused to be bothered with any nice punctilios of sentiment, that now blent with the tramp of the soldiers from the barracks and the intermittent drum of the band from North Square.

"I wish Lovie was here!" our friend thought, her fingers still clutched tight to the sleeve of No-man's coat. "It's nice in this town on Sunday." And while they all waited for the soldiers to pass into the church and for the band to disappear down High East Street, there stole into Wizzie's heart, forcing its way through her irritation with No-man's fuss about his stick, a new and curious feeling.

The girl herself, with a feminine instinct to reduce all lovely sensations to something personal, linked it at once with the fact that though he remained by Thuella's side in her colloquy with the laughing philosopher, Nancy Quirm's husband kept turning his great black head—the man wore his usual dirty clothes and in spite of the hot day had no hat—in her direction.

"He likes me better than Thuella," she said to herself. "He talks and walks with her, but he looks at me." And it was the delicious perception of a growing attraction between herself and this singular person that she took for granted must explain the sudden rush of happiness that so unexpectedly warmed her blood. But it had—she admitted to herself—something to do, too, with the day and the hour.

What was going on, she wondered, between D. No-man and her mysterious "Black Man" that had made them so much more intimate during the last month? It must have to do, she decided, with the fact that they were both working for Mr. Cumber.

But why was D. No-man always so "funny" when she questioned him about Uryen? She hadn't questioned him much. She had been shy herself over that; but there always seemed some queer barrier that rose up between them when his name was mentioned.

"All right then! I'll come without it. I *could* have caught you up; but if you feel like that about it—let it go! There, my dear, take my arm. I won't run away." Why did D. No-man have to say all this so loudly? Did he want everyone to know how trying he could be? But she took his arm, and tried to be as sweet to him as she could. She smiled at him as much as to say, "Look at 'Thel' fussing over that old man!" and with her free hand— while she leant on him with the other—she pushed her jersey under her broad leather belt, calling his attention to the prancing horse on its polished buckle, and hoping all the while that Uryen was watching these intimacies.

The little party walked down South Street in a loose, casual group. They could really have walked side by side down the middle of the road, so quiet was the town and so few were the people visible. The Fordington bells had stopped; but those in St. Peter's tower were ringing beautifully, and the sound made Wizzie's mood grow tenderer and tenderer. "It's funny how I like holding D.'s arm," she thought: "and looking at Uryen! It makes me feel safe. I really don't know whether I'd *want* to hold Uryen's arm. I'd be so nervous, it would spoil everything."

Up and down on the sound of St. Peter's bells her spirit floated, like a boat on a brimming tide. How massive and compact all the houses were in this old town! How they seemed to settle their patient stones into the solid earth just as if they were searching for the foundations of older buildings, which in their turn were reaching down to yet older ones.

"Mercy! I believe I'd even enjoy Icen Way to-day," she thought. "I must be getting soft like Nance. What a lot of people there must be just out of bed and having breakfast! The houses have a look as if they were full of people." And the fancy came to her as she walked along clutching D.'s arm that what made the town so still was purely the sound of these bells. Everything was listening to them. Not only the people, but their furniture; and not only the furniture, but the geraniums and calceolarias in the window-boxes!

"I used to feel like this," she thought, "waking up in that house in London when I was little. I used to feel like it when I played with my doll's house on the landing where the blue vase stood, as if everything was yours and you belonged to everything; to the stones outside and the chairs and tables inside, and the playthings in their boxes and the fires in their kitchens, and the cats on their rugs and the canaries in their cages and the pots on their kitchen-ranges! It's like the air and the warmth in the air knowing about you, and everything being nice because of that, and because of the rooks cawing and because of those milk-bottles being outside that door! It's the quietness of it, with these crowded houses listening to every step, and the pavements hot with sunshine and the roads all still, enjoying themselves; enjoying a little peace."

Her mounting happiness became so intense as she went along, gazing at Uryen's huge slouching back and dusky head, and thinking to herself: "He isn't listening to what 'Thel's' saying. He's thinking of me!" that when they reached the South Walk she felt, since Lovie wasn't there to be hugged, she'd have to do something to please D. No-man!

"I don't mind waiting for you here, D." she said. "I couldn't in the town. Besides, it bothered them all, your going back. But I'll sit down over there. You can run round by your Icen Way. *I* don't mind! I really honestly don't. We'll soon overtake them. I do wish to goodness we *had* brought Lovie!"

No-man removed his cap and wiped his forehead with his hand. He dropped her arm and stood still. He looked perplexed and worried, hesitating what to do, miserable without his great cudgel, but evidently unwilling to leave her.

"Well?" she repeated. "Aren't you going? There's a seat over there—you won't be long. We'll soon catch them up."

She looked steadily at him and their eyes clung to each other. They were standing by the railings, close to the cenotaph. The others were already crossing the road, Claudius and Mr. Wye in front, Uryen and Thuella following them.

Neither of the two seemed to wish to be the first to look away; but the girl didn't feel as if either of them were thinking solely of the other. They each seemed to be looking *through* the other, down some long receding vista of future days.

Almost as instinctively as if No-man had been Lovie, the girl suddenly put out her hand to straighten the collar of his coat. There must have been something about this natural gesture that struck the man as unusual; for the character of the expression in his eyes completely changed and in its changing caused a change in hers, too. They no longer looked through each other, thinking of their own lives. They looked *at* each other, wondering, confused, embarrassed, and with a sort of tentative shyness.

The bells at this point changed their "tempo," no doubt to indicate that there was only five minutes left before the beginning of the morning service, while a couple of tall choir-boys, hurrying past them, cast the same sort of covetous look at Wizzie's perfectly modelled hips and flanks as an older church-goer might have done.

The girl herself, so accustomed had she grown in the Circus to these anonymous recognitions of the desirability of her person, didn't give the boys' clinging glance a thought, but she detected in a second how a magnetic current passed into No-man's erotic nerves, and well did the girl know the appraising look with which he surveyed her, from the collar of her jersey to her belt and thence down her side. She knew that at that moment he would have been ready to burn a whole page of *Mary Channing* on condition that he might fondle her then and there to his heart's content!

But she frowned and sighed and looked away. Their significant moment had quite gone, killed by those choir-boys' effrontery, but the very last thing she wanted just then was to give him an opportunity for that cold-blooded dalliance which seemed the only passion of which he was capable.

Oh, she knew him so well! For when, after a nervous opening and shutting of the fingers of his right hand, as if to grasp the handle of that stick he had forgotten, he gave a little jerk to her wrist and whispered hurriedly. "Come back with me, sweetheart! They'll not worry, they'll just go on; and we'll catch

345

them up before they get to Maiden Castle; or, if we don't, we'll find them there. Come along, my pet!"

The dark wave of anger that mounted up in her against him at this moment showed itself in her eyes. Was this the way he was going to take her to his lodging in High East Street *for the first time?* Just because he hadn't seen her before in jersey and trousers!

He had hardly touched her hand when he dropped it hurriedly, catching sight of her face. "You don't want to? Oh, well, oh, well—then I won't go myself. To the devil with my stick, sweetheart! Don't 'ee look like that. I won't go at all! Come on, we'll soon catch them up. I didn't mean to spoil the day like this—and such a perfect day as it is! Come on, old girl."

Wizzie turned with him in silence, and they followed the path beside the row of villas that border the Weymouth Road as far as the Brewery.

It was impossible for them to avoid turning to look at the familiar fair-field when they came opposite to it. There was a great show of some kind there; but it was one of the ordinary big English circuses, and the name of its proprietor—a thoroughly English name—was displayed in large letters on its whirligigs and caravans. A curious Sunday calm hung over the glittering engine and the great show-tent—a somewhat desolate calm, characteristic of most places of human entertainment when under a temporary religious ban. A few men were strolling about among the closed booths and a group of children were peering at them through the rails, hoping evidently to snatch some unofficial glimpse of the open-mouthed lions and tigers advertised on the billboard.

"I expect our friends have left that foreigner," said D. Noman, "and gone back to a gipsy life again. I expect your foreign Circus itself has gone back where it came from—to Prague perhaps!" Wizzie quickened her steps. She could just see a good way ahead, over against the railings of Maumbury Rings, the slouching form of the bare-headed Uryen and Thuella's yellow dress and big-brimmed hat.

The sight of the fair-field and the familiar circus-erections brought back to her her insane desperation at Lovie's birth. But these things couldn't hurt her as they had done once. Away with them into the furnace of foul memories!

346

Her anger against D. No-man ebbed away rapidly as they went on; and they gradually drew nearer to Uryen and Thuella.

They were at the Amphitheatre now and the sunshine lay warm and bright on the slope of the near bank of that ancient circle of cruel sport and inhuman punishment. The man at her side gave the place a hurried excited glance, and then turned sharp upon her thrusting his hands deep into his pockets in an obvious effort to forget the absence of his familiar stick.

"Do you know, Wizz," he began, and then as he always did when his mind was full of something—and she sighed as he did it now—he stood stock-still, so that she was forced to pause, too.

"I'm going to make this old place of cruelty," he went on, "such a wound on the conscience of everyone that the ripples of what I say'll go on expanding, till—till——"

"Till what?" she said, watching him with her usual puzzled frown.

"Till they touch a few horrors of *our* time, my dear, such as——" He stopped, while an expression she had never noticed before came into his face. "Do you know," he went on slowly, and as if it wasn't easy for him to say the words, "that these mad scientists torture animals in their laboratories for what they call 'knowledge' just as the Romans did for what they called 'pleasure'?"

It was the tone of his voice rather than the gist of his words that made the girl's eyes grow startled and round. "Yes, and our stupid public opinion is just as indifferent—just as *gulled* into indifference—as it was then, and as it was when ten thousand people came here to see my Mary burnt!"

It was curious how she couldn't help the skin under a part of her boy's clothes turning into what is called "goose-flesh" under his words. He had talked to her about vivisection before, but never quite in this tone. Not that her mind was impressed. It was her body that felt that spasm of shivering. In her mind she reassured herself. She remembered the extravagant heroics that the girl in her story-book had to put up with for *her* eloquent lover.

Wizzie's conscience in these things was not, it must be admitted, any striking compliment to the influence of that early

347

bringing-up of which she was so proud. She was no fool, but in certain directions her mind was almost as undeveloped as Popsy's.

D. No-man sighed. He had evidently transgressed in this outburst some long-standing rule of his, and the girl felt vaguely that she hadn't distinguished herself in his eyes by the feeble : "Yes, D., yes, I see!" with which she received his words.

They moved on again but their delay had put a considerable distance between them and that slouching figure and the yellow dress by its side. Indeed, by the time they reached the cemetery gates Uryen and Thuella had turned into the Maiden Castle road and were out of sight.

Opposite the entrance to the cemetery, however, her incorrigible companion stopped again. "If he mentions Mary Channing now," the girl thought, "I'll just run on after Uryen, and he'll have to catch me by running!"

But it was about Uryen, not Mary Channing, that the man wanted to talk to her; and she listened with some apprehension. "Have you noticed anything?" he began very gravely, while the irrelevant thought flitted like a swift bird through the girl's head, "he's never taken me to see his mother's grave, any more than he's taken me to his room! He treats me like his 'tart,' not like his wife."

"Noticed what?"

"Anything about me and Enoch Quirm?"

"You and Uryen?"

"Yes."

"What about you and Uryen?"

"Have you noticed anything lately, very lately—anything different?"

"You've gone about a lot together. You've taken a fancy to each other. But why not? You gave him a share of the Cumber work. You got him out of a ticklish place. He's grateful, I expect."

"I don't mean that. I mean something else, Wizz."

There was no need for him to take her by the wrist now, for she had lifted up her face with breathless interest and was giving him a tremulous and concentrated hearing.

"Is he," she thought. "going to warn me that Uryen and I are too thick? Is he going to tell me that those Glymes people have begun to talk? I don't care if they have! I'll tell him what Jenny says about Nance and him."

"You remember that time in February, Wizz, when we went to Glymes, and he gave me that 'Head' for my bed? The thing you hated so when I put it on our chimney-piece?"

"Yes, yes, of course. Go *on*, for pity's sake!" For some reason she felt a fantastic alarm at what he might say. The idea that he was going to scold her about Uryen died down. But she still felt a tension of her nerves that made her extremely uncomfortable. "Tell me, tell me quick! Don't torment me, D.! What is it?"

"You remember how I've said that you and I are so like each other in so many ways?"

The girl nodded. She would have made a wry face at this point, if she hadn't been so intensely interested; for it was to the tune of these precious resemblances that he made love to her in the way she disliked most.

"And that it seemed like a kind of fate bring us together, that we both should have lost our mothers and never seen our fathers?"

"I *saw* my father!" she cried; and at the word she felt an almost complete liberation from her nervous tension that had been mounting up in her. In her relief she permitted her eyes to wander over the crowded cemetery at their side, wondering where D.'s mother's grave was among such a multitude, and what *her* mother would have thought of D. had she ever met him!

"But you don't *remember* seeing him," argued No-man stubbornly, evidently prepared to let the most life-and-death subject go when the question arose of his ideal "resemblance" to his Bronze-Age captive.

Wizzie shook her head and smiled at him happily. She felt so relieved that what he was making all this fuss about had only to do with their parents, and had no connection with her interest in Uryen, that she no longer hung on his words. In fact, as he went on to tell her about his mother, and about some affair his mother had had with Uryen before Nance came on the scene, her attention began to wander.

But men are all like that! The nuns had looked at each other when their priest was talking. She and Grummer had looked at

each other a thousand times when Old Funky was talking. She
and Jenny had looked at each other when Claudius was talking,
and how often must "Thel" and Nance have looked at each
other in that dirty study at Glymes!

While she kept saying: "Yes, yes, yes," D. went on, and he
seemed surprised she wasn't more astonished when he told her so
solemnly about his mother having let Uryen embrace her in the
bed with the heraldic heads. She was more interested in the
people who passed just then than in Uryen's early love-affairs;
and she noticed how silent these young men became in the
intensity of their desire for her. She noticed how they stopped
talking and laughing—just stared in dazed absorption till they
had passed. None of them, however, dared to look back; and it
wasn't as if D. had his great stick!

No, she couldn't understand their not looking back—but let
them go! It wasn't for men, not for *any* man, she'd put on these
things; not even for her "Black Man of Glymes." For herself,
alone!

But what was this? Mercy! what was D. telling her now?
Her mouth as well as her eyes opened as the import of his words
reached her, and her hands, which had been rather awkwardly
pressed low down into her boy's pockets, began unconsciously to
clasp each other, squeezing her knuckles white.

"But—you are—*sure*, D.?" she gasped in a low voice. "They
may have had a child, but are you sure it was *you*?" No-man
who had been astonished and a little hurt at her previous calmness, couldn't prevent a flicker of satisfaction in the presence of
her agitation, the satisfaction a person naturally feels when
startling news produces its proper effect.

"There can be no possible doubt," he said dryly. "The man's
my father. I've got to make the best of it."

"Do you—like him?"

No-man gave vent to a grim chuckle. "It's not a question of
that, my dear. It's a question of—it's a—different question,
Wizz."

"And Jenny says Nance has got fond of *you*; and I——"

He caught her up. "And you, I suppose, have got, as you say,
'fond' of him! It seems a peculiarity of girls to do that. Thuella
appears altogether——"

He stopped abruptly, aware of the deep trouble in her face.

Then he laid his hand on her shoulder. "Don't 'ee take it too hard, old girl," he whispered gently. "Perhaps it's just as well you *do* like him—since I'm his son."

"Oh, why, why, didn't you tell me this before?"

He made a vague gesture of helplessness.

"You knew in February, didn't you?" she said sharply.

"No, I didn't know then."

"But *that* was when—wasn't it?"

"I didn't know then."

She was silent, letting her eyes wander to the headstones that were visible through the iron gates.

"I don't see," he said slowly, "why you should take this so hard. It's me—it's I—not you— who's got to deal with it."

Her reply came quickly. "You ought to have told me from the start. You're not open with me, D.—not only about him, but about everything—oh, why did I ever——?" and her mouth drew down ominously. "You've not been open with me," she repeated, swallowing the lump in her throat.

"Were you so open with me then, my girl? A lot you ever told me about——"

"Stop!" she cried sharply. "No more of that! I won't *have* it—do you understand? If I agreed to live with you—if I went on living with you after I found——"

"Found *what*? Go on! We may as well have it all out, now we've begun. This isn't a bad place for you and me to come to an understanding. I don't know whether I ever told you; but it was here—by their graves down there—that I first met Nance, before we found you—and those people—behind the tent——"

She gave him one startled outraged look, a look from the depths of her woman's nature. "D.!" she murmured in a different voice, a subdued, weak, unsteady voice, "I never thought you would speak of *that* in this tone."

His face became drawn and tense and his mouth twitched. "You've never talked freely to me," he said. "You've never taken me into your confidence. You've kept that for your friend Jenny. Even *now* I don't know—I've not the least idea—what's really going on in your mind. You keep yourself as far from me as if—as if our room—our bed—our life together, were no more to you than—your life with *them*, before I took you away."

A spectator of this scene would have found it pathetic, the way in which in her boy's costume she made the little movements that a woman makes at a moment of stress. She herself was unconscious of what she did with her hands, feeling for her pockets, fumbling at her belt, plucking at the front of her jersey. She knew him so little that her ignorance closed in upon her self-pity, narrowing its channel, building a barrier between them.

She didn't even know—since in her self-colloquies she had got into the habit of assuming that the only bond between them was his cold-blooded sensuality—why it was that his words, his tone, hurt her like this, or why beneath her anger and grievance a strange cold, lost feeling began to invade her heart. Some deep instinctive assumption she had slipped into with him, far below her nervous irritations, began to crack and fall apart, as if that familiar Weymouth Road under her feet had broken into fissures and yawning crevices.

It never occurred to her to suspect that the sweet exciting glow about Uryen's interest in her was like the dallying of a rock-plant with the caresses of the wooing sun—dalliance that was impossible save for its root in the stone out of which it grew.

Her pride was so much greater than her knowledge, her conscious understanding so far inferior to her blind feminine instincts, that even now, in spite of the deathly chill that invaded her under his unexpected attack, she clung obstinately with her story-book intelligence to the fixed idea that there was no "real love" between them, that "real love" belonged to that picture-show world of her imagination, that world of magnetic glances from mysterious personages like the Glymes man, that world where she was brought back from her Circus-triumphs by a passionate admirer's limousine to a resplendent Lovie under a rosy porch!

"So Nance is 'fond' of *me,* is she?" he brought out with bitter sarcasm. "And *you* find yourself quite upset when you know who the man is you're so attracted to—and don't think I've not seen it—I saw it on Candlemas night when he made that stuff you and 'Thel' liked drinking! It's unlucky, isn't it, that he likes Thuella so much? But come on; let's hurry and catch them up! I've known, all the time, how annoyed you've been to hang back for me, with such exciting people ahead. I saw why you didn't want me to get my stick. Come on; let's catch them up! He'll love to have you with him as well as Thuella."

No-man might just as well have been repeating his own name: "Dud, Dud, Dud, Dud, Dud," over and over again, as indulging in all this elaborate sarcasm. Since his first words she hadn't listened to a thing he said. That deadly chill air from the crack in the security under her feet had numbed her whole being. She didn't care what he thought, or what he said, or for any reasonings he used. All she wanted was for the ground under her feet to stop swaying and cracking, to stop letting through those death-airs. So she kept staring and staring at him, her eyes brimming, her throat swelling, her lips sucked in against her teeth, and her nose, for all the sunshine that played upon it, showing white and pinched.

He must have seen that his sarcasms were paper darts sinking into a wooden post, for he suddenly changed his tune. He began talking to her in a low whisper, a whisper into which he threw every grievance against her that had been accumulating since November.

"How far have you gone with him, you and Thuella? Or perhaps I ought to say how far have you let *him* go? It's a shame I don't feel proud of a father—isn't it?—who likes 'em in pairs, like partridges. But how far has this thing gone? I knew there was something. You didn't fool me *altogether*. But all these things are so laughable—aren't they?—that it's hard to be serious about them. But you didn't fool me altogether! But what's so amusing about it is to think that he was just the same to mother as he is to you! That's what I've been thinking about lately—the amusingness of it all—*his* body and hers and now yours; and how funny that both mother and you should like men with hairy chests and men who aren't particularly keen on washing. *Can't you speak?* I know it's a shock to you to find out how old he is—well over sixty, anyway—I'm the one to know that much—*but can't you speak?*"

She straightened herself where she stood, clasped her hands behind her back, swallowed her tears, and faced him boldly. "I—simply—don't—know—what you're—talking about, D.," she said slowly. "There's *nothing at all* between Uryen and me, and let me tell you this too, you've no right to say that there's anything between him and 'Thel'! He's a peculiar man, he's a wonderful man; and I don't deny he's been kind to me and to 'Thel,' too. What's the matter with you, D.? What's come over you, that you act like this? You've never done it before. You've never before interfered with me. You've let me have everything I wanted. And now you suddenly turn on me like a madman! If you didn't want me to go to Glymes, if you didn't want me to see Mr. Quirm, why didn't you tell me so? I was happy enough in Friary Lane with Jenny. I didn't need to go to Glymes, or to take Lovie to Glymes. What *is* it? What's come over you? You must know perfectly well in your heart that I've not let any man but you—old *or* young—touch me since I've belonged to you. Has Jenny been putting things into your head? Do be sensible, D.—*don't* get such wild ideas!"

No-man's face changed a lot during this appeal. It lost its tension. Something resembling the pallid ghost of a smile flickered across it.

And Wizzie, whose penetration into the depths of human feeling had sharpened a good deal during this agitating scene, had the wit to see that he believed her, and the wit too to see that this reassurance was an incredible relief to him! Who on earth had put it into his head that she had gone such lengths with the "Black Man of Glymes"? As to what he told her about Uryen and him and their being father and son, she simply didn't believe it. D. *couldn't* be so much younger than Uryen. In all his ways D. was like an old man. Secretly she'd suspected from the first that he was much older than he pretended, just as Old Funky was much younger. No—no. Uryen was up to something with D. as everybody else was! D. was the most hopelessly stupid man in the whole world.

"Well, kid, let's go now, anyway. We can talk as we go," he had murmured awkwardly; and it was to the rhythm of their two pairs of feet on the Maiden Castle road that he gave her the rest of his evidence about the Glymes man and tried to show her that there could be no mistake in his conclusion. To all this she scarcely listened. What she kept wondering was how he had got it lodged in his mind that there "was something between" her and Uryen.

With her fixed idea of his pathetic stupidity it seemed to her unthinkable that he could really have noticed her girlish tremors in Uryen's presence. Her relief at his faith in her denial, the closing up of that terrible crack in the ground under her feet, her surprised recognition that he *could* get angry with her in the jealous fashion of an ordinary lover, all these things so restored her good spirits that she began to feel not only much wiser and cleverer than her old D. but easier in her mind about the excited feelings that the Glymes man had aroused.

It was not long before No-man, captivated as he had been all that morning, by the appeal of her boy's clothes, slipped his arm about her waist and began a sort of perambulatory love-making as they moved forward. She soon felt his fingers sliding from her waist to her side, and under his touch the swing of her limbs as she walked became a mechanical response to his amorous pressure. Cold as she was left as a rule by No-man's caresses there was something in the impregnating warmth of this June day that made her feel abnormally receptive, and thus it came about, for what was really the first time in all these months, that this pressure of his hand against her side as she moved proved to be, what no toyings or dallyings in the secure retreat of their Friary Lane room had ever been—a real provocation to her senses.

To the end of her life she never forgot that walk to the foot of Maiden Castle. All the way along that straight white hedge-less road, as it crossed the unenclosed pasture-lands and arable lands, which rolled off on both sides to their remote upland horizons, she yielded herself to a delicious orgy of nervous sensuality. Her relief in escaping from that ice-cold feeling of being an outcast in the world endowed the pressure of No-man's satyr-ish fingers with an unwonted human warmth.

But what was that? Her companion's voice, piercing the languorous trance of her wanton feelings, was talking now about something different from these diggings for dead idols.

"May I ask you something, something very particular, my precious?" he whispered, pulling her so close to him that she had to skip a step or two to get into rhythm with his strides.

And then, taking her yielding person as a symbol of a yielded personality, he admitted that what he would give a great deal to know if she didn't mind telling him—but if she *did* she must just say so and he wouldn't be offended—was whether, if she *had* by any chance got fond of Uryen, or had had what they call "an affair" with Uryen, she would have felt a curious loath-

355

ing for such an entanglement now he'd told her who the man was.

"You mean who *you* are," she said with rather a silly little laugh; but feeling reassured as she did now, she felt it hard to be serious.

"Don't 'ee try and be funny, child!" he retorted. "If it *isn't* as sickening to me as it would be to some, it isn't very nice. You mustn't think I'm entirely philosophical about it—I mean that I'm his son and he's my father."

"No, dear. I know how you feel."

"But would *you* have felt upset over it, Wizz, if you had—I know you haven't, but if you had—let him make love to you?"

"I don't see——"

"You mean you'd feel the same as if we weren't related at all?"

"I don't see——"

"You don't see that it makes any difference?" He looked at her gravely, half-humorously. "I always thought *I* was pretty detached in things like this, but on my soul, old girl, you beat me at it! I suppose it's only my bookishness, but when I think of those old Greek plays making so much of——"

"Oh, what, D.? What on earth are you talking about now? Gracious! I've never read a Greek play in my life. You'd better talk to Mr. Wye! Popsy told me she knew a father and son who lived with the same girl for years. She was his step-mother, of course, and there used to be rows; but in the end, when the father died, he left them all his money, and Popsy said the girl wasn't so nice to him when the old man was gone as she was before; and she never would marry him."

No-man couldn't help smiling at this. "But what would your convent people have thought, Wizz?"

"I'm sure *I* don't know! Not the same as your old Greeks, anyway!"

A flock of starlings swept down upon the edge of the field at their side where there was some newly sprouting corn, and then, disturbed by their advance, whirled away again, with a confused chattering, the sunshine heavy on their swaying mass of clumsy wings.

A man whose occupation it was impossible to guess, but whose attire was neutral, his expression impenetrable, his tie modest, his boots polished, his hands in his pockets, overtook them at this juncture, walking with brisk steps, his eyes on the road. No sooner had he passed them than he began whistling, in a faint flat monotone, a few bars from the familiar song. "Daisy, Daisy, give me your answer, do! I'm half-crazy, all for the love of you!"

No-man's arm fell incontinently to his side; and Wizzie could see from the savage wrinkling of his profile, which seemed snarling like a dog whose bone is taken away, that he could hardly restrain his anger.

A dead rook with a look in its eye as if it were thankful to be dead, and its few remaining feathers discoloured by dust, offered itself, however, as a humble distraction; and No-man, stooping down, picked it up by its tail, muttered some gibberish over it that she couldn't catch, and flung it into the young green wheat. To her present mood, the neutral pedestrian, with his half-hearted whistling, was a pleasing episode, while her companion's fuss over those dusty bones struck her as a most dreary affectation; but she could see that his face had resumed its equanimity as he paused to let the impertinent personage get ahead.

"What I mean is, Wizz," he went on. "Suppose you *had* started an affair with my father, would it have weighed on your mind when I told you who he was?"

She tried submissively to catch his drift, but she tried in vain. His own obvious absorption in the irresistible appeal of her figure in those tight trousers added the last note to the exultant trance of well-being in which she moved; and this matter of Uryen and he being father and son seemed totally irrelevant, even if it *were* true, to her relation either to the one or the other.

There was a groan of real trouble in the sigh with which he received her vague expression of uncertainty, her feeble: "I don't see, D., *why* it would have been so awful," but he let the matter drop after that, and they moved on slowly, keeping well to the rear of the brisk-stepping citizen with his hands in his pockets.

It was not long before No-man expressed his feelings about this easy gentleman in plain words——

"God damn this chap! Why can't he go slower or faster?

357

What does a person like that, anyway, think is going on at Maiden Castle?"

"Oh, shut up, D., do!" she protested. "We don't own the whole road." Womanlike she accepted this neutral person's presence as she accepted the dead rook and the hovering starlings; but the presence of a low bank at their side with an amazing variety of feathery grasses made her think how Lovie would have liked this walk. "She'd have wanted to get out and run along that bank," she thought, and she longed to be able to share her good spirits with her offspring.

"I'd like to know," said No-man presently, when they had nearly reached the gate where the road ended, and nothing but a lightly trodden field-track led up to the sacred earthworks, "what that fellow gets out of coming here?"

"Much the same as ourselves," she retorted turning to glance behind them. "There are people all the way along the road now! Dorchester people love an excuse to come out on Sunday."

But they both instinctively paused at this point, for the man in front of them had taken off his new bowler hat and was apparently examining the label inside it, as he leaned over the gate.

"I can't understand how anyone like you, who's writing books about people"—Wizzie had no idea she was going to blurt this out, but the thought seemed to have go so heavy in her mind that it slipped out and fell of its own accord, like a ripe pear— "can hate everyone like you do, D.! The world has to have all sorts, hasn't it? I know you don't think you're like anyone else, but *really*, you're just like those patronizing upper-class people who want to keep everyone at a distance." She felt his blank astonishment at her audacity in the way he looked at her; but he only said: "Come on, child! We must hurry up. They're waiting for us up there."

They had to pass the man at the gate; and in place of opening it to let them through he stepped back a pace or two and stared intently as they opened it for themselves. No-man haughtily averted his eyes from the irrelevant personage as he closed the gate after them, but Wizzie met the fellow's glance and no sooner had she done so than she realized that all this manoeuvring was simply to get a good, undisturbed stare at herself in her jersey and trousers. The normal "set" expression of the man's face changed as his eyes met hers into a relaxed and maudlin leer—not so much a leer, perhaps, as a fatuous, desire-drunk spasm of obsessed gazing—and afterwards, as they proceeded towards the entrance of the mysterious *Polis,* she knew perfectly well that the besotted individual was walking as closely as he dared behind them! She could even hear him pant—for he was not an athletic figure—and tap his knees, as he walked, with the hard brim of his bowler hat.

But *there* were all their four friends waiting for them on the extreme top of the first rampart of turf! No-man waved his arm to greet them and Wizzie was struck by the solemn and dramatic manner in which he did this; not just perfunctorily and casually, but exaggeratedly, just as Popsy used to do to the Circus-audience, when, after some difficulty with her balancing, she had at last got through her "turn."

He let her climb the hill a good deal ahead of the rest of them and none of the four at the crest of the highest ridge could see anything of her as she climbed, but in her mind she saw them, at least she saw Uryen and "Thel."

It was no great distance from the foot of Mai-Dun to the summit, but the final slope was steep, and not even in the Circus had Wizzie's spirits risen to the pitch they rose to now, or the exultant power of her body been more ready for anything. Her boy's attire offered no feminine impediment to her breathless rush, as she climbed the face of the final bulwark, but though the distance was negligible and her speed was beyond the power of any ordinary girl, she experienced for that brief epoch—for nothing is less of an absolute than time—some of the most radiant and exultant moments in her whole life.

Light-winged butterflies—but since neither at the convent nor in the Circus had Wizzie learnt any natural history, their names were nothing to her—fluttered against her face. Tiny little moths of various shades of pallid brown appeared and disappeared under her very fingers.

There was a scent in her nostrils as of grass upon which the sun had been shining so long that from every particular blade above the ground and from every rooty fibre beneath the ground something of the earth's most intimate sweat seemed to evaporate in the hot amorous air. She derived a curious sensual pleasure, every time she stooped in her ascent, from contact with the sun-warmed grass; and once or twice, as she bent down, she actually dug her nails into the thick-growing, honey-sweet turf. "I want to be myself," she thought as she scrambled up the slope with that hay-sweet scent in her nostrils, "I don't want to belong to either of them!"

But in the play of her limbs as she climbed she found it impossible not to yield more and more to that dangerous magnetic pull of Uryen's personality. "I may have a funny face," she thought, "but I am beautiful to-day."

Her appearance, hot and breathing hard after her rapid climb, but charmingly flushed and radiant, produced an electric effect upon the four persons seated on the top of the ridge.

Thuella jumped up at once. "We were waiting for you, my dear," she cried. "We thought you and D. might be totally lost! But sit down and rest yourself. We'll wait for D. here. Uryen has to go on now, to see what's happening at the excavations; but when he's found out how things are over there he'll come back and tell us. What are *you* doing, Father?" This last remark was addressed to Teucer Wye who was trying to catch a languid butterfly in his thin fingers.

"I'm going with Mr. Quirm," the professor brought out, letting the butterfly escape. "Won't *you* come too, Cask?"

"Hadn't we better wait for No-man?" said Claudius with no sign of rising.

But Teucer Wye scrambled up at once and laid his hand on his shoulder. "Come along, Cask," he said. "They can follow us, if they want to. No-man'll need a rest after his climb. We can report progress when we get back."

Wizzie noticed that Thuella gave her father an appreciative glance as Claudius rose stiffly to his feet. She seemed in as good a temper with her parent to-day as he was with her. "There, my dear, *there*!" she said to Wizzie. "Do as you're told, like a good child," and collapsing again upon the turf, she pulled her down at her side. Almost everything that our friend had hoped for was in the quick exchange of looks that now passed between Uryen and herself as she stretched herself, still breathing hard, by the prostrate girl.

The man's glance seemed to her to say : "Do as they tell you. Don't worry about me. We understand each other perfectly," and when the three of them went off at a leisurely pace, she deliberately refrained from following them with her eyes, but turned, with more sympathy in her flushed face than usual, to the wearer of the yellow dress.

"You darling," Thuella murmured, "now at last I've got you to myself!" And then with the particular look of narrow-lidded concentrated mischief, with which from time immemorial the harem has conspired against its possessor, she whispered in hurried eagerness: "How far did you leave him behind? How soon will he be here?"

For answer Wizzie merely shrugged her shoulders and rolling over with her face against the sweet-scented turf began plucking little blades of grass and drawing them negligently between her teeth. She knew exactly how "Thel" was sitting—for the girl too had changed her pose after that furtive question—by the feel of a foot against her side and a hand on her shoulder. Clearly she could visualize that upright cross-legged figure in the yellow dress, the long limbs bent beneath the flimsy skirt and the flapping hat concealing the bright hair. She felt wonderfully older than "Thel" as she tasted the bitter-sweetness of those small grass-blades. Somehow she felt as if her own unfulfilled and perhaps never-to-be-fulfilled ambitions, that image of herself balanced in radiant poise on her old horse's back and leaping forward, with that strong back always beneath her, through all the starry hoops of the world, placed her, even in her very renunciation, on a higher level than "Thel's" cloud-creating claims.

But had D., or Uryen himself, perhaps, told the girl, long before this, of their men's astonishing relationship? And, if "Thel" did know, did it set up in *her* eyes, as apparently it had done in his, some shocking barrier, a barrier only to be passed by an unthinkable sacrilege, between Uryen and any girl who lived with D.?

No, no. "Thel" was no more like an ordinary woman than she was herself. These artists were free of such scruples, and the wild clouds on "Thel's" canvas were like the glittering spangles of her own starry rush through the air—something that crossed these things on a magic tight-rope! But "Thel" was talking to her now, talking in a low excited voice, and Wizzie could feel, not only those electric fingers through her jersey, as the girl's

361

hand caressed her shoulder, but the troubled intensity with which she was looking down upon her prostrate form.

"Yes," she was saying, "and I'm not a bit jealous of you with him, and never shall be; but I am—oh, Wizzie darling!—and you know it, only you don't *want* to know it—terribly jealous of him with you! I'm jealous of everybody with you, of old D. even, silly though that may sound, and I'm wickedly—do you hear, you dangerous, silent girl—I'm wickedly jealous of Lovie."

Still drawing the little grasses through her teeth and making a faint sound that only herself could hear as she drew a drop of sweetness from each of them before she threw it away, Wizzie continued to feel so much older than the breather of these impassioned sentences that she found it impossible to take them seriously.

Her convent-school and her Circus-school had set such a gulf between men and women, and she herself—for all Jenny's talk of her "corruption"—was so eminently normal in these things, that all she said to herself was: " 'Thel's' too demonstrative. I *must* make her tell me which of her boys I remind her of!"

"It's Uryen's *ideas* that fascinate me," Thuella went on. "I can't bear the smelly clothes. He's more like a Chinaman than a Welshman. How on earth Nance can bear it when he takes off——"

"Don't be disgusting, 'Thel'!" our friend protested, spitting out a fragment of chalk-grit that had got into her mouth. "Of course you'll say it's my Circus-life; but it *isn't* that, at all. I don't care a damn how dirty a man is, or what his ideas are either! It's something quite different. By the way, 'Thel'—what *are* Uryen's ideas? I've heard him talk, and I like listening to him, but it seems to me it's all perfectly crazy. If Lovie were a man, instead of a baby girl, she'd have 'ideas' exactly like——"

"Who would Lovie have ideas like?"

Both the girls gave a start, and Thuella uttered a shrill little noise like the cry of a frightened moor-hen. But their disturber was only D. No-man, reaching them from an angle rather different from the one where they would naturally have looked for him.

"Well? Who *has* got Lovie's ideas?" he repeated brusquely, sitting down on Wizzie's further side. He was evidently delighted to come upon them like this; and to Wizzie, though she

362

still continued lying on her stomach, sucking grasses, it was a pleasant surprise that he was so gratified. "He can't like Thuella *very* much," she thought, "or he'd be annoyed by finding us together."

"Wizzie says," began Thuella, removing as she did so her big hat and tossing it on the grass, "that though she respects Uryen very much she thinks nothing of his ideas. She thinks his ideas are childish. What do you think about *that*, Master?"

He mumbled some incoherent sentence in reply to this, which Wizzie thought was a quotation from Shakespeare, but it left the younger girl as much in the dark as before as to whether "Thel" knew, or did not know, about D. and Uryen.

There was a silence after that between the three of them, till the man inquired what had happened to the rest of the party.

"Oh, don't worry about them, D.," Wizzie answered. "They know where we are."

"It was Claudius," threw in Thuella. "He couldn't wait; and he dragged Father and Uryen with him."

Another silence ensued which was broken by a noisy group of young people passing just below their resting-place. Of these new-comers it was possible only to see the heads and the hats, objects that belonged, it seemed, to three lads and a couple of women.

"Did you have a good breakfast in your attic, D.?" inquired Thuella. "Or did you get cross with 'the Royal Martyr' this morning?"

The effect of this question upon Wizzie's mind surprised herself, and while No-man began some long-winded rigmarole about what he'd seen from his kitchen-window yesterday or the day before, she rolled over and lay on her back between them, her head raised a little and her hands clasped behind it.

"What's this?" she thought. "He never tells *me* these things. But I'm not going to ask him what she's talking about." She had scarcely made this wise resolution, however, than she heard herself saying: "I wouldn't cross the threshold of D.'s room up there, 'Thel,' for fifty pounds! He brought one of those monsters —the one he got from Glymes—into *our* room and I made him take it away. He's got a pair of them up there now! I wouldn't sleep with such things at the foot of my bed—not if he paid me!"

363

She was certain she saw No-man at that second dodge a look that swept across her from the sunlit figure at her side. But he hurriedly began talking to them both in his most tiresome vein.

"You women are too practical," he told them, his eyes turning hastily from one to the other. "When Wizz wakes up she thinks only of what she's done or is going to do, or what Lovie's done or is going to do. *I* keep my mind——" He paused for a second under the look Wizzie gave him. "I'll pay you out for this," was what her look said.

And then her thoughts went back to Uryen and his being this tedious man's father. "It's all nonsense! Uryen can't be as old as that. But if he is, *I* don't care! I wouldn't care if the Devil was the father of both of them!"

But as she cogitated in this way, with her eyes half-closed, it began to dawn on her that some sort of emotional drama was going on across her grey trousers.

No-man kept fidgetting uneasily as he talked, and through the dazzling sun-spangles, that did not so much hide the two of them from her as metamorphose them into a blinding transfiguration, she seemed to detect—for she compensated for her want of responsiveness to symbolic figures like D.'s ditch-digger by being abnormally alive to the psychic currents between men and women—that Thuella was exercising some kind of sensual witchcraft over No-man. The second she realized this she became vividly alert to every word he was uttering, and not only so but she gave him one of those inspired smiles that women have the power of conjuring up, a smile whose falsity no man can fathom, for it has behind it the treachery of Nature herself.

But it must not be supposed that Wizzie for one second felt that there was anything extraordinary in all these criss-cross love-makings. Like most women, moving, as we all have to do, in the midst of a flickering cat's cradle of erotic currents, she took the most fantastic complications, that life so delights to improvise, in a spirit of practical and literal simplicity.

Left to herself, a natural daughter, as Uryen might have put it, of the earth-goddess Caridwen, it would never have occurred to her that any emotion, as long as it could somehow be squeezed into the category of love, could be regarded as "piquant" or "ironic" or "grotesque."

It was as much a part of life, this gipsy emotion, as a stickleback among minnows, or a puff-ball among cowslips, and to regard it as a mixture of the monstrous and the humorous instead of taking it simply and sadly as the way life was, struck her as childish.

She could tell from D.'s tone at this moment that he was in some deep internal excitement, though he was talking in his habitual vein. But there was a hollow space, full of an undercurrent of feeling that had nothing to do with his words, *between* his words and what they served to screen.

"What I can't get you people to see," D. was saying, "is that when, in that bit of road, for instance, between the barracks and Poundbury, which is now one of my favourite walks, I come on a patch of green moss on a grey wall, or catch the peculiar scent of trodden grass, I get a sensation that's more important than what you call 'love,' or anything else, nearer the secret of things too! It *is* 'Love' in a certain sense; but it's love of life itself and of something that comes to us through life! I don't know about Nancy or Jenny, but I've an idea that neither of *you* get these feelings, or you wouldn't look like you do when I talk about them. But, of course, you're an artist, 'Thel,' and Wizz is too, in her way, I suppose; but I'm not talking about that. I'm talking —hullo! *There* you are! Well? What news? Have you seen the grand discovery?"

As he spoke he scrambled to his feet, and the young women rose too; but for a moment the old gentleman—for it was Teucer Wye who had caught them napping—could only make whistling sounds through his toothless gums. He was panting and exhausted and he had apparently been running, but he waved Thuella aside when she tried to make him sit down. "Whew! Whew! I'll tell—you—whew!—as—we—go. *It's there* —they're showing it to everybody! They're quarrelling about it—but come—whew! whew! I've come to get you—you'll, whew! see—for—yourselves."

Wizzie saw No-man, who had a dazed and shame-faced look as he rose to his feet, like a boy caught in the act of "cribbing," contemplating with evident astonishment the dutiful way Thuella offered her parent her arm which the panting Mr. Wye was only too thankful to take.

"How stupid D. is!" she thought. "He can't understand the simplest event. He thinks a miracle has happened because 'Thel' and her father are friendly. Can't he see that when a person's free of her home and getting a little pleasure, a father becomes a different thing?"

But the Professor of Greek "at the small Midland college" did seem different enough to justify No-man's surprise, even if he had no explanation of the phenomenon. The old man hopped along so happily on Thuella's arm, flourishing his cane so gaily and digging it so wantonly into the mole-hills, that he resembled a sprightly wagtail under the escort of a considerate yellow-hammer. Out of breath though he was, he discoursed volubly all the way; and Wizzie—who advanced with *her* arm in that of D. side by side with the father and daughter—could hear all he was saying. The fact that she was being hurried to a spot where she would see Uryen again put her into such good spirits that even when No-man, taking advantage of the situation, began to squeeze her wrist against his ribs it didn't get on her nerves.

Old Teucer Wye was so excited that he forgot to give his side-pockets, where his precious text-books were, the usual reassuring pats. But he talked shrilly on the topic of how this great discovery appeared in the eyes of a true Platonist. And as far as Wizzie could gather it appeared very small and unimportant indeed; which was so exactly her own view that her heart warmed to the gesticulating little man. To *her* mind, as to the intelligence of one who was still called "professor" in Derbyshire, these broken images from the dust-bins of antiquity meant nothing but desolate bits of pottery labelled with paper tags. Wizzie had been taken once by Sister Bridget to visit a provincial museum and she remembered how, as she followed the heavy black robes of the nun, the whole place had smelt of a sepulchre, and had suggested at the same time a conspiracy of one's godfathers and godmothers to take away even what excitement the bones of death possessed by putting them under glass cases.

Thus our friend, buoyed up by the thought that in a minute or two she'd be seeing Uryen, kept smiling and nodding to old Teucer across the agitated D. who himself all this while was atoning for his recent shame by squeezing her arm with ferocious remorse.

"It's a beautiful image," Mr. Wye was saying. "It reminds *me* of the enthroned Demeter in the British Museum; and

Quirm himself admits that the cult of the chthonian divinities from Samothrace certainly spread to these islands ; but what I feel"—and here he permitted to the handle of his dark-coloured cane the privilege of tapping against one of the faded volumes hidden in his tweed-cloth pocket—"is that it's all so utterly unimportant! They weren't so wonderful in their lifetimes, these religious rituals, only reflections in water, only flickering shapes on the faces of clouds, but *now*—when they're historical curiosities or bits of doubtful evidence in support of questionable theories—they've no serious power over our souls. No, no, my boys—I mean, my girls—the soul feeds on invisible, not visible things! The soul is a wayfarer *through* matter only to learn the trick of shaking matter off! Of course matter affords symbols of the soul, and of the soul's journey from one level of spiritual beauty to another, but there's nothing divine in matter, *except the Divine*! The symbols that matter casts up are like the bubbles cast up to the surface of a stream when a glittering fish passes by. It's because of the passage of the soul through its inert resistance that matter produces symbols at all! No, no, this image isn't really important to us, not to our souls, you understand, for our souls are off and away, like—like a shoal—like a shoal of—of—of——"

"Of great white whales, Dad!" threw in Thuella.

"Well—why not? That's not a bad image of yours, Thuella. That wasn't a bad simile of Thuella's was it, No-man? Did you catch what my daughter said, Miss Ravelston? Shoals of white whales? Yes, my dear, why not? Shoals of whales voyaging on and on and on, over seas and seas, and beyond all seas, till they reach—whew! whew! But where have we got to? I wasn't looking! *This* isn't the way." Thus speaking, the excited little man stopped, jerked his arm away from Thuella's support, and leaning on his cane looked about him. Instead of the excavations what he saw before him was the deep trench to the east of Mai-Dun, the identical trench in which D. and Uryen had lingered when the latter revealed to the former those weird "ideas" that Wizzie so lightly discounted.

"We've gone the wrong way. I wasn't looking," the little man repeated. "I think it must be—more—more *over there*," and he lifted his cane and waved it vaguely in a northerly direction.

"This way—this is the way," threw in No-man. "I'm sure we

shall soon——" And dragging Wizzie off, in advance this time of the others, he began to ascend the slope leading to the northern extremity of the earthworks.

As they moved over the hot sweet-scented turf, the metallic sky above them quivering with distant lark-music, and the air about them disturbed by no nearer sound than the occasional droning flight of a bluebottle fly, whose passage across her ear-drum seemed to Wizzie charged with memories of her child-hood, they came upon an ancient dew-pond in whose dry circular hollow the delicate grass had been burnt by the heat to a faint sedge-colour.

In the centre of this tawny bowl, which resembled a hollow concave shield, they noticed a heap of firewood, only barely charred by fire and evidently left in haste by persons interrupted in some projected picnic.

"We must tell them about this," murmured D., pausing on the brink of the hollow place. "It would be nice to celebrate Midsummer Eve in the old heathen way."

Wizzie made no comment on this, but she thought in her heart: "They're all the same, these men! They *can't* take things as they are. They have to link them up with what other men have done and said and fussed about in the olden days. I'm getting sick of it." And with the weight of the burning sun on her head there came over her a fierce revulsion against all these thick, crushing, heavy burdens of cruel antiquity.

Suddenly without warning the girl was seized with a wild rush of emotion from some deep part of her being that she had been successfully suppressing for some time. "I'd like," she thought, "to fly to America in one of Claudius's airplanes, and leave them all—yes, leave even Lovie! As it is, she's fonder of D. than she is of me. I'd get a job in a real great Circus over there—the greatest of all! And then—and *then*—hard and clear and free—and with a body limber and bare, untouched by any man, and on a horse, just like my old horse—no! *my old horse himself,* come over the sea like a white whale—I'd show them, I'd show them!"

No-man turned out to be a better guide than Teucer Wye and it was not long before they were all four jostling and pushing and arguing along with the rest of their party, in the crowded interior of a little wooden shed where the overseer of

Maiden Castle, assisted on this particular occasion by a couple of uniformed policemen, was having all he could do to keep people from touching with their hands an object that rested on a rough wooden bench at the back of the hut. The small building was packed with people, most of them young, some of them passionately interested in the object before them, and all eager to propound their own especial theories as to the identity of this extraordinary thing.

D. kept Wizzie by his side, retaining a tight hold on her arm, while Uryen, who had easily and naturally joined them at their first appearance, was now wedged in against the girl's other side.

The packed little crowd in the shed kept heaving this way and that, while new people came and others pushed their way out. Everybody was talking at once, so that there was a hubbub of excited voices some of which were listened to by a larger group than others, but save for the overseer and the two policemen there was no authority present; none, that is, at that midmorning hour, of the principal chiefs of the excavation work.

One disturbing element was present, in the form of a large and extremely ugly Irish terrier, whose owner, a lanky youth not much more amiable in aspect than the beast itself, hovered about at the entrance, deriving an imbecile and apparently a malicious satisfaction from the confusion caused by the dog's proceedings.

Something about the Great Discovery, as "It"—or "They"—rested there on that crude bench, evidently excited a fearful but fascinated frenzy in this unappealing animal, for he kept making short runs towards the thing between the legs and skirts around him, barking furiously and then retiring in terror. Now and then his tail would wag with extreme delight as if the whole matter were a lively game; then he would be seized with panic, real or assumed, and would back away, or sink down on his hind legs.

Wizzie was too absorbed in watching Uryen's face to pay much attention to the thing before her. She gave it one quick surprised glance, and then, twisting her head round, away from D. who was too preoccupied to notice what she was doing, stared in wonder, and something like awe, at the great dark countenance by her side.

The Glymes man's massive lineaments seemed to her absolutely transformed by the Object on that rude wooden stand. His eyes blazed with an interior emotion that held the girl spellbound; but unlike No-man, who seemed completely to have forgotten her, though he held her arm in an almost savage grip, she felt sure that Uryen was not only conscious of her presence—had he not moved up to her the second they came in?—but was making various impatient movements to arrange matters according to some overpowering secret intention of his own.

Amid the loud excited voices arguing, disputing, exclaiming round her she felt nothing but Uryen's presence. It was he, it was his hand upon her shoulder, that was sending these delicious shivers through her, not the extraordinary Image about which that roomful of people was gathered. But mingled with the sweet and disturbing elation that filled her because of Uryen's proximity, she was not unaware of a jealous trouble in her heart which rose from the fact that he had wanted both of them near him in this mystical crisis. It was therefore with a feeling that was almost relief that she caught Claudius's familiar voice saying something to Teucer Wye above the hub-bub.

"No! I don't call it at all the Demeter," she heard the coal-yard amateur say. "The expression's much rougher, and the features less correct; but it's a wonderful achievement. I've no doubt it was done by some Roman soldier from the East, from some Greek colony that the Empire had civilized."

"What *are* you talking about, Cask?" she heard the shrill voice of Teucer Wye protesting. "A *Greek* colony civilized by the Romans? My dear man, look at the moulding of that brow, look at those deep-hollowed eye-sockets. The thing's from Samothrace; there's no doubt about it! It's earlier than Scopas, though, earlier than Praxiteles, but it's Greek through and through! It's one of those *kai alloi theoi* that Socrates invoked on the bank of the Ilyssus, along with Pan."

"But it's a group, Mr. Wye," she heard Claudius protesting. "The local authorities wanted to take it away—these officers tell me they watched it by turns all night—only they were afraid to touch it till an expert from London had seen it. That torso without a head—are you going to tell us that that's Persephone? It's a man, Mr. Wye, it's a man! And from his bust I would certainly say a Roman Emperor, one of those great civilizing Caesars who——"

He was interrupted from the threshold of the place by the voice of Dunbar Wye, who, with Mrs. Dunbar, had been standing outside the crowd for several minutes. They had reached Maiden Castle thus early by reason of Madam's desire to give her maid at least sixteen hours in which to dust and scrub and bustle about where it was torture to Dumbell to catch the swish of a skirt.

"Mr. Cask! Mr. Cask! Do I hear you mention the Caesars, Mr. Cask? It's a Caesar we want in England today! Just glance —any of you people—at *this*—and *this*—and *this*——No! they cost nothing, my lad, they cost nothing, sir, nothing at all; and you'll soon see the danger of all this Communistic——"

Here Dumbell hesitated, and for two good reasons. For one thing his wife, with a shrewd Cumber instinct for season and occasion, figuratively clapped her hand over his mouth, and for another he couldn't recall the latest Black-Shirt slogan. Guileless but obscure syllables burst the barrier of Dumbell's teeth; but with his lady's help he got his leaflets back into the botanical tin that hung round his shoulders, and they both tried to push their way toward Uryen, who had turned quickly round at the voice of Mr. Cumber's son-in-law.

Though she could only just catch his profile, Wizzie was amazed at the change in Uryen's face. It was as if he were applying the whole machinery of his personality to the business of burying his intellect, his pride, his very soul at the bottom of an interior pit! He allowed his chin to sink down upon his chest. His eyes grew so dead as to resemble opaque pieces of glass in the eyes of a South Sea idol; and removing his hands from both the girl's shoulders he let them hang loose by his side, like the hands of an idiot. Wizzie was not a little shocked by this transformation in her formidable "Black Man." What was the cause of it? It was inconceivable that Dumbell Wye— the greatest simpleton she had ever met—could scare Uryen Quirm.

She came to the conclusion that it was Cumber himself, represented by the practical Mrs. Wye, who had the power to take the magnetic heart out of her hero. She had plenty of time to ponder on the matter, for the shed was so packed that it took quite a while for the Wyes to reach him. "It must be the money he gets from them," she shrewdly surmised. "I know exactly how he feels. It's how I used to feel after I surpassed myself in the ring and Old Funky would send the hat round. Yes, it's the money! Wherever money enters it kills life! That's really what's the matter with D. and me. If I were working, and coming home every night to Lovie and him—how different it would be! It isn't Dumbell; it isn't *you* either, you fuzzy-wuzzy chit of a pin-head! It's the Cumber purse, that's done it." And she gazed up at Uryen's great hang-dog face with her own features all pinched and strained in sympathy, and her eyes brimming with tears. "Oh, you great one, you mysterious one," her heart groaned, "I know you because I love you; and when you started writing those articles for Cumber you blew your soul away like a dandelion-seed—yes—no—yes—no—yes—no! You gave him your ideas—one by one for his money—and now when you see those two fools, squeezing through to get at you, you feel—oh, I know how you feel!"

Her cheeks went hot and cold, and she found herself pressing the hand which No-man had left free against one of her breasts. For the first time in her life Wizzie knew what love meant in a woman. Those warm sensual feelings she had felt at first under Uryen's spell had transformed themselves completely. Strange and wild thoughts rushed through her brain. "If he is D.'s father," she said to herself: "why can't we go—all three of us—and live with him and Nance at Glymes? Jenny says Nance has got fond of D., so she'd be happy, and I wouldn't want anything but to see him every day, to be near him, to watch him, to comfort him about the Cumbers, to tell him it doesn't matter; to tell him to think—like I did in the Circus—that it's for life we work, not for Old Funky, not for those staring boys, not for the Cumbers, because they're all outside! Oh, my great one, my wonderful one, I don't mind your not washing! I don't mind your dirty clothes! It's *you yourself* I love—inside all that. Yes, yes, if you are D.'s father I'll be your girl, your daughter—I'll be your servant—I'll be anything to you you like!"

She kept making little unconscious movements with her free hand as she gazed up at that great, lowering, unhappy, drooping head, and finally she found herself, as the pressure increased around her due to the Wyes' squeezing themselves forward, holding tight to a fold of the man's jersey.

She had to swallow desperately to keep back her emotion. "He's unhappy, he's misunderstood by them all," she thought. "*He's like my old horse.*"

All this while it never entered her head to wonder what these "ideas" *were* which were the man's soul and which he was selling to the Cumbers. The extreme femininity of Wizzie's mind in regard to philosophical notions and all moral or immoral habits of thought had been left incredibly pure and unperverted both by convent and Circus.

Glancing for the first time with a flicker of interest at the strange group before her, round which the chalky rubble clung so thick and had been left so intact that it still obscured their outlines, she seemed to trace an odd resemblance between the rough-hewn object at the two figures' knees and that bed-post carving that had repulsed her so when D. put it on their chimney-piece.

But Mrs. Wye now bustled up; and after greeting No-man and Uryen inquired of the world in general whether Lord Fordington was there. "*Is* Lord Fordington here?" And she lifted her head like a bird looking for a crumb.

Dumbell's anxious fish-mouth too turned inquiringly round, while the persons nearest him nudged each other and gazed about them, and stared at the policemen, as if the well-known personage referred to might pop out at any moment from some official pocket.

But Dumbell began appealing in a loud voice to his father: "What do *you* say it is, Dad? Mr. Quirm says Mr. No-man knows what it is, and ought to be the one to write about it. What do you say it is, Dad?"

Wizzie felt really sorry for old Teucer Wye at that moment, for all the heads in the place were craning towards him and he had got himself wedged in among a group of noisy young prentices who displayed a tendency to push him to the front.

"Give us a speech, Professor!" one of them shouted. "Tell us what kind of a dog it is that the angel's kneeling on!"

"Thank you, Mr. Quirm," said Dumbell gravely, as Uryen muttered a few words in his ear. "It's all right, Dad!" he called out. "Don't disturb yourself. Stay where you are. Mr.

373

Quirm says it's not Demetrea, but the same thing in Welsh."

But Teucer Wye continued to disturb himself and allowed himself to be pushed forward towards the policemen, until at last, "dared," defied, hustled, and with his own excitement at fever pitch, he actually began, to Thuella's horrified disgust, a sort of public harangue.

Few of those present could see the speaker, so diminutive was his stature, but his shrill voice carried such a vibrating quiver of emotion that most of them stopped talking and set themselves to listen.

"My friends," cried the Midland professor : "oh, my dear Dorchester friends, this is an occasion———"

"Three cheers for the mayor !" interrupted a child's voice, repeating a lesson learnt for a quite different group of persons.

"———An occasion when we ought to take stock of ourselves and of our lives. My friends, these figures represent the religion of people four thousand years ago and to-day is Sunday, a day we owe to *our* religion. But what I want to say to you is this. On the top of this ancient earthwork, in this amazing weather, on the eve of the greatest of all heathen celebrations, the mysterious day which our church has dedicated to Saint John the Baptist, we must remember—oh, my friends we *must* remember !—that our souls are bound by no tradition, by no religion; that our souls have the power of separating themselves from matter altogether, the power of shaking off altogether this whole astronomical world, and of entering that higher, that purer level of existence where dwells the Eternal"—here the little man whistled through his gums—"and the—and the Unspeakable ! These precious discoveries must not bind us to earth. We must not think that because it is Sunday———"

But Thuella, who had been pushing and squeezing all this time to get near him, now indignantly seized him by the arm and soon reduced him to sulky and shamefaced silence.

But, "Three cheers for Mr. Wye !" cried one of the boys, the one who had been the worst in badgering the old man, but who now was profoundly impressed by the tone if not by the substance of these earnest words; but the elder of the two policemen intervened. Making a step in the boys' direction he gravely raised his hand. This was enough. The eyes that had been turned towards that shrill impassioned voice now returned guiltily and self-consciously towards the unearthed objects. Official decorum, on the top of Maiden Castle, had indicated that the path of discretion for the obedient commonality of Durnovaria lay in the direction of discreet idol-worship rather than of spiritual exaltation. To raise a cheer for an old gentleman whistling "Whew! whew!" through his gums and talking of the flight of the soul presented itself now as a serious lapse in good manners.

The only person present who disregarded the policeman was the supposed goddess from Samothrace. Her hollow eyes continued to stare straight in front of them as they had done under the chalk for four thousand years.

Wizzie on the contrary felt that if she and Thuella looked at each other they would have a giggling fit. That gravely uplifted hand seemed to say: "Everything dug up belongs to the Crown. This is not the place for a rumpus."

But the Irish terrier, having been quiescent for a long time, considered this a dedicated moment to bestir himself once more. He consequently resumed his game of hurried rushes and agitated retirements, and not content with this, what must the profane animal do but in the sight of all of them advance to the bench whereon the Discovery reposed, and deliberately lifting a shameless leg, proceed in all calmness to relieve nature!

In the confusion created by the ejection of the animal Wizzie turned to Thuella, and both the young people relieved the long tension of their nervous restraint in all this antiquity worship by a burst of girlish merriment. One last glance did Wizzie give at the *third* of these heathen apparitions, awaiting their "christening" by his Lordship.

"It's not the bed-post head," she said to herself, "though it's the same sort of thing. How disappointed old D. must be!" And with a shrug of her shoulders she let herself be dragged away.

The gathering of all our friends from Glymes and Friary Lane outside the excavation-shed was Dumbell's grand opportunity; and he hastened to disburden himself to both Uryen and No-man of the instructions he had brought from Mr. Cumber.

It soon transpired that the young Wyes were anxious now to carry off both the son and the father to the rooms they had taken at the Antelope; there, doubtless, to apportion them both

375

the exact limits of the aspect of the Great Discovery which it would be their task to handle.

D. at once suggested that instead of doing this they should all seek that dried-up dew-pond he and she had found, and there, *in situ*, have a thorough blood-and-iron discussion of what was to be telephoned. To this proposal Mr. and Mrs. Wye willingly consented; not so much—as Wizzie saw—with the idea of calling in the elder Mr. Wye to their discussion, as of avoiding any risk of their evasive correspondents escaping, or their "impressions" cooling off before they were officially registered.

It was a cruel disappointment to the girl when she found herself once more led off by No-man, in advance of the rest, across the central plateau of Mai-Dun. She tried to hang back, casting sympathetic looks at Uryen as he slouched wearily along between the two Wyes; but it was no use. No-man remorselessly dragged her on. Her only comfort was that Thuella was a good way behind, walking with her father again, and accompanied by the silent Claudius.

The thought of going back to Friary Lane after all this, the thought of resuming her normal life, of wheeling Lovie in the perambulator, of listening to Jenny's piled-up wrongs, of submitting to No-man's caresses night after night, seemed just then more than she could endure. How that image had stared past her, out and away, beyond them all! Yes, that stone woman's stare seemed to have broken up her resolution to be docile to fate. How *could* she leave him to that Glymes life with Nance? Oh, what *was* going to be the upshot of it all? "No, I can't stand it!" she said to herself. "I *know* he knows how much I care. But day will follow day, just as they always do. I shall be a good mother to Lovie, and a docile plaything for D., and you, my strange one, my unhappy one, my wonderful one, *you'll* try to console yourself with 'Thel'! Oh! Oh! Oh! What a thing, what a thing life is!"

As she now rubbed her knuckles together against her jersey, treating his arm as if it were a fetter she'd got so used to that she could reduce it to non-existence, she felt an intense longing to bring down this mood of self-satisfied complacency in which he strode along. Oh, she knew him through and through! His happiness just now was partly caused by that stone woman's head, with which he'd no doubt fallen in love simply because

376

she'd been buried for a thousand years, and partly by a childish longing—D. was much more childish than Lovie, for Lovie played at serious things—to light a bonfire in a dew-pond!

But whatever was the cause of his complacency, oh, how she longed to bring it down with a jerk! She longed to trouble it, to agitate it, to break it up; for she knew exactly how it made him feel from the look of his profile. It made him feel superior to Uryen, to Mr. Wye, to Claudius, and, of course, to herself.

"I told Jenny," she began, feeling almost as irritated by the noise the larks made over her head as by the heat of the burning sunshine : "that I didn't believe Nance was really so infatuated with you as she made out. What do you think yourself?"

No-man evidently regarded this question as of absurdly minor importance, and of no interest at all between him and her; for instead of stopping—that teasing trick of his when he wanted to think—he only went faster. "What's that?" he said. "What do I think about Nance and me?" He turned his eyes away from her to watch a butterfly. "Well, old girl, to tell you the truth I think I'd feel a bit funny if I were to make love to Nance. I wouldn't *mind* doing it! I've always thought there was something about Nance like a great white soft musk-rose with hardly a thorn on its twigs. But, God! my dear, it's too late. I might once have enjoyed making my little Stone-Age girl jealous; but I've got too fond of her now."

Wizzie almost drew blood from her lower lip so fiercely did she bite it; but he went on, totally oblivious.

"Besides, I'd feel funny, and that's the plain truth—I'd have an unpleasant sensation—if I made up to my father's wife."

Wizzie could hardly contain herself any longer, and the gall of her restraint transformed itself into the most corrosive sarcasm that he had ever brought down upon his head. She felt herself as if all the poison with which Mary Channing killed *her* old man were condensed into the syllables.

"What a good thing you've only got your sensations to think of, as against your 'funny' feelings, D.! It must make everything so wonderfully simple." Her bitter words did bring his stride to a pause then, and swinging round her he looked her up and down.

"What is it, kid?" he asked gravely. "You're upset about something."

"Oh, don't mind me!" she retorted. "Go on thinking about Mary Channing's wrongs!"

A look of real outrage came into his face, which in her anger she felt a malicious pleasure to have caused. She could hurt him where his book was concerned. She'd found that out, anyway!

But now, driven by the demon that possessed her, she tried another track. "He—your father—doesn't seem to like this work for Cumber. It doesn't bother *you* much, I see."

"Still harping on *him* then?"

"Why not, if he *is* your father?"

"Wizz, Wizz, what on earth's the matter with you? Have I done anything? Have I annoyed you?"

"*Annoyed me!*" The savage stress she laid upon this made him drop her arm. "Come on," she cried. "For God's sake, shut up, and come on! Do you think I want *him* to hear us wrangling?"

As she spoke she started off at such a pace that he was hard put to it to keep up with her.

"I hope Lovie's all right with Jenny," he murmured, as they approached the empty dew-pond with its unused heap of wood and kindling.

The girl was silent; and he tried again, for Old Funky's child still seemed to him the only safe topic with her in her present mood. "It's certainly a shame, as you said," he went on, "that we couldn't bring her with us, but it would never have done."

"That's a word you love, isn't it? 'Never would do'—'never would have done'— Well—don't mind me—set a match to your midsummer fire! I know how much you've been looking forward to *that* sensation!"

"*Damn you, Wizz!*" The words were out before he could hold them back; but immediately afterwards she could see how ashamed and remorseful he was. "Forgive me, sweetheart!" he whispered. "I don't know how we've slipped into all this. There, there, my treasure, don't 'ee be cross any more with your old kidnapper." As he spoke he laid both hands on her shoulders. "Wizz," he said, "little Wizz. I don't believe you've the smallest idea how fond I am of you. And you're really—down in your deep heart—just as fond of me. We didn't meet in that caravan and recognize each other at once for nothing. There! I won't say another word. You're just being childish about him. You

378

must really feel, just as I do, that if he *is* my father, it's sheer madness to be silly like this. You don't know him as well as I do. Neither of us knows him as well as poor Nance does. That boy of hers——" But he broke off suddenly and allowed his hands to sink down from her shoulders. She knew he had caught a look on her face that she had never let him see there before, a look of actual physical shrinking from his touch.

"All right, my dear," he said hurriedly, "I won't bother you now. We'll talk of this later." If she had longed to make him suffer she got little satisfaction from the grim hardening process through which his features now passed.

But leaving her side without further words he ran down to the dew-pond, knelt on the grass by the heap of wood, and producing matches and some crumpled papers from his pocket, set himself to start a blaze.

This evidently proved more difficult than he anticipated, and sitting down on the edge of the grassy hollow she watched his clumsy fumblings with lack-lustre eyes.

"Lovie would be all right with him," she thought. "He'd pay someone—Jenny herself very likely—to look after her; and old Claudius would be there. The child would probably bring those two together. No, I can't stand it any more. This is the end. I'll go off—to Bristol—to London—to America—and start working again. 'Thel' was quite right—when a person can do what I can do it's crazy to let it go."

But no sooner had these thoughts raced through her brain than she heard the voices of the Wyes approaching. "He's coming," she said to herself. "He'll be here in a minute. If I go to America I may never see him again. He'll be with 'Thel,' and he'll never know!"

No-man succeeded at last in getting his Midsummer Eve bonfire lit. When once it started the flames rose high ; for there was enough wind stirring to help the blaze, and yet, since the whole thing took place in so deep a concavity, not enough to disturb or carry away the burning pieces of wood.

It was not long before the whole party was grouped on the northerly rim of this grassy basin, from the centre of which, like some gigantic spike of fiery blossoms from a sunburnt calyx, the red flames wavered upward.

Most of the time while No-man kept tossing fuel upon the

heap—and he went on till he had exhausted all there was—the fire retained its original pyramidal shape; but there did come moments when the wind blew strong enough across this small crater to sweep the whole living mass, the red flames along with the clouds of ash-grey smoke, towards the particular segment of the enclosing circle where our friends were sitting.

When this happened they were all completely hidden in smoke, not only hidden from any passing stranger, but hidden from one another; a state of things which, curiously enough, seemed to lend itself to the mood of them all, except young Mrs. Wye, whose lively little screams, alternating with Dumbell's solemn protestations, made up a sort of comic-opera orchestration to the excited murmurings of the rest.

Wizzie had been to picnics before in full daylight when a fire had to be lit to boil a kettle, but those little gipsy flames were nothing to this flare. It was impossible not to be interested in the spectacle; and though she made up her mind not to bestow on D.'s silly idea the least word of commendation she found herself deriving an unexpected satisfaction from the crackling of sticks, the roaring of flames, the eddying of smoke, and the weird alternations of illumination and obscurity. Uryen was separated from her by both Thuella and her father, while between "Thel" and herself reclined old Claudius, who was now gazing at her and talking to her with infinite content after the hubbub in that excavation-shed.

"What a thing fire is, Miss Wizzie!" he was murmuring now, "and doesn't it give you a queer feeling to see it in this blazing sunshine? I can see Thuella is absorbed in it all and we mustn't disturb her"—here his voice became so low that Wizzie could scarcely hear it in the roaring of the flames—"or I'd like to ask her, and I warrant we all would, if there exists in the world any really good picture of this weird struggle between sun and fire. Some would say the fire was defeated; but I don't think so. It's not as yellow as at night but I think it's redder in some odd way, and I think it has a more supernatural and *impossible* look, if you can follow me, as if it really had the personality of one of those old four elements they worshipped, before the Romans used——"

"Well done for you, Claudius!" came the voice of No-man from out of the smoke, as like some lumbering aboriginal he moved round the bonfire he had lit. "If I hadn't left my old stick behind I'd stir up redder flames than these for you! I'm glad you're *worshipping* fire for once, instead of only—Uryen! Here's Mr. Cask ready to worship fire."

It was out of a thick rush of smoke that Uryen's voice came then. So thick indeed was the smoke that Teucer Wye scrambled to his feet and would have retreated; but it soon rolled away, and after coughing a little and spluttering a protest to his daughter, who continued to hug her thin knees as one impervious to such things, he turned back, and leaning on his cane gave an ear to what his Glymes neighbour was saying.

Wizzie couldn't catch Uryen's first words; but it soon became clear to her that he was resuming an argument he and Claudius had already begun.

"Not only Romans," she heard him say as the cloud of smoke rolled aside. "All ancient busts—— But what you thought was an armoured breastplate on his chest, like those on the coins of the Caesars, was something quite different. No-man knows what it was; No-man knows—No-man knows!" There was an almost tragic appeal in his voice as he raised it then, and Wizzie glanced at D. to see if he would respond.

But that gaunt figure, with his cap pulled low over his eyes, moved round and round his sinking fire, paying not the slightest heed.

The girl longed to call out: "Don't ask him again! Don't humiliate yourself before him!" But once more the man cried out: "No-man knows what it was!"

"He knows what you *think* it was!" she heard D. mutter grimly; and Dumbell must needs at that moment try to bring to the agitated man's notice some tiny little plant he had picked on their way to the place.

"It's still in bud, Mr. Quirm," she heard the man persist, "for it's early for them yet; but would you call it a sheep's-bit, or a devil's-bit? They're not both scabiouses you know. One is a——"

"You mustn't mind what I said, Quirm," pleaded Claudius gently, twisting his neck round and blinking from the sunshine while he still coughed from the effect of the smoke. "I see it hurts you to agree with me. I see that you're vexed about it, and I think"—he hesitated and rubbed his face with both his hands—"I think there's something else on your mind. Aye, man, man," and Wizzie looked sharply at him as his voice sank, for he suddenly spoke hoarsely and with deep feeling, "you're not the only one! Here we are, watching our friend's fire, and I wish your little girl could see it"—this he threw in *sotto voce* to Wizzie, catching her look—"but we've all got a hurt of some kind at the heart. It's because we won't—forgive me for saying it, Quirm!—shake off the past, shake off our personal feelings, and work for the future! I've been thinking a lot about this Discovery, that goddess's head, and that headless one, and that— other thing; and what I feel, Quirm, is, and I think I know you well enough to say this, that things like that, brought into the air after being buried so long, have an evil effect! Yes, an evil effect on all of us, Quirm. They're full of the old self, full of the old subjective personal lie, that we must shake off if the world's to go on and get better. Don't interrupt me, Dunbar! I'm not dragging up our dispute now. The thing is we *must* get rid of this perpetual 'I, I, I' with all its cravings and hurt feelings! We must live in the race and in helping the race forward. Man, man," and once more Wizzie caught something like a groan beneath his words, "don't you see it's nothing whether I'm right or you're right about that thing? Where we're all wrong is that we live by our personal feelings, instead of living——"

But Wizzie lost what he said at that point, though in spite of many indignant whistles from Dumbell's father and an outburst of spiteful giggling from Dumbell's wife, he went on for some while in the same strain, still addressing his remarks to Uryen, who stood as if sunk into a trance, not unlike the trance that was rendering Thuella so motionless and silent, as she sat hunched-up on the brink of the hollow.

But what distracted Wizzie at that moment was No-man's coming up to her and throwing himself down at her side. His fire was low and smouldering now. The smoke had vanished; and all the fuel was exhausted.

The tremendous force of the midsummer sun, for it must have been at least one o'clock by this time, seemed to be sucking up, as if with a gigantic tongue, all the life, all the vitality, all the character from those dying flames. If they were red before, they were a mockery of redness now. Some of them, in fact, as they rose into a momentary flare from the fiery heap, took to themselves the colour of fading crocuses. Others became pallid as summer lightning. One or two, just because this blazing sun and this burning metallic sky had sucked all the devilry out of them, and all the piracy, and all the life-lust, became spiritualized and etherealized, became like candle-flames, those purest of all forms of fire, those guileless sisterhoods of fire.

There were even some—but this may have had to do with the wavering edge between the grass that had been burned by the sun, that shaped itself into little straw-coloured estuaries and promontories round the place of burning, and the grass that had been burned black by the fire—that presented the appearance of *invisible fire*—fire that was almost as colourless as water.

Maiden Castle was undoubtedly doing what she must have done more than four thousand years ago, when that woman's head, along with those other things, looked into eternity across the land of the Durotriges—lifting up this blackened circle of burnt grass, the work of the fire-substance produced by man, towards the far-off living body of the greatest fire-mystery we know.

Round the dying flames of No-man's bonfire, on the rim of a dew-pond that now offered itself as a target for the sun's rays with what must soon be a bull's-eye of black annihilation, sat and stood, each with their own peculiar sense of the significance of the occasion, our group of enemy-friends. None of them could shake off a vague impression of something momentous in this death of fire beneath this majesty of burning light, none of them, unless it were Mr. Cumber's daughter, could dismiss the image of what the excavators had unearthed. That woman's head, that headless torso, that eyeless and earless beast-god— these things had been under the chalk when Caesar landed, under the chalk when the Conqueror landed, under the chalk when Victoria was crowned! They had been storing up in that long darkness all the wild prayers, all the desperate imprecations that had been addressed to them on the summit of Mai-Dun before the last stone had been added to Stonehenge.

And yet descendants of the same feathered tribes as had dashed their wings against the temple that housed these entities hovered still about the spot where after their long sojourn in darkness they saw the light again. And the great turf promontory, lifting up to the burning sun this blackened bowl of smouldering flame, lifted up also to the metallic sky the invisible thoughts about those weird *revenants* that each of these human skulls concealed.

It was not only No-man's lying down by her side that made Wizzie stop listening. Heedless of the blazing exposure of the least move that any of them made in that tremendous glare, D. laid his hand familiarly and possessively on the girl's thigh, just above the knee that was nearest him. "Don't 'ee be cross with me, my treasure!" he whispered. "I *swear* I won't be jealous with him any more." She didn't dare to make a proclamation of their quarrel by shaking off his hand; for though Claudius, as he talked, had turned away his head, almost everyone there could see them clearly.

But she cast about for a diversion so as to avoid answering him; nor had she any difficulty in finding what she wanted. To her absolute amazement, as she glanced at Thuella who was sitting bolt-upright in her yellow dress hugging her knees, she saw that the tall girl's face was convulsed with sobs and big tears were rolling down her cheeks.

No one else but she and No-man could see this, for they alone were between the girl and the smouldering flames at which she was staring, but the sight of her tears filled Wizzie with astonishment, for it was the first time, since she had known Thuella, that she had ever seen her weep.

"Look at 'Thel,' D.!" she whispered to him. No-man was evidently as much amazed as she was and he leapt instantly to his feet and offering his hand to Wizzie pulled her up too. They hurried past Claudius, who scarcely glanced at them from where he sat, and both sank down at the girl's side.

"What is it, 'Thel'?" whispered Wizzie in a low voice.

The weeping girl was so slow in answering, and the deep shadow of her big hat made it so hard to see with what expression she regarded her would-be comforters, that our friend had time, as she still felt the imprint of D.'s fingers on her thigh, to turn her pity into a fierce pulse of revolt against masculine possessiveness. How *dared* he lay his hand on her like that in this exposed place? It was therefore with a malicious sympathy that she heard "Thel" murmur at last, in a choking voice and evidently addressing No-man rather than herself: "Not—one—of you—cares—anything! I—I could—paint such—

384

pictures—if I had one single person who—who—none of you know, none! I'm—I'm more alone than if *I'd* been buried for four thousand years!"

Then Wizzie saw No-man, who had sat down a little farther from the agitated girl than she had done herself, shuffle across the grass till he could touch her and lay his hand on her knee. "I hope she'll enjoy *that*," she thought angrily.

But Thuella seemed totally indifferent. "Not one of you knows," she gasped again, "not one of you cares! I go on—working—in a void. It—was—it was this fire—in the sun—and I thought—I thought—what I could make of it—and then I thought—but no one cares!" and once more her sobs choked her.

For a second Wizzie was really touched by the spectacle of this passionate grief emerging from beneath that great flapping hat. " 'Thel' darling, don't you——" she began.

"It's like poisoned blood!" cried the girl, pointing at the bonfire, whose flames rising up before they died had caught the last fragment of unburnt fuel.

"Don't 'ee, 'Thel,' don't 'ee, child," said No-man calmly, pressing his fingers still more closely round her curved knee. "Do try, my dear, and change the current of your way of taking life. Concentrate on your own mind instead of on your work. It's your mind that's important, not what you do!"

Something about the tone in which he uttered these words seemed to fill Thuella with fury. She scrambled hurriedly to her feet, gave her yellow skirt an angry shake, and pointing a quivering finger at No-man, careless of the presence of the others, burst into a bitter invective.

The man rose too and so did Wizzie; and Wizzie herself was astonished at the uprush of evil pleasure that flooded her being as she watched D.'s babyish bewilderment under the girl's torrent of words.

"She's not well to-day. That's what it is," she thought. "She oughtn't to have come. I could see she wasn't herself. But all the better! If she'd been herself she'd never have said these things. Oh, I'm so glad she came. He'll hear *something,* anyway!"

And then Wizzie was aware of a savage impulse. "I'd like everyone here to attack D.!" she thought ."I hope Uryen does. I hope Claudius does, and Dumbell, too! Oh, I know so well what D.'s thinking now. He's thinking, 'I'm a good, quiet man, working at my book, going on my walks, enjoying my sensations, being kind to the girl I rescued. I am strong. I am self-controlled. I am dependent on nobody. I can get my own breakfast in my own attic. I am happy in myself, especially when I have a harmless amusement like making a bonfire'."

"Concentrate on my own mind?" Thuella was now screaming in hysterical shrillness, as with the brim of her hat pushed back and her eyes gleaming like a demon's she poured out her pent-up feelings on the bewildered D. "*His* own mind, *my* own mind, *all* our own minds! Why, it would be like that stream by your coal-yard, Mr. Cask, where those ducks stand on their heads all day long to get at the mud! My mind, *of* my mind, *to* my mind, *by, with,* or *from* my mind! I know what you think—— What contemptible teaching! You talk as if our minds were cheeses. I agree with you entirely, Mr. Cask. Let's burn our cheeselike minds, clean these maggotty sensations! Every noble person has ideas beyond himself, ideas that are dangerous to himself; but you dodge all that! It's round and round with you, isn't it? Count on your fingers; count on your toes; canter and caper and down he goes! Oh, how I despise you—how I *despise* you!" She stopped exhausted, staring at D. with flashing eyes.

By some chance No-man had been isolated from the rest as they crowded round; and he now stood close to his bonfire, whose flames, pale red "like poisoned blood," as Thuella had said, and looking shockingly unnatural in the bright sunshine, emphasized in some queer way the leanness and gauntness of his figure.

"How babyish he looks without his stick!" Wizzie thought. "With it he looks like a selfish old man; without it like a selfish child! But that's all *his* mind does when it gets out of itself. It goes into his stick!"

The dew-pond where No-man had made his bonfire was well out of the track to the excavation-shed so that only a few strangers came even within sight of this group of friends, and those who did were in too much fear of missing his lordship's "christening" of the great Discovery to yield to their curiosity. Thus it was brought about, either by the great goddess Chance, or by those occult fatalities of character that are often stronger than Chance, that while that southern promontory of Maiden

Castle held up to the burning sun this unnatural bonfire, whose flame looked like poisoned blood, it also held up a half-circle of highly strung men and women, their nerves wrought upon by the weird images that had been unearthed, who, through the medium of a girl in a yellow dress, were swept forward by some sudden psychic wave of irrational hostility towards their lonely bonfire maker. Any collection of human beings, however casually gathered, takes upon itself the nature of a living entity, but when the component members of such an entity have not been gathered casually, when there has been a united and premeditated object in such a gathering and above all when the separate units making up the resultant entity are well-acquainted with one another, and have been previously linked to one another by endless subtle relations, the most surprising and unpredictable behaviour may be expected of the multiple Being thus created. Individually, there was not a member of this group, except perhaps Dumbell and his young wife, who was not friendly to D. No-man. Uryen was more than friendly to him; and it was alien to the whole nature of Claudius to be seized with sudden malice against anyone. Teucer Wye had been all that day only waiting for an opportunity to tell No-man about the respectful memory of people in Derbyshire.

And yet, as they all listened now to Thuella's indignant reproaches, and it was only a woman friend who could know anything about the part played in such an outburst by sick nerves, it was easy for Wizzie to detect that her malevolent wish was actually, beyond her hope, being fulfilled. Had they been contemporaries of those images, No-man at that moment would probably have been flung into his own flames; and civilized as they were it was still plain that some morbid magnetic sympathy with Thuella's emotion had isolated the bonfire-maker. They had all been long without food. The unusual heat of the sun in that exposed spot had fevered their blood; and that staring stone head, that headless torso, that shapeless beast-form, though interpreted so differently by all of them, were still at work in the secret places of their minds, and anyone could see that the disturbing and even shocking sight of these flames in sunlight was rousing some sort of devilry in them.

What Wizzie felt herself just then, and she felt it with a sort of evil triumph, was that they couldn't help sharing Thuella's feelings, couldn't help feeling just as she did at that moment towards D. And though it was all instinct with her, and she would have been puzzled to explain it, she had an obscure sense that something she had always been aware of in D. was itself drawing towards him this psychic wave of hostility.

It was his habitual propitiation, his curious love of putting himself in the wrong, of bringing down on himself reproaches and abuse. Other people, men who *were* men, hit back openly and honestly when they were attacked. D. never did. Never once, till that scene to-day by the cemetery gate, had she known him to stand up for himself as people should! He led you on to make a fool of him. He seemed to *like* looking a fool with you.

In the depths of her mind Wizzie knew that one of her chief grievances against him was that she couldn't make him angry. It was like living with a tree rather than a man to live with D.—a tree that enjoyed having its branches mauled and cut! And now at this moment the man looked as if nothing would please him more than for them all to leap on him and throw him into those red embers.

"He's like a malicious scapegoat!" she thought, remembering the old scriptural phrase from her convent lessons. "And how silly he looks," she said to herself, "just like Lovie when I burnt her paper doll. And yet how pleased with himself he looks, just like he did that first night when he found me undressed by the fire! He's got nothing on his mind, as 'Thel' says, but his walks and his sensations. All the rest of us are unhappy—Uryen most of all. And there he stands, enjoying himself; enjoying—oh, how well I know him!—even being shown up by 'Thel'! Yes, you *may* look at me. It's true, it's true what I've told you. I *hate* you. Do you understand that? Put *that* among your sensations! I hate you; and I hate your book and both your dead bitches! And I'm glad 'Thel's' cursing you, and I'm glad the others feel the same. You're the Guy Fawkes of Maiden Castle!"

And then, while she saw D. looking foolishly north and south and east and west, as he stood there: "Is it for your stick you're looking, you great baby, or is it for you dear Nancy, for the sweet clinging Nancy, who loves you so?"

At that moment a startling thing happened, completely destroying the psychic suspense that held them all. Uryen suddenly rushed forward, seized Thuella, and dragging her to

388

Wizzie clutched both girls by the hand, one on each side of him. In a voice of forced facetiousness, that jarred oddly on Wizzie's ears, he cried out to No-man. "Get out of the way, lad! These girls and I want to pass through your fire!" and heedless of the indignant protests of the ex-professor, whose countenance at that moment assumed an almost shocking resemblance to Dumbell's, the unwieldy man, pulling the two girls with him, actually plunged down the slope of the pond, passed No-man in the descent, and rushed with his startled companions clear through the fiery embers.

Wizzie, who had never been in contact with the man before, except for a few conventional hand shakes, gave herself up to the magnetism of his grasp with the elation of a little girl; and when they were safe on the other side, and he released them both, she gasped with delight and uttered a quaint little circus-cry, the cry with which she was wont to respond to applause in the old Urgan tent.

Thuella on the contrary seemed ashamed and sobered; and when No-man, who negligently followed them across his fire, trampling as he went on what was still smouldering, bent down to brush some sparks from her yellow skirt, the girl laid her hand on his head. "Sorry, my friend," Wizzie heard her whisper. "You didn't mind so terribly much, did you? It was *everybody* I was cross with—not particularly you."

Scarcely three-quarters of an hour after the extinction of No-man's fire our whole party was passing the cemetery on their way back to Dorchester. It was now a little after two, but Wizzie was aware that Mrs. Dearth hadn't expected her and D. much sooner; and neither the Wye family nor Mr. Quirm seemed inclined to hurry back to Glymes, where they knew Nance would have some sort of meal for them however late they appeared. From various whispers exchanged between Dumbell and his wife as they went along Wizzie gathered that the Cumber girl was inclined to share the Quirms' hospitality rather than go to the expense of treating her husband's relations at the Antelope.

The return down the Weymouth Road coincided with the hour in which the burgesses of the town were lingering over their Sunday dinner, so that there was nothing to distract our friends from one another as they drifted *en masse* past the rail-

ings of the Amphitheatre. The massively-built old town, surrounded four-square by her umbrageous avenues, seemed to welcome their approach with her promise of shady coolness and
bodily refreshment. The absence of the weekly traffic had the
effect of attenuating to a minimum all the usual vibrations interposed between humanity and the mellow identity of the place.

Like the balmy air of a placid valley drifting over the grazing
backs of the multitudinous cattle : "All feeding like one," the
combined scent of foliage and flowers, of dust and chimney-
smoke, of sun-warmed masonry and mossy walls, came forth to
meet them. But it was as if this "Sunday smell" of Dorchester
contained something quite beyond all these familiar scents. It
seemed to bring with it—as if the whole ancient place had been
one deep vase of thick-pressed *pot-pourri*—a subtle perfume
that was like the sweet dust of long-buried generations, a consecrated secular dust from which all that was foul in mortality
had long since evaporated, leaving only a thrice-purged residue,
a holy deposit, the dust of what was inviolable in ashes, indestructible in embers, destined to perish only with our human
senses.

In a straggling shifting group they moved on until they
reached the bottom of South Street. Here after a brief discussion
between Thuella and Uryen the suggestion was made that to
finish their discussion and avoid the town they should all go
together by Bowling Alley and the West Walks to the Hangman's Cottage, and separate there.

Turning to the left, therefore, the whole *cortège* drifted down
the shady seclusion of the Alley, and made their way, still
through a branching aisle of trees, to where, near the top of
High West Street, are the railed-in fragments of Roman wall.

"You and Quirm," said Claudius to No-man, turning round as
he spoke, and sweeping his hawk's eye over the whole company,
to make sure Wizzie as well as the other two women heard him :
"are agreed then that what we saw is a pre-Roman image representing three mythological figures : a woman, a man, and a
beast. Uryen suggests that the woman is the goddess Caridwen,
that the headless man, which I took for a Roman Emperor,
is——"

Here Uryen himself hurriedly interrupted him, though Wizzie
received the impression that her "Black Man of Glymes" only

broke his gloomy silence under some strong interior compulsion. "I don't suggest," the man almost groaned. "I know."

"*Who* do you say it is?" inquired the Cumber girl sharply. And turning upon No-man she added in the brisk tone in which she had told her maid to dust Dumbell's treasures : "Father won't like it if you and Mr. Quirm take different views !"

"*Who* is the headless one?" cried Dumbell, taking the cue from his wife and precipitating himself towards Uryen in such haste that his botanical tin emitted a metallic tinkle. "*Who* is the headless one?"

For the first time in her knowledge of him Wizzie saw a flash of real anger in Enoch Quirm's eyes. Heavily he swung round and faced poor Dumbell. "Who?" he growled. "Did you say 'who?' Who, who, *who*—that's the word—and 'Who cares?' is another word !"

"But who *is* he?" repeated the searcher after the hundred-and-twentieth variety of British blackberry, "Who *is* he, Mr. Quirm?"

At that the Glymes man lost all control of himself. "He's *the Devil!*" he roared out; and turning away began hitting his chest and mumbling something in Welsh. This outcry of Uryen's, made more resonant by the presence of that ancient wall, caused a general disturbance.

Teucer Wye impatiently drew his cane along the railings that protected the imperial masonry, causing an unpleasant "tick—tick—tick" as the ferule struck each iron bar. Then he looked his Glymes neighbour up and down, as if he would have liked to have extracted the same sound from that lumbering body by a similar method.

Wizzie caught this look in Mr. Wye's face, and it made her dislike him more than ever. For her own part, when her Glymes man cried : "He's the Devil !" she would have done anything for him, anything to comfort him ! Her sense of fear was still there, but had the man been seated at that moment she would have willingly slid down upon his knees.

Thuella, when *she* heard this unhappy outburst, impatiently pushed her brother aside and began tucking in with her fingers the big man's baggy jersey, which was protruding in an unseemly fashion from his belt.

This, it may well be believed, caused Wizzie a spasm of

jealousy, but it was upon No-man that her anger fell. She caught on D.'s face, as he too approached Uryen, a look she had come especially to loathe. It was a look that to her mind seemed to say : "I am made of granite. These nervous attacks are beyond my comprehension."

So strong was her feeling that she jerked him back by the arm. "Leave him alone! Can't you see we're only making him worse?" Neither the emotion in her voice nor the violence with which she pulled him back had any effect on No-man; but they had an immediate effect on Thuella, who, swinging round, gave vent to a ringing peal of shrill malicious laughter. After which, clutching at her hat—for a hot dusty wind was now blowing on them from the road up to the barracks—she cried out impatiently : "Come on, Uryen! Come on, all of you! I want to show you something I've discovered in the Hardy statue. I told *you* about it, Wizz; but the others don't know."

It was an added blow to Wizzie when she saw Uryen shake himself like a great sick bear and stride off at a great pace by Thuella's side.

It is one of Nature's favourite tricks with a man and a woman who live together to intermit their bitterest quarrels with moments when, contrary to their own will perhaps, they find themselves as much united against the outer world as if they were the most passionate of lovers.

"Look at 'Thel,' " whispered No-man. "She's taken off her hat. Look at the sun on her head against old Hardy's knee! I wonder which he'd have been most interested in—you or her?" He became silent; staring, as Wizzie could see, not at Thuella's golden head, but into vacancy.

"Don't let's wait a single minute with them," she whispered eagerly, looking up into his face : "Just hullo! and good-bye!"

With a slow smile he returned from his interior contemplation. "Sure, my sweet!" he said. "Good-bye, and off we go."

When, however, they reached the statue they found it harder than they had expected to follow this drastic resolution. Straight towards the barracks as if he were acting as umpire in some invisible aerial tournament gazed with fixed stare the great sculptor in words. His bronze legs in their serviceable stockings, were crossed restfully at the knee, and his compact head, poised above his upright shoulders, was held as alert and as raptorial towards the cunning masks of the Immanent Will, as it had been held in life for the best part of a century.

"Hullo! you look as if you were all gathered round the figure-head of a ship!" cried No-man in his abrupt way, as they joined the others; and though as a rule Wizzie deliberately closed her mind to his offhand imaginings, this time, in her unexpected mood of taking refuge with him, she gave herself up completely to this fancy of his. Their friends were too occupied to bother about the way he greeted them, so that she had time to feel as if the old town lying round them were actually and indeed some huge phantasmal ship, loaded to the bulkheads with the perilous cargoes of the generations, and voyaging to its unknown port behind that forward-gazing bronze figure.

"Come here a second, No-man!" cried Dumbell. "No, wait a moment, Father! Let him see it! I'm not hurting Mr. Hardy."

The ex-professor ceased his efforts to snatch from that bronze back—so characteristic still, even in metal—a blank page from one of his son's Black-Shirt tracts. This fly-leaf the sacrilegious youth had spread out on that almost living surface and was using as a note-book.

As far as Wizzie could gather he was engaged in making a rough sketch with hurried strokes of his pencil, of the great Discovery they had just seen. Dumbell's gift for such rough drawings was not contemptible, and Wizzie was astonished at the crude verisimilitude of the scrawl. There, if her Glymes man was right, was the great Goddess Caridwen. There was the headless Unknown with what looked like Egyptian hieroglyphics on his breast; and there was the eyeless, earless Beast-snout! Once more that disturbing feeling that had something to do with her passage through the bonfire came over her; but very faintly this time, for she was clinging to D.'s arm as she leaned forward. It assumed too a rather different form at this minute possibly due to the fact that up the deeply-cut highway, flanked by houses with a rich Balzacian look of old romance, the cool airs from the river could reach her face, for she fancied herself wading through water in place of fire and aware of this demon beast as a great slippery fish-head swimming between her knees.

It annoyed her a good deal afterwards that so much of her consciousness should have been preoccupied just then with herself, for a curious event now occurred about every detail of which she would have liked to have been absolutely certain; but, as fate, would have it, she was doomed to be uncertain about the whole business.

D. had dropped her arm. Of *that* at least she was sure. And after dropping it he had taken the pencil from Dumbell to make some alteration. Whether he too was seized with dizziness then from lack of food, or whether—well! she never knew, then or later, what really happened. D. himself always swore to her "on his dying oath" that the last touch he gave with Dumbell's pencil was on the snout of the Beast, which he was anxious to make resemble still more closely his heraldic bed-posts. But what at any rate was certain was that after Mr. Wye or Claudius had snatched the leaflet away from the great man's back and they were all examining it, not without uneasy glances at each other, D. suddenly seized it and tore it into bits. But he had not done this before she had seen what was there—the name "Mona," in a shaky hand, written clear across the sketch!

PART THREE

9

FULL CIRCLE

THE unusually fine weather continued, with only brief intermissions, all through the summer. Indeed, it was not till the beginning of October that the rains began. When, however, they *did* come they avenged the long months of drought with such a constant downpour that conditions of life in Dorchester were completely changed.

One result of this incessant rain was the collapse of Claudius, whose health, already undermined by his labours in the coalyard, now broke down. The end of the second week in October found him laid up in his house in Friary Lane with a complication of obstinate ailments that threatened to be serious.

Mrs. Dearth, however, remained obdurate. Do what they could to persuade her to forgive her old friend, now that he was so ill, the indignant protests of both No-man and Wizzie were always received in the same way, by an implacable refusal to submit to what the aggrieved woman called "putting weakness before principle." What had fixed the final seal upon Jenny's perversity was her discovery—and our friends soon recognized that concealment was impossible—of the fact that the sick man was constantly being visited by youthful members of "the Movement" in Dorchester.

The relentless "Horse-Head"—and how cross Wizzie became when D. indulged his tedious love of nicknames !—had marked down among these young revolutionaries one or two who were not only feminine in sex but endowed with a charm that fell in most fatally with her preconceived ideas. She did once go so far as to invite the doctor who visited the ex-philanthropist into her front room to ask his opinion of the patient's condition ; but, as Wizzie and No-man knew too well, the one person who might have shocked and startled her into a more generous mood was not the doctor, a laconic optimist, but the district nurse, only she unfortunately was almost as comely in appearance as the young revolutionaries!

Talking it over together No-man and Wizzie came to the conclusion that their friend had obstinately closed her mind to any possible issue to Mr. Cask's illness but a favourable one.

"She thinks of it," No-man would say: "as a game of 'bluff' between them. She feels that he would have made a fool of her if he melted her heart by taking to his bed."

"It's the doctor," Wizzie would reply. "He's a first-rate man, but he'd be cheerful if the town was full of the Black Death."

Agreed as they were about Jenny and Claudius it cannot be said that No-man and his girl had grown any closer during these summer months. The presence of Lovie had pushed them further apart rather than brought them together, and of this the child seemed dimly aware; for they had both caught her in various irritating devices to bridge the rift.

Wizzie still brooded over the protracted wrong done to her about the attic on High East Street, and though it was plain he had to have a place to work in, and plain too that if he delayed his breakfast long enough to share it with her his morning's work would have to be curtailed, it was still a rooted grievance that this book of his always loomed up as more important than their life together.

All this summer her devotion to Enoch Quirm had been the chief outlet for that vein in her of girlish romance that was always being fed by her story-books; but something or other—some teasing obstacle—seemed always to turn up to prevent her being alone with him.

Over and over again, while the air was full of flower-pollen and grass-seed and humming insects she had wheeled the perambulator over the Blue Bridge and up the lane to Glymes, only to find Uryen away at Maiden Castle. And when she *had* caught him in his house it seemed difficult to get a moment with him alone. Nance wasn't the difficulty. Nance always seemed ready to leave them together. The trouble came from Thuella. The girl invariably came out when she saw Lovie's perambulator; and Wizzie even noticed that when she didn't join them, either Nance or Uryen himself would make some excuse to bring her on the scene. It was as if it needed the presence of the two of them together to liberate him from his growing gloom.

This gloominess was a new thing, and it evidently was a worry to Nance. Wizzie suspected that Nance's warm greetings had to do with the lifting of this cloud, and she came to the conclusion that the woman must have had the wit to notice that his spirits rose to their old pitch only when both the young women were with him.

The chief reason for his gloom seemed to be a very definite one ; and Nance often talked to Wizzie about it. This was some hurt to his inner nature done by his weekly articles on Welsh mythology for Mr. Cumber's paper. Nance told her that she'd implored him to get out of it. She confessed that she'd offered to get some daily job in the town to keep them going, if he'd only consent to give it up.

Wizzie herself had felt from the beginning that she understood perfectly what the man suffered in having to work for Mr. Cumber. She was still in the dark, and content to be in the dark, about these "ideas" of his, but she told herself it was as if she'd had to do her "turn" in the Circus-ring for the pleasure and under the censorship of Lord Fordington and his private guests.

Everybody by this time, both in Friary Lane and at Glymes, knew that D. was her "Black Man's" son. The story had even begun to leak out in the town ; and the two tall men—both of them striking figures, the one in his faded jersey, and the other with his familiar cudgel—were followed sometimes by inquisitive looks when together in the Dorchester streets. Her private feeling was that Uryen was fonder of D. than D. was of him ; but then D., though propitiatory to everyone, was fond of no one, while Uryen had become more vulnerable and human since the discovery at Maiden Castle.

Of one result of his connection with the Cumbers Wizzie couldn't help approving. The indefatigable Mrs. Wye, as much without reverence as she was without fear, and with no more sense of a person's feelings than of the feelings of a carpet that had to be beaten, drove the man into going to the barber's, with the result that his head no longer had an African look. Older he undoubtedly became under the scissors of the barber, but he acquired a more normal and natural appearance and his head ceased to resemble the woolly topknot of a mammoth ram. The little autocrat of Beulah Lodge hadn't scrupled to badger him about his clothes, too, but here he proved incorrigible.

"If she takes away his jersey," D. told Wizzie one night by their upper-room fire: "he'll go dotty, just as I would if you took away my stick."

All the first week of October it rained incessantly; but the heaviest rain Wizzie had ever known in her life was the rain that swept down the panes of Claudius's room when she and D. went in to see him on the afternoon of the eleventh.

Claudius confessed to them he had been worse in the night.

He told them he had had a violent shivering fit just before dawn and had tried to reach his fire, which the district nurse had made up in the hope that it might last till she came back in the morning.

"She rated me well, you may believe," he told them: "when she did come. She wouldn't have known about it though if Katie and Edith hadn't looked in on their way to work."

"Known about what?" inquired Wizzie anxiously. "You don't mean to say you couldn't get back to bed?"

Claudius worked himself up a bit higher on his pillows and chuckled. "I'm right as a trivet now," he said. "I'm far better than yesterday afternoon. Look at the rain! Listen to it." He was silent for a moment watching the streaming pane. Then, with a change of expression: "*She* doesn't know about last night, does she?"

"*We* don't know about last night," cried Wizzie, very much perturbed. "Did your Katies and Ediths find you out of bed?"

He surveyed her troubled face with a look of childish satisfaction. "How kind you are!" he murmured, stretching out his arm and touching her sleeve. Then drawing his hand back, he sighed heavily.

"No-man, my friend," he said: "this business must end well *this* time"—the rest of the sentence came slowly and emphatically—"for it wouldn't do for me to kick the bucket till she came round."

"But you *are* better to-day," said Wizzie gravely. "Your face shows it. Did the nurse let you have that stuff that I made D. buy at Boon's?"

But the man closed his eyes with a worried frown. His childish pleasure in frightening her about "last night" changed to weariness as her question about his food hung in the air. "It *must* end well *this* time," he repeated, without opening his eyes:

400

"but after she's come round and we're happy again——"

Wizzie and No-man exchanged glances as his voice sank.

"She's not the only one, Claudius," broke from the girl's lips; but No-man took him up in a tone that was almost argumentative. "I don't blame you, old man, for wanting to be out of it all, when you lay such burdens on yourself; but how on earth can a way of life be right when it makes a fellow like you talk of your end in that tone?"

The man on the bed opened his eyes and fixed them gravely on the speaker. "You—don't—understand—No-man," he said slowly. "A person can find life hard and look forward to being released just as a—as a soldier——" He hesitated a moment, while a charming and quaintly deprecatory smile flickered over his mouth. "A *Roman* soldier, might—want—his—discharge—even though——" and he closed his eyes again.

Wizzie gave D. a quick reproachful look and bending over the bed pulled the counterpane more closely round the man's shoulders. Then while No-man, moving to the window, stared at the streaming rain, she went into the kitchen and opened the stove to see how the fire was.

Putting on some coal she lifted the kettle, made a little clicking sound between her tongue and her teeth when she found it empty, filled it at the sink and taking up a tin of invalid's food that stood unopened on the shelf, proceeded to open it and transfer some of its contents to a saucepan.

"Wizzie!" called out the sick man from the bed in a faint and worried tone.

"He's calling you, Wizz!" echoed No-man from the window.

She hurried to his side, where he was craning his neck round to discover what she was doing.

"I don't—*want*—you to do anything in there," he murmured peevishly. "Nurse is a good nurse. She brings me broth from over the way. There's no need for you to do anything in there."

"All right," she replied. "I was only looking at the fire. I won't touch a thing if it worries you."

"Listen to me, Wizzie!"

She saw that it had become an effort to him to talk, and she bent down till her head was close to his.

"The doctor said yesterday," he whispered: "that if I didn't get someone to be with me at night I'd have to go to the hospital. I told him how good the nurse was; but he said she had other cases, and couldn't give me enough time. Wizzie, listen! I don't *want* to go to the hospital. In fact I *won't* go; and that's the truth. But I'm afraid he may get an ambulance when I'm too weak to resist. Wizzie! If I went there—*she* would be shy of coming to see me and I—know—she—may—take—into her head—to come any minute! So—get me some woman—an old woman, mind!—she wouldn't like it if it wasn't an old woman—will you, Wizzie? You will? You promise? Oh, how good you are to me, Wizzie!" and he sank back with his eyes shut and an expression of blissful satisfaction on his face. The girl left him and went over to D. at the window.

No-man began whispering to her at once. "But you do everything as it is, Wizz! You're always in here. He doesn't know half you do! Besides, there *aren't* old women like that. He's thinking of years ago."

Wizzie pondered, staring through the window at the torrents of rain. It was as if she were looking through *two* windows, both made of some substance less transparent than glass and both in the state in which the whole universe was to the eye of Heraclitus. And if the window of glass and the mock-window of water were both to them, in the grey corpse-flesh pallor that had substituted itself for daylight, spectral epitomes of the flowing away of all things, the wall of the King's Arms' stables opposite, usually so mellow and friendly, showed like the side of a drowning galleon, while the path beneath the wall was no longer a road for solid people to walk upon, but a phantasmal river for ghosts to gather at, a river where a crowd of Limbo-weary spirits might wave beseeching arms. The only substantial thing Wizzie could see as she looked out was a tradesman's boy, wearing a man's mackintosh, who was pushing his bicycle against the torrential flood. This lad's face—for the boy didn't know he was being overlooked or he would have pulled himself together—wore an expression of woebegone desolation.

Following that piteous white face with her eyes as it melted into the rain, she felt as if it were drifting on the same fatal tide that was bearing her own life into the unknown. D. had always told her that the first syllable of the word Dorchester meant "water." He had always said that there came moments in the place when the waters "under the firmament," rose to meet the waters "above the firmament, "and Deep called to Deep.

Only a night or two ago, in intervals of that love-making which left her so stiff and cold, she had had to listen, till she hated these things as much as she hated the touch of his bony fingers, to vague murmurings from him about difficulties between people having to do with the opposition of the elements to which they were attracted—fire against air, water against earth and so forth. "I hope *I* shan't die on a night like this!" she thought, as she turned to No-man, who, judging by his expression, was deriving some weird pleasure of his own from the corpse-grey deluge.

"I shall do for him myself," she whispered. "He won't know! He doesn't know now who empties his slops or fills his hot bottle. He thinks it's the nurse. Lovie will be all right with Jenny. You must look in in the morning to see how he is; and I'll get up earlier. What are you smiling at?"

No-man became grave at once. "But the nights, the nights, sweetheart," he whispered. "He oughtn't to be left alone at night. You heard what he said about those girls finding him? He ought to have a trained nurse. I'll talk to the doctor."

Wizzie frowned. She saw in her mind's eye, clear as a map, the upshot of this talk of D.'s with the doctor. They'd take him straight off to the hospital—the one thing she'd promised to prevent.

"What," she whispered, after listening intently for a second to the patient's loud and troubled breathing : "could a person sleep *on* here, if they did stay all night?"

No-man gave her a quick surprised look. He was evidently being shown an aspect of his "neolithic captive's" character that was new to him. Nor did Wizzie miss the full significance of this look. What it said to her was : "Can *this* be my selfish, touchy, spoilt, wayward Wizz, this practical helper of broken-down eccentrics?"

In a flash it shot through her head while her frown deepened till it deformed her whole face : "He has no idea that it's only *him—him and his ways*—that I can't——"

"He's got a room upstairs, hasn't he?" No-man whispered.

"Only with a big bed in it that he never uses. *That's* his bed. He's sleeping on it now."

They both gazed hopelessly round the littered room, which

403

might have been the office of some overworked agent of a foreign "airways" company in Bangkok or Honolulu.

To Wizzie's mind the only friendly objects to be seen in the whole place were the steaming kettle, visible through the open kitchen door, and Claudius's own head on his pillow. She was now seized with an inspiration. "I'll bring down his mattress from upstairs," she whispered: "just for to-night, and I'll take the rug and a blanket from *our* bed. I don't want to speak of it to Jenny if I can help—but she's bound to find out. Well, there it is! We must do what we can, day by day. If he gets worse *he'll have* to go to the hospital."

No-man nodded; and it was her turn now to feel surprised. She had supposed that at the mere idea of having to sleep alone he would have raised the devil.

"The rain's stopping!" he now whispered eagerly. "Look at that gutter, look at those drops, look at that roof!"

But while the girl obediently considered these objects, what No-man looked at was his watch.

"It's nearly four," he announced softly. "I think I'll go for an hour's walk and come back *here* for tea. You get tea ready for us all three; and I'll tell Jenny to give Lovie hers. I'll tell her we're going out. She'll guess where we are—but nothing said, nothing felt!"

Wizzie's face brightened. She knew that Claudius would be overjoyed at this arrangement. "All right. Get a few buns at Mrs. Major's will you? You know? Those old Dorchester ones. Don't get soaking wet now! I won't have this place dripping with water. And clean your boots on Jenny's door-mat. Do you understand? Don't forget now, and come rushing straight in here from your 'drowner's' ditches! I'll be——" and she looked round, clicking her tongue against her teeth—"I'll be clearing up some of this clutter."

No-man began hurriedly putting on his overcoat. It was absurdly obvious to Wizzie that his chief anxiety now was to get well away before she changed her mind. But nothing as she knew—hardly the torrential deluge that had just ceased—could stop him from snatching a walk before tea—— This particular contrast, the tension of his walk and the relaxation of his tea, was, next to his pleasure in caressing her in bed, his greatest daily sensation.

404

She watched him therefore with feelings that were only too familiar, as clutching his cudgel in a hand that was not yet lodged in the sleeve of his great-coat, and with that garment trailing loosely over his shoulder and the stick colliding against the door, he took himself off.

"I can't stand it! I can't stand it!" she repeated to herself in a kind of desperate chant as she went to get the broom from the kitchen. Her thoughts became less hopeless but more drastic after she had lit a couple of candles; for as they had begun to say in the Dorchester shops, with that curious satisfaction in *all* weather-changes that townsfolk have : "The evenings are closing in."

Their patient did not awaken that afternoon till No-man had been back for nearly half an hour. She decided to let him sleep as long as possible though she caught D. in several shamefaced glances at his watch.

To make up to her pedestrian for this delay she permitted him to relate to her in a whisper, as they stood by the stove, all the events of his walk. This was such a rare privilege to No-man that he soon became voluble, forgetting where they were, forgetting Claudius, forgetting everything, except to move the kettle and stir up the flames in the stove with the iron poker.

"He's enjoying his damned elements to-day, anyway," thought Wizzie, as she saw him refrain from replacing the kettle and extend his bony fingers over the fiery aperture.

"I went clear round Poundbury," he whispered proudly, and she thought to herself : "He talks of Poundbury as if it were the Cape of Good Hope."

"You know that steep copse on the other side, before you get to the old farm?"

Wizzie nodded smilingly, as much as to say : "Oh, yes, dear D., I am as familiar with that spot as I am with my own bedroom." But in her heart she sighed : "Oh, what *is* he talking about?" And she tried to conjure up this umbrageous precipice where all she had ever seen were grassy banks, like those of Maiden Castle.

"It's on a day like this," he went on, "that I can imagine the Roman sentries challenging any stray wanderer. Coming back, along the south of the hill, where there's a row of old thorn-bushes, I actually got a shock, and thought——"

She forced herself to smile. "You saw a Roman ghost?"

"Well, no! not *quite* that. But do you know what it was?"

"What, D.?"

"A black heifer! They like lying down under those old bushes. The trunks are worn smooth by the way they rub against them. You can believe how dripping-wet it all was—and the grey mist—and the mud——and the dung under those bushes."

She pretended to give a little shudder. Oh, how well she knew his childlike desire to enhance the contrast between her cosy warmth in Claudius's kitchen and his own encounters with thorn-bushes and heifers. She could humour him at these moments, especially on an evening like this, just as she did Lovie when the child was pretending there was a wolf behind the curtain.

"Yes, it's an odd thing, but I feel a much stronger Roman aura on Poundbury than at Maiden Castle, or even at Maum-bury Rings. They must have used Poundbury more consecu-tively I think. It must have been a permanent camp, whereas——"

He was interrupted by Claudius's voice. "*Who's there?*" came from the bed in the front room.

"Why, you said that," cried No-man, hurrying to his side, "exactly like my Roman sentry on Poundbury! I've just come back from up there," he added in a lower voice, ashamed of having forgotten the man's state and spoken so loudly.

But Claudius was evidently refreshed by his sleep; and the pleasure with which she found him contemplating her prepara-tions for tea gave the girl a pang as she joined her friend at his side. She had got the little fire to burn more brightly too, and its pleasant blaze, combined with the light of the candles, made a delicious contrast with the premature twilight framed in the uncurtained window. "Shall I pull down the blind?" she asked.

Claudius nodded, and while No-man shut out the moribund day, he whispered to Wizzie: "If only the door were to open now and *she*——"

Wizzie helped him to raise himself up on his pillows, made No-man retire into the kitchen while she aided him in a yet more personal way, and then, long before the familiar cry of "*Ech-o! Ech-o!*" sounded from the entrance to the King's Arms' tap they were all enjoying themselves, just as if he had not been ill at all, over their tea and their talk and the buns from Mrs. Major's. For a while their conversation remained peaceful and unexciting; but do what the girl could it was impossible with these two, to keep them from the wretched topics that had become the bane of her life.

Suddenly Claudius hoisted himself up from his pillows and, thrusting out a long arm in the direction of the two candles which were now burning low, lifted up his voice like a prophet. "I tell you," he cried : "none of you can stop it. It's coming on the world like shock after shock of electric light! Our candles will burn out, our pride will fail, our personal life will dissolve away ; but the new order is coming! Strong and terrible and impersonal, it's coming; a new good, a new evil, a new hope! Let those who cling to what they call 'Nature' look to it! The new age is the age of man conquering Nature. It is power *over* Nature, it is power *over* great men. It's the life—*it's the life of the Masses!* And I say to you, No-man, just as those candles——" He stopped with a sudden quiver of all his body. He uttered a low, sobbing gasp while his outstretched arm dropped down like a cut branch and his head fell on the pillow. His eyes seemed now to double-shut themselves, as if not only their outward flame, but the inner flame that had gleamed through them, had become extinct.

And following that first gasp there came a sound from his throat that made Wizzie's heart grow cold.

They both rose to their feet. Wizzie gave No-man one fierce reproachful look, and pushing back the tea-table, moved close up to his side. Here she stood for a second, gazing at him with round eyes and open mouth, in frozen immobility. Then she swung round and gave No-man such a look of concentrated hatred that she could see him wince under it and turn his eyes away. Very slowly and softly, having whispered to him not to stir, she moved on tiptoe towards the door.

Before she reached it, however, she caught a sound from the bed and turned back quickly. That terrifying sound in the man's throat had ceased and his eyes had opened. Not only so but he was smiling reassuringly at D. whose expression of childish dismay must have struck him.

When they were both at his side again he looked almost quizzically from one to the other. "How nice you two look

407

together!" he murmured, and then he sighed heavily. "Do you know," he said, "I sometimes take the auspices, quite in the old Roman way, about her and me. I look out of that window and watch for birds; not sparrows, for I don't count sparrows, but any other birds. And if the first one I see flies to the right I say to myself: 'She'll come round in the end,' but if it flies to the left I say to myself"—here that peculiarly sweet smile of which he had the secret crossed his face—"what I really say to myself, No-man, if it flies to the left, is: 'It's all childish nonsense!'"

"How do you feel *now*?" inquired Wizzie gravely. "You frightened me stiff a minute ago!"

"Oh, I'll be all right now," he said, composing his face and stretching out his legs as if for a familiar ordeal. "But I'll have to go through a bout of the pain now. So I'm afraid we'd better say good-bye for a while. When I get like that it always comes —just here." And he jabbed with his great, spatulate thumb, a thumb that could be bent backwards further than any thumb in Dorchester, the spot in the counterpane that covered the centre of his body. "What I think it is," he said, "is pleurisy. But the nurse won't have it. She says it's something else. But, whatever it is, it's hardly weakened me at all. Do you know what I told Edith when she said I fell down from weakness? I told her I fell down from dizziness, not weakness; I told her I was strong enough to beget a child! She *did* laugh at that. But I always talk freely to those girls. I like to make them laugh."

"Does it hurt much?" asked Wizzie.

"No, no, little one! Not as bad as all that. It takes most of my energy to cope with it. But I *can* cope with it. It's sharp; but it's not acute; it's not unbearable. Only I can't think of much else, while it's going on. Much better be off, you two! I don't like having visitors when I can't amuse them. But don't look like that, you darling girl! I'm not going to make faces, or make noises. I swear to you it isn't so bad."

"I wouldn't think of leaving you, Claudius," said Wizzie quietly, "but don't worry about me. I'll find lots to do. I'll treat your house like my own."

"I'll stay—a bit—longer—too," murmured No-man humbly, resuming his former seat and stretching out his legs again, "but I won't talk. I'll think. I'll think about my book."

After carrying the tea-things away Wizzie joined in this silent

408

vigil. An occasional faint twinge in his face and a few spasmodic jerks of his knees were the only signs of what the sick man was enduring; but he evidently had removed his consciousness from their presence as completely as if he were a thousand miles away.

Since that look of unequivocal hatred he had caught on her face D. had avoided Wizzie's eyes. But with this single exception he seemed wholly himself, serene, friendly, quite at ease, and enjoying to the full the sensation of the red coals, the guttering candles, the darkening window.

"I suppose he'd enjoy himself like this," the girl thought, "if Claudius were dying, and I'd run away, and Lovie were howling with that stitch in her side!"

"*Ech-o! Ech-o!*" came distinctly now from the end of Friary Lane; and in spite of the wretchedness of the evening there was faintly audible from the top of High East Street that warm stir, that rich vibration, that glowing movement of life in Dorchester, which always seems to rise to an intenser pitch when the wealthier Durnovarians have had *their* tea and the poorer ones are preparing to go home to theirs. The actual *volume* of sound, no doubt, is greater at half-past four, or even at half-past three, but when five o'clock strikes at the Guildhall some magnetic current of psychic sympathy seems to pour into the old place from all the country round, till from Piddle-Trenthide on the east, to Martin's Town on the west, a thicker smoke from human chimneys and a quicker pulse in human bodies carries into Dorchester a fresh awareness that the happiest hour in the whole Durotrigean day—the hour of tea—has come round again!

The man's pain—as first one candle and then the other guttered down and was extinguished—became to her a living presence in the fire-light. It was actually there among them, waiting in silence just as she and D. were waiting while the fatal tide flowed past them! It had "no form or comeliness," this pain-presence, by which it could be palpably felt, and yet it was the opposite of an evil thing, as it shared their silence.

How long they waited like this the girl could not have told. It seemed to her afterwards, judged by the sinking of the fire, to have been a good deal more than an hour.

At any rate it was her practical sense that the fire must not be allowed to go out that brought that curious vigil to an end. But she had no sooner got up and lit the kitchen-lamp and brought in a couple of fresh candles along with the coal than No-man scrambled to his feet.

"There are people stopping—outside!" he said. "I believe they're——" He was interrupted by a sharp knock at the house-door.

"Are—you—sure—it's *this* house?" murmured Wizzie; turning round as she lit the candles. "It may be ours!"

But a repetition of the knocking made her open the door into the passageway, and stand listening. "It *is* this door," she cried. "I must go and see!" So remote from everything outside that fire-lit room had her mind been that it gave her an almost painful shock, like being suddenly aroused from a deep sleep when she opened the door.

"I've come to see Mr. Roger Cask," said one of the three figures standing outside. "I'm the district——" but another of the figures, that of a man, came forward, and it did not lessen Wizzie's feeling of dazed confusion when she saw it was old Teucer Wye.

"I—was—in—town," stuttered the old man: "and—I—thought I'd just ask how our friend—was—but if——"

"Oh, no! Come in, Mr. Wye!" cried Wizzie.

"Come in, Nurse!" and she stared almost impolitely—so dazed she felt—at the third of the visitors.

This was a tall, excessively plain woman, with a big nose surmounted by glasses, and with something queer—at least so it seemed to Wizzie in that faint light—about her chin.

"Constancia," said the nurse abruptly, turning to this person with the vague intention of introducing her, "this is, I feel sure, Miss Ravelston from next door, who's been so kind to our patient. This is Miss Ferneau, Miss Ravelston, who's come to look after Mr. Cask. They are, I believe, well acquainted already, but I think Miss Ferneau will keep him in order. You *will* keep him in order, won't you, Constancia?"

Wizzie kept smiling and nodding in complete bewilderment while all this went on, and then, drawing back against the wide-open door, she made way for Constancia and the nurse to enter the narrow passage.

"Won't *you* come in, Mr. Wye?"

"No, no, whew! No, my dear miss, no, I won't come in. But you'll tell him I called? That's the chief thing, that he should know I called! Oh, no! I wouldn't disturb anyone now. Besides"—and he called Wizzie towards him while the nurse took Constancia into Claudius's room—"what I've really come to do is to tell my girl Jenny that she *must* make it up with our friend now that he's so ill. I've been thinking what to say for a whole week; and I've got the passages marked"—here he tapped his pocket. "That will settle it! I'm going to speak plain to her, Miss Ravelston. It's all here—and *here*"—and this time he tapped—though this second fountain of justice received but a feeble flick in comparision with the other—his forehead as well as his pocket.

"We'll come *with* you, Mr. Wye; one minute!"—and she called down the passage: "D.! D.! D!" for she said to herself: "He'll stay there, the stupid, while the nurse is taking—but I'm glad she's brought that woman for the night. He won't think *she'll* carry him off to the hospital. I only hope she won't forget—but the nurse *must* have told her—yes, come along, D.! Here's Mr. Wye come to *make* Jenny behave; and he wants us to hear what he'll say!"

This last remark of hers caused the old Platonist to shuffle with his feet for pride and joy. Wizzie could see how it pleased him by the way he fidgetted while he shook No-man's hand. He evidently could not wait to unburden himself of his week's meditations, while the presence of these two witnesses made him feel as if Friary Lane did after all possess some resemblance to Athens.

Their knocking soon brought the not-entirely-unprepared Jenny to her door and they all went straight into her kitchen, where Lovie, sitting in solitary state on a high chair, was having her tea.

Lovie put down her mug and held out her hands with such joy to greet No-man that Wizzie felt a momentary pang; but her spasm of jealousy was speedily forgotten in her intense curiosity and, to confess the truth, in a malicious hope against hope concerning "the plain words" her friend was to hear. Wizzie had always disliked old Teucer Wye. She completely understood the way he got upon his younger daughter's nerves. But her recent vigil with Claudius made her feel so indignant with Jenny that she prayed to God this horrid little man would make her sit up, and would say things to her that neither D. nor herself had dared to say. "But he won't," she thought. "He's one of these dreary talkers, and he'll go on and on; and he'll read his lesson-books to her; and Jenny will simply smile at me!"

But Wizzie soon discovered to her delight that she was completely wrong. In her ignorance of the ways of idealists, for neither in convent or Circus had she met such people, she did not allow for the astonishing lapses into gross realism, into shocking materialism, that seem Nature's revenge upon these rebels against her delicate adjustments.

But this gap in our friend's knowledge of life was destined now, in Mrs. Dearth's kitchen, to be amply filled.

She waited till the riotous greeting between No-man and Lovie was over, and then, drawing up a chair near the child's table, began encouraging her to get on with her meal.

But the ex-professor refused to sit down, while Mrs. Dearth, after refilling Lovie's mug, and catching the ominous trend of her father's harangue, stood erect and defiant on the side of the stove opposite to the one where No-man had taken refuge.

"It's a disgrace to me as your father, and to your mother who brought you up!" cried the old gentleman, not so much tapping as thumping the books in his pockets. "Do you know what I saw just now, and Miss Ravelston can bear me out"—here Wizzie bent low over Lovie's bowl of bread and milk—"I saw some terrible person brought in by the nurse to spend the night with that poor fellow! And here are you to all intents and purposes his wife—yes! I repeat it—his wife, refusing to lift a finger to help! Why, the man may die! I didn't see him but I saw enough. The man may die to-night, with no one with him but the awful individual I saw just now. It's not *my* affair, you say? God help you, woman, it's everyone's affair! All the town knows of it—he so ill in there and you!——"

He stopped for breath, but Wizzie noticed that on this occasion—in his role of a father rebuking his favourite daughter—he kept unusual control over himself and showed no sign of hysterical weakness. He never once whistled through his gums, and after that first thump at his side he never, till the end, so much as touched his pockets.

"We're all friends here," he continued, advancing to the table and resting his hand on its edge, while Lovie, pushing her mother's fingers away, dropped her spoon and stared at him with fascinated wonder, "and so I can speak plainly to you, my girl. The truth is—you've never grown up! You're behaving like a woman *who's never lived with a man*. It's—yes, I've made up my mind to say it and I will say it—you've grown into an unnatural old maid, Jenny, and it's because of *that,* because of your not living with him as a woman ought to live with an honest man who loves her, that you can keep up a silly quarrel with him like this! I begin to think that it was this old-maidishness of yours and not your wild notions of women's rights that drove Tom Dearth away. Your're a bigoted old maid, Jenny— that's what you are, and I'm ashamed of you! I've been thinking of this all the week. It's because you've not lived with Cask, as a woman should, I tell you, that you are acting in this obstinate, wicked way. You're only *half* a woman. If you'd"— here he did give a glance round him and pull himself up—"if you'd gone to bed with the man, Jenny, this old-maidish silliness would never have———"

But Mrs. Dearth had leapt forward with her hands clenched. "*Father!*" she cried; and the extremity of her indignation so scared the child at the table that she began to cry and hid her face against Wizzie's shoulder. "How can you, how *dare* you, say these things to me? Isn't it you who've always told me, since I was *her* age"—and she pointed at the sobbing Lovie—"that real love had no need of—of what you're talking about? Isn't it you who've always said that when two people love—oh, it's too much, it's too much, for *you* to turn against me. I've expected it from the rest—yes! and I've had it, too, all these cruel months, from those nearest to me"—and she swept her blazing eyes across Wizzie's averted face—"but that you, *you* from whom I've learnt what real, pure, spiritual love is, should now"—and she pressed her clenched fists against her mouth, while her bosom heaved with deep dry sobs.

"I—tell—you—you unhappy girl," brought out the little man, taking his hand from the table and raising himself automatically on his toes, "I tell you, you've misunderstood me all along—like everybody else. What I say is that we must free our souls from *all* these material things. While we're on earth our bodies must have their natural satisfaction, but this doesn't touch the soul.

413

It's nothing to the soul. The soul has no part in it. We're only here, imprisoned in matter, so that our souls should learn how to be free—you do the senses too much honour, you think too much about them, when you deny them like this. The soul should be indifferent, aloof, free of the whole business! When you play the angry virgin with this good man, you're not making less of your miserable senses, you're making more! Go to bed with him, girl, in this little house, in this little lane, but let your soul rise to the eternal, rise to the——"

But Jenny suddenly snatched her fists from her mouth—and Wizzie saw she had pressed them there so savagely that there was blood on her lips—and coming straight up to her father, hissed out at him in a low terrible voice, that made even D. draw up his muddy feet beneath his seat: "If you mean what you say, Father, *throw those books of yours into my stove!*"

At first the old gentleman, as he sank back on his heels and withdrew a step or two from her, could only whistle through his gums in the old familiar way. Then, as Wizzie stared in wonder at what she could see, half-hidden by Jenny's shoulder, of the man's face, she saw an extraordinary change pass over it and a look come into it as if he were another Teucer Wye, a Teucer Wye who had no daughter at all, a Teucer Wye, who had never been a professor "in a small Midland college," a Teucer Wye who did not know whether Glymes or Friary Lane, whether Dorchester or Athens was his abiding-place, a Teucer Wye who had—and yet had not—slept with the woman who gazed down on them out of that little picture. And it was while this other Teucer Wye, now looking forth from his face, gave a completely different air to his high forehead, to his toothless mouth, to his diminutive frame, that the man drew from his side-pockets both of his old school-texts and pushing his daughter aside went straight up to her stove and moved away the kettle from the fiery red opening.

Human gestures between four walls have the peculiarity sometimes of gathering to themselves such intense emotional magnetism that they are palpably felt, like the reaction to a physical shock, not only by the persons concerned, but by alien persons, and, it may chance, also by foreign substances.

It was certain at any rate that Wizzie felt compelled to rise to her feet and move forward towards the man as he held those books. It was plain to her that No-man too was driven by the same psychic force to do the same thing. As for little Lovie she managed to scramble down unaided from her high chair to the floor, where Jenny, not knowing in the least what she was doing, untied and took off the child's bib.

But not only have these tense moments within human walls and under human ceilings the power of generating palpable electric force, they seem also to have the power of retarding the movement of time.

Anyway, what Wizzie felt, though she couldn't have put it into words, was a sensation as if the whole of Jenny's kitchen— with all four of them standing there, staring and petrified—had been lowered by some eternal hand into a timeless vacuum. Her legs began to feel ice-cold, as if the passage from time to time-lessness meant the ebbing away of all bodily warmth.

Such effects sometimes outlast their cause; and so it is per-haps fortunate therefore that both Jenny's and Claudius's houses have long since been pulled down, and that where old Teucer Wye on this October evening moved his daughter's kettle to expose the red-hot interior of her stove, the sparrows from the cheerful tap-yard of the King's Arms can hop in peace, among nothing more ghostly than a few weather-beaten flagstones.

When it became clear, even to Lovie's mind, that this neatly-attired little man with the well-brushed hair actually intended to throw into that fiery furnace what was more precious to him than food and drink or human affection, the little girl rushed up to him screaming: "Not put books in fire! Not put nothing in fire!" and began tugging at his coat. The transfigured expres-sion on his countenance had been until then concealed from Jenny herself, but when he turned now with the books in his hands and faced her and it became clear to all of them, she suddenly began to tremble.

"It's a bargain, Jenny," he said solemnly; and Wizzie was struck by the quiet, self-controlled tone in which he spoke. "Give yourself to your man; throw this cruel virginity of yours into the fire, and I'll throw these books, which are my life, into your stove! Will you do it, Jenny my girl? The word was yours. It was you who said: 'Throw your books, your life, into my fire.' I'm serious, my child. This is a—a covenant between us. You've always been my dearest. You know *that*; and now I'm giving my best for you, more than my best! Shall we take"—he spoke almost exultingly at that moment—"the *Sortes Platonienses?* Shall we see what they say before they die? Mark you, my girl. This isn't only your father's sacrifice speaking, this is your proud virginity speaking—before we give them both to the fire!'"

Little Lovie, with a face blubbered with tears, stopped pulling at his coat. Wizzie could see that the child thought the man was going to read a story from the pretty books instead of throwing them into the flames.

"O beloved Pan," the old man translated, in a low intense voice, "and all ye other gods of this place, grant to me that I"—here he paused and looked straight at Mrs. Dearth who was trembling violently from head to foot while her fingers plucked at the fastening of her black blouse—"*and my dear daughter here,* may be made beautiful in our souls within!"

Wizzie, who was watching him intently, saw him fumble perceptibly with the second little book. "If he waits a second longer," she thought, "he won't do it!"

But Teucer Wye did not wait. Mumbling something that the girl couldn't catch he rushed to the stove, flung both volumes into its fiery heart, and clamped the kettle over the opening.

There was a deep hush in that kitchen then; and for an instant even Lovie held her breath. But she only held it, as children do, before a passionate burst of sobbing; and, when this came at last, she ran, not to Wizzie, but to Mrs. Dearth, and buried her face in the woman's dress.

"In our souls within!" repeated Teucer Wye in a whisper that was scarcely audible above the child's desperate sobbing; and touching lightly with his lips his daughter's head, which was bent low down over the clinging child, he picked up his hat—he hadn't taken off his overcoat—made two formal little bows, one to Wizzie and one to No-man, and hurried out of the room.

Wizzie remained staring at the door he had closed behind him till the sound of the street-door opening and shutting released the tension. Then she and No-man exchanged a long wordless look. It was not till much later, not indeed till they were both of them in bed in their upper room, with the fire-light flickering reassuringly over its familiar furniture, making the girl among

416

the water-lilies blush rosy-red and Thuella's picture of her father look forth with the lineaments of Pico della Mirandola, that they expressed their impressions of that scene in the kitchen.

"Do you think it *will* make any difference?" murmured No-man, taking the advantage of the chance that so pregnant a question gave him to slip his arm beneath her supine form.

"How can I tell? Don't, D.!—she only talked about Lovie afterwards when I was helping her wash up. She's got awfully fond of Lovie, D. If anything happened to—to me, I think she'd be almost glad."

"Don't 'ee say such things, my treasure."

"But she would! I *know* she would. At first she made—you remember?—all that fuss over me. But it's Lovie now. He said she was an old maid; but *I* think she'd like to have a lot of children——She's lonely; that's what it is."

"Maybe she'll come back to him now, and then perhaps——"

"How long can women have children, D.? Don't—I won't have it!"

He chuckled. "Oh, it all depends—how unkind you are to me, Wizz!—Certainly till forty, and over that, too! She's some years off forty yet."

There was a silence for a time between them, Wizzie meditating on the subject of women with "forty" in sight, and No-man trying to get the feeling that he was caressing her out of the bare fact of their inevitable contact as they lay side by side.

Then Wizzie said: "I don't see how you could have written your wife's name that day without knowing you did it if you're not always thinking about her."

"Good Lord, kid! Have we gone back to *that*? I tell you I *didn't* write it! Can't you take a plain answer? I don't know, any more than you do, how it got there."

"I suppose you want me to believe *she* wrote it—after being dead for ten years!"

He was silent; and she went on: "Grummer used to tell of a man she knew whose dead wife never left his girl a moment's peace. She said that in the night——"

"Now that's enough, Wizz! If you won't let me touch you, you needn't start—but you're only saying it to tease. You *know* you're not really jealous of—of those days."

"Who wrote it then on that bit of paper and why did you tear it up so quickly?"

He made no reply to this. "And what's more," she went on, "you went back there next morning to pick up those bits of paper!"

"*Wizzie!*"

She certainly had roused him now, for he raised his head from the pillow and glanced at the window, where the string of the blind was making a faint tapping as the wind blew. But he sank down again with a sigh; and again there was silence in that upper front room of Friary Lane.

"I know what you're thinking now, D."

"Oh, for God's sake, Wizz, don't go on with this! Do let's go to sleep."

"You're thinking, like you always say, about two skeletons, lying side by side on the surface of the earth, and neither knowing a thing of what's in the other's head."

"I'm thinking of something much more to the point than that, though it proves it about our two skulls. Do you know, Wizz, I saw *him* to-day in High East Street."

It was Wizzie's turn to be startled now; and she did more than just lift her head from the pillow. She sat straight up in the bed.

"Saw *him*? Old Funky? Why didn't you tell me before?"

"My dear child"—and he pulled the clothes round his exposed shoulder—"what time have I had for telling you anything? Besides—I thought we'd enjoy ourselves a little first, before we——"

"*Enjoy* ourselves!" She couldn't help throwing into this bitter exclamation all the complicated trouble his news brought her. She felt overpowered by a great wave of self-pity——Wasn't it just like her fate to have *him* reappearing, on the top of everything?

"Is the Circus here?"

"I've no idea. I haven't been that way for weeks. I suppose it is; or he wouldn't be in town."

"You don't think he's up to something new, D.—wanting more money or anything?"

"Oh, I don't suppose so. Just wandering about, looking at the shops. He didn't see me. At least he pretended not to."

"What'll you do if he speaks to you?"

"Well—find out what he wants, I suppose."

"Yes! that's just what you *would* do! Talk to him till he finds out everything! I suppose you'd bring him in here to see Lovie if he asked you to?"

No-man was silent. With a feeling of absolute hopelessness she sank down again on her pillow, and pulling the bed-clothes with a vicious twitch to her side of the bed, turned her back to her companion.

"He doesn't care what I feel," she thought, "any more than Old Funky does!" And she made, as she curled up on the extreme edge of the bed, with her knees almost touching her bosom, reverting in fact to the position in which she had lain before she was born, a vow that that very next day she would go out to Glymes and pour out all her troubles to Uryen. "Ordinary men don't understand women," she said to herself, "but *he* may, if only he lets me talk to him. But it'll be the same as it always is! He'll get Nance to fetch 'Thel' from next door and 'Thel' will act silly and make a fuss over me, like she always does, and he'll just sit and stare at us."

So thought Wizzie, hugging her rounded knees on the extreme edge of the bed, nor did the other "skeleton" make any attempt to disturb her, but over them both as they lay there, and it was not long before they were asleep, the wind began to shift, blowing now from south-south-west, straight across Maiden Castle from Chesil; and as its palpable but invisible form swept inland from the beach across the earthworks, there adhered to the substance of its presence particles and flakes, atoms and notes, gathered up from the surface of that huge parapet of pebbles and from the heaps of stranded seaweed left to perish there between its shelving ridges.

These particles and flakes, sea-soaked, sea-perforated, sea-born sea-bitten, became now as much part and parcel of the pressure of the life-mystery in Durnovaria as was the steady breathing of Miss Ravelston, or as were the intermittent heavings and spasmodic jerks with which the muscles and nerves of D. No-man recovered their equilibrium after the excitement of the day.

And since what exists in the macrocosm exists also in the microcosm, it may well be that these journeying sea-particles carried on the wind exercised upon these two sleeping forms the same sort of influence that the sea itself exercises on conscious minds, blighting and sterilizing in one sense, curing and restoring in another.

Over many another male and female pair in its air-voyage from the Atlantic must that south-west wind have blown, carrying the same influence of the salt sea, rousing far-off atavistic responses, making appeals where there could be no response, over furred couples, over feathered couples, under straw, under rustling leaves, under waving grasses, till it came to these two beneath their bed-clothes. Its effect upon the inanimate things it passed that night, we are forced in our ignorance to regard as nil, Hardy's bronze image unaffected, the brewery chimney unaffected, the bones of Mona and Cornelia unaffected, but that before the dawn came, at the hour when the magnetic pull of the solid earth is faintest, at the hour when all living things seem loosening their hold on the elements that sustain them, the sea wind found Wizzie's warm body in a yielding mood, not only allowing but encouraging No-man's caresses, while neither of them was fully awake, and all this may well have had to do with those salt-tasting atoms and the unbridled restlessness of the earth's great lover. This salt wind from Chesil Beach must have numbed and atrophied all those touchy centres of egotism in our friends, wherewith their personal minds spoilt their impersonal sensations; but when the interlude was over, and the depersonalized Wizzie, with hot cheeks and glowing limbs, had become the personal Wizzie with tantalized nerves and unsatisfied feelings, the wind dropped, and a pallid light, a light that was neither grey nor blue nor white nor yellow, the nameless light of the first vibration of dawn, that can be described only as a thinning of the "thick rotundity" of darkness, drew the girl's wide-opened eyes towards it in impatient longing for the day.

No-man, however, who had never been as fully awake as she, fell fast asleep now, and the girl was left to watch as calmly as she could the vast process of the earth's illumination. This huge creative act, in its detachment from all human troubles and in the implacable persistence of its cosmic cheerfulness, was far less sympathetic to her grievances and her fears than would have been the corresponding twilight of night-fall. But sympathetic or not, she had no wish just then to dwell upon it at all.

Wizzie was not of an introspective nature, nor was she the

kind of person to be vividly conscious of the non-human background of our life; and although, if left to herself, she couldn't be accused—few intelligent women can—of being totally blind to these recurrent phenomena, there were especial reasons why she instinctively discouraged her sensitiveness. She was not left long, however, to the risk of having to restrain any planetary emotion she might feel, for the dawn had not advanced very far before her nervously acute sense of hearing became aware of a distinct series of very human sounds in Jenny Dearth's bedroom.

Jenny was certainly up and dressing herself! Her first thought was of Lovie. It was Jenny who had begged her very soon after they first had Lovie with them, to move the child's cot into her room. As a rule Lovie was the first in that Friary Lane house to salute the sun; but closely as Wizzie listened now she could not hear a sound from her daughter—nothing but the creaking of the boards, and an occasional contact of glass with china that showed that Jenny was making her toilet. What was the woman up to, getting out of bed before it was light, before Lovie had lifted her voice, before a single sparrow had chirped? Intently did Wizzie listen, and as she listened she wondered more and more. Yes! Jenny was certainly dressing, and dressing, too— *that* her feminine eavesdropper detected from all sorts of subtle indications—with unusual nicety and care! Could it be that after sleepless hours spent in pondering on her father's gross and violent words she had decided to "give up her nonsense," and live with Claudius as his wife?

No sooner had this idea entered her head than she felt sure it *was* the true explanation of this early rising. Jenny was going to be on the watch, and the moment "that woman" went off duty she was going to take her place. Wizzie lay down again. If Jenny were going to wait till "that woman" went away she might have to wait till breakfast-time, till the time the nurse came.

But she jumped up now, quivering and tense with electric energy; for she heard Jenny's door softly open and shut, and then the stairs creaked under the woman's tread as she went down. Wizzie didn't hesitate a second. She slipped out of bed, snatched up the first garment that presented itself in the dim light, which turned out to be her own skirt; and with this clutched like a shawl round her shoulders, and with her bare feet emerging from her long old-fashioned night-gown, she opened the door without making a sound, left it ajar for her return, and tiptoed halfway downstairs. Here she paused and leaned over the banister. Yes! Jenny was in her kitchen now. She could tell exactly what she was doing. She was poking the coals, which, as Wizzie knew, were almost always still red in the morning, and throwing in certain bits of stick that it was her custom to keep all night close to the stove so that they might be especially dry when she came down.

Wizzie stretched as far as she could over the banister-rail and listened motionless. She kept well on the *qui vive,* however, so that the moment Jenny emerged from the kitchen she could be upstairs in a flash and back in her room, but she gave herself up to this eavesdropping with unmixed delight. If there was an element of malice in it, after the long vexation of Jenny's wilfulness, there was much more of excited sympathy for a woman's defiance of her own pride and prudery.

"She's not going to wait any longer," Wizzie thought. And she could feel through the pit of her own stomach, that was now pressed so tightly against the stair-rail, something of the wild beating of Jenny's heart and Jenny's pulses. Her instinct—which was almost telepathic—justified itself up to the hilt. She heard Jenny fill the kettle from the tap. She heard the unmistakable sound of iron on iron, as the woman placed it over the orifice of the stove. Then she heard a sound that caused a smile to cross her face and made her close her fingers still more tightly on the banister, for it was the sound of the tinkle of a wineglass against a salt-cellar. Now these objects always stood in front of a little round mirror, the shaving-mirror that had belonged to the vanished "Tom"; and to Wizzie, who knew by this time all the domestic recurrences in her friend's house, this sound meant one thing and one only, namely that Jenny Dearth was surveying her own appearance in the glass.

"She's going to him! She's going to him!" the girl thought, and drawing back from the banister she flattened herself against the wall and waited in breathless excitement. Yes! Apparently satisfied with the way she looked, Jenny now hurried with hasty steps to the entrance of the little back-yard that connected the two houses. A breath of chilly air struck Wizzie's thinly clad figure as this door opened letting her friend out; but heedless of this discomfort she hurried downstairs and rushing into the dining-room stationed herself at the window.

"If she's going to stay with him," she thought, "she'll bundle that woman into the street in no time." She waited for three—four—eight minutes without anything happening. Then she heard the Guildhall clock strike half-past something. But it was still dim outside, and the light in the King's Arms' tap-yard was still burning. How slowly the day came, in this part of the town! It used to come much more quickly in the old fair-field. Oh, how cold her bare legs had begun to feel, and her feet were icy, but a desperate obstinacy kept her there, and something else, too, something that she would have found it impossible to explain to anyone.

For as she stood clutching the curtain and staring across the narrow street at the stable-window opposite, through which she could see a lantern moving about that every now and then threw into distinction a bundle of loose hay that was pressing against the pane, her sympathy with what she imagined going on became almost morbid.

"She's giving herself to Claudius!" she thought. "She couldn't wait till he's well, and he'll be in a fever to respond. That crazy old man was right, and none of us thought of it. I was a fool not to think of it, and so was D.! Tom must have left her because all that suffrage talk on the top of her prudery was too much for him.

"And old Claudius must have been too tender and gentle, too. I suppose a woman's resistance is harder for a man to deal with than a girl's. I suppose if I'd been as old as Jenny—but then I'd never have had Lovie! Will Jenny have——"

But at this point her sympathy with Jenny's happiness transformed itself into a terrible craving for her Circus-life! To be on her old horse's back, to feel the tingling rapture of those balancings and leapings, those plunges and somersaults; to hear the cries—oh, how often she had suffered from bitter cold just like this while awaiting her turn in the tent!

As she hugged her skirt round her shoulders, and even went so far as to snatch up one of Jenny's woollen antimacassars and twist it round her waist, she noticed once more that moving lantern throwing a light on the wisp of hay that pressed against the stable-window, and she made up her mind that come what might she would leave both Lovie and D. and go back to her *work*.

But she was out into the hallway again now, for she had heard a sound upstairs. Yes! it was Lovie talking to herself, but apparently quite happily. "I declare," thought Lovie's mother, as she began to ascend the stairs, "that kid would be happy if it never saw a soul except when it was hungry. I—don't—believe—she'll—miss—me—one—bit!"

Each of these monosyllables was punctuated by the imprint of a bare foot on the staircase carpet, but in spite of their consolatory implication in the face of her recent resolve, it was with some degree of peevishness that after wrapping Jenny's bedclothes round her and sitting down on the edge of the bed near Lovie's cot, she endeavoured to recall the child's absorbed imagination from "Gwendolly's" successor to herself.

Lovie's new "Lovie" was a real doll, chosen for her by No-man with infinite care through at least half a dozen shops in Dorchester. She was a young doll—let us say a year old—but having been made in the Fatherland of Dolls her blue eyes and pounting lips possessed that fairylike beauty which few English doll-makers seem able to capture.

Every morning—about the time when the first cawing of the rooks was to be heard, as they flew from the elms in Frome House gardens to the elms in Acland House garden—Mrs. Dearth had to get out of bed to put on to the child a little woollen jacket, too thick for her to sleep in, but indispensable when she sat up with "Popsy." It was to "Popsy" that she was talking now, to "Popsy" that she'd been talking ever since Aunt Jenny had slipped the jacket over her sleepy head.

"Mummy's cold," said Wizzie trying to appeal to the little girl's sympathy. "Mummy didn't want to disturb D., so she came to see if her pretty one was all right."

" *'Popsy'* isn't cold."

"I should think not, with half your jacket twisted round her! You and 'Popsy' can't wear the same clothes at the same time. There—there—*that's* enough clothing for a doll. Dolls aren't—"

"*You've* got Aunt Jenny's things on. *You've* got D.'s money. *You* took old Funk's life and joy away!"

"*What's that?*" Wizzie jumped up from the bed and bending over the little girl seized her by the shoulders. This she did in

424

such a rush of agitation that "Popsy," who in her turn had been seized by *her* parent, uttered, under pressure of the child's fingers, a squeak like that of a new-born shrew-mouse and fell on the floor, where she lay with her eyes closed and her arms extended.

"When have you seen him? Tell me now! Tell me everything."

"Pick 'Popsy' up. 'Popsy's' deaded. *You've* deaded poor 'Popsy'."

"When did Old Funky speak to you, Lovie—yesterday? Remember now!"

But Lovie's head, in spite of the hands on her shoulders, was hanging over the edge of the cot, uttering consoling words to the fallen doll.

Something might easily just then have passed between these two feminine authorities at which even "Popsy" behind her diplomatically closed eyelids might have felt surprise, had not there come through Jenny's open window the distinct sound of a sharply closed street door.

Leaving the child's cot Wizzie flew to the window just in time to see, in the now quite transparent morning light, the upright form of Miss Ferneau, making its dignified and unhurried retreat down the hill towards the coal-yard. "Is she furious? Was there a scene? Did Jenny turn her out?"

These were questions that so absorbed the interest of our friend that when Miss Ferneau had vanished from her sight she picked up "Popsy" with her own hand and returned her to her offspring, merely remarking as she left the room: "If *you* can't remember who you meet when you're out, we'll see if D. can!"

It was after ten before Wizzie was ready to set off for Glymes. Her resolution to get a glimpse of Uryen that morning was finally sealed during a bitter quarrel with No-man over his allowing Old Funky to speak to his child. It had for some months been D.'s custom to take the child, without her perambulator, for little strolls down the street; but what especially hurt Wizzie's feelings in this case was that in mentioning the old man's presence in the town he had concealed the fact that he had a definite encounter with him. What *had* he actually said to the little girl? D. had got sulky under her anger, and would neither deny nor admit that the man had used the startling expression repeated so emphatically by Lovie.

425

Their quarrel had ended by No-man's going off in silence to High East Street, while she herself, in Jenny's continued absence, had had to get her own and Lovie's breakfast in the deserted kitchen.

This task accomplished, she settled the child on the kitchen rug, with the table between her and the stove; and before leaving her there she forced herself—though her head was throbbing with a whirl of conflicting emotions—to display a lively interest in "Popsy's" being put to bed in a miniature Great Western truck.

She soon realized, however, that Lovie was shrewd enough to divine something of the tragic tension of her mood; and every now and then, in the midst of their attendance on "Popsy's" siesta, she caught a pair of serious eyes fixed furtively on her face.

She got away at last; but she couldn't leave the child without telling Jenny that she was alone, and so after running upstairs to dress for going out, and after a final glance into the kitchen, she decided to visit the other house before setting forth.

Poor little Wizzie! For all her bitter experiences of what life can do to a spirited girl, she was not such an egoist as to find it altogether easy, on this particular morning, to leave Lovie by herself on the kitchen-floor. What she kept repeating in her heart, as with her hand on the door-handle she watched the child putting "Popsy" to sleep in the truck, was that it was fear of Old Funky that made it impossible to take her to Glymes. But below all that, she knew perfectly well that her real reason was her passionate feeling that she *must*, for once and at all costs, see D.'s father alone.

It was hard, all the same, to close that door on the child! Not that Lovie—though she knew her mother was standing there—showed the smallest interest in her presence. But the child's very lack of concern seemed to hold her all the more strongly, seemed to hold her as if, instead of being stationary on the floor, Lovie was being carried rapidly out of sight on a magic carpet.

She was certainly experiencing what D.'s poor Mary called, more than two hundred years ago: "being torn in half," and what she suffered was not the less acute for being unexpected. She felt so totally unable to move from that threshold that her mind began wandering about, just as if she had to wait till someone released her.

One of these wandering and drifting thoughts had to do with the new dress she had just put on. She became aware of a vague tickling sensation in her left breast, and she wondered if this feeling were the result of her dress being too tight.

She was still clinging to the door-handle and swaying from side to side on this terrible eel-bridge of destiny when the door into the yard opened and there, in the passage behind her, stood Jenny Dearth! Never in her life had she seen so transfigured a human face! It was a countenance of paradisic ecstasy. Had No-man seen her he would have been compelled to admit that extreme joy had the same effect on his "Horse-Head" as ex-treme agitation. It converted the bizarre into the extraordinary, the grotesque into the sublime.

In fact, Jenny's illuminated lineaments seemed more than human to Wizzie's startled eyes at that moment. It was like a face she had once seen outside the Circus-tent—the face of a woman who had won a lottery ticket. But the worst of it was that this illuminated woman's face, hovering before her—near her—and now pressed passionately against her own, while she knew that it brought the decisive settling-down to her dizzy trapeze of indecision, was prevented, by some diabolical non-conducting substance in herself, from delivering its message!

In fact, all the while her friend was hugging her to her heart, she was trying desperately but quite in vain, to take from her some final supernatural oracle. It had been a superstition of Grummer's that the first loss of a woman's virginity endowed her with magical and prophetic insight. Grummer had given many instances from her own experience of this species of second sight. " 'Tis the first 'a meets be the lucky oon, but 'taint all as knows it, more's the pity!" How she could hear the old woman's voice!

Once Grummer had even murmured something in this con-nection about "they Vestie Virgins in them Roman times," and though this particular example seemed a singular one there cer-tainly was something in Jenny's face. "But very likely," she said to herself, as she returned her friend's hug as warmly as she could, "very likely it's all my fancy. They've made it up—that's the great thing! And after all, Claudius is a sick man."

One thing it certainly did, this sudden reappearance of a transformed Jenny, it made it easy for Wizzie to set out alone. She took a new umbrella D. had given her on her birthday, which was on the twenty-seventh of July. This umbrella was the first really ladylike one that she'd ever had, and she was not a little proud of it. It had a round black handle with a solid silver band upon which D. had had her initials W.R. engraved, and she never let herself carry it unless she wore her best clothes. She had her best clothes on now, consisting of a navy blue tailor-made suit, with a neat blue hat trimmed with grey feathers. Nor would she like it if we forgot to mention her hand-bag which she had bought herself with Jenny's help and which both of them considered the finest flower of Durnovarian taste. Over her pretty clothes on a day of such doubtful prospects she was forced to throw a not very becoming raincoat, whose lack of style troubled her not a little; but she had bought it in her early Dorchester days, and D. was one "who never noticed such things."

Thus attired she set out; but instead of going the shortest way, which was down the hill to the coal-yard bridge, she turned, after a moment's hesitation into High East Street, and proceeded slowly along the near pavement towards D.'s lodgings. She was led to go this way, rather than the other, by one of those strange impulses that often remain, to the end of a person's life, so totally inscrutable that a superstitious mind might well be pardoned if it supplied the lack of any rational explanation by the idea of a supernatural hand laid on one's shoulder.

When she reached the door of No-man's lodging she stopped and under her ugly rain-coat and well-fitting blue dress her heart began to beat wildly. With a spasm of curious agitation she noticed that the door of the house had been left wide-open. There before her was the flight of stairs going up to D.'s attic! She advanced into the passage and stood at the foot of the stairs, thinking desperately. Her face was puckered into a concentrated frown, and her gloved hands fumbling at her hand-bag seemed as if they sought, independently of her consciousness, to slip into their old habit of chafing each other's knuckles.

Contrary to all her ways with D.—for she had long ago come to the conclusion that the more shabbily she was dressed the better he liked her—she instinctively bent her head and surveyed her appearance from head to foot. Then she twitched back the unsatisfactory ulster, and fidgeting a little and bending sideways gave her dress, at the place where it covered her hips, several cautious jerks. A crease in one of her stockings caught her eye next, necessitating the tightening of her suspenders, and to accomplish this manoeuvre unseen from the pavement, she was forced to ascend the staircase a step or two.

This small matter adjusted she pondered again, and this time her reflections led to her slipping off the offending rain-coat and hanging it across the arm that already held the umbrella and hand-bag.

"Damn this business of being a woman!" was what she thought as she ascended the stairs. "If D. came to surprise *me* he wouldn't have to give a thought to how he looked! And I declare *I* wouldn't either if I had my fling at the Circus!"

Arrived at the first landing without meeting a soul, she ascended the second flight much more rapidly. But at the foot of the third, the one that led direct to the attic, she paused again and rearranged her bag in relation to her cloak and her umbrella. In fact, she shifted these objects very much as a soldier, mounting a besieged wall, might take his dagger between his teeth.

All the while she was making these preparations she kept thinking: "What's the use? He'd be better pleased if I'd tumbled down and was all covered with mud!"

Biting her lower lip and moving so lightly that not the creak of a single step betrayed her approach, she now ascended the last flight to D.'s landing.

"What's *the matter* with my heart?" she said angrily to herself as she went up; and she became so aware, too, of that tickling sensation in her left breast that she pressed her free hand against it.

Once on the attic-landing she looked about her as furtively as a thief. "Yes, *that's* his room," she thought, but she felt she *must* delay for a second, for half a minute, before she surprised him.

Then suddenly, and without the least possibility of a doubt she heard the sound of a woman's voice inside the room. Her first instinct was to run down the stairs, run out of the house, run all the way to Glymes. But her second was to stand at the door and listen.

She did neither of these things. She went on tiptoe into D.'s kitchen.

She told herself often afterwards that she hadn't tried to listen a bit, not a little bit, to the voice of the woman in D.'s room.

It was only when the woman laughed at something D. said—and she could hear the low tones of his voice going on all the while—that she rushed out of the kitchen, across the landing, and into his room, with one sharp knock.

Yes! as she'd guessed from the tone of the laugh, from the low, sweet, milk-dripping, honey-oozing laugh, it was Nance who sprang away from him—Grummer would have said "like a cork from a bottle"—and came slithering towards her with out-stretched hand and two burning red spots on her cheeks! Yes, it was Nance who began at once, even, while Wizzie was pushing her hand aside and plunging a look she would have liked to have been that wall-scaler's dagger into what she'd have liked to have been D.'s heart: "Oh, that dress, my dear! I can't help saying it, even if you don't like to have your clothes mentioned, even if it gets on your nerves to be—oh, that dress is the loveliest thing I've seen!"

Wizzie had not grown accustomed, either in convent or Circus, to the peculiar archness that passes for a light social tone in certain feminine circles. Nancy Quirm was not, it must be confessed, any great adept at this airy art, but her manner of speech came nearer it than anyone else's Wizzie knew.

But what she felt towards Nance was nothing to what she felt against D. Never once—in all their days together—had he shown her this retreat of his; and now that she had come of her own accord it was to find his father's wife! She didn't care what they'd been doing, she told herself. She knew what Nance was, the sick cat! But that he should share with another woman——

The truth was that Wizzie was enough of a normal girl to feel defrauded of her rights by this exclusion. It hurt something in her that lay deeper than mere sex-instinct. It was treating her like a prostitute! Of course, she took no interest in his work. Why should she? But that he should have deliberately kept her out of this intimate side of his life, that he should have deliberately said to himself : "I won't have *her* in my attic !"—this was something far worse than just kissing, or whatever it was.

While all this bitterness surged up in her, D. was carrying the thing off with cold-blooded aplomb. In some odd way her contempt for Nance's "chatter" had staved off the outburst that she felt sure he had expected. She caught him looking at her, as she struggled with herself, her bosom swelling under her tight bodice, with puzzled astonishment. How little he knew her ! Did he think that to have caught him kissing Nance, or letting Nance kiss him, would make her make a scene, like a vulgar wife? She would show him ! If she couldn't chatter like Nance, she could hold her tongue and crush people by her dignity.

She said scarce anything—she couldn't trust herself to say anything—but she sank down on the chair he pulled over to the fire, letting her discomforted rival swing her legs awkwardly from its arm as she went on with her purring cajoleries. What *was* it about this soft feminine body as it leant over her, pretending to appraise the stuff of her blue suit, that made her feel sure she *had* interrupted something between them?

"No, I'm not going to bear it any longer. He'll have to give up this place, and find somewhere where we can live properly, or I've done with him. He can have Lovie, but I'll have my life."

"No, my dear, I'm *glad* to give it back to him, tell him," D. was now saying to Nance.

"Are you listening, Wizz?" he added, turning to her. "Nance and I are worried about my father. Dumbell and Fuzzy-wuzzy—isn't that a good name for the minx?—appeared last night, and they're sleeping in old Wye's room while he sleeps in the studio. They have driven my father distracted—it seems they're going to chuck him. His last articles have been too much for them. Nance simply doesn't know what's going to happen. Do you see *that?*" And he pointed to a roundish object rolled up in brown paper that lay in the middle of the bed. "That's my other head, the one he gave me, the one you hated so on your chimney-piece. It's nearly the same as my old one, see him? but not quite. 'Dor-Marth's' more like the Maiden Castle one, but they're all different. Devils differ as much as we do. It was what he said about these heads that did for him with old Cumber."

"What did he say?"

"He linked them up with Derfel's Horse, or with Derfel himself; didn't he, Nance? Derfel was a saint from the part of the country where his ancestors lived. In fact, as far as I can gather he was a good deal more than a saint. I suppose you might call him a saint-god; and Father thinks—aren't I right, Nance?—that in the end he was confused with his beast. He said that where he and Mother's people lived there was an avenue with these heads on the gate-posts—there's her picture of them, sweetheart, on that ottoman just behind you!—and people used to pray to Derfel's beast long after they burnt the image of Derfel."

"Is *that* all?" said Wizzie drily. "I don't see what Mr. Cumber could object to in that. He's not a Catholic, is he?"

"I'm afraid Enoch went a good deal further than that," said Nancy sadly, getting up from the chair's elbow and beginning slowly to gather her belongings together. She stood for quite a while with her back to the foot of the bed, putting on her old-fashioned hat; and Wizzie could not help noticing that she treated "Dor-Marth" with quite as little respect as she showed to bed-posts that had been left vacant.

"Uryen's things are nothing to her," thought our friend, as she watched the woman's figure outlined against the attic window; and she turned her eyes to the package on the bed with a new interest, now that she realized what it meant to her "Black Man of Glymes."

"What *are* Mr. Quirm's ideas about these things?" she asked abruptly.

No-man turned to her with a sharp surprised look as he rose to help Nance on with her ulster. "I'm afraid, my pretty one," he said, "you wouldn't be much the wiser if I tried to explain."

"I should say she wouldn't!" echoed Nance, turning round, too, and resting her hand on the solitary head, as she stooped to adjust the lower buttons of her rain-cloak. But her smile had faded when she straightened herself again and began pulling on her gloves. "It's all we can do," she remarked to D. sadly. "He's got the thing on his nerves. But he'd have never asked you if I hadn't——"

But No-man, who had been watching Wizzie with curious interest as she lay back in her chair with her brows knit and the fingers on her lap busy at their old trick, began to speak with

432

some eagerness. "It's no secret, my dear—besides, things have gone too far. Nance and I are worried about him. His idea is"—here he paused and glanced at Nance, as much as to say: "Stop me if I oughtn't to tell her"—"his idea is that *he himself* —and that's why he calls himself 'Uryen'— is in some way connected with our old mythology. I don't know whether you've every heard of what they call reincarnation? You have? Well, what my father's made himself believe, or come to believe, is that the supernatural Power, whatever it was, that incarnated itself in the Uryen of the legends—and it must have been a kind of Titan, if you know what I mean—not exactly an evil spirit, but not a good spirit, either—has now after all these centuries, come back to the world in him! In several of the old legends this Power was attended by some sort of beast—the whole thing's mixed up with sex and death and good and evil and all that's hardest in life to understand—and as far as I can make out it's with this beast, or *through* this beast—and that's where the sex part of it comes in—that we touch some great secret! It all sounds crazy, or as I put it it does; but so do all very ancient religions. But the thing that's worrying Nance and me now, and that's what she came to talk to me about, is that by letting himself go for these papers and openly discussing it he has shaken his own faith and got all confused, troubled, uncertain, *exposed* in some way, not knowing what he does believe or doesn't believe. Nance says she's only sure of one thing, and that's that he wants this head back. And it looks as if that were all we could do for him just now. Of course, it may end in his shaking off the whole business; but what we're afraid of is that it's gone too far; gone so far *that he couldn't go on with-out it*. Well, old girl, that's the situation! Of course what I've told you is between ourselves. He's my father, and I couldn't bear——"

But Wizzie interrupted him. "D.!" she brought out; and she uttered this syllable with such outraged indignation that Mrs. Quirm, who had wandered round the further side of the bed to reach for the package, paused in the act, to look at her.

"Well—anyhow, that's the situation," repeated No-man, "I've put it badly; but what it really amounts to is my father's life—I know it sounds perfectly crazy to you, Wizz; but, as it says at the end of *Faust*, all life is a symbol, and I suppose no religion that doesn't deal with sex-longing in *some* kind of way is much use to us."

Instead of replying, Wizzie glanced at Nance, and the two women exchanged a very complicated look in which not only quotations from *Faust* but all masculine philosophizing was put aside in the interest of something else.

Then while Nance was telling No-man what shops she had to go to, Wizzie began glancing critically about the room. How big the bed was! And this was the bed where for the last ten years D. had slept—not in Dorchester, of course, but somewhere—slept and thought of Mona! He had spoken about this bed, and about that ottoman, too, only a few weeks ago, when she inquired—thinking of her ideal little house—whether his mother had left him any furniture. "I expect," she said to herself bitterly, "his mother wouldn't like him to let *me* sleep in this bed!"

And then it came over her that this was probably the very bed where Uryen had seduced D.'s mother and where D. had been born.

"Well, good-bye, my dears!" murmured Nance quietly, moving to the door, with the sacred beast's head clutched as callously against her bosom as if it had been a bag of oranges, "I've got a lot of errands before I start back."

Wizzie jumped up at once. "Listen, Nance! I'm coming now straight over to your place. I haven't seen 'Thel' for an age. You don't want to carry that thing as well as a lot of parcels! Let *me* take it."

"But darling—" interposed No-man, and then, turning from her to Nance: "I want to show her everything now she's here. I never would let her come before because she can't bear those heads; and it's no good—but now she's here I'm going to show her everything."

Wizzie glanced at Nance again, and another look, not at all resembling the one exchanged before, passed between them. Wizzie said in this look: "He's trying to get round me. It's been a great blow to him that I've always refused to come up here," whereas Nance's look replied: "He wants to make you forget you found me here. I know this room as well as I know my own. It's a shame he's never let you come near it."

But No-man intervened at this point, addressing them both

with the complacent indulgence of a grown-up person putting right a couple of engaging children in an affair that required a mature mind. "Put that down, Nance!" he commanded, taking the package from her arms and laying it on his desk. "Wizzie shall bring it over a little later after I've enjoyed myself with her a bit!" The words struck Wizzie as designed to revenge something or other that Nance had done to him, or wouldn't do for him; but the woman showed no sign of taking the remark amiss.

"Very well—let's try and meet and walk *together!*" she said eagerly. "I'll be as quick as I can. I *shall* have a lot of parcels; so it *is* a comfort not to have this too. It's heavier than it looks! No—don't bother to come down. And don't forget to show Wizzie that house where you lived when you were Mary Channing's friend!" She shut the door behind her with one of her most pathetic society smiles, one of those smiles that always struck Wizzie as having something indecent about them, considering her spectacles and the weariness of the imprints in her face.

As soon as the door was closed there occurred between them that curious suspension of the stream of events which is an almost universal phenomenon when a couple who know each other intimately are suddenly left alone by the departure of a third. It is at such times as though this departing third, whose vanishing swells into so portentous a recession, actually raised as he departed an invisible dam of unearthly water that now flows between the two persons left behind, and across which they gaze helplessly at each other, each of them feeling as if the familiar objects round them had undergone some curious change. It is then that the pair seem suddenly grown shy of each other, gazing into each other's eyes across the last words of the departed, across his final gesture, across the diffused aura of his personality, each of them too shy to utter the magic word that shall break the spell. It even may occur that they feel a curious discomfort in looking at each other, as if something had happened to their familiar relation that had changed its quality, so that their common interests could only be referred to now in a whisper, as if the air were full of ears, or as if they were speaking before a corpse.

And not only so, but each material object in this transformed

435

spot, each chair, each rug, each cushion, each picture, gives the impression of having been drained of its customary spirit, of having been left a mere husk or mask or eidolon of itself, as though the departed one had carried away with him the living essence of these things, leaving them weary nonentities and insubstantial negations. Thus it was with our two friends while they stared blankly at each other listening to Nance's steps descending the stairs.

But Wizzie suddenly broke the silence. "Why!" she cried, stooping down by the bed, "she's dropped one of her gloves. One minute, D.; I'll soon catch her!" She jerked the door open and ran at top speed down the stairs. "Nance!" she cried, "Mrs. Quirm!" but it wasn't till she was out in the street that she overtook her.

Nance turned at her voice, and she handed her the glove, and for the third time that October morning an interchange of commentary on what was happening passed without words between them. And then, before she had the least notion of doing such a thing, an irresistible impulse of pure mischief, the sort of mischief that made the quietest sister in her convent flash out sometimes with a startling jest, forced Wizzie to fling back, as she turned to go: "Well! So long, till later! Isn't it a shame we're not allowed *to change our men*—you to look after D., and me to look after Uryen? We ought to make a little private plot about it, Nance Quirm! After all, we're all related now!"

Never had she seen behind poor Nance's spectacles such a look of bewildered simplicity as she caught at that moment. "She's stupid!" she cried to herself as she ran back. "No—I couldn't be jealous of *her*—even if I wanted to!"

She was confronted on her return to the attic by the sight of D. carrying a tray from the kitchen to the bedroom. On the tray was a tea-pot, two cups and saucers, and some milk and sugar. He looked extremely complacent and well-pleased with himself as he put down the tray on his mother's ottoman and hurried off to fetch some Osborne biscuits.

Wizzie re-seated herself in the arm-chair and accepted a cup from him with a biscuit in the saucer. She said to herself: "He's glad to have me here, I declare he is! Goodness, man! Why didn't you think of it before?"

436

"A cup of tea'll be just the thing for you, my lovely, before your walk. No! don't 'ee move! Here! put it down on this." He brought her a little stool, like a church hassock, and placed it carefully by her side, giving one of her legs, as he did so, a joyful squeeze.

With his own cup on the mantelpiece she felt him looking down upon her, sitting there, with profound satisfaction. "Take off your hat, my sweet," he said. "God! I feel as I did last November when I first carried you off."

She balanced her cup on the not over-attractive stool and began to lift her hands to her head. Then she changed her mind. "Oh, I can't bother," she said, "not now—but," and there was a certain wistfulness in her tone, as if she besought him to forgive her about the hat, "I'll take off my *gloves*—only I mustn't forget them, like Nance!"

He stooped down, and she felt that it gave him a thrill of pleasure to help her remove even these barriers. The minute they were off he lifted one of her hands to his lips; and then, bending down in front of her, pressed her knees together with his bony fingers.

"God!" he mumbled again, "but I'm as pleased as Punch to have you up here." Straightening his back again he remained opposite her, watching her drink her tea. "Wizz, old girl," he said. "*Think* of that first time I saw you in the caravan! We weren't long in understanding each other, were we?"

Her hand did not twitch as she held her cup, nor did the slightest vibration of response run through her, but deep in her heart this daughter of man cursed her Maker. Her curse was a woman's curse, not as articulate as his would have been; but if her Creator had possessed a human ear what he would have heard would have been something like this. "Damn you, God, for not fitting the love to the man!"

But D. suddenly hurried to the window and began rummaging in the drawer of his writing-table. "Thank the Lord!" she heard him mutter. "It *is* here." And when he came back to her side he thrust into her hand a tiny little roughly-taken photograph, one of the kind that beach photographers take at the seaside.

"What on earth's this, D.?" she murmured; and leaning forward—for the day was so cloudy that that side of his room

437

contained but a dim light—she held the little picture so that the flames flickered upon its glazed surface.

"Why!" she cried, in a rush of real pleasure. "It's Lovie! How *did* you get it taken?"

"Oh—just the other morning," he answered casually; but she could see he was thrilled by her surprise. "I was keeping it for All Souls' Day," he added in a low, half-apologetic voice.

"Why, it's lovely, D.!" she cried. "It's—it's *our*—Lovie—to the life! I can't think—what made you——" But here she couldn't go on, and with the little picture clutched between finger and thumb she bent her head on her knees in a fit of low-voiced crying. They were silent tears, and not the breath of a sob came with them; but this only affected D. the more, for having become a veritable expert in feminine emotion, he knew that loud sobs mean indignant self-pity, if not furious temper, whereas this silent rush of tears down a scarcely contorted face, means that one more tributary has begun to flow of that unceasing flood that from before the days of Niobe and Rachel has poured down the cheeks of women.

"What *is* it, my darling, my precious?" he cried, kneeling down in front of her. "Tell—your—old—D. what it is!"

But the delusion, full of the bitter-sweetness of love's treacherous sea, that she was simply weeping from the happiness of their love made No-man's own underlip begin to quiver. To recover himself and to give her a chance to do the same he now rose to his feet; and walking up to his original bed-post head, which showed not the remotest sign of disturbance at being deprived of its mate, he began to tap out a tune upon its sconce. The tune, of all tunes, that he selected, and that to effect some kind of cheerful diversion he must needs begin to drum, was none other than that familiar evangelical hymn: "Shall We Gather at the River?"—a composition that he had recently heard sung by a little group of revivalists upon High East Street.

Shall—we—gather—at—the Ri—ver, the Beautiful, the Beautiful Ri—ver, shall we gather at the Ri—ver, that flows by the throne of God?

And as if his tappings on "Dor-Marth's" head were not

438

emphatic enough to satisfy his desire for something normal and calming, he now began chanting aloud the actual words of the tune he tapped.

But Wizzie, who had not seen that quivering of his lip, at once assumed that this "Shall We Gather at the River?" was an impatient outburst of gross masculine ribaldry, indulged in at the expense of her silly girlish tears. In any case, even if she *had* seen his underlip tremble, she would still have been totally astray as to the nature of the relief he got from chanting "Shall We Gather at the River?" with such unnecessary vehemence. What she did, anyway, was to sit up at once, open her elegant hand-bag, take out from its silky recesses a handkerchief Popsy had given her on her twenty-second birthday, and proceed to dry her wet cheeks.

"What was it, sweetheart?" inquired D. tenderly; and leaving his beast, who certainly, in the dim light of that cloudy day, looked as if it well might be what he had told Nance it was, he went over to her side and stood, after his fashion, close to the mantelpiece, with his arm extended along half the length of its bare surface.

She did not reply at once, but stared, across his long legs, frowningly at the fire.

"God! what a brute I am!" he suddenly cried, clapping his hand to his pocket. "I never gave you a cigarette." This lapse in his hospitality having been rectified, and what was to her a quite irrelevant explanation gone into as to why he never smoked himself in the afternoon, she slowly lifted her small head and looked straight up at him.

"I was thinking of our life, D.," she said. "It's not what it ought to be—but I've never been——" she spoke in a low and intense voice, while what colour she had slowly left her cheeks in the effort her words cost her.

She saw that his face expressed bewildered astonishment and a miserable childish disappointment, and what she saw froze the words in her throat. How could she ever explain to a man like this? It was like snatching from Lovie, without a possibility of making her understand, something that she thought was hers to keep forever!

"Tell me what it is, Wizz! For God's sake, tell me what's wrong with you to-day? Is it *him*—is it Old Funky?"

She shook her head; and then with an impatient gesture threw her cigarette, only half-smoked, into the fire. How like him it was to drag in Old Funky—and how sick at heart it made her to have *that* worry brought up again! Oh, to get back to her real life, to get away from them all!

"What *is* it then?" he persisted. "Have I done anything? Is it because you found Nance here? If I thought for a minute that you were bothered about Nance I'd——"

But she interrupted him with a weary gesture. This was worse still. Would he never understand that it was *he himself*, not Old Funky, not Nance, not even her feeling for his father, that was at the bottom of it all?

"Don't you see, child, how unkind it is of you to go on like this and not even give a person a hint of what's the matter? What do you mean about 'something wrong with our life'?"

She felt so desperate and so driven, so torn and miserable, that her self-pity transformed itself into a rush of anger with him and his stupid badgering. "I mean you're *not a man*, D. That's the whole thing, if you *must* have it. No! I know what you're going to say—but I'm not thinking of *that*. You're not a man. You may be higher or lower. You may be an angel or you maybe—that beast over there! But a girl when she's my age, though I daresay when I'm as old as Nance or Jenny it'll be different, wants a companion, wants someone she can fuss with, be silly and gay with, take sides with, share things with, yes! and quarrel with! Do you realize, D., we've never once *made it up*? Why haven't we? Because you're not a man! Because——"

But at this point, in the tempest and whirl of her feelings, she suddenly remembered all the times he had responded to her outbursts with a placidity that was more maddening than if he'd hit her, and a confused sense came over her that by his open mouth and stupid bewilderment he was forcing her to say things quite different from what she meant! Her hopelessness of *ever* saying what she meant, while he looked at her like that, made her lips tremble and her eyes fill with angry tears.

"You oughtn't to forgive me like you do!" she cried in a strange husky voice. "You ought to shake me; you ought to curse me; you ought——Oh, D., I don't know what you are"—and her voice rose almost to a wail—"but you're not a man!"

440

She never forgot what his face looked like, after this cry of hers died away in the silence of that small room. It wasn't quite as tragic as the face of a wretched Guy Fawkes she once saw as it collapsed into the flames. It was more like the face of a terribly human scarecrow out of whose mouth, in one of their Sunday walks, she had seen Popsy knock the poor creature's pipe.

It was his overpowering astonishment that in a measure numbed the force of the blow, and he drew his arm from the chimney-piece, as if it were something that didn't belong to his body at all.

Then he stood for a second with his eyes fixed, not on her face, but on the hand-bag in her lap.

After that he began, with fingers that she could see were so deadened by her words that they could hardly obey his will, to button up, slowly and carefully, all the buttons of his coat. When his coat was buttoned up, he turned half-round and for another second stared in a puzzled way at his writing-table by the window, as if he were wondering what that round package was that he had taken from Nance and put down there! Then, turning again, like one of those hooded chimney-pots that some faint wind, felt by no other neighbouring object, seems to sway at its arbitrary whim, he fixed his eyes on the bed.

Wizzie was impelled, this time, to follow the direction of his benumbed stare, and she half-expected to see the phantom-shape of that wife of his, whose name had appeared so queerly on Dumbell's sketch, lying with her head on the pillow! "If he'd only snatch me up now," she thought, "and throw me down on that bed it would end all this nonsense!" She drew a deep angry breath. "But that bed's sacred to 'Mona,' *that's* why he'd never let me come up here." And once more her heart became cold as a stone.

But he moved across the room now, to where on a hook next to the cupboard hung his overcoat and cap, with his Cerne Giant's cudgel propped up beneath them against the panelling. "I think I'll go for a little walk," he murmured in a low sing-song voice: "a little walk, a little walk; yes, I think I'll go for a little walk, as the weather's so nice and fine!" He went to the door as soon as he'd got his overcoat and cap and taken his stick. "Don't forget the package," he remarked, forcing himself to give her a wry smile, "and I won't expect you till I see you.

They're certain to keep you to tea. But don't be *too* late—with *him* hanging round! Nance may overtake you, but I wouldn't stop about, waiting for her."

He paused for a second and then added, in a voice that was like the voice of a person watching a ship go down : "It may rain and then again it mayn't rain. We shall know if it comes; and if it doesn't come, we shall know it hasn't come. Don't worry about Lovie."

With that he was gone; and she heard his heavy steps, those steps that were neither fast nor slow, neither hurried nor lingering, sounding just as they always sounded, the steps of D. Noman going for his walk, going earlier than usual, but going for his walk, deliberately descending the stairs.

"I must be crazy, I declare!" she murmured aloud, as she caught herself making a hurried move forward, just as if, quite apart from her reasonable decision, something in her cried, "Run after him! Run after him! Stop him while you can!"

But it did give her a queer feeling to be left in possession—the very first day she had entered it—of this room of his! The first thing she did was to carry the tea-things back to the kitchen. Here, finding that "the Royal Martyr" had still a little hot water left, she cleaned their cups and deposited the tea-leaves under the lid of "Henry VIII."

Then returning to the bedroom she approached the "Questing Beast" at the foot of the bed and considered its appearance with some minuteness, running her fingers over its ambiguous physiognomy. Vaguely conscious, as she had been before that day of a faint tickling in her left breast, due perhaps to the tightness of her new dress, she instinctively pressed closer to the heraldic head, rubbing herself against it as an animal might rub itself against a tree.

As she did this her mind reverted to that inexplicable incident of the sudden scrawling of the name "Mona" across Dumbell's sketch.

"*She* can never have slept in this bed," she thought, "if it was his mother's. But he's slept in it ever since and thought about her. Oh deary I! I wish he was different, or I was different!"

But she moved away to the fire now, to pick up her gloves; and she only arrested herself in the act of putting on more coal by the thought : "But he'll be up there with Lovie." She contented herself, therefore, with hooking the "guard" carefully over what fire there was, and then, without further delay and having possessed herself of her various belongings, she picked up the paper parcel from D.'s table and ran downstairs.

Once on the pavement she decided that this time she *would* go the shortest way, whether the "invisible hand," that seemed directing all her motions this morning, approved or disapproved. The Guildhall clock was striking half-past twelve, and as she had only nibbled at D.'s Osborne biscuits she said to herself: "I'll run into the sweet-shop by St. Peter's, and buy some of that chocolate Jenny gets."

Possessed of the delicacy she desired, she was returning to North Square and the street leading to the little stream, when she happened to glance through the iron rails of the church at the statue of William Barnes.

She had often passed this statue before, but never till this moment had its mellow charm and the majestic benignity of its expression struck her as they did now. Wizzie's aesthetic taste was totally undeveloped but there was in this venerable old poet's look something beyond all "art," an effluence of peace, a spirit of benediction, a promise of comfort and of healing, that seemed to rise up in the centre of Dorchester life as if it sprang from some level of goodness in the deep earth below the town's oldest foundations.

So deeply did the mystical benignity of this hushed figure affect her that as she stood there, frowning and pondering, with that weird wrapped-up object in her gloved hands, for one passing second she actually forgot everything in a rush of melting sympathy for all the people in her confused life.

But the moment vanished as quickly as it came, vanished indeed in a sudden dread of encountering Nance, and of having her as a companion all the way to Glymes; and under the pressure of this fear, which quickly became something like a panic, she fled into North Square, hurried past the prison gate, and ran down the hill to the river-path at the bottom.

All the way to Hangman's Cottage, as she went along munching her chocolate, the image of that old poet by the church accompanied her, soothing her troubled mind. Everything she had come to like best in Dorchester seemed to be expressed in that calm figure.

"If I do go back to my life," she thought, "If I do leave D. and Lovie, I shan't forget what I felt just now!"

But she wasn't destined to leave the town in undisturbed peace. It had been—so she fancied—her fear of meeting Nance that had set her off at such a pace; and all the way to the Hangman's Cottage, in spite of the spiritual presence of William Barnes, she kept looking back : but oh! oh! oh! just before she reached that familiar landmark she was seized with a flash of conviction, a conviction as certain as if she had seen him following her, that Old Funky had watched her flight and would be on the look-out for her when she returned!

"He must have been watching for me," she thought, as she hurried on towards the Blue Bridge. "He must have seen me run down the hill! I *know* I wouldn't think of him like this for nothing."

But Wizzie was a brave and a resourceful girl, and she told herself that if Uryen wasn't in a fit state she would ask Mr. Wye, or even Dumbell, if he were out there still, to accompany her home. "He wouldn't dare to speak to me then," she told herself. "And if he did, I'd know what to say to him!" She had walked so fast all the way that when she finally reached the pond where Uryen had once rescued her and Lovie from the cows, she felt quite at ease in her mind about Old Funky following her.

"Let him wait for me, if he wants to!" she said to herself. "He'll get more than he bargains for!"

As fate would have it, although neither Old Funky nor Nance beset her approach to Glymes, she was not spared a troublesome companion. This came with a sudden change of the weather and took the form of a very formidable wind, blowing from the southwest.

And the nearer she drew to Glymes the stronger blew the wind; and it presently became necessary for her to button up her ugly ulster, clutch all she was carrying tight against her, pray that her grey-feathered hat wouldn't blow off, and hurry forward, like a little fishing-smack with all sails but one well furled.

When she arrived at the two houses, and had pushed open the garden-gate, she paused for a minute to take her breath and gather herself together. This delay, followed by her nervous and lingering approach to the Quirms' door—for her heart had begun, as it always did at the prospect of meeting Uryen, to tease her by its agitation—brought it about that her presence was observed from the front window of the Wye establishment, where the guileless Dumbell, weary of the wrangling between his wife and his father, was standing to watch the approach of the non-human storm. He must have called Thuella upon the scene at once, for while the visitor still stood at Nance's door waiting for an answer to her hesitant tap, that young woman, her painter's smock surmounted by a shawl, burst from their house and rushed across the flower-beds to greet her. "Oh, I'm so glad you've come! Oh, I've got such news for you, such incredible news!"

"How is Uryen?" was Wizzie's reply to this. "Has Nance come back? Will he come to the door? Is he still?——"

"Hush—he's coming *now*—oh, such news, my lovely one! You must come—*good*-bye!" And before the man inside had got the door open the excited girl was back again in her own house.

"How do you do, Mr. Quirm? I came to bring— Nance had too much to carry— I hope you don't mind——" She brought out these sentences in spasmodic jerks, while all he said was, "Come in, child, it's warmer in than out." This last sentence he repeated as he ushered her into their untidy room. "Warmer in—than out, in than out."

"How are you, Mr. Quirm?" she said, when the door was shut and she'd slipped off her ulster and laid down her things.

He made no attempt to help her in this, but stood with his back to the window gazing gloomily, and she fancied a little reproachfully, into her face. Without a second's hesitation she took off her hat, and throwing it down on the nearest chair, gave him the sweetest smile she had ever given to anyone in her life. A faint gleam came into his heavy-lidded eyes.

"How—pretty—you—are!" he murmured in a low whisper; and suddenly, to her intense surprise, he moved a step nearer, and taking her small head between his hands, he bent down and kissed it.

The touch of his hands, his breath on her hair, made Wizzie's heart beat furiously. Her legs too began to feel weak and shaky; and in the pit of her stomach she had the sensation she used to have as a little girl when she was being swung too high.

"Alone—with—him—at last," the pit of her stomach said. "Alone—with him—at last," repeated the trembling breasts under her tightly drawn dress. It was upon the latter that his eyes fell now as he released her head. "Pretty," he muttered again and this time his tone troubled and perplexed her.

There was something in it quite different from the tone of a normal grown-up man expressing sensual interest. But this very fact, that he was so different from his son in the way he acted, gave her a vibrant quiver of tenderness towards him. "Pretty," he repeated; and stretching out his hand he touched with his forefinger the tip of her left breast, the one she'd been conscious of all day, the one that had teased her by that tickling sensation. His gesture was the extreme opposite of a sensual one. An on-looker, who had been to Rome, would have been reminded of the outstretched finger of Michelangelo's Divinity putting life into the languid frame of the newly created parent of our race. But just because his touch was so strangely chaste Wizzie felt under its impact such a melting response that it was impossible to bear it. From the spot where he touched her there trembled through her whole body a tension that could only find relief by being taken into his arms.

"Let's—sit—down," she stammered: "no—*you*—and I'll—" and pushing him into his great armchair, a much more capacious piece of furniture than the one in D.'s attic, she slid down upon his lap. The warmth of her body, its electric pressure, the way she cuddled up against his chest, in blind contact with those garments whose state had shocked the fastidious D., the manner in which she caught up one of his hands and kissed it, as reverently as if he'd been some famous sage or formidable potentate, instead of a half-crazed fanatic, whose work wasn't good enough for a newspaper, all these things had a most releasing effect, not on the man's senses, but on his tongue.

But the flood of strange talk to which she now found herself half-listening—for she had never been one for taking the discourses of the sons of men with much seriousness—was nothing in intensity, or in abandonment, to her own feelings.

For the first time in her life Wizzie had round her the arms of a man she loved. It was no more to her than the howling of the

446

wind in the chimney that this man was her bedfellow's father. It was no more to her than the lashing of the rain on the pane that *another* father—the father of her own child—was waiting to intercept her return.

These "ironic" aspects of her situation, the scandal of which even the kindest of the kind priests of Durnovaria could not have condoned, no more bothered her than the fact that all those queer "ghost" noises that she'd heard on Candlemas night in the rafters of Glymes were now starting up again over her head! She had known what it was to feel herself yielding to her "Black Man" when she was no more than standing by his side and talking to him; but now she was between his hands; now she was lying on his knees; now her whole identity was being subdued to him, surrounded by him, dominated by him, and her emotion became so intense that his words, reaching her through a cloud of mist, through a vapour of smoke, through a medium that he would himself have compared with the sacred steam that rose from the life-giving Cauldron of Caridwen, might just as well have been "I love you, I love you, I love you" as anything that they actually were. She didn't even bother herself as to whether it gave him any pleasure to have her there like that.

He pressed her tightly to him in the pauses of his talk, but he always went on again, as if to talk to her, much more than to caress her, was his grand relief. It was not that he refrained from caressing her. Sometimes his hands were on her bosom, sometimes round her hips, sometimes against her flanks, as she cuddled up to him; but his mind was far away most of the time, absorbed in what she could see was more important to him than anything else, to pour out his thoughts into an ear that was ready to hear!

And the wind howled round the house as she had never heard a wind howl, and the rain dashed itself against the window. *This* rain did not fall in a continuous stream as it had done yesterday at Claudius's, but in furious intermittent gusts, under the impact of which it seemed sometimes as if the panes would be broken.

"I thought," he burst out, after a torrent of words that meant nothing to her : "that I'd only to tell them clearly what I was— the new medium, after all these years, of that great Power of

447

the Abyss that the bards and prophets of my race have groped for, for them—I won't say to accept—but to—to hear—to respect—not to turn *what is my life* into the—into the joke—oh, the Devil's joke!—of what they call scientific research." Here again he began to talk of things that the girl on his knees could make nothing of; but all of a sudden he stopped short, and a long terrible sigh, the sigh of a heart near its breaking-point convulsed his whole frame.

"You don't think," he said, in a very low but terrifyingly clear voice, "that"—and she could feel his whole body stiffen beneath her—"that—they're *right*—and that it's all—that it's all—*tommy-rot*?"

It may have been the combination of the tremendous gravity of his tone, the tragic desperation of that ultimate heart's cry, with the commonplace expression "tommy-rot" that hurt her so, but her nerves broke down at that point and she could bear no more.

Slipping from his lap, she ran across the room, picked up the package she had brought for him, and tearing off the paper and string as she returned, thrust the head into his hands. His delight was touching to see! He kissed the grotesque thing, he hugged it, he mumbled incoherent gibberish over it, he examined it, he turned it first one way and then another, he scrabbled over it, he scraped at it, he slobbered over it, he tapped it, he smelt it, he held it to his eyes, to his mouth, to his forehead, and even to his ears.

The girl stood in front of him, her fingers clasped behind her back, watching him with infinite sadness.

Presently, as he began chuckling to himself and behaving as an idiot might to whom someone has restored some lost and precious plaything, she became aware that there was a new sound audible somewhere that was struggling to make itself heard above the roaring of the wind and the weird noises in the roof. There was something about this extra sound added to all the rest that was too much for Wizzie's nerves; and the breaking-point of her tension, as was generally the case with her, showed itself in a burst of realistic anger.

What she felt now—it was a natural woman's instinct—was that Uryen was "giving way," that his loathsome fuss over a block of wood was just a fit of wilful hysterics out of which he "ought to be shaken." She found herself on the point of snatching the obscene thing from him. She did lay her hand on it; but he clutched it to him, and looked at her with a glance of heartbreaking supplication.

There was a momentary contest between them which was ended by Wizzie suddenly feeling that she was behaving as Mr. Cumber's daughter would have behaved. So she drew away. But that was her Uryen, her "Black Man of Glymes," sitting there before her, and it was unbelievable that her mind couldn't get into contact with his mind through all this nonsense.

"What *is* this thing?" she shouted at him just as if he had been deaf, while all the while that strange new sound kept hammering at her own consciousness. "What *is* this thing? What do you *want* with it? What good can it do you?"

She stood above him trembling with anger. She felt as if he were hugging this lump of wood out of deliberate devilishness, hugging it *instead of her,* hugging it to keep her away, just when fate and the storm and everything had given them this moment alone. There he was, her Glymes man, touching her, alone with her, she *herself,* he *himself,* and out of pure devilry he must play the imbecile and hug this loathsome thing!

"What are you doing with it? What *is* it?" she repeated hoarsely. Her hand was still on it as he clutched it against his jersey, but she no longer tried to take it from him, for somewhere at the back of her mind she could hear the voice of Dumbell's wife, telling the doctor that she'd "been forced to burn a horrid piece of wood."

"You—don't—understand," he said, still shrinking back in his chair with the same supplicating look. "It—He—I—always had some creature that was the body of our longing, of our *hiraeth,* of our desire, the incarnation of our power to break through and to pass——"

But Wizzie interrupted him. She felt like screaming at him! She felt as if she could only out-scream the storm, out-scream those noises in the roof, out-scream that *new* sound, which now struck her as a furious knocking at the outer door, she could get beyond this idiocy of his, back and behind it, where somewhere, in that majestic personality, abode the calm, unruffled Uryen she loved.

"To break through *what?*" she shrieked, swaying up and

down before him like a wounded pigeon and lowering her face till it almost touched his. "You can't break through life except by dying. And what's more if you don't stop this, if you don't drop that thing, you'll kill me !"

This last word of hers did seem to affect him; for making an obvious effort to satisfy her, he squeezed the creature into the space between his thigh and the chair and took her hands in his own.

"But, child," he said : "I think there's someone at the door. Do—you—mind—going to see?"

She straightened herself and listened. Yes, he was right. But to be heard in this wind, they must be knocking with a heavy stick ! And she thought of D.'s great cudgel. Was it D. come after her ? She hurried to the window and looked out, and the second her back was turned to him Uryen repossessed himself of the head and began to fondle it like an infant.

But there—outside the door—drenched to the skin—his long black coat clinging pitifully to his grotesque figure, without hat, without stick, without anything to mitigate the woefulness of his appearance, was Old Funky !

Driven by a kind of frenzy to get in out of the storm Mr. Urgan was striking at the door, kicking at the door, butting at the door, and raving at the door. The author of the first Gospel might have made him a symbol of the wicked man shut out of heaven. His coat-tails were so soaked with rain that the wind which whirled round him and seemed every minute about to lift him bodily off his feet, could do no better than hoist them up an inch or so, flap them against his rump for a minute, and then, dropping them, cause them to wrap themselves closely round his hips, in the reverse way to the manner in which the parade coats of the grenadiers of former times used to be folded back.

Wizzie gazed at him through the window with round eyes and rounder mouth. It was one of those spectacles that Chance and Nature combine to produce that are so evenly balanced between sickening pitifulness and monstrous humour that the same person could laugh or cry at the sight, according to the turn of a straw.

When the noise of the storm rose to such a pitch that the swinging of a battering-ram against the door would be no more than the tapping of a wren's beak, Mr. Urgan in his blind passion—for by this time the little man was well nigh beside himself—would draw back from the obdurate door, only to rush at it in the next lull like a beast with a pack of hounds behind him, when he would beat at it with his fists, and kick at it with his feet, and even pound at it with his head.

Now there was something about Old Funky's frantic fury to get in that excited in Wizzie, not fear—for at that moment she felt no more afraid of him than if he'd been a demented jackdaw—but a savage desire to keep him out.

The sight of him there, and she felt sure the room was too dark for him to see here, even though she pressed her face against the pane, raging so obstinately and so helplessly, had a most curious effect on her. It brought back, as if by a series of vivid lightning flashes, her struggle with him in the caravan. She *was* pressing her face now against the pane. Her thin nose, flattened at the tip, must have assumed, had Mr. Urgan been able to see it, the likeness of a crooked sixpence. And as she stared she seemed to engage again in that wild struggle.

"I *could* keep you out!" she kept repeating through her clenched teeth, while her face, pressed yet closer against the window, enlarged the blurred whiteness of that wicked sixpence.

But the wind began gathering in force just then to a pitch that made her draw back. The noises in the Glymes roof-top were increasing too, and the whole house seemed to rock and shake. She glanced at Uryen. He was still muttering and crooning over that beast-head, and it struck her that his great swarthy face had lost its accustomed restraint and had relaxed into a maudlin abandonment. What she saw now in his expression thoroughly shocked her. It was much worse than the tragic look he had worn when she first came in. The noises in the roof were so alarming now that she couldn't help glancing up at the ceiling.

"Don't you blow down!" she thought; and to her surprise she realized she had uttered this thought in audible words.

But there came a lull now, as if the storm were drawing back for a yet more terrible onslaught, and in that momentary cessation the frantic knocking at the door became audible to Uryen. He listened a moment, and looked at her with a puzzled expression.

"There's someone out there," he said peevishly. "Why don't you let them in?"

"Don't you move!" she cried. "I was *keeping* him out; but I'll let him in!" She opened the door, meeting as she did so a startling rush of cold air, and ran down the passage.

Uryen must have shot the bolt after he admitted her, and the pressure of the wind outside was so great that when she'd drawn it and turned the handle the door flew open with such a swing that it flung her against the wall and dashed Old Funky against her. She pushed him aside, however, and using all her strength got the thing shut and bolted.

As she did this the image of Nance rose up before her, but she said to herself : "She must have gone to Jenny's. It *must* have begun before she started."

"Come then," she said crossly. "Come in, now you're here!"

Mr. Urgan seemed too dazed to notice her crossness. He stood leaning against the wall recovering his breath, and fumbling, so it seemed to her, in an attempt to get something out from some inside pocket.

"Come in, now you're here," she repeated; and he followed her into the room.

He showed signs of suspicious alarm when he saw Uryen staring at him from above the object clutched in his hands.

But Wizzie's nerves rendered her desperate and shameless. "This is Lovie's father," she cried in an unnaturally high-pitched voice : "come to ask how his child is getting on."

But Uryen only nodded. Then he seemed to realize that something was required of him, and with a curious stiffening of his ravaged visage till it resumed something of its normal dignity he forced himself to speak quietly and naturally.

"I'm—not," he said, in a low far-away tone, like the voice of a living soul concealed behind a mask of decomposition. "I'm—not—myself—just now. Don't mind—talking—business—you two. I'm—not—very—well—to-day. Take—no—notice—of me."

This said, his whole countenance seemed to change before their eyes, becoming like the face of that "Ancient Anarch" so eloquently described by Milton; until, quite relapsed into his former condition, he fell to murmuring to himself, and finally to cuddling upon his lap the object that gave him such strange comfort.

The alarming noises in the roof above her, the tornado of

452

wind and rain, her heart-sick consciousness of Uryen's condition, made the presence of this dripping figure, under whose boots little pools were forming on the carpet, of less consequence to Wizzie than if he had been Lovie's doll. But it was not like a doll that he looked.

Never had Mr. Benjamin Urgan so closely resembled a monkey. He was like a monkey escaped in the storm from some barrel-organ that had been washed down the Frome! All the girl's heart and soul were set on that lamentable figure in the chair. Was it a relief to her, or was it not, that his trouble took the form of this maudlin, gloating pleasure? For himself it might be better, better than the despair from which it was an escape, but for her there was something degrading and sickening, something that made her loathe the whole business of life in seeing him like this.

She noticed as she watched him that his hair had grown perceptibly greyer. If in its tight negroid curls it had formerly resembled moss, it now resembled some species of lichen, lichen growing on a log that had been dead for a thousand years! "How *could* Nance leave him," she thought: "just to do some wretched shopping?" But then she remembered that, after all, the woman had come to fetch him the ghastly plaything he was now fondling with such satisfaction.

A singular peculiarity of the human mind is the power it has of hypnotizing itself or, perhaps one should say, of anaesthetizing itself at moments of great stress by the contemplation of small and insignificant details amid the whims and caprices of the inanimate. Thus it came about that when Wizzie turned away sick at heart from the spectacle of her hero's degradation, and began saying to herself: "It's all those Cumbers. This would never have happened if he hadn't worked for those Cumbers," instead of taking any notice of Mr. Urgan who was now unfolding with intense absorption some species of document he had at last extracted from the inner covering of his drenched person, she gazed with interest at the progress of a thin trickle of water, that, originating in one of the pools that had formed themselves at the man's feet, was making its way, with an apparent intention, along the pattern in an extremely dirty carpet.

For the girl's mind, the immediate pressing preoccupation was

453

to note if that trickle stopped, or didn't stop, till it reached the place where the pattern ended.

But Old Funky had now found what he sought. "Here—take this! Read this! 'Tis dry as a bone. I got 'un out here, no matter for this end-o-world 'urry-cain, and 'tisn't many what 'ud 'ave done it, not for love of a 'ard 'eart like the 'eart *some* 'ave got under their pretty titties!"

Lifting her eyes from the floor Wizzie took the envelope he handed to her and stared frowningly at it.

"Take off your coat and lay it over that chair," she said to him, letting the hand in which she held his document sink down wearily against her side.

But he waved this suggestion away. "Ben Urgan," he assured her: "weren't woon to rin arter a female 'ooman thro' a Come-to-Judgment 'urry-cain, only to dry his wold coat at her fire. What be writ in this 'ere dockymint be a matter for King's Jury. 'Tis to save 'ee from court and scandal I've a-follered 'ee here, and back Ole Ben don't stir, tho' the 'eavens fall, till you've a-seed un!"

Wizzie gave him a blank stare. Then glancing at Uryen, she found—and oh, she thanked the Lord for that!—that he'd fallen asleep, his massive head nodding and swaying over the object in his lap.

" 'Tis like this," said Mr. Urgan, catching at one of his dripping coat-tails and unceremoniously squeezing the water out of it where he stood, "and ye'll larn to hearken when ye larn me business! This 'ere dockymint, wot ye treats so light, be to tell all and sundry that me missus be a summoning of 'ee, calling of 'ee, that is, afore Court and Kingdom, to answer the charge"— here Old Funky shut his eyes, the better to recall what he had evidently, with the utmost difficulty, learnt by heart—"the charge of alienmating me affections. Her do say, nevertheless, and her lawyer do say arter her, that if your good man pay over to she summat in cash, and pay over to *he* summat in cash, this 'ere charge of alienmating, writ in this 'ere dockymint in King's Court Hebrew, can be nillified. The sum she *mentioned,* as settling thik little job to the peace of all, were fifteen guineas, and a trifle of a 'fiver' on top of that, for they as made out the same. Her *did* mention summat about taking a few pounds less, for old acquaintance sake, but that's 'atween she and thee wone

454

self! I washes me hands o' such meddlings wi' the course of Law and Government. What be doing of, ye mad 'ooman? 'Ere, 'ere! Gie 'un over to I—gie 'un over! Darn it, wench, what's come to 'ee then!"

This rush of protests was caused by the fact that Wizzie, her endurance quite at an end, was making an attempt to tear in half this formidable piece of foolscap, with the clear intention of throwing it into the fire! Two things, however, made it possible for Old Funky to rescue his "dockymint"; the first being that the paper was hard to tear, and the second that the fire in this house of confusion was nearly out.

But the scene was a sufficiently shameful one. It would have been still more so if the uncanny creakings and groanings above and the elemental hubbub outside the walls hadn't reduced to comparative negligibility all conflicts that were merely human. But they weren't an engaging sight just then—the proceedings in that front-room at Glymes: Old Funky, with his red wig awry—nor was it the first time that in a struggle with Wizzie this unholy topknot had been dis-arranged—with his thin, black, dripping form swaying about on the wet floor, struggling frantically to get the paper away from Wizzie, and Wizzie with a flush of dangerous anger on both cheeks and with her " 'lurin' " figure more " 'lurin' " than her antagonist had ever seen it, tugging at the paper so as to throw it on the fire!

If indeed there is any justification for our theory that by the intensity of the magnetism released in such scenes a lasting impression is made on the chemistry of the finer air, it might well happen that should any reader of this narrative take the trouble, on some dark stormy afternoon to visit the ploughed-over dump-heap by the gravel-pit, where the road from Piddle-Trenthide crosses the lane from Stinsford, he would become conscious, between pit and hedge, of the furious wrestling of a beautifully formed woman with a harlequinlike man, until with a leap and a cry a third figure, more startling than either, dissolves these "eidola of emotion" into the damp air around them!

For it was Enoch Quirm himself and none other who brought this shameful scene to an end. The shock of their physical contest must have roused him, in a way their voices, however raised, were unable to do. At any rate he awoke from his coma to see what looked to him like actual violence being offered to

455

Wizzie by a veritable rain-goblin, from whose black, tight-waisted, struggling form the water trickled to the floor.

Leaping up so suddenly that the head fell from his lap and went rolling along the carpet, Enoch Quirm, or, to be kind to him in his downfall, Uryen of "yr Echwyd," came lurching towards them with such a terrible gleam in his dead eyes that Old Funky in a paroxysm of panic tottered backwards, tottered in fact so blindly that he tripped up over the beast's head, which had come to rest in a pool of water, and fell to the floor. In falling, though luckily he was no heavy weight, he struck the back of his head such a violent blow on the iron fender that he lay stunned.

For a second Wizzie thought he was killed, and a queer reaction came over her. Forgetting all about her ally, she knelt down by the fallen man's side and set herself to examine his hurt. As she bent over him, and pushed back his wig, which was already bloodied into a new shade of red, she was no more conscious of Uryen picking up his fallen fetish and hurrying out into the passage than she was conscious of a lull in the storm and the sound of a car in the road outside.

An emotion stranger than any she had ever had, or than she was ever destined to have, flooded her being at the sight of that white skull with the blood oozing from its wound. The past swept over her with an overwhelming rush; and it came into her mind that the last time she had touched that slippery surface it was from the marks of her own nails that the blood had come. Indescribable emotions welled up in her breast and shivered through her. Kneeling there, over that blood-stained skull, she reached the tragic level of mortal feeling, where love and hate, blind savagery and infinite tenderness, melt into something for which there is no name.

What she had suffered, in shock and pain and outrage, when she yielded her maidenhood to this grotesque creature, seemed to return upon her, and to return in quite a different way from what she felt just now as she pressed her hot face against the window, watching his fury at the door.

It returned softened, transformed, dissolved; no longer as a brutal violation, but as something in which, with a wild self-laceration, she could even exult !

And what she felt now as she pushed aside his repulsive wig

456

and examined his scalp-wound, was something that never for one instant she had felt for her old D. How *could* a girl have any human feelings, good or bad, for a person like D., who if you tickled him didn't laugh and if you pricked him didn't bleed? How it all came back, that wild struggle in the caravan, that had ended in giving her Lovie! And curiously enough she now clearly remembered, as the dishevelled wig brought everything back, a detail of that scene that had sunk into complete oblivion. She remembered how at the very moment she was digging her nails into this brittle death's head, she was sure she heard—for he was stabled nearer to them then—the frightened neighing of her old horse!

As she thought of this she suddenly stopped examining his cut, and inserting her hand under his soaked clothes groped for his heart. Her joy to feel it beating was so intense that she was deaf to the hooting of the car in the road, deaf to the sound of Uryen's voice in the garden, and thrusting her fingers into her mouth, she began to bite them.

Whatever her guardian angel, if Wizzie had one, thought of the way her mind worked as she bit her blood-stained fingers, what the girl said to herself, or rather what she said to the unconscious form beneath her, was something like this—and as the words took shape in her breast she stared at him with that intense, round-eyed look that had excited No-man when he first saw her. "You taught me my job. You taught me my power. You taught me my life. You re-created my body!"

The salt taste of Old Funky's blood in her mouth still remained with her, as, scrambling to her feet, she ran to where she had left her things, and returning to his side with a clean handkerchief folded it into a little pad and pushed it under the wig where the scalp had been injured.

Old Funky's eyelids now began to quiver, and by the time she'd adjusted the handkerchief and placed a cushion beneath his head, he opened his eyes and gazed into her face with the dazed confusion of someone "coming round" after an anaesthetic. His first words were enough to show how much alive he was. "Where—be—me dockymint, wenchie?"

And then, after a pause, and a feeble effort to turn his head: "He ain't a-stole 'un, 'ave 'ee?"

But Wizzie, now that it was clear that the old rogue had

suffered no serious injury, became a completely different girl. She jumped to her feet and gave him a look of disgusted contempt. "You stay just where you are!" she said. "Wait a minute, though! I'm going to dry *this* at any rate." Thus speaking, in spite of his feeble resistance, she managed to pull off his drenched coat. She then gazed round the room till she caught sight of a not over-clean rug spread out on a dingy sofa, and having wrapped this, in spite of his protests, round the exposed person of the unfrocked Mr. Urgan, she gave heed, for the first time, to what was going on outside the house.

The storm had abated. The noises in the roof had ceased. But other sounds—sounds that had reached her ears before, but without carrying the faintest ripple of a reflex to her brain—were now entering the house from the wide-open front-door. She stood for a second listening. Then, catching sight on the floor of Old Funky's "dockymint," she picked it up and tucking it under his rug watched grimly the ecstatic delight with which the old wretch received it.

Events began now to follow one another in this ceasing of the storm with the precipitation of a stir in a cage of birds from which the covering has been removed.

Running out into the passage Wizzie could see, framed in the open doorway, surrounded by a spectral afternoon light, from which the storm, ere it went seemed to have sucked all natural livingness, leaving it wan and ghastly like the skin of a corpse, the towering figure of Enoch Quirm, assisted by a stranger, half-carrying, half-supporting the collapsed form of Nance.

"The storm frightened her," Uryen found time to call out as their eyes met, and she noticed that he had actually propped his heraldic monster on the top of the umbrella-stand, where "what seemed its head" lay tilted against the wall. "It's the old trouble," he said when they'd got her through the door, and he spoke as naturally and quietly as Wizzie had ever heard him speak. "It's her heart. But I'll soon get her round."

Hearing him speak like this, Wizzie couldn't help thinking: "He can shake it off for *her,* though he can't for me!" and as they carried Nance in and laid her on the wretched sofa from which she had herself just snatched the rug, it was upon him, and not upon Nance or Old Funky, that she kept her eyes fixed. She and the stranger—who was clearly the taxi-driver—now

458

stood side by side as Uryen attended to the collapsed woman. Watching him as he prepared his drug she uttered a prayer of intense gratitude to her convent's God, for it seemed certain to her now that his malady was a temporary one. She began talking quite garrulously to the taxi-man, so immeasurable was her relief; but alas! it didn't take long for her heart to sink again. She had scarcely been called to Nance's side by a smile and a whisper from the recovered woman, and had only just bent over her in response, when she knew by instinct, without actually seeing his face, that he was only waiting for an opportunity to slip out into the passage. Yes! when she lifted her head from her talk with Nance he had already been out to the umbrella-stand; and now, with his fetish under his arm and craftily avoiding her eye, he was fidgeting about the room. "He's looking for a place to put it," she thought, as she pretended not to notice him. "If I'd been that Cumber girl I'd have got rid of it while he was fussing over Nance."

Had the shameless No-man been present while his father, looking like a blasphemous sacristan, made a pile of his old Welsh books and balanced "Dor-Marth's" mate with exquisite nicety on the top of them, and while Old Funky squatting like a baboon in shirt and braces, peeped under the rug that covered his knees to see with his own eyes that Wizzie hadn't stolen the paper he had apparently braved the storm to give her, it may well have occurred to him that these obscure abortions, the wooden heraldic one and the parchment legal one, were striking modern instances of the ancient primitive belief in what recent research has come to name "exteriorized souls."

Meanwhile Wizzie, though in a quieter and sadder key, had resumed her conversation with the elderly taxi-driver, lending a grave ear to his impressive account of his drive through the storm, and indeed of other drives through many other storms, in a receding perspective of catastrophic motoring. The man was an elderly Dorset man of not a little personal dignity, who in his day had been a family coachman; and Wizzie couldn't help being struck by the discretion with which he suppressed the curiosity he *must* have felt about the singular appearance presented by Old Funky, and about the childish preoccupation of the master of the house with a pedestal of books upon which he was trying to balance a wooden idol.

459

"It's Mr. Urgan from the fair-field," she explained to him at the first opportunity she got. "He was caught in the storm, and had a bad fall. Yes—this storm has upset us terribly. We thought the house was coming down! Mr. Quirm is a nervous gentleman anyway"—here she lowered her voice to an appropriate whisper—"and all this"—and she glanced at the unfrocked ring-master—"has upset him. Oh, yes—and I'd be so grateful, Mr. Netherby, if you'd take the old man back—his coat's drying—you see how upset we've been—we've let the fire out—back to the fair-ground? Could you do that for me?" She paused to open her purse and to hand him a pound note. "No, never mind the change, Mr. Netherby! Only get him safe into his caravan. Will you do that? And if you would do something else for me"—and she smiled confidently—"we live at Mrs. Dearth's in Friary Lane—No-man the name is. And I want to send a note to *Mr.* No-man. Could you go round that way, and leave it? Mrs. Dearth will give it to him if he's not in. Sit down, won't you? I shan't be a moment."

Too polite to sit down, but noticing that Nance from her sofa was nodding encouragement to him, as much as to say, "Do whatever the young lady's asking you," the ex-family coachman, who in his time had seen such amazing scenes between aristocratic four walls that the spectacle of Mr. Urgan in his shirt and Mr. Quirm building pedestals for beast-heads must have presented itself as a simple vignette of ordinary middle-class life, stepped forward to within a couple of yards of the sofa of his recent fare, and joined respectfully in the amiable commiseration she was extending to Old Funky.

As Wizzie sat down to compose her letter at his writing-table, Uryen's pile of books collapsed for the tenth time, and the poor man cast upon his idol a look of hopeless apology, as though he heard the very voice of this brutish image of human desire assuring him: "If I'm not housed to my taste in a very few minutes the curse of Math the son of Mathonwy and of Gwydion the son of Don and of Manawyddan the son of Llyr be on you! May you do nothing else to your dying day but love *me* in place of your God, cherish *me* in place of your Love, and look for the secret of life and of death in *me* alone!"

In contemptuous disregard of both the prophet and his beast, Wizzie disentangled a pen and an ink-pot from the litter in front of her and composed the following letter. "He followed me out here but your father frightened him and he's gone. Am staying the night. Come over and fetch me if you like to-morrow afternoon. Not earlier though, as we shall all sleep late. I think your father's a *little* better. Don't worry. Love to Lovie. Your escaped What's—her—name, Wizz." She had only just signed her name when she became aware that Uryen, having given up for the nonce his struggle with the books, was watching her with an expression of diabolical cunning.

She found an envelope, however, and got her letter fastened up and addressed before she betrayed that she knew he was watching her; but when their eyes did meet the gleam of fero-cious craftiness with which he whispered his request startled her not a little.

"Run in next door for me, will you, child, and get Thuella to come? But don't go away yourself! *I want you both.* But tell Thuella to make the excuse of cooking something for Nance. Do you see? I want us all three to meet in the kitchen—it'll be quite easy; you needn't look like that!—while Nance is still out here."

To say that Wizzie was startled by the treacherous cunning in the majestic features of her "Black Man," as he bent down and whispered these words, would be to understate it. She was out-raged and made furious. The mortuary smell of his breath, which, if his wife's was like the fragrance of cow-slips, may be said to have resembled an emanation from long-dead seaweed, did not lessen her feeling; and with an expression in her face that D. knew only too well, but that Uryen had never seen before, she answered coldly, and no doubt more loudly than was necessary: "Certainly: I'll be seeing 'Thel' soon; but whether we'll come over here to-night, I'm sure I can't say! No doubt *she'll* come sooner or later. But it's too early yet to say what *we'll* do."

With this remark she left him to his obsession, and crossing the room gave her letter into the care of Mr. Netherby.

Until she began to have this romantic feeling for Uryen she had no idea from her own experience what it was like to be in love; and it had been her ignorance of this emotion that had tossed her first into Old Funky's arms and then into No-man's. Even now she was far more in the dark with regard to "her real

461

feelings," as the heroines in her story-books called it, towards D. and the Circus-man, than towards Uryen.

As she turned her eyes from one to another she felt as if she had been stripped, not only of her pretty, tight-fitting dress, but of her skin. She felt raw and aching all over. A morbid minuteness of observation, a savage realism, dominated her impression of all these people. Mr. Netherby had a drop of rheum hanging from his nose; and she wondered when it would fall. Old Funky's wig had got disarranged again and she could see the edge of her blood-stained handkerchief. Nance, in the process of being restored by Uryen, had suffered such a ruffling of her toilet that a couple of hairpins trailed across one of her ears at the end of a dishevelled wisp of hair. Uryen's own wretched clothes, always untidy, had recently become so rumpled that there had appeared a grotesquely flapping end of a not over-clean shirt between his jersey and trousers.

So exhausted did she feel in mind and body that when Old Funky, who as he set forth under the careful escort of Mr. Netherby, poked his tightly buttoned rain-soaked garment and whispered in her ear: "For another twenty quid, wenchie, tell your good man, and that'll make a snug 'arf 'undred, I'd let 'ee have the old hoss. He ain't what 'a were, and our Pop's got afeer'd o' he; so 'twould be a kindness to take 'un off us," she hadn't the heart to respond.

A dead sea of such weary distaste for the whole business of life, distaste for man and beast, distaste for the smallest effort to change the drift of fate, took possession of her that she let Mr. Netherby help the little man to shuffle across to his taxi without so much as a word of farewell.

Half an hour later, leaving Nance still on her sofa and Uryen back again in his chair, Wizzie did what she'd never done before, made her way alone through the passage between the two houses and knocked at the Wyes' door. Thuella herself opened. The girl held her finger to her lip to enjoin caution and began whispering eagerly to her.

"They're all in the studio. Let's go into the kitchen and lock the door! That's what I *have* to do now when I want to be alone. Father was bad enough—but, my dear!—it's far worse with these two. You know what poor Dumbell is—but *she*—oh, my precious!—*she*—why, I even felt sorry for Dad this morning when she went at him! And Dad came back so excited from Jenny's. He said he'd given her a proper fright. He didn't say much, because of *them* being here; but I've never seen him like he was last night. I really felt—oh, I don't know!—but he seemed *more of a person* when he came back last night. And do you know what? I took his side against *her,* and he was as pleased as if I'd given him a kiss! So when he went to bed I *did* give him a kiss, and, do you know, he gave me *such* a look, and then, all low and solemn, he gave me his blessing! I didn't know whether to laugh or cry. Listen, Wizz—oh, I can't *wait* to tell you my great news!—but do *you* think he did any good with Jenny?"

By this time the two young women—and Wizz began to feel her spirits rapidly coming back under the spell of her friend's excitement—were safe in "Thel's" cosy kitchen, where it was an indescribable relief to the younger girl to warm herself at the glowing stove. But for some reason she felt reluctant to tell her friend all she knew about the effect of Mr. Wye's visit to Friary Lane. She was no sentimentalist; but there had been a note struck in her morning's encounter with Jenny that made her prefer to keep her and Claudius out of this particular conversation. So, to change the topic as they sat facing the open stove, she asked her friend how they'd got on during the storm.

"Wasn't it awful?" replied Thuella, and then held her peace for an instant, while an almost mystical look came into her expressive face. "But—I'll tell you—all about that—later. How's Uryen now? I suppose Nance was in that taxi we heard?" She fell into silence again; and Wizzie thought: "She's keeping back something about Uryen, just as I am about Jenny. Oh, dear! What people we all are!"

But the other went on now in a low musing tone, as if talking to herself. "It was my fault at the start. It put it into D.'s head to introduce him to the Cumbers. It all began at that Antelope party."

Wizzie looked at her closely. "Do you think, 'Thel,' " she said gravely, "that he'll be himself again, after a time? Nance came to D.'s to-day—did you know that?—to get him one of those damned heads. I couldn't bear to see him with it. It was like Sister Agatha, when she got queer about the image of the Blessed Infant. I wish now that D. hadn't let him have it."

463

This time it was the elder girl who changed their topic of conversation. "Yes—it was the worst storm I've ever known here. How quiet everything seems now! Dad thinks there's a chimney, or a piece of the roof, blown down. Our fire, in there, smoked terribly. We could hardly see in the room. But Dumbell's been out, and can't see anything wrong. We've always called those noises our 'Glymes ghost,' and we'd look silly—oh, my sweet one, how lovely you are in that dress!—if it turns out that there's been something wrong with the roof all these years. But you wait—my angel—till you hear my great news! I've not told a soul yet. You'll be the first."

At this she bent down and pulled up first one and then the other of the most scarlet stockings that Wizzie had ever seen. Her stockings were the only finery Thuella had on that day. For the rest she wore her working-smock and a long faded skirt.

"Tell me about it now," whispered Wizzie, trying to throw more eagerness into her tone than she felt.

"No, no—it's too important for now. I've got to get them their tea in a minute. Look at the clock!"

"Listen, 'Thel,'" said Wizzie abruptly. "May I stay the night with you? I've told D. I might?"

The elder girl jumped to her feet and clapped her hands. "Have you really? Oh what joy, what joy! We'll talk and talk! *That's* when I'll tell you what's happened—when we're in bed and all's quiet—oh, you *dear,* how sweet of you!" And she threw her arms round her.

Their embrace, to which Wizzie, in her present mood of warmth and nervous recovery, responded more sympathetically than usual, was interrupted by two distinct knocks at the door in the hallway, followed by a third, a little louder. "It's Uryen!" cried Thuella. "That's his signal!" Leaving the door open behind her, so that Wizzie saw all she did, she answered the three knocks by three quick taps from her side and, admitting the man into the hallway, led him straight into the kitchen. Here, the minute he was safely inside, and they were all three together, she locked the door again.

The big man was in a terribly excited state. "Don't let me—" he gasped as soon as he was inside. "But it's a good thing"—and he lowered his voice to an inaudible whisper—"that I'm the——" Wizzie felt completely at a loss what to say to him, at

464

a loss to understand what had brought him here or what notion he'd got now into his disordered brain. She was also completely in the dark as to how far Thuella comprehended his manias. They all three hesitated for the flicker of a second, standing together in front of the warm stove; and then, in the spontaneous and instinctive way natural enough when a couple of young women are standing in a formidable man's presence, Thuella took possession of Wizzie's hand.

Wizzie, however, who never liked it when her friend became what she always thought of as "too demonstrative," frowned nervously and pulled her hand away. For some reason this harmless gesture, which at the worst was a thing of overstrained nerves, seemed to hoist up the dam and release the sluice of their visitor's feelings.

"Don't 'ee mind her," he said hurriedly, laying his hand consolingly on Thuella's shoulder. "It's the same all over the world! We may beg and beg but it's no avail! The thing to do"—and he bent down towards Thuella, totally disregarding Wizzie—"is to let your love transform itself into—into the force that makes the mystery tremble!" Uryen seemed so helpless and so agitated as he stood before them there, mumbling about unreturned love, and his form seemed to unwieldy and so much too big for the little kitchen, that the two girls exchanged glances wondering where to seat him.

"Let's get the one in the hall," Thuella whispered, and unlocking the door she succeeded with Wizzie's help in carrying in the old rusty iron garden-chair that nobody had bothered that year to drag into the garden. Unhooking from its peg her own domestic "over-all" she threw this over the iron-work to lessen its chill and persuaded the big man to trust the chair with his full weight.

Wizzie never forgot the tragic look of supplication that he threw—and he looked his full age to-night, looked as if he might be her grandfather—first at one of them, and then at the other. He made little groping movements, too, with his hands towards them as they leaned over the backs of their chairs.

"He wants *me* to sit on his knee," thought Wizzie; but immediately afterwards the ridiculous notion entered her tired head that he wanted *both* of them to sit on his knee!

It was queer how in her nervous state her consciousness of the least physical movement that anyone made became twice as intense as it would normally have been; but it was queerer still that her impressions in this unnatural condition reverted to old obscene talks between the Urgans over their caravan-fire! What would *those* two have made of this scene in "Thel's" kitchen?

Uryen all this time seemed struggling against some weight upon his spirit that was pressing him down. Even those groping movements with his hands, directed first to one of them and then to the other, had ceased, and certain spasmodic shivers and jerks of his big frame—resembling what we so calmly call the "automatic movements" of the animal we are killing—had taken their place.

But great incalculable Nature, who is often so much kinder to her misfits than any of their fellow mortals, chose, in her arbitrary waywardness, that Uryen should catch a quick feminine glance that now passed between the two girls.

But the naturalness of the spark does not lessen the force of the conflagration that follows it; and both the girls drew back in dismay at what they now saw and heard. Enoch leapt from his iron chair and rose towering above them, his striking lineaments convulsed with passion. His dead eyes flashed as Wizzie had never supposed they could; nor did the grotesque detail that Thuella's "over-all" continued to cling to his unwieldy bulk bring the least flicker of amusement into their frightened faces.

"So that's it—*you women!*" he broke out, and the instinctive cunning of his possessed spirit was shown in the way, for all his fury, he kept his tone low so that it should not reach the Glymes parlour. "It's nothing to you that I've put my last hope upon this moment! It's nothing to you that I've taken *your*"—and he fixed his flaming eyes on Thuella—"feeling for *you*"—and he turned them on Wizzie—"to break through into the Mystery that maddens me!"

Speaking in a lower and lower voice, as he went on, but more and more rapidly and passionately, he now bent his great head and moved his swaying bulk nearer and nearer to the two girls. Unconscious of what they did as they drew away, they pressed close to each other, Thuella clutching Wizzie's arm, and Wizzie clinging to Thuella's smock. "Nothing," he went on, his fingers closing and unclosing round the iron rim of the chair from which he had risen and at one second actually lifting it from the ground, "nothing, *nothing* to either of you, any more than it is to them! Well! it's over now. Between you all—you and these Cumbers and *he,* my own son, and Nance my own wife—you've done it at last; done what you've all been trying to do ever since I told you—fool, fool, fool, to tell you—what I know and what I am! If John Rhys were alive I'd have left you all, years ago, and gone to tell *him* the whole thing. He'd have understood, for he put me on the track of it. *He* knew how all Taliesin's prophecies were about me. He knew how all the old bards worshipped what works through me. *He* knew the mysterious secret of my race, of *his* race; that straining, that longing, that yearning, that craving, that madness to break through! *Hiraeth* is our word for it—no other tongue on earth has a word like that!— and *he* knew what it meant. Desire, but not ordinary desire. Desire grown beside itself! Desire driven against custom, driven against habit, driven against the cowardice of mankind. . . . . That's what *Hiraeth* is!" He paused; and Wizzie felt as though "Thel's" hot fingers clutching her wrist had pulses in them like burning fever. She herself was having to swallow and swallow; for there was a lump in her throat that she hadn't felt since the day she said good-bye to her horse. As is generally the case when women listen to the passionate madness of a man's life-illusion, what both the girls were feeling, what was making Wizzie swallow that lump and "Thel" grip her wrist till it hurt, was their own life-burden, their own self-pity. This lump in Wizzie's throat was called up by Enoch's tone, but the form it took, the picture reflected in its crystal globe, had no connection with anything he was saying. It wasn't his demented *Hiraeth* that brought that lump. It was her own practical, definite, professional *Hiraeth,* her longing to be whirling round the ring!

"What you women can't see," the voice of their deranged giant was now whispering, and his voice was so low and yet so intense that it was like the wind lifting the tapestry in a royal death-chamber, "and what those fools can't see, and what my son *won't* see, is that the Power of the Underworld that our old Bards worshipped, *though it was always defeated,* is the Power of the Golden Age! Yes, it's the Power our race adored when they built Avebury and Maiden Castle and Stonehenge and Caer Drwyn, when there were no wars, no vivisection, no

467

money, no ten-thousand-times accursed *nations*! They twisted it all round later, the sly children of gold and of burning, turning the dew of darkness into evil, and Bran the Blessed into a demon; but the Power that rushes through me when I go out *there*"—and he gave a jerk of his shoulder towards Maiden Castle—"the Power that I *am* under my name Uryen lies too deep for them to destroy. Whether I'm Uryen or not—'for all my mind is clouded with a doubt'—this *Hiraeth* of my race, this baffled, this thwarted, this hopeless desire, that from the beginning of things has defied morality, custom, convention, usage, comfort, and all the wise and prudent of the world, can never be destroyed out of the human heart now it has once appeared! It moves from the impossible to the impossible. It abolishes cause and effect. It strides from world to world creating new things out of nothing! It takes Nature between its fingers and Evolution in the palm of its hand. It's more than desire. It's all the defeated longing, all the baffled longing, all the forbidden longing, all the beating against the walls, that makes the wind howl and the rain cry! And it will break through. I tell you girls this, as I've told it to Nance and as I've told it to my son. It'll break through. And when it breaks through, these four thousand years wherein the world has been deceived and has left the way will be redeemed, and what was intended to happen will be allowed to happen, and the superstition of science will be exploded forever!"

His huge physiognomy was softening now, as the breath of his inspiration died down, but his unwieldy figure still bowed, still stooped, still swayed forward towards them, and his hands still kept clasping and unclasping over the rim of the iron chair. "But," he went on, "this—fulfilment—of—my—desire—I—shall —never see. Those people"—and he jerked his shoulder towards the parlour—"and you women and Nance and my"—here a great sob rose in his gullet—"and my son, too—even my own son—have killed my chance of ever seeing it—I mean in my soul"—and he struck himself on his chest—"where the only reality do bide."

Enoch's use of words as a rule was that of the upper middle-class, so that when he said "do bide" he was proving the depth of his emotion; for "bide" must have been a frequent expression on the lips of that Quirm family who had—unless he was lying to his son on the top of Mai-Dun—adopted him at Shaftesbury. "Yes, I shall—never—feel that Power—any—more. It came on the wind; and on the wind it has gone away. When I kept my secret here"—and again he struck himself on the chest—"where I've had it written from my birth, as *she* knew, and as Nance knows, I was strong in my faith. When I told my son I was strong in my faith. But when I wrote of it for the world the virtue went out of me! And now—you women, you women! Your hearts may love, but it's not with *Hiraeth,* they may ache, but it's not with *Hiraeth,* they may break, but they can never break as mine is breaking!

"But listen——" He dropped the iron chair he was tilting, as he bowed himself towards them, and it was as if his whole frame crumpled, wilted, and shrank. His features too lost their nobility, lost their massiveness, lost their very shape, and became decomposed like the face of a corpse. "The wind from yr Echwyd," he murmured in a far-off voice that seemed to come *through* him rather than from him, "the wind that—made my Uryen—has carried Uryen away. You women, you women, you care for none of these things! The *Hiraeth* of the mystery doesn't touch you, never has touched you. It's your men and your children and your play you want, not to *break through,* not to—to—take Life by the hair of its head, and wring the secret out of it!"

His last words were spoken so low as to be scarcely audible; and after uttering them he was silent. The two girls, who were now shamelessly clinging to each other in scared bewilderment, noticed that the great drops of perspiration which had been slowly forming across his forehead like bubbles of turpentine oozing from a fir-trunk had taken to themselves, by reason doubtless of the upleaping of the flames in the open stove, a curious reddish tinge. But he turned away from them now and moved towards the door.

Wizzie made a slight step forward with the feeling that she must, she *must* help him, but Thuella pulled her back, and she lacked the spirit to break away.

But all the human life appeared to have gone out of Enoch Quirm. He seemed to grope with his hands, as a beast might do who was standing on his hind legs. He seemed also, in some manner that was shocking to see, to be pawing with his feet, as his great slippers scraped along the floor. This trouble with his slippers was understandable enough as he had long since trodden down their heels and it was hard for him under normal conditions to keep them on; but Wizzie had the sharpest stab she was destined to know that night when she saw him go out in this manner.

But the strange thing was the depth of the anger she still felt against him for refusing to respond to her devotion except by this crazy dragging in of "Thel." With this anger she killed her pity. She felt as if his very madness were something he deliberately put on; part of his preference for "Thel"! "You've been strangling my love," she thought with a proud sob, as the door closed on him: "inch by inch ever since it was born; and now I've done with you! You've been playing with me from the start. You've always liked 'Thel' the best! You and 'Thel' must have a complete understanding. Let 'Thel' take care of you! I wash my hands of you!" And throwing off her friend's hand she stood absolutely still and did not move a step, even though she heard him fumbling and groping, like an animal without hands, to open the door into the passage between the two houses.

Thuella drew a deep breath. "You see?" she whispered. "I've known it was coming; and so has Nance. He's never been right since he worked for Cumber. I don't know what they'll do now, though, without that money."

Wizzie looked at her in silence; and then, like a hand striking her in the face out of the Invisible, the abominable loneliness of every single person in the world, the loneliness of our pain, of our despair, of our insanity, sent a shiver through her that made her feel sick and weak. She found herself trying to say something to Thuella, but though her lips moved, not a syllable could she utter.

She turned away and remained motionless for a second, staring at the door, her mouth open, her hands hanging loose. Then something outside the Wizzie she knew took possession of her.

"Stay where you are!" she said in a tone like the fall of some small heavy object into water, and rushing to the door she opened it, and closed it, crossed the hallway, and ran down the passage after him. The place was dim, but there was light enough to see what made her knees knock together and her heart almost stop. She saw Enoch Quirm on his hands and knees. The man was moving down the passage, slowly and heavily *on all fours.*

She was too paralysed to move. She just stood there and watched him. It wasn't until he reached the door at the other end that he rose unsteadily to his feet. Then with a sound that seemed to herself like a piercing cry but was in reality a hardly audible whistling through her teeth she ran after him and caught him up just as he was opening the door. Together they confronted the unperturbed figure of Nance, who was passing at that moment from kitchen to study with the tea-tray in her hands.

Only partially turning her head, she said quite quietly over her shoulder : "Oh, there you are ! I was *just* ready for you. Come in, Wizzie dear ! I hoped he'd manage to get you. Isn't Thuella coming?"

The familiar presence of his wife, the familiar look of the tea-tray, perhaps even—Heaven knows !—the piled-up pedestal of familiar books on which rested the head, seemed to bring the man back to his normal state.

Wizzie was the victim of such a whirl of indescribable relief mixed with proud anger, that she began to feel sick in her stomach. Both relief and anger must have appeared in the look she gave the man when their eyes met, for he removed his with an almost hand-dog expression. They all sat down at once round the table and like a child who turns from his nurse to his mother Enoch felt for his wife's hand, and when he got hold of it, held it so tightly that the woman had to make a sign to the girl to pour out the tea.

"But you're ill," she gasped as soon as she saw Wizzie's face more clearly. "You're white as a sheet !"

"Don't tease her. She'll soon be all right," grumbled the master of the house. "Drink your tea, child !"

Wizzie obeyed, and her colour slowly came back; but in a minute or two—though she saw that he was eating and drinking greedily—she had to beg Nance to let her go out for a second; and she had hardly shut herself into their lavatory than she was violently sick.

After that she felt better, though she vomited nothing but a little chocolate-coloured fluid; and on returning, though she re-

471

fused to eat anything or to smoke a cigarette, she drank several cups of strong tea.

"*I'll* have a cigarette, my chuck!" murmured Enoch to his wife the instant he'd finished. He pushed away his cup and plate then, but though he lit his cigarette there was something unnatural about the manner in which he leant his arms on the table and bowed his head over them. He was like a man who began to be overpowered by some secret drug that nobody had seen him take.

Wizzie thought she could detect—though the woman's spectacles always made it hard to catch the niceties of her expression —a look of terror in Nance's eyes. He seemed himself to be struggling against this seizure, for every now and then he would jerk his head up and take a whiff of his cigarette; only, however, to let it sink down again, till the fingers that held it hung finally at arm's length by his side.

At last, as the two women watched him—both of them thoroughly frightened now—the cigarette slipped from his fingers and fell on the floor, where, taking advantage of the human trouble in the air, it set itself to satisfy its own private and inanimate *Hiraeth* by making fiery love to the poor faded carpet.

"Uryen!" cried Nance jumping up from her seat. "Uryen, what is it? What's the matter?"

He made a feeble gesture to raise his head.

"*Enoch*—my chuck!" he murmured, and then, making what was evidently an heroic effort of his will, he heaved himself up almost straight in his chair, and looked at his wife with one of the most natural smiles Wizzie had ever seen on his sombre face.

"*Enoch*—dabchick—not Uryen! I have forgot—as it says somewhere—'that name and that name's'—" And once more his head sank on his arms.

Both the women were at his side now in consternation. "Let's get him to the couch," whispered Wizzie hoarsely, growing almost as pale as she had been before.

"We—can't! He's too heavy," cried Nance. "Oh, my God— what *shall* we do?"

"Shall I run across for Dunbar?" whispered Wizzie.

"Let's try first," said the other. And the support of their

combined weight, the pressure of their hands, along with a half-conscious craving in the man's own body to be in a horizontal position, evoked just enough impetus to get him to the sofa. Once there, however, he sank down with a weight that seemed almost superhuman, as if his form were responding to the gravitational pull of the earth's centre with a more than normal response, and lay motionless with closed eyes.

It was with a gasp of relief that Wizzie watched his massive chest under his rumpled jersey rise and fall gently with his breathing. "He's asleep," she whispered to Nance. "He was just worn out—with all this."

The older woman made a gesture as if to lay her hand on his heart, but Wizzie caught her arm.

"Don't touch him. He's all right now. For pity's sake don't wake him! It's the effect of—of the storm."

For a while they stood by his side, watching him intently; but his breathing continued quiet and natural, and at last turning to each other they drew a long deep sigh of relief.

"Shall I put this over him?" said Nance picking up the rug that had covered Old Funky.

But Wizzie shook her head. "For God's sake," she whispered crossly, "don't bother him! If he has a good sleep now—no! Don't touch the fire! Let him sleep. It's sleep he wants." She moved on tiptoe to one of the chairs by the table and carrying it to the side of the sofa settled herself there as if she intended to repeat yesterday's vigil over the bed of Claudius.

Nance shrugged her shoulders and taking off her spectacles held them up between her eyes and the lamp. Then she licked her thumb and rubbed some speck or other from one of their glasses.

Wizzie could see she was quite reassured now and had begun not only to feel a little ashamed of her own recent agitation but to feel that Wizzie's present concern about him was being carried too far. Putting on her spectacles again she began, moving quietly but without any excessive caution, to clear away the tea-things, while our friend, left on her uncomfortable seat at the unconscious man's side, was able to sink into her own thoughts. These took, as it may easily be imagined, a none too cheerful form. She saw again that huge beastlike figure on all fours advancing with such unnatural speed down that dim pas-

473

sage. She began to feel sick again in her stomach as that sight recurred. What on earth had made him do that?

In her present position she sat almost directly opposite that accursed head, propped up on its pedestal of ancient volumes and in the stillness and warmth of the room—for Nance's fire was now a mass of deep red coals—her fancy conjured up a sinister connection between the way he had hugged that evil thing and the way he had come down that passage.

Of his outburst against "Thel" and herself she did not think at all. All *that* she put down to his "ideas," to that remote realm of masculine infatuation, about which there was no need for a sensible person to trouble her mind.

But she did think long and deeply, while her fingers, clasped in her lap, played undisturbed their old game, about his preference for "Thel" over her.

"How silly I've been!" she thought. "I suppose that's always the way it is when you get fond of anyone. You think they *must* be feeling all you're feeling! But that's—" and the disillusioned young woman made a face at the unconscious Enoch. "Well! Whether it's 'Thel,' or whether it isn't 'Thel,' I was a fool to think it was me! I expect it isn't *us* at all; no, nor Nance either! I expect"—and she gazed with a sort of humorous peevishness at the countenance at her side—"he's like D.; and the only woman he ever really thinks about is D.'s mother!"

What began to disturb her just a little at this moment, as she tried to look humorously and indifferently at him, was the fact that in its present repose Enoch Quirm's face had once more become dignified and noble. How strange it was that her "Black Man of Glymes" should look so beautiful when he was asleep!

But even as she pondered on those quiet lineaments, so solemn and inviolable on that filthy sofa, that other image of him took their place; she saw again that bestial figure swaying and heaving as it fled from her on all fours down that Glymes passage. Clear through those majestic features the girl now stared into remote vacancy, the man's nose, eyes, mouth, chin, all growing vaporous and unreal, until they melted quite away. And it seemed to her as if both he and she were figures in some ghastly moving-picture where she could feel herself following him, as he moved like a beast, following him without cessation, up one diminishing perspective, and down another, until her stomach

474

grew so sick that she was always having to stop to retch and vomit, so that she was never able to get near to him, any more than he was able to get out of sight of *her*.

Her thoughts had carried her so far that it came with a startling jerk to her consciousness to find that his eyes were open and looking straight into her own. She was pulled back to reality with such a shock that she couldn't even smile at him, far less utter a word; and this numbness of her faculties was not lessened when she realized that he didn't know her, that he was thinking of someone else and addressing someone else, in her form.

"Cornie," he murmured, "I forgive you. You forgive me. That's enough, isn't it? And now they can do all." Once more his eyes closed; and an expression of impenetrable serenity came into his face.

"It's D.'s mother," thought Wizzie. "And how like D.! yes, they're both the same! Their life, their women, their work, their love—all nothing to them unless far away, far off in the past. I declare, it makes me want to live with old Claudius! He knows what women are. He knows it's the *present* we've got to have— or turn into shrews like Jenny, or softies like Nance!"

It was several hours after this, having left Enoch asleep on his sofa and Nance asleep in Enoch's chair, that Wizzie herself lay unconscious by Thuella's side. Perhaps the one point—save their love for Lovie—where Wizzie and D. were completely agreed was their loathing and contempt for dreams.

Instead of "Good night and sweet dreams!" the most amiable wave of the hand that these two queer ones ever gave each other before they slept was, "Sleep well—and don't dream!"

But the secret of that great underworld sea, into the bosom of which, at that hour, after the tumult, so many human consciousnesses, from Portland Bill to Stonehenge, had sunk, was independent of the demon-shoals of dreams that troubled it. It was an element *sui generis*, an unfathomable dimension peculiar to itself, the everlasting *other side* of the turmoil of life, a state of being that resembled death in one of its aspects and life in another; and was indeed life with something removed, and death with something added. And though independent of those troublesome shoals of demon-fish that dart through it, wretched intruders, phantom half-lives, chaotic eidola from the muddy

475

inland streams of consciousness, this great undersea takes many
shifting lights, many variations of density and volume, from the
accidents of time and place and neighbourhood. To a girl asleep
by a man those mysterious waters are not the same in their
lulling flow as to a child asleep by its parent. A woman asleep
by another woman draws from this mysterious sea ebbings and
flowings of magnetic currents different altogether from those
that reach her when she lies by a man.

The same unfathomable redemption lulls and soothes her, but
the mystic chemistry of that sublunary immersion, that baptism
in the flow of this life-death, has its own peculiar quality, a
quality as different from the other as the nearness and neighbourhood of a man is different from the nearness and neighbourhood of a woman.

It was not till after they had slept for several hours that,
awake together in the darkness, Thuella told Wizzie her great
secret.

"And you haven't let a soul know? And you've been arranging everything? And you've got the money? And you're off to-
morrow?"

And then it was that the voice out of the darkness uttered the
word with which the whole of the space-gulfs round them had
been palpitating for some minutes.

In those deep gulfs Wizzie had felt that fatal word taking
visible, though not yet *audible* shape; but her heart knew, and
the throbbing in her pulses knew, and the drops of sweat on her
forehead knew, and her occult soul, in its instincts and premoni-
tions, had known the longest of all—what that word was to be.

"It's the way they do things there," Thuella was whispering
now. "They don't write, as we do, and give people time. They
cable—and you've got to cable back. Well? Will you come,
Wizz?"

As must have happened so often in these turning-points in
women's lives no breath from Wizzie's lips actually formed the
syllable "yes." D. would have made her utter this word of fate
and would have told her it was the most important word a
woman *could* utter. Indeed, he would not have stopped there.
He would have gone on to wonder which of all the affirmative
syllables in the history of humanity—all equally drenched with
the saliva-dew of destiny—had been the first to pass what

Homer calls "the barrier our teeth." "Think, kid," he would have murmured into Wizzie's annoyed ears: "just think! At *some* actual moment in time, in *some* hollow cave, *somewhere* on the earth's surface, the particular sound destined to mean 'yes' for the whole race who inhabited Maiden Castle must have been heard *for the first time!*"

But Thuella, not being a man and not having a mind for which words, as words, whether affirmative or negative, are the best indication of the way the wind blows, was quite content with other than spoken signs as to how her friend received her generous offer.

Be it enough to say that when the two girls fell asleep for the second time that night it was clearly understood between them that no weakness at the last moment, no remorseful drawing back for any conceivable reason, should interfere with their daring and audacious plan. Wizzie was, as may be supposed, the first to awake; and she was no sooner awake than, after a wide-eyed stare at the vaguely outlined window, and with only the faintest puckering of her small face, a stream of tears began rolling down her cheeks.

It was silly. It was soft. It was, she told herself, "like Nance." But she couldn't help it. Her one hope was that "Thel" when *she* waked, as she was bound to do soon, would not try to comfort her. And it wasn't long before she became conscious that her companion *was* awake. And yet she was sure she hadn't made any noise.

Well! It didn't matter now! Now she could "lift up her voice," as the Bible says, and really weep. If only "Thel" would leave her alone—wouldn't ask her, now or ever, why she was crying, or for whom she was crying.

And "Thel" did leave her alone. She would never have thought that such a girl like "Thel"—and what an artist she must be to have such a thing happen to her!—could be like this and just leave her to herself. Popsy couldn't have stayed so still. Sister Bridget couldn't. Only her mother! and with that thought it became impossible to keep her sobs from shaking her and even shaking their bed.

But they stopped at last, stopped before there was light enough to see "Thel's" face; and it was she herself and not "Thel" who broke the silence that followed.

"Do—you—think," she said, "that if I do get work over there and get on at all I could have my old horse sent over? They'd sell him, I think, if I paid enough; for he's getting old and crochety and Popsy never could manage him. I don't mean at once; but later on. Do you think I *could* have him over?"

Thuella replied sympathetically to this question, but our friend could catch in her tone a faint ambiguity, as if she thought it very unlikely as the world went round, that the old Circus-horse would be welcome in the new hemisphere. They lay side by side in silence then, while the outline of the window grew slowly more distinct. Like two figures on a raft of fate they lay, half-tragic, half-exultant, till the morning's tide should carry them out.

"We wouldn't go by that nine train—would we—unless he was better?"

"Oh, he'll be better! Besides—remember what you promised last night!" And "Thel," who now looked, Wizzie thought in that dawn light, like one of the coldly beautiful inhuman angels who used to prop up the austere Madonna over the doorway that led to the convent lavatory, made it clear, once and for all, that for no earthly reason—not even if Uryen were much worse, could they afford to miss that train at the Southern Station.

"I've got the money; and as soon as we get to Southampton we'll buy everything. Nobody here'll be up till late, and we needn't carry a thing! Don't look like that. You're not going to turn on me now, are you?"

As Wizzie looked at the white figure by her side sitting up in bed, its face a blur, its hair a blur, but the tension of its will taut as a tight-rope, it presented itself to her consciousness that the act of running away when you had a child—"Thel" hadn't got a child!—was like feeling yourself slipping—everything going black in front of you—when you *had* to jump. She began to feel sick in her stomach like she'd felt last night.

Through the blur of "Thel's" face she could see the Great Western truck on Jenny's floor and Lovie's plump hands squeezing her doll into it. What it was that influenced Thuella to say what she said now—and Wizzie divined she realized fully that the compass-point of the decision was quivering—she never discovered to the end of her days. Was it some devilry in the girl? Was it the bottom-dregs of her contempt?

478

"We can't,"—she must have been saying, "We can't go back on it now"—but Wizzie was only dragged away from the truck on the floor in time to catch the end of her sentence—"because —don't you remember?—in the fortune we got that day in the slot-machine at Weymouth, my paper said: 'What you do, do quick!' and yours said: 'Don't stop to think before you leap!' so it's the same for both of us!"

Whatever consolation Wizzie may have derived from the fact that her flight was in harmony with the slot-machine's prejudice against "the pale cast of thought," it was not till the day after their boat sailed that Dud was able to get *his* thoughts about this event into any kind of order. He was helped to see matters in a clearer light by quite a long letter from Wizzie, a letter in which—though half of it consisted of a series of instructions as to his sounding the Urgans about the selling of the old horse— the girl went fully into her chief motive for running away.

"Everything," she wrote, "was too mixed-up. I simply couldn't stand it any more. I leave you quite free. It'll be only what I deserve if you get another girl. Only, if you do, I advise you"—here there was a sentence crossed out on which Dud pondered in vain. "And if you do," the letter continued, "I think I'd let Lovie stay on with Jenny and Claudius. I don't want to defend myself, D. I know I haven't been as nice to you as I should, and you've always been"—she had put "nice" first, but crossing it out, had substituted "good" instead—"and considerate to me. It was my longing to get back to the Circus and my work that made me do it—and other things too, but that was the chief thing. If I'd been cleverer, about books and all, it would have been different. If I'd got work at once when you took me away it would have been different. Don't be sorry or sad, and don't let Lovie feel bad, or think bad of me. You *were* good, about Lovie. No one but you would have been like that. Don't think I don't know it. I wouldn't like any other girl to see my things all about. Give them to Jenny, and if she doesn't want them, let her give them away. They know a lot of poor people. When I was in a bad mood the other night I hid all your bootlaces—those you bought from that tramp—under the mattress. And those bits of paper by the statue which you *did* go and pick up, for I found them in the drawer where your shirts

479

are, I threw into the fire. I'm sorry, D., I ever said I hated you. It isn't true"—this last sentence was underlined several times—"and perhaps some day we may meet again. But don't think about me"—here there were more scatchings out; but No-man, after long puzzling over these erasures, concluded that the sentence went on, "as you did about," but he could not decide whether the final word was "Mona" or "Mary"—"and don't let Lovie forget me. I'm sorry I was angry that night when Claudius was talking; and I'm sorry about *all* the times I was angry. 'Thel' has been seasick, but I haven't at all, *not once*. Kiss Lovie from her affectionate Mummy. And don't wish you'd never seen me—Wizz. P.S. Write me a line how your father is, to General Delivery, New York."

It was in Jenny's kitchen, three days after the flight of the two young women, that Dud finally deciphered all that was decipherable in this letter. Jenny was at the table giving Lovie her tea preparatory to getting it for the rest of them in the dining-room, where Claudius was now ensconced in his old place by the fire. Dud had found himself clinging a good deal to Mrs. Dearth these last days, for something had held him back from going over to Glymes; but as he thrust these crumpled and pondered-over sheets into his pocket he came to the conclusion that he really *must* walk over there that evening. He kept thrusting his hand into the inside pocket of his coat to make sure that Wizzie's letter, which it would be intolerable for any eyes but his own to see, was safe where he had placed it, but even while he did this he began another of the mental struggles he had been making for the last couple of days to shake off the numbness and inertia that had fallen on him.

"I must go over to Glymes," he kept saying to himself. "I must go over to Glymes to-night. I must go directly after tea." They had just had a visit from Dumbell who was unaccompanied this time by his fuzzy-headed lady, and Jenny had been revealing to Dud the direction of various straws on the life-stream at Beulah Lodge which surprised him not a little.

Jenny said that Dunbar had told her himself that he was giving their servant notice. This he told her he had been compelled to do because of her lack of proper respect for his botanical collection. "And that—you may mark my words,"—said Jenny, "is the beginning of the end. The next thing he'll do'll be

480

to give Madame notice! When a man dares to go as far as to pack off a woman's pet servant, they won't hang on much longer; and I wouldn't wonder if it won't be Dumbell who'll make the move. She's humiliated him to the limit over his Black-Shirt pranks, and he's taken it like a lamb; but botany's a different story—I believe he'd walk over both the father and the daughter to reach a new blackberry."

But it wasn't of these heroic deeds of poor Dumbell in a cause older than Fascism that Dud was musing now. He was going over in his mind all the upheavals out there at Glymes that their ambassador had been recording. Uryen was still in the same state of helpless apathy, lying all day without taking notice of anyone. Nance was still nursing him, helped now and then, much against her will, by the intrusive Mrs. Wye; but the most dramatic news brought by Mrs. Wye's husband was that old Teucer Wye had decided to leave Glymes at once for good and all.

Dud had been impressed by Jenny's reception of this news, which meant, of course, that the ex-professor was intending to plant himself on her and Claudius. "We'll be glad to have him," she'd told Dumbell bravely. "After all, if it hadn't been for him—" and she'd explained frankly to her brother how Claudius would now give up his place next door and live alto-gether with her, and how Mr. No-man, who couldn't bear to sleep alone in Miss Ravelston's room, was already spending his nights in his attic.

"I *must* get over to Glymes after tea, Jenny," was Dud's refrain to-night, but he seemed thankful that a good long time had yet to elapse before he would have to pull himself together for this duty.

As a matter of fact on this particular evening he never did go to Glymes and as the autumn went on he found that this ten-dency of his to sit brooding over Jenny's kitchen-fire became a recurrent habit. He had finished *Mary Channing* and his pub-lishers were "considering" it—had been "considering" it for more than a month already; and he found himself unable to make the effort of beginning a new book.

He walked even more than in the old days and further afield but with nothing approaching his former delight in these excur-sions. Little as Wizzie had been interested in what he called his "adventures," half the pleasure he got from them was to know

481

that he would find her there when he returned, and it wasn't the same thing to tell Jenny.

As October drew to its end he rarely went to Jenny's for any meal; for by this time her father had moved from Glymes and now occupied, in visible presence and in happier reality, the room dominated by Thuella's wicked picture, and it struck Dud as unfair to inflict upon the woman a third hungry man.

But this self-denying ordinance in respect to imposing on Jenny meant that if he didn't want to have his meals out he had to get all three of them in his own attic. And the result of this hugger-mugger method of feeding was that he soon began to suffer from vicious attacks of acute dyspepsia. In the long lonely years before he knew Wizzie he had got his meals out with normal regularity; but now, after his life with her, he found he had acquired a nervous aversion to entering the most harmless restaurant.

Less and less, too, after Teucer Wye's move into town, did Dud go out to Glymes. Unable, as we naturally are, to put down the singular behaviour of those who have had the privilege of living with us to a physical revulsion from ourselves, Dud was often tempted, as he went over and over in his mind every possible motive for Wizzie's leaving him, to attribute it, in *some* measure, to her jealousy of Nance. This thought made him extremely reluctant to have, just at present, any tête-à-tête interviews with his father's wife; and as such interviews were the only ones he *could* have—for in those last weeks of October Enoch seemed oblivious to everything—he made his visits to Glymes as brief and few as was compatible with a decent display of sympathy.

Uryen was indeed as good as dead; and though medical science gave a different name to his disorder, Dud agreed with Nance that by publishing his life-illusion he had "killed his heart."

The only exceptions to his withdrawn and comatose state during his son's visits seemed to Dud to resemble faint spasms of distaste for his presence. There were times when he thought the man knew him, and deliberately, in scriptural language, "turned his face to the wall." He spoke of this to Nance, suggesting that his father was concealing some mad suspicion that it was he who had spirited the girls away; but Nance wouldn't hear of this, and assured him with a sad smile that the runaways always overrated, "as young girls will," the interest her husband took in them.

It was a day or two before October was over that the end came. Nance had been forced to accept financial help from him, and forced also—and here he had the doctor's support—to call in the aid of a trained nurse; but by one of those accidents that can always happen in a sick-chamber it was when he was alone with him that Enoch died.

He was thinking of Wizzie as he kept guard while Nance and the nurse had their meal in the kitchen, and he had been staring gloomily out of the window wondering if she would reply to a letter he had written, when a sudden movement from the sofa— for they had left the man in peace where he first fell ill—made him swing quickly round.

Enoch's great heavy-lidded eyes were wide open and fixed with clear intelligence upon his own. And it was not any self-deception in our friend's mind, but he knew at once, with every faculty he possessed, that it was death and not life that brought this change. And as he answered his father's look, everything he was aware of, his own identity, the identity of the dying man, the untidy room, the "head" on the pile of books, the window through which his thoughts had flown so far, the image of Wizzie, receded, dwindled, melted, fused themselves together, reduced themselves to a faint remote pressure of something imponderable and far away!

And in the place of these things thus withdrawn, thus rendered vague and tenuous, a completely new reality, a reality that was himself and yet not himself, that was his father and yet not his father, pressed upon him and surrounded him.

The mysterious "yr Echwyd," of which the man was always talking, had no need now to be besieged by violence! It was here, it was around them both, it *was* them both, and all their accumulated experience with it. But this experience of theirs, their piled-up life-sensation, floated far-off on this new reality which now "undulated," as the poet says, so closely round them and absorbed them.

Dud tried to speak, but it was as if the air that carries articulate sound had suddenly been removed; and though his lips and his tongue were ready to obey him, not a word came from his mouth.

But Enoch spoke. "*I am*," he said with extraordinary natural-ness and quietness and without any particular emotion, while an expression, which neither then nor later could his hearer interpret, crossed his face, "*what I am*. So it's all right. It doesn't matter."

How the son wished afterwards that the man had been able to die as easily as those words had been spoken! But it was as if the terrible vitality that had always smouldered in that heavy frame couldn't give up its old desperation. His soul had spoken; but it was with a violent and spasmodic jerk of his prostrate frame, as if the vital spark, whether it called itself Enoch or Uryen, were wrenching itself from its bondage, were really "breaking" with a last desperate *Hiraeth* of its whole life-essence into the secret already known to his spirit, that the man tore himself out of life

The days that followed his death were days of labour and trouble for poor Dud. Wizzie would have been amused, if not annoyed, by the number of times—sometimes to himself and sometimes to Claudius, who was now his chief confidant—No-man used the word "ironical" about the matter of his father's interment.

He was buried on the last day of October in that very place, by the mounds of Cornelia and Mona, upon which our friend had had his eye as his own resting-place; and it was this fact, along with the chain of events connected with it, those fatal and grotesque links that bound them together, that made Dud envisage the whole business as a perfect example of Nature's humorous ways with man.

When November came, however, and brought with it the anniversary of their first meeting, Dud's thoughts, as he waited for Nance in his familiar attic-room, were of the grimmest and most bed-rock kind. If there was any of this ironical detachment, that used to make his girl so angry, left in his mood now it had been reduced to something more like the polish upon bare bones than the glow upon flesh and blood.

As he crouched over his fire the soul within sank down to its ultimate ledge of resistant power. "I'll hold her tight," he thought, "tight under my ribs, whether she hates me or not! To the end of my days where *I* go she'll go, and what *I* do she'll do." But even as he thought of this there came over him, like the slow drifting in of a vast, terrible, irresistible tide, the temptation to drop his personal life, to let it pass from him, to toss it overboard with all its sacred "sensations," and to treat himself, as Claudius did *himself*, as a mere objective bridge to the world's future.

But gathering up all his forces, No-man resisted this. "It can take my work," he thought in his desperation, "and my life but my soul it shall never take!" And against that insidiously seeping tide he felt as if he were stretching forth his arms and clutching at the great cloud of witnesses that emanated from the very foundations of this old Durnovaria. How they floated round him! And how, if he only clung to them through thick and thin, they could bear him up—clouds and vapours though they were! For they were the residue—immortal, indestructible —of all the personal souls that had held to their identity in the midst of the flowing away, an identity that rested on what all the while was behind this universal flux.

"What's behind it is *in* us," he thought, "not outside us. And all this 'progress' that old Claudius praises is only a return, a return *with a difference* but still a return, to the centre from which we spring!" He thrust his fists against the pit of his stomach, for his dyspepsia became sharp at that moment, but using his very discomfort as a *point d'appui* for intenser thought, he plunged like a diver into the mystery of the old town about him, whose mellow murmur came up from the street into his ears; and as he sank into its undersea of the long generations, he felt as if he were touching some calm undying presence down there, whose secret was that of the individual soul, not of the passing of any present into any future.

He undid the buttons of his braces now, so as the more easily to press his knuckles against his navel, and as he did this all his strength seemed suddenly to drain out of him, and a dull inert weariness of the whole struggle descended on him. This "whoreson lethargy" was the worst form that his nostalgia for Wizzie took. He missed her in every possible way. He missed her as the general background of his life, and this perhaps troubled him the most; but he also was perpetually receiving sideway thrusts of a sickening poignancy from all manner of unexpected little things.

And instead of missing her less, as day followed day, his

longing for her increased. The very absence of emotional passion from his nature, his very lack of feelings that depend on a certain virile energy, made it worse for him, for it deprived him of the relief that passionate hearts find in anger and pride and thoughts of revenge; while his grand cult of sensations, though it didn't altogether fail him, lost in some subtle way much of its finer edge.

What he discovered in fact, was something he had never realized before, the crucial role played in this life of sensation by contrast with something else! What he had really done—and the girl had known it—was to use the living Wizzie as he had used the dead Mona. It meant nothing to her that there was in this a proof of the intensity of his feeling, a proof of its ether-realized sensuality, of its all pervasiveness and absorbing diffusion.

It was no consolation to her that he thought of the modelling of her limbs as he walked round Poundbury, or that he mingled the curves of her " 'lurin' figure" with the *valla* and *fossae* of Maiden Castle! But this diffusion of her desirability through the earth he walked on, through the grass and the rocks and the stones and the trees he passed, became, now that he had lost her, a perpetual reminder of her, and an increasing craving for her presence. His Mona-wraith had not been the real Mona at all. She had been a creation of anonymous desire; but never was there a girl, he thought, more vitally alive than Wizzie. And it wasn't only in his walks, which she had not shared, that he pined for her. He had never believed that a girl's body could diffuse itself as Wizzie's did—quite apart from her mind— through the fabric of chairs, through the stuff of tablecloths, through the polish of door-handles, through the angles of looking-glasses, through the reflections on glass bottles, through the flickerings on coal-scuttles, and through all those meaning-less scrolls and scrawls that the elfish artistry of time leaves upon walls and ceilings.

He missed Uryen too, but not very much! He decided on general grounds that it's impossible to miss a man as much as you miss a girl, because a girl's body passes into everything round her, whereas the body of a man stays inside his clothes.

It was Enoch's voice, Enoch's turns of speech, Enoch's expressions when he was speaking, that he missed in that direction. He hoped devoutly that he never *would* see again any of the objects in that filthy study.

But he found it was cruelly difficult to do what Wizzie had told him to in her letter and give her things to Jenny! Her things were herself. While he still had her things, something, some essence of her personality, stayed with him. In fact, so much of her stayed with him that he once found himself wondering if she mightn't be conscious over there of how he was still clinging to her and hate him for it, no! not "hate" him, for she said she didn't do that, but feel cross and angry with him for it. Would she have been pleased or annoyed—he simply had not the least idea!—had she known how her going had changed everything for him?

Less than a month ago his escapes to this attic had been moments of stolen bliss, whereas now it was hard for him to realize what on earth there was in the place that had pleased him so much. He made a mental resolution that never again would he let himself fret or rebel against the contrast that lay at the bottom of all. How heavenly had been that passing backwards and forwards between Wizzie and his attic! That was the whole secret; though there was no need to go as far as the old monks and monkish scholars, and make Wizzie and her ways a temptation of the devil.

But to pass from your girl to your work, and then, back again, from your work to your girl—that was the way to live! As he now sat by his fire, waiting for Nance, and staring at the two bed-post heads—for she had made him take back the one Wizzie had carried away—he went over in his mind certain troublesome events that had occurred the day before, the day dedicated to All Saints. Nance had come to see him in great trouble early in the morning—that was the first thing—with the news that the workmen called in to examine the Glymes roof had announced that without extensive repairs the place was no longer safe for human habitation. Dumbell's verdict about such danger had thus proved superficial, and Uryen's "ghost-wind" had done damage of a more material sort than generally follows such phantom visitations.

Nance's early appearance, with a suit-case in her hand, after a panic-stricken night under the condemned roof, had necessitated his finding for her some immediate lodging, and this he had done through a good-natured acquaintance of his, the land-lord of the Phoenix, who caused a fire to be lit for her at once in a pleasant room of that romantic hostelry, looking out on his own High East Street.

But the disposal of Nance had been only the first of a series of sharp tests for our friend's philosophy. On returning to his attic, after leaving Nance to recover her equilibrium, and possibly to get some sleep after her agitated night, he found that some relative of his landlord's, in that sagacious man's absence, had allowed an obviously questionable visitor to ascend his stairs, for no sooner had he pushed open the door of his room than he was confronted by none other than Grummer Urgan and by Grummer in the highest feather of loquacity and greed. Her outer garment would have disgraced the most disreputable of "Madames," but when she threw back this piece of filthy finery her capacious bosom revealed a wealth of black satin, worthy of Lord Fordington's housekeeper.

We need not enlarge on the super-Rabelaisian dance which Dud's imagination—that of an innocent child combined with that of a sensual dotard—led this satin bosom and these clinking jet beads; but, as he worked it out afterwards, a certain sympathetic pity, doubtless the inverse side of his loathing of the preposterous woman, mingled with his almost malicious eagerness to be robbed.

After all, she did reveal to him that Old Funky was dangerously ill, that Popsy had had a final quarrel with the horse, and that they had received notice from the foreign Circus-owner that they must quit, but what made it possible for Grummer to carry off the *whole* contents of the cash-box in his mother's ottoman was undoubtedly, he decided, what usually makes us submit to spoliation, just an exaggerated fear of the power of the aggressor! He could not now recall whether he had *asked* her to sit down; but at one point in their extraordinary talk she certainly did sit down, for he remembered how especially head-strong his monstrous imaginations had become when he saw her in his chair.

It was congestion of the lungs, she told him, that her husband suffered from "mainly"; but she went into lively details about other ailments that had a less euphonious sound. She had heard, she said, of Miss Ravelston's departure, and had at once felt it to be her melancholy duty to come to assure him of her "kindly feelin's"—especially "as that gal had rinned off."

Remembering Wizzie's letter Dud had interrupted at that point to murmur something about hoping, as time went on, to be able to buy their horse from them, but Grummer's eyes gleamed with such lambent avarice at this that he contented himself with adding: "But one thing at a time, Mrs. Urgan, though I see you *would* sell him, if we agreed on the price."

And it was at that pregnant moment that the lady had presented him with the precious "dockymint." Now Dud being as ignorant of the mysterious processes of the law as was Wizzie herself, the terrifying number of "Whereases" and the still more alarming phrase "alienation of affection," on this piece of paper, very quickly caused him to open his mother's ottoman. Unfortunately he had only just withdrawn from the bank—so as to be ready for Nance's necessities—almost the whole of his balance; and if he didn't smile now to think of the ease with which this Gargamelle in satin disappeared with his savings, it was only because the third blow he received on this All Devils' Sunday, the one upon which he was pondering now, was more serious still. But what *had* the shameless old trollop hinted at as she departed?

He tried to remember her exact words. "Me and me 'usband don't 'old nothink but kind feelin's," was *one* of her final remarks; but her grand *esprit d'escalier,* as he bowed her out, consisted of an obscure hint as to a new form that these "kind feelin's" might eventually take, something to the effect that if he required any further feminine society Popsy had several amiable friends in Dorchester who would be very pleased to "see" such a liberal gentleman. He had only just begun to confide to his two "Questing Beasts" his reaction to this handsome hint, when as if All Saints' had really turned into All Devils' his eyes fell upon several unopened letters that had come by the last post on the day before.

Turning these over—as he did all his letters now—with a fantastic hope that there might be another from Wizzie, he had found that the only important one was from his publishers, and upon opening this communication he had learned to his dismay that "the reports of our Readers on *Mary Channing* have been so unfavourable that we feel obliged, much to our regret——"

489

In plain words, his book was rejected. This final blow on the top of the rest, and the fact that it had fallen just when his father's wife had become dependent on him, did come near to breaking down his fortitude.

Well! He must bestir himself. "I must go to the bank," he thought, "after we come back from the cemetery, and find out the worst. If I *am* overdrawn—well, I'll have to wire for an advance from Cumber, and just do nothing but write articles. One thing's certain; I won't start sponging on Claudius and Jenny!"

It occurred to him now to wonder what he would do, supposing old Cumber, in a rage with them all because of Dumbell's revolt against the fuzzy-head, stopped giving him any work. He hadn't received a word since the man had disposed so abruptly of Enoch and his mystic contributions. He would certainly be in a nice fix then, with his savings carried off by Grummer, and no money left in the bank! What *would* he do?

What he did at the moment was to pull his chair close to the fire and rub his hands up and down his shins. This was certainly a different kind of All Souls' Day from the one he had known a year ago! Instinctively idealizing his troubles, he began a childish and masculine attempt to make Wizzie and her running away responsible for the death of Enoch, for Nance being thrown on his hands, for Grummer's carrying off his savings, for the rejection of *Mary Channing,* and for his wretched dyspepsia.

Closer and closer he bent over his fire, putting his trousers tightly round his shins and passing his bony fingers up and down their nearly scorched surface. "Never has any girl," he thought, "left such a gap behind!"

And then suddenly, without any warning, just as though it had flown across his senses with the low hum of a shardborne beetle, came the memory of that maddening orgy of delicious viciousness, that he had enjoyed with his "Venetian Post" by the scummy pond.

Even at that moment, just when his whole being was crying out for Wizzie and Wizzie alone, the mere approach of this memory made his pulses beat and the blood rush to his head. "It's a madness," he thought; and he began to wonder whether he were alone in such madness, or whether, reaching out through the nerves of all the sons of man from some electric scummy pond at the heart of the cosmos, there was for every

490

man alive some peculiar impersonal lust that made the knees knock together and the hands shake.

"It's the *sharing of it*," he said to himself, "it's the sharing of this black electricity! Thuella and I must be exactly alike in that." And he fell, while the mere contemplation of it brought back the mad excitement, to speculating as to how long this thing would have lasted had he and Thuella lived together.

"What she and I feel," he thought—and it came over him that for a whole year, ever since he had first set eyes on her, he had really known it—"isn't passion, isn't *love* in any sort of sense; it's a black jet, a black spout, from the most dangerous madness there is! It's something that simply sweeps you away!" And with one of his outrageous flights of fancy Dud allowed himself to wonder if the appalling power of this insanity didn't spring from the fact that there was a paternity for it in the supernatural world.

He drew back now rather quickly from the bars of his small grate—he had long ago come to the conclusion that the reason Dorchester had the nicest hearths in the country was due to ancient Rome—for he thought he detected, rising from his trousers, the unmistakable smell of scorched cloth.

"I wonder if everybody," he said to himself, "is as immersed in the elements as I am? By God, I believe if I hadn't wanted to carry Wizzie off I might——" And the thought came into his head, even as the smell of the scorched trousers came into his nostrils, that in mediaeval times his dalliance with his Mona-wraith would have been regarded as an affair with an Elemental.

"But why was my conscience free over *that*," he wondered, "and so terribly stirred about Thuella? Does our *real* conscience only get roused by a madness that reduced the pleasure of life itself to cold, stale, wet ashes in comparison with it?"

Another odd thing was that for some reason—and his feeling here was very complicated—he found himself scrupulously avoiding any thought of the two girls being together. When he thought of Wizzie in America it was always as being alone, or as being alone in an American circus.

Staring into his fire, but no longer warming his shins, it came over him now with a curious chill to think of those Glymes houses completely deserted—Nance had said that it was more than likely that the whole place would be pulled down. He remembered the queer feelings he had that day of Thuella's party when he kept listening for Uryen's knock and imagining his figure outside the door.

Damn! But it was hard to think of Glymes without Thuella! Quite against his will—for he was the old shameless Dud still—he suddenly wondered what his life would have been if he'd never seen Wizzie! He would certainly have gone far with Thuella. "Maybe they'd have——"

But he pulled himself up on that point, and asked himself once more what he'd do, supposing Cumber *didn't* give him any more articles to write.

"What of that decent old chap," he thought, "who gave Claudius work?" And it made him feel contemptible and ashamed when he realized how scared he was of manual labour. And what of those dignified and quaint characters that he was always meeting down by the bridge, by the White Hart?

"But unsuccessful novelists," he said to himself, "don't get on the dole."

Just then he caught from the street below his window the familar sound of that Shakespearean mummer's dramatic voice, advertising some new attraction come to town. "I'll stick to old Durnovaria," he said to himself, "whatever becomes of me. By God, it's the most English town in England, and by far the best! I'd sooner be a door-keeper in Dorchester than——" And he thought of how he had felt the roots of this ancient mellow place sinking down to the very nadir of the earth—full of the magic of the generations! He thought of that refined young person who carried the Sunday-papers on her bicycle. He thought of the unconquerable laugh of the old *Echo*-seller. He thought of the mysteriously sweet smile of his friend the "Drowner." He thought of his tragic Mary Channing, of whose fate he had written—probably too well! No, no, whatever happened to him he must hang on here. Where else should he be when Wizzie returned, a famous circus "star," from over the water?

"I'm not going to give up," he said to himself, "because Wizz got bored with me. And I'm not going to become 'objective,' either, for all old Claudius' eloquence. I've got hold of something; and if people don't want what I've got hold of now—they'll come to it—sooner or later!"

492

He pushed back his chair still farther from the fire, and turning round glanced at the two heraldic heads. And the thought came to him, as he contemplated their obscene beast-faces, that all this talk of Enoch's about the prophets and their non-human "familiars" applied in his own case to what he got out of the Inanimate. "Yes," he thought, "that's what you are, you two, you're all the Inanimates on earth in which man's love-longing loses itself, and in which it finds itself. There's not a stick or stone in this place into which some lonely spirit hasn't poured the tragedy of his unsatisfied desire. *He* thought this 'groaning and travailing' of the longing in us could break through the barrier. But there *is* no barrier! We couldn't think of a barrier if there weren't something in us *already outside it!*

"Yes, you can leer at me, you two! If I hadn't found you out I'd be scared of you; and if I were scared of you—whether you were Mother's or not—I'd throw you into the Frome! But you can stay where you are. I'm not going to think of my girl here. I'm going to think of her in every stick and stone I pass, till she comes back. I'm alone with you again. But there are two of you, and *I'm two,* wherever I go, whether she hates me or not!"

But the carved heads stinted not or abated one jot of their inscrutable derision, and as he went on surveying them he began to feel not only a vicious twinge of his dyspepsia, but the same weary and hopeless lethargy as had been weighing him down ever since Wizzie went away.

He must have indeed fallen asleep soon after that, for he didn't hear Nance's steps or even her knock. and as she stood in the doorway watching him there her spectacles grew blurred with tears, for there was that in his unconscious pose that made her think of Enoch.

As they set out to the cemetery down Acland Road—for it was characteristic of Dud's present mood that he lacked the heart to insist on the Icen Way—poor Nance, who was in a sufficiently shaky state herself, was shocked to see him pause so often and bend low down, supporting himself on his cudgel and thrusting his fist into the pit of his stomach.

"It's nothing," he said, when, with the tips of her gloved fingers laid with infinite gentleness, for fear of hurting his feelings, upon his arm, she begged him to tell her what was wrong. "It's nothing," he said peevishly. "It'll pass in a moment. I can't

493

help it. My friends'll just have to get used to my acting like this! It's all nerves; but nerves generate acids." And as they went on and turned into the South Walks opposite Rothesay House, he imagined to himself, on the high wall before them there, a grotesque and terrifying fresco in rich colours—like the inferno on the wall at Pisa—representing the persecution of a human stomach by a demon-nerve. It was a monstrous inferno of his own that he mentally projected upon the garden-wall of that solidly-built mansion of the early eighties, but it was a wondrous comfort to him to see it there, and it gave him just the spirit he needed to straighten his back and trudge on.

And, as often happened with Dud, whose physical sensations, originating in the chemistry of his body, became the battle-field of his soul, this victory over the downward drag of his dyspepsia gave a zest to the more spiritual struggle of his whole identity with the present crisis in his life.

Thus he found himself able to jest quite lightly to his companion, as they passed the cenotaph, reminding her of her collapse on this spot exactly a year ago.

"Take care," she said with a tender smile, "you may make me collapse again!"

But he forced himself after that to glance boldly at the foreign Circus-name on the boardings along the fence where the fair-field was.

"Perhaps she'll come back famous and rich," he said to Nance, "and Lovie and I will go to see her and sit in the front row."

What did, however, give his philosophy a blow that made it stagger was the sight of Maumbury Rings.

"How the devil," he thought, "can I start another book, with Mary still unchampioned?"

But Nance had her own secret worries that she had been longing all day to confide in him. "What do you suppose he really did feel," she suddenly asked him, "when he went to such lengths to bring those two girls together?"

Dud was nonplussed at this: not because he hadn't thought over it himself, and come to his own conclusion, but because he found it so hard to explain his conclusion to his father's wife. He walked in silence for a little while, and then he said slowly and gravely: "He and I, my dear, are"—he hesitated for a

494

second before the word "are" but brought it out firmly enough—
"very alike in certain things. We both live at a somewhat
different level from most people. Mind you, I don't say at a
higher level, but a *different* one. With us, if I may say so, the
actual substance of our planet down to the centre of the earth,
with all the elements that work on it out of space, is something
—its mystery, its power for good and evil—that we can't take.
as most people do, just for granted! We think of it all the time,
if you get what I mean, and to him it always meant—this vast
weight of matter—something separating us from the real reality.
Old Wye feels much the same, and that's where"—he hesitated
again and again overcame his hesitation—"where Uryen and he
differ from Claudius. I don't know whether you've read *Faust*,
my dear, but, if you have, you'll remember that he has to 'break
through'—and that's the word *he* was always using—into the
underworld, or the overworld, or whatever you like to call it, to
reach the secret—'the Mothers,' as the book says. Enoch's idea
was, I think, that frustrated love—unreturned love, I mean— was
the strongest magnetic force in the world. Mephistopheles gives
Faust a key by which he 'breaks through.' Do 'ee see now what
I'm driving at? To Enoch this 'key' was frustrated love; and for
some reason he got into his head that 'Thel's' love for Wizz was
like that! Neither of them, of course, had the least notion of
what he was up to. No sane person, *could* have had. How he
supposed he could 'break through,' as he called it, on the
strength of another person's feelings is more than I can follow.
But of course some sort of *vicariousness* does appear in all the
old mystical cults. His mania for those damned beast-heads of
my mother's—and *that* I know, as I tried to explain to you and
Wizz the other day—was the same sort of thing. And *there* I'm
rather like him. It all comes from living, as he and I do, more
in the great cosmic forces—forgive the way I'm talking, my
dear!—than in ordinary human interests. I take these things
historically—what *would* old Claudius say if he heard me?—but
he took them literally. And it was when he read what Rhys says
about Uryen that he began pretending to himself, for he
couldn't have altogether believed it, or he wouldn't have broken
his heart when he *wrote* about it, that he was himself the mysterious Being of those old legends."

Dud stopped at this point. They had crossed the railway

bridge and were already at the entrance to the cemetery. Not the smallest comment did his "cemetery-woman" make upon his long discourse. Whether she followed it or not he couldn't tell, and her silence made him feel something of a fool; but the mere putting of all this into words had been a comfort to him; and now, as they threaded their way between the mounds and the cypress-trees, he couldn't help drawing her arm through his own.

What a sequence of events in those crowded twelve months had linked him with this sad, soft, much-enduring creature! Well, *there* they were; they were coming to them now, his graves and her graves.

For a minute or two they stood hand in hand by the freshly turned mould. Then the woman whispered: "I forgave him when he didn't know it. But he knows it now." And Dud realized what was in her mind when, with a faint smile, she drew her hand from his and moved away to the grave of her son.

And an apathy, a numbness, a strange quiescence descended upon D. No-man; not the same apathy that had been weighing him down all these last days, but the apathy that comes on a person when his soul, removing itself to a distance from his body, faces without flinching but with an immense weariness the long ascending path up which it has to drag that mortal companion of its wayfaring. Which of those two—his mother, with her inhuman egoism or Mona, with her weird unselfishness—held the secret that prevailed? Well! He must go on as best he could in his own way. He must be decent to Nance. He must be faithful, after his fashion, to Wizzie. He must hold fiercely to all those "sensations" of his! It was no good. He could *not* live, as this dead man had done, in a wild search for the life behind life.

One life at a time! But neither would he close one single cranny or crevice of his mind to the "intimations of immortality" that in this place and at this hour were so thick about him. And then a well-known sound in the air above him made him glance upwards. One of old Claudius's airplanes! "Hold to the centre," he said to himself, "as you move on. The future's *not* everything." And he dug his stick into the earth, with his eyes on the ground. Then, pulling it out with a jerk, he went to meet Nance.

THE END